THE CONSTANT PRINCESS

Philippa Gregory is an established writer and broadcaster for radio and television. She holds a PhD in eighteenth-century literature from the University of Edinburgh. She has been widely praised for her historical novels, including *Earthly Joys, Virgin Earth, A Respectable Trade, The Other Boleyn Girl,* (which was adapted for BBC television), *The Queen's Fool* and *The Virgin's Lover.* Philippa Gregory lives in the North of England with her family. For more information, visit www.philippagregory.com and for automatic updates about this author, go to www.harpercollins.co.uk and register for AuthorTracker.

PHILIPPA GREGORY

THE CONSTANT PRINCESS

HarperCollins*Publishers*

HarperCollins*Publishers*
77–85 Fulham Palace Road,
Hammersmith, London W6 8JB

www.harpercollins.co.uk

Published by HarperCollins*Publishers* 2005
1 3 5 7 9 8 6 4 2

A catalogue record for this book
is available from the British Library

ISBN 0 00 721278 X

Set in Minion by Palimpsest Book Production Limited,
Polmont, Stirlingshire

Printed and bound in Great Britain by
Clays Ltd, St Ives plc

For Anthony

Princess of Wales

Granada, 1491

There was a scream, and then the loud roar of fire enveloping silken hangings, then a mounting crescendo of shouts of panic that spread and spread from one tent to another as the flames ran too, leaping from one silk standard to another, running up guy ropes and bursting through muslin doors. Then the horses were neighing in terror and men shouting to calm them, but the terror in their own voices made it worse, until the whole plain was alight with a thousand raging blazes, and the night swirled with smoke and rang with shouts and screams.

The little girl, starting up out of her bed in her fear, cried out in Spanish for her mother and screamed: 'The Moors? Are the Moors coming for us?'

'Dear God, save us, they are firing the camp!' her nurse gasped. 'Mother of God, they will rape me, and spit you on their sickle blades.'

'Mother!' cried the child, struggling from her bed. 'Where is my mother?'

She dashed outside, her nightgown flapping at her legs, the hangings of her tent now alight and blazing up behind her in an inferno

3

of panic. All the thousand, thousand tents in the camp were ablaze, sparks pouring up into the dark night sky like fiery fountains, blowing like a swarm of fireflies to carry the disaster onwards.

'Mother!' She screamed for help.

Out of the flames came two huge, dark horses, like great, mythical beasts moving as one, jet black against the brightness of the fire. High up, higher than one could dream, the child's mother bent down to speak to her daughter who was trembling, her head no higher than the horse's shoulder. 'Stay with your nurse and be a good girl,' the woman commanded, no trace of fear in her voice. 'Your father and I have to ride out and show ourselves.'

'Let me come with you! Mother! I shall be burned. Let me come! The Moors will get me!' The little girl reached her arms up to her mother.

The firelight glinted weirdly off the mother's breastplate, off the embossed greaves of her legs, as if she were a metal woman, a woman of silver and gilt, as she leaned forwards to command. 'If the men don't see me, then they will desert,' she said sternly. 'You don't want that.'

'I don't care!' the child wailed in her panic. 'I don't care about anything but you! Lift me up!'

'The army comes first,' the woman mounted high on the black horse ruled. 'I have to ride out.'

She turned her horse's head from her panic-stricken daughter. 'I will come back for you,' she said over her shoulder. 'Wait there. I have to do this now.'

Helpless, the child watched her mother and father ride away. 'Madre!' she whimpered. 'Madre! Please!' but the woman did not turn.

'We will be burned alive!' Madilla, her servant, screamed behind her. 'Run! Run and hide!'

'You can be quiet.' The child rounded on her with sudden angry spite. 'If I, the Princess of Wales herself, can be left in a burning campsite, then you, who are nothing but a Morisco anyway, can certainly endure it.'

She watched the two horses go to and fro among the burning tents. Everywhere they went the screams were stilled and some discipline returned to the terrified camp. The men formed lines, passing buckets all the way to the irrigation channel, coming out of terror back into order. Desperately, their general ran among his men, beating them with the side of his sword into a scratch battalion from those who had been fleeing only a moment before, and arrayed them in defence formation on the plain, in case the Moors had seen the pillar of fire from their dark battlements, and sallied out to attack and catch the camp in chaos. But no Moors came that night; they stayed behind the high walls of their castle and wondered what fresh devilry the mad Christians were creating in the darkness, too fearful to come out to the inferno that the Christians had made, suspecting that it must be some infidel trap.

The five-year-old child watched her mother's determination conquer fire itself, her queenly certainty douse panic, her belief in success overcome the reality of disaster and defeat. The little girl perched on one of the treasure chests, tucked her nightgown around her bare toes, and waited for the camp to settle.

When the mother rode back to her daughter she found her dry-eyed and steady.

'Catalina, are you all right?' Isabella of Spain dismounted and turned to her youngest, most precious daughter, restraining herself from pitching to her knees and hugging the little girl. Tenderness would not raise this child as a warrior for Christ, weakness must not be encouraged in a princess.

The child was as iron-spined as her mother. 'I am all right now,' she said.

'You weren't afraid?'

'Not at all.'

The woman nodded her approbation. 'That is good,' she said. 'That is what I expect of a princess of Spain.'

'And Princess of Wales,' her daughter added.

This is me, this little five-year-old girl, perching on the treasure chest with a face white as marble and blue eyes wide with fear, refusing to tremble, biting my lips so I don't cry out again. This is me, conceived in a camp by parents who are rivals as well as lovers, born in a moment snatched between battles in a winter of torrential floods, raised by a strong woman in armour, on campaign for all of my childhood, destined to fight for my place in the world, to fight for my faith against another, to fight for my word against another's: born to fight for my name for my faith and for my throne. I am Catalina, Princess of Spain, daughter of the two greatest monarchs the world has ever known: Isabella of Castile and Ferdinand of Aragon. Their names are feared from Cairo to Baghdad to Constantinople to India and beyond by all the Moors in all their many nations: Turks, Indians, Chinamen; our rivals, admirers, enemies till death. My parents' names are blessed by the Pope as the finest kings to defend the faith against the might of Islam, they are the greatest crusaders of Christendom as well as the first kings of Spain; and I am their youngest daughter, Catalina, Princess of Wales, and I will be Queen of England.

Since I was a child of three I have been betrothed in marriage to Prince Arthur, son of King Henry of England, and when I am fifteen I shall sail to his country in a beautiful ship with my standard flying at the top of the mast, and I shall be his wife and then his queen. His country is rich and fertile – filled with fountains and the sound of dripping water, ripe with warm fruits and scented with flowers; and it will be my country, I shall take care of it. All this has been arranged almost since my birth, I have always known it will be; and though I shall be sorry to leave my mother and my home, after all, I was born a princess, destined to be queen, and I know my duty.

I am a child of absolute convictions. I know that I will be Queen of England because it is God's will, and it is my mother's order. And I believe, as does everyone in my world, that God and my mother are generally of the same mind; and their will is always done.

In the morning the campsite outside Granada was a dank mess of smouldering hangings, destroyed tents, heaps of smoky forage, everything destroyed by one candle carelessly set. There could be nothing but retreat. The Spanish army had ridden out in its pride to set siege to the last great kingdom of the Moors in Spain, and had been burned to nothing. It would have to ride back again, to regroup.

'No, we don't retreat,' Isabella of Spain ruled.

The generals, called to a makeshift meeting under a singed awning, batted away the flies that were swarming around the camp, feasting off the wreckage.

'Your Majesty, we have lost for this season,' one of the generals said gently to her. 'It is not a matter of pride nor of willingness. We have no tents, we have no shelter, we have been destroyed by ill luck. We will have to go back and provision ourselves once more, set the siege again. Your husband –' he nodded to the dark, handsome man who stood slightly to one side of the group, listening '– he knows this. We all know this. We will set the siege again, they will not defeat us. But a good general knows when he has to retreat.'

Every man nodded. Common sense dictated that nothing could be done but release the Moors of Granada from their siege for this season. The battle would keep. It had been coming for seven centuries. Each year had seen generations of Christian kings increase their lands at the cost of the Moors. Every battle had pushed back the time-honoured Moorish rule of al Andalus a little further to the south. Another year would make no difference. The little girl, her back against a damp tent post that smelled of wet embers, watched her mother's serene expression. It never changed.

'Indeed it *is* a matter of pride,' she corrected him. 'We are fighting an enemy who understands pride better than any other. If we crawl away in our singed clothes, with our burned carpets rolled up under our arms, they will laugh themselves to al-Yanna, to their paradise. I cannot permit it. But more than all of this: it is God's will that we fight the Moors, it is God's will that we go forwards. It is not God's will that we go back. So we must go forwards.'

The child's father turned his head with a quizzical smile but he did not dissent. When the generals looked to him he made a small gesture with his hand. 'The queen is right,' he said. 'The queen is always right.'

'But we have no tents, we have no camp!'

He directed the question to her. 'What do you think?'

'We shall build one,' she decided.

'Your Majesty, we have laid waste to the countryside for miles all around. I daresay we could not sew so much as a kamiz for the Princess of Wales. There is no cloth. There is no canvas. There are no watercourses, no crops in the fields. We have broken the canals and ploughed up the crops. We have laid them waste; but it is we that are destroyed.'

'So we build in stone. I take it we have stone?'

The king turned a brief laugh into clearing his throat. 'We are surrounded by a plain of arid rocks, my love,' he said. 'One thing we do have is stone.'

'Then we will build, not a camp, but a city of stone.'

'It cannot be done!'

She turned to her husband. 'It will be done,' she said. 'It is God's will and mine.'

He nodded. 'It will be done.' He gave her a quick, private smile. 'It is my duty to see that God's will is done; and my pleasure to enforce yours.'

The army, defeated by fire, turned instead to the elements of earth and water. They toiled like slaves in the heat of the sun and the chill of the evenings. They worked the fields like peasants where they had thought they would triumphantly advance. Everyone, cavalry officers, generals, the great lords of the country, the cousins of kings, was expected to toil in the heat of the sun and lie on hard, cold ground at night. The Moors, watching from the high, impenetrable battlements of the red fort on the hill above Granada, conceded that the Christians had courage. No-one could say that they were not determined. And equally, everyone knew that they were doomed. No force could take the red fort at Granada, it had never fallen in two centuries. It was placed high on a cliff, overlooking a plain that was itself a wide, bleached bowl. It could not be surprised by a hidden attack. The cliff of red rock that towered up from the plain became imperceptibly the walls of red stone of the castle, rising high and higher; no scaling ladders could reach the top, no party could climb the sheer face.

Perhaps it could be betrayed by a traitor; but what fool could be found who would abandon the steady, serene power of the Moors, with all the known world behind them, with an undeniable faith to support them, to join the rabid madness of the Christian army whose kings owned only a few mountainous acres of Europe and who were hopelessly divided? Who would want to leave al-Yanna, the garden, which was the image of paradise itself, inside the walls of the most beautiful palace in Spain, the most beautiful palace in Europe, for the rugged anarchy of the castles and fortresses of Castile and Aragon?

Reinforcements would come for the Moors from Africa, they had kin and allies from Morocco to Senegal. Support would come for them from Baghdad, from Constantinople. Granada might look small compared with the conquests that Ferdinand and Isabella had made, but standing behind Granada was the greatest empire in the world – the empire of the Prophet, praise be his name.

But, amazingly, day after day, week after week, slowly, fighting the heat of the spring days and the coldness of the nights, the Christians did the impossible. First there was a chapel built in the round like a mosque, since the local builders could do that most quickly; then, a small house, flat-roofed inside an Arabic courtyard, for King Ferdinand, Queen Isabella and the royal family: the Infante, their precious son and heir, the three older girls, Isabel, Maria, Juana, and Catalina the baby. The queen asked for nothing more than a roof and walls, she had been at war for years, she did not expect luxury. Then there were a dozen stone hovels around them where the greatest lords reluctantly took some shelter. Then, because the queen was a hard woman, there were stables for the horses and secure stores for the gunpowder and the precious explosives for which she had pawned her own jewels to buy from Venice; then, and only then, were built barracks and kitchens, stores and halls. Then there was a little town, built in stone, where once there had been a little camp. No-one thought it could be done; but, bravo! it was done. They called it Santa Fe and Isabella had triumphed over misfortune once again. The doomed siege of Granada by the determined, foolish Christian kings would continue.

Catalina, Princess of Wales, came upon one of the great lords of the Spanish camp in whispered conference with his friends. 'What are you doing, Don Hernando?' she asked with all the precocious confidence of a five-year-old who had never been far from her mother's side, whose father could deny her very little.

'Nothing, Infanta,' Hernando Perez del Pulgar said with a smile that told her that she could ask again.

'You are.'

'It's a secret.'

'I won't tell.'

'Oh! Princess! You would tell. It is such a great secret! Too big a secret for a little girl.'

'I won't! I really won't! I truly won't!' She thought. 'I promise upon Wales.'

'On Wales! On your own country?'

'On England?'

'On England? Your inheritance?'

She nodded. 'On Wales and on England, and on Spain itself.'

'Well, then. If you make such a sacred promise I will tell you. Swear that you won't tell your mother?'

She nodded, her blue eyes wide.

'We are going to get into the Alhambra. I know a gate, a little postern gate, that is not well guarded, where we can force an entry. We are going to go in, and guess what?'

She shook her head vigorously, her auburn plait swinging beneath her veil like a puppy's plump tail.

'We are going to say our prayers in their mosque. And I am going to leave an Ave Maria stabbed to the floor with my dagger. What d'you think of that?'

She was too young to realise that they were going to a certain death. She had no idea of the sentries at every gate, of the merciless rage of the Moors. Her eyes lit up in excitement. 'You are?'

'Isn't it a wonderful plan?'

'When are you going?'

'Tonight! This very night!'

'I shan't sleep till you come back!'

'You must pray for me, and then go to sleep, and I will come myself, Princess, and tell you and your mother all about it in the morning.'

She swore she would never sleep and she lay awake, quite rigid in her little cot-bed, while her maid tossed and turned on the rug at the door. Slowly, her eyelids drooped until the lashes lay on the round cheeks, the little plump hands unclenched and Catalina slept.

But in the morning, he did not come, his horse was missing from its stall and his friends were absent. For the first time in her life, the little girl had some sense of the danger he had run – mortal danger, and for nothing but glory and to be featured in some song.

'Where is he?' she asked. 'Where is Hernando?'

The silence of her maid, Madilla, warned her. 'He will come?' she asked, suddenly doubtful. 'He will come back?'

Slowly, it dawns on me that perhaps he will not come back, that life is not like a ballad, where a vain hope is always triumphant and a handsome man is never cut down in his youth. But if he can fail and die, then can my father die? Can my mother die? Can I? Even I? Little Catalina, Infanta of Spain and Princess of Wales?

I kneel in the sacred circular space of my mother's newly built chapel; but I am not praying. I am puzzling over this strange world that is suddenly opening up before me. If we are in the right – and I am sure of that; if these handsome young men are in the right – and I am sure of that – if we and our cause are under the especial hand of God, then how can we ever fail?

But if I have misunderstood something, then something is very wrong, and we are all indeed mortal, perhaps we can fail. Even hand-some Hernando Perez del Pulgar and his laughing friends, even my mother and father can fail. If Hernando can die, then so too can my mother and father. And if this is so, then what safety is there in the world? If Madre can die, like a common soldier, like a mule pulling a baggage cart, as I have seen men and mules die, then how can the world go on? How could there be a God?

Then it was time for her mother's audience for petitioners and friends, and suddenly he was there, in his best suit, his beard combed, his eyes dancing, and the whole story spilled out: how they had dressed in their Arab clothes so as to pass for townspeople in the darkness, how they had crept in through the postern gate, how they had dashed up to the mosque, how they had kneeled and gabbled an Ave Maria and stabbed the prayer into the floor of the mosque, and then, surprised by guards, they had fought their way, hand to hand, thrust and parry, blades flashing in the moonlight; back down the narrow street, out of the door that they had forced only moments earlier, and were away into the night before the full alarm had been sounded. Not a scratch on them, not a man lost. A triumph for them and a slap in the face for Granada.

It was a great joke to play on the Moors, it was the funniest thing in the world to take a Christian prayer into the very heart of their holy place. It was the most wonderful gesture to insult them. The queen was delighted, the king too, the princess and her sisters looked at their champion, Hernando Perez del Pulgar, as if he were a hero from the romances, a knight from the time of Arthur at Camelot. Catalina clapped her hands in delight at the story, and commanded that he tell it and re-tell it, over and over again. But in the back of her mind, pushed far away from thought, she remembered the chill she had felt when she had thought that he was not coming back.

Next, they waited for the reply from the Moors. It was certain to happen. They knew that their enemy would see the venture as the challenge that it was, there was bound to be a response. It was not long in coming.

The queen and her children were visiting Zubia, a village near to Granada, so Her Majesty could see the impregnable walls of the fort herself. They had ridden out with a light guard and the commander was white with horror when he came dashing up to them in the little village square and shouted that the gates of the red fort had opened and the Moors were thundering out, the full army, armed for attack. There was no time to get back to camp, the queen and the three princesses could never outrun Moorish horsemen on Arab stallions, there was nowhere to hide, there was nowhere even to make a stand.

In desperate haste Queen Isabella climbed to the flat roof of the nearest house, pulling the little princess by her hand up the crumbling stairs, her sisters running behind. 'I have to see! I have to see!' she exclaimed.

'Madre! You are hurting me!'

'Quiet, child. We have to see what they intend.'

'Are they coming for us?' the child whimpered, her little voice muffled by her own plump hand.

'They may be. I have to see.'

It was a raiding party, not the full force. They were led by their champion, a giant of a man, dark as mahogany, a glint of a smile beneath his helmet, riding a huge black horse as if he were Night riding to overwhelm them. His horse snarled like a dog at the watching guard, its teeth bared.

'Madre, who is that man?' the Princess of Wales whispered to her mother, staring from the vantage point of the flat roof of the house.

'That is the Moor called Yarfe, and I am afraid he has come for your friend, Hernando.'

'His horse looks so frightening, like it wants to bite.'

'He has cut off its lips to make it snarl at us. But we are not made fearful by such things. We are not frightened children.'

'Should we not run away?' asked the frightened child.

Her mother, watching the Moor parade, did not even hear her daughter's whisper.

'You won't let him hurt Hernando, will you? Madre?'

'Hernando laid the challenge. Yarfe is answering it. We will have to fight,' she said levelly. 'Yarfe is a knight, a man of honour. He cannot ignore the challenge.'

'How can he be a man of honour if he is a heretic? A Moor?'

'They are most honourable men, Catalina, though they are unbelievers. And this Yarfe is a hero to them.'

'What will you do? How shall we save ourselves? This man is as big as a giant.'

'I shall pray,' Isabella said. 'And my champion Garallosco de la Vega will answer Yarfe for Hernando.'

As calmly as if she were in her own chapel at Cordoba, Isabella kneeled on the roof of the little house and gestured that her daughters should do the same. Sulkily, Catalina's older sister, Juana, dropped to her knees, the princesses Isabel and Maria, her other two older sisters, followed suit. Catalina saw, peeping through her clasped hands as she kneeled in prayer, that Maria was shaking with fear, and that Isabel, in her widow's gown, was white with terror.

'Heavenly Father, we pray for the safety of ourselves, of our cause, and of our army.' Queen Isabella looked up at the brilliantly blue sky. 'We pray for the victory of Your champion, Garallosco de la Vega, at this time of his trial.'

'Amen,' the girls said promptly, and then followed the direction of their mother's gaze to where the ranks of the Spanish guard were drawn up, watchful and silent.

'If God is protecting him . . .' Catalina started.

'Silence,' her mother said gently. 'Let him do his work, let God do His, and let me do mine.' She closed her eyes in prayer.

Catalina turned to her eldest sister and pulled at her sleeve. 'Isabel, if God is protecting him, then how can he be in danger?'

Isabel looked down at her little sister. 'God does not make the way smooth for those He loves,' she said in a harsh whisper. 'He sends hardships to try them. Those that God loves the best are those who suffer the worst. I know that. I, who lost the only man that I will ever love. You know that. Think about Job, Catalina.'

'Then how shall we win?' the little girl demanded. 'Since God loves Madre, won't He send her the worst hardships? And so how shall we ever win?'

'Hush,' their mother said. 'Watch. Watch and pray with faith.'

Their small guard and the Moorish raiding party were drawn up opposite each other, ready for battle. Then Yarfe rode forwards on his great black charger. Something white bobbed at the ground, tied to the horse's glossy black tail. There was a gasp as the soldiers in the front rank recognised what he had. It was the Ave Maria that Hernando had left speared to the floor of the mosque. The Moor had tied it to the tail of his horse as a calculated insult, and now rode the great creature forwards and back before the Christian ranks, and smiled when he heard their roar of rage.

'Heretic,' Queen Isabella whispered. 'A man damned to hell. God strike him dead and scourge his sin.'

The queen's champion, de la Vega, turned his horse and rode towards the little house where the royal guards ringed the court-yard, the tiny olive tree, the doorway. He pulled up his horse beside the olive tree and doffed his helmet, looking up at his queen and the princesses on the roof. His dark hair was curly and sparkling with sweat from the heat, his dark eyes sparkled with anger. 'Your Grace, do I have your leave to answer his challenge?'

'Yes,' the queen said, never shrinking for a moment. 'Go with God, Garallosco de la Vega.'

'That big man will kill him,' Catalina said, pulling at her mother's long sleeve. 'Tell him he must not go. Yarfe is so much bigger. He will murder de la Vega!'

'It will be as God wills,' Isabella maintained, closing her eyes in prayer.

'Mother! Your Majesty! He is a giant. He will kill our champion.'

Her mother opened her blue eyes and looked down at her daughter

16

and saw her little face was flushed with distress and her eyes were filling with tears. 'It will be as God wills it,' she repeated firmly. 'You have to have faith that you are doing God's will. Sometimes you will not understand, sometimes you will doubt, but if you are doing God's will you cannot be wrong, you cannot go wrong. Remember it, Catalina. Whether we win this challenge or lose it, it makes no difference. We are soldiers of Christ. You are a soldier of Christ. If we live or die, it makes no difference. We will die in faith, that is all that matters. This battle is God's battle, He will send a victory, if not today, then tomorrow. And whichever man wins today, we do not doubt that God will win, and we will win in the end.'

'But de la Vega . . .' Catalina protested, her fat lower lip trembling.

'Perhaps God will take him to His own this afternoon,' her mother said steadily. 'We should pray for him.'

Juana made a face at her little sister, but when their mother kneeled again the two girls clasped hands for comfort. Isabel kneeled beside them, Maria beside her. All of them squinted through their closed eyelids to the plain where the bay charger of de la Vega rode out from the line of the Spaniards, and the black horse of the Moor trotted proudly before the Saracens.

The queen kept her eyes closed until she had finished her prayer, she did not even hear the roar as the two men took up their places, lowered their visors, and clasped their lances.

Catalina leapt to her feet, leaning over the low parapet so that she could see the Spanish champion. His horse thundered towards the other, racing legs a blur, the black horse came as fast from the opposite direction. The clash when the two lances smacked into solid armour could be heard on the roof of the little house, as both men were flung from their saddles by the force of the impact, the lances smashed, their breastplates buckled. It was nothing like the ritualised jousts of the court. It was a savage impact designed to break a neck or stop a heart.

'He is down! He is dead!' Catalina cried out.

'He is stunned,' her mother corrected her. 'See, he is getting up.'

The Spanish knight staggered to his feet, unsteady as a drunkard from the heavy blow to his chest. The bigger man was up already, helmet and heavy breastplate cast aside, coming for him with a huge sickle sword at the ready, the light flashing off the razor-sharp edge. De la Vega drew his own great weapon. There was a tremendous crash as the swords smacked together and then the two men locked blades and struggled, each trying to force the other down. They circled clumsily, staggering under the weight of their armour and from their concussion; but there could be no doubt that the Moor was the stronger man. The watchers could see that de la Vega was yielding under the pressure. He tried to spring back and get free; but the weight of the Moor was bearing down on him and he stumbled and fell. At once the black knight was on top of him, forcing him downwards. De la Vega's hand closed uselessly on his long sword, he could not bring it up. The Moor raised his sword to his victim's throat, ready to give the death blow, his face a black mask of concentration, his teeth gritted. Suddenly he gave a loud cry and fell back. De la Vega rolled up, scrabbled to his feet, crawling on his hands and knees like a rising dog.

The Moor was down, plucking at his breast, his great sword dropped to one side. In de la Vega's left hand was a short stabbing dagger stained with blood, a hidden weapon used in a desperate riposte. With a super-human effort the Moor got to his feet, turned his back on the Christian and staggered towards his own ranks. 'I am lost,' he said to the men who ran forwards to catch him. 'We have lost.'

At a hidden signal the great gates of the red fort opened and the soldiers started to pour out. Juana leapt to her feet. 'Madre, we must run!' she screamed. 'They are coming! They are coming in their thousands!'

Isabella did not rise from her knees, even when her daughter dashed across the roof and ran down the stairs. 'Juana, come back,' she ordered in a voice like a whip crack. 'Girls, you will pray.'

She rose and went to the parapet. First she looked to the marshalling of her army, saw that the officers were setting the men into formation ready for a charge as the Moorish army, terrifying in their forward rush, came pouring on. Then she glanced down to see Juana, in a frenzy of fear, peeping around the garden wall, unsure whether to run for her horse or back to her mother.

Isabella, who loved her daughter, said not another word. She returned to the other girls and kneeled with them. 'Let us pray,' she said and closed her eyes.

'She didn't even look!' Juana repeated incredulously that night when they were in their room, washing their hands and changing their dirty clothes, Juana's tear-streaked face finally clean. 'There we are, in the middle of a battle, and she closes her eyes!'

'She knew that she would do more good appealing for the intercession of God than running around crying,' Isabel said pointedly. 'And it gave the army better heart than anything else to see her, on her knees, in full sight of everyone.'

'What if she had been hit by an arrow or a spear?'

'She was not. We were not. And we won the battle. And you, Juana, behaved like a half-mad peasant. I was ashamed of you. I don't know what gets into you. Are you mad or just wicked?'

'Oh, who cares what you think, you stupid widow?'

6th January 1492

Day by day the heart went out of the Moors. The Queen's Skirmish turned out to be their last battle. Their champion was dead, their city encircled, they were starving in the land that their fathers had made fertile. Worse, the promised support from Africa had failed them, the Turks had sworn friendship but the janissaries did not come, their king had lost his nerve, his son was a hostage with the Christians, and before them were the Princes of Spain, Isabella and Ferdinand, with all the power of Christendom behind them, with a holy war declared and a Christian crusade gathering pace with the scent of success. Within a few days of the meeting of the champions, Boabdil, the King of Granada, had agreed terms of peace, and a few days after, in the ceremony planned with all the grace that was typical of the Moors of Spain, he came down on foot to the iron gates of the city with the keys to the Alhambra Palace on a silken pillow and handed them over to the King and Queen of Spain in a complete surrender.

Granada, the red fort that stood above the city to guard it, and the gorgeous palace which was hidden inside the walls – the Alhambra – were given to Ferdinand and to Isabella.

Dressed in the gorgeous silks of their defeated enemy, turbaned, slippered, glorious as caliphs, the Spanish royal family, glittering with the spoils of Spain, took Granada. That afternoon Catalina, the Princess of Wales, walked with her parents up the winding, steep path through the shade of tall trees, to the most beautiful palace in Europe, slept that night in the brilliantly tiled harem and woke to the sound of rippling water in marble fountains, and thought herself a Moorish princess born to luxury and beauty, as well as a Princess of England.

And this is my life, from this day of victory. I had been born as a child of the camp, following the army from siege to battle, seeing things that perhaps no child should see, facing adult fears every day. I had marched past the bodies of dead soldiers rotting in the spring heat because there was no time to bury them, I had ridden behind mules whipped into

staggering bloodstained corpses, pulling my father's guns through the high passes of the Sierra. I saw my mother slap a man's face for weeping with exhaustion. I heard children of my own age crying for their parents burned at the stake for heresy; but at this moment, when we dressed ourselves in embroidered silk and walked into the red fort of Granada and through the gates to the white pearl that is the Alhambra Palace, at this moment I became a princess for the first time.

I became a girl raised in the most beautiful palace in Christendom, protected by an impregnable fort, blessed by God among all others, I became a girl of immense, unshakeable confidence in the God that had brought us to victory, and in my destiny as His most favourite child and my mother's most favourite daughter.

Alhambra proved to me, once and for all, that I was uniquely favoured by God, as my mother had been favoured by God. I was his chosen child, raised in the most beautiful palace in Christendom, and destined for the highest things.

The Spanish family with their officers ahead and the royal guard behind, glorious as Sultans, entered the fort through the enormous square tower known as the Justice Gate. As the shadow of the first arch of the tower fell on Isabella's upturned face the trumpeters played a great shout of defiance, like Joshua before the walls of Jericho, as if they would frighten away the lingering devils of the infidel. At once there was an echo to the blast of sound, a shuddering sigh, from everyone gathered inside the gateway, pressed back against the golden walls, the women half-veiled in their robes, the men standing tall and proud and silent, watching, to see what the conquerors would do next. Catalina looked above the sea of heads and saw the flowing shapes of Arabic script engraved on the gleaming walls.

'What does that say?' she demanded of Madilla, her nursemaid.

Madilla squinted upwards. 'I don't know,' she said crossly. She always denied her Moorish roots. She always tried to pretend that she knew nothing of the Moors or their lives though she had been born and bred a Moor herself and only converted – according to Juana – for convenience.

'Tell us, or we'll pinch you,' Juana offered sweetly.

The young woman scowled at the two sisters. 'It says: "May God allow the justice of Islam to prevail within".'

Catalina hesitated for a moment, hearing the proud ring of certainty, a determination to match her own mother's voice.

'Well, He hasn't,' Juana said smartly. 'Allah has deserted the Alhambra and Isabella has arrived. And if you Moors knew Isabella like we do, you would know that the greatest power is coming in and the lesser power going out.'

'God save the queen,' Madilla replied quickly. 'I know Queen Isabella well enough.'

As she spoke the great doors before them, black wood studded with black nails, swung open on their black hammered hinges, and with another blast of trumpets the king and queen strode into the inner courtyard.

Like dancers rehearsed till they were step-perfect, the Spanish guard peeled off to right and left inside the town walls, checking that the place was safe, and no despairing soldiers were preparing a last ambush. The great fort of the Alcazaba, built like the prow of a ship, jutting out over the plain of Granada, was to their left, and the men poured into it, running across the parade square, ringing the walls, running up and down the towers. Finally, Isabella the queen looked up to the sky, shaded her eyes with her hand clinking with Moorish gold bracelets, and laughed aloud to see the sacred banner of St James and the silver cross of the crusade flying where the crescent had been.

Then she turned to see the domestic servants of the palace slowly approaching, their heads bowed. They were led by the Grand Vizier, his height emphasised by his flowing robes, his piercing black eyes meeting hers, scanning King Ferdinand at her side, and the royal family behind them: the prince and the four princesses. The king and the prince were dressed as richly as sultans, wearing rich, embroidered tunics over their trousers, the queen and the princesses were wearing the traditional kamiz tunics made from the finest silks, over white linen trousers, with veils falling from their heads held back by filets of gold.

'Your Royal Highnesses, it is my honour and duty to welcome you to the Alhambra Palace,' the Grand Vizier said, as if it were the most ordinary thing in the world to hand over the most beautiful palace in Christendom to armed invaders.

The queen and her husband exchanged one brief glance. 'You can take us in,' she said.

The Grand Vizier bowed and led the way. The queen glanced back at her children. 'Come along, girls,' she said and went ahead of them, through the gardens surrounding the palace, down some steps and into the discreet doorway.

'This is the main entrance?' She hesitated before the small door set in the unmarked wall.

The man bowed. 'Your Highness, it is.'

Isabella said nothing but Catalina saw her raise her eyebrows as if she did not think much of it, and then they all went inside.

But the little doorway is like a keyhole to a treasure chest of boxes, the one opening out from another. The man leads us through them like a slave opening doors to a treasury. Their very names are a poem: the Golden Chamber, the Courtyard of the Myrtles, the Hall of the Ambassadors, the Courtyard of the Lions, or the Hall of the Two Sisters. It will take us weeks to find our way from one exquisitely tiled room to another. It will take us months to stop marvelling at the pleasure of

the sound of water running down the marble gulleys in the rooms, flowing to a white marble fountain that always spills over with the cleanest, freshest water of the mountains. And I will never tire of looking through the white stucco tracery to the view of the plain beyond, the mountains, the blue sky and golden hills. Every window is like a frame for a picture, they are designed to make you stop, look and marvel. Every window frame is like white-work embroidery – the stucco is so fine, so delicate, it is like sugar-work by confectioners, not like anything real.

We move into the harem as the easiest and most convenient rooms for my three sisters and me, and the harem servants light the braziers in the cool evenings, and scatter the scented herbs as if we were the sultanas who lived secluded behind the screens for so long. We have always worn Moorish dress at home and sometimes at great state occasions so still there is the whisper of silks and the slap of slippers on marble floors, as if nothing has changed. Now, we study where the slave girls read, we walk in the gardens that were planted to delight the favourites of the sultan. We eat their fruits, we love the taste of their sherbets, we tie their flowers into garlands for our own heads, and we run down their allées where the heavy scent of roses and honeysuckle is sweet in the cool of the morning.

We bathe in the hammam, standing stock still while the servants lather us all over with a rich soap that smells of flowers. Then they pour golden ewer after golden ewer of hot water over us, splashing from head to toe, to wash us clean. We are soothed with rose oil, wrapped in fine sheets and lie, half-drunk with sensual pleasure, on the warm marble table that dominates the entire room, under the golden ceiling where the star-shaped openings admit dazzling rays of sunlight into the shadowy peace of the place. One girl manicures our toes while another works on our hands, shaping the nails and painting delicate patterns of henna. We let the old woman pluck our eyebrows, paint our eyelashes. We are served as if we are sultanas, with all the riches of Spain and all the luxury of the East, and we surrender utterly to the delight of the palace. It captivates us, we swoon into submission; the so-called victors.

Even Isabel, grieving for the loss of her husband, starts to smile again. Even Juana, who is usually so moody and so sulky, is at peace. And I become the pet of the court, the favourite of the gardeners who let me pick my own peaches from the trees, the darling of the harem where I am taught to play and dance and sing, and the favourite of the kitchen where they let me watch them preparing the sweet pastries and dishes of honey and almonds of Arabia.

My father meets with foreign emissaries in the Hall of the Ambassadors, he takes them to the bath house for talks, like any leisurely sultan. My mother sits cross-legged on the throne of the Nasrids who have ruled here for generations, her bare feet in soft leather slippers, the drapery of her kamiz falling around her. She listens to the emissaries of the Pope himself, in a chamber that is walled with coloured tiles and dancing with pagan light. It feels like home to her, she was raised in the Alcazar in Seville, another Moorish palace. We walk in their gardens, we bathe in their hammam, we step into their scented leather slippers and we live a life that is more refined and more luxurious than they could dream of in Paris or London or Rome. We live graciously. We live, as we have always aspired to do, like Moors. Our fellow Christians herd goats in the mountains, pray at roadside cairns to the Madonna, are terrified by superstition and lousy with disease, live dirty and die young. We learn from Moslem scholars, we are attended by their doctors, study the stars in the sky which they have named, count with their numbers which start at the magical zero, eat of their sweetest fruits and delight in the waters which run through their aqueducts. Their architecture pleases us, at every turn of every corner we know that we are living inside beauty. Their power now keeps us safe; the Alcazabar is, indeed, invulnerable to attack once more. We learn their poetry, we laugh at their games, we delight in their gardens, in their fruits, we bathe in the waters they have made flow. We are the victors but they have taught us how to rule. Sometimes

I think that we are the barbarians, like those who came after the Romans or the Greeks, who could invade the palaces and capture the aqueducts, and then sit like monkeys on a throne, playing with beauty but not understanding it.

We do not change our faith, at least. Every palace servant has to give lip service to the beliefs of the One True Church. The horns of the mosque are silenced, there is to be no call to prayer in my mother's hearing. And anyone who disagrees can either leave for Africa at once, convert at once, or face the fires of the Inquisition. We do not soften under the spoils of war, we never forget that we are victors and that we won our victory by force of arms and by the will of God. We made a solemn promise to poor King Boabdil, that his people, the Moslems, should be as safe under our rule as the Christians were safe under his. We promise the convivencia – a way of living together – and they believe that we will make a Spain where anyone, Moor or Christian or Jew, can live quietly and with self-respect since all of us are 'People of the Book'. Their mistake is that they meant that truce, and they trusted that truce, and we – as it turns out – do not.

We betray our word in three months, expelling the Jews and threatening the Moslems. Everyone must convert to the True Faith and then, if there is any shadow of doubt, or any suspicion against them, their faith will be tested by the Holy Inquisition. It is the only way to make one nation: through one faith. It is the only way to make one people out of the great varied diversity which had been al Andalus. My mother builds a chapel in the council chamber and where it had once said 'Enter and ask. Do not be afraid to seek justice for here you will find it', in the beautiful shapes of Arabic, she prays to a sterner, more intolerant God than Allah; and no-one comes for justice any more.

But nothing can change the nature of the palace. Not even the stamp of our soldiers' feet on the marble floors can shake the centuries-old sense of peace. I make Madilla teach me what the flowing inscriptions mean in every room, and my favourite is not the promises of justice, but the words written in the Courtyard of the Two Sisters which says:

26

'Have you ever seen such a beautiful garden?' and then answers itself: 'We have never seen a garden with greater abundance of fruit, nor sweeter, nor more perfumed.'

It is not truly a palace, not even as those we had known at Cordoba or Toledo. It is not a castle, nor a fort. It was built first and foremost as a garden with rooms of exquisite luxury so that one could live outside. It is a series of courtyards designed for flowers and people alike. It is a dream of beauty: walls, tiles, pillars melting into flowers, climbers, fruit and herbs. The Moors believe that a garden is a paradise on earth, and they have spent fortunes over the centuries to make this 'al-Yanna': the word that means garden, secret place, and paradise.

I know that I love it. Even as a little child I know that this is an exceptional place; that I will never find anywhere more lovely. And even as a child I know that I cannot stay here. It is God's will and my mother's will that I must leave al-Yanna, my secret place, my garden, my paradise. It is to be my destiny that I should find the most beautiful place in all the world when I am just six years old, and then leave it when I am fifteen; as homesick as Boabdil, as if happiness and peace for me will only ever be short-lived.

Dogmersfield Palace, Hampshire, Autumn 1501

'I say, you cannot come in! If you were the King of England himself – you could not come in.'

'I *am* the King of England,' Henry Tudor said, without a flicker of amusement. 'And she can either come out right now, or I damned well will come in and my son will follow me.'

'The Infanta has already sent word to the king that she cannot see him,' the duenna said witheringly. 'The noblemen of her court rode out to explain to him that she is in seclusion, as a lady of Spain. Do you think the King of England would come riding down the road when the Infanta has refused to receive him? What sort of a man do you think he is?'

'Exactly like this one,' he said and thrust his fist with the great gold ring towards her face. The Count de Cabra came into the hall in a rush, and at once recognised the lean forty-year-old man threatening the Infanta's duenna with a clenched fist, a few aghast servitors behind him, and gasped out: 'The king!'

At the same moment the duenna recognised the new badge of England, the combined roses of York and Lancaster, and recoiled. The count skidded to a halt and threw himself into a low bow.

'It is the king,' he hissed, his voice muffled by speaking with his head on his knees. The duenna gave a little gasp of horror and dropped into a deep curtsey.

'Get up,' the king said shortly. 'And fetch her.'

'But she is a princess of Spain, Your Grace,' the woman said, rising but with her head still bowed low. 'She is to stay in seclusion. She cannot be seen by you before her wedding day. This is the tradition. Her gentlemen went out to explain to you . . .'

'It's *your* tradition. It's not *my* tradition. And since she is my daughter-in-law in my country, under my laws, she will obey my tradition.'

'She has been brought up most carefully, most modestly, most properly . . .'

'Then she will be very shocked to find an angry man in her bedroom. Madam, I suggest that you get her up at once.'

'I will not, Your Grace. I take my orders from the Queen of Spain herself and she charged me to make sure that every respect was shown to the Infanta and that her behaviour was in every way . . .'

'Madam, you can take your working orders from me; or your marching orders from me. I don't care which. Now send the girl out or I swear on my crown I will come in and if I catch her naked in bed then she won't be the first woman I have ever seen in such a case. But she had better pray that she is the prettiest.'

The Spanish duenna went quite white at the insult.

'Choose,' the king said stonily.

'I cannot fetch the Infanta,' she said stubbornly.

'Dear God! That's it! Tell her I am coming in at once.'

She scuttled backwards like an angry crow, her face blanched with shock. Henry gave her a few moments to prepare, and then called her bluff by striding in behind her.

The room was lit only by candles and firelight. The covers of the bed were turned back as if the girl had hastily jumped up. Henry registered the intimacy of being in her bedroom, with her sheets still warm, the scent of her lingering in the enclosed space, before he looked at her. She was standing by the bed, one small white hand on the carved wooden post. She had a cloak of dark blue thrown over her shoulders and her white nightgown trimmed with priceless lace peeped through the opening at the front. Her rich auburn hair, plaited for sleep, hung down her back, but her face was completely shrouded in a hastily thrown mantilla of dark lace.

Dona Elvira darted between the girl and the king. 'This is the Infanta,' she said. 'Veiled until her wedding day.'

'Not on my money,' Henry Tudor said bitterly. 'I'll see what I've bought, thank you.'

He stepped forwards. The desperate duenna nearly threw herself to her knees. 'Her modesty . . .'

'Has she got some awful mark?' he demanded, driven to voice his deepest fear. 'Some blemish? Is she scarred by the pox and they did not tell me?'

'No! I swear.'

Silently, the girl put out her white hand and took the ornate lace hem of her veil. Her duenna gasped a protest but could do nothing to stop the princess as she raised the veil, and then flung it back. Her clear blue eyes stared into the lined, angry face of Henry Tudor without wavering. The king drank her in, and then gave a little sigh of relief at the sight of her.

She was an utter beauty: a smooth, rounded face, a straight, long nose, a full, sulky, sexy mouth. Her chin was up, he saw; her gaze challenging. This was no shrinking maiden fearing ravishment. This was a fighting princess standing on her dignity even in this most appalling moment of embarrassment.

He bowed. 'I am Henry Tudor, King of England,' he said.

She curtseyed.

He stepped forwards and saw her curb her instinct to flinch away. He took her firmly at the shoulders, and kissed one warm, smooth cheek and then the other. The perfume of her hair and the warm, female smell of her body came to him and he felt desire pulse in his groin and at his temples. Quickly he stepped back and let her go.

'You are welcome to England,' he said. He cleared his throat. 'You will forgive my impatience to see you. My son too is on his way to visit you.'

'I beg your pardon,' she said icily, speaking in perfectly phrased French. 'I was not informed until a few moments ago that Your Grace was insisting on the honour of this unexpected visit.'

Henry fell back a little from the whip of her temper. 'I have a right . . .'

She shrugged, an absolutely Spanish gesture. 'Of course. You have every right over me.'

At the ambiguous, provocative words, he was again aware of his closeness to her: of the intimacy of the small room, the tester bed hung with rich draperies, the sheets invitingly turned back, the pillow still impressed with the shape of her head. It was a scene for ravishment, not for a royal greeting. Again he felt the secret thud-thud of lust.

'I'll see you outside,' he said abruptly, as if it was her fault that he could not rid himself of the flash in his mind of what it would be like to have this ripe little beauty that he had bought. What would it be like if he had bought her for himself, rather than for his son?

'I shall be honoured,' she said coldly.

He got himself out of the room briskly enough, and nearly collided with Prince Arthur, hovering anxiously in the doorway.

'Fool,' he remarked.

Prince Arthur, pale with nerves, pushed his blond fringe back from his face, stood still and said nothing.

'I'll send that duenna home at the first moment I can,' the king said. 'And the rest of them. She can't make a little Spain in England, my son. The country won't stand for it, and I damned well won't stand for it.'

31

'People don't object. The country people seem to love the princess,' Arthur suggested mildly. 'Her escort says . . .'

'Because she wears a stupid hat. Because she is odd: Spanish, rare. Because she is young and –' he broke off '– pretty.'

'Is she?' he gasped. 'I mean: is she?'

'Haven't I just gone in to make sure? But no Englishman will stand for any Spanish nonsense once they get over the novelty. And neither will I. This is a marriage to cement an alliance; not to flatter her vanity. Whether they like her or not, she's marrying you. Whether you like her or not, she's marrying you. Whether she likes it or not, she's marrying you. And she'd better get out here now or I won't like her and that will be the only thing that can make a difference.'

I have to go out, I have won only the briefest of reprieves and I know he is waiting for me outside the door to my bedchamber and he has demonstrated, powerfully enough, that if I do not go to him, then the mountain will come to Mohammed and I will be shamed again.

I brush Dona Elvira aside as a duenna who cannot protect me now, and I go to the door of my rooms. My servants are frozen, like slaves enchanted in a fairy tale by this extraordinary behaviour from a king. My heart hammers in my ears and I know a girl's embarrassment at having to step forwards in public, but also a soldier's desire to let battle be joined, the eagerness to know the worst, to face danger rather than evade it.

Henry of England wants me to meet his son, before his travelling party, without ceremony, without dignity as if we were a scramble of peasants. So be it. He will not find a princess of Spain falling back for fear. I grit my teeth, I smile as my mother commanded me.

I nod to my herald, who is as stunned as the rest of my companions. 'Announce me,' I order him.

His face blank with shock, he throws open the door. 'The Infanta
Catalina, Princess of Spain and Princess of Wales,' he bellows.
   This is me. This is my moment. This is my battle cry.
   I step forwards.

The Spanish Infanta – with her face naked to every man's gaze –
stood in the darkened doorway and then walked into the room, only
a little flame of colour in both cheeks betraying her ordeal.

At his father's side, Prince Arthur swallowed. She was far more
beautiful than he had imagined, and a million times more haughty.
She was dressed in a gown of dark black velvet, slashed to show an
undergown of carnation silk, the neck cut square and low over her
plump breasts, hung with ropes of pearls. Her auburn hair, freed
from the plait, tumbled down her back in a great wave of red-gold.
On her head was a black lace mantilla flung determinedly back. She
swept a deep curtsey and came up with her head held high, graceful
as a dancer.

'I beg your pardon for not being ready to greet you,' she said in
French. 'If I had known you were coming I would have been
prepared.'

'I'm surprised you didn't hear the racket,' the king said. 'I was
arguing at your door for a good ten minutes.'

'I thought it was a pair of porters brawling,' she said coolly.

Arthur suppressed a gasp of horror at her impertinence; but his
father was eyeing her with a smile as if a new filly was showing
promising spirit.

'No. It was me; threatening your lady-in-waiting. I am sorry that
I had to march in on you.'

She inclined her head. 'That was my duenna, Dona Elvira. I am
sorry if she displeased you. Her English is not good. She cannot
have understood what you wanted.'

'I wanted to see my daughter-in-law, and my son wanted to see his bride, and I expect an English princess to behave like an English princess, and not like some damned sequestered girl in a harem. I thought your parents had beaten the Moors. I didn't expect to find them set up as your models.'

Catalina ignored the insult with a slight turn of her head. 'I am sure that you will teach me good English manners,' she said. 'Who better to advise me?' She turned to Prince Arthur and swept him a royal curtsey. 'My lord.'

He faltered in his bow in return, amazed at the serenity that she could muster in this most embarrassing of moments. He reached into his jacket for her present, fumbled with the little purse of jewels, dropped them, picked them up again and finally thrust them towards her, feeling like a fool.

She took them and inclined her head in thanks, but did not open them. 'Have you dined, Your Grace?'

'We'll eat here,' he said bluntly. 'I ordered dinner already.'

'Then can I offer you a drink? Or somewhere to wash and change your clothes before you dine?' She examined the long, lean length of him consideringly, from the mud spattering his pale, lined face to his dusty boots. The English were a prodigiously dirty nation, not even a great house such as this one had an adequate hammam or even piped water. 'Or perhaps you don't like to wash?'

A harsh chuckle was forced from the king. 'You can order me a cup of ale and have them send fresh clothes and hot water to the best bedroom and I'll change before dinner.' He raised a hand. 'You needn't take it as a compliment to you. I always wash before dinner.'

Arthur saw her nip her lower lip with little white teeth as if to refrain from some sarcastic reply. 'Yes, Your Grace,' she said pleasantly. 'As you wish.' She summoned her lady-in-waiting to her side and gave her low-voiced orders in rapid Spanish. The woman curtseyed and led the king from the room.

The princess turned to Prince Arthur.

'*Et tu?*' she asked in Latin. 'And you?'

'I? What?' he stammered.

He felt that she was trying not to sigh with impatience.

'Would you like to wash and change your coat also?'

'I've washed,' he said. As soon as the words were out of his mouth he could have bitten off his own tongue. He sounded like a child being scolded by a nurse, he thought. 'I've washed', indeed. What was he going to do next? Hold out his hands palms-upwards so that she could see he was a good boy?

'Then will you take a glass of wine? Or ale?'

Catalina turned to the table, where the servants were hastily laying cups and flagons.

'Wine.'

She raised a glass and a flagon and the two chinked together, and then chink-chink-chinked again. In amazement, he saw that her hands were trembling.

She poured the wine quickly and held it to him. His gaze went from her hand and the slightly rippled surface of the wine to her pale face.

She was not laughing at him, he saw. She was not at all at ease with him. His father's rudeness had brought out the pride in her, but alone with him she was just a girl, some months older than him, but still just a girl. The daughter of the two most formidable monarchs in Europe; but still just a girl with shaking hands.

'You need not be frightened,' he said very quietly. 'I am sorry about all this.'

He meant – your failed attempt to avoid this meeting, my father's brusque informality, my own inability to stop him or soften him, and, more than anything else, the misery that this business must be for you: coming far from your home among strangers and meeting your new husband, dragged from your bed under protest.

She looked down. He stared at the flawless pallor of her skin, at the fair eyelashes and pale eyebrows.

Then she looked up at him. 'It's all right,' she said. 'I have seen far worse than this, I have been in far worse places than this, and I have known worse men than your father. You need not fear for me. I am afraid of nothing.'

No-one will ever know what it cost me to smile, what it cost me to stand before your father and not tremble. I am not yet sixteen, I am far from my mother, I am in a strange country, I cannot speak the language and I know nobody here. I have no friends but the party of companions and servants that I have brought with me, and they look to me to protect them. They do not think to help me.

I know what I have to do. I have to be a Spanish princess for the English, and an English princess for the Spanish. I have to seem at ease where I am not, and assume confidence when I am afraid. You may be my husband, but I can hardly see you, I have no sense of you yet. I have no time to consider you, I am absorbed in being the princess that your father has bought, the princess that my mother has delivered, the princess that will fulfil the bargain and secure a treaty between England and Spain.

No-one will ever know that I have to pretend to ease, pretend to confidence, pretend to grace. Of course I am afraid. But I will never, never show it. And, when they call my name I will always step forwards.

The king, having washed and taken a couple of glasses of wine before he came to his dinner, was affable with the young princess, determined to overlook their introduction. Once or twice she caught him glancing at her sideways, as if to get the measure of her, and she turned to look at him, full on, one sandy eyebrow slightly raised as if to interrogate him.

'Yes?' he demanded.

'I beg your pardon,' she said equably. 'I thought Your Grace needed something. You glanced at me.'

'I was thinking you're not much like your portrait,' he said.

She flushed a little. Portraits were designed to flatter the sitter, and when the sitter was a royal princess on the marriage market, even more so.

'Better-looking,' Henry said begrudgingly, to reassure her. 'Younger, softer, prettier.'

She did not warm to the praise as he expected her to do. She merely nodded as if it were an interesting observation.

'You had a bad voyage,' Henry remarked.

'Very bad,' she said. She turned to Prince Arthur. 'We were driven back as we set out from Corunna in August and we had to wait for the storms to pass. When we finally set sail it was still terribly rough, and then we were forced into Plymouth. We couldn't get to Southampton at all. We were all quite sure we would be drowned.'

'Well, you couldn't have come overland,' Henry said flatly, thinking of the parlous state of France and the enmity of the French king. 'You'd be a priceless hostage for a king who was heartless enough to take you. Thank God you never fell into enemy hands.'

She looked at him thoughtfully. 'Pray God I never do.'

'Well, your troubles are over now,' Henry concluded. 'The next boat you are on will be the royal barge when you go down the Thames. How shall you like to become Princess of Wales?'

'I have been the Princess of Wales ever since I was three years old,' she corrected him. 'They always called me Catalina, the Infanta, Princess of Wales. I knew it was my destiny.' She looked at Arthur, who still sat silently observing the table. 'I have known we would be married all my life. It was kind of you to write to me so often. It made me feel that we were not complete strangers.'

He flushed. 'I was ordered to write to you,' he said awkwardly. 'As part of my studies. But I liked getting your replies.'

'Good God, boy, you don't exactly sparkle, do you?' asked his father critically.

Arthur flushed scarlet to his ears.

'There was no need to tell her that you were ordered to write,' his father ruled. 'Better to let her think that you were writing of your own choice.'

'I don't mind,' Catalina said quietly. 'I was ordered to reply. And, as it happens, I should like us always to speak the truth to each other.'

The king barked out a laugh. 'Not in a year's time you won't,' he predicted. 'You will be all in favour of the polite lie then. The great saviour of a marriage is mutual ignorance.'

Arthur nodded obediently, but Catalina merely smiled, as if his observations were of interest, but not necessarily true. Henry found himself piqued by the girl, and still aroused by her prettiness.

'I daresay your father does not tell your mother every thought that crosses his mind,' he said, trying to make her look at him again.

He succeeded. She gave him a long, slow, considering gaze from her blue eyes. 'Perhaps he does not,' she conceded. 'I would not know. It is not fitting that I should know. But whether he tells her or not: my mother knows everything anyway.'

He laughed. Her dignity was quite delightful in a girl whose head barely came up to his chest. 'She is a visionary, your mother? She has the gift of Sight?'

She did not laugh in reply. 'She is wise,' she said simply. 'She is the wisest monarch in Europe.'

The king thought he would be foolish to bridle at a girl's devotion to her mother, and it would be graceless to point out that her mother might have unified the kingdoms of Castile and Aragon but that she was still a long way from creating a peaceful and united Spain. The tactical skill of Isabella and Ferdinand had forged a single country from the Moorish kingdoms, they had yet to make everyone accept their peace. Catalina's own journey to London had been disrupted by rebellions of Moors and Jews who could not bear the tyranny of the Spanish kings. He changed the subject. 'Why don't you show us a dance?' he demanded, thinking that he would like to see her move. 'Or is that not allowed in Spain either?'

'Since I am an English princess I must learn your customs,' she said. 'Would an English princess get up in the middle of the night and dance for the king after he forced his way into her rooms?'

Henry laughed at her. 'If she had any sense she would.'

She threw him a small, demure smile. 'Then I will dance with my ladies,' she decided, and rose from her seat at the high table and went down to the centre of the floor. She called one by name, Henry noted, Maria de Salinas, a pretty, dark-haired girl who came quickly to stand beside Catalina. Three other young women, pretending shyness but eager to show themselves off, came forwards.

Henry looked them over. He had asked Their Majesties of Spain that their daughter's companions should all be pretty, and he was pleased to see that however blunt and ill-mannered they had found his request, they had acceded to it. The girls were all good-looking but none of them outshone the princess who stood, composed, and then raised her hands and clapped, to order the musicians to play.

He noticed at once that she moved like a sensual woman. The dance was a pavane, a slow ceremonial dance, and she moved with her hips swaying and her eyes heavy-lidded, a little smile on her face. She had been well-schooled, any princess would be taught how to dance in the courtly world where dancing, singing, music and poetry mattered more than anything else; but she danced like a woman who let the music move her, and Henry, who had some experience, believed that women who could be summoned by music were the ones who responded to the rhythms of lust.

He went from pleasure in watching her to a sense of rising irritation that this exquisite piece would be put in Arthur's cold bed. He could not see his thoughtful, scholarly boy teasing and arousing the passion in this girl on the edge of womanhood. He imagined that Arthur would fumble about and perhaps hurt her, and she would grit her teeth and do her duty as a woman and a queen must, and then, like as not, she would die in childbirth; and the whole performance of finding a bride for Arthur would have to be under-gone again, with no benefit for himself but only this irritated, frus-trated arousal that she seemed to inspire in him. It was good that she was desirable, since she would be an ornament to his court; but it was a nuisance that she should be so very desirable to him.

Henry looked away from her dancing and comforted himself with the thought of her dowry which would bring him lasting benefit and come directly to him, unlike this bride who seemed bound to unsettle him and must go, however mismatched, to his son. As soon as they were married her treasurer would hand over the first payment of her dowry: in solid gold. A year later he would deliver the second part in gold and in her plate and jewels. Having fought his way to the throne on a shoestring and uncertain credit, Henry trusted the power of money more than anything in life; more even than his throne, for he knew he could buy a throne with money, and far more than women, for they are cheaply bought; and far, far more than the joy of a smile from a virgin princess who stopped her dance now, swept him a curtsey and came up smiling.

'Do I please you?' she demanded, flushed and a little breathless.

'Well enough,' he said, determined that she should never know how much. 'But it's late now and you should go back to your bed. We'll ride with you a little way in the morning before we go ahead of you to London.'

She was surprised at the abruptness of his reply. Again, she glanced towards Arthur as if he might contradict his father's plans; perhaps stay with her for the remainder of the journey, since his father had bragged of their informality. But the boy said nothing. 'As you wish, Your Grace,' she said politely.

The king nodded and rose to his feet. The court billowed into deep curtseys and bows as he stalked past them, out of the room. 'Not so informal, at all,' Catalina thought as she watched the King of England stride through his court, his head high. 'He may boast of being a soldier with the manners of the camp, but he insists on obedience and on the show of deference. As indeed, he should,' added Isabella's daughter to herself.

Arthur followed behind his father with a quick 'Goodnight' to the princess as he left. In a moment all the men in their train had gone too, and the princess was alone but for her ladies.

'What an extraordinary man,' she remarked to her favourite, Maria de Salinas.

'He liked you,' the young woman said. 'He watched you very closely, he liked you.'

'And why should he not?' she asked with the instinctive arrogance of a girl born to the greatest kingdom in Europe. 'And even if he did not, it is all already agreed, and there can be no change. It has been agreed for almost all my life.'

He is not what I expected, this king who fought his way to the throne and picked up his crown from the mud of a battlefield. I expected him to be more like a champion, like a great soldier, perhaps like my father. Instead he has the look of a merchant, a man who puzzles over profit indoors, not a man who won his kingdom and his wife at the point of a sword.

I suppose I hoped for a man like Don Hernando, a hero that I could look up to, a man I would be proud to call father. But this king is lean and pale like a clerk, not a knight from the romances at all.

I expected his court to be more grand, I expected a great procession and a formal meeting with long introductions and elegant speeches, as we would have done it in the Alhambra. But he is abrupt; in my view he is rude. I shall have to become accustomed to these northern ways, this scramble to do things, this brusque ordering. I cannot expect things to be done well or even correctly. I shall have to overlook a lot until I am queen and can change things.

But, anyway, it hardly matters whether I like the king or he likes me. He has engaged in this treaty with my father and I am betrothed to his son. It hardly matters what I think of him, or what he thinks of me. It is not as if we will have to deal much together. I shall live and rule Wales and he will live and rule England, and when he dies it will be my husband on his throne and my son will be the next Prince of Wales, and I shall be queen.

As for my husband-to-be – oh! – he has made a very different first impression. He is so handsome! I did not expect him to be so hand-some! He is so fair and slight, he is like a page boy from one of the old romances. I can imagine him waking all night in a vigil, or singing up to a castle window. He has pale, almost silvery skin, he has fine golden hair, and yet he is taller than me and lean and strong like a boy on the edge of manhood.

He has a rare smile, one that comes reluctantly and then shines. And he is kind. That is a great thing in a husband. He was kind when he took the glass of wine from me, he saw that I was trembling, and he tried to reassure me.

I wonder what he thinks of me? I do so wonder what he thinks of me?

Just as the king had ruled, he and Arthur went swiftly back to Windsor the next morning and Catalina's train, with her litter carried by mules, with her trousseau in great travelling chests, her ladies-in-waiting, her Spanish household, and the guards for her dowry treasure, laboured up the muddy roads to London at a far slower pace.

She did not see the prince again until their wedding day, but when she arrived in the village of Kingston-upon-Thames her train halted in order to meet the greatest man in the kingdom, the young Edward Stafford, Duke of Buckingham, and Henry, Duke of York, the king's second son, who were appointed to accompany her to Lambeth Palace.

'I'll come out,' Catalina said hastily, emerging from her litter and walking quickly past the waiting horses, not wanting another quarrel with her strict duenna about young ladies meeting young men before their wedding day. 'Dona Elvira, say nothing. The boy is a child of ten years old. It doesn't matter. Not even my mother would think that it matters.'

'At least wear your veil!' the woman implored. 'The Duke of Buck … Buck … whatever his name, is here too. Wear your veil when you go before him, for your own reputation, Infanta.'

'Buckingham,' Catalina corrected her. 'The Duke of Buckingham. And call me Princess of Wales. And you know I cannot wear my veil because he will have been commanded to report to the king. You know what my mother said: that he is the king's mother's ward, restored to his family fortunes, and must be shown the greatest respect.'

The older woman shook her head, but Catalina marched out barefaced, feeling both fearful and reckless at her own daring, and saw the duke's men drawn up in array on the road and before them, a young boy: helmet off, bright head shining in the sunshine.

Her first thought was that he was utterly unlike his brother. While Arthur was fair-haired and slight and serious-looking, with a pale complexion and warm brown eyes, this was a sunny boy who looked as if he had never had a serious thought in his head. He did not take after his lean-faced father, he had the look of a boy for whom life came easily. His hair was red-gold, his face round and still baby-plump, his smile when he first saw her was genuinely friendly and bright, and his blue eyes shone as if he was accustomed to seeing a very pleasing world.

'Sister!' he said warmly, jumped down from his horse with a clatter of armour, and swept her a low bow.

'Brother Henry,' she said, curtseying back to him to precisely the right height, considering that he was only a second son of England, and she was an Infanta of Spain.

43

'I am so pleased to see you,' he said quickly, his Latin rapid, his English accent strong. 'I was so hoping that His Majesty would let me come to meet you before I had to take you into London on your wedding day. I thought it would be so awkward to go marching down the aisle with you, and hand you over to Arthur, if we hadn't even spoken. And call me Harry. Everyone calls me Harry.'

'I too am pleased to meet you, Brother Harry,' Catalina said politely, rather taken-aback at his enthusiasm.

'Pleased! You should be dancing with joy!' he exclaimed buoyantly. 'Because Father said that I could bring you the horse which was to be one of your wedding-day presents and so we can ride together to Lambeth. Arthur said you should wait for your wedding day, but I said, why should she wait? She won't be able to ride on her wedding day. She'll be too busy getting married. But if I take it to her now we can ride at once.'

'That was kind of you.'

'Oh, I never take any notice of Arthur,' Harry said cheerfully.

Catalina had to choke down a giggle. 'You don't?'

He made a face and shook his head. 'Serious,' he said. 'You'll be amazed how serious. And scholarly, of course, but not gifted. Everyone says I am very gifted, languages mostly, but music also. We can speak French together if you wish, I am extraordinarily fluent for my age. I am considered a pretty fair musician. And of course I am a sportsman. Do you hunt?'

'No,' Catalina said, a little overwhelmed. 'At least, I only follow the hunt when we go after boar or wolves.'

'Wolves? I should so like to hunt wolves. D'you really have bears?'

'Yes, in the hills.'

'I should so like to hunt a bear. Do you hunt wolves on foot like boar?'

'No, on horseback,' she said. 'They're very fast, you have to take very fast dogs to pull them down. It's a horrid hunt.'

44

'I shouldn't mind that,' he said. 'I don't mind anything like that. Everyone says I am terribly brave about things like that.'

'I am sure they do,' she said, smiling.

A handsome man in his mid-twenties came forwards and bowed. 'Oh, this is Edward Stafford, the Duke of Buckingham,' Harry said quickly. 'May I present him?'

Catalina held out her hand and the man bowed again over it. His intelligent, handsome face was warm with a smile. 'You are welcome to your own country,' he said in faultless Castilian. 'I hope everything has been to your liking on your journey? Is there anything I can provide for you?'

'I have been well cared for indeed,' Catalina said, blushing with pleasure at being greeted in her own language. 'And the welcome I have had from people all along the way has been very kind.'

'Look, here's your new horse,' Harry interrupted, as the groom led a beautiful black mare forwards. 'You'll be used to good horses, of course. D'you have Barbary horses all the time?'

'My mother insists on them for the cavalry,' she said.

'Oh,' he breathed. 'Because they are so fast?'

'They can be trained as fighting horses,' she said, going forwards and holding out her hand, palm upwards, for the mare to sniff at and nibble at her fingers with a soft, gentle mouth.

'Fighting horses?' he pursued.

'The Saracens have horses which can fight as their masters do, and the Barbary horses can be trained to do it too,' she said. 'They rear up and strike down a soldier with their front hooves, and they will kick out behind, too. The Turks have horses that will pick up a sword from the ground and hand it back to the rider. My mother says that one good horse is worth ten men in battle.'

'I should so like to have a horse like that,' Harry said longingly. 'I wonder how I should ever get one?'

He paused, but she did not rise to the bait. 'If only someone would give me a horse like that, I could learn how to ride it,' he said transparently. 'Perhaps for my birthday, or perhaps next week, since it is not me getting married, and I am not getting any wedding gifts. Since I am quite left out, and quite neglected.'

'Perhaps,' said Catalina, who had once seen her own brother get his way with exactly the same wheedling.

'I should be trained to ride properly,' he said. 'Father has promised that though I am to go into the church I shall be allowed to ride at the quintain. But My Lady the King's Mother says I may not joust. And it's really unfair. I should be allowed to joust. If I had a proper horse I could joust, I am sure I would beat everyone.'

'I am sure you would,' she said.

'Well, shall we go?' he asked, seeing that she would not give him a horse for asking.

'I cannot ride, I do not have my riding clothes unpacked.'

He hesitated. 'Can't you just go in that?'

Catalina laughed. 'This is velvet and silk. I can't ride in it. And besides, I can't gallop around England looking like a mummer.'

'Oh,' he said. 'Well, shall you go in your litter then? Won't it make us very slow?'

'I am sorry for that, but I am ordered to travel in a litter,' she said. 'With the curtains drawn. I can't think that even your father would want me to charge around the country with my skirts tucked up.'

'Of course the princess cannot ride today,' the Duke of Buckingham ruled. 'As I told you. She has to go in her litter.'

Harry shrugged. 'Well, I didn't know. Nobody told me what you were going to wear. Can I go ahead then? My horses will be so much faster than the mules.'

'You can ride ahead but not out of sight,' Catalina decided. 'Since you are supposed to be escorting me you should be with me.'

'As I said,' the Duke of Buckingham observed quietly and exchanged a little smile with the princess.

'I'll wait at every crossroads,' Harry promised. 'I am escorting you, remember. And on your wedding day I shall be escorting you again. I have a white suit with gold slashing.'

'How handsome you will look,' she said, and saw him flush with pleasure.

'Oh, I don't know . . .'

'I am sure everyone will remark what a handsome boy you are,' she said, as he looked pleased.

'Everyone always cheers most loudly for me,' he confided. 'And I like to know that the people love me. Father says that the only way to keep a throne is to be beloved by the people. That was King Richard's mistake, Father says.'

'My mother says that the way to keep the throne is to do God's work.'

'Oh,' he said, clearly unimpressed. 'Well, different countries, I suppose.'

'So we shall travel together,' she said. 'I will tell my people that we are ready to move on.'

'I will tell them,' he insisted. 'It is me who escorts you. I shall give the orders and you shall rest in your litter.' He gave one quick side-ways glance at her. 'When we get to Lambeth Palace you shall stay in your litter till I come for you. I shall draw back the curtains and take you in, and you should hold my hand.'

'I should like that very much,' she assured him, and saw his ready rush of colour once again.

He bustled off and the duke bowed to her with a smile. 'He is a very bright boy, very eager,' he said. 'You must forgive his enthusiasm. He has been much indulged.'

'His mother's favourite?' she asked, thinking of her own mother's adoration for her only son.

'Worse still,' the duke said with a smile. 'His mother loves him as she should; but he is the absolute apple of his grandmother's eye, and it is she who rules the court. Luckily he is a good boy, and well-mannered. He has too good a nature to be spoiled, and the king's mother tempers her treats with lessons.'

'She is an indulgent woman?' she asked.

He gave a little gulp of laughter. 'Only to her son,' he said. 'The rest of us find her – er – more majestic than motherly.'

'May we talk again at Lambeth?' Catalina asked, tempted to know more about this household that she was to join.

'At Lambeth and London, I shall be proud to serve you,' the young man said, his eyes warm with admiration. 'You must command me as you wish. I shall be your friend in England, you can call on me.'

I must have courage, I am the daughter of a brave woman and I have prepared for this all my life. When the young duke spoke so kindly to me there was no need for me to feel like weeping, that was foolish. I must keep my head up and smile. My mother said to me that if I smile no-one will know that I am homesick or afraid, I shall smile and smile however odd things seem.

And though this England seems so strange now, I will become accustomed. I will learn their ways and feel at home here. Their odd ways will become my ways, and the worst things – the things that I utterly cannot bear – those I shall change when I am queen. And anyway, it will be better for me than it was for Isabel, my sister. She was only married a few months and then she had to come home, a widow. Better for me than for Maria, who had to follow in Isabel's footsteps to Portugal, better for me than for Juana, who is sick with love for her husband Philip. It must be better for me than it was for Juan, my poor brother, who died so soon after finding happiness. And always better for me than for my mother, whose childhood was lived on a knife edge.

My story won't be like hers, of course. I have been born to less exciting times. I shall hope to make terms with my husband Arthur and with his odd, loud father, and with his sweet little braggart brother. I shall hope that his mother and his grandmother will love me or at the very least teach me how to be a Princess of Wales, a Queen of England. I shall not have to ride in desperate dashes by night from one besieged fortress to another, as my mother did. I shall not have to pawn my own jewels to pay mercenary soldiers, as she did. I shall not have to ride out in my own armour to rally my troops. I shall not be threatened by the wicked French on one side and the heretic Moors on the other, as my mother was. I shall marry Arthur and when his father dies – which must be soon, for he is so very old and so very bad-tempered – then we shall be King and Queen of England and my mother will rule in Spain as I rule in England and she will see me keep England in alliance with Spain as I have promised her, she will see me hold my country in an unbreakable treaty with hers, she will see I shall be safe forever.

London, 14th November 1501

On the morning of her wedding day Catalina was called early; but she had been awake for hours, stirring as soon as the cold, wintry sun had started to light the pale sky. They had prepared a great bath – her ladies told her that the English were amazed that she was going to wash before her wedding day and that most of them thought that she was risking her life. Catalina, brought up in the Alhambra where the bath houses were the most beautiful suite of rooms in the palace, centres of gossip, laughter and scented water, was equally amazed to hear that the English thought it perfectly adequate to bathe only occasionally, and that the poor people would bathe only once a year.

She had already realised that the scent of musk and ambergris which had wafted in with the king and Prince Arthur had underlying notes of sweat and horse, and that she would live for the rest of her life among people who did not change their underwear from

49

one year to the next. She had seen it as another thing that she must learn to endure, as an angel from heaven endures the privations of earth. She had come from al Yanna – the garden, the paradise – to the ordinary world. She had come from the Alhambra Palace to England, she had anticipated some disagreeable changes.

'I suppose it is always so cold that it does not matter,' she said uncertainly to Dona Elvira.

'It matters to us,' the duenna said. 'And you shall bathe like an Infanta of Spain though all the cooks in the kitchen have had to stop what they are doing to boil up water.'

Dona Elvira had commanded a great tureen from the flesh kitchen which was usually deployed to scald beast carcases, had it scoured by three scullions, lined it with linen sheets and filled it to the brim with hot water scattered with rose petals and scented with oil of roses brought from Spain. She lovingly supervised the washing of Catalina's long white limbs, the manicuring of her toes, the filing of her fingernails, the brushing of her teeth and finally the three-rinse washing of her hair. Time after time the incredulous English maids toiled to the door to receive another ewer of hot water from exhausted page boys, and tipped it in the tub to keep the temperature of the bath hot.

'If only we had a proper bath house,' Dona Elvira mourned. 'With steam and a tepidarium and a proper clean marble floor! Hot water on tap and somewhere for you to sit and be properly scrubbed.'

'Don't fuss,' Catalina said dreamily as they helped her from the bath and patted her all over with scented towels. One maid took her hair, squeezed out the water and rubbed it gently with red silk soaked in oil to give it shine and colour.

'Your mother would be so proud of you,' Dona Elvira said as they led the Infanta towards her wardrobe and started to dress her in layer after layer of shifts and gowns. 'Pull that lace tighter, girl, so that the skirt lies flat. This is her day, as well as yours, Catalina. She said that you would marry him whatever it cost her.'

Yes, but she did not pay the greatest price. I know they bought me this wedding with a king's ransom for my dowry, and I know that they endured long and hard negotiations, and I survived the worst voyage anyone has ever taken, but there was another price paid that we never speak of – wasn't there? And the thought of that price is in my mind today, as it has been on the journey, as it was on the voyage, as it has been ever since I first heard of it.

There was a man of only twenty-four years old, Edward Plantagenet, the Duke of Warwick and a son of the kings of England, with – truth be told – a better claim to the throne of England than that of my father-in-law. He was a prince, nephew to the king, and of blood royal. He committed no crime, he did nothing wrong, but he was arrested for my sake, taken to the Tower for my benefit, and finally killed, beheaded on the block, for my gain, so that my parents could be satisfied that there were no pretenders to the throne that they had bought for me.

My father himself told King Henry himself that he would not send me to England while the Duke of Warwick was alive, and so I am like Death himself, carrying the scythe. When they ordered the ship for me to come to England: Warwick was a dead man.

They say he was a simpleton. He did not really understand that he was under arrest, he thought that he was housed in the Tower as a way of giving him honour. He knew he was the last of the Plantagenet princes, and he knew that the Tower has always been royal lodgings as well as a prison. When they put a pretender, a cunning man who had tried to pass himself off as a royal prince, into the room next door to poor Warwick, he thought it was for company. When the other man invited him to escape, he thought it was a clever thing to do, and like the innocent he was, he whispered of their plans where his guards could hear. That gave them the excuse they needed for a charge of treason.

They trapped him very easily, they beheaded him with little protest from anyone.

The country wants peace and the security of an unchallenged king. The country will wink at a dead claimant or two. I am expected to wink at it also. Especially as it is done for my benefit. It was done at my father's request, for me. To make my way smooth.

When they told me that he was dead, I said nothing, for I am an Infanta of Spain. Before anything else, I am my mother's daughter. I do not weep like a girl and tell all the world my every thought. But when I was alone in the gardens of the Alhambra in the evening with the sun going down and leaving the world cool and sweet, I walked beside a long canal of still water, hidden by the trees, and I thought that I would never walk in the shade of trees again and enjoy the flicker of hot sunshine through cool green leaves without thinking that Edward, Duke of Warwick, will see the sun no more, so that I might live my life in wealth and luxury. I prayed then that I might be forgiven for the death of an innocent man.

My mother and father have fought down the length of Castile and Aragon, have ridden the breadth of Spain to make justice run in every village, in the smallest of hamlets – so that no Spaniard can lose his life on the whim of another. Even the greatest lords cannot murder a peasant; they have to be ruled by the law. But when it came to England and to me, they forgot this. They forgot that we live in a palace where the walls are engraved with the promise: 'Enter and ask. Do not be afraid to seek justice for here you will find it.' They just wrote to King Henry and said that they would not send me until Warwick was dead, and in a moment, at their expressed wish, Warwick was killed.

And sometimes, when I do not remember to be Infanta of Spain nor Princess of Wales but just the Catalina who walked behind her mother through the great gate into the Alhambra Palace, and knew that her mother was the greatest power the world had ever known; sometimes I wonder childishly, if my mother has not made a great mistake? If she has not driven God's will too far? Farther even than

God would want? For this wedding is launched in blood, and sails in a sea of innocent blood. How can such a wedding ever be the start of a good marriage? Must it not – as night follows sunset – be tragic and bloody too? How can any happiness ever come to Prince Arthur and to me that has been bought at such a terrible price? And if we could be happy would it not be an utterly sinfully-selfish joy?

Prince Harry, the ten-year-old Duke of York, was so proud of his white taffeta suit that he scarcely glanced at Catalina until they were at the west doors of St Paul's Cathedral and then he turned and stared, trying to see her face through the exquisite lace of the white mantilla. Ahead of them stretched a raised pathway, lined with red cloth, studded with golden nails, running at head height from the great doorway of the church where the citizens of London crowded to get a better view, up the long aisle to the altar where Prince Arthur stood, pale with nerves, six hundred slow ceremonial paces away.

Catalina smiled at the young boy at her side, and he beamed with delight. Her hand was steady on his proffered arm. He paused for a moment more, until everyone in the enormous church realised that the bride and prince were at the doorway, waiting to make their entrance, a hush fell, everyone craned to see the bride, and then, at the precise, most theatrical moment, he led her forwards.

Catalina felt the congregation murmur around her feet as she went past them, high on the stage that King Henry had ordered to be built so that everyone should see the flower of Spain meet the rosebush of England. The prince turned as she came towards him, but was blinded for a moment by irritation at the sight of his brother, leading the princess as if he himself were the bridegroom, glancing around as he walked, acknowledging the doffing of caps and the whispering of curtseys with his smug little smile, as if it were him that everyone had come to see.

Then they were both at Arthur's side and Harry had to step back, however reluctantly, as the princess and prince faced the archbishop together and kneeled together on the specially embroidered white taffeta cushions.

'Never has a couple been more married,' King Henry thought sourly, standing in the royal pew with his wife and his mother. 'Her parents trusted me no further than they would a snake, and my view of her father has always been that of a half-Moor huckster. Nine times they have been betrothed. This will be a marriage that nothing can break. Her father cannot wriggle from it, whatever second thoughts he has. He will protect me against France now; this is his daughter's inheritance. The very thought of our alliance will frighten the French into peace with me, and we must have peace.'

He glanced at his wife at his side. Her eyes were filled with tears, watching her son and his bride as the archbishop raised their clasped hands and wrapped them in his holy stole. Her face, beautiful with emotion, did not stir him. Who ever knew what she was thinking behind that lovely mask? Of her own marriage, the union of York and Lancaster which put her as a wife on the throne that she could have claimed in her own right? Or was she thinking of the man she would have preferred as a husband? The king scowled. He was never sure of his wife, Elizabeth. In general, he preferred not to consider her.

Beyond her, his flint-faced mother, Margaret Beaufort, watched the young couple with a glimmer of a smile. This was England's triumph, this was her son's triumph, but far more than that, this was *her* triumph – to have dragged this base-born bastard family back from disaster, to challenge the power of York, to defeat a reigning king, to capture the very throne of England against all the odds. This was her making. It was her plan to bring her son back from France at the right moment to claim his throne. They were her alliances who gave him the soldiers for the battle. It was her battle plan which left the usurper Richard to despair on the field at

Bosworth, and it was her victory that she celebrated every day of her life. And this was the marriage that was the culmination of that long struggle. This bride would give her a grandson, a Spanish–Tudor king for England, and a son after him, and after him: and so lay down a dynasty of Tudors that would be never-ending.

Catalina repeated the words of the marriage vow, felt the weight of a cold ring on her finger, turned her face to her new husband and felt his cool kiss, in a daze. When she walked back down that absurd walkway and saw the smiling faces stretching from her feet to the walls of the cathedral she started to realise that it was done. And when they went from the cool dark of the cathedral to the bright wintry sunlight outside and heard the roar of the crowd for Arthur and his bride, the Prince and Princess of Wales, she realised that she had done her duty finally and completely. She had been promised to Arthur from childhood, and now, at last, they were married. She had been named the Princess of Wales since she was three years old and now, at last, she had taken her name, and taken her place in the world. She looked up and smiled and the crowd, delighted with the free wine, with the prettiness of the young girl, with the promise of safety from civil war that could only come with a settled royal succession, roared their approval.

They were husband and wife; but they did not speak more than a few words to each other for the rest of the long day. There was a formal banquet, and though they were seated side by side, there were healths to be drunk and speeches to be attended to, and musicians playing. After the long dinner of many courses there was an entertainment with poetry and singers and a tableau. No-one had ever seen so much money flung at a single occasion. It was a greater celebration than the king's own wedding, greater even than his own coronation. It was a redefinition of the English kingly state, and it told the world that this marriage of the Tudor rose to the Spanish princess was one of the greatest events of the new age. Two new dynasties were proclaiming themselves by this union: Ferdinand and Isabella of the new country that they were forging from al Andalus, and the Tudors who were making England their own.

The musicians played a dance from Spain and Queen Elizabeth, at a nod from her mother-in-law, leaned over and said quietly to Catalina, 'It would be a great pleasure for us all if you would dance.'

Catalina, quite composed, rose from her chair and went to the centre of the great hall as her ladies gathered around her, formed a circle and held hands. They danced the pavane, the same dance that Henry had seen at Dogmersfield, and he watched his daughter-in-law through narrowed eyes. Undoubtedly, she was the most bed-dable young woman in the room. A pity that a cold fish like Arthur would be certain to fail to teach her the pleasures that could be had between sheets. If he let them both go to Ludlow Castle she would either die of boredom or slip into complete frigidity. On the other hand, if he kept her at his side she would delight his eyes, he could watch her dance, he could watch her brighten the court. He sighed. He thought he did not dare.

'She is delightful,' the queen remarked.

'Let's hope so,' he said sourly.

'My lord?'

He smiled at her look of surprised inquiry. 'No, nothing. You are right, delightful indeed. And she looks healthy, doesn't she? As far as you can tell?'

'I am sure she is, and her mother assured me that she is most regular in her habits.'

He nodded. 'That woman would say anything.'

'But surely not; nothing that would mislead us? Not on a matter of such importance?' she suggested.

He nodded and let it go. The sweetness of his wife's nature and her faith in others was not something he could change. Since she had no influence on policy, her opinions did not matter. 'And Arthur?' he said. 'He seems to be growing and strong? I would to God he had the spirits of his brother.'

They both looked at young Harry who was standing, watching the dancers, his face flushed with excitement, his eyes bright.

'Oh, Harry,' his mother said indulgently. 'But there has never been a prince more handsome and more full of fun than Harry.'

The Spanish dance ended and the king clapped his hands. 'Now Harry and his sister,' he commanded. He did not want to force Arthur to dance in front of his new bride. The boy danced like a clerk, all gangling legs and concentration. But Harry was raring to go and was on the floor with his sister Princess Margaret in a moment. The musicians knew the young royals' taste in music and struck up a lively galliard. Harry tossed his jacket to one side and threw himself into the dance, stripped down to his shirtsleeves like a peasant.

There was a gasp from the Spanish grandees at the young prince's shocking behaviour, but the English court smiled with his parents at his energy and enthusiasm. When the two had romped their way through the final turns and gallop, everyone applauded, laughing. Everyone but Prince Arthur, who was staring into the middle distance, determined not to watch his brother dance. He came to with a start only when his mother put her hand on his arm.

'Please God he's daydreaming of his wedding night,' his father remarked to Lady Margaret his mother. 'Though I doubt it.'

She gave a sharp laugh. 'I can't say I think much of the bride,' she said critically.

'You don't?' he asked. 'You saw the treaty yourself.'

'I like the price but the goods are not to my taste,' she said with her usual sharp wit. 'She is a slight, pretty thing, isn't she?'

'Would you rather a strapping milkmaid?'

'I'd like a girl with the hips to give us sons,' she said bluntly. 'A nursery-full of sons.'

'She looks well enough to me,' he ruled. He knew that he would never be able to say how well she looked to him. Even to himself he should never even think it.

Catalina was put into her wedding bed by her ladies, Maria de Salinas kissed her goodnight, and Dona Elvira gave her a mother's blessing; but Arthur had to undergo a further round of backslapping ribaldry, before his friends and companions escorted him to her door. They put him into bed beside the princess, who lay still and silent as the strange men laughed and bade them goodnight, and then the arch-bishop came to sprinkle the sheets with holy water and pray over the young couple. It could not have been a more public bedding unless they had opened the doors for the citizens of London to see the young people side by side, awkward as bolsters, in their marital bed. It seemed like hours to both of them until the doors were finally closed on the smiling, curious faces and the two of them were quite alone, seated upright against the pillows, frozen like a pair of shy dolls.

There was silence.

'Would you like a glass of ale?' Arthur suggested in a voice thin with nerves.

'I don't like ale very much,' Catalina said.

'This is different. They call it wedding ale, it's sweetened with mead and spices. It's for courage.'

'Do we need courage?'

He was emboldened by her smile and got out of bed to fetch her a cup. 'I should think we do,' he said. 'You are a stranger in a new land, and I have never known any girls but my sisters. We both have much to learn.'

She took the cup of hot ale from him and sipped the heady drink. 'Oh, that *is* nice.'

Arthur gulped down a cup and took another. Then he came back to the bed. Raising the cover and getting in beside her seemed an imposition; the idea of pulling up her night shift and mounting her was utterly beyond him.

'I shall blow out the candle,' he announced.

The sudden dark engulfed them, only the embers of the fire glowed red.

'Are you very tired?' he asked, longing for her to say that she was too tired to do her duty.

'Not at all,' she said politely, her disembodied voice coming out of the darkness. 'Are you?'

'No.'

'Do you want to sleep now?' he asked.

'I know what we have to do,' she said abruptly. 'All my sisters have been married. I know all about it.'

'I know as well,' he said, stung.

'I didn't mean that you don't know, I meant that you need not be afraid to start. I know what we have to do.'

'I am not afraid, it is just that I . . .'

To his absolute horror he felt her hand pull his nightshirt upwards, and touch the bare skin of his belly.

'I did not want to frighten you,' he said, his voice unsteady, desire rising up even though he was sick with fear that he would be incompetent.

'I am not afraid,' said Isabella's daughter. 'I have never been afraid of anything.'

In the silence and the darkness he felt her take hold of him and grasp firmly. At her touch he felt his desire well up so sharply that he was afraid he would come in her hand. With a low groan he rolled over on top of her and found she had stripped herself naked to the waist, her nightgown pulled up. He fumbled clumsily and felt her flinch as he pushed against her. The whole process seemed quite impossible, there was no way of knowing what a man was supposed to do, nothing to help or guide him, no knowing the mysterious geography of her body, and then she gave a little cry of pain, stifled with her hand, and he knew he had done it. The relief was so great that he came at once, a half-painful, half-pleasurable rush which told him that, whatever his father thought of him, whatever his brother Harry thought of him, the job was done and he was a man and a husband; and the princess was his wife and no longer a virgin untouched.

Catalina waited till he was asleep and then she got up and washed herself in her privy chamber. She was bleeding but she knew it would stop soon, the pain was no worse than she had expected, Isabel her sister had said it was not as bad as falling from a horse, and she had been right. Margot, her sister-in-law, had said that it was paradise; but Catalina could not imagine how such deep embarrassment and discomfort could add up to bliss – and concluded that Margot was exaggerating, as she often did.

Catalina came back to the bedroom. But she did not go back to the bed. Instead she sat on the floor by the fire, hugging her knees and watching the embers.

'Not a bad day,' I say to myself, and I smile; it is my mother's phrase. I want to hear her voice so much that I am saying her words to myself. Often, when I was little more than a baby, and she had spent a long day in the saddle, inspecting the forward scouting parties, riding back to chivvy up the slower train, she would come into her tent, kick off her riding boots, drop down to the rich Moorish rugs and cushions by the fire in the brass brazier and say: 'Not a bad day.'

'Is there ever a bad day?' I once asked her.

'Not when you are doing God's work,' she replied seriously. 'There are days when it is easy and days when it is hard. But if you are on God's work then there are never bad days.'

I don't for a moment doubt that bedding Arthur, even my brazen touching him and drawing him into me, is God's work. It is God's work that there should be an unbreakable alliance between Spain and England. Only with England as a reliable ally can Spain challenge the spread of France. Only with English wealth, and especially English ships, can we Spanish take the war against wickedness to the very heart of the Moorish empires in Africa and Turkey. The Italian princes are a muddle of rival ambitions, the French are a danger to every neighbour, it has to be England who joins the crusade with Spain to maintain the defence of Christendom against the terrifying might of the Moors; whether they be black Moors from Africa, the bogeymen of my childhood, or light-skinned Moors from the dreadful Ottoman Empire. And once they are defeated, then the crusaders must go on, to India, to the East, as far as they have to go to challenge and defeat the wickedness that is the religion of the Moors. My great fear is that the Saracen kingdoms stretch forever, to the end of the world and even Cristóbal Colón does not know where that is.

'What if there is no end to them?' I once asked my mother, as we leaned over the sun-warmed walls of the fort and watched the despatch of a new group of Moors leaving the city of Granada, their baggage loaded on mules, the women weeping, the men with their heads bowed low, the flag of St James now flying over the red fort where the crescent had rippled for seven centuries, the bells ringing for Mass where once horns had blown for heretic prayers. 'What if now we have defeated these, they just go back to Africa and in another year, they come again?'

'That is why you have to be brave, my Princess of Wales,' my mother had answered. 'That is why you have to be ready to fight them whenever they come, wherever they come. This is war till the end of the world, till the end of time when God finally ends it. It will take many shapes. It will never cease. They will come again and again, and you will have to be ready in Wales as we will be ready in Spain. I bore you to be a fighting princess as I am a Queen Militant. Your father and I placed you in England as Maria is placed in Portugal, as Juana is

placed with the Hapsburgs in the Netherlands. You are there to defend the lands of your husbands, and to hold them in alliance with us. It is your task to make England ready and keep it safe. Make sure that you never fail your country, as your sisters must never fail theirs, as I have never failed mine.'

Catalina was awakened in the early hours of the morning by Arthur gently pushing between her legs. Resentfully, she let him do as he wanted, knowing that this was the way to get a son and make the alliance secure. Some princesses, like her mother, had to fight their way in open warfare to secure their kingdom. Most princesses, like her, had to endure painful ordeals in private. It did not take long, and then he fell asleep. Catalina lay as still as a frozen stone in order not to wake him again.

He did not stir until daybreak, when his grooms of the bedchamber rapped brightly on the door. He rose up with a slightly embarrassed 'Good morning' to her; and went out. They greeted him with cheers and marched him in triumph to his own rooms. Catalina heard him say, vulgarly, boastfully, 'Gentlemen, this night I have been in Spain,' and heard the yell of laughter that applauded his joke. Her ladies came in with her gown and heard the men's laughter. Dona Elvira raised her thin eyebrows to heaven at the manners of these English.

'I don't know what your mother would say,' Dona Elvira remarked.

'She would say that words count less than God's will, and God's will has been done,' Catalina said firmly.

It was not like this for my mother. She fell in love with my father on sight and she married him with great joy. When I grew older I began to understand that they felt a real desire for each other – it was not

just a powerful partnership of a great king and queen. My father might take other women as his lovers; but he needed his wife, he could not be happy without her. And my mother could not even see another man. She was blind to anybody but my father. Alone, of all the courts in Europe, the court of Spain had no tradition of love-play, of flirtation, of adoration of the queen in the practice of courtly love. It would have been a waste of time. My mother simply did not notice other men and when they sighed for her and said her eyes were as blue as the skies she simply laughed and said, 'What nonsense,' and that was an end to it.

When my parents had to be apart they wrote every day, he would not move one step without telling her of it, and asking for her advice. When he was in danger she hardly slept.

He could not have got through the Sierra Nevada if she had not been sending him men and digging teams to level the road for him. No-one else could have driven a road through there. He would have trusted no-one else to support him, to hold the kingdom together as he pushed forwards. She could have conquered the mountains for no-one else, he was the only one that could have attracted her support. What looked like a remarkable unity of two calculating players was deceptive – it was their passion which they played out on the political stage. She was a great queen because that was how she could evoke his desire. He was a great general in order to match her. It was their love, their lust, which drove them; almost as much as God.

We are a passionate family. When Isabel, my sister, now with God, came back from Portugal a widow she swore that she had loved her husband so much that she would never take another. She had been with him for only six months but she said that without him, life had no meaning. Juana, my second sister, is so in love with her husband Philip that she cannot bear to let him out of her sight, when she learns that he is interested in another woman she swears that she will poison her rival, she is quite mad with love for him. And my brother . . . my darling brother Juan . . . simply died of love. He and his beautiful wife

Margot were so passionate, so besotted with each other, that his health failed, he was dead within six months of their wedding. Is there anything more tragic than a young man dying six months into his marriage? I come from passionate stock – but what about me? Shall I ever fall in love?

Not with this clumsy boy, for a certainty. My early liking for him has quite melted away. He is too shy to speak to me, he mumbles and pretends he cannot think of the words. He forced me to command in the bedroom, and I am ashamed that I had to be the one to make the first move. He makes me into a woman without shame, a woman of the marketplace when I want to be wooed like a lady in a romance. But if I had not invited him – what could he have done? I feel a fool now, and I blame him for my embarrassment. 'In Spain,' indeed! He would have got no closer than the Indies if I had not showed him how to do it. Stupid puppy.

When I first saw him I thought he was as beautiful as a knight from the romances, like a troubadour, like a poet. I thought I could be like a lady in a tower and he could sing beneath my window and persuade me to love him. But although he has the looks of a poet he doesn't have the wit. I can never get more than two words out of him, and I begin to feel that I demean myself in trying to please him.

Of course, I will never forget that it is my duty to endure this youth, this Arthur. My hope is always for a child, and my destiny is to keep England safe against the Moors. I shall do that; whatever else happens, I shall be Queen of England and protect my two countries: the Spain of my birth and the England of my marriage.

London, Winter 1501

Arthur and Catalina, standing stiffly side by side on the royal barge, but not exchanging so much as one word, led a great fleet of gaily painted barges downriver to Baynard's Castle, which would be their London home for the next weeks. It was a huge, rectangular palace of a house overlooking the river, with gardens running down to the water's edge. The Mayor of London, the councillors, and all the court followed the royal barge; and musicians played as the heirs to the throne took up residence in the heart of the City.

Catalina noticed that the Scots envoys were much in attendance, negotiating the marriage of her new sister-in-law, Princess Margaret. King Henry was using his children as pawns in his game for power, as every king must do. Arthur had made the vital link with Spain, Margaret, though only twelve years old, would make Scotland into a friend, rather than the enemy that it had been for generations. Princess Mary also would be married, when her time came, either to the greatest enemy that the country faced, or the greatest friend that they hoped to keep. Catalina was glad that she had known from childhood that she should be the next Queen of England. There had been no changes of policy and no shifting alliances. She had been

Queen of England-to-be almost from birth. It made the separation from her home and from her family so much easier.

She noticed that Arthur was very restrained in his greeting when he met the Scots lords at dinner at the Palace of Westminster.

'The Scots are our most dangerous enemies,' Edward Stafford, the Duke of Buckingham, told Catalina in whispered Castilian, as they stood at the back of the hall, waiting for the company to take their seats. 'The king and the prince hope that this marriage will make them our friend forever, will bind the Scots to us. But it is hard for any of us to forget how they have constantly harried us. We have all been brought up to know that we have a most constant and malignant enemy to the north.'

'Surely they are only a poor little kingdom,' she queried. 'What harm can they do us?'

'They always ally with France,' he told her. 'Every time we have a war with France they make an alliance and pour over our northern borders. And, they may be small and poor but they are the doorway for the terrible danger of France to invade us from the north. I think Your Grace knows from your own childhood that even a small country on your frontier can be a danger.'

'Well, the Moors had only a small country at the end,' she observed. 'My father always said that the Moors were like a disease. They might be a small irritation but they were always there.'

'The Scots are our plague,' he agreed. 'Once every three years or so, they invade and make a little war, and we lose an acre of land or win it back again. And every summer they harry the border countries and steal what they cannot grow or make themselves. No northern farmer has ever been safe from them. The king is determined to have peace.'

'Will they be kind to the Princess Margaret?'

'In their own rough way.' He smiled. 'Not as you have been welcomed, Infanta.'

Catalina beamed in return. She knew that she was warmly

welcomed in England. Londoners had taken the Spanish princess to their hearts, they liked the gaudy glamour of her train, the oddness of her dress, and they liked the way the princess always had a smile for a waiting crowd. Catalina had learned from her mother that the people are a greater power than an army of mercenaries and she never turned her head away from a cheer. She always waved, she always smiled, and if they raised a great bellow of applause she would even bob them a pretty little curtsey.

She glanced over to where the Princess Margaret, a vain, precocious girl, was smoothing down her dress and pushing back her headdress before going into the hall.

'Soon you will be married and going away, as I have done,' Catalina remarked pleasantly in French. 'I do hope it brings you happiness.'

The younger girl looked at her boldly. 'Not as you have done, for you have come to the finest kingdom in Europe, whereas I have to go far away into exile,' she said.

'England may be fine to you; but it is still strange to me,' Catalina said, trying not to flare up at the rudeness of the girl. 'And if you had seen my home in Spain you would be surprised at how fine our palace is there.'

'There is nowhere better than England,' Margaret said with the serene conviction of one of the spoiled Tudor children. 'But it will be good to be queen. While you are still only a princess, I shall be queen. I shall be the equal of my mother.' She thought for a moment. 'Indeed, I shall be the equal of your mother.'

The colour rushed into Catalina's face. 'You would never be the equal of my mother,' she snapped. 'You are a fool to even say it.'

Margaret gasped.

'Now, now, Your Royal Highnesses,' the duke interrupted quickly. 'Your father is ready to take his place. Will you please to follow him into the hall?'

Margaret turned and flounced away from Catalina.

'She is very young,' the duke said soothingly. 'And although she would never admit to it, she is afraid to leave her mother and her father and go so far away.'

'She has a lot to learn,' Catalina said through gritted teeth. 'She should learn the manners of a queen if she is going to be one.' She turned to find Arthur at her side, ready to conduct her into the hall behind his parents.

The royal family took their seats. The king and his two sons sat at the high table under the canopy of state, facing out over the hall, to their right sat the queen and the princesses. My Lady, the King's Mother, Margaret Beaufort, was seated beside the king, between him and his wife.

'Margaret and Catalina were having cross words as they came in,' she observed to him with grim satisfaction. 'I thought that the Infanta would irritate our Princess Margaret. She cannot bear to have too much attention shown to another, and everyone makes such a fuss over Catalina.'

'Margaret will soon be gone,' Henry said shortly. 'Then she can have her own court, and her own honeymoon.'

'Catalina has become the very centre of the court,' his mother complained. 'The palace is crowded out with people coming to watch her dine. Everyone wants to see her.'

'She's a novelty only, a seven-day wonder. And anyway, I want people to see her.'

'She has charm of a sort,' the older woman noted. The groom of the ewer presented a golden bowl filled with scented water and Lady Margaret dipped her fingertips and then wiped them on the napkin.

'I think her very pleasing,' Henry said as he dried his own hands. 'She went through the wedding without one wrong step, and the people like her.'

His mother made a small, dismissive gesture. 'She is sick with her own vanity, she has not been brought up as I would bring up a child of mine. Her will has not been broken to obedience. She thinks that she is something special.'

Henry glanced across at the princess. She had bent her head to listen to something being said by the youngest Tudor princess, Princess Mary; and he saw her smile and reply. 'D'you know? *I* think she is something special,' he said.

The celebrations continued for days and days, and then the court moved on to the new-built, glamorous palace of Richmond, set in a great and beautiful park. To Catalina, in a swirl of strange faces and introductions, it felt as if one wonderful joust and fete merged into another, with herself at the very centre of it all, a queen as celebrated as any sultana with a country devoted to her amusement. But after a week the party was concluded with the king coming to the princess and telling her that it was time for her Spanish companions to go home.

Catalina had always known that the little court which had accompanied her through storms and near-shipwreck to present her to her new husband would leave her once the wedding was done and the first half of the dowry paid; but it was a gloomy couple of days while they packed their bags and said goodbye to the princess. She would be left with her small domestic household, her ladies, her chamberlain, her treasurer, and her immediate servants, but the rest of her entourage must leave. Even knowing as she did that this was the way of the world, that the wedding party always left after the wedding, did not make her feel any less bereft. She sent them with messages to everyone in Spain and with a letter for her mother.

From her daughter, Catalina, Princess of Wales, to Her Royal Highness
of Castile and Aragon, and most dearest Madre,
   Oh, Madre!
   As these ladies and gentlemen will tell you, the prince and I have a

good house near the river. It is called Baynard's Castle although it is not a castle but a palace and newly built. There are no bath houses, for either ladies or men. I know what you are thinking. You cannot imagine it.

Dona Elvira has had the blacksmith make a great cauldron which they heat up on the fire in the kitchen and six serving men heave it to my room for my bath. Also, there are no pleasure gardens with flowers, no streams, no fountains, it is quite extraordinary. It all looks as if it is not yet built. At best, they have a tiny court which they call a knot garden where you can walk round and round until you are dizzy. The food is not good and the wine very sour. They eat nothing but preserved fruit and I believe they have never heard of vegetables.

You must not think that I am complaining, I wanted you to know that even with these small difficulties I am content to be the princess. Prince Arthur is kind and considerate to me when we meet, which is generally at dinner. He has given me a very beautiful mare of Barbary stock mixed with English, and I ride her every day. The gentlemen of the court joust (but not the princes); my champion is often the Duke of Buckingham who is very kind to me, he advises me as to the court and tells me how to go on. We all often dine in the English style, men and women together. The women have their own rooms but men visitors and male servants come and go out of them as if they were public, there is no seclusion for women at all. The only place I can be sure to be alone is if I lock myself in the necessary house – otherwise there are people everywhere.

Queen Elizabeth, though very quiet, is very kind to me when we meet and I like being in her company. My Lady the King's Mother is very cold; but I think she is like that with everyone except the king and the princes. She dotes on her son and grandsons. She rules the court as if she were queen herself. She is very devout and very serious. I am sure she is very admirable in every way.

You will want to know if I am with child. There are no signs yet. You will want to know that I read my Bible or holy books for two hours every day, as you ordered, and that I go to Mass three times a day and I take communion every Sunday also. Father Alessandro Geraldini is well, and *as great a spiritual guide and advisor in England as he was in Spain, and I trust to him and to God to keep me strong in the faith to do God's work in England as you do in Spain. Dona Elvira keeps my ladies in good order and I obey her as I would you. Maria de Salinas is my best friend, here as at home, though nothing here is like Spain, and I cannot bear her to talk of home at all.*

I will be the princess that you want me to be. I shall not fail you or God. I will be queen and I will defend England against the Moors.

Please write to me soon and tell me how you are. You seemed so sad and low when I left, I hope that you are better now. I am sure that the darkness that you saw in your mother will pass over you, and not rest on your life as it did on hers. Surely, God would not inflict sadness on you, who has always been His favourite? I pray for you and for Father every day. I hear your voice in my head, advising me all the time. Please write soon to your daughter who loves you so much,

Catalina

PS Although I am glad to be married, and to be called to do my duty for Spain and God, I miss you very much. I know you are a queen before a mother but I would be so glad to have one letter from you. C

The court bade a cheerful farewell to the Spanish but Catalina found it hard to smile and wave. After they had gone she went down to the river to see the last of the barges shrink and then disappear in the distance and King Henry found her there, a lonely figure, on the pier looking downstream, as if she wished she were going too.

He was too skilled with women to ask her what was wrong. He knew very well what was wrong: loneliness, and homesickness natural enough in a young woman of nearly sixteen years old. He had been an exile from England for almost all his own life, he knew very well the rise and fall of yearning that comes with an unexpected scent, the change of seasons, a farewell. To invite an explanation

71

would only trigger a flood of tears and achieve nothing. Instead, he tucked her cold little hand under his arm and said that she must see his library which he had newly assembled at the palace and she could borrow books to read at any time. He threw an order over his shoulder to one of his pages as he led the princess to the library and walked her round the beautiful shelves, showing her not only the classical authors and the histories that were his own interest, but also the stories of romance and heroism which he thought more likely to divert her.

She did not complain, he noticed with pleasure, and she had rubbed her eyes dry as soon as she had seen him coming towards her. She had been raised in a hard school. Isabella of Spain had been a soldier's wife and a soldier herself, she did not raise any of her girls to be self-indulgent. He thought there was not a young woman in England who could match this girl for grit. But there were shadows under the princess's blue eyes and though she took the proffered volumes with a word of thanks she still did not smile.

'And do you like maps?' he asked her.

She nodded. 'Of course,' she said. 'In my father's library we have maps of the whole world, and Cristóbal Colón made him a map to show him the Americas.'

'Does your father have a large library?' he asked, jealous of his reputation as a scholar.

Her polite hesitation before she replied told him everything, told him that his library here, of which he had been so proud, was nothing to the learning of the Moors of Spain. 'Of course my father has inherited many books, they are not all his own collection,' Catalina said tactfully. 'Many of them are Moorish authors, from Moorish scholars. You know that the Arabs translated the Greek authors before they were ever made into French or Italian, or English. The Arabs had all the sciences and all the mathematics when they were forgotten in Christendom. He has all the Moorish translations of Aristotle and Sophocles and everyone.'

He could feel his longing for the new learning like a hunger. 'He has many books?'

'Thousands of volumes,' she said. 'Hebrew and Arabic, Latin, and all the Christian languages too. But he doesn't read them all, he has Arab scholars to study them.'

'And the maps?' he asked.

'He is advised mostly by Arab navigators and map-makers,' she said. 'They travel so far overland, they understand how to chart their way by the stars. The sea voyages are just the same to them as a journey through the desert. They say that a watery waste is the same as a plain of sand, they use the stars and the moon to measure their journey in both.'

'And does your father think that much profit will come from his discoveries?' the king asked curiously. 'We have all heard of these great voyages of Cristóbal Colón and the treasures he has brought back.'

He admired how her eyelashes swept down to hide the gleam. 'Oh, I could not say.' Cleverly, she avoided the question. 'Certainly, my mother thinks that there are many souls to save for Jesus.'

Henry opened the great folder with his collection of maps and spread them before her. Beautifully illuminated sea monsters frolicked in the corners. He traced for her the coastline of England, the borders of the Holy Roman Empire, the handful of regions of France, the new widening borders of her own country of Spain and the papal lands in Italy. 'You see why your father and I have to be friends,' he said to her. 'We both face the power of France on our doorstep. We cannot even trade with each other unless we can keep France out of the narrow seas.'

'If Juana's son inherits the Hapsburg lands then he will have two kingdoms,' she indicated. 'Spain and also the Netherlands.'

'And your son will have all of England, an alliance with Scotland, and all our lands in France,' he said, making a sweep with his spread palm. 'They will be a powerful pair of cousins.'

She smiled at the thought of it, and Henry saw the ambition in her. 'You would like to have a son who would rule half of Christendom?'

'What woman would not?' she said. 'And my son and Juana's son could surely defeat the Moors, could drive them back and back beyond the Mediterranean Sea?'

'Or perhaps you might find a way to live in peace,' he suggested. 'Just because one man calls Him Allah, and another calls him God is no reason for believers to be enemies, surely?'

At once Catalina shook her head. 'It will have to be a war forever, I think. My mother says that it is the great battle between Good and Evil which will go on until the end of time.'

'Then you will be in danger forever,' he started, when there was a tap on the great wooden door of the library. It was the page that Henry had sent running, bringing a flustered goldsmith who had been waiting for days to show his work to the king and was rather surprised to be summoned in a moment.

'Now,' Henry said to his daughter-in-law, 'I have a treat for you.'

She looked up at him. 'Good God,' he thought. 'It would be a man of stone who did not want this little flower in his bed. I swear that I could make her smile, and at any rate, I would enjoy trying.'

'Have you?'

Henry gestured to the man who flapped out a cloth of maroon velvet from his pocket, and then spilled the contents of his knapsack on to the scarlet background. A tumble of jewels, diamonds, emeralds, rubies, pearls, chains, lockets, earrings and brooches was swiftly spread before Catalina's widening gaze.

'You shall have your pick,' Henry said, his voice warm and intimate. 'It is my private gift to you, to bring the smile back to your pretty face.'

She hardly heard him, she was at the table in a moment, the goldsmith holding up one rich item after another. Henry watched her indulgently. So she might be a princess with a pure blood line of

Castilian aristocrats, while he was the grandson of a working man; but she was a girl as easily bought as any other. And he had the means to please her.

'Silver?' he asked.

She turned a bright face to him. 'Not silver,' she said decisively.

Henry remembered that this was a girl who had seen the treasure of the Incas cast at her feet.

'Gold then?'

'I do prefer gold.'

'Pearls?'

She made a little moue with her mouth.

'My God, she has a kissable mouth,' he thought. 'Not pearls?' he asked aloud.

'They are not my greatest favourite,' she confided. She smiled up at him. 'What is your favourite stone?'

'Why, she is flirting with me,' he said to himself, stunned at the thought. 'She is playing me like she would an indulgent uncle. She is reeling me in like a fish.'

'Emeralds?'

She smiled again.

'No. This,' she said simply.

She had picked out, in a moment, the most expensive thing in the jeweller's pack, a collar of deepest blue sapphires with a matching pair of earrings. Charmingly, she held the collar against her smooth cheeks so that he could look from the jewels to her eyes. She took a step closer towards him so that he could smell the scent on her hair, orange-blossom water from the gardens of the Alhambra. She smelled as if she were an exotic flower herself. 'Do they match my eyes?' she asked him. 'Are my eyes as blue as sapphires?'

He took a little breath, surprised at the violence of his response. 'They are. You shall have them,' he said, almost choking on his desire for her. 'You shall have this and anything else you like. You shall name your . . . your . . . wish.'

The look she threw up at him was of pure delight. 'And my ladies too?'

'Call your ladies, they shall have their pick.'

She laughed with pleasure and ran to the door. He let her go. He did not trust himself to stay in the room without chaperones. Hastily, he took himself out into the hall and met his mother, returning from hearing Mass.

He kneeled and she put her fingers on his head in her blessing. 'My son.'

'My lady mother.'

He rose to his feet. She quickly took in the flush of his face and his suppressed energy. 'Has something troubled you?'

'No!'

She sighed. 'Is it the queen? Is it Elizabeth?' she asked wearily. 'Is she complaining about the Scots' marriage for Margaret again?'

'No,' he said. 'I have not seen her today.'

'She will have to accustom herself,' she said. 'A princess cannot choose whom she marries and when she leaves home. Elizabeth would know that if she had been properly brought up. But she was not.'

He gave his crooked smile. 'That is hardly her fault.'

His mother's disdain was apparent. 'No good would ever have come from her mother,' she said shortly. 'Bad breeding, the Woodvilles.'

Henry shrugged and said nothing. He never defended his wife to his mother – her malice was so constant and so impenetrable that it was a waste of time to try to change her mind. He never defended his mother to his wife; he never had to. Queen Elizabeth never commented on her difficult mother-in-law or her demanding husband. She took him, his mother, his autocratic rule, as if they were natural hazards, as unpleasant and as inevitable as bad weather.

'You should not let her disturb you,' his mother said.

'She has never disturbed me,' he said, thinking of the princess who did.

I am certain now that the king likes me, above all his daughters, and I am so glad of it. I am used to being the favourite daughter, the baby of the family. I like it when I am the favourite of the king, I like to feel special.

When he saw that I was sad at my court going back to Spain and leaving me in England he spent the afternoon with me, showing me his library, talking about his maps, and finally, giving me an exquisite collar of sapphires. He let me pick out exactly what I wanted from the goldsmith's pack, and he said that the sapphires were the colour of my eyes.

I did not like him very well at first, but I am becoming accustomed to his abrupt speech and his quick ways. He is a man whose word is law in this court and in this land and he owes thanks to no-one for anything, except perhaps his Lady Mother. He has no close friends, no intimates but her and the soldiers who fought with him, who are now the great men of his court. He is not tender to his wife nor warm to his daughters, but I like it that he attends to me. Perhaps I will come to love him as a daughter. Already I am glad when he singles me out. In a court such as this, which revolves around his approval, it makes me feel like a princess indeed when he praises me, or spends time with me.

If it were not for him then I think I would be even more lonely than I am. The prince my husband treats me as if I were a table or a chair. He never speaks to me, he never smiles at me, he never starts a conversation, it is all he can do to find a reply. I think I was a fool when I thought he looked like a troubadour. He looks like a milksop and that is the truth. He never raises his voice above a whisper, he never says anything of any interest. He may well speak French and Latin and half a dozen languages, but since he has nothing to say – what good are they? We live as strangers and if he did not come to my bedchamber at night, once a week as if on duty, I would not know I was married at all.

I show the sapphires to his sister, the Princess Margaret, and she is eaten up with jealousy. I shall have to confess to the sin of vanity and of pride. It is not right for me to flaunt them before her; but if she had ever been kind to me by word or deed then I would not have showed her. I want her to know that her father values me, even if she and her grandmother and her brother do not. But now all I have done is upset her and put myself in the wrong, and I will have to confess and make a penance.

Worst of all, I did not behave with the dignity that a princess of Spain should always show. If she were not such a fishwife's apprentice then I could have been better. This court dances around the king as if nothing matters more in the world than his favour, and I should know better than to join in. At the very least I should not be measuring myself against a girl four years younger than me and only a princess of England, even if she calls herself Queen of Scotland at every opportunity.

The young Prince and Princess of Wales finished their visit to Richmond and started to make their own royal household in Baynard's Castle. Catalina had her rooms at the back of the house, overlooking the gardens and the river, with her household, her Spanish ladies, her Spanish chaplain, and duenna, and Arthur's rooms overlooked the City, with his household, his chaplain, and his tutor. They met formally only once a day for dinner, when the two households sat at opposite sides of the hall and stared at each other with mutual suspicion, more like enemies in the middle of a forced truce than members of a united home.

The castle was run according to the commands of Lady Margaret, the king's mother. The feast days and fast days, the entertainments and the daily timetable were all commanded by her. Even the nights when Arthur was to visit his wife in her bedchamber had been appointed by her. She did not want the young people becoming exhausted, nor did she want them neglecting their duties. So once a week the prince's household and friends solemnly escorted him to the princess's rooms and left him there overnight. For both young people the experience was an ordeal of embarrassment. Arthur became no more skilled, Catalina endured his silent determination as politely as she could. But then, one day in early December, Catalina's monthly course started and she told Dona Elvira. The duenna at once told the prince's groom of the bedchamber that the prince could not come to the Infanta's bed for a week; the Infanta was indisposed. Within half an hour, everyone from the king at Whitehall to the spit boy at Baynard's Castle knew that the Princess of Wales was having her course and so no child had yet been conceived; and everyone from the king to the spit boy wondered, since the girl was lusty and strong and since she was bleeding – obviously fertile – if Arthur was capable of doing his side of their duty.

In the middle of December, when the court was preparing for the great twelve-day feast of Christmas, Arthur was summoned by his father and ordered to prepare to leave for his castle at Ludlow.

'I suppose you'll want to take your wife with you,' the king said, smiling at his son in an effort to seem unconcerned.

'As you wish, sir,' Arthur replied carefully.

'What would you wish?'

After enduring a week's ban from Catalina's bed, with everyone remarking among themselves that no child had been made – but to be sure, it was early days yet, and it might be nobody's fault – Arthur felt embarrassed and discouraged. He had not gone back to her bedroom and she had sent no message to invite him. He could not expect an invitation – he knew that was ridiculous – a princess of Spain could hardly send for the prince of England; but she had not smiled or encouraged him in any way at all. He had received no message to tell him to resume his visits, and he had no idea how long these mysteries usually took. There was no-one that he could ask, and he did not know what he should do.

'She does not seem very merry,' Arthur observed.

'She's homesick,' his father said briskly. 'It's up to you to divert her. Take her to Ludlow with you. Buy her things. She's a girl like any other. Praise her beauty. Tell her jokes. Flirt with her.'

Arthur looked quite blank. 'In Latin?'

His father barked his harsh laugh. 'Lad. You can do it in Welsh if your eyes are smiling and your cock is hard. She'll know what you mean. I swear it. She's a girl who knows well enough what a man means.'

There was no answering brightness from his son. 'Yes, sir.'

'If you don't want her with you, you're not obliged to take her this year, you know. You were supposed to marry and then spend the first year apart.'

'That was when I was fourteen.'

'Only a year ago.'

'Yes, but . . .'

'So you do want her with you?'

His son flushed. The father regarded the boy with sympathy. 'You want her, but you are afraid she will make a fool of you?' he suggested.

The blond head drooped, nodded.

'And you think if you and she are far from court and from me, then she will be able to torment you.'

Another small nod. 'And all her ladies. And her duenna.'

'And time will hang heavy on your hands.'

The boy looked up, his face a picture of misery.

'And she will be bored and sulky and she will make your little court at Ludlow a miserable prison for both of you.'

'If she dislikes me . . .' he started, his voice very low.

Henry rested a heavy hand on his boy's shoulder. 'Oh, my son.

It doesn't matter what she thinks of you,' he said. 'Perhaps your mother was not my choice, perhaps I was not hers. When a throne is involved the heart comes in second place if it ever matters at all. She knows what she has to do; and that is all that counts.'

'Oh, she knows all about it!' the boy burst out resentfully. 'She has no . . .'

His father waited. 'No . . . what?'

'No shame at all.'

Henry caught his breath. 'She is shameless? She is passionate?' He tried to keep the desire from his voice, a sudden lascivious picture of his daughter-in-law, naked and shameless, in his mind.

'No! She goes at it like a man harnessing a horse,' Arthur said miserably. 'A task to be done.'

Henry choked down a laugh. 'But at least she does it,' he said. 'You don't have to beg her, or persuade her. She knows what she has to do?'

Arthur turned from him to the window and looked out of the arrow slit to the cold river Thames below. 'I don't think she likes me. She only likes her Spanish friends, and Mary, and perhaps Henry. I see her laughing with them and dancing with them as if she were very merry in their company. She chatters away with her own people, she is courteous to everyone who passes by. She has a smile for everyone. I hardly ever see her, and I don't want to see her, either.'

Henry dropped his hand on his son's shoulder. 'My boy, she doesn't know what she thinks of you,' he assured him. 'She's too busy in her own little world of dresses and jewels and those damned gossipy Spanish women. The sooner you and she are alone together, the sooner you two will come to terms. You can take her with you to Ludlow and you can get acquainted.'

The boy nodded, but he did not look convinced. 'If it is your wish, sire,' he said formally.

'Shall I ask her if she wants to go?'

81

The colour flooded into the young man's cheeks. 'What if she says no?' he asked anxiously.

His father laughed. 'She won't,' he promised. 'You'll see.'

Henry was right. Catalina was too much of a princess to say either yes or no to a king. When he asked her if she would like to go to Ludlow with the prince she said that she would do whatever the king wished.

'Is Lady Margaret Pole still at the castle?' she asked, her voice a little nervous.

He scowled at her. Lady Margaret was now safely married to Sir Richard Pole, one of the solid Tudor warhorses, and warden of Ludlow Castle. But Lady Margaret had been born Margaret Plantagenet, beloved daughter of the Duke of Clarence, cousin to King Edward and sister to Edward of Warwick whose claim to the throne had been so much greater than Henry's own.

'What of it?'

'Nothing,' she said hastily.

'You have no cause to avoid her,' he said gruffly. 'What was done, was done in my name, by my order. You don't bear any blame for it.'

She flushed as if they were talking of something shameful. 'I know.'

'I can't have anyone challenging my right to the throne,' he said abruptly. 'There are too many of them, Yorks and Beauforts, and Lancasters too, and endless others who fancy their chances as pretenders. You don't know this country. We're all married and intermarried like so many coneys in a warren.' He paused to see if she would laugh, but she was frowning, following his rapid French. 'I can't have anyone claiming by their pretended right what I have won by conquest,' he said. 'And I won't have anyone else claiming by conquest either.'

'I thought you were the true king,' Catalina said hesitantly.

'I am now,' said Henry Tudor bluntly. 'And that's all that matters.'

'You were anointed.'

'I am now,' repeated with a grim smile.

'But you are of the royal line?'

'I have royal blood in my veins,' he said, his voice hard. 'No need to measure how much or how little. I picked up my crown off the battlefield, literally, it was at my feet in the mud. So I knew; everyone knew – everyone saw God give me the victory because I was his chosen king. The archbishop anointed me because he knew that too. I am as much king as any in Christendom, and more than most because I did not just inherit as a baby, the fruit of another man's struggle – God gave me my kingdom when I was a man. It is my just desert.'

'But you had to claim it . . .'

'I claimed my own,' he said finally. 'I won my own. God gave my own to me. That's an end to it.'

She bowed her head to the energy in his words. 'I know, sire.'

Her submissiveness, and the pride that was hidden behind it, fascinated him. He thought that there had never been a young woman whose smooth face could hide her thoughts like this one.

'D'you want to stay here with me?' Henry asked softly, knowing that he should not ask her such a thing, praying, as soon as the words were out of his mouth, that she would say 'no' and silence his secret desire for her.

'Why, I wish whatever Your Majesty wishes,' she said coolly.

'I suppose you want to be with Arthur?' he asked, daring her to deny it.

'As you wish, sire,' she said steadily.

'Tell me! Would you like to go to Ludlow with Arthur, or would you rather stay here with me?'

She smiled faintly, and would not be drawn. 'You are the king,' she said quietly. 'I must do whatever you command.'

Henry knew he should not keep her at court beside him but he could not resist playing with the idea. He consulted her Spanish advisors, and found them hopelessly divided and squabbling among themselves. The Spanish ambassador, who had worked so hard to deliver the intractable marriage contract, insisted that the princess should go with her new husband, and that she should be seen to be a married woman in every way. Her confessor, who alone of all of them seemed to have a tenderness for the little princess, urged that the young couple should be allowed to stay together. Her duenna, the formidable and difficult Dona Elvira, preferred not to leave London. She had heard that Wales was a hundred miles away, a mountainous and rocky land. If Catalina stayed in Baynard's Castle and the household was rid of Arthur, then they would make a little Spanish enclave in the heart of the City, and the duenna's power would be unchallenged, she would rule the princess and the little Spanish court.

The queen volunteered her opinion that Catalina would find Ludlow too cold and lonely in mid-December and suggested that perhaps the young couple could stay together in London until spring.

'You just hope to keep Arthur with you, but he has to go,' Henry said brusquely to her. 'He has to learn the business of kingship and there is no better way to learn to rule England than to rule the Principality.'

'He's still young, and he is shy with her.'

'He has to learn to be a husband too.'

'They will have to learn to deal together.'

'Better that they learn in private then.'

In the end, it was the king's mother who gave the decisive advice. 'Send her,' she said to her son. 'We need a child off her. She won't make one on her own in London. Send her with Arthur to Ludlow.' She laughed shortly. 'God knows, they'll have nothing else to do there.'

'Elizabeth is afraid that she will be sad and lonely,' the king remarked. 'And Arthur is afraid that they will not deal well together.'

'Who cares?' his mother asked. 'What difference does that make? They are married and they have to live together and make an heir.'

He shot her a swift smile. 'She is only just sixteen,' he said, 'and the baby of her family, still missing her mother. You don't make any allowances for her youth, do you?'

'I was married at twelve years old, and gave birth to you in the same year,' she returned. 'No-one made any allowances for me. And yet I survived.'

'I doubt you were happy.'

'I was not. I doubt that she is. But that, surely, is the last thing that matters?'

Dona Elvira told me that I must refuse to go to Ludlow. Father Geraldini said that it was my duty to go with my husband. Dr de Puebla said that for certain my mother would want me to live with my husband, to do everything to show that the marriage is complete in word and deed. Arthur, the hopeless beanpole, said nothing, and his father seems to want me to decide; but he is a king and I don't trust him.

All I really want to do is to go home to Spain. Whether we are in London or whether we live in Ludlow it will be cold, and it will rain all the time, the very air feels wet, I cannot get anything good to eat, and I cannot understand a word anybody says.

I know I am Princess of Wales and I will be Queen of England. That is true, and it will be true. But, this day, I cannot feel very glad about it.

'We are to go to my castle at Ludlow,' Arthur remarked awkwardly to Catalina. They were seated side by side at dinner, the hall below them, the gallery above and the wide doors crowded with people who had come from the City for the free entertainment of watching the court dine. Most people were observing the Prince of Wales and his young bride.

She bowed her head but did not look at him. 'Is it your father's command?' she asked.

'Yes.'

'Then I shall be happy to go,' she said.

'We will be alone, but for the warden of the castle and his wife,' Arthur went on. He wanted to say that he hoped she would not mind, that he hoped she would not be bored, or sad or – worst of all – angry with him.

She looked at him without a smile. 'And so?'

'I hope you will be content,' he stumbled.

'Whatever your father wishes,' she said steadily, as if to remind him that they were merely prince and princess and had no rights and no power at all.

He cleared his throat. 'I shall come to your room tonight,' he asserted.

She gave him a look from eyes as blue and hard as the sapphires around her neck. 'Whatever you wish,' she said in the same neutral tone.

He came when she was in bed and Dona Elvira admitted him to the room, her face like a stone, disapproval in every gesture. Catalina sat up in bed and watched as his groom of the bedchamber took his gown from his shoulders and went quietly out, closing the door behind him.

'Wine?' Arthur asked. He was afraid his voice quavered slightly.

'No, thank you,' she said.

Awkwardly the young man came to the bed, turned back the sheets, got in beside her. She turned to look at him, and he knew he was blushing beneath her inquiring gaze. He blew out the candle so she could not see his discomfort. A little torchlight from the guard outside flickered through the slats of the shutters, and then was gone as the guard moved on. Arthur felt the bed move as she lay back and pulled her nightdress out of the way. He felt as if he were a thing to her, an object of no importance, something she had to endure in order to be Queen of England.

He threw back the covers and jumped from the bed. 'I'm not staying here. I'm going to my room,' he said tersely.

'What?'

'I shan't stay here. I'm not wanted . . .'

'Not wanted? I never said you were not . . .'

'It is obvious. The way you look . . .'

'It's pitch black! How d'you know how I look? And anyway, you look as if someone forced you here!'

'I? It isn't me who sent a message that half the court heard, that I was not to come to your bed.'

He heard her gasp. 'I did not say you were not to come. I had to tell them to tell you . . .' She broke off in embarrassment. 'It was my time . . . you had to know . . .'

'Your duenna told my steward that I was not to come to your bed. How do you think that made me feel? How d'you think that looked to everyone?'

'How else was I to tell you?' she demanded.

'Tell me yourself!' he raged. 'Don't tell everyone else in the world.'

'How could I? How could I say such a thing? I should be so embarrassed!'

'Instead it is me who is made to look a fool!'

Catalina slipped out of bed and steadied herself, holding the tall carved bedpost. 'My lord, I apologise if I have offended you, I don't know how such things are done here . . . In future I will do as you wish . . .'

He said nothing.

She waited.

'I'm going,' he said and went to hammer on the door for his groom to come to him.

'Don't!' The cry was forced out of her.

'What?' He turned.

'Everyone will know,' she said desperately. 'Know that there is something wrong between us. Everyone will know that you have just come to me. If you leave at once, everyone will think . . .'

'I won't stay here!' he shouted.

Her pride rushed up. 'You will shame us both!' she cried out. 'What do you want people to think? That I disgust you, or that you are impotent?'

'Why not? If both are true?' He hammered on the door even louder.

She gasped in horror and fell back against the bedpost.

'Your Grace?' came a shout from the outer chamber and the door opened to reveal the groom of the bedchamber and a couple of pages, and behind them Dona Elvira and a lady-in-waiting.

Catalina stalked over to the window and turned her back to the room. Uncertainly, Arthur hesitated, glancing back at her for help, for some indication that he could stay after all.

'For shame!' Dona Elvira exclaimed, pushing past Arthur and running to throw a gown around Catalina's shoulders. Once the woman was standing with her arm around Catalina, glaring at him, Arthur could not return to his bride; he stepped over the threshold and went to his own rooms.

I cannot bear him. I cannot bear this country. I cannot live here for the rest of my life. That he should say that I disgust him! That he should dare to speak to me so! Has he run mad like one of their filthy dogs that pant everywhere? Has he forgotten who I am? Has he forgotten himself?

I am so furious with him I should like to take a scimitar and slice his stupid head off. If he thought for a moment he would have known that everyone in the palace, everyone in London, probably everyone in this gross country, will laugh at us. They will say I am ugly and that I cannot please him.

I am crying with temper, it's not grief. I tuck my head into the pillow of my bed, so that no-one can hear me and tell everyone else that the princess cried herself to sleep because her husband would not bed her. I am choking on tears and temper, I am so angry with him.

After a little while I stop, I wipe my face, I sit up. I am a princess by birth and by marriage, I should not give way. I shall have some dignity even if he has none. He is a young man, a young English man at that – how should he know how to behave? I think of my home in the moonlight, of how the walls and the tracery gleam white and the yellow stone is bleached to cream. That is a palace, where people know how to behave with grace and dignity. I wish with all my heart that I was still there.

I remember that I used to watch a big yellow moon reflected in the water of the sultana's garden. Like a fool, I used to dream of being married.

Oxford, Christmas 1501

They set off a few days before Christmas. Resolutely, they spoke to each other in public with utter courtesy, and ignored each other completely when no-one was watching. The queen had asked that they might at least stay for the twelve-day feast but My Lady the King's Mother had ruled that they should take their Christmas at Oxford, it would give the country a chance to see the prince and the new Princess of Wales, and what the king's mother said was law.

Catalina travelled by litter, jolted mercilessly over the frozen roads, her mules foundering in the fords, chilled to the bone however many rugs and furs they packed around her. The king's mother had ruled that she should not ride for fear of a fall. The unspoken hope was that Catalina was carrying a child. Catalina herself said nothing to confirm or deny the hope. Arthur was silence itself.

They had separate rooms on the road to Oxford, and separate rooms at Magdalene College when they arrived. The choristers were ready, the kitchens were ready, the extraordinarily rich hospitality of Oxford was ready to make merry; but the Prince and Princess of Wales were as cold and as dull as the weather.

They dined together, seated at the great table facing down the hall, and as many of the citizens of Oxford who could get into the gallery took their seats and watched the princess put small morsels of food in her mouth, and turn her shoulder to her husband, while he looked around the hall for companions and conversation, as if he were dining alone.

They brought in dancers and tumblers, mummers and players. The princess smiled very pleasantly but never laughed, gave small purses of Spanish coins to all the entertainers, thanked them for their attendance; but never once turned to her husband to ask him if he was enjoying the evening. The prince walked around the room, affable and pleasant to the great men of the city. He spoke in English, all the time, and his Spanish-speaking bride had to wait for someone to talk to her in French or Latin, if they would. Instead, they clustered around the prince and chatted and joked and laughed, almost as if they were laughing at her, and did not want her to understand the jest. The princess sat alone, stiffly on her hard, carved wooden chair, her head held high and a small, defiant smile on her lips.

At last it was midnight and the long evening could end. Catalina rose from her seat and watched the court sink into bows and curtseys. She dropped a low Spanish curtsey to her husband, her duenna behind her with a face like flint. 'I bid you goodnight, Your Grace,' said the princess in Latin, her voice clear, her accent perfect.

'I shall come to your room,' he said. There was a little murmur of approval; the court wanted a lusty prince.

The colour rose in her cheeks at the very public announcement. There was nothing she could say. She could not refuse him; but the way she rose and left the room did not promise him a warm welcome when they were alone. Her ladies dipped their curtseys and followed her in a little offended flurry, swishing off like a many-coloured veil trailing behind her. The court smiled behind their hands at the high spirits of the bride.

Arthur came to her half an hour later, fired up by drink and resentment. He found her still dressed, waiting by the fire, her duenna at her side, her room ablaze with candles, her ladies still talking and playing cards as if it were the middle of the afternoon. Clearly, she was not a young woman on her way to bed.

'Sire, good evening,' she said and rose and curtseyed as he entered.

Arthur had to check his backwards step, in retreat at the first encounter. He was ready for bed, in his nightgown with only a robe thrown over his shoulders. He was acutely aware of his bare feet and vulnerable toes. Catalina blazed in her evening finery. The ladies all turned and looked at him, their faces unfriendly. He was acutely conscious of his nightgown and his bare legs and a chuckle of barely suppressed laughter from one of his men behind him.

'I expected you to be in bed,' he said.

'Of course, I can go to bed,' she returned with glacial courtesy. 'I was about to go to bed. It is very late. But when you announced so publicly that you would visit me in my rooms I thought you must be planning to bring all the court with you. I thought you were telling everyone to come to my rooms. Why else announce it at the top of your voice so that everybody could hear?'

'I did not announce it at the top of my voice!'

She raised an eyebrow in wordless contradiction.

'I shall stay the night,' he said stubbornly. He marched to her bedroom door. 'These ladies can go to their beds, it is late.' He nodded to his men. 'Leave us.' He went into her room and closed the door behind him.

She followed him and closed the door behind her, shutting out the bright, scandalised faces of the ladies. Her back to the door, she watched him throw off his robe and nightgown so he was naked, and climb into her bed. He plumped up the pillows and leaned back, his arms crossed against his narrow bare chest, like a man awaiting an entertainment.

It was her turn to be discomforted. 'Your Grace . . .'

'You had better get undressed,' he taunted her. 'As you say, it's very late.'

She turned one way, and then the other. 'I shall send for Dona Elvira.'

'Do. And send for whoever else undresses you. Don't mind me, please.'

Catalina bit her lip. He could see her uncertainty. She could not bear to be stripped naked in front of him. She turned and went out of the bedchamber.

There was a rattle of irritable Spanish from the room next door. Arthur grinned, he guessed that she was clearing the room of her ladies and undressing out there. When she came back, he saw that he was right. She was wearing a white gown trimmed with exquisite lace and her hair was in a long plait down her back. She looked more like a little girl than the haughty princess she had been only moments before, and he felt his desire rise up with some other feeling: a tenderness.

She glanced at him, her face unfriendly. 'I will have to say my prayers,' she said. She went to the prie-dieu and kneeled before it. He watched her bow her head over her clasped hands and start to whisper. For the first time his irritation left him, and he thought how hard it must be for her. Surely, his unease and fear must be nothing to hers: alone in a strange land, at the beck and call of a boy a few months younger than her, with no real friends and no family, far away from everything and everyone she knew.

The bed was warm. The wine he had drunk to give him courage now made him feel sleepy. He leaned back on the pillow. Her prayers were taking a long time but it was good for a man to have a spiritual wife. He closed his eyes on the thought. When she came to bed he thought he would take her with confidence but with gentleness. It was Christmas, he should be kind to her. She was probably lonely and afraid. He should be generous. He thought warmly of how loving he would be to her, and how grateful she would be. Perhaps they would learn to give each other pleasure, perhaps he would make her happy. His breathing deepened, he gave a tiny little snuffly snore. He slept.

Catalina looked around from her prayers and smiled in pure triumph. Then, absolutely silently, she crept into bed beside him and, carefully arranging herself so that not even of the hem of her nightgown could touch him, she composed herself for sleep.

You thought to embarrass me before my women, before all the court. You thought you could shame me and triumph over me. But I am a princess of Spain and I have known things and seen things that you, in this safe little country, in this smug little haven, would never dream of. I am the Infanta, I am the daughter of the two most powerful monarchs in the whole of Christendom who alone have defeated the greatest threat ever to march against it. For seven hundred years the Moors have occupied Spain, an empire mightier than that of the Romans, and who drove them out? My mother! My father! So you needn't think I am afraid of you – you rose-petal prince, or whatever they call you. I shall never stoop to do anything that a princess of Spain should not do. I shall never be petty or spiteful. But if you challenge me, I shall defeat you.

Arthur did not speak to her in the morning, his boy's high pride was utterly cut to the quick. She had shamed him at his father's court by denying him her rooms, and now she had shamed him in private. He felt that she had trapped him, made a fool of him, and was even now laughing at him. He rose up and went out in sullen silence. He went to Mass and did not meet her eyes, he went hunting and was gone all day. He did not speak to her at night. They watched a play, seated side by side, and not one word was exchanged all evening. A whole week they stayed at Oxford and they did not say more than a dozen words to each other every day. He swore a private bitter oath to himself that he would never, ever speak to her again. He would get a child on her, if he could, he would humiliate her in every way that he could, but he would never say one direct word to her, and he would never, never, never sleep again in her bed.

When the morning came for them to move on to Ludlow the sky was grey with clouds, fat-bellied with snow. Catalina came out of the doorway of the college and recoiled as the icy, damp air hit her in the face. Arthur ignored her.

She stepped out into the yard where the train was all drawn up and waiting for her. She hesitated before the litter. It struck him that she was like a prisoner, hesitating before a cart. She could not choose.

'Will it not be very cold?' she asked.

He turned a hard face to her. 'You will have to get used to the cold, you're not in Spain now.'

'So I see.'

She drew back the curtains of the litter. Inside there were rugs for her to wrap around herself and cushions for her to rest on, but it did not look very cosy.

'It gets far worse than this,' he said cheerfully. 'Far colder, it rains or sleets or snows, and it gets darker. In February we have only a couple of hours of daylight at best, and then there are the freezing fogs which turn day into night so it is forever grey.'

She turned and looked up at him. 'Could we not set out another day?'

'You agreed to come,' he taunted her. 'I would have been happy to leave you at Greenwich.'

'I did as I was told.'

'So here we are. Travelling on as we have been ordered to do.'

'At least you can move about and keep warm,' she said plaintively. 'Can I not ride?'

'My Lady the King's Mother said you could not.'

She made a little face but she did not argue.

'It's your choice. Shall I leave you here?' he asked briskly, as if he had little time for these uncertainties.

'No,' she said. 'Of course not,' and climbed into the litter and pulled the rugs over her feet and up around her shoulders.

Arthur led the way out of Oxford, bowing and smiling at the people who had turned out to cheer him. Catalina drew the curtains of her litter against the cold wind and the curious stares, and would not show her face.

They stopped for dinner at a great house on the way and Arthur went into dine without even waiting to help her from the litter. The lady of the house, flustered, went out to the litter and found Catalina stumbling out, white-faced and with red eyes.

'Princess, are you all right?' the woman asked her.

'I am cold,' Catalina said miserably. 'I am freezing cold. I think I have never been so cold.'

She hardly ate any dinner, they could not make her take any wine. She looked ready to drop with exhaustion; but as soon as they had eaten Arthur wanted to push on, they had twenty more miles to go before the early dusk of winter.

'Can't you refuse?' Maria de Salinas asked her in a quick whisper.

'No,' the princess said. She rose from her seat without another word. But when they opened the great wooden door to go out into the courtyard, small flakes of snow swirled in around them.

'We cannot travel in this, it will soon be dark and we shall lose the road!' Catalina exclaimed.

'I shall not lose the road,' Arthur said, and strode out to his horse. 'You shall follow me.'

The lady of the house sent a servant flying for a heated stone to put in the litter at Catalina's feet. The princess climbed in, hunched the rugs around her shoulders, and tucked her hands in deep.

'I am sure that he is impatient to get you to Ludlow to show you his castle,' the woman said, trying to put the best aspect on a miserable situation.

'He is impatient to show me nothing but neglect,' Catalina snapped; but she took care to say it in Spanish.

They left the warmth and lights of the great house and heard the doors bang behind them as they turned the horses' heads to the west, and to the white sun which was sinking low on the horizon. It was two hours past noon but the sky was so filled with snow clouds that there was an eerie grey glow over the rolling landscape. The road snaked ahead of them, brown tracks against brown fields, both of them bleaching to whiteness under the haze of swirling snow. Arthur rode ahead, singing merrily, Catalina's litter laboured along behind. At every step the mules threw the litter to one side and then the other, she had to keep a hand on the edge to hold herself in place, and her fingers became chilled and then cramped, blue from cold. The curtains kept out the worst of the snowflakes but not the insistent, penetrating draughts. If she drew back a corner to look out at the country she saw a whirl of whiteness as the snowflakes danced and circled the road, the sky seeming greyer every moment.

The sun set white in a white sky and the world grew more shadowy. Snow and clouds closed down around the little cavalcade which wound its way across a white land under a grey sky.

Arthur's horse cantered ahead, the prince riding easily in the saddle, one gloved hand on the reins, the other on his whip. He had stout woollen undergarments under his thick leather jerkin and soft, warm leather boots. Catalina watched him ride forwards. She was too cold and too miserable even to resent him. More than anything else she wished he would ride back to tell her that the journey was nearly over, that they were there.

An hour passed, the mules walked down the road, their heads bowed low against the wind that whirled flakes around their ears and into the litter. The snow was getting thicker now, filling the air and drifting into the ruts of the lane. Catalina had hunched up under the covers, lying like a child, the rapidly cooling stone at her belly, her knees drawn up, her cold hands tucked in, her face ducked down, buried in the furs and rugs. Her feet were freezing cold, there was a gap in the rugs at her back and now and then she shivered at a fresh draught of icy air.

All around, outside the litter, she could hear men chattering and laughing about the cold, swearing that they would eat well when the train got into Burford. Their voices seemed to come from far away; Catalina drifted into a sleep from coldness and exhaustion.

Groggily, she woke when the litter bumped down to the ground and the curtains were swept back. A wave of icy air washed over her and she ducked her head down and cried out in discomfort.

'Infanta?' Dona Elvira asked. The duenna had been riding her mule, the exercise had kept her warm. 'Infanta? Thank God, at last we are here.'

Catalina would not lift her head.

'Infanta, they are waiting to greet you.'

Still Catalina would not look up.

'What's this?' It was Arthur's voice, he had seen the litter put down and the duenna bending over it. He saw that the heap of rugs made no movement. For a moment, with a pang of dismay, he thought that the princess might have been taken ill. Maria de Salinas gave him a reproachful look. 'What's the matter?'

'It is nothing.' Dona Elvira straightened up and stood between the prince and his young wife, shielding Catalina as he jumped from his horse and came towards her. 'The princess has been asleep, she is composing herself.'

'I'll see her,' he said. He put the woman aside with one confident hand and kneeled down beside the litter.

'Catalina?' he asked quietly.

'I am frozen with cold,' said a little thread of voice. She lifted her head and he saw that she was as white as the snow itself and her

97

lips were blue. 'I am so c . . . cold that I shall die and then you will be happy. You can b . . . bury me in this horrible country and m . . . marry some fat, stupid Englishwoman. And I shall never see . . .' She broke off into sobs.

'Catalina?' He was utterly bemused.

'I shall never see my m . . . mother again. But she will know that you killed me with your miserable country and your cruelty.'

'I have not been cruel!' he rejoined at once, quite blind to the gathering crowd of courtiers around them. 'By God, Catalina, it was not me!'

'You have been cruel.' She lifted her face from the rugs. 'You have been cruel because –'

It was her sad, white, tearstained face that spoke to him far more than her words could ever have done. She looked like one of his sisters when their grandmother scolded them. She did not look like an infuriating, insulting princess of Spain, she looked like a girl who had been bullied into tears – and he realised that it was he who had bullied her, he had made her cry, and he had left her in the cold litter for all the afternoon while he had ridden on ahead and delighted in the thought of her discomfort.

He reached into the rugs and pulled out her icy hand. Her fingers were numb with cold. He knew he had done wrong. He took her blue fingertips to his mouth and kissed them, then he held them against his lips and blew his warm breath against them. 'God forgive me,' he said. 'I forgot I was a husband. I didn't know I had to be a husband. I didn't realise that I could make you cry. I won't ever do so again.'

She blinked, her blue eyes swimming in unshed tears. 'What?'

'I was wrong. I was angry but quite wrong. Let me take you inside and we will get warm and I shall tell you how sorry I am and I will never be unkind to you again.'

At once she struggled with her rugs and Arthur pulled them off her legs. She was so cramped and so chilled that she stumbled when she tried to stand. Ignoring the muffled protests of her duenna, he swept her up into his arms and carried her like a bride across the threshold of the hall.

Gently he put her down before the roaring fire, gently he put back her hood, untied her cloak, chafed her hands. He waved away the servants who would have come to take her cloak, offered her wine. He made a little circle of peace and silence around them, and he watched the colour come back to her pale cheeks.

'I am sorry,' he said, heartfelt. 'I was very, very angry with you but I should not have taken you so far in such bad weather and I should never have let you get cold. It was wrong of me.'

'I forgive you,' she whispered, a little smile lighting her face.

'I didn't know that I had to take care of you. I didn't think. I have been like a child, an unkind child. But I know now, Catalina. I will never be unkind to you again.'

She nodded. 'Oh, please. And you too must forgive me. I have been unkind to you.'

'Have you?'

'At Oxford,' she whispered, very low.

He nodded. 'And what do you say to me?'

She stole a quick upwards glance at him. He was not making a play of offence. He was a boy still, with a boy's fierce sense of fairness. He needed a proper apology.

'I am very, very sorry,' she said, speaking nothing but the truth. 'It was not a good thing to do, and I was sorry in the morning, but I could not tell you.'

'Shall we go to bed now?' he whispered to her, his mouth very close to her ear.

'Can we?'

'If I say that you are ill?'

She nodded, and said nothing more.

'The princess is unwell from the cold,' Arthur announced generally. 'Dona Elvira will take her to her room, and I shall dine there, alone with her, later.'

'But the people have come to see Your Grace . . .' his host pleaded. 'They have an entertainment for you, and some disputes they would like you to hear . . .'

'I shall see them all in the hall now, and we shall stay tomorrow also. But the princess must go to her rooms at once.'

'Of course.'

There was a flurry around the princess as her ladies, led by Dona Elvira, escorted her to her room. Catalina glanced back at Arthur. 'Please come to my room for dinner,' she said clearly enough for everyone to hear. 'I want to see you, Your Grace.'

It was everything to him: to hear her publicly avow her desire for him. He bowed at the compliment and then he went to the great hall and called for a cup of ale and dealt very graciously with the half-dozen men who had mustered to see him, and then he excused himself and went to her room.

Catalina was waiting for him, alone by the fireside. She had dismissed her women, her servants, there was no-one to wait on them, they were quite alone. He almost recoiled at the sight of the empty room; the Tudor princes and princesses were never left alone. But she had banished the servants who should wait at the table, she had sent away the ladies who should dine with them. She had even dismissed her duenna. There was no-one to see what she had done to her apartments, nor how she had set the dinner table.

She had swathed the plain wooden furniture in scarves of light cloth in vivid colours, she had even draped scarves from the tapestries to hide the cold walls, so the room was like a beautifully trimmed tent.

She had ordered them to saw the legs of the table down to stumps, so the table sat as low as a footstool, a most ridiculous piece of furniture. She had set big cushions at either end, as if they should recline like savages to eat. The dinner was set out on the table at knee level, drawn up to the warmth of the burning logs like some barbaric feast, there were candles everywhere and a rich smell like incense, as heady as a church on a feast day.

Arthur was about to complain at the wild extravagance of sawing up the furniture; but then he paused. This was, perhaps, not just some girlish folly; she was trying to show him something.

She was wearing a most extraordinary costume. On her head was a twist of the finest silk, turned and knotted like a coronet with a tail hanging down behind which she had tucked nonchalantly in one side of the headdress as if she would pull it over her face like a veil. Instead of a decent gown she wore a simple shift of the finest, lightest silk, smoky blue in colour, so fine that he could almost see through it, to glimpse the paleness of her skin underneath. He could feel his heartbeat thud when he realised she was naked beneath this wisp of silk. Beneath the chemise she was wearing a pair of hose – like men's hose – but nothing like men's hose, for they were billowy leggings which fell from her slim hips where they were tied with a drawstring of gold thread, to her feet where they were tied again, leaving her feet half bare in dainty crimson slippers worked with a gold thread. He looked her up and down, from barbaric turban to Turkish slippers, and found himself bereft of speech.

'You don't like my clothes,' Catalina said flatly, and he was too inexperienced to recognise the depth of embarrassment that she was ready to feel.

'I've never seen anything like them before,' he stammered. 'Are they Arab clothes? Show me!'

She turned on the spot, watching him over her shoulder and then coming back to face him again. 'We all wear them in Spain,' she said. 'My mother too. They are more comfortable than gowns, and cleaner. Everything can be washed, not like velvets and damask.'

He nodded, he noticed now a light rosewater scent which came from the silk.

'And they are cool in the heat of the day,' she added.

'They are . . . beautiful.' He nearly said 'barbaric' and was so glad that he had not, when her eyes lit up.

'Do you think so?'

'Yes.'

At once she raised her arms and twirled again to show him the flutter of the hose and the lightness of the chemise.

'You wear them to sleep in?'

She laughed. 'We wear them nearly all the time. My mother always wears them under her armour, they are far more comfortable than anything else, and she could not wear gowns under chain mail.'

'No . . .'

'When we are receiving Christian ambassadors, or for great state occasions, or when the court is at feast, we wear gowns and robes, especially at Christmas when it is cold. But in our own rooms, and always in the summer, and always when we are on campaign, we wear Morisco dress. It is easy to make, and easy to wash, and easy to carry, and best to wear.'

'You cannot wear it here,' Arthur said. 'I am so sorry. But My Lady the King's Mother would object if she knew you even had them with you.'

She nodded. 'I know that. My mother was against me even bringing them. But I wanted something to remind me of my home and I thought I might keep them in my cupboard and tell nobody. Then tonight, I thought I might show you. Show you myself, and how I used to be.'

Catalina stepped to one side and gestured to him that he should come to the table. He felt too big, too clumsy, and on an instinct, he stooped and shucked off his riding boots and stepped on to the rich rugs barefoot. She gave a little nod of approval and beckoned him to sit. He dropped to one of the gold-embroidered cushions.

Serenely, she sat opposite him and passed him a bowl of scented water, with a white napkin. He dipped his fingers and wiped them.

She smiled and offered him a gold plate laid with food. It was a dish of his childhood, roasted chicken legs, devilled kidneys, with white manchet bread: a proper English dinner. But she had made them serve only tiny portions on each individual plate, dainty bones artfully arranged. She had sliced apples served alongside the meat, and added some precious spiced meats next to sliced sugared plums. She had done everything she could to serve him a Spanish meal, with all the delicacy and luxury of the Moorish taste.

Arthur was shaken from his prejudice. 'This is . . . beautiful,' he said, seeking a word to describe it. 'This is . . . like a picture. You are like . . .' He could not think of anything that he had ever seen that was like her. Then an image came to him. 'You are like a painting I once saw on a plate,' he said. 'A treasure of my mother's from Persia. You are like that. Strange, and most lovely.'

She glowed at his praise. 'I want you to understand,' she said, speaking carefully in Latin. 'I want you to understand what I am. Cuiusmodi sum.'

'What you are?'

'I am your wife,' she assured him. 'I am the Princess of Wales, I will be Queen of England. I will be an Englishwoman. That is my destiny. But also, as well as this, I am the Infanta of Spain, of al Andalus.'

'I know.'

'You know; but you don't know. You don't know about Spain, you don't know about me. I want to explain myself to you. I want you to know about Spain. I am a princess of Spain. I am my father's favourite. When we dine alone, we eat like this. When we are on campaign, we live in tents and sit before the braziers like this, and we were on campaign for every year of my life until I was seven.'

'But you are a Christian court,' he protested. 'You are a power in Christendom. You have chairs, proper chairs, you must eat your dinner off a proper table.'

'Only at banquets of state,' she said. 'When we are in our private rooms we live like this, like Moors. Oh, we say grace; we thank the

One God at the breaking of the bread. But we do not live as you live here in England. We have beautiful gardens filled with fountains and running water. We have rooms in our palaces inlaid with precious stones and inscribed with gold letters telling beautiful truths in poetry. We have bath houses with hot water to wash in and thick steam to fill the scented room, we have ice houses packed in winter with snow from the sierras so our fruit and our drinks are chilled in summer.'

The words were as seductive as the images. 'You make yourself sound so strange,' he said reluctantly. 'Like a fairy tale.'

'I am only just realising now how strange we are to each other,' Catalina said. 'I thought that your country would be like mine but it is quite different. I am coming to think that we are more like Persians than like Germans. We are more Arabic than Visigoth. Perhaps you thought that I would be a princess like your sisters, but I am quite, quite different.'

He nodded. 'I shall have to learn your ways,' he proposed tentatively. 'As you will have to learn mine.'

'I shall be Queen of England, I shall have to become English. But I want you to know what I was, when I was a girl.'

Arthur nodded. 'Were you very cold today?' he asked. He could feel a strange new feeling, like a weight in his belly. He realised it was discomfort, at the thought of her being unhappy.

She met his look without concealment. 'Yes,' she said. 'I was very cold. And then I thought that I had been unkind to you and I was very unhappy. And then I thought that I was far away from my home and from the heat and the sunshine and my mother and I was very homesick. It was a horrible day, today. I had a horrible day, today.'

He reached his hand out to her. 'Can I comfort you?'

Her fingertips met his. 'You did,' she said. 'When you brought me in to the fire and told me you were sorry. You do comfort me. I will learn to trust that you always will.'

He drew her to him; the cushions were soft and easy, he laid her beside him and he gently tugged at the silk that was wrapped around her head. It slipped off at once and the rich red tresses tumbled down. He touched them with his lips, then her sweet slightly trembling mouth, her eyes with the sandy eyelashes, her light eyebrows, the blue veins at her temples, the lobes of her ears. Then he felt his desire rise and he kissed the hollow at the base of her throat, her thin collarbones, the warm, seductive flesh from neck to shoulder, the hollow of her elbow, the warmth of her palm, the erotically deep-scented armpit, and then he drew her shift over her head and she was naked, in his arms, and she was his wife, and a loving wife, at last, indeed.

I love him. I did not think it possible, but I love him. I have fallen in love with him. I look at myself in the mirror, in wonderment, as if I am changed, as everything else is changed. I am a young woman in love with my husband. I am in love with the Prince of Wales. I, Catalina of Spain, am in love. I wanted this love, I thought it was impossible, and I have it. I am in love with my husband and we shall be King and Queen of England. Who can doubt now that I am chosen by God for His especial favour? He brought me from the dangers of war to safety and peace in the Alhambra Palace and now He has given me England and the love of the young man who will be its king.

In a sudden rush of emotion I put my hands together and pray: 'Oh God, let me love him forever, do not take us from each other as Juan was taken from Margot, in their first months of joy. Let us grow old together, let us love each other for ever.'

Ludlow Castle, January 1502

The winter sun was low and red over the rounded hills as they rattled through the great gate that pierced the stone wall around Ludlow.

Arthur, who had been riding beside the litter, shouted to Catalina over the noise of the hooves on the cobbles. 'This is Ludlow, at last!'

Ahead of them the men-at-arms shouted: 'Make way for Arthur! Prince of Wales!' and the doors banged open and people tumbled out of their houses to see the procession go by.

Catalina saw a town as pretty as a tapestry. The timbered second storeys of the crowded buildings overhung cobbled streets with prosperous little shops and working yards tucked cosily underneath them on the ground floor. The shopkeepers' wives jumped up from their stools set outside the shops to wave to her and Catalina smiled, and waved back. From the upper storeys the glovers' girls and shoemakers' apprentices, the goldsmiths' boys and the spinsters leaned out and called her name. Catalina laughed, and caught her breath as one young lad looked ready to overbalance but was hauled back in by his cheering mates.

They passed a great bull ring with a dark-timbered inn, as the church bells of the half-dozen religious houses, college, chapels and hospital of Ludlow started to peal their bells to welcome the prince and his bride home.

Catalina leaned forwards to see her castle, and noted the unassailable march of the outer bailey. The gate was flung open, they went in, and found the greatest men of the town, the mayor, the church elders, the leaders of the wealthy trades guilds, assembled to greet them.

Arthur pulled up his horse and listened politely to a long speech in Welsh and then in English.

'When do we eat?' Catalina whispered to him in Latin and saw his mouth quiver as he held back a smile.

'When do we go to bed?' she breathed, and had the satisfaction of seeing his hand tremble on the rein with desire. She gave a little giggle and ducked back into the litter until finally the interminable speeches of welcome were finished and the royal party could ride on through the great gate of the castle to the inner bailey.

It was a neat castle, as sound as any border castle in Spain. The curtain wall marched around the inner bailey high and strong, made in a curious rosy-coloured stone that made the powerful walls more warm and domestic.

Catalina's eye, sharpened by her training, looked from the thick walls to the well in the outer bailey, the well in the inner bailey, took in how one defensible area led to another, thought that a siege could be held off for years. But it was small, it was like a toy castle, something her father would build to protect a river crossing or a vulnerable road. Something a very minor lord of Spain would be proud to have as his home.

'Is this it?' she asked blankly, thinking of the city that was housed inside the walls of her home, of the gardens and the terraces, of the hill and the views, of the teeming life of the town centre, all inside defended walls. Of the long hike for the guards: if they went all around the battlements they would be gone for more than an hour. At Ludlow a sentry would complete the circle in minutes. 'Is this it?'

At once he was aghast. 'Did you expect more? What were you expecting?'

She would have caressed his anxious face, if there had not been hundreds of people watching. She made herself keep her hands still. 'Oh, I was foolish. I was thinking of Richmond.' Nothing in the world would have made her say that she was thinking of the Alhambra.

He smiled, reassured. 'Oh, my love. Richmond is new-built, my father's great pride and joy. London is one of the greatest cities of Christendom, and the palace matches its size. But Ludlow is only a town, a great town in the Marches, for sure, but a town. But it is wealthy, you will see, and the hunting is good and the people are welcoming. You will be happy here.'

'I am sure of it,' said Catalina, smiling at him, putting aside the thought of a palace built for beauty, only for beauty, where the builders had thought firstly where the light would fall and what reflections it would make in still pools of marble.

She looked around her and saw, in the centre of the inner bailey, a curious circular building like a squat tower.

'What's that?' she asked, struggling out of the litter as Arthur held her hand.

He glanced over his shoulder. 'It's our round chapel,' he said negligently.

'A round chapel?'

'Yes, like in Jerusalem.'

At once she recognised with delight the traditional shape of the mosque – designed and built in the round so that no worshipper was better placed than any others, because Allah is praised by the poor man as well as the rich. 'It's lovely.'

Arthur glanced at her in surprise. To him it was only a round tower built with the pretty plum-coloured local stone, but he saw that it glowed in the afternoon light, and radiated a sense of peace.

'Yes,' he said, hardly noticing it. 'Now this,' he indicated the great building facing them, with a handsome flight of steps up to the open door, 'this is the great hall. To the left are the council chambers of Wales and, above them, my rooms. To the right are the guest bedrooms and chambers for the warden of the castle and his lady: Sir Richard and Lady Margaret Pole. Your rooms are above, on the top floor.'

He saw her swift reaction. 'She is here now?'

'She is away from the castle at the moment.'

She nodded. 'There are buildings behind the great hall?'

'No. It is set into the outer wall. This is all of it.'

Catalina schooled herself to keep her face smiling and pleasant.

'We have more guest rooms in the outer bailey,' he said defensively. 'And we have a lodge house, as well. It is a busy place, merry. You will like it.'

'I am sure I will,' she smiled. 'And which are my rooms?'

He pointed to the highest windows. 'See up there? On the right-hand side, matching mine, but on the opposite side of the hall.'

She looked a little daunted. 'But how will you get to my rooms?' she asked quietly.

He took her hand and led her, smiling to his right and to his left, towards the grand stone stairs to the double doors of the great hall. There was a ripple of applause and their companions fell in behind them. 'As My Lady the King's Mother commanded me, four times a month I shall come to your room in a formal procession through the great hall,' he said. He led her up the steps.

'Oh.' She was dashed.

He smiled down at her. 'And all the other nights I shall come to you along the battlements,' he whispered. 'There is a private door that goes from your rooms to the battlements that run all around the castle. My rooms go on to them too. You can walk from your rooms to mine whenever you wish and nobody will know whether we are together or not. They will not even know whose room we are in.'

He loved how her face lit up. 'We can be together, whenever we want?'

'We will be happy here.'

Yes I will, I will be happy here. I will not mourn like a Persian for the beautiful courts of his home and declare that there is nowhere else fit for life. I will not say that these mountains are a desert without oases like a Berber longing for his birthright. I will accustom myself to Ludlow, and I will learn to live here, on the border, and later in England. My mother is not just a queen, she is a soldier, and she raised me to know my duty and to do it. It is my duty to learn to be happy here and to live here without complaining.

I may never wear armour as she did, I may never fight for my country, as she did; but there are many ways to serve a kingdom, and to be a merry, honest, constant queen is one of them. If God does not call me to arms, He may call me to serve as a lawgiver, as a bringer of justice. Whether I defend my people by fighting for them against an enemy or by fighting for their freedom in the law, I shall be their queen, heart and soul, Queen of England.

It was night time, past midnight. Catalina glowed in the firelight. They were in bed, sleepy, but too desirous of each other for sleep.

'Tell me a story.'

'I have told you dozens of stories.'

'Tell me another. Tell me the one about Boabdil giving up the Alhambra Palace with the golden keys on a silk cushion and going away crying.'

'You know that one. I told it to you last night.'

'Then tell me the story about Yarfa and his horse that gnashed its teeth at Christians.'

'You are a child. And his name was Yarfe.'

'But you saw him killed?'

'I was there; but I didn't see him actually die.'

'How could you not watch it?'

'Well, partly because I was praying as my mother ordered me to, and because I was a girl and not a bloodthirsty, monstrous boy.'

Arthur tossed an embroidered cushion at her head. She caught it and threw it back at him.

'Well, tell me about your mother pawning her jewels to pay for the crusade.'

She laughed again and shook her head, making her auburn hair swing this way and that. 'I shall tell you about my home,' she offered.

'All right.' He gathered the purple blanket around them both and waited.

'When you come through the first door to the Alhambra it looks like a little room. Your father would not stoop to enter a palace like that.'

'It's not grand?'

'It's the size of a little merchant's hall in the town here. It is a good hall for a small house in Ludlow, nothing more.'

'And then?'

'And then you go into the courtyard and from there into the golden chamber.'

'A little better?'

'It is filled with colour, but still it is not much bigger. The walls are bright with coloured tiles and gold leaf and there is a high balcony, but it is still only a little space.'

'And then, where shall we go today?'

'Today we shall turn right and go into the Court of the Myrtles.'

He closed his eyes, trying to remember her descriptions. 'A courtyard in the shape of a rectangle, surrounded by high buildings of gold.'

'With a huge, dark wooden doorway framed with beautiful tiles at the far end.'

'And a lake, a lake of a simple rectangle shape, and on either side of the water, a hedge of sweet-scented myrtle trees.'

'Not a hedge like you have,' she demurred, thinking of the ragged edges of the Welsh fields in their struggle of thorn and weed.

'Like what, then?' he asked, opening his eyes.

'A hedge like a wall,' she said. 'Cut straight and square, like a block of green marble, like a living green sweet-scented statue. And the gateway at the end is reflected back in the water, and the arch around it, and the building that it is set in. So that the whole thing is mirrored in ripples at your feet. And the walls are pierced with light screens of stucco, as airy as paper, like white on white embroidery. And the birds . . .'

'The birds?' he asked, surprised, for she had not told him of them before.

She paused while she thought of the word. '*Apodes*?' she said in Latin.

'*Apodes*? Swifts?'

She nodded. 'They flow like a turbulent river of birds just above your head, round and round the narrow courtyard, screaming as they go, as fast as a cavalry charge, they go like the wind, round and round, as long as the sun shines on the water they go round, all day. And at night –'

'At night?'

She made a little gesture with her hands, like an enchantress. 'At night they disappear, you never see them settle or nest. They just disappear – they set with the sun, but at dawn they are there again, like a river, like a flood.' She paused. 'It is hard to describe,' she said in a small voice. 'But I see it all the time.'

'You miss it,' he said flatly. 'However happy I may make you, you will always miss it.'

She made a little gesture. 'Of course. It is to be expected. But I never forget who I am. Who I was born to be.'

Arthur waited.

She smiled at him, her face was warmed by her smile, her blue eyes shining. 'The Princess of Wales,' she said. 'From my childhood I knew it. They always called me the Princess of Wales. And so Queen of England, as destined by God. Catalina, Infanta of Spain, Princess of Wales.'

He smiled in reply and drew her closer to him, they lay back together, her head on his shoulder, her dark red hair a veil across his chest.

'I knew I would marry you almost from the moment I was born,' he said reflectively. 'I can't remember a time when I was not betrothed to you. I can't remember a time when I was not writing letters to you and taking them to my tutor for correction.'

'Lucky that I please you, now I am here.'

He put his finger under her chin and turned her face up towards him for a kiss. 'Even luckier, that I please you,' he said.

'I would have been a good wife anyway,' she insisted. 'Even without this . . .'

He pulled her hand down beneath the silky sheets to touch him where he was growing big again.

'Without this, you mean?' he teased.

'Without this . . . joy,' she said and closed her eyes and lay back, waiting for his touch.

Their servants woke them at dawn and Arthur was ceremonially escorted from her bed. They saw each other again at Mass but they were seated at opposite sides of the round chapel, each with their own household, and could not speak.

The Mass should be the most important moment of my day, and it should bring me comfort – I know that. But I always feel lonely during Mass. I do pray to God and thank Him for His especial care of me, but just being in this chapel – shaped like a tiny mosque – reminds me so much of my mother. The smell of incense is as evocative of her as if it were her perfume, I cannot believe that I am not kneeling beside her as I have done four times a day for almost every day of my life. When I say 'Hail Mary, full of grace' it is my mother's round, smiling, determined face that I see. And when I pray for courage to do my duty in this strange land with these dour, undemonstrative people, it is my mother's strength that I need.

I should give thanks for Arthur but I dare not even think of him when I am on my knees to God. I cannot think of him without the sin of desire. The very image of him in my mind is a deep secret, a pagan pleasure. I am certain that this is not the holy joy of matrimony. Such intense pleasure must be a sin. Such dark, deep desire and satisfaction cannot be the pure conception of a little prince that is the whole point and purpose of this marriage. We were put to bed by an archbishop but our passionate coupling is as animal as a pair of sun-warmed snakes twisted all around in their pleasure. I keep my joy in Arthur a secret from everyone, even from God.

I could not confide in anyone, even if I wanted to. We are expressly forbidden from being together as we wish. His grandmother, My Lady the King's Mother, has ordered this, as she orders everything, even everything here in the Welsh Marches. She has said that he should come to my room once a week every week, except for the time of my courses, he should arrive before ten of the clock and leave by six. We obey her of course, everybody obeys her. Once a week, as she has commanded, he comes through the great hall, like a young man reluctantly obedient, and in the morning he leaves me in silence and goes quietly away as a young man who has done his duty, not one that has been awake all night in breathless delight. He never boasts of pleasure, when they come to fetch him from my chamber he says nothing, nobody knows the joy we take in each other's passion. No-one will ever know that we are together every night. We meet on the battlements which run from his rooms to mine at the very top of the castle, grey-blue sky arching above us, and we consort like lovers in secret, concealed by the night, we go to my room, or to his, and we make a private world together, filled with hidden joy.

Even in this crowded small castle filled with busybodies and the king's mother's spies, nobody knows that we are together, and nobody knows how much we are in love.

After Mass the royal pair went to break their fast in their separate rooms, though they would rather have been together. Ludlow Castle was a small reproduction of the formality of the king's court. The king's mother had commanded that after breakfast Arthur must work with his tutor at his books or at sports as the weather allowed; and Catalina must work with her tutor, sew, or read, or walk in the garden.

'A garden!' Catalina whispered under her breath in the little patch of green with the sodden turf bench on one side of a thin border, set in the corner of the castle walls. 'I wonder if she has ever seen a real garden?'

In the afternoon they might ride out together to hunt in the woods around the castle. It was a rich countryside, the river fast-flowing through a wide valley with old thick woodlands on the sides of the hills. Catalina thought she would grow to love the pasture lands around the River Teme and, on the horizon, the way the darkness of the hills gave way to the sky. But in the mid-winter weather it was a landscape of grey and white, only the frost or the snow bringing brightness to the blackness of the cold woods. The weather was often too bad for the princess to go out at all. She hated the damp fog or when it drizzled with icy sleet. Arthur often rode alone.

'Even if I stayed behind I would not be allowed to be with you,' he said mournfully. 'My grandmother would have set me something else to do.'

'So go!' she said, smiling, though it seemed a long, long time until dinner and she had nothing to do but to wait for the hunt to come home.

They went out into the town once a week, to go to St Laurence's Church for Mass, or to visit the little chapel by the castle wall, to attend a dinner organised by one of the great guilds, or to see a cockfight, a bull baiting, or players. Catalina was impressed by the neat prettiness of the town; the place had escaped the violence of the wars between York and Lancaster that had finally been ended by Henry Tudor.

'Peace is everything to a kingdom,' she observed to Arthur.

'The only thing that can threaten us now is the Scots,' he said.

'The Yorkist line are my forebears, the Lancasters too, so the rivalry ends with me. All we have to do is keep the north safe.'

'And your father thinks he has done that with Princess Margaret's marriage?'

'Pray God he is right, but they are a faithless lot. When I am king I shall keep the border strong. You shall advise me, we'll go out together and make sure the border castles are repaired.'

'I shall like that,' she said.

'Of course, you spent your childhood with an army fighting for border lands, you would know better than I what to look for.'

She smiled. 'I am glad it is a skill of mine that you can use. My father always complained that my mother was making Amazons, not princesses.'

They dined together at dusk, and thankfully, dusk came very early on those cold winter nights. At last they could be close, seated side by side at the high table looking down the hall of the castle, the great hearth heaped with logs on the side wall. Arthur always put Catalina on his left, closest to the fire, and she wore a cloak lined with fur, and had layer upon layer of linen shifts under her ornate gown. Even so, she was still cold when she came down the icy stairs from her warm rooms to the smoky hall. Her Spanish ladies, Maria de Salinas, her duenna Dona Elvira and a few others, were seated at one table, the English ladies who were supposed to be her companions at another and her retinue of Spanish servants were seated at another. The great lords of Arthur's council, his chamberlain, Sir Richard Pole, warden of the castle, Bishop William Smith of Lincoln, his physician, Dr Bereworth, his treasurer Sir Henry Vernon, the steward of his household, Sir Richard Croft, his groom of the privy chamber, Sir William Thomas of Carmarthen, and all the leading men of the Principality, were seated in the body of the hall. At the back and in the gallery every nosy parker, every busybody in Wales could pile in to see the Spanish princess take her dinner, and speculate if she pleased the young prince or no.

There was no way to tell. Most of them thought that he had failed to bed her. For see! The Infanta sat like a stiff little doll and rarely leaned towards her young husband. The Prince of Wales spoke to her as if by rote, every ten minutes. They were little patterns of good behaviour, and they scarcely even looked at each other. The gossips said that he went to her rooms, as ordered, but only once a week and never of his own choice. Perhaps the young couple did not please each other. They were young, perhaps too young for marriage.

No-one could tell that Catalina's hands were gripped tight in her lap to stop herself from touching her husband, nor that every half-hour or so he glanced at her, apparently indifferent, and whispered so low that only she could hear: 'I want you right now.'

After dinner there would be dancing and perhaps mummers or a storyteller, a Welsh bard or strolling players to watch. Sometimes the poets would come in from the high hills and tell old, strange tales in their own tongue that Arthur could follow only with difficulty, but which he would try to translate for Catalina.

> 'When the long yellow summer comes and victory comes
>   to us,
> And the spreading of the sails of Brittany,
> And when the heat comes and when the fever is kindled
> There are portents that victory will be given to us.'

'What is that about?' she asked him.

'The long yellow summer is when my father decided to invade from Brittany. His road took him to Bosworth and victory.'

She nodded.

'It was hot, that year, and the troops came with the Sweat, a new disease, which now curses England as it does Europe with the heat of every summer.'

She nodded again. A new poet came forwards, played a chord on his harp and sang.

'And this?'

'It's about a red dragon that flies over the Principality,' he said. 'It kills the boar.'

'What does it mean?' Catalina asked.

'The dragon is the Tudors: us,' he said. 'You'll have seen the red dragon on our standard. The boar is the usurper, Richard. It's a compliment to my father, based on an old tale. All their songs are ancient songs. They probably sang them in the ark.' He grinned. 'Songs of Noah.'

'Do they give you Tudors credit for surviving the flood? Was Noah a Tudor?'

'Probably. My grandmother would take credit for the Garden of Eden itself,' he returned. 'This is the Welsh border, we come from Owen ap Tudor, from Glendower, we are happy to take the credit for everything.'

As Arthur predicted, when the fire burned low they would sing the old Welsh songs of magical doings in dark woods that no man could know. And they would tell of battles and glorious victories won by skill and courage. In their strange tongue they would tell stories of Arthur and Camelot, and Merlin the prince, and Guinevere: the queen who betrayed her husband for a guilty love.

'I should die if you took a lover,' he whispered to her as a page shielded them from the hall and poured wine.

'I can never even see anyone else when you are here,' she assured him. 'All I see is you.'

Every evening there was music or some entertainment for the Ludlow court. The king's mother had ruled that the prince should keep a merry house – it was a reward for the loyalty of Wales that had put her son Henry Tudor on an uncertain throne. Her grandson must pay the men who had come out of the hills to fight for the Tudors and remind them that he was a Welsh prince, and he would go on counting on their support to rule the English, whom no-one could count on at all. The Welsh must join with England and together, the two of them could keep out the Scots, and manage the Irish.

When the musicians played the slow formal dances of Spain, Catalina would dance with one of her ladies, conscious of Arthur's gaze on her, keeping her face prim, like a little mummer's mask of respectability; though she longed to twirl around and swing her hips like a woman in the seraglio, like a Moorish slave girl dancing for a sultan. But My Lady the King's Mother's spies watched everything, even in Ludlow, and would be quick to report any indiscreet behaviour by the young princess. Sometimes, Catalina would slide a glance at her husband and see his eyes on her, his look that of a man in love. She would snap her fingers as if part of the dance, but in fact to warn him that he was staring at her in a way that his grandmother would not like; and he would turn aside and speak to someone, tearing his gaze away from her.

Even after the music was over and the entertainers gone away, the young couple could not be alone. There were always men who sought council with Arthur, who wanted favours or land or influence, and they would approach him and talk low-voiced, in English, which Catalina did not yet fully understand, or in Welsh, which she thought no-one could ever understand. The rule of law barely ran in the border lands, each landowner was like a war-lord in his own domain. Deeper in the mountains there were people who still thought that Richard was on the throne, who knew nothing of the changed world, who spoke no English, who obeyed no laws at all.

Arthur argued, and praised, and suggested that feuds should be forgiven, that trespasses should be made good, that the proud Welsh chieftains should work together to make their land as prosperous as their neighbour England, instead of wasting their time in envy. The valleys and coastal lands were dominated by a dozen petty lords, and in the high hills the men ran in clans like wild tribes. Slowly, Arthur was determined to make the law run throughout the land.

'Every man has to know that the law is greater than his lord,'

Catalina said. 'That is what the Moors did in Spain, and my mother and father followed them. The Moors did not trouble themselves to change people's religions nor their language, they just brought peace and prosperity and imposed the rule of law.'

'Half of my lords would think that was heresy,' he teased her. 'And your mother and father are now imposing their religion, they have driven out the Jews already, the Moors will be next.'

She frowned. 'I know,' she said. 'And there is much suffering. But their intention was to allow people to practise their own religion. When they won Granada that was their promise.'

'D'you not think that to make one country, the people must always be of one faith?' he asked.

'Heretics can live like that,' she said decidedly. 'In al Andalus the Moors and Christians and Jews lived in peace and friendship alongside one another. But if you are a Christian king, it is your duty to bring your subjects to God.'

Catalina would watch Arthur as he talked with one man and then another, and then, at a sign from Dona Elvira, she would curtsey to her husband and withdraw from the hall. She would read her evening prayers, change into her robe for the night, sit with her ladies, go to her bedroom and wait, and wait and wait.

'You can go, I shall sleep alone tonight,' she said to Dona Elvira.

'Again?' The duenna frowned. 'You have not had a bed companion since we came to the castle. What if you wake in the night and need some service?'

'I sleep better with no-one else in the room,' Catalina would say. 'You can leave me now.'

The duenna and the ladies would bid her goodnight and leave, the maids would come and unlace her bodice, unpin her headdress, untie her shoes and pull off her stockings. They would hold out her warmed linen nightgown and she would ask for her cape and say she would sit by the fire for a few moments, and then send them away.

In the silence, as the castle settled for the night, she would wait for him. Then, at last she would hear the quiet sound of his foot-fall at the outer door of her room, where it opened on to the battlements that ran between his tower and hers. She would fly to the door and unbolt it, he would be pink-cheeked from the cold, his cape thrown over his own nightshirt as he tumbled in, the cold wind blowing in with him as she threw herself into his arms.

'Tell me a story.'

'Which story tonight?'

'Tell me about your family.'

'Shall I tell you about my mother when she was a girl?'

'Oh yes. Was she a princess of Castile like you?'

Catalina shook her head. 'No, not at all. She was not protected or safe. She lived in the court of her brother, her father was dead, and her brother did not love her as he should. He knew that she was his only true heir. He favoured his daughter; but everyone knew that she was a bastard, palmed off on him by his queen. She was even nicknamed by the name of the queen's lover. They called her La Beltraneja after her father. Can you think of anything more shameful?'

Arthur obediently shook his head. 'Nothing.'

'My mother was all but a prisoner at her brother's court; the queen hated her, of course, the courtiers were unfriendly and her brother was plotting to disinherit her. Even their own mother could not make him see reason.'

'Why not?' he asked, and then caught her hand when he saw the shadow cross her face. 'Ah, love, I am sorry. What is the matter?'

'Her mother was sick,' she said. 'Sick with sadness. I don't understand quite why, or why it was so very bad. But she could hardly speak or move. She could only cry.'

'So your mother had no protector?'

'No, and then the king her brother ordered that she should be betrothed to Don Pedro Giron.' She sat up a little and clasped her hands around her knees. 'They said he had sold his soul to the devil, a most wicked man. My mother swore that she would offer her soul to God and God would save her, a virgin, from such a fate. She said that surely no merciful God would take a girl like her, a princess, who had survived long years in one of the worst courts of Europe, and then throw her at the end into the arms of a man who wanted her ruin, who desired her only because she was young and untouched, who wanted to despoil her?'

Arthur hid a grin at the romantic rhythm of the story. 'You do this awfully well,' he said. 'I hope it ends happily.'

Catalina raised her hand like a troubadour calling for silence. 'Her greatest friend and lady-in-waiting Beatriz had taken up a knife and sworn that she would kill Don Pedro before he laid hands on Isabella; but my mother kneeled before her prie-dieu for three days and three nights and prayed without ceasing to be spared this rape.

'He was on his journey towards her, he would arrive the very next day. He ate well and drank well, telling his companions that tomorrow he would be in the bed of the highest-born virgin of Castile.

'But that very night he died.' Catalina's voice dropped to an awed whisper. 'Died before he had finished his wine from dinner. Dropped dead as surely as if God had reached down from the heavens and pinched the life out of him as a good gardener pinches out a greenfly.'

'Poison?' asked Arthur, who knew something of the ways of determined monarchs, and who thought Isabella of Castile quite capable of murder.

'God's will,' Catalina answered seriously. 'Don Pedro found, as everyone else has found, that God's will and my mother's desires always run together. And if you knew God and my mother as I know them, you would know that their will is always done.'

He raised his glass and drank a toast to her. 'Now that is a good story,' he said. 'I wish you could tell it in the hall.'

'And it is all true,' she reminded him. 'I know it is. My mother told me it herself.'

'So she fought for her throne too,' he said thoughtfully.

'First for her throne, and then to make the kingdom of Spain.'

He smiled. 'For all that they tell us that we are of royal blood, we both come from a line of fighters. We have our thrones by conquest.'

She raised her eyebrows. 'I come from royal blood,' she said. 'My mother has her throne by right.'

'Oh yes. But if your mother had not fought for her place in the world she would have been Dona whatever his name was –'

'Giron.'

'Giron. And you would have been born a nobody.'

Catalina shook her head. The idea was quite impossible for her to grasp. 'I should have been the daughter of the sister of the king whatever happened. I should always have had royal blood in my veins.'

'You would have been a nobody,' he said bluntly. 'A nobody with royal blood. And so would I if my father had not fought for his throne. We are both from families who claim their own.'

'Yes,' she conceded reluctantly.

'We are both the children of parents who claim what rightfully belongs to others.' He went further.

Her head came up at once. 'They do not! At least my mother did not. She was the rightful heir.'

Arthur disagreed. 'Her brother made his daughter his heir, he recognised her. Your mother had the throne by conquest. Just as my father won his.'

Her colour rose. 'She did not,' she insisted. 'She is the rightful heir to the throne. All she did was defend her right from a pretender.'

'Don't you see?' he said. 'We are all pretenders until we win. When we win, we can rewrite the history and rewrite the family trees, and execute our rivals, or imprison them, until we can argue that there was always only one true heir: ourselves. But before then, we are one of many claimants. And not even always the best claimant with the strongest claim.'

She frowned. 'What are you saying?' she demanded. 'Are you saying that I am not the true princess? That you are not the true heir to England?'

He took her hand. 'No, no. Don't be angry with me,' he soothed her. 'I am saying that we have and we hold what we claim. I am saying that we make our own inheritance. We claim what we want, we say that we are Prince of Wales, Queen of England. That we decide the name and the title we go by. Just like everyone else does.'

'You are wrong,' she said. 'I was born Infanta of Spain and I will die Queen of England. It is not a matter of choice, it is my destiny.'

He took her hand and kissed it. He saw there was no point pursuing his belief that a man or a woman could make their own destiny with their own conviction. He might have his doubts; but with her the task was already done. She had complete conviction, her destiny was made. He had no doubt that she would indeed defend it to death. Her title, her pride, her sense of self were all one. 'Katherine, Queen of England,' he said, kissing her fingers, and saw her smile return.

I love him so deeply, I did not know that I could ever love anyone like this. I can feel myself growing in patience and wisdom, just through my love for him. I step back from irritability and impatience, I even bear my homesickness without complaint. I can feel myself becoming a better woman, a better wife, as I seek to please him and make him

proud of me. I want him always to be glad that he married me. I want us always to be as happy as we are today. There are no words to describe him . . . there are no words.

A messenger came from the king's court bringing the newlyweds some gifts: a pair of deer from the Windsor forest, a parcel of books for Catalina, letters from Elizabeth the queen, and orders from My Lady the King's Mother who had heard, though no-one could imagine how, that the prince's hunt had broken down some hedges, and who commanded Arthur to make sure that they were restored and the landowner compensated.

He brought the letter to Catalina's room when he came at night. 'How can she know everything?' he demanded.

'The man will have written to her,' she said ruefully.

'Why not come direct to me?'

'Because he knows her? Is he her liege man?'

'Could be,' he said. 'She has a network of alliances like spider threads across the country.'

'You should go to see him,' Catalina decided. 'We could both go. We could take him a present, some meat or something, and pay what we owe.'

Arthur shook his head at the power of his grandmother. 'Oh yes, we can do that. But how can she know everything?'

'It's how you rule,' she said. 'Isn't it? You make sure that you know everything and that anyone with a trouble comes to you. Then they take the habit of obedience and you take the habit of command.'

He chuckled. 'I can see I have married another Margaret Beaufort,' he said. 'God help me with another one in the family.'

Catalina smiled. 'You should be warned,' she admitted. 'I am the daughter of a strong woman. Even my father does as he is bid by her.'

He put down the letter and gathered her to him. 'I have longed for you all day,' he said into the warm crook of her neck.

She opened the front of his nightshirt so she could lay her cheek against his sweet-smelling skin. 'Oh, my love.'

With one accord they moved to the bed. 'Oh, my love.'

'Tell me a story.'

'What shall I tell you tonight?'

'Tell me about how your father and mother were married. Was it arranged for them, as it was for us?'

'Oh no,' she exclaimed. 'Not at all. She was quite alone in the world, and though God had saved her from Don Pedro she was still not safe. She knew that her brother would marry her to anyone who would guarantee to keep her from inheriting his throne.

'They were dark years for her, she said that when she appealed to her mother it was like talking to the dead. My grandmother was lost in a world of her own sorrow, she could do nothing to help her own daughter.

'My mother's cousin, her only hope, was the heir to the neighbouring kingdom: Ferdinand of Aragon. He came to her in disguise. Without any servants, without any soldiers, he rode through the night and came to the castle where she was struggling to survive. He had himself brought in, and threw off his hat and cape so she saw him, and knew him at once.'

Arthur was rapt. 'Really?'

Catalina smiled. 'Isn't it like a romance? She told me that she loved him at once, fell in love on sight like a princess in a poem. He proposed marriage to her then and there, and she accepted him then and there. He fell in love with her that night, at first sight, which is something that no princess can expect. My mother, my father, were blessed by God. He moved them to love and their hearts followed their interests.'

'God looks after the kings of Spain,' Arthur remarked, half-joking.

She nodded. 'Your father was right to seek our friendship. We are making our kingdom from al Andalus, the lands of the Moorish princes. We have Castile and Aragon, now we have Granada and we will have more. My father's heart is set on Navarre, and he will not stop there. I know he is determined to have Naples. I don't think he will be satisfied until all the south and western regions of France are ours. You will see. He has not made the borders he wants for Spain yet.'

'They married in secret?' he asked, still amazed at this royal couple who had taken their lives into their own hands and made their own destiny.

She looked slightly sheepish. 'He told her he had a dispensation, but it was not properly signed. I am afraid that he tricked her.'

He frowned. 'Your wonderful father lied to his saintly wife?'

She gave a little rueful smile. 'Indeed, he will do anything to get his own way. You quickly learn it when you have dealings with him. He always thinks ahead, two, perhaps three, steps ahead. He knew my mother was devout and would not marry without the dispensation and *ole!* – there is a dispensation in her hand.'

'But they put it right later?'

'Yes, and though his father and her brother were angry, it was the right thing to do.'

'How could it be the right thing to do? To defy your family? To disobey your own father? That's a sin. It breaks a commandment. It is a cardinal sin. No Pope could bless such a marriage.'

'It was God's will,' she said confidently. 'None of them knew that it was God's will. But my mother knew. She always knows what God wills.'

'How can she be so sure? How could she be so sure then, when she was only a girl?'

She chuckled. 'God and my mother have always thought alike.'

He laughed and tweaked the lock of her hair. 'She certainly did the right thing in sending you to me.'

'She did,' Catalina said. 'And we shall do the right thing by the country.'

'Yes,' he said. 'I have such plans for us when we come to the throne.'

'What shall we do?'

Arthur hesitated. 'You will think me a child, my head filled with stories from books.'

'No I shan't, tell me!'

'I should like to make a council, like the first Arthur did. Not like my father's council, which is just filled with his friends who fought for him, but a proper council of all the kingdom. A council of knights, one for each county. Not chosen by me because I like their company, but chosen by their own county – as the best of men to represent them. And I should like them to come to the table and each of them should know what is happening in their own county, they should report. And so if a crop is going to fail and there is going to be hunger we should know in time and send food.'

Catalina sat up, interested. 'They would be our advisors. Our eyes and ears.'

'Yes. And I should like each of them to be responsible for building defences, especially the ones in the north and on the coasts.'

'And for mustering troops once a year, so we are always ready for attack,' she added. 'They will come, you know.'

'The Moors?'

She nodded. 'They are defeated in Spain for now, but they are as strong as ever in Africa, in the Holy Lands, in Turkey and the lands beyond. When they need more land they will move again into Christendom. Once a year in the spring, the Ottoman sultan goes to war, like other men plough the fields. They will come against us. We cannot know when they will come, but we can be very certain that they will do so.'

128

'I want defences all along the south coast against France, and against the Moors,' Arthur said. 'A string of castles, and beacons behind them, so that when we come under attack in – say – Kent, we can know about it in London, and everyone can be warned.'

'You will need to build ships,' she said. 'My mother commissioned fighting ships from the dockyard in Venice.'

'We have our own dockyards,' he said. 'We can build our own ships.'

'How shall we raise the money for all these castles and ships?' Isabella's daughter asked the practical question.

'Partly from taxing the people,' he said. 'Partly from taxing the merchants and the people who use the ports. It is for their safety, they should pay. I know people hate the taxes but that is because they don't see what is done with the money.'

'We will need honest tax collectors,' Catalina said. 'My father says that if you can collect the taxes that are due and not lose half of them along the way it is better than a regiment of cavalry.'

'Yes, but how d'you find men that you can trust?' Arthur thought aloud. 'At the moment, any man who wants to make a fortune gets himself a post of collecting taxes. They should work for us, not for themselves. They should be paid a wage and not collect on their own account.'

'That has never been achieved by anyone but the Moors,' she said. 'The Moors in al Andalus set up schools and even universities for the sons of poor men, so that they had clerks that they could trust. And their great offices of court are always done by the young scholars, sometimes the young sons of their king.'

'Shall I take a hundred wives to get a thousand clerks for the throne?' he teased her.

'Not another single one.'

'But we have to find good men,' he said thoughtfully. 'You need loyal servants to the crown, those who owe their salary to the crown and their obedience to the crown. Otherwise they work for themselves and they take bribes and all their families become over-mighty.'

'The church could teach them,' Catalina suggested. 'Just as the imam teaches the boys for the Moors. If every parish church was as learned as a mosque with a school attached to it, if every priest knew he had to teach reading and writing, then we could found new colleges at the universities, so that boys could go on and learn more.'

'Is it possible?' he asked. 'Not just a dream?'

She nodded. 'It could be real. To make a country is the most real thing anyone can do. We will make a kingdom that we can be proud of, just as my mother and father did in Spain. We can decide how it is to be, and we can make it happen.'

'Camelot,' he said simply.

'Camelot,' she repeated.

Ludlow Castle, Spring 1502

It snowed for a sennight in February, and then came a thaw and the snow turned to slush and now it is raining again. I cannot walk in the garden, nor go out on a horse, nor even ride out into the town by mule. I have never seen such rain in my life before. It is not like our rain that falls on the hot earth and yields a rich, warm smell as the dust is laid and the plants drink up the water. But this is cold rain on cold earth, and there is no perfume and only standing pools of water with dark ice on it like a cold skin.

I miss my home with an ache of longing in these cold dark days. When I tell Arthur about Spain and the Alhambra it makes me yearn that he should see it for himself, and meet my mother and father. I want them to see him, and know our happiness. I keep wondering if his father would not allow him out of England . . . but I know I am dreaming. No king would ever let his precious son and heir out of his lands.

Then I start to wonder if I might go home for a short visit on my own. I cannot bear to be without Arthur for even a night, but then I think that unless I go to Spain alone I will never see my mother again, and the thought of that, never feeling the touch of her hand on my hair or seeing her smile at me – I don't know how I would bear to never see her again.

I am glad and proud to be Princess of Wales and the Queen of England-to-be, but I did not think, I did not realise – I know, how silly this is of me – but I did not quite understand that it would mean that I would live here forever, that I would never come home again. Somehow, although I knew I would be married to the Prince of Wales and one day be Queen of England, I did not fully understand that this would be my home now and forever; and that I may never see my mother or my father or my home again.

I expected at least that we would write, I thought I would hear from her often. But it is as she was with Isabel, with Maria, with Juana; she sends instructions through the ambassador, I have my orders as a princess of Spain. But as a mother to her daughter, I hear from her only rarely.

I don't know how to bear it. I never thought such a thing could happen. My sister Isabel came home to us after she was widowed, though she married again and had to leave again. And Juana writes to me that she will go home on a visit with her husband. It isn't fair that she should go and I not be allowed to. I am only just sixteen. I am not ready to live without my mother's advice. I am not old enough to live without a mother. I look for her every day to tell me what I should do – and she is not there.

My husband's mother, Queen Elizabeth, is a cipher in her own household. She cannot be a mother to me, she cannot command her own time, how should she advise me? It is the king's mother, Lady Margaret, who rules everything; and she is a most well-thought-of, hard-hearted woman. She cannot be a mother to me, she couldn't be a mother to anyone. She worships her son because thanks to him she is the mother of the king; but she does not love him, she has no tenderness. She does not even love Arthur and if a woman could not love him she must be utterly without a heart. Actually, I am quite sure that she dislikes me, though I don't know why she should.

And anyway, I am sure my mother must miss me as I miss her? Surely, very soon, she will write to the king and ask him if I can come home for a visit? Before it gets much colder here? And it is terribly cold and wet already. I am sure I cannot stay here all the long winter. I am sure I will be ill. I am sure she must want me to come home . . .

Catalina, seated at the table before the window, trying to catch the failing light of a grey February afternoon, took up her letter, asking her mother if she could come for a visit to Spain, and tore it gently in half and then in half again and fed the pieces into the fire in her room. It was not the first letter she had written to her mother asking to come home, but – like the others – it would never be sent. She would not betray her mother's training by turning tail and running from grey skies and cold rain and people whose language no-one could ever understand and whose joys and sorrows were a mystery.

She was not to know that even if she had sent the letter to the Spanish ambassador in London, then that wily diplomat would have opened it, read it, and torn it up himself, and then reported the whole to the King of England. Rodrigo Gonsalvi de Puebla knew, though Catalina did not yet understand, that her marriage had forged an alliance between the emerging power of Spain and the emerging power of England against the emerging power of France. No homesick princess wanting her mother would be allowed to unbalance that.

'Tell me a story.'

'I am like Scheherazade, you want a thousand stories from me.'

'Oh yes!' he said. 'I will have a thousand and one stories. How many have you told me already?'

'I have told you a story every night since we were together, that first night, at Burford,' she said.

'Forty-nine days,' he said.

'Only forty-nine stories. If I was Scheherazade I would have nine hundred and fifty-two to go.'

He smiled at her. 'Do you know, Catalina, I have been happier in these forty-nine days than ever in my life before?'

She took his hand and put it to her lips.

'And the nights!'

Her eyes darkened with desire. 'Yes, the nights,' she said quietly.

'I long for every nine hundred and fifty-two more,' he said. 'And then I will have another thousand after that.'

'And a thousand after that?'

'And a thousand after that forever and ever until we are both dead.'

She smiled. 'Pray God we have long years together,' she said tenderly.

'So what will you tell me tonight?'

She thought. 'I shall tell you of a Moor's poem.'

Arthur settled back against the pillows as she leaned forwards and fixed her blue gaze on the curtains of the bed, as if she could see beyond them, to somewhere else.

'He was born in the deserts of Arabia,' she explained. 'So when he came to Spain he missed everything about his home. He wrote this poem.

"A palm tree stands in the middle of Rusafa,
Born in the west, far from the land of palms.
I said to it: How like me you are, far away and in exile
In long separation from your family and friends.
You have sprung from soil in which you are a stranger
And I, like you, am far from home."'

He was silent, taking in the simplicity of the poem. 'It is not like our poetry,' he said.

'No,' she replied quietly. 'They are a people who have a great love of words, they love to say a true thing simply.'

He opened his arms to her and she slid alongside him so that they were lying, thigh to thigh, side to side. He touched her face, her cheek was wet.

'Oh my love! Tears?'

She said nothing.

'I know that you miss your home,' he said softly, taking her hand in his and kissing the fingertips. 'But you will become accustomed to your life here, to your thousand, thousand days here.'

'I am happy with you,' Catalina said quickly. 'It is just . . .' Her voice trailed away. 'My mother,' she said, her voice very small. 'I miss her. And I worry about her. Because . . . I am the youngest, you see. And she kept me with her as long as she could.'

'She knew you would have to leave.'

'She's been much . . . tried. She lost her son, my brother, Juan, and he was our only heir. It is so terrible to lose a prince, you cannot imagine how terrible it is to lose a prince. It is not just the loss of him, but the loss of everything that might have been. His life has gone, but his reign and his future have gone too. His wife will no longer be queen, everything that he hoped for will not happen. And then the next heir, little Miguel, died at only two years old. He was all we had left of my sister Isabel, his mother, and then it pleased God to take him from us too. Poor Maria died far away from us in Portugal, she went away to be married and we never saw her again. It was natural that my mother kept me with her for comfort. I was her last child to leave home. And now I don't know how she will manage without me.'

Arthur put his arm around her shoulders and drew her close. 'God will comfort her.'

'She will be so lonely,' she said in a little voice.

'Surely she, of all women in the world, feels God's comfort?'

'I don't think she always does,' Catalina said. 'Her own mother was tormented by sadness, you know. Many of the women of our family can get quite sick with sorrow. I know that my mother fears sinking into sadness just like her mother: a woman who saw things so darkly that she would rather have been blind. I know she fears that she will never be happy again. I know that she liked to have me with her so that I could make her happy. She said that I was a child born for joy, that she could tell that I would always be happy.'

'Does your father not comfort her?'

'Yes,' she said uncertainly. 'But he is often away from her. And anyway, I should like to be with her. But you must know how I feel. Didn't you miss your mother when you were first sent away? And your father and your sisters and your brother?'

'I miss my sisters; but not my brother,' he said so decidedly that she had to laugh.

'Why not? I thought he was such fun.'

'He is a braggart,' Arthur said irritably. 'He is always pushing himself forwards. Look at our wedding, he had to be at the centre of the stage all the time, look at our wedding feast when he had to dance so that all eyes were on him. Pulling Margaret up to dance and making a performance of himself.'

'Oh no! It was just that your father told him to dance, and he was merry. He's just a boy.'

'He wants to be a man. He tries to be a man, he makes a fool of all of us when he tries. And nobody ever checks him! Did you not see how he looked at you?'

'I saw nothing at all,' she said truthfully. 'It was all a blur for me.'

'He fancies himself in love with you, and dreamed that he was walking you up the aisle on his own account.'

She laughed. 'Oh! How silly!'

'He's always been like that,' he said resentfully. 'And because he is the favourite of everyone he is allowed to say and do exactly as

136

he wants. I have to learn the law, and languages, and I have to live here and prepare myself for the crown; but Harry stays at Greenwich or Whitehall at the centre of court as if he were an ambassador; not an heir who should be trained. He has to have a horse when I have a horse – though I had been kept on a steady palfrey for years. He has a falcon when I have my first falcon – nobody makes him train a kestrel and then a goshawk for year after year, then he has to have my tutor and tries to outstrip me, tries to outshine me whenever he can, and always takes the eye.'

Catalina saw he was genuinely irritated. 'But he is only a second son,' she observed.

'He is everyone's favourite,' Arthur said glumly. 'He has everything for the asking and everything comes easily to him.'

'He is not the Prince of Wales,' she pointed out. 'He may be liked; but he is not important. He only stays at court because he is not important enough to be sent here. He does not have his own Principality. Your father will have plans for him. He will probably be married and sent away. A second son is no more important than a daughter.'

'He is to go into the church,' he said. 'He is to be a priest. Who would marry him? So he will be in England forever. I daresay I shall have to endure him as my archbishop, if he does not manage to make himself Pope.'

Catalina laughed at the thought of the flushed-faced blond, bright boy as Pope. 'How grand we shall all be when we are grown up,' she said. 'You and me, King and Queen of England, and Harry, archbishop; perhaps even a cardinal.'

'Harry won't ever grow up,' he insisted. 'He will always be a selfish boy. And because my grandmother – and my father – have always given him whatever he wanted, just for the asking, he will be a greedy, difficult boy.'

'Perhaps he will change,' she said. 'When my oldest sister, poor Isabel, went away to Portugal the first time, you would have thought her the vainest, most worldly girl you could imagine. But when her husband died and she came home she cared for nothing but to go into a convent. Her heart was quite broken.'

'Nobody will break Harry's heart,' his older brother asserted. 'He hasn't got one.'

'You'd have thought the same of Isabel,' Catalina argued. 'But she fell in love with her husband on her wedding day and she said she would never love again. She had to marry for the second time, of course. But she married unwillingly.'

'And did you?' he asked, his mood suddenly changing.

'Did I what? Marry unwillingly?'

'No! Fall in love with your husband on your wedding day?'

'Certainly not on my wedding day,' she said. 'Talk about a boastful boy! Harry is nothing to you! I heard you tell them all the next morning that having a wife was very good sport.'

Arthur had the grace to look abashed. 'I may have said something in jest.'

'That you had been in Spain all night?'

'Oh, Catalina. Forgive me. I knew nothing. You are right, I was a boy. But I am a man now, your husband. And you did fall in love with your husband. So don't deny it.'

'Not for days and days,' she said dampeningly. 'It was not love at first sight at all.'

'I know when it was, so you can't tease me. It was the evening at Burford when you had been crying and I kissed you for the first time properly, and I wiped your tears away with my sleeves. And then that night I came to you, and the house was so quiet that it was as if we were the only people alive in the whole world.'

She snuggled closer into his arms. 'And I told you my first story,' she said. 'But do you remember what it was?'

'It was the story of the fire at Santa Fe,' he said. 'When the luck was against the Spanish for once.'

She nodded. 'Normally, it was us who brought fire and the sword. My father has a reputation of being merciless.'

'Your father was merciless? Though it was land he was claiming for his own? How did he hope to bring the people to his will?'

'By fear,' she said simply. 'And anyway, it was not his will. It was God's will, and sometimes God is merciless. This was not an ordinary war, it was a crusade. Crusades are cruel.'

He nodded.

'They had a song about my father's advance. The Moors had a song.'

She threw back her head and in a haunting, low voice, translating the words into French, she sang to him:

'Riders gallop through the Elvira gate, up to the Alhambra,
Fearful tidings they bring the king,
Ferdinand himself leads an army, flower of Spain,
Along the banks of the Jenil; with him comes
Isabel, Queen with the heart of a man.'

Arthur was delighted. 'Sing it again!'

She laughed and sang again.

'And they really called her that: "Queen with the heart of a man"?'

'Father says that when she was in camp it was better than two battalions for strengthening our troops and frightening the Moors. In all the battles they fought, she was never defeated. The army never lost a battle when she was there.'

'To be a king like that! To have them write songs about you.'

'I know,' Catalina said. 'To have a legend for a mother! It's not surprising I miss her. In those days she was never afraid of anything. When the fire would have destroyed us, she was not afraid then. Not of the flames in the night and not of defeat. Even when my father and all the advisors agreed that we would have to pull back to Toledo and re-arm, come again next year, my mother said no.'

'Does she argue with him in public?' Arthur asked, fascinated at the thought of a wife who was not a subject.

139

'She does not exactly argue,' she said thoughtfully. 'She would never contradict him or disrespect him. But he knows very well when she doesn't agree with him. And mostly, they do it her way.'

He shook his head.

'I know what you're thinking, a wife should obey. She would say so herself. But the difficulty is that she's always right,' said her daughter. 'All the times I can think of, whenever it has been a great question as to whether the army should go on, or whether something can be done. It's as if God advises her, it really is; she knows best what should be done. Even Father knows that she knows best.'

'She must be an extraordinary woman.'

'She is queen,' Catalina said simply. 'Queen in her own right. Not a mere queen by marriage, not a commoner raised to be queen. She was born a princess of Spain like me. Born to be a queen. Saved by God from the most terrible dangers to be Queen of Spain. What else should she do but command her kingdom?'

That night I dream I am a bird, an apus, a swift, flying high and fearless over the kingdom of new Castile, south from Toledo, over Cordoba, south to the kingdom of Granada; the ground below me laid out like a tawny carpet, woven from the gold-fleeced sheep of the Berbers, the brass earth pierced by bronze cliffs, the hills so high that not even olive trees can cling to their steep slopes. On I fly, my little bird-heart thudding until I see the rosy walls of the Alcazar, the great fort which encloses the palace of the Alhambra, and flying low and fast, I skim the brutal squareness of the watchtower where the flag of the sickle moon once waved, to plunge down towards the Court of Myrtles to fly round and around in the warm air, enclosed by dainty buildings of stucco and tile, looking down on the mirror of water, and seeing at last the one I am looking for: my mother, Isabella of Spain,

walking in the warm evening air, and thinking of her daughter in
faraway England.

Ludlow Castle, March 1502

'I want to ask you to meet a lady who is a good friend of mine and is ready to be a friend of yours,' Arthur said, choosing his words with care.

Catalina's ladies-in-waiting, bored on a cold afternoon with no entertainment, craned forwards to listen while trying to appear engaged in their needlework.

At once she blanched as white as the linen she was embroidering. 'My lord?' she asked anxiously. He had said nothing of this in the early hours of the morning when they had woken and made love. She had not expected to see him until dinner. His arrival in her rooms signalled that something had happened. She was wary, waiting to know what was going on.

'A lady? Who is she?'

'You may have heard of her from others, but I beg you to remember that she is eager to be your friend, and she has always been a good friend to me.'

Catalina's head flew up, she took a breath. For a moment, for a dreadful moment, she thought that he was introducing a former mistress into her court, begging a place among ladies-in-waiting for some woman who had been his lover, so that they might continue their affair.

If this is what he is doing, I know what part I must play. I have seen my mother haunted by the pretty girls that my father, God forgive him,

cannot resist. Again and again we would see him pay attention to some new face at court. Each time my mother behaved as if she had noticed nothing, dowered the girl handsomely, married her off to an eligible courtier, and encouraged him to take his new bride far, far away. It was such a common occurrence that it became a joke: that if a girl wanted to marry well with the queen's blessing, and travel to some remote province, all she had to do was to catch the eye of the king, and in no time she would find herself riding away from the Alhambra on a fine new horse with a set of new clothes.

I know that a sensible woman looks the other way and tries to bear her hurt and humiliation when her husband chooses to take another woman to his bed. What she must not do, what she absolutely must never do, is behave like my sister Juana, who shames herself and all of us by giving way to screaming fits, hysterical tears, and threats of revenge.

'It does no good,' my mother once told me when one of the ambassadors relayed to us some awful scene at Philip's court in the Netherlands: Juana threatening to cut off the woman's hair, attacking her with a pair of scissors, and then swearing she would stab herself.

'It only makes it worse to complain. If a husband goes astray you will have to take him back into your life and into your bed, whatever he has done; there is no escape from marriage. If you are queen and he is king you have to deal together. If he forgets his duty to you, that is no reason to forget yours to him. However painful, you are always his queen and he is always your husband.'

'Whatever he does?' I asked her. 'However he behaves? He is free though you are bound?'

She shrugged. 'Whatever he does cannot break the marriage bond. You are married in the sight of God: he is always your husband, you are always queen. Those whom God has joined together, no man can put asunder. Whatever pain your husband brings you, he is still your husband. He may be a bad husband; but he is still your husband.'

'What if he wants another?' I asked, sharp in my young girl's curiosity.

'If he wants another he can have her or she can refuse him, that is *between them. That is for her and her conscience,' my mother had said steadily. 'What must not change is you. Whatever he says, whatever she wants: you are still his wife and his queen.'*

Catalina summoned this bleak counsel and faced her young husband. 'I am always glad to meet a friend of yours, my lord,' she said levelly, hoping that her voice did not quaver at all. 'But, as you know, I have only a small household. Your father was very clear that I am not allowed any more companions than I have at present. As you know, he does not pay me any allowance. I have no money to pay another lady for her service. In short, I cannot add any lady, even a special friend of yours, to my court.'

Arthur flinched at the reminder of his father's mean haggling over her train. 'Oh no, you mistake me. It is not a friend who wants a place. She would not be one of your ladies-in-waiting,' he said hastily. 'It is Lady Margaret Pole, who is waiting to meet you. She has come home here at last.'

Holy Mary, Mother of God, pray for us. This is worse than if it was his mistress. I knew I would have to face her one day. This is her home, but she was away when we got here and I thought she had deliberately snubbed me by being away and staying away. I thought she was avoiding me out of hatred, as I would avoid her from shame. Lady Margaret Pole is sister to that poor boy, the Duke of Warwick, beheaded to make the succession safe for me, and for my line. I have been dreading the moment when I would have to meet her. I have been praying to the saints that she would stay away, hating me, blaming me, but keeping her distance.

Arthur saw her quick gesture of rejection, but he had known of no way to prepare her for this. 'Please,' he said hurriedly. 'She has been away caring for her children or she would have been here with her husband to welcome you to the castle when we first arrived. I told you she would return. She wants to greet you now. We all have to live together here. Sir Richard is a trusted friend of my father, the lord of my council and the warden of this castle. We will all have to live together.'

Catalina put out a shaking hand to him and at once he came closer, ignoring the fascinated attention of her ladies.

'I cannot meet her,' she whispered. 'Truly, I can't. I know that her brother was put to death for my sake. I know my parents insisted on it, before they would send me to England. I know he was innocent, innocent as a flower, kept in the Tower by your father so that men should not gather round him and claim the throne in his name. He could have lived there in safety all his life but for my parents demanding his death. She must hate me.'

'She doesn't hate you,' he said truthfully. 'Believe me, Catalina, I would not expose you to anyone's unkindness. She does not hate you, she doesn't hate me, she doesn't even hate my father who ordered the execution. She knows that these things happen. She is a princess, she knows as well as you do that it is not choice but policy that governs us. It was not your choice, nor mine. She knows that your father and mother had to be sure that there were no rival princes to claim the throne, that my father would clear my way, whatever it cost him. She is resigned.'

'Resigned?' she gasped incredulously. 'How can a woman be resigned to the murder of her brother, the heir of the family? How can she greet me with friendship when he died for my convenience? When we lost my brother our world ended, our hopes died with him. Our future was buried with him. My mother, who is a living saint, still cannot bear it. She has not been happy since the day of his death. It is unbearable to her. If he had been executed for some

144

stranger I swear she would have taken a life in return. How could Lady Margaret lose her brother and bear it? How can she bear me?'

'She has resignation,' he said simply. 'She is a most spiritual woman and if she looked for reward, she has one in that she is married to Sir Richard Pole, a man most trusted by my father, and she lives here in the highest regard and she is my friend and I hope will be yours.'

He took her hand and felt it tremble. 'Come, Catalina. This isn't like you. Be brave, my love. She won't blame you.'

'She must blame me,' she said in an anguished whisper. 'My parents insisted that there should be no doubt over your inheritance. I know they did. Your own father promised that there would be no rival princes. They knew what he meant to do. They did not tell him to leave an innocent man with his life. They let him do it. They wanted him to do it. Edward Plantagenet's blood is on my head. Our marriage is under the curse of his death.'

Arthur recoiled, he had never before seen her so distressed. 'My God, Catalina, you cannot call us accursed.'

She nodded miserably.

'You have never spoken of this.'

'I could not bear to say it.'

'But you have thought it?'

'From the moment they told me that he was put to death for my sake.'

'My love, you cannot really think that we are accursed?'

'In this one thing.'

He tried to laugh off her intensity. 'No. You must know we are blessed.' He drew closer and said very quietly, so that no-one else could hear, 'Every morning when you wake in my arms, do you feel accursed then?'

'No,' she said unwillingly. 'No, I don't.'

'Every night when I come to your rooms, do you feel the shadow of sin upon you?'

'No,' she conceded.

'We are not cursed,' he said firmly. 'We are blessed with God's favour. Catalina, my love, trust me. She has forgiven my father, she certainly would never blame you. I swear to you, she is a woman with a heart as big as a cathedral. She wants to meet you. Come with me and let me present her to you.'

'Alone then,' she said, still fearing some terrible scene.

'Alone. She is in the castle warden's rooms now. If you come at once, we can leave them all here, and go quietly by ourselves and see her.'

She rose from her seat and put her hand on the crook of his arm. 'I am walking alone with the princess,' Arthur said to her ladies. 'You can all stay here.'

They looked surprised to be excluded, and some of them were openly disappointed. Catalina went past them without looking up.

Once out of the door he preceded her down the tight spiral staircase, one hand on the central stone post, one on the wall. Catalina followed him, lingering at every deep-set arrowslit window, looking down into the valley where the Teme had burst its banks and was like a silver lake over the water meadows. It was cold, even for March in the Borders, and Catalina shivered as if a stranger was walking on her grave.

'My love,' he said, looking back up the narrow stairs towards her. 'Courage. Your mother would have courage.'

'She ordered this thing,' she said crossly. 'She thought it was for my benefit. But a man died for her ambition, and now I have to face his sister.'

'She did it for you,' he reminded her. 'And nobody blames you.' They came to the floor below the princess's suite of rooms and without hesitation, Arthur tapped on the thick wooden door of the warden's apartments and went in.

The square room overlooking the valley was the match of Catalina's presence chamber upstairs, panelled with wood and hung with bright tapestries. There was a lady waiting for them, seated by the fireside, and when the door opened she rose. She was dressed in a pale grey gown with a grey hood on her hair. She was about thirty years of age; she looked at Catalina with friendly interest, and then she sank into a deep, respectful curtsey.

Disobeying the nip of his bride's fingers, Arthur withdrew his arm and stepped back as far as the doorway. Catalina looked back at him reproachfully and then bobbed a small curtsey to the older woman. They rose up together.

'I am so pleased to meet you,' Lady Pole said sweetly. 'And I am sorry not to have been here to greet you. But one of my children was ill and I went to make sure that he was well nursed.'

'Your husband has been very kind,' Catalina managed to say.

'I hope so, for I left him a long list of commandments; I so wanted your rooms to be warm and comfortable. You must tell me if there is anything you would like. I don't know Spain, so I didn't know what things would give you pleasure.'

'No! It is all . . . absolutely.'

The older woman looked at the princess. 'Then I hope you will be very happy here with us,' she said.

'I hope to . . .' Catalina breathed. 'But I . . . I . . .'

'Yes?'

'I was very sorry to hear of the death of your brother.' Catalina dived in. Her face, which had been white with discomfort, now flushed scarlet. She could feel her ears burning, and to her horror she heard her voice tremble. 'Indeed, I was very sorry. Very . . .'

'It was a great loss to me, and to mine,' the woman said steadily. 'But it is the way of the world.'

'I am afraid that my coming . . .'

'I never thought that it was any choice or any fault of yours, Princess. When our dear Prince Arthur was to be married his father was bound to make sure that his inheritance was secured. I know that my brother would never have threatened the peace of the

147

Tudors, but they were not to know that. And he was ill-advised by a mischievous young man, drawn into some foolish plot...' She broke off as her voice shook; but rapidly she recovered herself. 'Forgive me. It still grieves me. He was an innocent, my brother. His silly plotting was proof of his innocence, not of his guilt. There is no doubt in my mind that he is in God's keeping now, with all innocents.'

She smiled at the princess. 'In this world, we women often find that we have no power over what men do. I am sure you would have wished my brother no harm, and indeed, I am sure that he would not have stood against you or against our dearest prince here – but it is the way of the world that harsh measures are sometimes taken. My father made some bad choices in his life, and God knows he paid for them in full. His son, though innocent, went the way of his father. A turn of the coin and it could all have been different. I think a woman has to learn to live with the turn of the coin even when it falls against her.'

Catalina was listening intently. 'I know my mother and father wanted to be sure that the Tudor line was without challenge,' she breathed. 'I know that they told the king.' She felt as if she had to make sure that this woman knew the depth of her guilt.

'As I might have done if I had been them,' Lady Margaret said simply. 'Princess, I do not blame you, nor your mother or father. I do not blame our great king. Were I any one of them, I might have behaved just as they have done, and explained myself only to God. All I have to do, since I am not one of these great people but merely the humble wife to a fine man, is to take care how I behave, and how I will explain myself to God.'

'I felt that I came to this country with his death on my conscience,' Catalina admitted in a sudden rush.

The older woman shook her head. 'His death is not on your conscience,' she said firmly. 'And it is wrong to blame yourself for another's doing. Indeed, I would think your confessor would tell you: it is a form of pride. Let that be the sin that you confess, you need not take the blame for the sins of others.'

Catalina looked up for the first time and met the steady eyes of Lady Pole, and saw her smile. Cautiously she smiled back, and the older woman stretched out her hand, as a man would offer to shake on a bargain. 'You see,' she said pleasantly. 'I was a Princess Royal myself once. I was the last Plantagenet princess, raised by King Richard in his nursery with his son. Of all the women in the world, I should know that there is more to life than a woman can ever control. There is the will of your husband, and of your parents, and of your king, and of your God. Nobody could blame a princess for the doings of a king. How could one ever challenge it? Or make any difference? Our way has to be obedience.'

Catalina, her hand in the warm, firm grasp, felt wonderfully reassured. 'I am afraid I am not always very obedient,' she confessed.

The older woman laughed. 'Oh yes, for one would be a fool not to think for oneself,' she allowed. 'True obedience can only happen when you secretly think you know better, and you choose to bow your head. Anything short of that is just agreement, and any ninny-in-waiting can agree. Don't you think?'

And Catalina, giggling with an English woman for the first time, laughed aloud and said: 'I never wanted to be a ninny-in-waiting.'

'Neither did I,' gleamed Margaret Pole, who had been a Plantagenet, a Princess Royal and was now a mere wife buried in the fastness of the Tudor Borders. 'I always know that I am myself, in my heart, whatever title I am given.'

I am so surprised to find that the woman whose presence I have dreaded is making the castle at Ludlow feel like a home for me. Lady Margaret Pole is a companion and friend to comfort me for the loss of my mother and sisters. I realise now that I have always lived in a

world dominated by women: the queen my mother, my sisters, our ladies- and maids-in-waiting, and all the women servants of the seraglio. In the Alhambra we lived almost withdrawn from men, in rooms built for the pleasure and comfort of women. We lived almost in seclusion, in the privacy of the cool rooms, and ran through the courtyards and leaned on the balconies secure in the knowledge that half the palace was exclusively in the ownership of us women.

We would attend the court with my father, we were not hidden from sight; but the natural desire of women for privacy was served and emphasised by the design of the Alhambra where the prettiest rooms and the best gardens were reserved for us.

It is strange to come to England and find the world dominated by men. Of course I have my rooms and my ladies, but any man can come and ask for admittance at any time. Sir Richard Pole or any other of Arthur's gentlemen can come to my rooms without notice and think that they are paying me a compliment. The English seem to think it right and normal that men and women should mix. I have not yet seen a house with rooms that are exclusive to women, and no woman goes veiled as we sometimes did in Spain, not even when travelling, not even among strangers.

Even the royal family is open to all. Men, even strangers, can stroll through the royal palaces as long as they are smart enough for the guards to admit them. They can wait around in the queen's presence chamber and see her any time she walks by, staring at her as if they were family. The great hall, the chapel, the queen's public rooms are open to anyone who can find a good hat and a cape and pass as gentry. The English treat women as if they are boys or servants, they can go anywhere, they can be looked at by anyone. For a while I thought this was a great freedom, and for a while I revelled in it; then I realised the English women may show their faces but they are not bold like men, they are not free like boys; they still have to remain silent and obey.

Now with Lady Margaret Pole returned to the warden's rooms it feels as if this castle has come under the rule of women. The evenings in the hall are less hearty, even the food at dinner has changed. The troubadours sing of love and less of battles, there is more French spoken and less Welsh.

My rooms are above, and hers are on the floor below, and we go up and down stairs all day to see each other. When Arthur and Sir Richard are out hunting, the castle's mistress is still at home and the place does not feel empty any more. Somehow, she makes it a lady's castle, just by being here. When Arthur is away, the life of the castle is not silent, waiting for his return. It is a warm, happy place, busy in its own day's work.

I have missed having an older woman to be my friend. Maria de Salinas is a girl as young and silly as I am, she is a companion, not a mentor. Dona Elvira was nominated by my mother the queen to stand in a mother's place for me; but she is not a woman I can warm to, though I have tried to love her. She is strict with me, jealous of her influence over me, ambitious to run the whole court. She and her husband, who commands my household, want to dominate my life. Since that first evening at Dogmersfield when she contradicted the king himself, I have doubted her judgement. Even now she continually cautions me against becoming too close with Arthur, as if it were wrong to love a husband, as if I could resist him! She wants to make a little Spain in England, she wants me to still be the Infanta. But I am certain that my way ahead in England is to become English.

Dona Elvira will not learn English. She affects not to be able to understand French when it is spoken with an English accent. The Welsh she treats with absolute contempt as barbarians on the very edge of civilisation, which is not very comfortable when we are visiting the townspeople of Ludlow. To be honest, sometimes she behaves more grandly than any woman I have ever known, she is prouder than my mother herself. She is certainly grander than me. I have to admire her, but I cannot truly love her.

But Margaret Pole was educated as the niece of a king and is as

fluent in Latin as me. We speak French easily together, she is teaching
me English, and when we come across a word we don't know in any
of our shared languages, we compose great mimes that set us wailing
with giggles. I made her cry with laughing when I tried to demon-
strate indigestion, and the guards came running, thinking we were
under attack when she used all the ladies of the court and their maid-
servants to demonstrate to me the correct protocol for an English hunt
in the field.

With Margaret, Catalina thought she could raise the question of her
future, and her father-in-law of whom she was frankly nervous.

'He was displeased before we came away,' she said. 'It is the question of the dowry.'

'Oh, yes?' Margaret replied. The two women were seated in a
window, waiting for the men to come back from hunting. It was
bitterly cold and damp outside, neither of them had wanted to go
out. Margaret thought it better to volunteer nothing about the vexed
question of Catalina's dowry; she had already heard from her husband
that the Spanish king had perfected the art of double dealing. He
had agreed a substantial dowry for the Infanta, but then sent her to
England with only half the money. The rest, he suggested, could be
made up with the plate and treasure that she brought as her household goods. Outraged, King Henry had demanded the full amount.
Sweetly Ferdinand of Spain replied that the Infanta's household had
been supplied with the very best, Henry could take his pick.

It was a bad way to start a marriage that was, in any case, founded
only on greed and ambition, and a shared fear of France. Catalina
was caught between the determination of two cold-hearted men.
Margaret guessed that one of the reasons that Catalina had been
sent to Ludlow Castle with her husband was to force her to use her
own household goods and so diminish their value. If King Henry

had kept her at court in Windsor or Greenwich or Westminster, she would have eaten off his plates and her father could have argued that the Spanish plate was as good as new, and must be taken as the dowry. But now, every night they ate from Catalina's gold plates and every scrape of a careless knife knocked a little off the value. When it was time to pay the second half of the dowry, the King of Spain would find he would have to pay cash. King Ferdinand might be a hard man and a cunning negotiator but he had met his match in Henry Tudor of England.

'He said that I should be a daughter to him,' Catalina started carefully. 'But I cannot obey him as a daughter should, if I am to obey my own father. My father tells me not to use my plate and to give it to the king. But he won't accept it. And since the dowry is unpaid the king sends me away with no provision, he doesn't even pay my allowance.'

'Does the Spanish ambassador not advise you?'

Catalina made a little face. 'He is the king's own man,' she said. 'No help to me. I don't like him. He is a Jew, but converted. An adaptable man. A Spaniard, but he has lived here for years. He is become a man for the Tudors, not for Aragon. I shall tell my father that he is poorly served by Dr de Puebla, but in the meantime, I have no good advice, and in my household Dona Elvira and my treasurer never stop quarrelling. She says that my goods and my treasure must be loaned to the goldsmiths to raise money, he says he will not let them out of his sight until they are paid to the king.'

'And have you not asked the prince what you should do?'

Catalina hesitated. 'It is a matter between his father and my father,' she said cautiously. 'I didn't want to let it disturb us. He has paid for all my travelling expenses here. He is going to have to pay for my ladies' wages at midsummer, and soon I will need new gowns. I don't want to ask him for money. I don't want him to think me greedy.'

'You love him, don't you?' Margaret asked, smiling, and watched the younger woman's face light up.

'Oh yes,' the girl breathed. 'I do love him so.'

The older woman smiled. 'You are blessed,' she said gently. 'To be a princess and to find love with the husband you are ordered to marry. You are blessed, Catalina.'

'I know. I do think it is a sign of God's especial favour to me.'

The older woman paused at the grandness of the claim, but did not correct her. The confidence of youth would wear away soon enough without any need for warnings. 'And do you have any signs?'

Catalina looked puzzled.

'Of a child coming? You do know what to look for?'

The young woman blushed. 'I do know. My mother told me. There are no signs yet.'

'It's early days,' Lady Margaret said comfortingly. 'But if you had a child on the way I think there would be no difficulty with a dowry. I think nothing would be too good for you if you were carrying the next Tudor prince.'

'I ought to be paid my allowance whether I have a child or not,' Catalina observed. 'I am Princess of Wales, I should have an allowance to keep my state.'

'Yes,' said Margaret drily. 'But who is going to tell the king that?'

'Tell me a story.'

They were bathed in the dappled gold of candlelight and fire-light. It was midnight and the castle was silent but for their low voices, all the lights were out but for the blaze of Catalina's chambers where the two young lovers were resisting sleep.

'What shall I tell you about?'

'Tell me a story about the Moors.'

She thought for a moment, throwing a shawl around her bare shoulders against the cold. Arthur was sprawled across the bed but when she moved he gathered her to him so her head rested on his naked chest. He ran his hand through her rich red hair and gathered it into his fist.

'I will tell you a story about one of the sultanas,' she said. 'It is not a story. It is true. She was in the harem; you know that the women live apart from the men in their own rooms?'

He nodded, watching the candlelight flicker on her neck, on the hollow at her collarbone.

'She looked out of the window and the tidal river beneath her window was at low ebb. The poor children of the town were playing in the water. They were on the slipway for the boats and they had spread mud all around and they were slipping and sliding, skating in the mud. She laughed while she watched them and she said to her ladies how she wished that she could play like that.'

'But she couldn't go out?'

'No, she could never go out. Her ladies told the eunuchs who guarded the harem and they told the Grand Vizier and he told the sultan, and when she left the window and went to her presence chamber, guess what?'

He shook his head, smiling. 'What?'

'Her presence chamber was a great marble hall. The floor was made of rose-veined marble. The sultan had ordered them to bring great flasks of perfumed oils and pour them on the floor. All the perfumiers in the town had been ordered to bring oil of roses to the palace. They had brought rose petals and sweet-smelling herbs and they had made a thick paste of oil of roses and rose petals and herbs and spread it, one foot thick, all across the floor of her presence chamber. The sultana and her ladies stripped to their chemises and slid and played in the mud, threw rose water and petals and all the afternoon played like the mudlarks.'

He was entranced. 'How glorious.'

She smiled up at him. 'Now it is your turn. You tell me a story.'

'I have no stories like that. It is all fighting and winning.'

'Those are the stories you like best when I tell them,' she pointed out.

'I do. And now your father is going to war again.'

'He is?'

'Did you not know?'

Catalina shook her head. 'The Spanish ambassador sometimes sends me a note with the news, but he has told me nothing. Is it a crusade?'

'You are a bloodthirsty soldier of Christ. I should think the infidels shake in their sandals. No, it is not a crusade. It is a far less heroic cause. Your father, rather surprisingly to us, has made an alliance with King Louis of France. Apparently they plan to invade Italy together and share the spoils.'

'King Louis?' she asked in surprise. 'Never! I had thought they would be enemies until death.'

'Well, it seems that the French king does not care who he allies with. First the Turks and now your father.'

'Well, better that King Louis makes alliance with my father than with the Turks,' she said stoutly. 'Anything is better than they are invited in.'

'But why would your father join with our enemy?'

'He has always wanted Naples,' she confided to him. 'Naples and Navarre. One way or another he will have them. King Louis may think he has an ally but there will be a high price to pay. I know him. He plays a long game but he usually gets his own way. Who sent you the news?'

'My father. I think he is vexed not to be in their counsel. He fears the French worse only than the Scots. It is a disappointment for us that your father would ally with them on anything.'

'On the contrary, your father should be pleased that my father is keeping the French busy in the south. My father is doing him a service.'

He laughed at her. 'You are a great help.'

'Will your father not join with them?'

Arthur shook his head. 'Perhaps, but his one great desire is to keep England at peace. War is a terrible thing for a country. You are a soldier's daughter and you should know. My father says it is a terrible thing to see a country at war.'

'Your father only fought one big battle,' she said. 'Sometimes you have to fight. Sometimes you have to beat your enemy.'

'I wouldn't fight to gain land,' he said. 'But I would fight to defend our borders. And I think we will have to fight against the Scots unless my sister can change their very nature.'

'And is your father prepared for war?'

'He has the Howard family to keep the north for him,' he said. 'And he has the trust of every northern landlord. He has reinforced the castles and he keeps the Great North Road open so that he can get his soldiers up there if needs be.'

Catalina looked thoughtful. 'If he has to fight he would do better to invade them,' she said. 'Then he can choose the time and the place to fight and not be forced into defence.'

'Is that the better way?'

She nodded. 'My father would say so. It is everything to have your army moving forwards and confident. You have the wealth of the country ahead of you, for your supplies; you have the movement forwards: soldiers like to feel that they are making progress. There is nothing worse than being forced to turn and fight.'

'You are a tactician,' he said. 'I wish to God I had your childhood and knew the things you know.'

'You do have,' she said sweetly. 'For everything I know is yours, and everything I am is yours. And if you and our country ever need me to fight for you then I will be there.'

It has become colder and colder and the long week of rain has turned into showers of hail and now snow. Even so it is not bright, cold wintry weather but a low, damp mist with swirling cloud and flurries of slush

which clings in clumps to trees and turrets and sits in the river like old sherbet.

When Arthur comes to my room he slips along the battlements like a skater and this morning, as he went back to his room, we were certain we would be discovered because he slid on fresh ice and fell and cursed so loud that the sentry on next tower put his head out and shouted 'Who goes there?' and I had to call back that it was only me, feeding the winter birds. So Arthur whistled at me and told me it was the call of a robin and we both laughed so much that we could barely stand. I am certain that the sentry knew anyway, but it was so cold he did not come out.

Now today Arthur has gone out riding with his council, who want to look at a site for a new corn mill while the river is in spate and partly blocked by snow and ice, and Lady Margaret and I are staying at home and playing cards.

It is cold and grey, it is wet all the time, even the walls of the castle weep with icy moisture, but I am happy. I love him, I would live with him anywhere, and spring will come and then summer. I know we will be happy then too.

The tap on the door came late at night. She threw it open.

'Ah love, my love! Where have you been?'

He stepped into the room and kissed her. She could taste the wine on his breath. 'They would not leave,' he said. 'I have been trying to get away to be with you for three hours at the very least.'

He picked her up off her feet and carried her to the bed. 'But Arthur, don't you want . . . ?'

'I want you.'

'Tell me a story.'

'Are you not sleepy now?'

'No. I want you to sing me the song about the Moors losing the battle of Malaga.'

Catalina laughed. 'It was the battle of Alhama. I shall sing you some of the verses; but it goes on and on.'

'Sing me all of them.'

'We would need all night,' she protested.

'We have all night, thank God,' he said, his joy in his voice. 'We have all night and we have every night for the rest of our lives, thank God for it.'

'It is a forbidden song,' she said. 'Forbidden by my mother herself.'

'So how did you learn it?' Arthur demanded, instantly diverted.

'Servants,' she said carelessly. 'I had a nursemaid who was a Morisco and she would forget who I was, and who she was, and sing to me.'

'What's a Morisco? And why was the song banned?' he asked curiously.

'A Morisco means "little Moor" in Spanish,' she explained. 'It's what we call the Moors who live in Spain. They are not really Moors like those in Africa. So we call them little Moors, or Moros. As I left, they were starting to call themselves Mudajjan – one allowed to remain.'

'One allowed to remain?' he asked. 'In their own land?'

'It's not their land,' she said instantly. 'It's ours. Spanish land.'

'They had it for seven hundred years,' he pointed out. 'When you Spanish were doing nothing but herding goats in the mountains, they were building roads and castles and universities. You told me so yourself.'

'Well, it's ours now,' she said flatly.

He clapped his hands like a sultan. 'Sing the song, Scheherazade. And sing it in French, you barbarian, so I can understand it.'

Catalina put her hands together like a woman about to pray and bowed low to him.

'Now that is good,' Arthur said, revelling in her. 'Did you learn that in the harem?'

She smiled at him and tipped up her head and sang.

'An old man cries to the king: Why comes this sudden calling?
*   – Alas! Alhama!*
Alas my friends, Christians have won Alhama – Alas! Alhama!
A white-bearded imam answers: This has thou merited, oh King!
*   – Alas! Alhama!*
In an evil hour thou slewest the Abencerrages, flower of Granada
*   – Alas! Alhama!*
Not Granada, not kingdom, not thy life shall long remain – Alas!
*   Alhama!'*

She fell silent. 'And it was true,' she said. 'Poor Boabdil came out of the Alhambra Palace, out of the red fort that they said would never fall, with the keys on a silk cushion, bowed low and gave them to my mother and my father and rode away. They say that at the mountain pass he looked back at his kingdom, his beautiful kingdom, and wept, and his mother told him to weep like a woman for what he could not hold as a man.'

Arthur let out a boyish crack of laughter. 'She said what?'

Catalina looked up, her face grave. 'It was very tragic.'

'It is just the sort of thing my grandmother would say,' he said delightedly. 'Thank God my father won his crown. My grandmother would be just as sweet in defeat as Boabdil's mother. Good God: "weep like a woman for what you cannot hold as a man." What a thing to say to a man as he walks away in defeat!'

Catalina laughed too. 'I never thought of it like that,' she said. 'It isn't very comforting.'

'Imagine going into exile with your mother, and she so angry with you!'

'Imagine losing the Alhambra, never going back there!'

160

He pulled her to him and kissed her face. 'No regrets!' he commanded.

At once she smiled for him. 'Then divert me,' she ordered. 'Tell me about your mother and father.'

He thought for a moment. 'My father was born an heir to the Tudors, but there were dozens in line for the throne before him,' he said. 'His father wanted him called Owen, Owen Tudor, a good Welsh name, but his father died before his birth, in the war. My grandmother was only a child of twelve when he was born, but she had her way and called him Henry – a royal name. You can see what she was thinking even then, even though she was little more than a child herself, and her husband was dead.

'My father's fortunes soared up and down with every battle of the civil war. One time he was a son of the ruling family, the next they were on the run. His uncle Jasper Tudor – you remember him – kept faith with my father and with the Tudor cause, but there was a final battle and our cause was lost, and our king executed. Edward came to the throne and my father was the last of the line. He was in such danger that Uncle Jasper broke out of the castle where they were being held and fled with him out of the country to Brittany.'

'To safety?'

'Of a sort. He told me once that he woke every morning expecting to be handed over to Edward. And once, King Edward said that he should come home and there would be a kind welcome and a wedding arranged for him. My father pretended to be ill on the road and escaped. He would have come home to his death.'

Catalina blinked. 'So he was a pretender too, in his time.'

He grinned at her. 'As I said. That is why he fears them so much. He knows what a pretender can do if the luck is with him. If they had caught him they would have brought him home to his death in the Tower. Just like he did to Warwick. My father would have been put to death the moment King Edward had him. But he pretended to be ill and got away, over the border into France.'

'They didn't hand him back?'

Arthur laughed. 'They supported him. He was the greatest challenge to the peace of England, of course they encouraged him. It suited the French to support him then: when he was not king but pretender.'

She nodded, she was a child of a prince praised by Machiavelli himself. Any daughter of Ferdinand was born to double-dealing. 'And then?'

'Edward died young, in his prime, with only a young son to inherit. His brother Richard first held the throne in trust and then claimed it for himself and put his own nephews, Edward's sons, the little princes, in the Tower of London.'

She nodded, this was a history she had been taught in Spain, and the greater story – of deadly rivalry for a throne – was a common theme for both young people.

'They went into the Tower and never came out again,' Arthur said bleakly. 'God bless their souls, poor boys, no-one knows what happened to them. The people turned against Richard, and summoned my father from France.'

'Yes?'

'My grandmother organised the great lords one after another, she was an arch-plotter. She and the Duke of Buckingham put their heads together and had the nobles of the kingdom in readiness. That's why my father honours her so highly: he owes her his throne. And he waited until he could get a message to my mother to tell her that he would marry her if he won the throne.'

'Because he loved her?' Catalina asked hopefully. 'She is so beautiful.'

'Not he. He hadn't even seen her. He had been in exile for most of his life, remember. It was a marriage cobbled together because his mother knew that if she could get those two married then everyone would see that the heir of York had married the heir of Lancaster and the war could be over. And her mother saw it as her

162

only way out to safety. The two mothers brokered the deal together like a pair of crones over a cauldron. They're both women you wouldn't want to cross.'

'He didn't love her?' She was disappointed.

Arthur smiled. 'No. It's not a romance. And she didn't love him. But they knew what they had to do. When my father marched in and beat Richard and picked the crown of England out of the bodies and the wreckage of the battlefield, he knew that he would marry the princess, take the throne, and found a new line.'

'But wasn't she next heir to the throne anyway?' she asked, puzzled. 'Since it was her father who had been King Edward? And her uncle who had died in the battle, and her brothers were dead?'

He nodded. 'She was the oldest princess.'

'So why didn't she claim the throne for herself?'

'Aha, you are a rebel!' he said. He took a handful of her hair and pulled her face towards him. He kissed her mouth, tasting of wine and sweetmeats. 'A Yorkist rebel, which is worse.'

'I just thought she should have claimed the throne for herself.'

'Not in this country,' Arthur ruled. 'We don't have reigning queens in this England. Girls don't inherit. They cannot take the throne.'

'But if a king had only a daughter?'

He shrugged. 'Then it would be a tragedy for the country. You have to give me a boy, my love. Nothing else will do.'

'But if we only had a girl?'

'She would marry a prince and make him King Consort of England, and he would rule alongside her. England has to have a king. Like your mother did. She reigns alongside her husband.'

'In Aragon she does, but in Castile he rules alongside her. Castile is her country and Aragon his.'

'We'd never stand for it in England,' Arthur said.

She drew away from him in indignation. She was only half-pretending. 'I tell you this, if we have only one child and she is a girl then she will rule as queen and she will be a queen as good as any man can be king.'

'Well, she will be a novelty,' he said. 'We don't believe a woman can defend the country as a king needs to do.'

'A woman can fight,' she said instantly. 'You should see my mother in armour. Even I could defend the country. I have seen warfare, which is more than you have done. I could be as good a king as any man.'

He smiled at her, shaking his head. 'Not if the country was invaded. You couldn't command an army.'

'I could command an army. Why not?'

'No English army would be commanded by a woman. They wouldn't take orders from a woman.'

'They would take orders from their commander,' she flashed out. 'And if they don't then they are no good as soldiers and they have to be trained.'

He laughed. 'No Englishman would obey a woman,' he said. He saw by her stubborn face that she was not convinced.

'All that matters is that you win the battle,' she said. 'All that matters is that the country is defended. It doesn't matter who leads the army as long as they follow.'

'Well, at any rate, my mother had no thought of claiming the throne for herself. She would not have dreamed of it. She married my father and became Queen of England through marriage. And because she was the York Princess and he was the Lancaster heir my grandmother's plan succeeded. My father may have won the throne by conquest and acclaim; but we will have it by inheritance.'

Catalina nodded. 'My mother said there was nothing wrong with a man who is new-come to the throne. What matters is not the winning but the keeping of it.'

'We shall keep it,' he said with certainty. 'We shall make a great country here, you and me. We shall build roads and markets, churches and schools. We shall put a ring of forts around the coast-line and build ships.'

'We shall create courts of justice as my mother and father have done in Spain,' she said, settling back into the pleasure of planning a future on which they could agree. 'So that no man can be cruelly treated by another. So that every man knows that he can go to the court and have his case heard.'

He raised his glass to her. 'We should start writing this down,' he said. 'And we should start planning how it is to be done.'

'It will be years before we come to our thrones.'

'You never know. I don't wish it – God knows, I honour my father and my mother and I would want nothing before God's own time. But you never know. I am Prince of Wales, you are Princess. But we will be King and Queen of England. We should know who we will have at our court, we should know what advisors we will choose, we should know how we are going to make this country truly great. If it is a dream, then we can talk of it together at nighttime, as we do. But if it is a plan, we should write it in the daytime, take advice on it, think how we might do the things we want.'

Her face lit up. 'When we have finished our lessons for the day, perhaps we could do it then. Perhaps your tutor would help us, and my confessor.'

'And my advisors,' he said. 'And we could start here. In Wales. I can do what I want, within reason. We could make a college here, and build some schools. We could even commission a ship to be built here. There are shipwrights in Wales, we could build the first of our defensive ships.'

She clapped her hands like the girl she was. 'We could start our reign!' she said.

'Hail Queen Katherine! Queen of England!' Arthur said playfully, but at the ring of the words he stopped and looked at her more seriously. 'You know, you will hear them say that, my love. Vivat! Vivat Catalina Regina, Queen Katherine, Queen of England.'

It is like an adventure, wondering what sort of country we can make, what sort of king and queen we will be. It is natural we should think of Camelot. It was my favourite book in my mother's library and I found Arthur's own well-thumbed copy in his father's library.

I know that Camelot is a story, an ideal, as unreal as the love of a troubadour, or a fairy-tale castle or legends about thieves and treasure and genies. But there is something about the idea of ruling a kingdom with justice, with the consent of the people, which is more than a fairy tale.

Arthur and I will inherit great power, his father has seen to that. I think we will inherit a strong throne and a great treasure. We will inherit with the goodwill of the people; the king is not loved but he is respected, and nobody wants a return to endless battles. These English have a horror of civil war. If we come to the throne with this power, this wealth, and this goodwill, there is no doubt in my mind that we can make a great country here.

And it shall be a great country in alliance with Spain. My parents' heir is Juana's son, Charles. He will be Holy Roman Emperor and King of Spain. He will be my nephew and we will have the friendship of kinsmen. What a powerful alliance this will be: the great Holy Roman Empire and England. Nobody will be able to stand against us, we might divide France, we might divide most of Europe. Then we will stand, the empire and England against the Moors, then we will win and the whole of the East, Persia, the Ottomans, the Indies, even China will be laid open to us.

The routine of the castle changed. In the days which were starting to become warmer and brighter the young Prince and Princess of

Wales set up their office in her rooms, dragged a big table over to the window for the afternoon light, and pinned up maps of the Principality on the linenfold panelling.

'You look as if you are planning a campaign,' Lady Margaret Pole said pleasantly.

'The princess should be resting,' Dona Elvira remarked resentfully to no-one in particular.

'Are you unwell?' Lady Margaret asked quickly.

Catalina smiled and shook her head, she was becoming accustomed to the obsessive interest in her health. Until she could say that she was carrying England's heir she would have no peace from people asking her how she did.

'I don't need to rest,' she said. 'And tomorrow, if you will take me, I should like to go out and see the fields.'

'The fields?' asked Lady Margaret, rather taken aback. 'In March? They won't plough for another week or so, there is almost nothing to see.'

'I have to learn,' Catalina said. 'Where I live, it is so dry in summer that we have to build little ditches in every field, to the foot of every tree, to channel water to the plants to make sure that they can drink and live. When we first rode through this country and I saw the ditches in your fields, I was so ignorant I thought they were bringing water in.' She laughed aloud at the memory. 'And then the prince told me they were drains to take the water away. I could not believe it! So we had better ride out and you must tell me everything.'

'A queen does not need to know about fields,' Dona Elvira said in muted disapproval from the corner. 'Why should she know what the farmers grow?'

'Of course a queen needs to know,' Catalina replied, irritated. 'She should know everything about her country. How else can she rule?'

'I am sure you will be a very fine Queen of England,' Lady Margaret said, making the peace.

Catalina glowed. 'I shall be the best Queen of England that I can be,' she said. 'I shall care for the poor and assist the church, and if we are ever at war I shall ride out and fight for England just as my mother did for Spain.'

Planning for the future with Arthur, I forget my homesickness for Spain. Every day we think of some improvement we could make, of some law that should be changed. We read together, books of philosophy and politics, we talk about whether people can be trusted with their freedom, of whether a king should be a good tyrant or should step back from power. We talk about my home: of my parents' belief that you make a country by one church, one language, and one law. Or whether it could be possible to do as the Moors did: to make a country with one law but with many faiths and many languages, and assume that people are wise enough to choose the best.

We argue, we talk. Sometimes we break up in laughter, sometimes we disagree. Arthur is my lover always, my husband, undeniably. And now he is becoming my friend.

Catalina was in the little garden of Ludlow Castle, which was set along the east wall, in earnest conversation with one of the castle gardeners. In neat beds around her were the herbs that the cooks used, and some herbs and flowers with medicinal properties grown by Lady Margaret. Arthur, seeing Catalina as he walked back from confession in the round chapel, glanced up to the great hall to check that no-one would prevent him, and slipped off to be with her. As he drew up she was gesturing, trying to describe something. Arthur smiled.

'Princess,' he said formally in greeting.

She swept him a low curtsey, but her eyes were warm with pleasure at the sight of him. 'Sire.'

The gardener had dropped to his knees in the mud at the arrival of the prince. 'You can get up,' Arthur said pleasantly. 'I don't think you will find many pretty flowers at this time of year, Princess.'

'I was trying to talk to him about growing salad vegetables,' she said. 'But he speaks Welsh and English and I have tried Latin and French and we don't understand each other at all.'

'I think I am with him. I don't understand either. What is salad?'

She thought for a moment. '*Acetaria*.'

'*Acetaria*?' he queried.

'Yes, salad.'

'What is it, exactly?'

'It is vegetables that grow in the ground and you eat them without cooking them,' she explained. 'I was asking if he could plant some for me.'

'You eat them raw? Without boiling?'

'Yes, why not?'

'Because you will be dreadfully ill, eating uncooked food in this country.'

'Like fruit, like apples. You eat them raw.'

He was unconvinced. 'More often cooked, or preserved or dried. And anyway, that is a fruit and not leaves. But what sorts of vegetables do you want?'

'*Lactuca*,' she said.

'*Lactuca*?' he repeated. 'I have never heard of it.'

She sighed. 'I know. You none of you seem to know anything of vegetables. *Lactuca* is like . . .' She searched her mind for the truly terrible vegetable that she had been forced to eat, boiled into a pulp at one dinner at Greenwich. 'Samphire,' she said. 'The closest thing you have to *lactuca* is probably samphire. But you eat *lactuca* without cooking and it is crisp and sweet.'

'Vegetables? Crisp?'

'Yes,' she said patiently.

'And you eat this in Spain?'

She nearly laughed at his appalled expression. 'Yes. You would like it.'

'And can we grow it here?'

'I think he is telling me: no. He has never heard of such a thing. He has no seeds. He does not know where we would find such seeds. He does not think it would grow here.' She looked up at the blue sky with the scudding rain clouds. 'Perhaps he is right,' she said, a little weariness in her voice. 'I am sure that it needs much sunshine.'

Arthur turned to the gardener. 'Ever heard of a plant called *lactuca*?'

'No, Your Grace,' the man said, his head bowed. 'I'm sorry, Your Grace. Perhaps it is a Spanish plant. It sounds very barbaric. Is Her Royal Highness saying they eat grass there? Like sheep?'

Arthur's lip quivered. 'No, it is a herb, I think. I will ask her.'

He turned to Catalina and took her hand and tucked it in the crook of his arm. 'You know sometimes in summer, it is very sunny and very hot here. Truly. You would find the midday sun was too hot. You would have to sit in the shade.'

She looked disbelievingly from the cold mud to the thickening clouds.

'Not now, I know; but in summer. I have leaned against this wall and found it warm to the touch. You know, we grow strawberries and raspberries and peaches. All the fruit that you grow in Spain.'

'Oranges?'

'Well, perhaps not oranges,' he conceded.

'Lemons? Olives?'

He bridled. 'Yes, indeed.'

She looked suspiciously at him. 'Dates?'

'In Cornwall,' he asserted, straight-faced. 'Of course it is warmer in Cornwall.'

'Sugar cane? Rice? Pineapples?'

He tried to say yes, but he could not repress the giggles and she crowed with laughter, and fell on him.

When they were steady again he glanced around the inner bailey and said, 'Come on, nobody will miss us for a while,' and led her down the steps to the little sally-port and let them out of the hidden door.

A small path led them to the hillside which fell away steeply from the castle down to the river. A few lambs scampered off as they approached, a lad wandering after them. Arthur slid his arm around her waist and she let herself fall into pace with him.

'We do grow peaches,' he assured her. 'Not the other things, of course. But I am sure we can grow your *lactuca*, whatever it is. All we need is a gardener who can bring the seeds and who has already grown the things you want. Why don't you write to the gardener at the Alhambra and ask him to send you someone?'

'Could I send for a gardener?' she asked incredulously.

'My love, you are going to be Queen of England. You can send for a regiment of gardeners.'

'Really?'

Arthur laughed at the delight dawning on her face. 'At once. Did you not realise it?'

'No! But where should he garden? There is no room against the castle wall, and if we are to grow fruit as well as vegetables . . .'

'You are Princess of Wales! You can plant your garden wherever you please. You shall have all of Kent if you want it, my darling.'

'Kent?'

'We grow apples and hops there, I think we might have a try at *lactuca*.'

Catalina laughed with him. 'I didn't think. I didn't dream of sending for a gardener. If only I had brought one in the first place. I have all these useless ladies-in-waiting and I need a gardener.'

'You could swap him for Dona Elvira.'

She gurgled with laughter.

'Ah God, we are blessed,' he said simply. 'In each other and in our lives. You shall have anything you want, always. I swear it. Do you want to write to your mother? She can send you a couple of good men and I will get some land turned over at once.'

'I will write to Juana,' she decided. 'In the Netherlands. She is in the north of Christendom like me. She must know what will grow in this weather. I shall write to her and see what she has done.'

'And we shall eat *lactuca*!' he said, kissing her fingers. 'All day. We shall eat nothing but *lactuca*, like sheep grazing grass, whatever it is.'

'Tell me a story.'

'No, you tell me something.'

'If you will tell me about the fall of Granada, again.'

'I will tell you. But you have to explain something to me.'

Arthur stretched out and pulled her so that she was lying across the bed, her head on his shoulder. She could feel the rise and fall of his smooth chest as he breathed and hear the gentle thud of his heartbeat, constant as love.

'I shall explain everything.' She could hear the smile in his voice. 'I am extraordinarily wise today. You should have heard me after dinner tonight dispensing justice.'

'You are very fair,' she conceded. 'I do love it when you give a judgement.'

'I am a Solomon,' he said. 'They will call me Arthur the Good.'

'Arthur the Wise,' she suggested.

'Arthur the Magnificent.'

Catalina giggled. 'But I want you to explain to me something that I heard about your mother.'

'Oh yes?'

'One of the English ladies-in-waiting told me that she had been betrothed to the tyrant Richard. I thought I must have misunderstood her. We were speaking French and I thought I must have had it wrong.'

'Oh, that story,' he said with a little turn of the head.

'Is it not true? I hope I have not offended you?'

'No, not at all. It's a tale often told.'

'It cannot be true?'

'Who knows? Only my mother and Richard the tyrant can know what took place. And one of them is dead and the other is silent as the grave.'

'Will you tell me?' she asked tentatively. 'Or should we not speak of it at all?'

He shrugged. 'There are two stories. The well-known one, and its shadow. The story that everyone knows is that my mother fled into sanctuary with her mother and sisters, they were hiding in a church altogether. They knew if they left they would be arrested by Richard the Usurper and would disappear into the Tower like her young brothers. No-one knew if the princes were alive or dead, but nobody had seen them, everyone feared they were dead. My mother wrote to my father – well, she was ordered to by her mother – she told him that if he would come to England, a Tudor from the Lancaster line, then she, a York princess, would marry him, and the old feud between the two families would be over forever. She told him to come and save her, and know her love. He received the letter, he raised an army, he came to find the princess, he married her and brought peace to England.'

'That is what you told me before. It is a very good story.'

Arthur nodded.

'And the story you don't tell?'

Despite himself he giggled. 'It's rather scandalous. They say that she was not in sanctuary at all. They say that she left the sanctuary and her mother and sisters. She went to court. King Richard's wife was dead and he was looking for another. She accepted the proposal of King Richard. She would have married her uncle, the tyrant, the man who murdered her brothers.'

Catalina's hand stole over her mouth to cover her gasp of shock, her eyes were wide. 'No!'

'So they say.'

'The queen, your mother?'

'Herself,' he said. 'Actually, they say worse. That she and Richard were betrothed as his wife lay dying. That is why there is always such enmity between her and my grandmother. My grandmother does not trust her; but she will never say why.'

'How could she?' she demanded.

'How could she not?' he returned. 'If you look at it from her point of view, she was a princess of York, her father was dead, her mother was the enemy of the king trapped in sanctuary, as much in prison as if she was in the Tower. If she wanted to live, she would have to find some way into the favour of the king. If she wanted to be acknowledged as a princess at all, she would have to have his recognition. If she wanted to be Queen of England she would have to marry him.'

'But surely, she could have . . .' she began and then she fell silent.

'No.' He shook his head. 'You see? She was a princess, she had very little choice. If she wanted to live she would have to obey the king. If she wanted to be queen she would have to marry him.'

'She could have raised an army on her own account.'

'Not in England,' he reminded her. 'She would have to marry the King of England to be its queen. It was her only way.'

Catalina was silent for a moment. 'Thank God that for me to be queen I had to marry you, that my destiny brought me so easily here.'

He smiled. 'Thank God we are happy with our destiny. For we would have married, and you would have been Queen of England, whether you had liked me or not. Wouldn't you?'

'Yes,' she said. 'There is never a choice for a princess.'

He nodded.

'But your grandmother, My Lady the King's Mother, must have planned your mother's wedding to your father. Why does she not forgive her? She was part of the plan.'

'Those two powerful women, my father's mother and my mother's mother, brokered the deal between them like a pair of washerwomen selling stolen linen.'

She gave a little squeak of shock.

Arthur chuckled, he found that he dearly loved surprising her. 'Dreadful, isn't it?' he replied calmly. 'My mother's mother was probably the most hated woman in England at one time.'

'And where is she now?'

He shrugged. 'She was at court for a while, but My Lady the King's Mother disliked her so much she got rid of her. She was famously beautiful, you know, and a schemer. My grandmother accused her of plotting against my father and he chose to believe her.'

'She is never dead? They never executed her!'

'No. He put her into a convent and she never comes to court.'

She was aghast. 'Your grandmother had the queen's own mother confined in a convent?'

He nodded, his face grave. 'Truly. You be warned by this, beloved. My grandmother welcomes no-one to court that might distract from her own power. Make sure you never cross her.'

Catalina shook her head. 'I never would. I am absolutely terrified of her.'

'So am I!' he laughed. 'But I know her, and I warn you. She will stop at nothing to maintain the power of her son, and of her family. Nothing will distract her from this. She loves no-one but him. Not me, not her husbands, no-one but him.'

'Not you?'

He shook his head. 'She does not even love him, as you would understand it. He is the boy that she decided was born to be king. She sent him away when he was little more than a baby for his safety. She saw him survive his boyhood. Then she ordered him into the face of terrible danger to claim the throne. She could only love a king.'

She nodded. 'He is her pretender.'

175

'Exactly. She claimed the throne for him. She made him king. He is king.'

He saw her grave face. 'Now, enough of this. You have to sing me your song.'

'Which one?'

'Is there another one about the fall of Granada?'

'Dozens, I should think.'

'Sing me one,' he commanded. He piled a couple of extra cushions behind his head, and she knelt up before him, tossed back her mane of red hair and began to sing in a low sweet voice:

*'There was crying in Granada when the sun was going down
Some calling on the Trinity, some calling on Mahoun,
Here passed away the Koran and therein the Cross was borne,
And here was heard the Christian bell and there the Moorish horn.*
Te Deum Laudamus! *Was up the Alcala sung:
Down from the Alhambra minarets were all the crescents flung,
The arms thereon of Aragon, they with Castile display
One king comes in in triumph, one weeping goes away.'*

He was silent for long minutes. She stretched out again beside him on her back, looking, without seeing, the embroidered tester of the bed over their heads.

'It's always like that, isn't it?' he remarked. 'The rise of one is the fall of another. I shall be king but only at my father's death. And at my death, my son will reign.'

'Shall we call him Arthur?' she asked. 'Or Henry for your father?'

'Arthur is a good name,' he said. 'A good name for a new royal family in Britain. Arthur for Camelot, and Arthur for me. We don't want another Henry; my brother is enough for anyone. Let's call him Arthur, and his older sister will be called Mary.'

'Mary? I wanted to call her Isabella, for my mother.'

'You can call the next girl Isabella. But I want our first-born to be called Mary.'

'Arthur must be first.'

He shook his head. 'First we will have Mary so that we learn how to do it all with a girl.'

'How to do it all?'

He gestured. 'The christening, the confinement, the birthing, the whole fuss and worry, the wet nurse, the rockers, the nursemaids. My grandmother has written a great book to rule how it shall be done. It is dreadfully complicated. But if we have our Mary first then our nursery is all ready, and in your next confinement we shall put our son and heir into the cradle.'

She rose up and turned on him in mock indignation. 'You would practise being a father on my daughter!' she exclaimed.

'You wouldn't want to start with my son,' he protested. 'This will be the rose of the rose of England. That's what they call me, remember: "the rose of England". I think you should deal with my little rosebud, my little blossom, with great respect.'

'She is to be Isabella then,' Catalina stipulated. 'If she comes first, she shall be Isabella.'

'Mary, for the queen of heaven.'

'Isabella for the Queen of Spain.'

'Mary, to give thanks for you coming to me. The sweetest gift that heaven could have given me.'

Catalina melted into his arms. 'Isabella,' she said as he kissed her.

'Mary,' he whispered into her ear. 'And let us make her now.'

It is morning. I lie awake, it is dawn and I can hear the birds slowly starting to sing. The sun is coming up and through the lattice window I can see a glimpse of blue sky. Perhaps it will be a warm day, perhaps the summer is coming at last.

Beside me, Arthur is breathing quietly and steadily. I can feel my heart swell with love for him, I put my hand on the fair curls of his head and wonder if any woman has ever loved a man as I love him.

I stir and put my other hand on the warm roundness of my belly. Can it be possible that last night we made a child? Is there already, safe in my belly, a baby who will be called Mary, Princess Mary, who will be the rose of the rose of England?

I hear the footsteps of the maid moving about in my presence chamber, bringing wood for the fire, raking up the embers. Still Arthur does not stir. I put a gentle hand on his shoulder. 'Wake up, sleepy-head,' I say, my voice warm with love. 'The servants are outside, you must go.'

He is damp with sweat, the skin of his shoulder is cold and clammy.

'My love?' I ask. 'Are you well?'

He opens his eyes and smiles at me. 'Don't tell me it's morning already. I am so weary I could sleep for another day.'

'It is.'

'Oh, why didn't you wake me earlier? I love you so much in the morning and now I can't have you till tonight.'

I put my face against his chest. 'Don't. I slept late too. We keep late hours. And you will have to go now.'

Arthur holds me close, as if he cannot bear to let me go; but I can hear the groom of the chamber open the outside door to bring hot water. I draw myself away from him. It is like tearing off a layer of my own skin. I cannot bear to move away from him.

Suddenly, I am struck by the warmth of his body, the tangled heat of the sheets around us. 'You are so hot!'

'It is desire,' he says, smiling. 'I shall have to go to Mass to cool down.'

He gets out of bed and throws his gown around his shoulders. He gives a little stagger.

'Beloved, are you all right?' I ask.

'A little dizzy, nothing more,' he says. 'Blind with desire, and it is

178

all your fault. See you in chapel. Pray for me, sweetheart.'

I get up from bed, and unbolt the battlements door to let him out. He sways a little as he goes up the stone steps, then I see him straighten his shoulders to breathe in the fresh air. I close the door behind him, and then go back to my bed. I glance round the room, nobody could know that he has been here. In a moment, Dona Elvira taps on my door and comes in with the maid-in-waiting and behind them a couple of maids with the jug of hot water, and my dress for the day.

'You slept late, you must be overtired,' Dona Elvira says disapprovingly; but I am so peaceful and so happy that I cannot even be troubled to reply.

In the chapel they could do no more than exchange hidden smiles. After Mass, Arthur went riding and Catalina went to break her fast. After breakfast was her time to study with her chaplain and Catalina sat at the table in the window with him, their books before them, and studied the letters of St Paul.

Margaret Pole came in as Catalina was closing her book. 'The prince begs your attendance in his rooms,' she said.

Catalina rose to her feet. 'Has something happened?'

'I think he is unwell. He has sent away everyone but the grooms of the body and his servers.'

Catalina left at once, followed by Dona Elvira and Lady Margaret. The prince's rooms were crowded by the usual hangers-on of the little court: men seeking favour or attention, petitioners asking for justice, the curious come to stare, and the host of lesser servants and functionaries. Catalina went through them all to the double doors of Arthur's private chamber, and went in.

He was seated in a chair by the fire, his face very pale. Dona Elvira and Lady Margaret waited at the door as Catalina went quickly towards him.

'Are you ill, my love?' she asked quickly.

He managed a smile but she saw it was an effort. 'I have taken some kind of chill, I think,' he said. 'Come no closer, I don't want to pass it to you.'

'Are you hot?' she asked fearfully, thinking of the Sweat which came on like a fever and left a corpse.

'No, I feel cold.'

'Well, it is not surprising in this country where it either snows or rains all the time.'

He managed another smile.

Catalina looked around and saw Lady Margaret. 'Lady Margaret, we must call the prince's physician.'

'I sent my servants to find him already,' she said, coming forwards.

'I don't want a fuss made,' Arthur said irritably. 'I just wanted to tell you, Princess, that I cannot come to dinner.'

Her eyes went to his. 'How shall we be alone?' was the unspoken question.

'May I dine in your rooms?' she asked. 'Can we dine alone, privately, since you are ill?'

'Yes, let's,' he ruled.

'See the doctor first,' Lady Margaret advised. 'If Your Grace permits. He can advise what you should eat, and if it is safe for the princess to be with you.'

'He has no disease,' Catalina insisted. 'He says he just feels tired. It is just the cold air here, or the damp. It was cold yesterday and he was riding half the day.'

There was a tap on the door and a voice called out. 'Dr Bereworth is here, Your Grace.'

Arthur raised his hand in permission, Dona Elvira opened the door and the man came into the room.

'The prince feels cold and tired.' Catalina went to him at once, speaking rapidly in French. 'Is he ill? I don't think he's ill. What do you think?'

The doctor bowed low to her and to the prince. He bowed to Lady Margaret and Dona Elvira.

'I am sorry, I don't understand,' he said uncomfortably in English to Lady Margaret. 'What is the princess saying?'

Catalina clapped her hands together in frustration. 'The prince . . .' she began in English.

Margaret Pole came to her side. 'His Grace is unwell,' she said.

'May I speak with him alone?' he asked.

Arthur nodded. He tried to rise from the chair but he almost staggered. The doctor was at once at his side, supporting him, and led him into his bedchamber.

'He cannot be ill.' Catalina turned to Dona Elvira and spoke to her in Spanish. 'He was well last night. Just this morning he felt hot. But he said he was only tired. But now he can hardly stand. He cannot be ill.'

'Who knows what illness a man might take in this rain and fog?' the duenna replied dourly. 'It's a wonder that you are not sick yourself. It is a wonder that any of us can bear it.'

'He is not sick,' Catalina said. 'He is just overtired. He rode for a long time yesterday. And it was cold, there was a very cold wind. I noticed it myself.'

'A wind like this can kill a man,' Dona Elvira said gloomily. 'It blows so cold and so damp.'

'Stop it!' Catalina said, clapping her hands to her ears. 'I won't hear another word. He is just tired, overtired. And perhaps he has taken a chill. There is no need to speak of killing winds and damp.'

Lady Margaret stepped forwards and gently took Catalina's hands. 'Be patient, Princess,' she counselled. 'Dr Bereworth is a very good doctor, and he has known the prince from childhood. The prince is a strong young man and his health is good. It is probably nothing to worry about at all. If Dr Bereworth is concerned we will send for the king's own physician from London. We will soon have him well again.'

Catalina nodded, and turned to sit by the window and look out. The sky had clouded over, the sun was quite gone. It was raining again, the raindrops chasing down the small panes of glass. Catalina watched them. She tried to keep her mind from the death of her brother who had loved his wife so much, who had been looking forward to the birth of their son. Juan had died within days of taking sick, and no-one had ever known what was wrong with him.

'I shan't think of him, not of poor Juan,' Catalina whispered to herself. 'The cases are not alike at all. Juan was always slight, little; but Arthur is strong.'

The physician seemed to take a long time and when he came out of the bedchamber, Arthur was not with him. Catalina who had risen from her seat as soon as the door opened, peeped around him to see Arthur lying on the bed, half-undressed, half-asleep.

'I think his grooms of the body should prepare him for bed,' the doctor said. 'He is very weary. He would be better for rest. If they take care, they can get him into bed without waking him.'

'Is he ill?' Catalina demanded speaking slowly in Latin. '*Aegrotat?* Is he very ill?'

The doctor spread his hands. 'He has a fever,' he said cautiously in slow French. 'I can give him a draught to bring down his fever.'

'Do you know what it is?' Lady Margaret asked, her voice very low. 'It's not the Sweat, is it?'

'Please God it is not. And there are no other cases in the town, as far as I know. But he should be kept quiet and allowed to rest. I shall go and make up this draught and I will come back.'

The low-voiced English was incomprehensible to Catalina. 'What does he say? What did he say?' she demanded of Lady Margaret.

'Nothing more than you heard,' the older woman assured her. 'He has a fever and needs rest. Let me get his men to undress him and put him properly to bed. If he is better tonight, you can dine with him. I know he would like that.'

182

'Where is he going?' Catalina cried out as the doctor bowed and went to the door. 'He must stay and watch the prince!'

'He is going to make a draught to bring down his fever. He will be back at once. The prince will have the best of care, Your Grace. We love him as you do. We will not neglect him.'

'I know you would not . . . it is only . . . Will the doctor be long?'

'He will be as quick as he can. And see, the prince is asleep. Sleep will be his best medicine. He can rest and grow strong and dine with you tonight.'

'You think he will be better tonight?'

'If it is just a little fever and fatigue then he will be better in a few days,' Lady Margaret said firmly.

'I will watch over his sleep,' Catalina said.

Lady Margaret opened the door and beckoned to the prince's chief gentlemen. She gave them their orders and then she drew the princess through the crowd to her own rooms. 'Come, Your Grace,' she said. 'Come for a walk in the inner bailey with me and then I shall go back to his rooms and see that everything is comfortable for him.'

'I shall go back now,' Catalina insisted. 'I shall watch over his sleep.'

Margaret glanced at Dona Elvira. 'You should stay away from his rooms in case he does have a fever,' she said speaking slowly and clearly in French, so that the duenna could understand her. 'Your health is most important, Princess. I would not forgive myself if anything happened to either of you.'

Dona Elvira stepped forwards and narrowed her lips. Lady Margaret knew she could be relied on to keep the princess from danger.

'But you said he only had a slight fever. I can go to him?'

'Let us wait to see what the doctor has to say.' Lady Margaret lowered her voice. 'If you should be with child, dear Princess, we would not want you to take his fever.'

'But I will dine with him.'

'If he is well enough.'

'But he will want to see me!'

'Depend upon it,' Lady Margaret smiled. 'When his fever has broken and he is better this evening and sitting up and eating his dinner he will want to see you. You have to be patient.'

Catalina nodded. 'If I go now, do you swear that you will stay with him all the time?'

'I will go back now, if you will walk outside and then go to your room and read or study or sew.'

'I'll go!' said Catalina, instantly obedient. 'I'll go to my rooms if you will stay with him.'

'At once,' Lady Margaret promised.

This small garden is like a prison yard, I walk round and round in the herb garden, and the rain drizzles over everything like tears. My rooms are no better, my privy chamber is like a cell, I cannot bear to have anyone with me, and yet I cannot bear to be alone. I have made the ladies sit in the presence chamber, their unending chatter makes me want to scream with irritation. But when I am alone in my room I long for company. I want someone to hold my hand and tell me that everything will be all right.

I go down the narrow stone stairs and across the cobbles to the round chapel. A cross and a stone altar is set in the rounded wall, a light burning before it. It is a place of perfect peace; but I can find no peace. I fold my cold hands inside my sleeves and hug myself and I walk around the circular wall, it is thirty-six steps to the door and then I walk the circle again, like a donkey on a treadmill. I am praying; but I have no faith that I am heard.

'I am Catalina, Princess of Spain and of Wales,' I remind myself. 'I am Catalina, beloved of God, especially favoured by God. Nothing can

go wrong for me. Nothing as bad as this could ever go wrong for me. It is God's will that I should marry Arthur and unite the kingdoms of Spain and England. God will not let anything happen to Arthur nor to me. I know that He favours my mother and me above all others. This fear must be sent to try me. But I will not be afraid because I know that nothing will ever go wrong for me.'

Catalina waited in her rooms, sending her women every hour to ask how her husband did. The first few hours they said he was still sleeping, the doctor had made his draught and was standing by his bed, waiting for him to wake. Then, at three in the afternoon, they said that he had wakened but was very hot and feverish. He had taken the draught and they were waiting to see his fever cool. At four he was worse, not better, and the doctor was making up a different prescription.

He would take no dinner, he would just drink some cool ale and the doctor's cures for fever.

'Go and ask him if he will see me?' Catalina ordered one of her English women. 'Make sure you speak to Lady Margaret. She promised me that I should dine with him. Remind her.'

The woman went and came back with a grave face. 'Princess, they are all very anxious,' she said. 'They have sent for a physician from London. Dr Bereworth, who has been watching over him, does not know why the fever does not cool down. Lady Margaret is there and Sir Richard Pole, Sir William Thomas, Sir Henry Vernon, Sir Richard Croft, they are all waiting outside his chamber and you cannot be admitted to see him. They say he is wandering in his mind.'

'I must go to the chapel. I must pray,' Catalina said instantly.

She threw a veil over her head and went back to the round chapel. To her dismay, Prince Arthur's confessor was at the altar, his head bowed low in supplication, some of the greatest men of the town and castle were seated around the wall, their heads bowed. Catalina slipped into the room, and fell to her knees. She rested her chin on her hands and scrutinised the hunched shoulders of the priest for any sign that his prayers were being heard. There was no way of telling. She closed her eyes.

Dearest God, spare Arthur, spare my darling husband, Arthur. He is only a boy, I am only a girl, we have had no time together, no time at all. You know what a kingdom we will make if he is spared. You know what plans we have for this country, what a holy castle we will make from this land, how we shall hammer the Moors, how we shall defend this kingdom from the Scots. Dear God, in your mercy spare Arthur and let him come back to me. We want to have our children: Mary, who is to be the rose of the rose, and our son Arthur who will be the third Holy Roman Catholic Tudor king for England. Let us do as we have promised. Oh dear Lord, be merciful and spare him. Dear Lady, intercede for us, and spare him. Sweet Jesus, spare him. It is I, Catalina, who asks this, and I ask in the name of my mother, Queen Isabella, who has worked all her life in your service, who is the most Christian queen, who has served on your crusades. She is beloved of You, I am beloved of You. Do not, I beg You, disappoint me.

It grew dark as Catalina prayed but she did not notice. It was late when Dona Elvira touched her gently on the shoulder and said, 'Infanta, you should have some dinner and go to bed.'

Catalina turned a white face to her duenna. 'What word?' she asked.

'They say he is worse.'

Sweet Jesus, spare him, sweet Jesus, spare me, sweet Jesus, spare England.
Say that Arthur is no worse.

In the morning they said that he had passed a good night, but the gossip among the servers of the body was that he was sinking. The fever had reached such a height that he was wandering in his mind, sometimes he thought he was in his nursery with his sisters and his brother, sometimes he thought he was at his wedding, dressed in brilliant white satin, and sometimes, most oddly, he thought he was in a fantastic palace. He spoke of a courtyard of myrtles, a rectangle of water like a mirror reflecting a building of gold, and a circular sweep of flocks of swifts who went round and round all the sunny day long.

'I shall see him,' Catalina announced to Lady Margaret at noon.

'Princess, it may be the Sweat,' her ladyship said bluntly. 'I cannot allow you to go close to him. I cannot allow you to take any infection. I should be failing in my duty if I let you go too close to him.'

'Your duty is to me!' Catalina snapped.

The woman, a princess herself, never wavered. 'My duty is to England,' she said. 'And if you are carrying a Tudor heir then my duty is to that child, as well as to you. Do not quarrel with me please, Princess. I cannot allow you to go closer than the foot of his bed.'

'Let me go there, then,' Catalina said, like a little girl. 'Please just let me see him.'

Lady Margaret bowed her head and led the way to the royal chambers. The crowds in the presence chamber had swollen in numbers as the word had gone around the town that their prince was fighting for his life; but they were silent, silent as a crowd in mourning. They were waiting and praying for the rose of England. A few men saw Catalina, her face veiled in her lace mantilla, and called out a blessing on her, then one man stepped forwards and dropped to his knee. 'God bless you, Princess of Wales,' he said. 'And may the prince rise from his bed and be merry with you again.'

'Amen,' Catalina said through cold lips, and went on.

The double doors to the inner chamber were thrown open and Catalina went in. A makeshift apothecary's room had been set up in the prince's privy chamber, a trestle table with large glass jars of ingredients, a pestle and mortar, a chopping board, and half a dozen men in the gaberdine gowns of physicians were gathered together. Catalina paused, looking for Dr Bereworth.

'Doctor?'

He came towards her at once, and dropped to his knee. His face was grave. 'Princess.'

'What news of my husband?' she said, speaking slowly and clearly for him in French.

'I am sorry, he is no better.'

'But he is not worse,' she suggested. 'He is getting better.'

He shook his head. '*Il est très malade*,' he said simply.

Catalina heard the words but it was as if she had forgotten the language. She could not translate them. She turned to Lady Margaret. 'He says that he is better?' she asked.

Lady Margaret shook her head. 'He says that he is worse,' she said honestly.

'But they will have something to give him?' She turned to the doctor. '*Vous avez un médicament?*'

He gestured at the table behind him, at the apothecary.

'Oh, if only we had a Moorish doctor!' Catalina cried out. 'They have the greatest skill, there is no-one like them. They had the best universities for medicines before . . . If only I had brought a doctor with me! Arab medicine is the finest in the world!'

'We are doing everything we can,' the doctor said stiffly.

Catalina tried to smile. 'I am sure,' she said. 'I just so wish . . . Well! Can I see him?'

A quick glance between Lady Margaret and the doctor showed that this had been a matter of some anxious discussion.

'I will see if he is awake,' he said, and went through the door.

Catalina waited. She could not believe that only yesterday morning Arthur had slipped from her bed complaining that she had not woken him early enough to make love. Now, he was so ill that she could not even touch his hand.

The doctor opened the door. 'You can come to the threshold, Princess,' he said. 'But for the sake of your own health, and for the health of any child you could be carrying, you should come no closer.'

Catalina stepped up quickly to the door. Lady Margaret pressed a pomander stuffed with cloves and herbs in her hand. Catalina held it to her nose. The acrid smell made her eyes water as she peered into the darkened room.

Arthur was sprawled on the bed, his nightgown pulled down for modesty, his face flushed with fever. His blond hair was dark with sweat, his face gaunt. He looked much older than his fifteen years. His eyes were sunk deep into his face, the skin beneath his eyes stained brown.

'Your wife is here,' the doctor said quietly to him.

Arthur's eyes fluttered open and she saw them narrow as he tried to focus on the bright doorway and Catalina, standing before him, her face white with shock.

'My love,' he said. '*Amo te.*'

'*Amo te,*' she whispered. 'They say I cannot come closer.'

'Don't come closer,' he said, his voice a thread. 'I love you.'

'I love you too!' She could hear that her voice was strained with tears. 'You will be well?'

He shook his head, too weary to speak.

'Arthur?' she said, demandingly. 'You will get better?'

He rested his head back on his hot pillow, gathering his strength. 'I will try, beloved. I will try so hard. For you. For us.'

'Is there anything you want?' she asked. 'Anything I can get for you?' She glanced around. There was nothing that she could do for him. There was nothing that would help. If she had brought a Moorish doctor with her, if her parents had not destroyed the learning of the Arab universities, if the church had allowed the study of medicine, and not called knowledge heresy . . .

'All I want is to live with you,' he said, his voice a thin thread.

She gave a little sob. 'And I you.'

'The prince should rest now, and you should not linger here.' The doctor stepped forwards.

'Please, let me stay!' she cried in a whisper. 'Please allow me. I beg you. Please let me be with him.'

Lady Margaret put a hand around her waist and drew her back. 'You shall come again, if you leave now,' she promised. 'The prince needs to rest.'

'I shall come back,' Catalina called to him, and saw the little gesture of his hand which told her that he had heard her. 'I shall not fail you.'

Catalina went to the chapel to pray for him, but she could not pray. All she could do was think of him, his white face on the white pillows. All she could do was feel the throb of desire for him. They had been married only one hundred and forty days, they had been passionate lovers for only ninety-four nights. They had promised that they would have a lifetime together, she could not believe that she was on her knees now, praying for his life.

This cannot be happening, he was well only yesterday. This is some terrible dream and in a moment I will wake up and he will kiss me and call me foolish. Nobody can take sick so quickly, nobody can go from strength and beauty to being so desperately ill in such a short time. In a moment I will wake up. This cannot be happening. I cannot pray, but it does not matter that I cannot pray because it is not really happening. A dream prayer would mean nothing. A dream illness means nothing. I am not a superstitious heathen to fear dreams. I shall wake up in a moment and we will laugh at my fears.

At dinner time she rose up, dipped her finger in the holy water, crossed herself, and with the water still wet on her forehead went back to his chambers, with Dona Elvira following, close behind.

The crowds in the halls outside the rooms and in the presence chamber were thicker than ever, women as well as men, silent with inarticulate grief. They made way for the princess without a word but a quiet murmur of blessings. Catalina went through them, looking neither to left nor right, through the presence chamber, past the apothecary bench, to the very door of his bedchamber.

The guard stepped to one side. Catalina tapped lightly on the door and pushed it open.

They were bending over him on the bed. Catalina heard him cough, a thick cough as though his throat was bubbling with water.

'*Madre de Dios*,' she said softly. 'Holy Mother of God, keep Arthur safe.'

The doctor turned at her whisper. His face was pale. 'Keep back!' he said urgently. 'It is the Sweat.'

At that most feared word Dona Elvira stepped back and laid hold of Catalina's gown as if she would drag her from danger.

'Loose me!' Catalina snapped and tugged her gown from the duenna's hands. 'I will come no closer, but I have to speak with him,' she said steadily.

The doctor heard the resolution in her voice. 'Princess, he is too weak.'

'Leave us,' she said.

'Princess.'

'I have to speak to him. This is the business of the kingdom.'

One glance at her determined face told him that she would not be denied. He went past her with his head low, his assistants following behind him. Catalina made a little gesture with her hand and Dona Elvira retreated. Catalina stepped over the threshold and pushed the door shut on them.

She saw Arthur stir in protest.

'I won't come any closer,' she assured him. 'I swear it. But I have to be with you. I cannot bear . . .' She broke off.

His face when he turned it to her was shiny with sweat, his hair as wet as when he came in from hunting in the rain. His young round face was strained as the disease leached the life out of him.

'*Amo te*,' he said through lips that were cracked and dark with fever.

'*Amo te*,' she replied.

'I am dying,' he said bleakly.

Catalina did not interrupt nor deny him. He saw her straighten a little, as if she had staggered beneath a mortal blow.

He took a rasping breath. 'But you must still be Queen of England.'

'What?'

He took a shaky breath. 'Love – obey me. You have sworn to obey me.'

'I will do anything.'

192

'Marry Harry. Be queen. Have our children.'

'What?' She was dizzy with shock. She could hardly make out what he was saying.

'England needs a great queen,' he said. 'Especially with him. He's not fit to rule. You must teach him. Build my forts. Build my navy. Defend against the Scots. Have my daughter Mary. Have my son Arthur. Let me live through you.'

'My love –'

'Let me do it,' he whispered longingly. 'Let me keep England safe through you. Let me live through you.'

'I am your wife,' she said fiercely. 'Not his.'

He nodded. 'Tell them you are not.'

She staggered at that, and felt for the door to support her.

'Tell them I could not do it.' A hint of a smile came to his drained face. 'Tell them I was unmanned. Then marry Harry.'

'You hate Harry!' she burst out. 'You cannot want me to marry him. He is a child! And I love you.'

'He will be king,' he said desperately. 'So you will be queen. Marry him. Please. Beloved. For me.'

The door behind her opened a crack and Lady Margaret said quietly, 'You must not exhaust him, Princess.'

'I have to go,' Catalina said desperately to the still figure in the bed.

'Promise me . . .'

'I will come back. You will get better.'

'Please.'

Lady Margaret opened the door wider and took Catalina's hand. 'For his own good,' she said quietly. 'You have to leave him.'

Catalina turned away from the room, she looked back over her shoulder. Arthur lifted a hand a few inches from the rich coverlet. 'Promise,' he said. 'Please. For my sake. Promise. Promise me now, beloved.'

'I promise,' burst out of her.

His hand fell, she heard him give a little sigh of relief.

They were the last words they said to each other.

Ludlow Castle, 2nd April 1502

At six o'clock, Vespers, Arthur's confessor, Dr Eldenham, adminis-
tered extreme unction and Arthur died soon after. Catalina knelt on
the threshold as the priest anointed her husband with the oil and
bowed her head for the blessing. She did not rise from her knees
until they told her that her boy-husband was dead and she was a
widow of sixteen years old.

Lady Margaret on one side and Dona Elvira on the other half-
carried and half-dragged Catalina to her bedchamber. Catalina
slipped between the cold sheets of her bed and knew that however
long she waited there, she would not hear Arthur's quiet footstep
on the battlements outside her room, and his tap on the door. She
would never again open her door and step into his arms. She would
never again be snatched up and carried to her bed, having wanted
all day to be in his arms.

'I cannot believe it,' she said brokenly.

'Drink this,' Lady Margaret said. 'The physician left it for you. It
is a sleeping draught. I will wake you at noon.'

'I cannot believe it.'

'Princess, drink.'

Catalina drank it down, ignoring the bitter taste. More than
anything else she wanted to be asleep and never wake again.

*That night I dreamed I was on the top of the great gateway of the red
fort that guards and encircles the Alhambra palace. Above my head*

194

the standards of Castile and Aragon were flapping like the sails on Cristóbal Colón's ships. Shading my eyes from the autumn sun, looking out over the great plain of Granada, I saw the simple, familiar beauty of the land, the tawny soil intersected by a thousand little ditches carrying water from one field to another. Below me was the white-walled town of Granada, even now, ten years on from our conquest, still, unmistakably a Moorish town: the houses all arranged around shady courtyards, a fountain splashing seductively in the centre, the gardens rich with the perfume of late flowering roses, and the boughs of the trees heavy with fruit.

Someone was calling for me: 'Where is the Infanta?'

And in my dream I answered: 'I am Katherine, Queen of England. That is my name now.'

They buried Arthur, Prince of Wales, on St George's Day, this first prince of all England, after a nightmare journey from Ludlow to Worcester when the rain lashed down so hard that they could barely make way. The lanes were awash, the water meadows knee-high in flood water and the Teme had burst its banks and they could not get through the fords. They had to use bullock carts for the funeral procession, horses could not have made their way through the mire on the lanes, and all the plumage and black cloth was sodden by the time they finally straggled into Worcester.

Hundreds turned out to see the miserable cortege go through the streets to the cathedral. Hundreds wept for the loss of the rose of England. After they lowered his coffin into the vault beneath the choir, the servants of his household broke their staves of office and threw them into the grave with their lost master. It was over for them. Everything they had hoped for, in the service of such a young and promising prince was finished. It was over for Arthur. It felt as if everything was over and could never be set right again.

No, no, no.

For the first month of mourning Catalina stayed in her rooms. Lady Margaret and Dona Elvira gave out that she was ill, but not in danger. In truth they feared for her reason. She did not rave or cry, she did not rail against fate or weep for her mother's comfort, she lay in utter silence, her face turned towards the wall. Her family tendency to despair tempted her like a sin. She knew she must not give way to weeping and madness, for if she once let go she would never be able to stop. For the long month of seclusion Catalina gritted her teeth and it took all her willpower and all her strength to stop herself from screaming out in grief.

When they woke her in the morning she said she was tired. They did not know that she hardly dared to move for fear that she would moan aloud. After they had dressed her, she would sit on her chair like a stone. As soon as they allowed it, she would go back to bed, lie on her back, and look up at the brightly coloured tester that she had seen with eyes half-closed by love, and know that Arthur would never pull her into the crook of his arm again.

They summoned the physician, Dr Bereworth, but when she saw him her mouth trembled and her eyes filled with tears. She turned her head away from him and she went swiftly into her bedchamber and closed the door on them all. She could not bear to see him, the doctor who had let Arthur die, the friends who had watched it happen. She could not bear to speak to him. She felt a murderous rage at the sight of the doctor who had failed to save the boy. She wished him dead, and not Arthur.

'I am afraid her mind is affected,' Lady Margaret said to the doctor as they heard the latch click on the privy chamber door. 'She does not speak, she does not even weep for him.'

'Will she eat?'

'If food is put before her and if she is reminded to eat.'

'Get someone, someone familiar – her confessor perhaps – to read to her. Encouraging words.'

'She will see no-one.'

'Might she be with child?' he whispered. It was the only question that now mattered.

'I don't know,' she replied. 'She has said nothing.'

'She is mourning him,' he said. 'She is mourning like a young woman, for the young husband she has lost. We should let her be. Let her grieve. She will have to rise up soon enough. Is she to go back to court?'

'The king commands it,' Lady Margaret said. 'The queen is sending her own litter.'

'Well, when it comes she will have to change her ways then,' he said comfortably. 'She is only young. She will recover. The young have strong hearts. And it will help her to leave here, where she has such sad memories. If you need any advice please call me. But I will not force myself into her presence, poor child.'

No, no, no.

But Catalina did not look like a poor child, Lady Margaret thought. She looked like a statue, like a stone princess carved from grief. Dona Elvira had dressed her in her new dark clothes of mourning, and persuaded her to sit in the window where she could see the green trees and the hedges creamy with may blossom, the sun on the fields, and hear the singing of the birds. The summer had come as Arthur had promised her that it would, it was warm as he had sworn it would be; but she was not walking by the river with him, greeting the swifts as they flew in from Spain. She was not planting salad vegetables in the gardens of the castle and persuading him to try them. The summer was here, the sun was here, Catalina was here, but Arthur was cold in the dark vault of Worcester Cathedral.

Catalina sat still, her hands folded on the black silk of her gown, her eyes looking out of the window, but seeing nothing, her mouth folded tight over her gritted teeth as if she were biting back a storm of words.

'Princess,' Lady Margaret started tentatively.

Slowly, the head under the heavy black hood turned towards her. 'Yes, Lady Margaret?' Her voice was hoarse.

'I would speak with you.'

Catalina inclined her head.

Dona Elvira stepped back and went quietly out of the room.

'I have to ask you about your journey to London. The royal litter has arrived and you will have to leave here.'

There was no flicker of animation in Catalina's deep blue eyes. She nodded again, as if they were discussing the transport of a parcel.

'I don't know if you are strong enough to travel.'

'Can I not stay here?' Catalina asked.

'I understand the king has sent for you. I am sorry for it. They write that you may stay here until you are well enough to travel.'

'Why, what is to become of me?' Catalina asked, as if it was a matter of absolute indifference. 'When I get to London?'

'I don't know.' The former princess did not pretend for one moment that a girl of a royal family could choose her future. 'I am sorry. I do not know what is planned. My husband has been told nothing except to prepare for your journey to London.'

'What do you think might happen? When my sister's husband

died, they sent her back to us from Portugal. She came home to Spain again.'

'I would expect that they will send you home,' Lady Margaret said.

Catalina turned her head away once more. She looked out of the window but her eyes saw nothing. Lady Margaret waited, she wondered if the princess would say anything more.

'Does a Princess of Wales have a house in London as well as here?' she asked. 'Shall I go back to Baynard's Castle?'

'You are not the Princess of Wales,' Lady Margaret started. She was going to explain but the look that Catalina turned on her was so darkly angry that she hesitated. 'I beg your pardon,' she said. 'I thought perhaps you did not understand . . .'

'Understand what?' Catalina's white face was slowly flushing pink with temper.

'Princess?'

'Princess of what?' Catalina snapped.

Lady Margaret dropped into a curtsey, and stayed low.

'Princess of what?' Catalina shouted loudly, and the door opened behind them and Dona Elvira came quickly into the room and then checked as she saw Catalina on her feet, her cheeks burning with temper, and Lady Margaret on her knees. She went out again without a word.

'Princess of Spain,' Lady Margaret said very quietly.

There was intense silence.

'I am the Princess of Wales,' Catalina said slowly. 'I have been the Princess of Wales all my life.'

Lady Margaret rose up and faced her. 'Now you are the Dowager Princess.'

Catalina clapped a hand over her mouth to hold back a cry of pain.

'I am sorry, Princess.'

Catalina shook her head, beyond words, her fist at her mouth muffling her whimpers of pain. Lady Margaret's face was grim. 'They will call you Dowager Princess.'

'I will never answer to it.'

'It is a title of respect. It is only the English word for widow.'

Catalina gritted her teeth and turned away from her friend to look out of the window. 'You can get up,' she said through her teeth. 'There is no need for you to kneel to me.'

The older woman rose to her feet and hesitated. 'The queen writes to me. They want to know of your health. Not only if you feel well, and strong enough to travel; they really need to know if you might be with child.'

Catalina clenched her hands together, turned away her face so that Lady Margaret should not see her cold rage.

'If you are with child and that child is a boy then he will be the Prince of Wales, and then King of England, and you would be My Lady the King's Mother,' Lady Margaret reminded her quietly.

'And if I am not with child?'

'Then you are the Dowager Princess, and Prince Harry is Prince of Wales.'

'And when the king dies?'

'Then Prince Harry becomes king.'

'And I?'

Lady Margaret shrugged in silence. 'Next to nothing', said the gesture. Aloud she said, 'You are the Infanta still.' Lady Margaret tried to smile. 'As you will always be.'

'And the next Queen of England?'

'Will be the wife of Prince Harry.'

The anger went out of Catalina, she walked to the fireplace, took hold of the high mantelpiece and steadied herself with it. The little fire burning in the grate threw out no heat that she could feel through the thick black skirt of her mourning gown. She stared at the flames as if she would understand what had happened to her.

'I am become again what I was, when I was a child of three,' she said slowly. 'The Infanta of Spain, not the Princess of Wales. A baby. Of no importance.'

Lady Margaret, whose own royal blood had been carefully diluted by a lowly marriage so that she could pose no threat to the Tudor throne of England, nodded. 'Princess, you take the position of your husband. It is always thus for all women. If you have no husband and no son, then you have no position. You have only what you were born to.'

'If I go home to Spain as a widow, and they marry me to an arch-duke, I will be Archduchess Catalina, and not a princess at all. Not Princess of Wales, and never Queen of England.'

Lady Margaret nodded. 'Like me,' she said.

Catalina turned her head. 'You?'

'I was a Plantagenet princess, King Edward's niece, sister to Edward of Warwick, the heir to King Richard's throne. If King Henry had lost the battle at Bosworth Field it would have been King Richard on the throne now, my brother as his heir and Prince of Wales, and I should be Princess Margaret, as I was born to be.'

'Instead you are Lady Margaret, wife to the warden of a little castle, not even his own, on the edge of England.'

The older woman nodded her assent to the bleak description of her status.

'Why did you not refuse?' Catalina asked rudely.

Lady Margaret glanced behind her to see that the door to the presence chamber was shut and none of Catalina's women could hear.

'How could I refuse?' she asked simply. 'My brother was in the Tower of London, simply for being born a prince. If I had refused to marry Sir Richard, I should have joined him. My brother put his dear head down on the block for nothing more than bearing his name. As a girl, I had the chance to change my name. So I did.'

'You had the chance to be Queen of England!' Catalina protested.

Lady Margaret turned away from the younger woman's energy.

'It is as God wills,' she said simply. 'My chance, such as it was, has gone. Your chance has gone too. You will have to find a way to live the rest of your life without regrets, Infanta.'

Catalina said nothing, but the face that she showed to her friend was closed and cold. 'I will find a way to fulfil my destiny,' she said. 'Ar –' She broke off, she could not name him, even to her friend. 'I once had a conversation about claiming one's own,' she said. 'I understand it now. I shall have to be a pretender to myself. I shall insist on what is mine. I know what is my duty and what I have to do. I shall do as God wills, whatever the difficulties for me.'

The older woman nodded. 'Perhaps God wills that you accept your fate. Perhaps it is God's will that you be resigned,' she suggested.

'He does not,' Catalina said firmly.

I will tell no-one what I promised. I will tell no-one that in my heart I am still Princess of Wales, I will always be Princess of Wales until I see the wedding of my son and see my daughter-in-law crowned. I will tell no-one that I understand now what Arthur told me: that even a princess born may have to claim her title.

I have told no-one whether or not I am with child. But I know, well enough. I had my course in April, there is no baby. There is no Princess Mary, there is no Prince Arthur. My love, my only love, is dead and there is nothing left of him for me, not even his unborn child.

I will say nothing, though people constantly pry and want to know. I have to consider what I am to do, and how I am to claim the throne that Arthur wanted for me. I have to think how to keep my promise to him, how to tell the lie that he wanted me to tell. How I can make it convincing, how I can fool the king himself, and his sharp-witted, hard-eyed mother.

But I have made a promise, I do not retract my word. He begged me for a promise and he dictated the lie I must tell, and I said 'yes'. I will not fail him. It is the last thing he asked of me, and I will do it. I will do it for him, and I will do it for our love.

Oh my love, if you knew how much I long to see you.

Catalina travelled to London with the black-trimmed curtains of the litter closed against the beauty of the countryside, as it came into full bloom. She did not see the people doff their caps or curtsey as the procession wound through the little English villages. She did not hear the men and women call 'God bless you, Princess!' as the litter jolted slowly down the village streets. She did not know that every young woman in the land crossed herself and prayed that she should not have the bad luck of the pretty Spanish princess who had come so far for love and then lost her man after only five months.

She was dully aware of the lush green of the countryside, of the fertile swelling of the crops in the fields and the fat cattle in the water-meadows. When their way wound through the thick forests, she noticed the coolness of the green shade, and the thick interleaving of the canopy of boughs over the road. Herds of deer vanished into the dappled shade and she could hear the calling of a cuckoo and the rattle of a woodpecker. It was a beautiful land, a wealthy land, a great inheritance for a young couple. She thought of Arthur's desire to protect this land of his against the Scots, against the Moors. Of his will to reign here better and more justly than it had ever been done before.

She did not speak to her hosts on the road who attributed her silence to grief, and pitied her for it. She did not speak to her ladies, not even to Maria who was at her side in silent sympathy, nor to Dona Elvira who, at this crisis in Spanish affairs, was everywhere; her husband organising the houses on the road, she herself ordering the princess's food, her bedding, her companions, her diet. Catalina said nothing and let them do as they wished with her.

Some of her hosts thought her sunk so deep in grief that she was beyond speech, and prayed that she should recover her wits again, and go back to Spain and make a new marriage that would bring her a new husband to replace the old. What they did not know was that Catalina was holding her grief for her husband in some hidden place deep inside her. Deliberately, she delayed her mourning until she had the safety to indulge in it. While she jolted along in the litter she was not weeping for him, she was racking her brains how to fulfil his dream. She was wondering how to obey him, as he had demanded. She was thinking how she should fulfil her deathbed promise to the only young man she had ever loved.

I shall have to be clever. I shall have to be more cunning than King Henry Tudor, more determined than his mother. Faced with those two, I don't know that I can get away with it. But I have to get away with it. I have given my promise, I will tell my lie. England shall be ruled as Arthur wanted. The rose will live again, I shall make the England that he wanted.

I wish I could have brought Lady Margaret with me to advise me, I miss her friendship, I miss her hard-won wisdom. I wish I could see her steady gaze and hear her counsel to be resigned, to bow to my destiny, to give myself to God's will. I would not follow her advice – but I wish I could hear it.

Summer 1502

Croydon, May 1502

The princess and her party arrived at Croydon Palace and Dona Elvira led Catalina to her private rooms. For once, the girl did not go to her bedchamber and close the door behind her, she stood in the sumptuous presence chamber, looking around her. 'A chamber fit for a princess,' she said.

'But it is not your own,' Dona Elvira said, anxious for her charge's status. 'It has not been given to you. It is just for your use.'

The young woman nodded. 'It is fitting,' she said.

'The Spanish ambassador is in attendance,' Dona Elvira told her. 'Shall I tell him that you will not see him?'

'I will see him,' Catalina said quietly. 'Tell him to come in.'

'You don't have to . . .'

'He may have word from my mother,' she said. 'I should like her advice.'

The duenna bowed and went to find the ambassador. He was deep in conversation in the gallery outside the presence chamber with Father Alessandro Geraldini, the princess's chaplain. Dona

Elvira regarded them both with dislike. The chaplain was a tall, handsome man, his dark good looks in stark contrast to those of his companion. The ambassador, Dr de Puebla, was tiny beside him, leaning against a chair to support his misshaped spine, his damaged leg tucked behind the other, his bright little face alight with excitement.

'She could be with child?' the ambassador confirmed in a whisper. 'You are certain?'

'Pray God it is so. She is certainly in hopes of it,' the confessor confirmed.

'Dr de Puebla!' the duenna snapped, disliking the confidential air between the two men. 'I shall take you to the princess now.'

De Puebla turned and smiled at the irritable woman. 'Certainly, Dona Elvira,' he said equably. 'At once.'

Dr de Puebla limped into the room, his richly trimmed black hat already in his hand, his small face wreathed in an unconvincing smile. He bowed low with a flourish, and came up to inspect the princess.

At once he was struck by how much she had changed in such a short time. She had come to England a girl, with a girl's optimism. He had thought her a spoilt child, one who had been protected from the harshness of the real world. In the fairy-tale palace of the Alhambra this had been the petted youngest daughter of the most powerful monarchs in Christendom. Her journey to England had been the first real discomfort she had been forced to endure, and she had complained about it bitterly, as if he could help the weather. On her wedding day, standing beside Arthur and hearing the cheers for him, had been the first time she had taken second place to anyone but her heroic parents.

But before him now was a girl who had been hammered by unhappiness into a fine maturity. This Catalina was thinner, and paler, but with a new spiritual beauty, honed by hardship. He drew his breath. This Catalina was a young woman with a queenly presence. She had become through grief not only Arthur's widow, but her mother's daughter. This was a princess from the line that had defeated the most powerful enemy of Christendom. This was the very bone of the bone and blood of the blood of Isabella of Castile. She was cool, she was hard. He hoped very much that she was not going to be difficult.

De Puebla gave her a smile that he meant to be reassuring and saw her scrutinise him with no answering warmth in her face. She gave him her hand and then she sat in a straight-backed wooden chair before the fire. 'You may sit,' she said graciously, gesturing him to a lower chair, further away.

He bowed again, and sat.

'Do you have any messages for me?'

'Of sympathy, from the king and Queen Elizabeth and from My Lady the King's Mother, and from myself of course. They will invite you to court when you have recovered from your journey and are out of mourning.'

'How long am I to be in mourning?' Catalina inquired.

'My Lady the King's Mother has said that you should be in seclusion for a month after the burial. But since you were not at court during that time, she has ruled that you will stay here until she commands you to return to London. She is concerned for your health . . .'

He paused, hoping that she would volunteer whether or not she was with child, but she let the silence stretch.

He thought he would ask her directly. 'Infanta . . .'

'You should call me princess,' she interrupted. 'I am the Princess of Wales.'

He hesitated, thrown off course. 'Dowager Princess,' he corrected her quietly.

Catalina nodded. 'Of course. It is understood. Do you have any letters from Spain?'

He bowed and gave her the letter he was carrying in the hidden pocket in his sleeve. She did not snatch it from him like a child and open it, then and there. She nodded her head in thanks and held it.

'Do you not want to open it now? Do you not want to reply?'

'When I have written my reply, I will send for you,' she said simply, asserting her power over him. 'I shall send for you when I want you.'

'Certainly, Your Grace.' He smoothed the velvet nap of his black breeches to hide his irritation but inwardly he thought it an impertinence that the Infanta, now a widow, should command where before the Princess of Wales had politely requested. He thought he perhaps did not like this new, finer Catalina, after all.

'And have you heard from Their Majesties in Spain?' she asked. 'Have they advised you as to their wishes?'

'Yes,' he said, wondering how much he should tell her. 'Of course, Queen Isabella is anxious that you are not unwell. She asked me to inquire after your health and to report to her.'

A secretive shadow crossed Catalina's face. 'I shall write to the queen my mother and tell her my news,' she said.

'She was anxious to know . . .' he began, probing for the answer to the greatest question: was there an heir? Was the princess with child?

'I shall confide in no-one but my mother.'

'We cannot proceed to the settlement of your jointure and your arrangements until we know,' he said bluntly. 'It makes a difference to everything.'

She did not flare up as he had thought she would do. She inclined her head, she had herself under tight control. 'I shall write to my mother,' she repeated, as if his advice did not much matter.

He saw he would get nothing more from her. But at least the chaplain had told him she could be with child, and he should know. The king would be glad to know that there was at least a possibility of an heir. At any rate she had not denied it. There might be capital to make from her silence. 'Then I will leave you to read your letter.' He bowed.

She made a casual gesture of dismissal and turned to look at the flames of the little summertime fire. He bowed again and, since she was not looking at him, scrutinised her figure. She had no bloom of early pregnancy but some women took it badly in the first months. Her pallor could be caused by morning sickness. It was impossible for a man to tell. He would have to rely on the confessor's opinion, and pass it on with a caution.

I open my mother's letter with hands that are trembling so much that I can hardly break the seals. The first thing I see is the shortness of the letter, only one page.

'Oh, Madre,' I breathe. 'No more?'

Perhaps she was in haste; but I am bitterly hurt to see that she has written so briefly! If she knew how much I want to hear her voice she would have written at twice the length. As God is my witness I don't think I can do this without her; I am only sixteen and a half, I need my mother.

I read the short letter through once, and then, almost incredulously, I read it through again.

It is not a letter from a loving mother to her daughter. It is not a letter from a woman to her favourite child, and that child on the very edge of despair. Coldly, powerfully, she has written a letter from a queen to a princess. She writes of nothing but business. We could be a pair of merchants concluding a sale.

She says that I am to stay in whatever house is provided for me until I have had my next course and I know that I am not with child. If that is the case I am to command Dr de Puebla to demand my join-ture as Dowager Princess of Wales and as soon as I have the full money and <u>not before</u> (underlined so there can be no mistake), I am to take ship for Spain.

If, on the other hand, God is gracious, and I am with child, then I am to assure Dr de Puebla that the money for my dowry will be paid in cash and at once, he is to secure me my allowance as Dowager Princess of Wales, and I am to rest and hope for a boy.

I am to write to her at once and tell her if I think I am with child. I am to write to her as soon as I am certain, one way or the other, and I am to confide also in Dr de Puebla and to maintain myself under the chaperonage of Dona Elvira.

I fold the letter carefully, matching the edges one to another as if tidiness matters very much. I think that if she knew of the despair that laps at the edges of my mind like a river of darkness she would have written to me more kindly. If she knew how very alone I am, how grieved I am, how much I miss him, she would not write to me of settlements and jointures and titles. If she knew how much I loved him and how I cannot bear to live without him she would write and tell me that she loves me, that I am to go home to her at once, without delay.

I tuck the letter into the pocket at my waist, and I stand up, as if reporting for duty. I am not a child any more. I will not cry for my mother. I see that I am not in the especial care of God since he could let Arthur die. I see that I am not in the especial love of my mother, since she can leave me alone, in a strange land.

She is not only a mother, she is Queen of Spain, and she has to ensure that she has a grandson, or failing a grandson, a watertight treaty. I am not just a young woman who has lost the man she loves. I am a Princess of Spain and I have to produce a grandson, or failing that a watertight treaty. And in addition, I am now bound by a promise. I have promised that I will be Princess of Wales again, and Queen of England. I have promised this to the young man to whom I promised everything. I will perform it for him, whatever anyone else wants.

The Spanish ambassador did not report at once to Their Majesties of Spain. Instead, playing his usual double game, he took the chaplain's opinion first to the King of England.

'Her confessor says that she is with child,' he remarked.

For the first time in days King Henry felt his heart lighten. 'Good God, if that were so, it would change everything.'

'Please God it is so. I should be glad of it,' de Puebla agreed. 'But I cannot guarantee it. She shows no sign of it.'

'Could be early days,' Henry agreed. 'And God knows, and I know, a child in the cradle is not a prince on the throne. It's a long road to the crown. But it would be a great comfort to me if she was with child – and to the queen,' he added as an afterthought.

'So she must stay here in England until we know for sure,' the ambassador concluded. 'And if she is not with child we shall settle our accounts, you and I, and she shall go home. Her mother asks for her to be sent home at once.'

'We'll wait and see,' Henry said, conceding nothing. 'Her mother will have to wait like the rest of us. And if she is anxious to have her daughter home she had better pay the rest of the dowry.'

'You would not delay the return of the princess to her mother over a matter of money,' the ambassador suggested.

'The sooner everything is settled the better,' the king said smoothly. 'If she is with child then she is our daughter and the mother of our heir; nothing would be too good for her. If she is not, then she can go home to her mother as soon as her dowry is paid.'

I know that there is no Mary growing in my womb, there is no Arthur; but I shall say nothing until I know what to do. I dare say nothing until I am sure what I should do. My mother and father will be planning for the good of Spain, King Henry will be planning for the good

of England. Alone, I will have to find a way to fulfil my promise. Nobody will help me. Nobody can even know what I am doing. Only Arthur in heaven will understand what I am doing and I feel far, far away from him. It is so painful, a pain I could not imagine. I have never needed him more than now, now that he is dead, and only he can advise me how to fulfil my promise to him.

Catalina had spent less than a month of seclusion at Croydon Palace when the king's chamberlain came to tell her that Durham House in the Strand had been prepared for her and she could go there at her convenience.

'Is this where a Princess of Wales would stay?' Catalina demanded urgently of de Puebla, who had been immediately summoned to her privy chamber. 'Is Durham House where a princess would be housed? Why am I not to live in Baynard's Castle again?'

'Durham House is perfectly adequate,' he stammered, taken aback by her fervour. 'And your household is not diminished at all. The king has not asked you to dismiss anyone. You are to have an adequate court. And he will pay you an allowance.'

'My jointure as the prince's widow?'

He avoided her gaze. 'An allowance at this stage. He has not been paid your dowry from your parents, remember, so he will not pay your jointure. But he will give you a good sum, one that will allow you to keep your state.'

'I should have my jointure.'

He shook his head. 'He will not pay it until he has the full dowry. But it is a good allowance, you will keep a good state.'

He saw that she was immensely relieved. 'Princess, there is no question but that the king is respectful of your position,' he said carefully. 'You need have no fears of that. Of course, if he could be assured as to your health . . .'

Again the shuttered look closed down Catalina's face. 'I don't know what you mean,' she said shortly. 'I am well. You can tell him that I am well. Nothing more.'

I am buying time, letting them think that I am with child. It is such agony, knowing that my time of the month has come and gone, that I am ready for Arthur's seed, but he is cold and gone and he will never come to my bed again, and we will never make his daughter Mary and his son Arthur.

I cannot bear to tell them the truth: I am barren, without a baby to raise for him. And while I say nothing they have to wait too. They will not send me home to Spain while they hope that I might still be My Lady the Mother of the Prince of Wales. They have to wait.

And while they wait I can plan what I shall say, and what I shall do. I have to be wise as my mother would be, and cunning as the fox, my father. I have to be determined like her, and secretive like him. I have to think how and when I shall start to tell this lie, Prince Arthur's great lie. If I can tell it so that it convinces everyone, if I can place myself so that I fulfil my destiny, then Arthur, beloved Arthur, can do as he wished. He can rule England through me, I can marry his brother and become queen. Arthur can live through the child I conceive with his brother, we can make the England we swore that we would make, despite misfortune, despite his brother's folly, despite my own despair.

I shall not give myself to heartbreak, I shall give myself to England. I shall keep my promise. I shall be constant to my husband and to my destiny. And I shall plan and plot and consider how I shall conquer this misfortune and be what I was born to be. How I shall be the pretender who becomes the queen.

London, June 1502

The little court moved to Durham House in late June and the remainder of Catalina's court straggled in from Ludlow Castle, speaking of a town in silence and a castle in mourning. Catalina did not seem particularly pleased at the change of scene, though Durham House was a pretty palace with lovely gardens running down to the river, with its own stairs and a pier for boats. The ambassador came to visit and found her in the gallery at the front of the house, which overlooked the front courtyard below and Ivy Lane beyond.

She let him stand before her.

'Her Grace, the queen your mother, is sending an emissary to escort you home as soon as your widow's jointure is paid. Since you have not told us that you are with child she is preparing for your journey.'

De Puebla saw her press her lips together as if to curb a hasty reply. 'How much does the king have to pay me, as his son's widow?'

'He has to pay you a third of the revenues of Wales, Cornwall and Chester,' he said. 'And your parents are now asking, in addition, that King Henry return all of your dowry.'

Catalina looked aghast. 'He never will,' she said flatly. 'No emissary will be able to convince him. King Henry will never pay such sums to me. He didn't even pay my allowance when his son was alive. Why should he repay the dowry and pay a jointure when he has nothing to gain from it?'

The ambassador shrugged his shoulders. 'It is in the contract.'

'So too was my allowance, and you failed to make him pay that,' she said sharply.

'You should have handed over your plate as soon as you arrived.'

'And eat off what?' she blazed out.

Insolently, he stood before her. He knew, as she did not yet understand, that she had no power. Every day that she failed to announce

214

she was with child her importance diminished. He was certain that she was barren. He thought her a fool now; she had bought herself a little time by her discretion – but for what? Her disapproval of him mattered very little; she would soon be gone. She might rage but nothing would change.

'Why did you ever agree to such a contract? You must have known he would not honour it.'

He shrugged. The conversation was meaningless. 'How should we think there would ever be such a tragic occurrence? Who could have imagined that the prince would die, just as he entered into adult life? It is so very sad.'

'Yes, yes,' said Catalina. She had promised herself she would never cry for Arthur in front of anyone. The tears must stay back. 'But now, thanks to this contract, the king is deep in debt to me. He has to return the dowry that he has been paid, he cannot have my plate, and he owes me this jointure. Ambassador, you must know that he will never pay this much. And clearly he will never give me the rents of – where? – Wales and, and Cornwall? – forever.'

'Only until you remarry,' he observed. 'He has to pay your jointure until you remarry. And we must assume that you will remarry soon. Their Majesties will want you to return home in order to arrange a new marriage for you. I imagine that the emissary is coming to fetch you home just for that. They probably have a marriage contract drawn up for you already. Perhaps you are already betrothed.'

For one moment de Puebla saw the shock in her face then she turned abruptly from him to stare out of the window on the court-yard before the palace and the open gates to the busy streets outside.

He watched the tightly stretched shoulders and the tense turn of her neck, surprised that his shot at her second marriage had hit her so hard. Why should she be so shocked at the mention of marriage? Surely she must know that she would go home only to be married again?

Catalina let the silence grow as she watched the street beyond the Durham House gate. It was so unlike her home. There were no dark men in beautiful gowns, there were no veiled women. There were no street sellers with rich piles of spices, no flower sellers staggering under small mountains of blooms. There were no herbalists, physicians, or astronomers, plying their trade as if knowledge could be freely available to anyone. There was no silent movement to the mosque for prayer five times a day, there was no constant splash of fountains. Instead there was the bustle of one of the greatest cities in the world, the relentless, unstoppable buzz of prosperity and commerce, and the ringing of the bells of hundreds of churches. This was a city bursting with confidence, rich on its own trade, exuberantly wealthy.

'This is my home now,' she said. Resolutely she put aside the pictures in her mind of a warmer city, of a smaller community, of an easier, more exotic world. 'The king should not think that I will go home and remarry as if none of this has happened. My parents should not think that they can change my destiny. I was brought up to be Princess of Wales and Queen of England. I shall not be cast off like a bad debt.'

The ambassador, from a race who had known disappointment, so much older and wiser than the girl who stood at the window, smiled at her unseeing back. 'Of course it shall be as you wish,' he lied easily. 'I shall write to your father and mother and say that you prefer to wait here, in England, while your future is decided.'

Catalina rounded on him. 'No, I shall decide my future.'

He had to bite the inside of his cheeks to hide his smile. 'Of course you will, Infanta.'

'Dowager Princess.'

'Dowager Princess.'

She took a breath; but when it came, her voice was quite steady. 'You may tell my father and mother, and you shall tell the king, that I am not with child.'

'Indeed,' he breathed. 'Thank you for informing us. That makes everything much clearer.'

'How so?'

'The king will release you. You can go home. He would have no claim on you, no interest in you. There can be no reason for you to stay. I shall have to make arrangements but your jointure can follow you. You can leave at once.'

'No,' she said flatly.

De Puebla was surprised. 'Dowager Princess, you can be released from this failure. You can go home. You are free to go.'

'You mean the English think they have no use for me?'

He gave the smallest of shrugs, as if to ask: what was she good for, since she was neither maid nor mother?

'What else can you do here? Your time here is over.'

She was not yet ready to show him her full plan. 'I shall write to my mother,' was all she would reply. 'But you are not to make arrangements for me to leave. It may be that I shall stay in England for a little while longer. If I am to be remarried, I could be remarried in England.'

'To whom?' he demanded.

She looked away from him. 'How should I know? My parents and the king should decide.'

I have to find a way to put my marriage to Harry into the mind of the king. Now that he knows I am not with child surely it will occur to him that the resolution for all our difficulties is to marry me to Harry?

If I trusted Dr de Puebla more, I should ask him to hint to the king that I could be betrothed to Harry. But I do not trust him. He muddled my first marriage contract, I don't want him muddling this one.

If I could get a letter to my mother without de Puebla seeing it then I could tell her of my plan, of Arthur's plan.

But I cannot. I am alone in this. I do feel so fearfully alone.

'They are going to name Prince Harry as the new Prince of Wales,' Dona Elvira said quietly to the princess as she was brushing her hair in the last week of June. 'He is to be Prince Harry, Prince of Wales.'

She expected the girl to break down at this last severing of her links with the past but Catalina did nothing but look around the room. 'Leave us,' she said shortly to the maids who were laying out her nightgown and turning down the bed.

They went out quietly and closed the door behind them. Catalina tossed back her hair and met Dona Elvira's eyes in the mirror. She handed her the hairbrush again and nodded for her to continue.

'I want you to write to my parents and tell them that my marriage with Prince Arthur was not consummated,' she said, smoothly. 'I am a virgin as I was when I left Spain.'

Dona Elvira was stunned, the hairbrush suspended in mid-air, her mouth open. 'You were bedded in the sight of the whole court,' she said.

'He was impotent,' Catalina said, her face as hard as a diamond.

'You were together once a week.'

'With no effect,' she said, unwavering. 'It was a great sadness to him, and to me.'

'Infanta, you never said anything. Why did you not tell me?'

Catalina's eyes were veiled. 'What should I say? We were newly wed. He was very young. I thought it would come right in time.'

Dona Elvira did not even pretend to believe her. 'Princess, there is no need for you to say this. Just because you have been a wife need not damage your future. Being a widow is no obstacle to a good marriage. They will find someone for you. They will find a good match for you, you do not have to pretend . . .'

'I don't want "someone",' Catalina said fiercely. 'You should know that as well as me. I was born to be Princess of Wales and Queen of England. It was Arthur's greatest wish that I should be Queen of England.' She pulled herself back from thinking of him, or saying more. She bit her lip; she should not have tried to say his name. She forced down the tears and took a breath. 'I am a virgin untouched, now, as I was in Spain. You shall tell them that.'

'But we need say nothing, we can go back to Spain, anyway,' the older woman pointed out.

'They will marry me to some lord, perhaps an archduke,' Catalina said. 'I don't want to be sent away again. Do you want to run my household in some little Spanish castle? Or Austria? Or worse? You will have to come with me, remember. Do you want to end up in the Netherlands, or Germany?'

Dona Elvira's eyes darted away, she was thinking furiously. 'No-one would believe us if we say you are a virgin.'

'They would. You have to tell them. No-one would dare to ask me. You can tell them. It has to be you to tell them. They will believe you because you are close to me, as close as a mother.'

'I have said nothing so far.'

'And that was right. But you will speak now. Dona Elvira, if you don't seem to know, or if you say one thing and I say another, then everyone will know that you are not in my confidence, that you have not cared for me as you should. They will think you are negligent of my interests, that you have lost my favour. I should think that my mother would recall you in disgrace if she thought that I was a virgin and you did not even know. You would never serve in a royal court again if they thought you had neglected me.'

'Everyone saw that he was in love with you.'

'No they didn't. Everyone saw that we were together, as a prince and princess. Everyone saw that he came to my bedroom only as he had been ordered. No more. No-one can say what went on behind the bedroom door. No-one but me. And I say that he was impotent. Who are you to deny that? Do you dare to call me a liar?'

The older woman bowed her head to gain time. 'If you say so,' she said carefully. 'Whatever you say, Infanta.'

'Princess.'

'Princess,' the woman repeated.

'And I do say it. It is my way ahead. Actually, it is your way ahead too. We can say this one, simple thing and stay in England; or we can return to Spain in mourning and become next to nobody.'

'Of course, I can tell them what you wish. If you wish to say your husband was impotent and you are still a maid then I can say that. But how will this make you queen?'

'Since the marriage was not consummated, there can be no objection to me marrying Prince Arthur's brother Harry,' Catalina said in a hard, determined voice.

Dona Elvira gasped with shock at this next stage.

Catalina pressed on. 'When this new emissary comes from Spain you may inform him that it is God's will and my desire that I be Princess of Wales again, as I always have been. He shall speak to the king. He shall negotiate, not my widow's jointure, but my next wedding.'

Dona Elvira gaped. 'You cannot make your own marriage!'

'I can,' Catalina said fiercely. 'I will, and you will help me.'

'You cannot think that they will let you marry Prince Harry?'

'Why should they not? The marriage with his brother was not consummated. I am a virgin. The dowry to the king is half-paid. He can keep the half he already has and we can give him the rest of it. He need not pay my jointure. The contract has been signed and sealed, they need only change the names, and here I am in England already. It is the best solution for everyone. Without it I become nothing; you certainly are nobody. Your ambition, your husband's ambition, will all come to nothing. But if we can win this then you will be the mistress of a royal household, and I will be as I should be: Princess of Wales and Queen of England.'

'They will not let us!' Dona Elvira gasped, appalled at her charge's ambition.

'They will let us,' Catalina said fiercely. 'We have to fight for it. We have to be what we should be; nothing less.'

Princess in Waiting

Winter 1503

King Henry and his queen, driven by the loss of their son, were expecting another child, and Catalina, hoping for their favour, was sewing an exquisite layette of baby clothes before a small fire in the smallest room of Durham Palace in the early days of February 1503. Her ladies, hemming seams according to their abilities, were seated at a distance; Dona Elvira could speak privately.

'This should be your baby's layette,' the duenna said resentfully under her breath. 'A widow for a year, and no progress made. What is going to become of you?'

Catalina looked up from her delicate black-thread work. 'Peace, Dona Elvira,' she said quietly. 'It will be as God and my parents and the king decide.'

'Seventeen, now,' Dona Elvira said, stubbornly pursuing her theme, her head down. 'How long are we to stay in this Godforsaken country, neither a bride nor a wife? Neither at court nor elsewhere? With bills mounting up and the jointure still not paid?'

'Dona Elvira, if you knew how much your words grieve me, I don't think you would say them,' Catalina said clearly. 'Just because you mutter them into your sewing like a cursing Egyptian doesn't

225

mean I don't hear them. If I knew what was to happen, I would tell you myself at once. You will not learn any more by whispering your fears.'

The woman looked up and met Catalina's clear gaze.

'I think of you,' she said bluntly. 'Even if no-one else does. Even if that fool ambassador and that idiot the emissary does not. If the king does not order your marriage to the prince then what is to become of you? If he will not let you go, if your parents do not insist on your return, then what is going to happen? Is he just going to keep you forever? Are you a princess or a prisoner? It is nearly a year. Are you a hostage for the alliance with Spain? How long can you wait? You are seventeen, how long can you wait?'

'I am waiting,' Catalina said calmly. 'Patiently. Until it is resolved.'

The duenna said nothing more, Catalina did not have the energy to argue. She knew that during this year of mourning for Arthur, she had been steadily pushed more and more to the margins of court life. Her claim to be a virgin had not produced a new betrothal as she had thought it would; it had made her yet more irrelevant. She was only summoned to court on the great occasions, and then she was dependent on the kindness of Queen Elizabeth.

The king's mother, Lady Margaret, had no interest in the impoverished Spanish princess. She had not proved readily fertile, she now said she had never even been bedded, she was widowed and brought no more money into the royal treasury. She was of no use to the house of Tudor except as a bargaining counter in the continuing struggle with Spain. She might as well stay at her house in the Strand, as be summoned to court. Besides, My Lady the King's Mother did not like the way that the new Prince of Wales looked at his widowed sister-in-law.

Whenever Prince Harry met her, he fixed his eyes on her with puppy-like devotion. My Lady the King's Mother had privately decided that she would keep them apart. She thought that the girl smiled on the young prince too warmly, she thought she encouraged his boyish adoration to serve her own foreign vanity. My Lady the King's Mother was resentful of anyone's influence on the only surviving son and heir. Also, she mistrusted Catalina. Why would the young widow encourage a brother-in-law who was nearly six years her junior? What did she hope to gain from his friendship? Surely she knew that he was kept as close as a child: bedded in his father's rooms, chaperoned night and day, constantly supervised? What did the Spanish widow hope to achieve by sending him books, teaching him Spanish, laughing at his accent and watching him ride at the quintain, as if he were in training as her knight errant?

Nothing would come of it. Nothing could come of it. But My Lady the King's Mother would allow no-one to be intimate with Harry but herself, and she ruled that Catalina's visits to court were to be rare and brief.

The king himself was kind enough to Catalina when he saw her, but she felt him eye her as if she were some sort of treasure that he had purloined. She always felt with him as if she were some sort of trophy – not a young woman of seventeen years old, wholly dependent on his honour, his daughter by marriage.

If she could have brought herself to speak of Arthur to her mother-in-law or to the king then perhaps they would have sought her out to share their grief. But she could not use his name to curry favour with them. Even a year since his death, she could not think of him without a tightness in her chest which was so great that she thought it could stop her breathing for very grief. She still could not say his name out loud. She certainly could not play on her grief to help her at court.

'But what will happen?' Dona Elvira continued.

Catalina turned her head away. 'I don't know,' she said shortly.

'Perhaps if the queen has another son with this baby, the king will send us back to Spain,' the duenna pursued.

Catalina nodded. 'Perhaps.'

The duenna knew her well enough to recognise Catalina's silent determination. 'Your trouble is, that you still don't want to go,' she whispered. 'The king may keep you as a hostage against the dowry money, your parents may let you stay; but if you insisted you could get home. You still think you can make them marry you to Harry; but if that was going to happen you would be betrothed by now. You have to give up. We have been here a year now and you make no progress. You will trap us all here while you are defeated.'

Catalina's sandy eyelashes swept down to veil her eyes. 'Oh no,' she said. 'I don't think that.'

There was a sharp rap at the door. 'Urgent message for the Dowager Princess of Wales!' the voice called out.

Catalina dropped her sewing and rose to her feet. Her ladies sprang up too. It was so unusual for anything to happen in the quiet court of Durham House that they were thrown into a flutter.

'Well, let him in!' Catalina exclaimed.

Maria de Salinas flung open the door and one of the royal grooms of the chamber came in and kneeled before the princess. 'Grave news,' he said shortly. 'A son, a prince, has been born of the queen and has died. Her Grace the Queen has died too. God pray for His Grace in his kingly grief.'

'What?' demanded Dona Elvira, trying to take in the astounding rush of events.

'God save her soul,' Catalina replied correctly. 'God save the King.'

'Heavenly Father, take Your daughter Elizabeth into Your keeping. You must love her, she was a woman of great gentleness and grace.'

I sit back on my heels and abandon the prayer. I think the queen's life, ended so tragically, was one of sorrow. If Arthur's version of the scandal were true, then she had been prepared to marry King Richard, however despicable a tyrant. She had wanted to marry him and be his queen. Her mother and My Lady the King's Mother and the victory of

Bosworth had forced her to take King Henry. She had been born to be Queen of England, and she had married the man who could give her the throne.

I thought that if I had been able to tell her of my promise then she would have known the pain that seeps through me like ice every time I think of Arthur, and know that I promised him I would marry Harry. I thought that she might have understood if you are born to be Queen of England you have to be Queen of England, whoever is king. Whoever your husband will have to be.

Without her quiet presence at court I feel that I am more at risk, further from my goal. She was kind to me, she was a loving woman. I was waiting out my year of mourning and trusting that she would help me into marriage with Harry, because he would be a refuge for me, and because I would be a good wife to him. I was trusting that she knew one could marry a man for whom one feels nothing but indifference and still be a good wife.

But now the court will be ruled by My Lady the King's Mother and she is a formidable woman, no friend to anyone but her own cause, no affection for anyone but her son Henry, and his son, Prince Harry.

She will help no-one but she will serve the interests of her own family first. She will consider me as only one candidate among many for his hand in marriage. God forgive her, she might even look to a French bride for him and then I will have failed not only Arthur but my own mother and father too, who need me to maintain the alliance between England and Spain and the enmity between England and France.

This year has been hard for me, I had expected a year of mourning and then a new betrothal; I have been growing more and more anxious since no-one seems to be planning such a thing. And now I am afraid that it will get worse. What if King Henry decides to surrender the second part of the dowry and sends me home? What if they betroth Harry, that foolish boy, to someone else? What if they just forget me? Hold me as a hostage to the good behaviour of Spain but neglect me?

229

Leave me at Durham House, a shadow princess over a shadow court, while the real world goes on elsewhere?

I hate this time of year in England, the way the winter lingers on and on in cold mists and grey skies. In the Alhambra the water in the canals will be released from frost and starting to flow again, icy cold, rushing deep with melt-water from the snows of the sierra. The earth will be starting to warm in the gardens, the men will be planting flowers and young saplings, the sun will be warm in the mornings and the thick hangings will be taken down from the windows so the warm breezes can blow through the palace again.

The birds of summer will come back to the high hills and the olive trees will shimmer their leaves of green and grey. Everywhere the farmers will be turning over the red soil, and there will be the scent of life and growth.

I long to be home; but I will not leave my post. I am not a soldier who forgets his duty, I am a sentry who wakes all night. I will not fail my love. I said 'I promise', and I do not forget it. I will be constant to him. The garden that is immortal life, al-Yanna, will wait for me, the rose will wait for me in al-Yanna, Arthur will wait for me there. I will be Queen of England as I was born to be, as I promised him I would be. The rose will bloom in England as well as in heaven.

There was a great state funeral for Queen Elizabeth, and Catalina was in mourning black again. Through the dark lace of her mantilla she watched the orders of precedence, the arrangements for the service, she saw how everything was commanded by the great book of the king's mother. Even her own place was laid down, behind the princesses, but before all the other ladies of the court.

Lady Margaret, the king's mother, had written down all the procedures to be followed at the Tudor court, from birth chambers to lying in state, so that her son and the generations which she prayed would come after him would be prepared for every occasion, so that each occasion would match another, and so that every occasion, however distant in the future, would be commanded by her.

Now her first great funeral, for her unloved daughter-in-law, went off with the order and grace of a well-planned masque at court, and as the great manager of everything she stepped up visibly, unquestionably, to her place as the greatest lady at court.

2nd April 1503

It was a year to the day that Arthur had died and Catalina spent the day alone in the chapel of Durham House. Father Geraldini held a memorial Mass for the young prince at dawn and Catalina stayed in the little church, without breaking her fast, without taking so much as a cup of small ale, all the day.

Some of the time she knelt before the altar, her lips moving in silent prayer, struggling with the loss of him with a grief which was as sharp and as raw as the day that she had stood on the threshold of his room and learned that they could not save him, that he would die, that she would have to live without him.

For some of the long hours, she prowled around the empty chapel, pausing to look at the devotional pictures on the walls or the exquisite carving of the pew ends and the rood screen. Her horror was that she was forgetting him. There were mornings when she woke and tried to see his face, and found that she could see nothing beneath her closed eyelids, or worse, all she could see was some rough sketch of him, a poor likeness: the simulacrum and no longer the real thing. Those mornings she would sit up quickly, clench her knees up to her belly, and hold herself tight so that she did not give way to her agonising sense of loss.

Then, later in the day she would be talking to her ladies, or sewing, or walking by the river, and someone would say something, or she would see the sun on the water and suddenly he would be there before her, as vivid as if he were alive, lighting up the afternoon. She would stand quite still for a moment, silently drinking him in, and then she would go on with the conversation, or continue her walk, knowing that she would never forget him. Her eyes had the print of him on their lids, her body had the touch of him on her skin, she was his, heart and soul, till death: not – as it turned out – till his death; but till her death. Only when the two of them were gone from this life would their marriage in this life be over.

But on this, the anniversary of his death, Catalina had promised herself that she should be alone, she would allow herself the indulgence of mourning, of railing at God for taking him.

'You know, I shall never understand Your purpose,' I say to the statue of the crucified Christ, hanging by His bloodstained palms over the altar. 'Can you not give me a sign? Can you not show me what I should do?'

I wait but He says nothing. I have to wonder if the God who spoke so clearly to my mother is sleeping, or gone away. Why should He direct her, and yet remain silent for me? Why should I, raised as a fervently Christian child, a passionately Roman Catholic child, have no sense of being heard when I pray from my deepest grief? Why should God desert me, when I need Him so much?

I return to the embroidered kneeler before the altar but I do not kneel on it in a position of prayer, I turn it around and sit on it, as if I were at home, a cushion pulled up to a warm brazier, ready to talk, ready to listen. But no-one speaks to me now. Not even my God.

'I know it is Your will that I should be queen,' I say thoughtfully, as if He might answer, as if He might suddenly reply in a tone as reasonable as my own. 'I know that it is my mother's wish too. I know

that my darling –' I cut short the end of the sentence. Even now, a year on, I cannot take the risk of saying Arthur's name, even in an empty chapel, even to God. I still fear an outpouring of tears, the slide into hysteria and madness. Behind my control is a passion for Arthur like a deep mill pond held behind a sluice gate. I dare not let one drop of it out. There would be a flood of sorrow, a torrent.

'I know that he wished I should be queen. On his deathbed, he asked for a promise. In Your sight, I gave him that promise. In Your name I gave it. I meant it. I am sworn to be queen. But how am I to do it? If it is Your will, as well as his, as I believe, if it is Your will as well as my mother's, as I believe, then, God: hear this. I have run out of stratagems. It has to be You. You have to show me the way to do it.'

I have been demanding this of God with more and more urgency for a year now; while the endless negotiations about the repayment of the dowry and the payment of the jointure drag on and on. Without one clear word from my mother I have come to think that she is playing the same game as me. Without doubt, I know that my father will have some long tactical play in mind. If only they would tell me what I should do! In their discreet silence I have to guess that they are leaving me here as bait for the king. They are leaving me here until the king sees, as I see, as Arthur saw, that the best resolution of this difficulty would be for me to marry Prince Harry.

The trouble is, that as every month goes by, Harry grows in stature and status at the court: he becomes a more attractive prospect. The French king will make a proposal for him, the hundred princelings of Europe with their pretty daughters will make offers, even the Holy Roman Emperor has an unmarried daughter Margaret, who might suit. We have to bring this to a decision now, this very month of April, as my first year of widowhood ends. Now that I am free from my year of waiting. But the balance of power has changed. King Henry is in no hurry, his heir is young – a boy of only eleven. But I am seventeen years old. It is time I was married. It is time I was Princess of Wales once more.

Their Majesties of Spain are demanding the moon: full restitution of their investment, and the return of their daughter, the full widow's jointure to be paid for an indefinite period. The great cost of this is designed to prompt the King of England to find another way. My parents' patience with negotiation allows England to keep both me and the money. They show that they expect the return of neither me nor the money. They are hoping that the King of England will see that he need return neither the dowry nor me.

But they underestimate him. King Henry does not need them to hint him to it. He will have seen perfectly well for himself. Since he is not progressing, he must be resisting both demands. And why should he not? He is in possession. He has half the dowry, and he has me.

And he is no fool. The calmness of the new emissary, Don Gutierre Gomez de Fuensalida, and the slowness of the negotiations has alerted this most acute king to the fact that my mother and father are content to leave me in his hands, in England. It does not take a Machiavelli to conclude that my parents hope for another English marriage – just as when Isabel was widowed they sent her back to Portugal to marry her brother-in-law. These things happen. But only if everyone is in agreement. In England, where the king is new-come to his throne and filled with ambition, it may take more skill than we can deploy to bring it about.

My mother writes to me to say she has a plan but it will take some time to come to fruition. In the meantime she tells me to be patient and never to do anything to offend the king or his mother.

'I am Princess of Wales,' I reply to her. 'I was born to be Princess of Wales and Queen of England. You raised me in these titles. Surely, I should not deny my own upbringing? Surely, I can be Princess of Wales and Queen of England, even now?'

'Be patient,' she writes back to me, in a travel-stained note which *takes weeks to get to me and which has been opened; anyone can have read it. 'I agree that your destiny is to be Queen of England. It is your destiny, God's will, and my wish. Be patient.'*

'How long must I be patient?' I ask God, on my knees to Him in His chapel on the anniversary of Arthur's death. 'If it is Your will, why do You not do it at once? If it is not Your will, why did You not destroy me with Arthur? If You are listening to me now – why do I feel so terribly alone?'

Late in the evening a rare visitor was announced in the quiet presence chamber of Durham House. 'Lady Margaret Pole,' said the guard at the door. Catalina dropped her Bible and turned her pale face to see her friend hesitating shyly in the doorway.

'Lady Margaret!'

'Dowager Princess!' She curtseyed low and Catalina went swiftly across the room to her, raised her up and fell into her arms.

'Don't cry,' Lady Margaret said quietly into her ear. 'Don't cry or I swear I shall weep.'

'I won't, I won't, I promise I won't.' Catalina turned to her ladies. 'Leave us,' she said.

They went reluctantly, a visitor was a novelty in the quiet house, and besides there were no fires burning in any of the other chambers. Lady Margaret looked around the shabby room.

'What is this?'

Catalina shrugged and tried to smile. 'I am a poor manager, I am afraid. And Dona Elvira is no help. And in truth, I have only the money the king gives me and that is not much.'

'I was afraid of this,' the older woman said. Catalina drew her to the fire and sat her down on her own chair.

'I thought you were still at Ludlow?'

'We were. We have been. Since neither the king nor the prince comes to Wales all the business has fallen on my husband. You would think me a princess again to see my little court there.'

Catalina again tried to smile. 'Are you grand?'

'Very. And mostly Welsh-speaking. Mostly singing.'

'I can imagine.'

'We came for the queen's funeral, God bless her, and then I wanted to stay for a little longer and my husband said that I might come and see you. I have been thinking of you all day, today.'

'I have been in the chapel,' Catalina said inconsequently. 'It doesn't seem like a year.'

'It doesn't, does it?' Lady Margaret agreed, though privately she thought that the girl had aged far more than one year. Grief had refined her girlish prettiness, she had the clear, decided looks of a woman who had seen her hopes destroyed. 'Are you well?'

Catalina made a little face. 'I am well enough. And you? And the children?'

Lady Margaret smiled. 'Praise God, yes. But do you know what plans the king has for you? Are you to . . .' She hesitated. 'Are you to go back to Spain? Or stay here?'

Catalina drew a little closer. 'They are talking, about the dowry, about my return. But nothing gets done. Nothing is decided. The king is holding me and holding my dowry, and my parents are letting him do it.'

Lady Margaret looked concerned. 'I had heard that they might consider betrothing you to Prince Harry,' she said. 'I did not know.'

'It is the obvious choice. But it does not seem obvious to the king,' Catalina said wryly. 'What do you think? Is he a man to miss an obvious solution, d'you think?'

'No,' said Lady Margaret, whose life had been jeopardised by the king's awareness of the obvious fact of her family's claim on his throne.

'Then I must assume that he has thought of this choice and is waiting to see if it is the best he can make,' Catalina said. She gave a little sigh. 'God knows, it is weary work, waiting.'

'Now your mourning is over, no doubt he will make arrangements,' her friend said hopefully.

'No doubt,' Catalina replied.

After weeks spent alone, mourning for his wife, the king returned to the court at Whitehall Palace, and Catalina was invited to dine with the royal family and seated with the Princess Mary and the ladies of the court. The young Harry, Prince of Wales, was placed securely between his father and grandmother. Not for this Prince of Wales the cold journey to Ludlow Castle and the rigorous training of a prince in waiting. Lady Margaret had ruled that this prince, their only surviving heir, should be brought up under her own eye, in ease and comfort. He was not to be sent away, he was to be watched all the time. He was not even allowed to take part in dangerous sports, jousting or fighting, though he was quite wild to take part, and a boy who loved activity and excitement. His grandmother had ruled that he was too precious to risk.

He smiled at Catalina and she shot him a look that she hoped was discreetly warm. But there was no opportunity to exchange so much as one word. She was firmly anchored further down the table and she could hardly see him thanks to My Lady the King's Mother, who plied him with the best of all foods from her own plate, and interposed her broad shoulder between him and the ladies.

Catalina thought that it was as Arthur had said, that the boy was spoiled by this attention. His grandmother leaned back for a moment to speak to one of the ushers and Catalina saw Harry's gaze flick towards her. She gave him a smile and then cast down her eyes. When she glanced up, he was still looking at her and then he blushed red to be caught. 'A child.' She shot a sideways little smile even as she silently criticised him. 'A child of eleven. All boasting and boyishness. And why should this plump, spoilt boy be spared when Arthur . . .' At once she stopped the thought. To compare Arthur with his brother was to wish the little boy dead, and she would not do that. To think of Arthur in public was to risk breaking down and she would never do that.

'A woman could rule a boy like that,' she thought. 'A woman could be a very great queen if she married such a boy. For the first ten years he would know nothing, and by then, perhaps he might be in such a habit of obedience that he would let his wife continue to rule. Or he might be, as Arthur told me, a lazy boy. A young man wasted. He might be so lazy that he could be diverted by games and hunting and sports and amusements, so that the business of the kingdom could be done by his wife.'

Catalina never forgot that Arthur had told her that the boy fancied himself in love with her. 'If they give him everything that he wants, perhaps he might be the one who chooses his bride,' she thought. 'They are in the habit of indulging him. Perhaps he could beg to marry me and they would feel obliged to say "yes".'

She saw him blush even redder, even his ears turned pink. She held his gaze for a long moment, she took in a little breath and parted her lips as if to whisper a word to him. She saw his blue eyes focus on her mouth and darken with desire, and then, calculating the effect, she looked down. 'Stupid boy,' she thought.

The king rose from the table and all the men and women on the crowded benches of the hall rose too, and bowed their heads.

'Give you thanks for coming to greet me,' King Henry said. 'Comrades in war and friends in peace. But now forgive me, as I wish to be alone.'

He nodded to Harry, he offered his mother his hand, and the royal family went through the little doorway at the back of the great hall to their privy chamber.

'You should have stayed longer,' the king's mother remarked as they settled into chairs by the fire and the groom of the ewery brought them wine. 'It looks bad, to leave so promptly. I had told the Master of Horse you would stay, and there would be singing.'

'I was weary,' Henry said shortly. He looked over to where Catalina and the Princess Mary were sitting together. The younger girl was red-eyed, the loss of her mother had hit her hard. Catalina was – as usual – cool as a stream. He thought she had great power of self-containment. Even this loss of her only real friend at court, her last friend in England, did not seem to distress her.

'She can go back to Durham House tomorrow,' his mother remarked, following the direction of his gaze. 'It does no good for her to come to court. She has not earned her place here with an heir, and she has not paid for her place here with her dowry.'

'She is constant,' he said. 'She is constant in her attendance on you, and on me.'

'Constant like the plague,' his mother returned.

'You are hard on her.'

'It is a hard world,' she said simply. 'I am nothing but just. Why don't we send her home?'

'Do you not admire her at all?'

She was surprised by the question. 'What is there to admire in her?'

'Her courage, her dignity. She has beauty, of course, but she also has charm. She is educated, she is graceful. I think, in other circumstances, she could have been merry. And she has borne herself, under this disappointment, like a queen.'

'She is of no use to us,' she said. 'She was our Princess of Wales; but our boy is dead. She is of no use to us now, however charming she may seem to be.'

Catalina looked up and saw them watching her. She gave a small, controlled smile and inclined her head. Henry rose, went to a window bay on his own, and crooked his finger for her. She did not jump to come to him, as any of the women of court would have jumped. She looked at him, she raised an eyebrow as if she were

239

considering whether or not to obey, and then she gracefully rose to her feet and strolled towards him.

'Good God, she is desirable,' he thought to himself. 'No more than seventeen. Utterly in my power, and yet still she walks across the room as if she were Queen of England crowned.'

'You will miss the queen, I daresay,' he said abruptly in French as she came up to him.

'I shall,' she replied clearly. 'I grieve for you in the loss of your wife. I am sure my mother and father would want me to give you their commiserations.'

He nodded, never taking his eyes from her face. 'We share a grief now,' he observed. 'You have lost your partner in life and I have lost mine.'

He saw her gaze sharpen. 'Indeed,' she said steadily. 'We do.'

He wondered if she was trying to unravel his meaning. If that quick mind was working behind that clear lovely face there was no sign of it. 'You must teach me the secret of your resignation,' he said.

'Oh, I don't think I resign myself.'

Henry was intrigued. 'You don't?'

'No. I think I trust in God that He knows what is right for all of us, and His will shall be done.'

'Even when His ways are hidden, and we sinners have to stumble about in the dark?'

'I know my destiny,' Catalina said calmly. 'He has been gracious to reveal it to me.'

'Then you're one of the very few,' he said, thinking to make her laugh at herself.

'I know,' she said without a glimmer of a smile. He realised that she was utterly serious in her belief that God had revealed her future to her. 'I am blessed.'

'And what is this great destiny that God has for you?' he said sarcastically. He hoped so much that she would say that she should be Queen of England, and then he could ask her, or draw close to her, or let her see what was in his mind.

'To do God's will, of course, and bring His kingdom to earth,' she said cleverly, and evaded him once more.

I speak very confidently of God's will, and I remind the king that I was raised to be Princess of Wales, but in truth God is silent to me. Since the day of Arthur's death I can have no genuine conviction that I am blessed. How can I call myself blessed when I have lost the one thing that made my life complete? How can I be blessed when I do not think I will ever be happy again? But we live in a world of believers – I have to say that I am under the especial protection of God, I have to give the illusion of being sure of my destiny. I am the daughter of Isabella of Spain. My inheritance is certainty.

But in truth, of course, I am increasingly alone. I feel increasingly alone. There is nothing between me and despair but my promise to Arthur, and the thin thread, like gold wire in a carpet, of my own determination.

May 1503

King Henry did not approach Catalina for one month for the sake of decency, but when he was out of his black jacket he made a formal visit to her at Durham House. Her household had been warned that he would come, and were dressed in their best. He saw the signs of wear and tear in the curtains and rugs and hangings and smiled to himself. If she had the good sense that he thought she had, she would be glad to see a resolution to this awkward position. He congratulated himself on not making it easier for her in this last year. She should know by now that she was utterly in his power and her parents could do nothing to free her.

His herald threw open the double doors to her presence chamber and shouted: 'His Grace, King Henry of England . . .'

Henry waved aside the other titles and went in to his daughter-in-law.

She was wearing a dark-coloured gown with blue slashings on the sleeve, a richly embroidered stomacher and a dark blue hood. It brought out the amber in her hair and the blue in her eyes and he smiled in instinctive pleasure at the sight of her as she sank into a deep formal curtsey and rose up.

'Your Grace,' she said pleasantly. 'This is an honour indeed.'

He had to force himself not to stare at the creamy line of her neck, at the smooth, unlined face that looked back up at him. He had lived all his life with a beautiful woman of his own age; now here was a girl young enough to be his daughter, with the rich-scented bloom of youth still on her, and breasts full and firm. She was ready for marriage, indeed, she was over-ready for marriage. This was a girl who should be bedded. He checked himself at once, and thought he was part lecher, part lover to look on his dead son's child-bride with such desire.

'Can I offer you some refreshment?' she asked. There was a smile in the back of her eyes.

He thought if she had been an older, a more sophisticated woman he would have assumed she was playing him, as knowingly as a skilled angler can land a salmon.

'Thank you. I will take a glass of wine.'

And so she caught him. 'I am afraid I have nothing fit to offer you,' she said smoothly. 'I have nothing left in my cellars at all, and I cannot afford to buy good wine.'

Henry did not show by so much as a flicker that he knew she had trapped him into hearing of her financial difficulties. 'I am sorry for that, I will have some barrels sent over,' he said. 'Your house-keeping must be very remiss.'

'It is very thin,' she said simply. 'Will you take a cup of ale? We brew our own ale very cheaply.'

'Thank you,' he said, biting his lip to hide a smile. He had not dreamed that she had so much self-confidence. The year of widowhood had brought out her courage, he thought. Alone in a foreign land she had not collapsed as other girls might have collapsed, she had gathered her power and become stronger.

'Is My Lady the King's Mother in good health and the Princess Mary well?' she asked, as confidently as if she were entertaining him in the gold room of the Alhambra.

'Yes, thank God,' he said. 'And you?'

She smiled and bowed her head. 'And no need to ask for your health,' she remarked. 'You never look any different.'

'Do I not?'

'Not since the very first time we met,' she said. 'When I had just landed in England and was coming to London and you rode to meet me.' It cost Catalina a good deal not to think of Arthur as he was on that evening, mortified by his father's rudeness, trying to talk to her in an undertone, stealing sideways looks at her.

Determinedly she put her young lover from her mind and smiled at his father and said: 'I was so surprised by your coming, and so startled by you.'

He laughed. He saw that she had conjured the picture of when he first saw her, a virgin by her bed, in a white gown with a blue cape with her hair in a plait down her back, and how he thought then that he had come upon her like a ravisher, he had forced his way into her bedchamber, he could have forced himself on to her.

He turned and took a chair to cover his thoughts, gesturing that she should sit down too. Her duenna, the same sour-faced Spanish mule, he noticed irritably, stood at the back of the room with two other ladies.

Catalina sat perfectly composed, her white fingers interlaced in her lap, her back straight, her entire manner that of a young woman

243

confident of her power to attract. Henry said nothing and looked at her for a moment. Surely she must know what she was doing to him when she reminded him of their first meeting? And yet surely the daughter of Isabella of Spain and the widow of his own son could not be wilfully tempting him to lust?

A servant came in with two cups of small ale. The king was served first and then Catalina took a cup. She took a tiny sip and set it down.

'D'you still not like ale?' He was startled at the intimacy in his own voice. Surely to God he could ask his daughter-in-law what she liked to drink?

'I drink it only when I am very thirsty,' she replied. 'But I don't like the taste it leaves in my mouth.' She put her hand to her mouth and touched her lower lip. Fascinated, he watched her fingertip brush the tip of her tongue. She made a little face. 'I think it will never be a favourite of mine,' she said.

'What did you drink in Spain?' He found he could hardly speak. He was still watching her soft mouth, shiny where her tongue had licked her lips.

'We could drink the water,' she said. 'In the Alhambra the Moors had piped clean water all the way from the mountains into the palace. We drank mountain spring water from the fountains, it was still cold. And juices from fruits of course, we had wonderful fruits in summer, and ices, and sherbets and wines as well.'

'If you come on progress with me this summer we can go to places where you can drink the water,' he said. He thought he was sounding like a stupid boy, promising her a drink of water as a treat. Stubbornly, he persisted. 'If you come with me we can go hunting, we can go to Hampshire, beyond, to the New Forest. You remember the country around there? Near where we first met?'

'I should like that so much,' she said. 'If I am still here, of course.'

'Still here?' He was startled, he had almost forgotten that she was his hostage, she was supposed to go home by summer. 'I doubt your father and I will have agreed terms by then.'

'Why, how can it take so long?' she asked, her blue eyes wide with assumed surprise. 'Surely we can come to some agreement?' She hesitated. 'Between friends? Surely if we cannot agree about the moneys owed, there is some other way? Some other agreement that can be made? Since we have made an agreement before?'

It was so close to what he had been thinking that he rose to his feet, discomfited. At once she rose too. The top of her pretty blue hood only came to his shoulder, he thought he would have to bend his head to kiss her, and if she were under him in bed he would have to take care not to hurt her. He felt his face flush hot at the thought of it. 'Come here,' he said thickly and led her to the window embrasure where her ladies could not overhear them.

'I have been thinking what sort of arrangement we might come to,' he said. 'The easiest thing would be for you to stay here. I should certainly like you to stay here.'

Catalina did not look up at him. If she had done so then, he would have been sure of her. But she kept her eyes down, her face downcast. 'Oh, certainly, if my parents agree,' she said, so softly that he could hardly hear.

He felt himself trapped. He felt he could not go forwards while she held her head so delicately to one side and showed him only the curve of her cheek and her eyelashes, and yet he could hardly go back when she had asked him outright if there was not another way to resolve the conflict between him and her parents.

'You will think me very old,' he burst out.

Her blue eyes flashed up at him and were veiled again. 'Not at all,' she said levelly.

'I am old enough to be your father,' he said, hoping she would disagree.

Instead she looked up at him. 'I never think of you like that,' she said.

Henry was silent. He felt utterly baffled by this slim young woman who seemed at one moment so deliciously encouraging and yet at another moment, quite opaque. 'What would you like to do?' he demanded of her.

At last she raised her head and smiled up at him, her lips curving up but no warmth in her eyes. 'Whatever you command,' she said. 'I should like most of all to obey you, Your Grace.'

What does he mean? What is he doing? I thought he was offering me Harry and I was about to say 'yes' when he said that I must think him very old, as old as my father. And of course he is, indeed, he looks far older than my father, that is why I never think of him like a father, a grandfather perhaps, or an old priest. My father is handsome; a terrible womaniser; a brave soldier; a hero on the battlefield. This king has fought one half-hearted battle and put down a dozen unheroic uprisings of poor men too sickened with his rule to endure it any more. So he is not like my father and I spoke only the truth when I said that I never see him like that.

But then he looked at me as if I had said something of great interest, and then he asked me what I wanted. I could not say to his face that I wanted him to overlook my marriage to his oldest son, and marry me anew to his youngest. So I said that I wanted to obey him. There can be nothing wrong with that. But somehow it was not what he wanted. And it did not get me to where I wanted.

I have no idea what he wants. Nor how to turn it to my own advantage.

Henry went back to Whitehall Palace, his face burning and his heart pounding, hammered between frustration and calculation. If he could persuade Catalina's parents to allow the wedding, he could claim the rest of her substantial dowry, be free of their claims for her jointure, reinforce the alliance with Spain at the very moment that he was looking to secure new alliances with Scotland and France, and perhaps, with such a young wife, get another son and heir on her. One daughter on the throne of Scotland, one daughter on the throne of France should lock both nations into peace for a lifetime. The Princess of Spain on the throne of England should keep the most Christian kings of Spain in alliance. He would have bolted the great powers of Christendom into peaceful alliance with England not just for a generation, but for generations to come. They would have heirs in common; they would be safe. England would be safe. Better yet, England's sons might inherit the kingdoms of France, of Scotland, of Spain. England might conceive its way into peace and greatness.

It made absolute sense to secure Catalina; he tried to focus on the political advantage and not think of the line of her neck nor the curve of her waist. He tried to steady his mind by thinking of the small fortune that would be saved by not having to provide her with a jointure nor with her keep, by not having to send a ship, several ships probably, to escort her home. But all he could think was that she had touched her soft mouth with her finger and told him that she did not like the lingering taste of ale. At the thought of the tip of her tongue against her lips he groaned aloud and the groom holding the horse for him to dismount looked up and said: 'Sire?'

'Bile,' the king said sourly.

It did feel like too rich a fare that was sickening him, he decided as he strode to his private apartments, courtiers eddying out of his way with sycophantic smiles. He felt that he must remember that she was little more than a child, she was his own daughter-in-law. If he listened to the good sense that had carried him so far, he should simply promise to pay her jointure, send her back to her parents, and then delay the payment till they had her married to some other kingly fool elsewhere, and he could get away with paying nothing.

But at the mere thought of her married to another man he had to stop and put his hand out to the oak panelling for support.

'Your Grace?' someone asked him. 'Are you ill?'

'Bile,' the king repeated. 'Something I have eaten.'

His chief groom of the body came to him. 'Shall I send for your physician, Your Grace?'

'No,' the king said. 'But send a couple of barrels of the best wine to the Dowager Princess. She has nothing in her cellar, and when I have to visit her I should like to drink wine and not ale.'

'Yes, Your Grace,' the man said, bowed, and went away. Henry straightened up and went to his rooms. They were crowded with people as usual: petitioners, courtiers, favour-seekers, fortune-hunters, some friends, some gentry, some noblemen attending on him for love or calculation. Henry regarded them all sourly. When he had been Henry Tudor on the run in Brittany he had not been blessed with so many friends.

'Where is my mother?' he asked one of them.

'In her rooms, Your Grace,' the man replied.

'I shall visit her,' he said. 'Let her know.'

He gave her a few moments to ready herself, and then he went to her chambers. On her daughter-in-law's death she had moved into the apartment traditionally given to the queen. She had ordered new tapestries and new furniture and now the place was more grandly furnished than any queen had ever had before.

'I'll announce myself,' the king said to the guard at her door, and stepped in without ceremony.

Lady Margaret was seated at a table in the window, the household accounts spread before her, inspecting the costs of the royal court as if it were a well-run farm. There was very little waste and no extravagance allowed in the court run by Lady Margaret, and royal servants who had thought that some of the payments which passed through their hands might leave a little gold on the side were soon disappointed.

Henry nodded his approval at the sight of his mother's supervision of the royal business. He had never rid himself of his own anxiety that the ostentatious wealth of the throne of England might prove to be hollow show. He had financed a campaign for the throne on debt and favours; he never wanted to be cap in hand again.

She looked up as he came in. 'My son.'

He kneeled for her blessing as he always did when he first greeted her every day, and felt her fingers gently touch the top of his head.

'You look troubled,' she remarked.

'I am,' he said. 'I went to see the Dowager Princess.'

'Yes?' A faint expression of disdain crossed her face. 'What are they asking for now?'

'We –' He broke off and then started again. 'We have to decide what is to become of her. She spoke of going home to Spain.'

'When they pay us what they owe,' she said at once. 'They know they have to pay the rest of her dowry before she can leave.'

'Yes, she knows that.'

There was a brief silence.

'She asked if there could not be another agreement,' he said. 'Some resolution.'

'Ah, I've been waiting for this,' Lady Margaret said exultantly. 'I knew they would be after this. I am only surprised they have waited so long. I suppose they thought they should wait until she was out of mourning.'

'After what?'

'They will want her to stay,' she said.

Henry could feel himself beginning to smile and deliberately he set his face still. 'You think so?'

'I have been waiting for them to show their hand. I knew that they were waiting for us to make the first move. Ha! That we have made them declare first!'

He raised his eyebrows, longing for her to spell out his desire. 'For what?'

'A proposal from us, of course,' she said. 'They knew that we

249

would never let such a chance go. She was the right match then, and she is the right match now. We had a good bargain with her then, and it is still good. Especially if they pay in full. And now she is more profitable than ever.'

His colour flushed as he beamed at her. 'You think so?'

'Of course. She is here, half her dowry already paid, the rest we have only to collect, we have already rid ourselves of her escort, the alliance is already working to our benefit – we would never have the respect of the French if they did not fear her parents, the Scots fear us too – she is still the best match in Christendom for us.'

His sense of relief was overwhelming. If his mother did not oppose the plan then he felt he could push on with it. She had been his best and safest advisor for so long that he could not have gone against her will.

'And the difference in age?'

She shrugged. 'It is what? Five, nearly six years? That is nothing for a prince.'

He recoiled as if she had slapped him in the face. 'Six years?' he repeated.

'And Harry is tall for his age and strong. They will not look mismatched,' she said.

'No,' he said flatly. 'No. Not Harry. I did not mean Harry. I was not speaking of Harry!'

The anger in his voice alerted her. 'What?'

'No. No. Not Harry. Damn it! Not Harry!'

'What? Whatever can you mean?'

'It is obvious! Surely it is obvious!'

Her gaze flashed across his face, reading him rapidly, as only she could. 'Not Harry?'

'I thought you were speaking of me.'

'Of you?' She quickly reconsidered the conversation. 'Of you for the Infanta?' she asked incredulously.

He felt himself flush again. 'Yes.'

250

'Arthur's widow? Your own daughter-in-law?'

'Yes! Why not?'

Lady Margaret stared at him in alarm. She did not even have to list the obstacles.

'He was too young. It was not consummated,' he said, repeating the words that the Spanish ambassador had learned from Dona Elvira, which had been spread throughout Christendom.

She looked sceptical.

'She says so herself. Her duenna says so. The Spanish say so. Everybody says so.'

'And you believe them?' she asked coldly.

'He was impotent.'

'Well . . .' It was typical of her that she said nothing while she considered it. She looked at him, noting the colour in his cheeks and the trouble in his face. 'They are probably lying. We saw them wedded and bedded and there was no suggestion then that it had not been done.'

'That is their business. If they all tell the same lie and stick to it, then it is the same as the truth.'

'Only if we accept it.'

'We do,' he ruled.

She raised her eyebrows. 'It is your desire?'

'It is not a question of desire. I need a wife,' Henry said coolly, as though it could be anyone. 'And she is conveniently here, as you say.'

'She would be suitable by birth,' his mother conceded, 'but for her relationship to you. She is your daughter-in-law even if it was not consummated. And she is very young.'

'She is seventeen,' he said. 'A good age for a woman. And a widow. She is ready for a second marriage.'

'She is either a virgin or she is not,' Lady Margaret observed waspishly. 'We had better agree.'

'She is seventeen,' he corrected himself. 'A good age for marriage. She is ready for a full marriage.'

251

'The people won't like it,' she observed. 'They will remember her wedding to Arthur, we made such a show of it. They took to her. They took to the two of them. The pomegranate and the rose. She caught their fancy in her lace mantilla.'

'Well, he is dead,' he said harshly. 'And she will have to marry someone.'

'People will think it odd.'

He shrugged. 'They will be glad enough if she gives me a son.'

'Oh yes, if she can do that. But she was barren with Arthur.'

'As we have agreed, Arthur was impotent. The marriage was not consummated.'

She pursed her lips but said nothing.

'And it gains us the dowry and removes the cost of the jointure,' he pointed out.

She nodded. She loved the thought of the fortune that Catalina would bring.

'And she is here already.'

'A most constant presence,' she said sourly.

'A constant princess,' he smiled.

'Do you really think her parents would agree? Their Majesties of Spain?'

'It solves their dilemma as well as ours. And it maintains the alliance.' He found he was smiling, and tried to make his face stern, as normal. 'She herself would think it was her destiny. She believes herself born to be Queen of England.'

'Well then, she is a fool,' his mother remarked smartly.

'She was raised to be queen since she was a child.'

'But she will be a barren queen. No son of hers will be any good. He could never be king. If she has one at all, he will come after Harry,' she reminded him. 'He will even come after Harry's sons. It's a far poorer alliance for her than marriage to a Prince of Wales. The Spanish won't like it.'

'Oh, Harry is still a child. His sons are a long way ahead. Years.'

'Even so. It would weigh on her parents. They will prefer Prince Harry for her. That way, she is queen and her son is king after her. Why would they agree to anything less?'

Henry hesitated. There was nothing he could say to fault her logic, except that he did not wish to follow it.

'Oh. I see. You want her,' she said flatly when the silence extended so long that she realised there was something he could not let himself say. 'It is a matter of your desire.'

He took the plunge. 'Yes,' he confirmed.

Lady Margaret looked at him with calculation in her gaze. He had been taken from her as little more than a baby for safekeeping. Since then she had always seen him as a prospect, as a potential heir to the throne, as her passport to grandeur. She had hardly known him as a baby, never loved him as a child. She had planned his future as a man, she had defended his rights as a king, she had mapped his campaign as a threat to the House of York – but she had never known tenderness for him. She could not learn to feel indulgent towards him this late in her life; she was hardly ever indulgent to anyone, not even to herself.

'That's very shocking,' she said coolly. 'I thought we were talking of a marriage of advantage. She stands as a daughter to you. This desire is a carnal sin.'

'It is not and she is not,' he said. 'There is nothing wrong in honourable love. She is not my daughter. She is his widow. And it was not consummated.'

'You will need a dispensation, it is a sin.'

'He never even had her!' he exclaimed.

'The whole court put them to bed,' she pointed out levelly.

'He was too young. He was impotent. And he was dead, poor lad, within months.'

She nodded. 'So she says now.'

'But you do not advise me against it,' he said.

'It is a sin,' she repeated. 'But if you can get dispensation and her parents agree to it, then –' She pulled a sour face. 'Well, better her than many others, I suppose,' she said begrudgingly. 'And she can live at court under my care. I can watch over her and command her more easily than I could an older girl, and we know that she behaves herself well. She is obedient. She will learn her duties under me. And the people love her.'

'I shall speak to the Spanish ambassador today.'

She thought she had never seen such a bright gladness in his face. 'I suppose I can teach her.' She gestured to the books before her. 'She will have much to learn.'

'I shall tell the ambassador to propose it to Their Majesties of Spain and I shall talk to her tomorrow.'

'You will go again so soon?' she asked curiously.

Henry nodded. He would not tell her that even to wait till tomorrow seemed too long. If he had been free to do so, he would have gone back straight away and asked her to marry him that very night, as if he were a humble squire and she a maid, and not King of England and Princess of Spain; father and daughter-in-law.

Henry saw that Dr de Puebla the Spanish ambassador was invited to Whitehall in time for dinner, given a seat at one of the top tables, and plied with the best wine. Some venison, hanged to perfection and cooked in a brandywine sauce, came to the king's table, he helped himself to a small portion and sent the dish to the Spanish ambassador. De Puebla, who had not experienced such favours since first negotiating the Infanta's marriage contract, loaded his plate with a heavy spoon and dipped the best manchet bread into the gravy, glad to eat well at court, wondering quietly behind his avid smile what it might mean.

The king's mother nodded towards him, and de Puebla rose up

from his seat to bow to her. 'Most gracious,' he remarked to himself as he sat down once more. 'Extremely. Exceptionally.'

He was no fool, he knew that something would be required for all these public favours. But given the horror of the past year – when the hopes of Spain had been buried beneath the nave in Worcester Cathedral – at least these were straws in a good wind. Clearly, King Henry had a use for him again as something other than a whipping boy for the failure of the Spanish sovereigns to pay their debts.

De Puebla had tried to defend Their Majesties of Spain to an increasingly irritable English king. He had tried to explain to them in long, detailed letters that it was fruitless asking for Catalina's widow's jointure if they would not pay the remainder of the dowry. He tried to explain to Catalina that he could not make the English king pay a more generous allowance for the upkeep of her household, nor could he persuade the Spanish king to give his daughter financial support. Both kings were utterly stubborn, both quite determined to force the other into a weak position. Neither seemed to care that in the meantime Catalina, only seventeen, was forced to keep house with an extravagant entourage in a foreign land on next to no money. Neither king would take the first step and undertake to be responsible for her keep, fearing that this would commit him to keeping her and her household forever.

De Puebla smiled up at the king, seated on his throne under the canopy of state. He genuinely liked King Henry, he admired the courage with which he had seized and held the throne, he liked the man's direct good sense. And more than that, de Puebla liked living in England, he was accustomed to his good house in London, to the importance conferred on him by representing the newest and most powerful ruling house in Europe. He liked the fact that his Jewish background and recent conversion were utterly ignored in England, since everyone at this court had come from nowhere and changed their name or their affiliation at least once. England suited de Puebla, and he would do his best to remain. If it meant serving the King of

England better than the King of Spain, he thought it was a small compromise to make.

Henry rose from the throne and gave the signal that the servers could clear the plates. They swept the board and cleared the trestle tables, and Henry strolled among the diners, pausing for a word here and there, still very much the commander among his men. All the favourites at the Tudor court were the gamblers who had put their swords behind their words and marched into England with Henry. They knew their value to him, and he knew his to them. It was still a victors' camp rather than a softened civilian court.

At length Henry completed his circuit and came to de Puebla's table. 'Ambassador,' he greeted him.

De Puebla bowed low. 'I thank you for your gift of the dish of venison,' he said. 'It was delicious.'

The king nodded. 'I would have a word with you.'

'Of course.'

'Privately.'

The two men strolled to a quieter corner of the hall while the musicians in the gallery struck a note and began to play.

'I have a proposal to resolve the issue of the Dowager Princess,' Henry said as drily as possible.

'Indeed?'

'You may find my suggestion unusual, but I think it has much to recommend it.'

'At last,' de Puebla thought to himself. 'He is going to propose Harry. I thought he was going to let her sink a lot lower before he did that. I thought he would bring her down so that he could charge us double for a second try at Wales. But, so be it. God is merciful.'

'Ah yes?' de Puebla said aloud.

'I suggest that we forget the issue of the dowry,' Henry started. 'Her goods will be absorbed into my household. I shall pay her an appropriate allowance, as I did for the late Queen Elizabeth – God bless her. I shall marry the Infanta myself.'

De Puebla was almost too shocked to speak. 'You?'

'I. Is there any reason why not?'

The ambassador gulped, drew a breath, managed to say, 'No, no, at least . . . I suppose there could be an objection on the grounds of affinity.'

'I shall apply for a dispensation. I take it that you are certain that the marriage was not consummated?'

'Certain,' de Puebla gasped.

'You assured me of that on her word?'

'The duenna said . . .'

'Then it is nothing,' the king ruled. 'They were little more than promised to one another. Hardly man and wife.'

'I will have to put this to Their Majesties of Spain,' de Puebla said, desperately trying to assemble some order to his whirling thoughts, striving to keep his deep shock from his face. 'Does the Privy Council agree?' he asked, playing for time. 'The Archbishop of Canterbury?'

'It is a matter between ourselves at the moment,' Henry said grandly. 'It is early days for me as a widower. I want to be able to reassure Their Majesties that their daughter will be cared for. It has been a difficult year for her.'

'If she could have gone home . . .'

'Now there will be no need for her to go home. Her home is England. This is her country,' Henry said flatly. 'She shall be queen here, as she was brought up to be.'

De Puebla could hardly speak for shock at the suggestion that this old man, who had just buried his wife, should marry his dead son's bride. 'Of course. So, shall I tell Their Majesties that you are quite determined on this course? There is no other arrangement that we should consider?' De Puebla racked his brains as to how he could bring in the name of Prince Harry, who was surely Catalina's most appropriate future husband. Finally, he plunged in. 'Your son, for instance?'

'My son is too young to be considered for marriage as yet,' Henry disposed of the suggestion with speed. 'He is eleven and a strong, forward boy but his grandmother insists that we plan nothing for him for another four years. And by then, the Princess Dowager would be twenty-one.'

'Still young,' gasped de Puebla. 'Still a young woman, and near him in age.'

'I don't think Their Majesties would want their daughter to stay in England for another four years without husband or household of her own,' Henry said with unconcealed threat. 'They could hardly want her to wait for Harry's majority. What would she do in those years? Where would she live? Are they proposing to buy her a palace and set up a household for her? Are they prepared to give her an income? A court, appropriate to her position? For four years?'

'If she could return to Spain to wait?' de Puebla hazarded.

'She can leave at once, if she will pay the full amount of her dowry, and find her own fortune elsewhere. Do you really think she can get a better offer than Queen of England? Take her away if you do!'

It was the sticking point that they had reached over and over again in the past year. De Puebla knew he was beaten. 'I will write to Their Majesties tonight,' he said.

I dreamed I was a swift, flying over the golden hills of the Sierra Nevada. But this time, I was flying north, the hot afternoon sun was on my left, ahead of me was a gathering of cool cloud. Then suddenly, the cloud took shape, it was Ludlow Castle, and my little bird heart fluttered at the sight of it and at the thought of the night that would come when he would take me in his arms and press down on me, and I would melt with desire for him.

Then I saw it was not Ludlow but the great grey walls were those of Windsor Castle, and the curve of the river was the great grey glass of the river Thames, and all the traffic plying up and down and the great ships at anchor were the wealth and the bustle of the English. I knew I was far from my home, and yet I was at home. This would be my home, I would build a little nest against the grey stone of the towers here, just as I would have done in Spain. And here they would call me a swift; a bird which flies so fast that no-one has ever seen it land, a bird that flies so high that they think it never touches the ground. I shall not be Catalina, the Infanta of Spain. I shall be Katherine of Aragon, Queen of England, just as Arthur named me: Katherine, Queen of England.

'The king is here again,' Dona Elvira said, looking out of the window. 'He has ridden here with just two men. Not even a standard bearer or guards.' She sniffed. The widespread English informality was bad enough but this king had the manners of a stable boy.

Catalina flew to the window and peered out. 'What can he want?' she wondered. 'Tell them to decant some of his wine.'

Dona Elvira went out of the room in a hurry. In the next moment Henry strolled in, unannounced. 'I thought I would call on you,' he said.

Catalina sank into a deep curtsey. 'Your Grace does me much honour,' she said. 'And at least now I can offer you a glass of good wine.'

Henry smiled and waited. The two of them stood while Dona Elvira returned to the room with a Spanish maid-in-waiting carrying a tray of Morisco brassware with two Venetian glasses of red wine. Henry noted the fineness of the workmanship and assumed correctly that it was part of the dowry that the Spanish had withheld.

'Your health,' he said, holding up his glass to the princess.

To his surprise she did not simply raise her glass in return, she raised her eyes and gave him a long, thoughtful look. He felt himself tingle, like a boy, as his eyes met hers. 'Princess?' he said quietly.

'Your Grace?'

They both of them glanced towards Dona Elvira, who was standing uncomfortably close, quietly regarding the floorboards beneath her worn shoes.

'You can leave us,' the king said.

The woman looked at the princess for her orders, and made no move to leave.

'I shall talk in private with my daughter-in-law,' King Henry said firmly. 'You may go.'

Dona Elvira curtseyed and left, and the rest of the ladies swept out after her.

Catalina smiled at the king. 'As you command,' she said.

He felt his pulse speed at her smile. 'Indeed, I do need to speak to you privately. I have a proposal to put to you. I have spoken to the Spanish ambassador and he has written to your parents.'

'At last. This is it. At last,' Catalina thought. 'He has come to propose Harry for me. Thank God, who has brought me to this day. Arthur, beloved, this day you will see that I shall be faithful to my promise to you.'

'I need to marry again,' Henry said. 'I am still young –' He thought he would not say his age of forty-six. 'It may be that I can have another child or two.'

Catalina nodded politely; but she was barely listening. She was waiting for him to ask her to marry Prince Harry.

'I have been thinking of all the princesses in Europe who would be suitable partners for me,' he said.

Still the princess before him said nothing.

'I can find no-one I would choose.'

She widened her eyes to indicate her attention.

Henry ploughed on. 'My choice has fallen on you,' he said bluntly, 'for these reasons. You are here in London already, you have become accustomed to living here. You were brought up to be Queen of England, and you will be queen as my wife. The difficulties with the dowry can be put aside. You will have the same allowance that I paid to Queen Elizabeth. My mother agrees with this.'

At last his words penetrated her mind. She was so shocked that she could barely speak. She just stared at him. 'Me?'

'There is a slight objection on the grounds of affinity but I shall ask the Pope to grant a dispensation,' he went on. 'I understand that your marriage to Prince Arthur was never consummated. In that case, there is no real objection.'

'It was not consummated.' Catalina repeated the words by rote, as if she no longer understood them. The great lie had been part of a plot to take her to the altar with Prince Harry, not with his father. She could not now retract it. Her mind was so dizzy that she could only cling to it. 'It was not consummated.'

'Then there should be no difficulty,' the king said. 'I take it that you do not object?'

He found that he could hardly breathe, waiting for her answer. Any thought that she had been leading him on, tempting him to this moment, had vanished when he looked into her bleached, shocked face.

He took her hand. 'Don't look so afraid,' he said, his voice low with tenderness. 'I won't hurt you. This is to resolve all your problems. I will be a good husband to you. I will care for you.' Desperately, he racked his brains for something that might please her. 'I will buy you pretty things,' he said. 'Like those sapphires that you liked so much. You shall have a cupboard full of pretty things, Catalina.'

She knew she had to reply. 'I am so surprised,' she said.

'Surely you must have known that I desired you?'

I stopped my cry of denial. I wanted to say that of course I had not known. But it was not true. I had known, as any young woman would have known, from the way he had looked at me, from the way that I

had responded to him. From the very first moment that I met him there was this undercurrent between us. I ignored it. I pretended it was something easier than it was, I deployed it. I have been most at fault.

In my vanity, I thought that I was encouraging an old man to think of me kindly, that I could engage him, delight him, even flirt with him, first as a fond father-in-law and then to prevail upon him to marry me to Harry. I had meant to delight him as a daughter, I had wanted him to admire me, to pet me. I wanted him to dote on me.

This is a sin, a sin. This is a sin of vanity and a sin of pride. I have deployed his lust and covetousness. I have led him to sin through my folly. No wonder God has turned His face from me and my mother never writes to me. I am most wrong.

Dear God, I am a fool, and a childish, vain fool at that. I have not lured the king into a trap of my own satisfaction, but merely baited his trap for me. My vanity and pride in myself made me think that I could tempt him to do whatever I want. Instead, I have tempted him only to his own desires, and now he will do what he wants. And what he wants is me. And it is my own stupid fault.

'You must have known.' Henry smiled down at her confidently. 'You must have known when I came to see you yesterday, and when I sent you the good wine?'

Catalina gave a little nod. She had known something – fool that she was – she had known something was happening; and praised her own diplomatic skills for being so clever as to lead the King of England by the nose. She had thought herself a woman of the world and thought her ambassador an idiot for not achieving this outcome from a king who was so easily manipulated. She had thought she had the King of England dancing to her bidding, when in fact he had his own tune in mind.

'I desired you from the moment I first saw you,' he told her, his voice very low.

She looked up. 'You did?'

'Truly. When I came into your bedchamber at Dogmersfield.'

She remembered an old man, travel-stained and lean, the father of the man she would marry. She remembered the sweaty male scent as he forced his way into her bedroom and she remembered standing before him and thinking: what a clown, what a rough soldier to push in where he is not wanted. And then Arthur arrived, his blond hair tousled, and with the brightness of his shy smile.

'Oh yes,' she said. From somewhere deep inside her own resolution, she found a smile. 'I remember. I danced for you.'

Henry drew her a little closer and slid his arm around her waist. Catalina forced herself not to pull away. 'I watched you,' he said. 'I longed for you.'

'But you were married,' Catalina said primly.

'And now I am widowed and so are you,' he said. He felt the stiffness of her body through the hard boning of the stomacher and let her go. He would have to court her slowly, he thought. She might have flirted with him, but now she was startled by the turn that things had taken. She had come from an absurdly sheltered upbringing and her innocent months with Arthur had hardly opened her eyes at all. He would have to take matters slowly with her. He would have to wait until she had permission from Spain, he would leave the ambassador to tell her of the wealth she might command, he would have to let her women urge the benefits of the match upon her. She was a young woman, by nature and experience she was bound to be a fool. He would have to give her time.

'I will leave you now,' he said. 'I will come again tomorrow.'

She nodded, and walked with him to the door of her privy chamber. There she hesitated. 'You mean it?' she asked him, her blue eyes suddenly anxious. 'You mean this as a proposal of marriage, not as a feint in a negotiation? You truly want to marry me? I will be queen?'

He nodded. 'I mean it.' The depth of her ambition began to dawn on him and he smiled as he slowly saw the way to her. 'Do you want to be queen so very much?'

Catalina nodded. 'I was brought up to it,' she said. 'I want nothing more.' She hesitated, for a moment she almost thought to tell him that it had been the last thought of his son, but then her passion for Arthur was too great for her to share him with anyone, even his father. And besides, Arthur had planned that she should marry Harry.

The king was smiling. 'So you don't have desire, but you do have ambition,' he observed a little coldly.

'It is nothing more than my due,' she said flatly. 'I was born to be a queen.'

He took her hand and bent over it. He kissed her fingers; and he stopped himself from licking them. 'Take it slowly,' he warned himself. 'This is a girl and possibly a virgin; certainly not a whore.' He straightened up. 'I shall make you Katherine of Aragon, Queen of England,' he promised her, and saw her blue eyes darken with desire at the title. 'We can marry as soon as we have the dispensation from the Pope.'

Think! Think! I urgently command myself. You were not raised by a fool to be a fool, you were raised by a queen to be a queen. If this is a feint you ought to be able to see it. If it is a true offer you ought to be able to turn it to your advantage.

It is not a true fulfilment of the promise I made to my beloved but it is close. He wanted me to be Queen of England and to have the children that he would have given me. So what if they will be his half-brother and half-sister rather than his niece and nephew? That makes no difference.

I shrink from the thought of marrying this old man, old enough to be my father. The skin at his neck is fine and loose, like that of a turtle. I cannot imagine being in bed with him. His breath is sour, an old man's breath; and he is thin, and he will feel bony at the hips and shoulders. But I shrink from the thought of being in bed with that child Harry. His face is as smooth and as rounded as a little girl's. In truth, I cannot bear the thought of being anyone's wife but Arthur's; and that part of my life has gone.

Think! Think! This might be the very right thing to do.

Oh God, beloved, I wish you were here to tell me. I wish I could just visit you in the garden for you to tell me what I should do. I am only seventeen, I cannot outwit a man old enough to be my father, a king with a nose for pretenders.

Think!

I will have no help from anyone. I have to think alone.

Dona Elvira waited until the princess's bedtime and until all the maids-in-waiting, the ladies and the grooms of the bedchamber had withdrawn. She closed the door on them all and then turned to the princess, who was seated in her bed, her hair in a neat plait, her pillows plumped behind her.

'What did the king want?' she demanded without ceremony.

'He proposed marriage to me,' Catalina said bluntly in reply. 'For himself.'

For a moment the duenna was too stunned to speak then she crossed herself, as a woman seeing something unclean. 'God save us,' was all she said. Then: 'God forgive him for even thinking it.'

'God forgive you,' Catalina replied smartly. 'I am considering it.'

'He is your father-in-law, and old enough to be your father.'

'His age doesn't matter,' Catalina said truly. 'If I go back to Spain they won't seek a young husband for me but an advantageous one.'

'But he is the father of your husband.'

Catalina nipped her lips together. 'My late husband,' she said bleakly. 'And the marriage was not consummated.'

Dona Elvira swallowed the lie; but her eyes flicked away, just once.

'As you remember,' Catalina said smoothly.

'Even so! It is against nature!'

'It is not against nature,' Catalina asserted. 'There was no consummation of the betrothal, there was no child. So there can be no sin against nature. And anyway, we can get a dispensation.'

Dona Elvira hesitated. 'You can?'

'He says so.'

'Princess, you cannot want this?'

The princess's little face was bleak. 'He will not betroth me to Prince Harry,' she said. 'He says the boy is too young. I cannot wait four years until he is grown. So what can I do but marry the king? I was born to be Queen of England and mother of the next King of England. I have to fulfil my destiny, it is my God-given destiny. I thought I would have to force myself to take Prince Harry. Now it seems I shall have to force myself to take the king. Perhaps this is God testing me. But my will is strong. I will be Queen of England, and the mother of the king. I shall make this country a fortress against the Moors, as I promised my mother, I shall make it a country of justice and fairness defended against the Scots, as I promised Arthur.'

'I don't know what your mother will think,' the duenna said. 'I should not have left you alone with him, if I had known.'

Catalina nodded. 'Don't leave us alone again.' She paused. 'Unless I nod to you,' she said. 'I may nod for you to leave, and then you must go.'

The duenna was shocked. 'He should not even see you before your wedding day. I shall tell the ambassador that he must tell the king that he cannot visit you at all now.'

Catalina shook her head. 'We are not in Spain now,' she said fiercely. 'D'you still not see it? We cannot leave this to the ambassador, not even my mother can say what shall happen. I shall have to make this happen. I alone have brought it so far, and I alone will make it happen.'

I hoped to dream of you, but I dreamed of nothing. I feel as if you have gone far, far away. I have no letter from my mother so I don't know what she will make of the king's wish. I pray, but I hear nothing from God. I speak very bravely of my destiny and God's will but they feel now quite intertwined. If God does not make me Queen of England then I do not know how I can believe in Him. If I am not Queen of England then I do not know what I am.

Catalina waited for the king to visit her as he had promised. He did not come the next day but Catalina was sure he would come the day after. When three days had elapsed she walked on her own by the river, chafing her hands in the shelter of her cloak. She had been so sure that he would come again that she had prepared herself to keep him interested, but under her control. She planned to lead him on, to keep him dancing at arm's length. When he did not come she realised that she was anxious to see him. Not for desire – she thought she would never feel desire again – but because he was her only way to the throne of England. When he did not come, she was mortally afraid that he had had second thoughts, and he would not come at all.

'Why is he not coming?' I demand of the little waves on the river, washing against the bank as a boatman rows by. 'Why would he come so passionate and earnest one day, and then not come at all?'

267

I am so fearful of his mother, she has never liked me and if she turns her face from me, I don't know that he will go ahead. But then I remember that he said that his mother had given her permission. Then I am afraid that the Spanish ambassador might have said something against the match – but I cannot believe that de Puebla would ever say anything to inconvenience the king, even if he failed to serve me.

'Then why is he not coming?' I ask myself. 'If he was courting in the English way, all rush and informality, then surely he would come every day?'

Another day went past, and then another. Finally, Catalina gave way to her anxiety and sent the king a message at his court, hoping that he was well.

Dona Elvira said nothing, but her stiff back as she supervised the brushing and powdering of Catalina's gown that night spoke volumes.

'I know what you are thinking,' Catalina said, as the duenna waved the maid of the wardrobe from the room and turned to brush Catalina's hair. 'But I cannot risk losing this chance.'

'I am thinking nothing,' the older woman said coldly. 'These are English ways. As you tell me, we cannot now abide by decent Spanish ways. And so, I am not qualified to speak. Clearly, my advice is not taken. I am an empty vessel.'

Catalina was too worried to soothe the older woman. 'It doesn't matter what you are,' she said distractedly. 'Perhaps he will come tomorrow.'

Henry, seeing her ambition as the key to her, had given the girl a few days to consider her position. He thought she might compare the life she led at Durham House, in seclusion with her little Spanish court, her furniture becoming more shabby and no new gowns, with the life she might lead as a young queen at the head of one of the richest courts in Europe. He thought she had the sense to think that through on her own. When he received a note from her, inquiring as to his health, he knew that he had been right; and the next day he rode down the Strand to visit her.

Her porter who kept the gate said that the princess was in the garden, walking with her ladies by the river. Henry went through the back door of the palace to the terrace, and down the steps through the garden. He saw her by the river, walking alone, ahead of her ladies, her head slightly bowed in thought, and he felt an old, familiar sensation in his belly at the sight of a woman he desired. It made him feel young again, that deep pang of lust, and he smiled at himself for feeling a young man's passion, for knowing again a young man's folly.

His page, running ahead, announced him and he saw her head jerk up at his name and she looked across the lawn and saw him. He smiled, he was waiting for that moment of recognition between a woman and a man who loves her – the moment when their eyes meet and they both know that intense moment of joy, that moment when the eyes say: 'Ah, it is you,' and that is everything.

Instead, like a dull blow, he saw at once that there was no leap of her heart at the sight of him. He was smiling shyly, his face lit up with anticipation; but she, in the first moment of surprise, was nothing more than startled. Unprepared, she did not feign emotion, she did not look like a woman in love. She looked up, she saw him – and he could tell at once that she did not love him. There was no shock of delight. Instead, chillingly, he saw a swift expression of calculation cross her face. She was a girl in an unguarded moment, wondering if she could have her own way. It was the look of a huckster, pricing a fool ready for fleecing. Henry, the father of two selfish girls, recognised it in a moment, and knew that whatever the princess might say, however sweetly she might say it, this would be a marriage of convenience to her, whatever it was to him. And more than that, he knew that she had made up her mind to accept him.

He walked across the close-scythed grass towards her and took her hand. 'Good day, Princess.'

Catalina curtseyed. 'Your Grace.'

She turned her head to her ladies. 'You can go inside.' To Dona Elvira she said, 'See that there are refreshments for His Grace when we come in.' Then she turned back to him. 'Will you walk, sire?'

'You will make a very elegant queen,' he said with a smile. 'You command very smoothly.'

He saw her hesitate in her stride and the tension leave her slim young body as she exhaled. 'Ah, you mean it then,' she breathed. 'You mean to marry me.'

'I do,' he said. 'You will be a most beautiful Queen of England.'

She glowed at the thought of it. 'I still have many English ways to learn.'

'My mother will teach you,' he said easily. 'You will live at court in her rooms and under her supervision.'

Catalina checked a little in her stride. 'Surely I will have my own rooms, the queen's rooms?'

'My mother is occupying the queen's rooms,' he said. 'She moved in after the death of the late queen, God bless her. And you will join her there. She thinks that you are too young as yet to have your own rooms and a separate court. You can live in my mother's rooms with her ladies and she can teach you how things are done.'

He could see that she was troubled, but trying hard not to show it.

'I should think I know how things are done in a royal palace,' Catalina said, trying to smile.

'An English palace,' he said firmly. 'Fortunately my mother has run all my palaces and castles and managed my fortune since I came to the throne. She shall teach you how it is done.'

Catalina closed her lips on her disagreement. 'When do you think we will hear from the Pope?' she asked.

'I have sent an emissary to Rome to inquire,' Henry said. 'We shall have to apply jointly, your parents and myself. But it should be resolved very quickly. If we are all agreed, there can be no real objection.'

'Yes,' she said.

'And we are completely agreed on marriage?' he confirmed.

'Yes,' she said again.

He took her hand and tucked it into his arm. Catalina walked a little closer and let her head brush against his shoulder. She was not wearing a headdress, only the hood of her cape covered her hair, and the movement pushed it back. He could smell the essence of roses on her hair, he could feel the warmth of her head against his shoulder. He had to stop himself from taking her in his arms. He paused and she stood close to him; he could feel the warmth of her, down the whole length of his body.

'Catalina,' he said, his voice very low and thick.

She stole a glance and saw desire in his face, and she did not step away. If anything, she came a little closer. 'Yes, Your Grace?' she whispered.

Her eyes were downcast but slowly, in the silence, she looked up at him. When her face was upturned to his, he could not resist the unstated invitation, he bent and kissed her on the lips.

There was no shrinking, she took his kiss, her mouth yielded under his, he could taste her, his arms came around her, he pressed her towards him, he could feel his desire for her rising in him so strongly that he had to let her go, that minute, or disgrace himself.

He released her and stood shaking with desire so strong that he could not believe its power as it washed through him. Catalina pulled her hood forwards as if she would be veiled from him, as if she were a girl from a harem with a veil hiding her mouth, only dark, promising eyes showing above the mask. That gesture, so foreign, so secretive, made him long to push back her hood and kiss her again. He reached for her.

'We might be seen,' she said coolly, and stepped back from him. 'We can be seen from the house, and anyone can go by on the river.'

Henry let her go. He could say nothing, for he knew his voice would tremble. Silently, he offered her his arm once more, and silently she took it. They fell into pace with each other, he tempering his longer stride to her steps. They walked in silence for a few moments.

'Our children will be your heirs?' she confirmed, her voice cool and steady, following a train of thought very far from his own whirl of sensations.

He cleared his throat. 'Yes, yes, of course.'

'That is the English tradition?'

'Yes.'

'They will come before your other children?'

'Our son will inherit before the Princesses Margaret and Mary,' he said. 'But our daughters would come after them.'

She frowned a little. 'How so? Why would they not come before?'

'It is first on sex, and then on age,' he said. 'The first-born boy inherits, then other boys, then girls according to age. Please God there is always a prince to inherit. England has no tradition of ruling queens.'

'A ruling queen can command as well as a king,' said the daughter of Isabella of Castile.

'Not in England,' said Henry Tudor.

She left it at that. 'But our oldest son would be king when you died,' she pursued.

'Please God I have some years left,' he said wryly.

She was seventeen, she had no sensitivity about age. 'Of course. But when you die, if we had a son, he would inherit?'

'No. The king after me will be Prince Harry, the Prince of Wales.'

She frowned. 'I thought you could nominate an heir? Can you not make it our son?'

He shook his head. 'Harry is Prince of Wales. He will be king after me.'

'I thought he was to go into the church?'

'Not now.'

'But if we have a son? Can you not make Harry king of your French dominions, or Ireland, and make our son King of England?'

Henry laughed shortly. 'No. For that would be to destroy my kingdom, which I have had some trouble to win and to keep together. Harry will have it all by right.' He saw she was disturbed. 'Catalina, you will be Queen of England, one of the finest kingdoms of Europe, the place your mother and father chose for you. Your sons and daughters will be princes and princesses of England. What more could you want?'

'I want my son to be king,' she answered him frankly.

He shrugged. 'It cannot be.'

She turned away slightly, only his grip on her hand kept her close.

He tried to laugh it off. 'Catalina, we are not even married yet. You might not even have a son. We need not spoil our betrothal for a child not yet conceived.'

'Then what would be the point of marriage?' she asked, direct in her self-absorption.

He could have said 'desire'. 'Destiny, so that you shall be queen.'

She would not let it go. 'I had thought to be Queen of England and see my son on the throne,' she repeated. 'I had thought to be a power in the court, like your mother is. I had thought that there are castles to build and a navy to plan and schools and colleges to found. I want to defend against the Scots on our northern borders and against the Moors on our coasts. I want to be a ruling queen in England, these are things I have planned and hoped for. I was named as the next Queen of England almost in my cradle, I have thought about the kingdom I would reign, I have made plans. There are many things that I want to do.'

He could not help himself, he laughed aloud at the thought of this girl, this child, presuming to make plans for the ruling of his kingdom. 'You will find that I am before you,' he said bluntly. 'This kingdom shall be run as the king commands. This kingdom is run as I command. I did not fight my way to the crown to hand it over to a girl young enough to be my daughter. Your task will be to fill the royal nurseries and your world will start and stop there.'

'But your mother . . .'

'You will find my mother guards her domains as I guard mine,' he said, still chuckling at the thought of this child planning her future at his court. 'She will command you as a daughter and you will obey. Make no mistake about it, Catalina. You will come into my court and obey me, you will live in my mother's rooms and obey her. You will be Queen of England and have the crown on your head. But you will be my wife, and I will have an obedient wife as I have always done.'

He stopped, he did not want to frighten her, but his desire for her was not greater than his determination to hold this kingdom that he had fought so hard to win. 'I am not a child like Arthur,' he said to her quietly, thinking that his son, a gentle boy, might have made all sorts of soft promises to a determined young wife. 'You will not rule beside me. You will be a child-bride to me. I shall love you and make you happy. I swear you will be glad that you married me. I shall be kind to you. I shall be generous to you. I shall give you anything you want. But I shall not make you a ruler. Even at my death you will not rule my country.'

That night I dreamed that I was a queen in a court with a sceptre in one hand and wand in the other and a crown on my head. I raised the sceptre and found it changed in my hand, it was a branch of a

tree, the stem of a flower, it was valueless. My other hand was no longer filled with the heavy orb of the sceptre, but with rose petals. I could smell their scent. I put my hand up to touch the crown on my head and I felt a little circlet of flowers. The throne room melted away and I was in the sultana's garden at the Alhambra, my sisters plaiting circlets of daisies for each other's heads.

'Where is the Queen of England?' someone called from the terrace below the garden.

I rose from the lawn of camomile flowers and smelled the bitter-sweet perfume of the herb as I tried to run past the fountain to the archway at the end of the garden. 'I am here!' I tried to call, but I made no noise above the splashing of the water in the marble bowl.

'Where is the Queen of England?' I heard them call again.

'I am here!' I called out silently.

'Where is Queen Katherine of England?'

'Here! Here! Here!'

The ambassador, summoned at daybreak to come at once to Durham House, did not trouble himself to get there until nine o'clock. He found Catalina waiting for him in her privy chamber with only Dona Elvira in attendance.

'I sent for you hours ago,' the princess said crossly.

'I was undertaking business for your father and could not come earlier,' he said smoothly, ignoring the sulky look on her face. 'Is there something wrong?'

'I spoke with the king yesterday and he repeated his proposal of marriage,' Catalina said, a little pride in her voice.

'Indeed.'

'But he told me that I would live at court in the rooms of his mother.'

'Oh.' The ambassador nodded.

'And he said that my sons would inherit only after Prince Harry.'

The ambassador nodded again.

'Can we not persuade him to overlook Prince Harry? Can we not draw up a marriage contract to set him aside in favour of my son?'

The ambassador shook his head. 'It's not possible.'

'Surely, a man can choose his heir?'

'No. Not in the case of a king come so new to his throne. Not an English king. And even if he could, he would not.'

She leapt from her chair and paced to the window. 'My son will be the grandson of the kings of Spain!' she exclaimed. 'Royal for centuries. Prince Harry is nothing more than the son of Elizabeth of York and a successful pretender.'

De Puebla gave a little hiss of horror at her bluntness and glanced towards the door. 'You would do better never to call him that. He is the King of England.'

She nodded, accepting the reprimand. 'But he has not my breeding,' she pursued. 'Prince Harry would not be the king that my boy would be.'

'That is not the question,' the ambassador observed. 'The question is of time and practice. The king's oldest son is always the Prince of Wales. He always inherits the throne. This king, of all the kings in the world, is not going to make a pretender of his own legitimate heir. He has been dogged with pretenders. He is not going to make another.'

As always, Catalina flinched at the thought of the last pretender, Edward of Warwick, beheaded to make way for her.

'Besides,' the ambassador continued, 'any king would rather have a sturdy eleven-year-old son as his heir than a new-born in the cradle. These are dangerous times. A man wants to leave a man to inherit, not a child.'

'If my son is not to be king, then what is the point of me marrying a king?' Catalina demanded.

'You would be queen,' the ambassador pointed out.

'What sort of a queen would I be with My Lady the King's Mother ruling everything? The king would not let me have my way in the kingdom, and she would not let me have my way in the court.'

'You are very young,' he started, trying to soothe her.

'I am old enough to know my own mind,' Catalina stated. 'And I want to be queen in truth as well as in name. But he will never let me be that, will he?'

'No,' de Puebla admitted. 'You will never command while he is alive.'

'And when he is dead?' she demanded, without shrinking.

'Then you would be the Dowager Queen,' de Puebla offered.

'And my parents might marry me once more to someone else, and I might leave England anyway!' she finished, quite exasperated.

'It is possible,' he conceded.

'And Harry's wife would be Princess of Wales, and Harry's wife would be the new queen. She would go before me, she would rule in my place, and all my sacrifice would be for nothing. And her sons would be Kings of England.'

'That is true.'

Catalina threw herself into her chair. 'Then I have to be Prince Harry's wife,' she said. 'I have to be.'

De Puebla was quite horrified. 'I understood you had agreed with the king to marry him! He gave me to believe that you were agreed.'

'I had agreed to be queen,' she said, white-faced with determination. 'Not some cat's-paw. D'you know what he called me? He said I would be his child-bride, and I would live in his mother's rooms, as if I were one of her ladies-in-waiting!'

'The former queen . . .'

'The former queen was a saint to put up with a mother-in-law like that one. She stepped back all her life. I can't do it. It is not what I want, it is not what my mother wants, and it is not what God wants.'

'But if you have agreed . . .'

'When has any agreement been honoured in this country?' Catalina demanded fiercely. 'We will break this agreement and make another. We will break this promise and make another. I shall not marry the king, I shall marry another.'

'Who?' he asked numbly.

'Prince Harry, the Prince of Wales,' she said. 'So that when King Henry dies I shall be queen in deed as well as name.'

There was a short silence.

'So you say,' said de Puebla slowly. 'Perhaps. But who is going to tell the king?'

God, if You are there, tell me that I am doing the right thing. If You are there, then help me. If it is Thy will that I am Queen of England, then I will need help to achieve it. It has all gone wrong now, and if this has been sent to try me, then see! I am on my knees and shaking with anxiety. If I am indeed blessed by You, destined by You, chosen by You, and favoured by You, then why do I feel so hopelessly alone?

Ambassador Dr de Puebla found himself in the uncomfortable position of having to bring bad news to one of the most powerful and irascible kings in Christendom. He had firm letters of refusal from Their Majesties of Spain in his hand, he had Catalina's determination to be Princess of Wales, and he had his own shrinking courage, screwed up to the tightest point for this embarrassing meeting.

The king had chosen to see him in the stable yard of Whitehall Palace, he was there looking at a consignment of new Barbary horses, brought in to improve English stock. De Puebla thought of making a graceful reference to foreign blood refreshing native strains, breeding best done between young animals; but he saw Henry's dark face and realised that there would be no easy way out of this dilemma.

'Your Grace,' he said, bowing low.

'De Puebla,' the king said shortly.

'I have a reply from Their Majesties of Spain to your most flattering proposal; but perhaps I should see you at a more opportune time?'

'Here is well enough. I can imagine from your tiptoeing in what they say.'

'The truth is . . .' de Puebla prepared to lie. 'They want their daughter home, and they cannot contemplate her marriage to you. The queen is particularly vehement in her refusal.'

'Because?' the king inquired.

'Because she wants to see her daughter, her youngest, sweetest daughter, matched to a prince of her own age. It is a woman's whim –' The diplomat made a little diffident gesture. 'Only a woman's whim. But we have to recognise a mother's wishes, don't we? Your Grace?'

'Not necessarily,' the king said unhelpfully. 'But what does the Dowager Princess say? I thought that she and I had an understanding. She can tell her mother of her preference.' The king's eyes were on the Arab stallion, walking proud-headed around the yard, his ears flickering backwards and forwards, his tail held high, his neck arched like a bow. 'I imagine she can speak for herself.'

'She says that she will obey you, as ever, Your Grace,' de Puebla said tactfully.

'And?'

'But she has to obey her mother.' He fell back at the sudden hard glance that the king threw at him. 'She is a good daughter, Your Grace. She is an obedient daughter to her mother.'

'I have proposed marriage to her and she has indicated that she would accept.'

'She would never refuse a king such as you. How could she? But

279

if her parents do not consent, they will not apply for dispensation. Without dispensation from the Pope, there can be no marriage.'

'I understand that her marriage was not consummated. We barely need a dispensation. It is a courtesy, a formality.'

'We all know that it was not consummated,' de Puebla hastily confirmed. 'The princess is a maid still, fit for marriage. But all the same the Pope would have to grant a dispensation. If Their Majesties of Spain do not apply for such a dispensation, then what can anyone do?'

The king turned a dark, hard gaze on the Spanish ambassador. 'I don't know, now. I thought I knew what we would do. But now I am misled. You tell me. What can anyone do?'

The ambassador drew on the enduring courage of his race, his secret Jewishness which he held to his heart in the worst moments of his life. He knew that he and his people would always, somehow, survive.

'Nothing can be done,' he said. He attempted a sympathetic smile and felt that he was smirking. He rearranged his face into the gravest expression. 'If the Queen of Spain will not apply for dispensation there is nothing that can be done. And she is inveterate.'

'I am not one of Spain's neighbours to be overrun in a spring campaign,' the king said shortly. 'I am no Granada. I am no Navarre. I do not fear her displeasure.'

'Which is why they long for your alliance,' de Puebla said smoothly.

'An alliance how?' the king asked coldly. 'I thought they were refusing me?'

'Perhaps we could avoid all this difficulty by celebrating another marriage,' the diplomat said carefully, watching Henry's dark face. 'A new marriage. To create the alliance we all want.'

'To whom?'

At the banked-down anger in the king's face the ambassador lost his words.

'Sire . . . I . . .'

'Who do they want for her now? Now that my son, the rose, is dead and buried? Now she is a poor widow with only half her dowry paid, living on my charity?'

'The prince,' de Puebla plunged in. 'She was brought to the kingdom to be Princess of Wales. She was brought here to be wife to the prince, and later – much later, please God – to be queen. Perhaps that is her destiny, Your Grace. She thinks so, certainly.'

'She thinks!' the king exclaimed. 'She thinks like that filly thinks! Nothing beyond the next minute.'

'She is young,' the ambassador said. 'But she will learn. And the prince is young, they will learn together.'

'And we old men have to stand back, do we? She has told you of no preference, no particular liking for me? Though she gave me clearly to understand that she would marry me? She shows no regret at this turn around? She is not tempted to defy her parents and keep her freely given word to me?'

The ambassador heard the bitterness in the old man's voice. 'She is allowed no choice,' he reminded the king. 'She has to do as she is bidden by her parents. I think, for herself, there was an attraction, perhaps even a powerful attraction. But she knows she has to go where she is bid.'

'I thought to marry her! I would have made her queen! She would have been Queen of England.' He almost choked on the title, all his life he had thought it the greatest honour that a woman could think of, just as his title was the greatest in his own imagination.

The ambassador paused for a moment to let the king recover.

'You know, there are other, equally beautiful young ladies in her family,' he suggested carefully. 'The young Queen of Naples is a widow now. As King Ferdinand's niece, she would bring a good dowry, and she has the family likeness.' He hesitated. 'She is said to be very lovely, and –' He paused. 'Amorous.'

'She gave me to understand that she loved me. Am I now to think her a pretender?'

The ambassador felt a cold sweat which seeped from every pore of his body at that dreadful word. 'No pretender,' he said, his smile quite ghastly. 'A loving daughter-in-law, an affectionate girl . . .'

There was an icy silence.

'You know how pretenders fare in this country,' the king said stiffly.

'Yes! But . . .'

'She will regret it, if she plays with me.'

'No play! No pretence! Nothing!'

The king let the ambassador stand, slightly shaking with anxiety.

'I thought to finish this whole difficulty with the dowry and the jointure,' Henry remarked, at length.

'And so it can be. Once the princess is betrothed to the prince, then Spain will pay the second half of the dowry and the widow's jointure is no more,' de Puebla assured him. He noticed he was talking too rapidly, took a breath, and went slower. 'All difficulties are finished. Their Majesties of Spain would be glad to apply for dispensation for their daughter to marry Prince Harry. It would be a good match for her and she will do as she is ordered. It leaves you free to look around for your wife, Your Grace, and it frees the revenues of Cornwall and Wales and Chester to your own disposal once more.'

King Henry shrugged his shoulders and turned from the schooling ring and the horse. 'So it is over?' he asked coldly. 'She does not desire me, as I thought she did. I mistook her attention to me. She meant to be nothing but filial?' He laughed harshly at the thought of her kiss by the river. 'I must forget my desire for her?'

'She has to obey her parents as a Princess of Spain,' de Puebla reminded him. 'On her own account, I know there was a preference. She told me so herself.' He thought that Catalina's double-dealing could be covered by this. 'She is disappointed, to tell you the truth.

282

But her mother is adamant. I cannot deny the Queen of Castile. She is utterly determined to have her daughter returned to Spain, or married to Prince Harry. She will brook no other suggestion.'

'So be it,' said the king, his voice like ice. 'I had a foolish dream, a desire. It can finish here.'

He turned and walked away from the stable yard, his pleasure in his horses soured.

'I hope that there is no ill feeling?' the ambassador asked, hobbling briskly behind him.

'None at all,' the king threw over his shoulder. 'None in the world.'

'And the betrothal with Prince Harry? May I assure Their Catholic Majesties that it will go ahead?'

'Oh, at once. I shall make it my first and foremost office.'

'I do hope there is no offence?' de Puebla called to the king's retreating back.

The king turned on his heel and faced the Spanish ambassador, his clenched fists on his hips, his shoulders square. 'She has tried to play me like a fool,' he said through thin lips. 'I don't thank her for it. Her parents have tried to lead me by the nose. I think they will find that they have a dragon, not one of their baited bulls. I won't forget this. You Spaniards, you will not forget it either. And she will regret the day she tried to lead me on as if I were a lovesick boy, as I regret it now.'

'It is agreed,' de Puebla said flatly to Catalina. He was standing before her – 'Like an errand boy!' he thought indignantly – as she was ripping the velvet panels out of a gown to re-model the dress.

'I am to marry Prince Harry,' she said in a tone as dull as his own. 'Has he signed anything?'

'He has agreed. He has to wait for a dispensation. But he has agreed.'

She looked up at him. 'Was he very angry?'

'I think he was even angrier than he showed me. And what he showed me was bad.'

'What will he do?' she asked.

He scrutinised her pale face. She was white but she was not fearful. Her blue eyes were veiled as her father's were veiled when he was planning something. She did not look like a damsel in distress, she looked like a woman trying to outwit a most dangerous protagonist. She was not endearing, as a woman in tears would have been endearing, he thought. She was formidable; but not pleasing.

'I don't know what he will do,' he said. 'His nature is vengeful. But we must give him no advantage. We have to pay your dowry at once. We have to complete our side of the contract to force him to complete his.'

'The plate has lost its value,' she said flatly. 'It is damaged by use. And I have sold some.'

He gasped. 'You have sold it? It is the king's own!'

She shrugged. 'I have to eat, Dr de Puebla. We cannot all go uninvited to court and thrust our way in to the common table. I am not living well, but I do have to live. And I have nothing to live on but my goods.'

'You should have preserved them intact!'

She shrugged 'I should never have been reduced to this. I have had to pawn my own plate to live. Whoever is to blame, it is not me.'

'Your father will have to pay the dowry and pay you an allowance,' he said grimly. 'We must give them no excuse to withdraw. If your dowry is not paid he will not marry you to the prince. Infanta, I must warn you, he will revel in your discomfort. He will prolong it.'

Catalina nodded. 'He is my enemy too then.'

'I fear it.'

'It will happen, you know,' she said inconsequentially.

'What?'

'I will marry Harry. I will be queen.'

'Infanta, it is my dearest wish.'

'Princess,' she replied.

Whitehall, June 1503

'You are to be betrothed to Catalina of Aragon,' the king told his son, thinking of the son who had gone before.

The blond boy flushed as pink as a girl. 'Yes, sire.'

He had been coached perfectly by his grandmother. He was prepared for everything but real life.

'Don't think the marriage will happen,' the king warned him.

The boy's eyes flashed up in surprise and were then cast down again. 'No?'

'No. They have robbed us and cheated us at every turn, they have rolled us over like a bawd in a tavern. They have cozened us and promised one thing after another like a cock-teaser in drink. They say –' He broke off, his son's wide-eyed gaze reminding him that he had spoken as a man to a man, and this was a boy. Also, his resentment should not show, however fiercely it burned.

'They have taken advantage of our friendship,' he summed up. 'And now we will take advantage of their weakness.'

'Surely we are all friends?'

Henry grimaced, thinking of that scoundrel Ferdinand, and of his daughter, the cool beauty who had turned him down. 'Oh, yes,' he said. 'Loyal friends.'

'So I am to be betrothed and later, when I am fifteen, we will be married?'

The boy had understood nothing. So be it. 'Say sixteen.'

'Arthur was fifteen.'

Henry bit down the reply that much good it had done Arthur. Besides, it did not matter since it would never happen. 'Oh, yes,' he said again. 'Fifteen, then.'

The boy knew that something was wrong. His smooth forehead was furrowed. 'We do mean this, don't we, Father? I would not mislead such a princess. It is a most solemn oath I will make?'

'Oh, yes,' the king said again.

The night before my betrothal to Prince Harry, I have a dream so lovely that I do not want to wake. I am in the garden of the Alhambra, walking with my hand in Arthur's, laughing up at him, and showing him the beauty around us: the great sandstone wall which encircles the fort, the city of Granada below us and the mountains capped with silvery snow on the horizon.

'I have won,' I say to him. 'I have done everything you wanted, everything that we planned. I will be princess as you made me. I will be queen as you wanted me to be. My mother's wishes are fulfilled, my own destiny will be complete, your desire and God's will. Are you happy now, my love?'

He smiles down at me, his eyes warm, his face tender, a smile he has only for me. 'I shall watch over you,' he whispers. 'All the time. Here in al-Yanna.'

I hesitate at the odd sound of the word on his lips, and then I realise that he has used the Moorish word: 'al-Yanna', which means both heaven, a cemetery, and a garden. For the Moors, heaven is a garden, an eternal garden.

'I shall come to you one day,' I whisper, even as his grasp on my hand becomes lighter, and then fades, though I try to hold him. 'I shall be with you again, my love. I shall meet you here in the garden.'

'I know,' he says, and now his face is melting away like mist in the morning, like a mirage in the hot air of the sierra. 'I know we will be together again, Catalina, my Katherine, my love.'

25th June 1503

It was a bright, hot June day. Catalina was dressed in a new gown of blue with a blue hood, the eleven-year-old boy opposite her was radiant with excitement, dressed in cloth of gold.

They were before the Bishop of Salisbury with a small court present: the king, his mother, the Princess Mary, and a few other witnesses. Catalina put her cold hand in the prince's warm palm and felt the plumpness of childhood beneath her fingers.

Catalina looked beyond the flushed boy to his father's grave face. The king had aged in the months since the death of his wife, and the lines in his face were more deeply grooved, his eyes shadowed. Men at the court said he was sick, some illness which was thinning his blood and wearing him out. Others said that he was sour with disappointment: at the loss of his heir, at the loss of his wife, at the frustration of his plans. Some said he had been crossed in love, outwitted by a woman. Only that could have unmanned him so bitterly.

Catalina smiled shyly at him, but there was no echoing warmth from the man who would be her father-in-law for the second time, but had wanted her for his own. For a moment, her confidence dimmed. She had allowed herself to hope that the king had surrendered to her determination, to her mother's ruling, to God's will. Now, seeing his cold look, she had a moment of fear that perhaps this ceremony – even something as serious and sacred as a betrothal – might perhaps be nothing more than a revenge by this most cunning of kings.

287

Chilled, she turned away from him to listen to the bishop recite the words of the marriage service and she repeated her part, making sure not to think of when she had said the words before, only a year and a half ago, when her hand had been cool in the grasp of the most handsome young man she had ever seen, when her bridegroom had given her a shy sideways smile, when she had stared at him through the veil of her mantilla and been aware of the thousands of silently watching faces beyond.

The young prince, who had been dazzled then by the beauty of his sister-in-law the bride, was now the bridegroom. His beam was the boisterous joy of a young boy in the presence of a beautiful older girl. She had been the bride of his older brother, she was the young woman he had been proud to escort on her wedding day. He had begged her for a present of a Barbary horse for his tenth birthday. He had looked at her at her wedding feast and that night prayed that he too might have a Spanish bride just like her.

When she had left the court with Arthur he had dreamed of her, he had written poems and love-songs, secretly dedicating them to her. He had heard of Arthur's death with a bright, fierce joy that now she was free.

Now, not even two years on, she was before him, her hair brushed out bronze and golden over her shoulders signifying her virgin state, her blue lace mantilla veiling her face. Her hand was in his, her blue eyes were on him, her smile was only for him.

Harry's braggart boyish heart swelled so full in his chest that he could scarcely reply to his part of the service. Arthur was gone, and he was Prince of Wales; Arthur was gone, and he was his father's favourite, the rosebush of England. Arthur was gone, and Arthur's bride was his wife. He stood straight and proud and repeated his oaths in his clear treble voice. Arthur was gone, and there was only one Prince of Wales and one Princess: Prince Harry and Princess Katherine.

Princess Again

1504

I may think that I have won; but still I have not won. I should have won; but I have not won. Harry reaches twelve, and they declare him Prince of Wales but they do not come for me, declare our betrothal or invest me as princess. I send for the ambassador. He does not come in the morning, he does not even come that day. He comes the day after, as if my affairs have no urgency, and he does not apologise for his delay. I ask him why I have not been invested as Princess of Wales alongside Harry and he does not know. He suggests that they are waiting for the payment of my dowry and without it, nothing can go ahead. But he knows, and I know, and King Henry knows, that I no longer have all my plate to give to them, and if my father will not send his share, there is nothing I can do.

My mother the queen must know that I am desolate; but I hear from her only rarely. It is as if I am one of her explorers, a solitary Cristóbal Colón with no companions and no maps. She has sent me out into the world and if I tumble off the edge or am lost at sea, there is nothing that anyone can do.

She has nothing to say to me. I fear that she is ashamed of me, as I wait at court like a supplicant for the prince to honour his promise.

In November I am so filled with foreboding that she is ill or sad that I write to her and beg her to reply to me, to send me at least one word. That, as it happens, was the very day that she died and so she never had my letter and I never had my one word. She leaves me in death as she left me in life: to silence and a sense of her absence.

I knew that I would miss her when I left home. But it was a comfort to me to know that the sun still shone in the gardens of the Alhambra, and she was still there beside the green-trimmed pool. I did not know that the loss of her would make my situation in England so much worse. My father, having long refused to pay the second half of my dowry as part of his game with the King of England, now finds his play has become a bitter truth – he cannot pay. He has spent his life and his fortune in ceaseless crusade against the Moors and there is no money left for anyone. The rich revenues of Castile are now paid to Juana, my mother's heir; and my father has nothing in the treasury of Aragon for my marriage. My father is now no more than one of the many kings of Spain. Juana is the great heiress of Castile and, if the gossips are to be believed, Juana has run as mad as a rabid dog, tormented by love and by her husband into insanity. Anyone looking at me now no longer sees a princess of a united Spain, one of the great brides of Christendom; but a widowed pauper with bad blood. Our family fortunes are cascading down like a house of cards without my mother's steady hand and watchful eye. There is nothing left for my father but despair; and that is all the dowry he can give me.

I am only nineteen. Is my life over?

1509

And then, I waited. Incredibly, I waited for a total of six years. Six years when I went from a bride of seventeen to a woman of twenty-three. I knew then that King Henry's rage against me was bitter, and effective, and long-lasting. No princess in the world had ever been made to wait so long, or treated so harshly, or left in such despair. I am not exaggerating this, as a troubadour might do to make a better story – as I might have told you, beloved, in the dark hours of the night. No, it was not like a story, it was not even like a life. It was like a prison sentence, it was like being a hostage with no chance of redemption, it was loneliness, and the slow realisation that I had failed.

I failed my mother and failed to bring to her the alliance with England that I had been born and bred to do. I was ashamed of my failure. Without the dowry payment from Spain I could not force the English to honour the betrothal. With the king's enmity I could force them to do nothing. Harry was a child of thirteen, I hardly ever saw him. I could not appeal to him to make his promise good. I was power-less, neglected by the court and falling into shameful poverty.

Then Harry was fourteen years of age and our betrothal was still not made marriage, and that marriage not celebrated. I waited a year, he reached fifteen years, and nobody came for me. So Harry reached his sixteenth and then his seventeenth birthday, and still nobody came for me. Those years turned. I grew older. I waited. I was constant. It was all I could be.

I turned the panels on my gowns and sold my jewels for food. I had to sell my precious plate, one gold piece at a time. I knew it was the property of the king as I sent for the goldsmiths. I knew that each time I pawned a piece I put my wedding back another day. But I had to eat, my household had to eat. I could pay them no wages, I could hardly ask them to beg for me as well as go hungry on their own account.

I was friendless. I discovered that Dona Elvira was plotting against my father in favour of Juana and her husband Philip and I dismissed her, in a rage, and sent her away. I did not care if she spoke against me, if she named me as a liar. I did not care even if she declared that Arthur and I had been lovers. I had caught her in treason against my father; did she truly think I would ally with my sister against the King of Aragon? I was so angry that I did not care what her enmity cost me.

Also, since I am not a fool, I calculated rightly that no-one would believe her word against mine. She fled to Philip and Juana in the Netherlands, and I never heard from her again, and I never complained of my loss.

I lost my ambassador, Dr de Puebla. I had often complained to my father of his divided loyalties, of his disrespect, of his concessions to the English court. But when he was recalled to Spain I found that he had known more than I had realised, he had used his friendship with the king to my advantage, he had understood his way around this most difficult court. He had been a better friend than I had known, and I was the poorer without him. I lost a friend and an ally, through my own arrogance; and I was sorry for his absence. His replacement: the emissary who had come to take me home, Don Gutierre Gomez de Fuensalida, was a pompous fool who thought the English were honoured by his presence. They sneered at his face and laughed behind his back and I was a ragged princess with an ambassador entranced by his own self-importance.

I lost my dear father in Christ, the confessor I trusted, appointed by my mother to guide me, and I had to find another for myself. I lost the ladies of my little court, who would not live in hardship and poverty, and I could not pay anyone else to serve me. Maria de Salinas stood by me, through all these long years of endurance, for love; but the other ladies wanted to leave. Then, finally, I lost my house, my lovely house on the Strand, which had been my home, a little safe place in this most foreign land.

The king promised me rooms at court and I thought that he had at last forgiven me. I thought he was offering me to come to court, to live in the rooms of a princess and to see Harry. But when I moved my household there I found that I was given the worst rooms, allocated the poorest service, unable to see the prince, except on the most formal of state occasions. One dreadful day, the court left on progress without telling us and we had to dash after them, finding our way down the unmarked country lanes, as unwanted and as irrelevant as a wagon filled with old goods. When we caught up, no-one had noticed that we were missing and I had to take the only rooms left: over the stables, like a servant.

The king stopped paying my allowance, his mother did not press my case. I had no money of my own at all. I lived despised on the fringe of the court, with Spaniards who served me only because they could not leave. They were trapped like me, watching the years slide by, getting older and more resentful till I felt like the sleeping princess of the fairy tale and thought that I would never wake.

I lost my vanity – my proud sense that I could be cleverer than that old fox who was my father-in-law, and that sharp vixen his mother. I learned that he had betrothed me to his son Prince Harry, not because he loved and forgave me, but because it was the cleverest and cruellest way to punish me. If he could not have me, then he could make sure that no-one had me. It was a bitter day when I realised that.

And then, Philip died and my sister Juana was a widow like me, and King Henry came up with a plan to marry her, my poor sister – driven from her wits by the loss of her husband – and put her over me, on the throne of England, where everyone would see that she was crazed, where everyone could see the bad blood which I share, where everyone would know that he had made her queen and thrown me down to nothing. It was a wicked plan, certain to shame and distress both me and Juana. He would have done it if he could, and he made me his pander as well – he forced me to recommend him to my father. Under my father's orders I spoke to the king of Juana's beauty; under the king's orders I urged my father to accept his suit, all the time knowing that I was betraying my very soul. I lost my ability to refuse King Henry my persecutor, my father-in-law, my would-be seducer. I was afraid to say 'no' to him. I was very much reduced, that day.

I lost my vanity in my allure, I lost my confidence in my intelligence and skills; but I never lost my will to live. I was not like my mother, I was not like Juana, I did not turn my face to the wall and long for my pain to be over. I did not slide into the wailing grief of madness nor into the gentle darkness of sloth. I gritted my teeth, I am the constant princess, I don't stop when everyone else stops. I carried on. I waited. Even when I could do nothing else, I could still wait. So I waited.

These were not the years of my defeat; these were the years when I grew up, and it was a bitter maturing. I grew from a girl of sixteen ready for love to a half-orphaned, lonely widow of twenty-three. These were the years when I drew on the happiness of my childhood in the Alhambra and my love for my husband to sustain me, and swore that whatever the obstacles before me, I should be Queen of England. These were the years when, though my mother was dead, she lived again through me. I found her determination inside me, I found her courage inside me, I found Arthur's love and optimism inside me. These were the years when although I had nothing left: no husband, no mother, no friends, no fortune and no prospects; I swore that however disregarded, however poor, however unlikely a prospect, I would still be Queen of England.

News, always slow to reach the bedraggled Spaniards on the fringe of the royal court, filtered through that Harry's sister the Princess Mary was to be married, gloriously, to Prince Charles, son of King Philip and Queen Juana, grandson to both the Emperor Maximilian and King Ferdinand. Amazingly, at this of all moments, King Ferdinand at last found the money for Catalina's dowry, and packed it off to London.

'My God, we are freed. There can be a double wedding. I can marry him,' Catalina said, heartfelt, to the Spanish emissary, Don Gutierre Gomez de Fuensalida.

He was pale with worry, his yellow teeth nipping at his lips. 'Oh, Infanta, I hardly know how to tell you. Even with this alliance, even with the dowry money – dear God, I fear it comes too late. I fear it will not help us at all.'

'How can it be? Princess Mary's betrothal only deepens the alliance with my family.'

'What if . . .' He started and broke off. He could hardly speak of the danger that he foresaw. 'Princess, all the English know that the dowry money is coming, but they do not speak of your marriage. Oh, Princess, what if they plan an alliance that does not include Spain? What if they plan an alliance between the emperor and King Henry? What if the alliance is for them to go to war against Spain?'

She turned her head. 'It cannot be.'

'What if it is?'

'Against the boy's own grandfather?' she demanded.

'It would only be one grandfather, the emperor, against another, your father.'

'They would not,' she said determinedly.

'They could.'

'King Henry would not be so dishonest.'

'Princess, you know that he would.'

She hesitated. 'What is it?' she suddenly demanded, sharp with irritation. 'There is something else. Something you are not telling me. What is it?'

He paused, a lie in his mouth; then he told her the truth. 'I am afraid, I am very afraid, that they will betroth Prince Harry to Princess Eleanor, the sister of Charles.'

'They cannot, he is betrothed to me.'

'They may plan it as part of a great treaty. Your sister Juana to marry the king, your nephew Charles for Princess Mary, and your niece Eleanor for Prince Harry.'

'But what about me? Now that my dowry money is on its way at last?'

He was silent. It was painfully apparent that Catalina was excluded by these alliances, and no provision made for her.

'A true prince has to honour his promise,' she said passionately. 'We were betrothed by a bishop before witnesses, it is a solemn oath.'

The ambassador shrugged, hesitated. He could hardly make himself tell her the worst news of all. 'Your Grace, Princess, be brave. I am afraid he may withdraw his oath.'

'He cannot.'

Fuensalida went further. 'Indeed, I am afraid it is already withdrawn. He may have withdrawn it years ago.'

'What?' she asked sharply. 'How?'

'A rumour, I cannot be sure of it. But I am afraid . . .' He broke off.

'Afraid of what?'

'I am afraid that the prince may be already released from his betrothal to you.' He hesitated at the sudden darkening of her face. 'It will not have been his choice,' he said quickly. 'His father is determined against us.'

'How could he? How can such a thing be done?'

'He could have sworn an oath that he was too young, that he was under duress. He may have declared that he did not want to marry you. Indeed, I think that is what he has done.'

'He was not under duress!' Catalina exclaimed. 'He was utterly delighted. He has been in love with me for years, I am sure he still is. He did want to marry me!'

'An oath sworn before a bishop that he was not acting of his own free will would be enough to secure his release from his promise.'

'So all these years that I have been betrothed to him, and acted on that premise, all these years that I have waited and waited and endured . . .' She could not finish. 'Are you telling me that for all these years, when I believed that we had them tied down, contracted, bound, he has been free?'

The ambassador nodded; her face was so stark and shocked that he could hardly find his voice.

'This is . . . a betrayal,' she said. 'A most terrible betrayal.' She choked on the words. 'This is the worst betrayal of all.'

He nodded again.

There was a long, painful silence. 'I am lost,' she said simply. 'Now I know it. I have been lost for years and I did not know. I have been fighting a battle with no army, with no support. Actually – with no cause. You tell me that I have been defending a cause that was gone long ago. I was fighting for my betrothal but I was not betrothed. I have been all alone, all this long time. And now I know it.'

Still she did not weep, though her blue eyes were horrified.

'I made a promise,' she said, her voice harsh. 'I made a solemn and binding promise.'

'Your betrothal?'

She made a little gesture with her hand. 'Not that. I swore a promise. A deathbed promise. Now you tell me it has all been for nothing.'

'Princess, you have stayed at your post, as your mother would have wanted you to do.'

'I have been made a fool!' burst out of her, from the depth of her shock. 'I have been fighting for the fulfilment of a vow, not knowing that the vow was long broken.'

He could say nothing, her pain was too raw for any soothing words.

After a few moments, she raised her head. 'Does everyone know but me?' she asked bleakly.

He shook his head. 'I am sure it was kept most secret.'

'My Lady the King's Mother,' she predicted bitterly. 'She will have known. It will have been her decision. And the king, the prince himself, and if he knew, then the Princess Mary will know – he would have told her. And his closest companions . . .' She raised her head. 'The king's mother's ladies, the princess's ladies. The bishop that he swore to, a witness or two. Half the court, I suppose.' She paused. 'I thought that at least some of them were my friends,' she said.

The ambassador shrugged. 'In a court there are no friends, only courtiers.'

'My father will defend me from this . . . cruelty!' she burst out. 'They should have thought of that before they treated me so! There will be no treaties for England with Spain when he hears about this. He will take revenge for this abuse of me.'

He could say nothing, and in the still silent face that he turned to her she saw the worst truth.

'No,' she said simply. 'Not him. Not him as well. Not my father. He did not know. He loves me. He would never injure me. He would never abandon me here.'

Still he could not tell her. He saw her take a deep breath.

'Oh. Oh. I see. I see from your silence. Of course. He knows, of course he knows, doesn't he? My father? The dowry money is just another trick. He knows of the proposal to marry Prince Harry to Princess Eleanor. He has been leading the king on to think that he can marry Juana. He ordered me to encourage the king to marry Juana. He will have agreed to this new proposal for Prince Harry. And so he knows that the prince has broken his oath to me? And is free to marry?'

'Princess, he has told me nothing. I think he must know. But perhaps he plans . . .'

Her gesture stopped him. 'He has given up on me. I see. I have failed him and he has cast me aside. I am indeed alone.'

'So shall I try to get us home now?' Fuensalida asked quietly. Truly, he thought, it had become the very pinnacle of his ambitions. If he could get this doomed princess home to her unhappy father and her increasingly deranged sister, the new Queen of Castile, he would have done the best he could in a desperate situation. Nobody would marry Catalina of Spain now she was the daughter of a divided kingdom. Everyone could see that the madness in her blood was coming out in her sister. Not even Henry of England could pretend that Juana was fit to marry when she was on a crazed progress across Spain with her dead husband's coffin. Ferdinand's tricky diplomacy had rebounded on him and now everyone in Europe was his enemy, with two of the most powerful men in Europe allied to make war against him. Ferdinand was lost, and going down. The best that this unlucky princess could expect was a scratch marriage to some Spanish grandee and retirement to the countryside, with a chance to escape the war that must come. The worst was to remain trapped and in poverty in England, a forgotten hostage that no-one would ransom. A prisoner who would be soon forgotten, even by her gaolers.

'What shall I do?' Finally she accepted danger. He saw her take it in. Finally, she understood that she had lost. He saw her, a queen in every inch, learn the depth of her defeat. 'I must know what I should do. Or I shall be hostage, in an enemy country, with no-one to speak for me.'

He did not say that he had thought her just that, ever since he had arrived.

'We shall leave,' he said decisively. 'If war comes they will keep you as a hostage and they will seize your dowry. God forbid that now the money is finally coming, it should be used to make war against Spain.'

'I cannot leave,' she said flatly. 'If I go, I will never get back here.'

'It is over!' he cried in sudden passion. 'You see it yourself, at last. We have lost. We are defeated. It is over for you and England. You have held on and faced humiliation and poverty, you have faced it like a princess, like a queen, like a saint. Your mother herself could not have shown more courage. But we are defeated, Infanta. You have lost. We have to get home as best we can. We have to run, before they catch us.'

'Catch us?'

'They could imprison us both as enemy spies and hold us to ransom,' he told her. 'They could impound whatever remains of your dowry goods and impound the rest when it arrives. God knows, they can make up a charge, and execute you, if they want to enough.'

'They dare not touch me! I am a princess of royal blood,' she flared up. 'Whatever else they can take from me, they can never take that! I am Infanta of Spain even if I am nothing else! Even if I am never Queen of England, at least I will always be Infanta of Spain.'

'Princes of royal blood have gone into the Tower of London before and not come out again,' the ambassador said bleakly. 'Princes of the royal blood of England have had those gates shut behind them and never seen daylight again. He could call you a pretender. You know what happens in England to pretenders. We have to go.'

Catalina curtseyed to My Lady the King's Mother and received not even a nod of the head in return. She stiffened. The two retinues had met on their way to Mass; behind the old lady was her granddaughter the Princess Mary and half a dozen ladies. All of them showed frosty faces to the young woman who was supposed to be betrothed to the Prince of Wales but who had been neglected for so long.

'My lady.' Catalina stood in her path, waiting for an acknowledgement.

The king's mother looked at the young woman with open dislike.

'I hear that there are difficulties over the betrothal of the Princess Mary,' she said.

Catalina looked towards the Princess Mary and the girl, hidden behind her grandmother, made an ugly grimace at her and broke off with a sudden snort of laughter.

'I did not know,' Catalina said.

'You may not know, but your father undoubtedly knows,' the old woman said irritably. 'In one of your constant letters to him you might tell him that he does his cause and your cause no good by trying to disturb our plans for our family.'

'I am very sure he does not . . .' Catalina started.

'I am very sure that he does; and you had better warn him not to stand in our way,' the old woman interrupted her sharply, and swept on.

'My own betrothal . . .' Catalina tried.

'Your betrothal?' The king's mother repeated the words as if she had never heard them before. 'Your betrothal?' Suddenly, she laughed, throwing her head back, her mouth wide. Behind her, the princess laughed too, and then all the ladies were laughing out loud at the thought of the pauper princess speaking of her betrothal to the most eligible prince in Christendom.

'My father is sending my dowry!' Catalina cried out.

'Too late! You are far too late!' the king's mother wailed, clutching at the arm of her friend.

Catalina, confronted by a dozen laughing faces, reduced to helpless hysteria at the thought of this patched princess offering her bits of plate and gold, ducked her head down, pushed through them, and went away.

That night the ambassador of Spain and an Italian merchant of some wealth and great discretion stood side by side on a shadowy quayside at a quiet corner of the London docks, and watched the quiet loading of Spanish goods on to a ship bound for Bruges.

'She has not authorised this?' the merchant whispered, his dark face lit by flickering torchlight. 'We are all but stealing her dowry! What will happen if the English suddenly say that the marriage is to go ahead and we have emptied her treasure room? What if they see that the dowry has come from Spain at last, but it never reached her treasure room? They will call us thieves. We will be thieves!'

'They will never say it is to go ahead,' the ambassador said simply. 'They will impound her goods and imprison her the moment that they declare war on Spain, and they could do that any day now. I dare not let King Ferdinand's money fall into the hands of the English. They are our enemies, not our allies.'

'What will she do? We have emptied her treasury. There is nothing in her strong-room but empty boxes. We have left her a pauper.'

The ambassador shrugged. 'She is ruined anyway. If she stays here when England is at war with Spain then she is an enemy hostage and they will imprison her. If she runs away with me she will have no kind welcome back at home. Her mother is dead and her family is ruined and she is ruined too. I would not be surprised if she did not throw herself into the Thames and drown. Her life is over. I cannot see what will become of her. I can save her money, if you will ship it out for me. But I cannot save her.'

I know I have to leave England; Arthur would not want me to stay to face danger. I have a terror of the Tower and the block that would be fitting only if I were a traitor, and not a princess who has never done anything wrong but tell one great lie, and that for the best. It would be the jest of all time if I had to put my head down on Warwick's block and die, a Spanish pretender to the throne where he died a Plantagenet.

That must not happen. I see that my writ does not run. I am not such a fool as to think I can command any more. I do not even pray any more. I do not even ask for my destiny. But I can run away. And I think the time to run away is now.

'You have done what?' Catalina demanded of her ambassador. The inventory in her hand trembled.

'I took it upon my own authority to move your father's treasure from the country. I could not risk . . .'

'*My* dowry.' She raised her voice.

'Your Grace, we both know it will not be needed for a wedding. He will never marry you. They would take your dowry and he would still not marry you.'

'It was my side of the bargain!' she shouted. 'I keep faith! Even if no-one else does! I have not eaten, I have given up my own house so as not to pawn that treasure. I make a promise and I keep to it, whatever the cost!'

'The king would have used it to pay for soldiers to fight against your father. He would have fought against Spain with your father's own gold!' Fuensalida exclaimed miserably. 'I could not let it happen.'

'So you robbed me!'

He stumbled over the words. 'I took your treasure into safe-keeping in the hopes that . . .'

'Go!' she said abruptly.

'Princess?'

'You have betrayed me, just as Dona Elvira betrayed me, just as everyone always betrays me,' she said bitterly. 'You may leave me. I shall not send for you again. Ever. Be very sure that I shall never speak to you again. But I shall tell my father what you have done. I shall write to him at once and tell him that you have stolen my dowry monies, that you are a thief. You will never be received at the court in Spain.'

He bowed, trembling with emotion, and then he turned to leave, too proud to defend himself.

'You are nothing more than a traitor!' Catalina cried as he reached the door. 'And if I were a queen with the power of the queen I would have you hanged for treason.'

He stiffened. He turned, he bowed again, his voice when he spoke was ice. 'Infanta, please do not make a fool of yourself by insulting me. You are badly mistaken. It was your own father who commanded me to return your dowry. I was obeying his direct order. Your own father wanted your treasury stripped of every valuable. It is he who decided to make you a pauper. He wanted the dowry money returned because he has given up all hope of your marriage. He wanted the money kept safe and smuggled safely out of England.

'But I must tell you,' he added with weighty malice, 'he did not order me to make sure that *you* were safe. He gave no orders to smuggle you safely out of England. He thought of the treasure but not of you. His orders were to secure the safety of the goods. He did not even mention you by name. I think he must have given you up for lost.'

As soon as the words were out he wished he had not said them. The stricken look on her face was worse than anything he had ever seen before. 'He told you to send back the gold but to leave me behind? With nothing?'

'I am sure . . .'

Blindly, she turned her back to him and walked to the window so that he could not see the blank horror on her face. 'Go,' she repeated. 'Just go.'

I am the sleeping princess in the story, a snow princess left in a cold land and forgetting the feel of the sun. This winter has been a long one, even for England. Even now, in April, the grass is so frosty in the

morning that when I wake and see the ice on my bedroom windows the light filtering through is so white that I think it has snowed overnight. The water in the cup by my bed is frozen by midnight, and we cannot now afford to keep the fire in through the night. When I walk outside on the icy grass, it crunches thickly under my feet and I can feel its chill through the thin soles of my boots. This summer, I know, will have all the mild sweetness of an English summer; but I long for the burning heat of Spain. I want to have my despair baked out of me once more. I feel as if I have been cold for seven years, and if nothing comes to warm me soon I shall simply die of it, just melt away under the rain, just blow away like the mist off the river. If the king is indeed dying, as the court rumour says, and Prince Harry comes to the throne and marries Eleanor, then I shall ask my father for permission to take the veil and retire to a convent. It could not be worse than here. It could not be poorer, colder or more lonely. Clearly my father has forgotten his love for me and given me up, just as if I had died with Arthur. Indeed, now, I acknowledge that every day I wish that I had died with Arthur.

I have sworn never to despair – the women of my family dissolve into despair like molasses into water. But this ice in my heart does not feel like despair. It feels as if my rock-hard determination to be queen has turned me to stone. I don't feel as if I am giving way to my feelings like Juana; I feel as if I have mislaid my feelings. I am a block, an icicle, a princess of constant snow.

I try to pray to God but I cannot hear Him. I fear He has forgotten me as everyone else has done. I have lost all sense of His presence, I have lost my fear of His will, and I have lost my joy in His blessing. I can feel nothing for Him. I no longer think I am His special child, chosen to be blessed. I no longer console myself that I am His special child, chosen to be tested. I think He has turned His face from me. I don't know why, but if my earthly father can forget me, and forget that I was his favourite child, as he has done, then I suppose my Heavenly Father can forget me too.

In all the world I find that I care for only two things now: I can still feel my love for Arthur, like a warm, still-beating heart in a little bird that has fallen from a frozen sky, chilled and cold. And I still long for Spain, for the Alhambra Palace, for al-Yanna; the garden, the secret place, paradise.

I endure my life only because I cannot escape it. Each year I hope that my fortunes will change; each year when Harry's birthday comes around and the betrothal is not made marriage, I know that another year of my fertile life has come and gone. Each midsummer day, when the dowry payment falls due and there is no draft from my father, I feel shame: like a sickness in my belly. And twelve times a year, for seven years, that is eighty-four times, my courses have come and gone. Each time I bleed I think, there is another chance to make a prince for England wasted. I have learned to grieve for the stain on my linen as if it is a child lost. Eighty-four chances for me to have a son, in the very flush of my youth; eighty-four chances lost. I am learning to miscarry. I am learning the sorrow of miscarriage.

Each day, when I go to pray I look up at the crucified Christ and say: 'Your will be done'. That is each day for seven years, that is two thousand, five hundred and fifty-six times. This is the arithmetic of my pain. I say: 'Your will be done'; but what I mean is: 'make Your will on these wicked English councillors and this spiteful, unforgiving English king, and his old witch of a mother. Give me my rights. Make me queen. I must be queen, I must have a son, or I will become a princess of snow'.

21st April 1509

'The king is dead,' Fuensalida the ambassador wrote briefly to Catalina, knowing that she would not receive him in person, knowing that she would never forgive him for stealing her dowry and naming her as a pretender, for telling her that her father had abandoned her. 'I know you will not see me but I have to do my duty and warn you that on his deathbed the king told his son that he was free to marry whoever he chooses. If you wish me to commission a ship to take you home to Spain, I have personal funds to do so. Myself, I cannot see that you will gain anything by staying in this country but insult, ignominy, and perhaps danger.'

'Dead,' Catalina said.

'What?' one of her ladies asked.

Catalina scrunched the letter into her hand. She never trusted anyone with anything now. 'Nothing,' she said. 'I am going for a walk.'

Maria de Salinas stood up and put Catalina's patched cloak about her shoulders. It was the same cloak that she had worn wrapped around in the winter cold when she and Arthur had left London for Ludlow, seven years earlier.

'Shall we come with you?' she offered, without enthusiasm, glancing at the grey sky beyond the windows.

'No.'

I pound alongside the river, the gravelled walk pricking the soles of my feet through the thin leather, as if I am trying to run away from hope itself. I wonder if there is any chance that my luck might change, might be changing now. The king who wanted me, and then hated me for refusing him, is dead. They said he was sick; but God knows, he never weakened. I thought he would reign forever. But now he is dead. Now he has gone. It will be the prince who decides.

I dare not touch hope. After all these years of fasting, I feel as if hope would make me drunk if I had so much of a drop of it on my lips. But I do hope for just a little taste of optimism, just a little flavour which is not my usual diet of grim despair.

Because I know the boy, Harry. I swear I know him. I have watched him as a falconer wakes with a tired bird. Watched him, and judged him, and checked my judgement against his behaviour again and again. I have read him as if I were studying my catechism. I know his strengths and his weaknesses, and I think I have faint, very faint, reason for hope.

Harry is vain, it is the sin of a young boy and I do not blame him for it, but he has it in abundance. On the one hand this might make him marry me, for he will want to be seen to be doing the right thing – honouring his promise, even rescuing me. At the thought of being saved by Harry, I have to stop in my stride and pinch my nails into the palms of my hands in the shelter of my cloak. This humiliation too I can learn to bear. Harry may want to rescue me and I shall have to be grateful. Arthur would have died of shame at the thought of his little braggart brother rescuing me; but Arthur died before this hour, my mother died before this hour; I shall have to bear it alone.

But equally, his vanity could work against me. If they emphasise the wealth of Princess Eleanor, the influence of her Hapsburg family, the glory of the connection to the Holy Roman Emperor – he may be seduced. His grandmother will speak against me and her word has been his law. She will advise him to marry Princess Eleanor and he will be attracted – like any young fool – to the idea of an unknown beauty.

But even if he wants to marry her, it still leaves him with the difficulty of what to do with me. He would look bad if he sent me home, surely he cannot have the gall to marry another woman with me still in attendance at court? I know that Harry would do anything rather than look foolish. If I can find a way to stay here until they have to consider his marriage, then I will be in a strong position indeed.

I walk more slowly, looking around me at the cold river, the passing boatmen huddled in their winter coats against the cold. 'God bless you, Princess!' calls out one man, recognising me. I raise my hand in reply. The people of this odd, fractious country have loved me from the moment they scrambled to see me in the little port of Plymouth. That will count in my favour too with a prince new-come to his throne and desperate for affection.

Harry is not mean with money. He is not old enough yet to know the value of it, and he has always been given anything he might want. He will not bicker over the dowry and the jointure. I am sure of that. He will be disposed to make a lordly gesture. I shall have to make sure that Fuensalida and my father do not offer to ship me home to make way for the new bride. Fuensalida despaired long ago of our cause. But now I do not. I shall have to resist his panic, and my own fears. I must stay here to be in the field. I cannot draw back now.

Harry was attracted to me once, I know that. Arthur told me of it first, said that the little boy liked leading me into my wedding, had been dreaming that he was the bridegroom and I was the bride. I have nurtured his liking, every time I see him I pay him particular attention. When his sister laughs at him and disregards him, I glance his way, ask him to sing for me, watch him dance with admiration. On the rare occasions that I have caught a moment with him in private I ask him to read to me and we discuss our thoughts on great writers. I make sure that he knows that I find him illuminating. He is a clever boy, it is no hardship to talk with him.

My difficulty always has been that everyone else admires him so greatly that my modest warmth can hardly weigh with him. Since his grandmother My Lady the King's Mother declares that he is the handsomest prince in Christendom, the most learned, the most promising, what can I say to compare? How can one compliment a boy who is already flattered into extreme vanity, who already believes that he is the greatest prince the world has known?

These are my advantages. Against them I could list the fact that he has been destined for me for six years and he perhaps sees me as his father's choice and a dull choice at that. That he has sworn before a bishop that I was not his choice in marriage and that he does not want to marry me. He might think to hold to that oath, he might think to *proclaim he never wanted me, and deny the oath of our betrothal. At the thought of Harry announcing to the world that I was forced on him and now he is glad to be free of me, I pause again. This too I can endure.*

These years have not been kind to me. He has never seen me laughing with joy, he has never seen me smiling and easy. He has never seen me dressed other than poorly, and anxious about my appearance. They have never called me forwards to dance before him, or to sing for him. I always have a poor horse when the court is hunting and sometimes I cannot keep up. I always look weary and I am always anxious. He is young and frivolous and he loves luxury and fineness of dress. He might have a picture of me in his mind as a poor woman, a drag upon his family, a pale widow, a ghost at the feast. He is a self-indulgent boy, he might decide to excuse himself from his duty. He is vain and light-hearted and might think nothing of sending me away.

But I have to stay. If I leave, he will forget me in a moment, I am certain of that, at least. I have to stay.

Fuensalida, summoned to the king's council, went in with his head held high, trying to seem unbowed, certain that they had sent for him to tell him to leave and take the unwanted Infanta with him. His high Spanish pride, which had so much offended them so very often in the past, took him through the door and to the Privy Council table. The new king's ministers were seated around the table, there was a place left empty for him in the plumb centre. He felt like a boy, summoned before his tutors for a scolding.

'Perhaps I should start by explaining the condition of the Princess of Wales,' he said diffidently. 'The dowry payment is safely stored, out of the country, and can be paid in . . .'

'The dowry does not matter,' one of the councillors said.

'The dowry?' Fuensalida was stunned into silence. 'But the princess's plate?'

'The king is minded to be generous to his betrothed.'

There was a stunned silence from the ambassador. 'His betrothed?'

'Of the greatest importance now is the power of the King of France and the danger of his ambitions in Europe. It has been thus since Agincourt. The king is most anxious to restore the glory of England. And now we have a king as great as that Henry, ready to make England great again. English safety depends on a three-way alliance between Spain and England, and the emperor. The young king believes that his wedding with the Infanta will secure the support of the King of Aragon to this great cause. This is, presumably, the case?'

'Certainly,' said Fuensalida, his head reeling. 'But the plate . . .'

'The plate does not matter,' one of the councillors repeated.

'I thought that her goods . . .'

'They do not matter.'

'I shall have to tell her of this . . . change . . . in her fortunes.'

The Privy Council rose to their feet. 'Pray do.'

'I shall return when I have . . . er . . . seen her.' Pointless, Fuensalida thought, to tell them that she had been so angry with him for what she saw as his betrayal that he could not be sure that she would see him. Pointless to reveal that the last time he had seen her he had told her that she was lost and her cause was lost and everyone had known it for years.

He staggered as much as walked from the room, and almost collided with the young prince. The youth, still not yet eighteen, was radiant. 'Ambassador!'

Fuensalida threw himself back and dropped to his knee. 'Your Grace! I must . . . condole with you on the death of . . .'

'Yes, yes.' He waved aside the sympathy. He could not make himself look grave. He was wreathed in smiles, taller than ever. 'You will wish to tell the princess that I propose that our marriage takes place as soon as possible.'

Fuensalida found he was stammering with a dry mouth. 'Of course, sire.'

'I shall send a message to her for you,' the young man said generously. He giggled. 'I know that you are out of favour. I know that she has refused to see you, but I am sure that she will see you for my sake.'

'I thank you,' the ambassador said. The prince waved him away. Fuensalida rose from his bow and went towards the Princess's chambers. He realised that it would be hard for the Spanish to recover from the largesse of this new English king. His generosity, his ostentatious generosity, was crushing.

Catalina kept her ambassador waiting, but she admitted him within the hour. He had to admire the self-control that set her to watch the clock when the man who knew her destiny was waiting outside to tell her.

'Emissary,' she said levelly.

He bowed. The hem of her gown was ragged. He saw the neat, small threads where it had been stitched up, and then worn ragged again. He had a sense of great relief that whatever happened to her after this unexpected marriage, she would never again have to wear an old gown.

'Dowager Princess, I have been to the Privy Council. Our troubles are over. He wants to marry you.'

Fuensalida had thought she might cry with joy, or pitch into his arms, or fall to her knees and thank God. She did none of these things. Slowly, she inclined her head. The tarnished gold leaf on the hood caught the light. 'I am glad to hear it,' was all she said.

'They say that there is no issue about the plate.' He could not keep the jubilation from his voice.

She nodded again.

'The dowry will have to be paid. I shall get them to send the money back from Bruges. It has been in safe-keeping, Your Grace. I have kept it safe for you.' His voice quavered, he could not help it.

Again she nodded.

He dropped to one knee. 'Princess, rejoice! You will be Queen of England.'

Her blue eyes when she turned them to him were hard, like the sapphires she had sold long ago. 'Emissary, I was always going to be Queen of England.'

I have done it. Good God, I have done it. After seven endless years of waiting, after hardship and humiliation, I have done it. I go into my bedchamber and kneel before my prie-dieu and close my eyes. But I speak to Arthur, not to the risen Lord.

'I have done it,' I tell him. 'Harry will marry me, I have done as you wished me to do.'

For a moment I can see his smile, I can see him as I did so often, when I glanced sideways at him during dinner and caught him smiling down the hall to someone. Before me again is the brightness of his face, the darkness of his eyes, the clear line of his profile. And more than anything else, the scent of him, the very perfume of my desire.

Even on my knees before a crucifix I give a little sigh of longing. 'Arthur, beloved. My only love. I shall marry your brother but I am always yours.' For a moment, I remember, as bright as the first taste of early cherries, the scent of his skin in the morning. I raise my face and it is as if I can feel his chest against my cheek as he bears down on me, thrusts towards me. 'Arthur,' I whisper. I am now, I will always be, forever his.

Catalina had to face one ordeal. As she went into dinner in a hastily tailored new gown, with a collar of gold at her neck and pearls in her ears, and was conducted to a new table at the very front of the hall, she curtseyed to her husband-to-be and saw his bright smile at her, and then she turned to her grandmother-in-law and met the basilisk gaze of Lady Margaret Beaufort.

'You are fortunate,' the old lady said afterwards, as the musicians started to play and the tables were taken away.

'I am?' Catalina replied, deliberately dense.

'You married one great prince of England and lost him; now it seems you will marry another.'

'This can come as no surprise,' Catalina observed in flawless French, 'since I have been betrothed to him for six years. Surely, my lady, you never doubted that this day would come? You never thought that such an honourable prince would break his holy word?'

The old woman hid her discomfiture well. 'I never doubted our intentions,' she returned. 'We keep our word. But when you withheld your dowry and your father reneged on his payments, I wondered as to your intentions. I wondered about the honour of Spain.'

'Then you were kind to say nothing to disturb the king,' Catalina said smoothly. 'For he trusted me, I know. And I never doubted your desire to have me as your granddaughter. And see! Now I will be your granddaughter, I will be Queen of England, the dowry is paid, and everything is as it should be.'

She left the old lady with nothing to say – and there were few that could do that. 'Well, at any rate, we will have to hope that you are fertile,' was all she sourly mustered.

'Why not? My mother had half a dozen children,' Catalina said sweetly. 'Let us hope my husband and I are blessed with the fertility of Spain. My emblem is the pomegranate – a Spanish fruit, filled with life.'

My Lady the King's Grandmother swept away, leaving Catalina alone. Catalina curtseyed to her departing back and rose up, her head high. It did not matter what Lady Margaret might think or say, all that mattered was what she could do. Catalina did not think she could prevent the wedding, and that was all that mattered.

Greenwich Palace, 11th June 1509

I was dreading the wedding, the moment when I would have to say the words of the marriage vows that I had said to Arthur. But in the end the service was so unlike that glorious day in St Paul's Cathedral that I could go through it with Harry before me, and Arthur locked away in the very back of my mind. I was doing this for Arthur, the very thing he had commanded, the very thing that he had insisted on – and I could not risk thinking of him.

There was no great congregation in a cathedral, there were no watching ambassadors, or fountains flowing with wine. We were married within the walls of Greenwich Palace in the church of the Friars Observant, with only three witnesses and half a dozen people present.

There was no rich feasting or music or dancing, there was no drunkenness at court or rowdiness. There was no public bedding. I had been afraid of that – the ritual of putting to bed and then the public showing of the sheets in the morning; but the prince – the king, I now have to say – is as shy as me, and we dine quietly before the court and withdraw together. They drink our healths and let us go. His grandmother is there, her face like a mask, her eyes cold. I show her every courtesy, it doesn't matter to me what she thinks now. She can do nothing. There is no suggestion that I shall be living in her chambers under her supervision. On the contrary she has moved out of her rooms for me. I am married to Harry. I am Queen of England and she is nothing more than the grandmother of a king.

My ladies undress me in silence, this is their triumph too, this is their escape from poverty as well as mine. Nobody wants to remember the night at Oxford, the night at Burford, the nights at Ludlow. Their fortunes as much as mine depend on the success of this great deception. If I asked them, they would deny Arthur's very existence.

Besides, it was all so long ago. Seven long years. Who but I can remember that far back? Who but I ever knew the delight of waiting for Arthur, the firelight on the rich-coloured curtains of the bed, the glow of candlelight on our entwined limbs? The sleepy whispers in the early hours of the morning: 'Tell me a story!'

They leave me in one of my dozen exquisite new nightgowns and withdraw in silence. I wait for Harry, as long ago I used to wait for Arthur. The only difference is the utter absence of joy.

The men-at-arms and the gentlemen of the bedchamber brought the young king to the queen's door, tapped on it and admitted him to her rooms. She was in her gown, seated by the fireside, a richly embroidered shawl thrown over her shoulders. The room was warm, welcoming. She rose as he came in and swept him a curtsey.

Harry lifted her up with a touch on her elbow. She saw at once that he was flushed with embarrassment, she felt his hand tremble.

'Will you take a cup of wedding ale?' she invited him, she made sure that she did not think of Arthur bringing her a cup and saying it was for courage.

'I will,' he said. His voice, still so young, was unsteady in its register. She turned away to pour the ale so he should not see her smile.

They lifted their cups to each other. 'I hope you did not find today too quiet for your taste,' he said uncertainly. 'I thought with my father newly dead we should not have too merry a wedding. I did not want to distress My Lady, his mother.'

She nodded but said nothing.

'I hope you are not disappointed,' he pressed on. 'Your first wedding was so very grand.'

Catalina smiled. 'I hardly remember it, it was so long ago.'

He looked pleased at her reply, she noted. 'It was, wasn't it? We were all little more than children.'

'Yes,' she said. 'Far too young to marry.'

He shifted in his seat. She knew that the courtiers who had taken Hapsburg gold would have spoken against her. The enemies of Spain would have spoken against her. His own grandmother had advised against this wedding. This transparent young man was still anxious about his decision, however bold he might try to appear.

'Not that young; you were fifteen,' he reminded her. 'A young woman.'

'And Arthur was the same age,' she said, daring to name him. 'But he was never strong, I think. He could not be a husband to me.'

Harry was silent and she was afraid she had gone too far. But then she saw the glimpse of hope in his face.

'It is indeed true then, that the marriage was never consummated?' he asked, colouring up in embarrassment. 'I am sorry . . . I wondered . . . I know they said . . . but I did wonder . . .'

'Never,' she said calmly. 'He tried once or twice but you will remember that he was not strong. He may have even bragged that he had done it, but, poor Arthur, it meant nothing.'

'I shall do this for you,' I say fiercely, in my mind, to my beloved. 'You wanted this lie. I shall do it thoroughly. If it is going to be done, it must be done thoroughly. It has to be done with courage, conviction; and it must never be undone.'

Aloud, Catalina said: 'We married in the November, you remember. December we spent most of the time travelling to Ludlow and were apart on the journey. He was not well after Christmas, and then he died in April. I was very sad for him.'

'He was never your lover?' Harry asked, desperate to be certain.

'How could he be?' She gave a pretty, deprecatory shrug that made the gown slip off one creamy shoulder a little. She saw his eyes drawn to the exposed skin, she saw him swallow. 'He was not strong. Your own mother thought that he should have gone back to Ludlow alone, for the first year. I wish we had done that. It would have made no difference to me, and he might have been spared. He was like a stranger to me for all our marriage. We lived like children in a royal nursery. We were hardly even companions.'

He sighed as if he were free of a burden, the face he turned to her was bright. 'You know, I could not help but be afraid,' he said. 'My grandmother said . . .'

'Oh! Old women always gossip in the corners,' she said, smiling. She ignored his widened eyes at her casual disrespect. 'Thank God we are young and need pay no attention.'

'So, it was just gossip,' he said, quickly adopting her dismissive tone. 'Just old women's gossip.'

'We won't listen to her,' she said, daring him to go on. 'You are king and I am queen and we shall make up our own minds. We hardly need her advice. Why – it is her advice that has kept us apart when we could have been together.'

It had not struck him before. 'Indeed,' he said, his face hardening. 'We have both been deprived. And all the time she hinted that you were Arthur's wife, wedded and bedded, and I should look elsewhere.'

'I am a virgin, as I was when I came to England,' she asserted boldly. 'You could ask my old duenna or any of my women. They all knew it. My mother knew it. I am a virgin untouched.'

He gave a little sigh as if released from some worry. 'You are kind to tell me,' he said. 'It is better to have these things in the light, so we know, so we both know. So that no-one is uncertain. It would be terrible to sin.'

'We are young,' she said. 'We can speak of such things between ourselves. We can be honest and straightforward together. We need not fear rumours and slanders. We need have no fear of sin.'

'It will be my first time too,' he admitted shyly. 'I hope you don't think the less of me?'

'Of course not,' she said sweetly. 'When were you ever allowed to go out? Your grandmother and your father had you mewed up as close as a precious falcon. I am glad that we shall be together, that it will be the first time, for both of us, together.'

Harry rose to his feet and held out his hand. 'So, we shall have to learn together,' he said. 'We shall have to be kind to each other. I don't want to hurt you, Catalina. You must tell me if anything hurts you.'

Easily she moved into his arms, and felt his whole body stiffen at her touch. Gracefully, she stepped back, as if modestly shrinking but kept one hand on his shoulder to encourage him to press forwards until the bed was behind her. Then she let herself lean back until she was on the pillows, smiling up at him, and she could see his blue eyes darken with desire.

'I have wanted you since I first saw you,' he said breathlessly. He stroked her hair, her neck, her naked shoulder, with a hurried touch, wanting all of her, at once.

She smiled. 'And I, you.'

'Really?'

She nodded.

'I dreamed that it was me that married you that day.' He was flushed, breathless.

Slowly, she untied the ribbons at the throat of her nightgown, letting the silky linen fall apart so that he could see her throat, her round, firm breasts, her waist, the dark shadow between her legs.

Harry gave a little groan of desire at the sight of her. 'It might as well have been,' she whispered. 'I have had no other. And we are married now, at last.'

'Ah God, we are,' he said longingly. 'We are married now, at last.'

He dropped his face into the warmth of her neck, she could feel his breath coming fast and urgent in her hair, his body was pushing against hers, Catalina felt herself respond. She remembered Arthur's touch and gently bit the tip of her tongue to remind herself never, never to say Arthur's name out loud. She let Harry push against her, force himself against her and then he was inside her. She gave a little rehearsed cry of pain but she knew at once, in a heart-thud of dread, that it was not enough. She had not cried out enough, her body had not resisted him enough. She had been too warm, too welcoming. It had been too easy. He did not know much, this callow boy; but he knew that it was not difficult enough.

He checked, even in the midst of his desire. He knew that something was not as it should be. He looked down at her. 'You *are* a virgin,' he said uncertainly. 'I hope that I do not hurt too much.'

But he knew that she was not. Deep down, he knew that she was no virgin. He did not know much, this over-protected boy, but he knew this. Somewhere in his mind, he knew that she was lying.

She looked up at him. 'I was a virgin until this moment,' she said, managing the smallest of smiles. 'But your potency has overcome me. You are so strong. You overwhelmed me.'

His face was still troubled, but his desire could not wait. He started to move again, he could not resist the pleasure. 'You have mastered me,' she encouraged him. 'You are my husband, you have taken your own.' She saw him forget his doubt in his rising desire. 'You have done what Arthur could not do,' she whispered.

They were the very words to trigger his desire. The young man gave a groan of pleasure and fell down on to her, his seed pumping into her, the deed undeniably done.

He doesn't question me again. He wants so much to believe me that he does not ask the question, fearing that he might get an answer he doesn't like. He is cowardly in this. He is accustomed to hearing the answers he wants to hear and he would rather an agreeable lie than an unpalatable truth.

Partly, it is his desire to have me, and he wants me as I was when he first saw me: a virgin in bridal white. Partly it is to disprove everyone who warned him against the trap that I had set for him. But more than anything else: he hated and envied my beloved Arthur and he wants me just because I was Arthur's bride, and – God forgive him for a spiteful, envious, second son – he wants me to tell him that he can do something that Arthur could not do, that he can have something that Arthur could not have. Even though my beloved husband is cold under the nave of Worcester Cathedral, the child that wears his crown still wants to triumph over him. The greatest lie is not in telling Harry that I am a virgin. The greatest lie is in telling him that he is a better man, more of a man than his brother. And I did that too.

In the dawn, while he is still sleeping, I take my pen-knife and cut the sole of my foot, where he will not notice a scar, and drip blood on the sheet where we had lain, enough to pass muster for an inspection by My Lady the King's Grandmother, or any other bad-tempered, suspicious enemy who might still seek to discomfort me. There is to be no showing of the sheets for a king and his bride; but I know that everyone will ask, and it is best that my ladies can say that they have all seen the smear of blood, and that I am complaining of the pain.

In the morning, I do everything that a bride should do. I say I am tired, and I rest for the morning. I smile with my eyes looking downwards as if I have discovered some sweet secret. I walk a little stiffly and I refuse to ride out to hunt for a week. I do everything to indicate

that I am a young woman who has lost her virginity. I convince
everyone. And besides, no-one wants to believe anything other.

The cut on my foot is sore for a long, long time. It catches me every
time I step into my new shoes, the ones with the great diamond buckles.
It is like a reminder to me of the lie I promised Arthur that I would
tell. Of the great lie that I will live, for the rest of my life. I don't mind
the sharp little nip of pain when I slide my right foot into my shoe. It
is nothing to the pain that is hidden deep inside me when I smile at
the unworthy boy who is king and call him, in my new admiring voice:
'husband'.

Harry woke in the night and his quiet stillness woke Catalina.

'My lord?' she asked.

'Go to sleep,' he said. 'It's not yet dawn.'

She slipped from the bed and lit a taper in the red embers of the fire, then lit a candle. She let him see her, nightgown half-open, her smooth flanks only half-hidden by the fall of the gown. 'Would you like some ale? Or some wine?'

'A glass of wine,' he said. 'You have one too.'

She put the candle in the silver holder and came back to the bed beside him with the wine glasses in her hand. She could not read his face, but suppressed her pang of irritation that, whatever it was, she had to be woken, she had to inquire what was troubling him, she had to demonstrate her concern. With Arthur she had known in a second what he wanted, what he was thinking. But anything could distract Harry, a song, a dream, a note thrown from the crowd. Anything could trouble him. He had been raised to be accustomed to sharing his thoughts, accustomed to guidance. He needed an entourage of friends and admirers, tutors, mentors, parents. He liked constant conversation. Catalina had to be everyone to him.

'I have been thinking about war,' he said.

'Oh.'

'King Louis thinks he can avoid us, but we will force war on him. They tell me he wants peace, but I will not have it. I am the King of England, the victors of Agincourt. He will find me a force to be reckoned with.'

She nodded. Her father had been clear that Harry should be encouraged in his warlike ambitions against the King of France. He had written to her in the warmest of terms as his dearest daughter, and advised her that any war between England and France should be launched, not on the north coast – where the English usually invaded – but on the borders between France and Spain. He suggested that the English should reconquer the region of Aquitaine which would be glad to be free of France and would rise up to meet its liberators. Spain would be in strong support. It would be an easy and glorious campaign.

'In the morning I am going to order a new suit of armour,' Harry said. 'Not a suit for jousting, I want heavy armour, for the battle-field.'

She was about to say that he could hardly go to war when there was so much to do in the country. The moment that an English army left for France, the Scots, even with an English bride on their throne, were certain to take advantage and invade the north. The whole tax system was riddled with greed and injustice and must be reformed, there were new plans for schools, for a king's council, for forts and a navy of ships to defend the coast. These were Arthur's plans for England, they should come before Harry's desire for a war.

'I shall make my grandmother regent when I go to war,' Harry said. 'She knows what has to be done.'

Catalina hesitated, marshalling her thoughts. 'Yes indeed,' she said. 'But the poor lady is so old now. She has done so much already. Perhaps it might be too much of a burden for her?'

He smiled. 'Not her! She has always run everything. She keeps the royal accounts, she knows what is to be done. I don't think anything would be too much for her as long as it kept us Tudors in power.'

'Yes,' Catalina said, gently touching on his resentment. 'And see how well she ruled you! She never let you out of her sight for a moment. Why, I don't think she would let you go out even now if she could prevent you. When you were a boy, she never let you joust, she never let you gamble, she never let you have any friends. She dedicated herself to your safety and your wellbeing. She could not have kept you closer if you had been a princess.' She laughed. 'I think she thought you were a princess and not a lusty boy. Surely it is time that she had a rest? And you had some freedom?'

His swift, sulky look told her that she would win this.

'Besides,' she smiled, 'if you give her any power in the country she will be certain to tell the council that you will have to come home, that war is too dangerous for you.'

'She could hardly stop me going to war,' he bristled. 'I am the king.'

Catalina raised her eyebrows. 'Whatever you wish, my love. But I imagine she will stop your funds, if the war starts to go badly. If she and the Privy Council doubt your conduct of the war they need do nothing but sit on their hands and not raise taxes for your army. You could find yourself betrayed at home – betrayed by her love, I mean – while you are attacked abroad. You might find that the old people stop you doing what you want. Like they always try to do.'

He was aghast. 'She would never work against me.'

'Never on purpose,' Catalina agreed with him. 'She would always think she was serving your interest. It is just that . . .'

'What?'

'She will always think that she knows your business best. To her, you will always be a little boy.'

She saw him flush with annoyance.

'To her you will always be a second son, the one who came after Arthur. Not the true heir. Not fitted for the throne. Old people cannot change their minds, cannot see that everything is different now. But really, how can she ever trust your judgement, when she has spent her life ruling you? To her, you will always be the youngest prince, the baby.'

'I shall not be limited by an old woman,' he swore.

'Your time is now,' Catalina agreed.

'D'you know what I shall do?' he demanded. 'I shall make you regent when I go to war! You shall rule the country for me while I am gone. You shall command our forces at home. I would trust no-one else. We shall rule together. And you will support me as I require. D'you think you could do that?'

She smiled at him. 'I know I can. I won't fail,' she said. 'I was born to rule England. I shall keep the country safe while you are away.'

'That's what I need,' Harry said. 'And your mother was a great commander, wasn't she? She supported her husband. I always heard that he led the troops but she raised the money and raised the army?'

'Yes,' she said, a little surprised at his interest. 'Yes, she was always there. Behind the lines, planning his campaigns, and making sure he had the forces he needed, raising funds and raising troops, and sometimes she was in the very forefront of the battles. She had her own armour, she would ride out with the army.'

'Tell me about her,' he said, settling himself down in the pillows. 'Tell me about Spain. About what it was like when you were a little girl in the palaces of Spain. What was it like? In – what is it called – the Alhambra?'

It was too close to what had been before. It was as if a shadow had stretched over her heart. 'Oh, I hardly remember it at all,' she said, smiling at his eager face. 'There's nothing to tell.'

'Go on. Tell me a story about it.'

'No. I can't tell you anything. D'you know, I have been an English princess for so long, I could not tell you anything about it at all.'

In the morning Harry was filled with energy, excited at the thought of ordering his suit of armour, wanting a reason to declare war at once. He woke her with kisses and was on her, like an eager boy, while she was waking. She held him close, welcomed his quick, selfish pleasure, and smiled when he was up and out of bed in a moment, hammering at the door and shouting for his guards to take him to his rooms.

'I want to ride before Mass today,' he said. 'It is such a wonderful day. Will you come with me?'

'I'll see you at Mass,' Catalina promised him. 'And then you can breakfast with me, if you wish.'

'We'll take breakfast in the hall,' he ruled. 'And then we must go hunting. It is too good weather not to take the dogs out. You will come, won't you?'

'I'll come,' she promised him, smiling at his exuberance. 'And shall we have a picnic?'

'You are the best of wives!' he exclaimed. 'A picnic would be wonderful. Will you tell them to get some musicians and we can dance? And bring ladies, bring all your ladies, and we shall all dance.'

She caught him before he went out of the door. 'Harry, may I send for Lady Margaret Pole? You like her, don't you? Can I have her as a lady-in-waiting?'

He stepped back into the room, caught her into his arms and kissed her heartily. 'You shall have whoever you want to serve you. Anyone you want, always. Send for her at once, I know she is the finest of women. And appoint Lady Elizabeth Boleyn too. She is returning to court after her confinement. She has had another girl.'

'What will she call her?' Catalina asked, diverted.

'Mary, I think. Or Anne. I can't remember. Now, about our dance . . .'

She beamed at him. 'I shall get a troupe of musicians and dancers and if I can order soft-voice zephyrs I will do that too.' She laughed at the happiness in his face. She could hear the tramp of his guard coming to the door. 'See you at Mass!'

I married him for Arthur, for my mother, for God, for our cause, and for myself. But in a very little while I have come to love him. It is impossible not to love such a sweet-hearted, energetic, good-natured boy as Harry, in these first years of his reign. He has never known anything but admiration and kindness, he expects nothing less. He wakes happy every morning, filled with the confident expectation of a happy day. And, since he is king, and surrounded by courtiers and flatterers, he always has a happy day. When work troubles him or people come to him with disagreeable complaints he looks around for someone to take the bother of it away from him. In the first few weeks it was his grandmother who commanded; slowly, I make sure that it is to me that he hands the burdens of ruling the kingdom.

The Privy Councillors learn to come to me to ascertain what the king would think. It is easier for them to present a letter or a suggestion, if he has been prepared by me. The courtiers soon know that anything that encourages him to go away from me, anything that takes the country away from the alliance with Spain will displease me, and Harry does not like it when I frown. Men seeking advantage, advocates seeking help, petitioners seeking justice, all learn that the quickest way to a fair, prompt decision is to call first at the queen's rooms and then wait for my introduction.

I never have to ask anyone to handle him with tact. Everyone knows that a request should come to him as it were fresh, for the first time. Everyone knows that the self-love of a young man is very new and very bright and should not be tarnished. Everyone takes a warning from the case of his grandmother who is finding herself put gently and implacably to one side, because she openly advises him, because she takes decisions without him, because once – foolishly – she scolded him. Harry is a king so careless that he will hand over the keys of his kingdom to anyone he trusts. The trick for me is to make sure that he trusts only me.

I make sure that I never blame him for not being Arthur. I taught myself – in the seven years of widowhood – that God's will was done when He took Arthur from me, and there is no point in blaming those who survive when the best prince is dead. Arthur died with my promise in his ears and I think myself very lucky indeed that marriage to his brother is not a vow that I have to endure; but one I can enjoy.

I like being queen. I like having pretty things and rich jewels and a lap dog, and assembling ladies-in-waiting whose company is a pleasure. I like paying Maria de Salinas the long debt of her wages and watching her order a dozen gowns and fall in love. I like writing to Lady Margaret Pole and summoning her to my court, falling into her arms and crying for joy to see her again, and having her promise that she will be with me. I like knowing that her discretion is absolute; she never says one word about Arthur. But I like it that she knows what this marriage has cost me, and why I have done it. I like her watching me make Arthur's England even though it is Harry on the throne.

The first month of marriage is nothing for Harry but a round of parties, feasts, hunts, outings, pleasure trips, boating trips, plays, and tournaments. Harry is like a boy who has been locked up in a school room for too long and is suddenly given a summer holiday. The world is so filled with amusement for him that the least experience gives him great pleasure. He loves to hunt – and he had never been allowed fast horses before. He loves to joust and his father and grandmother had never even allowed him in the lists. He loves the company of men of the world who carefully adapt their conversation and their amusements to divert him. He loves the company of women but – thank God – his childlike devotion to me holds him firm. He likes to talk to pretty women, play cards with them, watch them dance and reward them with great prizes for petty feats – but always he glances towards me to see that I approve. Always he stays at my side, looking down at me from his greater height with a gaze of such devotion that I can't help but be loving towards him for what he brings me; and in a very little while, I can't help but love him for himself.

He has surrounded himself with a court of young men and women who are such a contrast to his father's court that they demonstrate by their very being that everything has changed. His father's court was filled with old men, men who had been through hard times together, some of them battle-hardened; all of them had lost and regained their lands at least once. Harry's court is filled with men who have never known hardship, never been tested.

I have made a point of saying nothing to criticise either him or the group of wild young men that gather around him. They call themselves the 'Minions' and they encourage each other in mad bets and jests all the day and – according to gossip – half the night too. Harry was kept so quiet and so close for all his childhood that I think it natural he should long to run wild now, and that he should love the young men who boast of drinking bouts and fights, and chases and attacks, and girls who they seduce, and fathers who pursue them with cudgels. His best friend is William Compton, the two go about with their arms around each other's shoulders as if ready to dance or braced for a fight for half the day. There is no harm in William, he is as great a fool as the rest of the court, he loves Harry as a comrade, and he has a mock-adoration of me that makes us all laugh. Half of the Minions pretend to be in love with me and I let them dedicate verses and sing songs to me and I make sure that Harry always knows that his songs and poems are the best.

The older members of the court disapprove and have made stern criticisms of the king's boisterous lads; but I say nothing. When the councillors come to me with complaints I say that the king is a young man and youth will have its way. There is no great harm in any one of the comrades; when they are not drinking, they are sweet young men. One or two, like the Duke of Buckingham who greeted me long ago, or the young Thomas Howard, are fine young men who would be an ornament to any court. My mother would have liked them. But when the lads are deep in their cups they are noisy and rowdy and excitable as young men always are and when they are sober they talk *nonsense. I look at them with my mother's eyes and I know that they are the boys who will become the officers in our army. When we go to war their energy and their courage is just what we will need. The noisiest, most disruptive young men in peacetime are exactly the leaders I will need in time of war.*

Lady Margaret, the king's grandmother, having buried a husband or two, a daughter-in-law, a grandson and finally her own precious prince, was a little weary of fighting for her place in the world and Catalina was careful not to provoke her old enemy into open warfare. Thanks to Catalina's discretion, the rivalry between the two women was not played overtly – anyone hoping to see Lady Margaret abuse her granddaughter-in-law as she had insulted her son's wife was disappointed. Catalina slid away from conflict.

When Lady Margaret tried to claim precedence by arriving at the dining-hall door a few footsteps before Catalina, a Princess of the Blood, an Infanta of Spain and now Queen of England, Catalina stepped back at once and gave way to her with such an air of generosity that everyone remarked on the pretty behaviour of the new queen. Catalina had a way of ushering the older woman before her that absolutely denied all rules of precedence and instead somehow emphasised Lady Margaret's ungainly gallop to beat her granddaughter-in-law to the high table. They also saw Catalina pointedly step back, and everyone remarked on the grace and generosity of the younger woman.

The death of Lady Margaret's son, King Henry, had hit the old lady hard. It was not so much that she had lost a beloved child; it was more that she had lost a cause. In his absence she could hardly summon the energy to force the Privy Councillors to report to her before going to the king's rooms. Harry's joyful excusing of his father's debts and freeing of his father's prisoners she took as an insult to his father's memory, and to her own rule. The sudden leap of the court into youth and freedom and playfulness made her feel old and bad-tempered. She, who had once been the commander of the court and the maker of the rules, was left to one side. Her opinion no longer mattered. The great book by which all court events must be governed had been written by her; but suddenly, they were celebrating events that were not in her book, they invented pastimes and activities, and she was not consulted.

She blamed Catalina for all the changes she most disliked, and Catalina smiled very sweetly and continued to encourage the young king to hunt and to dance and to stay up late at night. The old lady grumbled to her ladies that the queen was a giddy, vain thing and would lead the prince to disaster. Insultingly, she even remarked that it was no wonder Arthur had died, if this was the way that the Spanish girl thought a royal household should be run.

Lady Margaret Pole remonstrated with her old acquaintance as tactfully as she could. 'My lady, the queen has a merry court but she never does anything against the dignity of the throne. Indeed, without her, the court would be far wilder. It is the king who insists on one pleasure after another. It is the queen who gives this court its manners. The young men adore her and nobody drinks or misbehaves before her.'

'It is the queen who I blame,' the old woman said crossly. 'Princess Eleanor would never have behaved like this. Princess Eleanor would have been housed in my rooms, and the place would have run by my rules.'

Tactfully, Catalina heard nothing; not even when people came to her and repeated the slanders. Catalina simply ignored her grandmother-in-law and the constant stream of her criticism. She could have done nothing that would irritate her more.

It was the late hours that the court now kept that were the old lady's greatest complaint. Increasingly, she had to wait and wait for dinner to be served. She would complain that it was so late at night that the servants would not be finished before dawn, and then she would retire before the court had even finished their dinner.

'You keep late hours,' she told Harry. 'It is foolish. You need your sleep. You are only a boy; you should not be roistering all night. I cannot keep hours like this, and it is a waste of candles.'

'Yes; but my lady grandmother, you are nearly seventy years old,' he said patiently. 'Of course you should have your rest. You shall retire whenever you wish. Catalina and I are only young. It is natural for us to want to stay up late. We like amusement.'

'She should be resting. She has to conceive an heir,' Lady Margaret said irritably. 'She's not going to do that bobbing about in a dance with a bunch of feather-heads. Masquing, every night. Whoever heard of such a thing? And who is to pay for all this?'

'We've been married less than a month!' he exclaimed, a little irritated. 'These are our wedding celebrations. I think we can enjoy good pastimes, and keep a merry court. I like to dance.'

'You act as if there was no end to money,' she snapped. 'How much has this dinner cost you? And last night's? The strewing herbs alone must cost a fortune. And the musicians? This is a country that has to hoard its wealth, it cannot afford a spendthrift king. It is not the English way to have a popinjay on the throne, a court of mummers.'

Harry flushed, he was about to make a sharp retort.

'The king is no spendthrift,' Catalina intervened quickly. 'This is just part of the wedding festivities. Your son, the late king, always thought that there should be a merry court. He thought that people should know that the court was wealthy and gay. King Harry is only following in the footsteps of his wise father.'

'His father was not a young fool under the thumb of his foreign wife!' the old lady said spitefully.

Catalina's eyes widened slightly and she put her hand on Harry's sleeve to keep him silent. 'I am his partner and his help-meet, as God has bidden me,' she said gently. 'As I am sure you would want me to be.'

334

The old lady grunted. 'I hear you claim to be more than that,' she began.

The two young people waited. Catalina could feel Harry shift restlessly under the gentle pressure of her hand.

'I hear that your father is to recall his ambassador. Am I right?' She glared at them both. 'Presumably he does not need an ambassador now. The King of England's own wife is in the pay and train of Spain. The King of England's own wife is to be the Spanish ambassador. How can that be?'

'My lady grandmother ...' Harry burst out; but Catalina was sweetly calm.

'I am a princess of Spain, of course I would represent the country of my birth to my country by marriage. I am proud to be able to do such a thing. Of course I will tell my father that his beloved son, my husband, is well, that our kingdom is prosperous. Of course I will tell my husband that my loving father wants to support him in war and peace.'

'When we go to war ...' Harry began.

'War?' the old lady demanded, her face darkening. 'Why should we go to war? We have no quarrel with France. It is only her father who wants war with France, no-one else. Tell me that not even you will be such a fool as to take us into war to fight for the Spanish! What are you now? Their errand boy? Their vassal?'

'The King of France is a danger to us all!' Harry stormed. 'And the glory of England has always been ...'

'I am sure My Lady the King's Grandmother did not mean to disagree with you, sire,' Catalina said sweetly. 'These are changing times. We cannot expect older people always to understand when things change so quickly.'

'I'm not quite in my dotage yet!' the old woman flared. 'And I know danger when I see it. And I know divided loyalties when I see them. And I know a Spanish spy ...'

'You are a most treasured advisor,' Catalina assured her. 'And my lord the king and I are always glad of your advice. Aren't we, Harry?'

He was still angry. 'Agincourt was . . .'

'I'm tired,' the old woman said. 'And you twist and twist things about. I'm going to my room.'

Catalina swept her a deep, respectful curtsey, Harry ducked his head with scant politeness. When Catalina came up the old woman had gone.

'How can she say such things?' Harry demanded. 'How can you bear to listen to her when she says such things? She makes me want to roar like a baited bear! She understands nothing, and she insults you! And you just stand and listen!'

Catalina laughed, took his cross face in her hands and kissed him on the lips. 'Oh, Harry, who cares what she thinks as long as she can do nothing? Nobody cares what she says now.'

'I am going to war with France whatever she thinks,' he promised.

'Of course you are, as soon as the time is right.'

I hide my triumph over her, but I know the taste of it, and it is sweet. I think to myself that one day the other tormentors of my widowhood, the princesses, Harry's sisters, will know my power too. But I can wait.

Lady Margaret may be old but she cannot even gather the senior people of court about her. They have known her forever, the bonds of kinship, wardship, rivalry and feud run through them all like veins through dirty marble. She was never well-liked: not as a woman, not as the mother of a king. She was from one of the great families of the country but when she leapt up so high after Bosworth she flaunted her importance. She has a great reputation for learning and for holiness but she is not beloved. She always insisted on her position as the king's mother and a gulf has grown between her and the other people of the court.

Drifting away from her, they are becoming friends of mine: Lady Margaret Pole of course, the Duke of Buckingham and his sisters, Elizabeth and Anne, Thomas Howard, his sons, Sir Thomas and Lady Elizabeth Boleyn, dearest William Warham, the Archbishop of Canterbury, George Talbot, Sir Henry Vernon that I knew from Wales. They all know that although Harry neglects the business of the realm, I do not.

I consult them for their advice, I share with them the hopes that Arthur and I had. Together with the men of the Privy Council I am bringing the kingdom into one powerful, peaceful country. We are starting to consider how to make the law run from one coast to another, through the wastes, the mountains and forests alike. We are starting to work on the defences of the coast. We are making a survey of the ships that could be commanded into a fighting navy, we are creating muster rolls for an army. I have taken the reins of the kingdom into my hands and found that I know how it is done.

Statecraft is my family business. I sat at my mother's feet in the throne room of the Alhambra Palace. I listened to my father in the beautiful golden Hall of the Ambassadors. I learned the art and the craft of kingship as I had learned about beauty, music, and the art of building, all in the same place, all in the same lessons. I learned a taste for rich tiling, for bright sunlight falling on a delicate tracery of stucco, and for power, all at the same time. Becoming a Queen Regnant is like coming home. I am happy as Queen of England. I am where I was born and raised to be.

The king's grandmother lay in her ornate bed, rich curtains drawn close so that she was lulled by shadows. At the foot of the bed an uncomplaining lady-in-waiting held up the monstrance for her to see the body of Christ in its white purity through the diamond-cut piece of glass. The dying woman fixed her eyes on it, occasionally looking to the ivory crucifix on the wall beside the bed, ignoring the soft murmur of prayers around her.

Catalina kneeled at the foot of the bed, her head bowed, a coral rosary in her hands, praying silently. My Lady Margaret, confident of a hard-won place in heaven, was sliding away from her place on earth.

Outside, in her presence chamber, Harry waited for them to tell him that his grandmother was dead. The last link to his subordinate, junior childhood would be broken with her death. The years in which he had been the second son – trying a little harder for attention, smiling a little brighter, working at being clever – would all be gone. From now on, everyone he would meet would know him only as the most senior member of his family, the greatest of his line. There would be no articulate, critical old Tudor lady to watch over this gullible prince, to cut him down with one quiet word in the very moment of his springing up. When she was dead he could be a man, on his own terms. There would be no-one left who knew him as a boy. Although he was waiting, outwardly pious, for news of her death, inside he was longing to hear that she was gone, that he was at last truly independent, at last a man and a king. He had no idea that he still desperately needed her counsel.

'He must not go to war,' the king's grandmother said hoarsely from the bed.

The lady-in-waiting gave a little gasp at the sudden clarity of her mistress's speech. Catalina rose to her feet. 'What did you say, my lady?'

'He must not go to war,' she repeated. 'Our way is to keep out of the endless wars of Europe, to keep behind the seas, to keep safe and far away from all those princeling squabbles. Our way is keep the kingdom at peace.'

'No,' Catalina said steadily. 'Our way is to take the crusade into the heart of Christendom and beyond. Our way is to make England a leader in establishing the church throughout Europe, throughout the Holy Land, to Africa, to the Turks, to the Saracens, to the edge of the world.'

'The Scots . . .'

'I shall defeat the Scots,' Catalina said firmly. 'I am well aware of the danger.'

'I did not let him marry you for you to lead us to war.' The dark eyes flared with fading resentment.

'You did not let him marry me at all. You opposed it from the first moment,' Catalina said bluntly. 'And I married him precisely so that he should mount a great crusade.' She ignored the little whimper from the lady-in-waiting, who believed that a dying woman should not be contradicted.

'You will promise me that you will not let him go to war,' the old lady breathed. 'My dying promise, my deathbed promise. I lay it on you from my deathbed, as a sacred duty.'

'No.' Catalina shook her head. 'Not me. Not another. I made one deathbed promise and it has cost me dearly. I will not make another. Least of all to you. You have lived your life and made your world as you wished. Now it is my turn. I shall see my son as King of England and perhaps King of Spain. I shall see my husband lead a glorious crusade against the Moors and the Turks. I shall see my country, England, take its place in the world, where it should be. I shall see England at the heart of Europe, a leader of Europe. And I shall be the one that defends it and keeps it safe. I shall be the one that is Queen of England, as you never were.'

'No . . .' the old woman breathed.

'Yes,' Catalina swore, without compromise. 'I am Queen of England now and I will be till my death.'

The old woman raised herself up, struggled for breath. 'You pray for me.' She laid the order on the younger woman almost as if it were a curse. 'I have done my duty to England, to the Tudor line. You see that my name is remembered as if I were a queen.'

Catalina hesitated. If this woman had not served herself, her son and her country, the Tudors would not be on the throne. 'I will pray for you,' she conceded grudgingly. 'And as long as there is a chantry in England, as long as the Holy Roman Catholic Church is in England, your name will be remembered.'

'Forever,' the old woman said, happy in her belief that some things could never change.

'Forever,' Catalina agreed.

Then, less than an hour later, she was dead; and I became queen, ruling queen, undeniably in command, without a rival, even before my coronation. No-one knows what to do in the court, there is no-one who can give a coherent order. Harry has never ordered a royal funeral, how should he know where to begin, how to judge the extent of the honour that should be given to his grandmother? How many mourners? How long the time of mourning? Where should she be buried? How should the whole ceremonial be done?

I summon my oldest friend in England, the Duke of Buckingham, who greeted me on my arrival all those years ago and is now Lord High Steward, and I ask for Lady Margaret Pole to come to me. My ladies bring me the great volume of ceremonial, The Royal Book, written by the king's dead grandmother herself, and I set about organising my first public English event.

I am lucky; tucked inside the cover of the book I find three pages of handwritten instructions. The vain old lady had laid out the order of the procession that she wanted for her funeral. Lady Margaret and I gasp at the numbers of bishops she would like to serve, the pall-bearers, the mutes, the mourners, the decorations on the streets, the duration of the mourning. I show them to the Duke of Buckingham, her one-time ward, who says nothing but in discreet silence just smiles and shakes his head. Hiding my unworthy sense of triumph I take a quill, dip it in black ink, cut almost everything by a half, and then start to give orders.

It was a quiet ceremony of smooth dignity, and everyone knew that it had been commanded and ordered by the Spanish bride. Those who had not known before realised now that the girl who had been waiting for seven years to come to the throne of England had not wasted her time. She knew the temperament of the English people, she knew how to put on a show for them. She knew the tenor of the court: what they regarded as stylish, what they saw as mean. And she knew, as a princess born, how to rule. In those days before her coronation, Catalina established herself as the undeniable queen, and those who had ignored her in her years of poverty now discovered in themselves tremendous affection and respect for the princess.

She accepted their admiration, just as she had accepted their neglect: with calm politeness. She knew that by ordering the funeral of the king's grandmother she established herself as the first woman of the new court, and the arbiter of all decisions of court life. She had, in one brilliant performance, established herself as the foremost leader of England. And she was certain that after this triumph no-one would ever be able to supplant her.

We decide not to cancel our coronation, though My Lady the King's Grandmother's funeral preceded it. The arrangements are all in place, we judge that we should do nothing to mar the joy of the City or of the people who have come from all over England to see the boy Harry take his father's crown. They say that some have travelled all the way from Plymouth, who saw me come ashore, a frightened seasick girl, all those years ago. We are not going to tell them that the great celebration of

Harry's coming to the throne, of my coronation, is cancelled because a cross old lady has died at an ill-judged time. We agree that the people are expecting a great celebration and we should not deny them.

In truth, it is Harry who cannot bear a disappointment. He had promised himself a great moment of glory and he would not miss it for the world. Certainly not for the death of a very old lady who spent the last years of her life preventing him from having his own way in anything.

I agree with him. I judge that the king's grandmother seized her power and enjoyed her time, and now it is time for us. I judge that it is the mood of the country and the mood of the court to celebrate the triumph of Harry's coming to the throne with me at his side. Indeed, for some of them, who have long taken an interest in me, there is the greatest delight that I shall have the crown at last. I decide – and there is no-one but me to decide – that we will go ahead. And so we do.

I know that Harry's grief for his grandmother is only superficial; his mourning is mostly show. I saw him when I came from her privy chamber, and he knew, since I had left her bedside, that she must be dead. I saw his shoulders stretch out and lift, as if he were suddenly free from the burden of her care, as if her skinny, loving, age-spotted hand had been a dead weight on his neck. I saw his quick smile – his delight that he was alive and young and lusty, and that she was gone. Then I saw the careful composing of his face into conventional sadness and I stepped forwards, with my face grave also, and told him that she was dead, in a low sad voice, and he answered me in the same tone.

I am glad to know that he can play the hypocrite. The court room in the Alhambra Palace has many doors; my father told me that a king should be able to go out of one and come in through another and nobody know his mind. I know that to rule is to keep your own counsel. Harry is a boy now, but one day he will be a man and he will have to make up his own mind and judge well. I will remember that he can say one thing and think another.

But I have learned something else about him too. When I saw that *he did not weep one real tear for his grandmother I knew that this king, our golden Harry, has a cold heart that no-one can trust. She had been as a mother to him; she had dominated his childhood. She had cared for him, watched over him, and taught him herself. She supervised his every waking moment and shielded him from every unpleasant sight, she kept him from tutors who would have taught him of the world, and allowed him to walk only in the gardens of her making. She spent hours on her knees in prayer for him and insisted that he be taught the rule and the power of the church. But when she stood in his way, when she denied him his pleasures, he saw her as his enemy; and he cannot forgive anyone who refuses him something he wants. I know from this that this boy, this charming boy, will grow to be a man whose selfishness will be a danger to himself, and to those around him. One day we may all wish that his grandmother had taught him better.*

24th June 1509

They carried Catalina from the Tower to Westminster as an English princess. She travelled in a litter made of cloth of gold, carried high by four white palfreys so everyone could see her. She wore a gown of white satin and a coronet set with pearls, her hair brushed out over her shoulders. Harry was crowned first and then Catalina bowed her head and took the holy oil of kingship on her head and breasts, stretched out her hand for the sceptre and the ivory wand, knew that, at last, she was a queen, as her mother had been: an anointed queen, a greater being than mere mortals, a step closer to the angels, appointed by God to rule His country, and under His especial protection. She knew that finally she had fulfilled the destiny that she had been born for, she had taken her place, as she had promised that she would.

She took a throne just a little lower than King Henry's, and the crowd that cheered for the handsome young king coming to his throne also cheered for her, the Spanish princess, who had been constant against the odds and was crowned Queen Katherine of England at last.

I have waited for this day for so long that when it comes it is like a dream, like the dreams I have had of my greatest desires. I go through the coronation ceremony: my place in the procession, my seat on the throne, the cool lightness of the ivory rod in my hand, my other hand tightly gripping the heavy sceptre, the deep, heady scent of the holy oil on my forehead and breasts, as if it is another dream of longing for Arthur.

But this time it is real.

When we come out of the Abbey and I hear the crowd cheer for him, for me, I turn to look at my husband beside me. I am shocked then, a sudden shock like waking suddenly from a dream – that he is not Arthur. He is not my love. I had expected to be crowned beside Arthur and for us to take our thrones together. But instead of the handsome, thoughtful face of my husband, it is Harry's round, flushed beam. Instead of my husband's shy, coltish grace, it is Harry's exuberant swagger at my side.

I realise at that moment, that Arthur really is dead, really gone from me. I am fulfilling my part of our promise, marrying the King of England, even though it is Harry. Please God, Arthur is fulfilling his part: to watch over me from al-Yanna, and to wait for me there. One day, when my work is done and I can go to my love, I will live with him forever.

'Are you happy?' the boy asks me, shouting to make himself heard above the pealing of the bells and the cheering of the crowds. 'Are you happy, Catalina? Are you glad that I married you? Are you glad to be Queen of England, that I have given you this crown?'

344

'I am very happy,' I promise him. 'And you must call me Katherine now.'

'Katherine?' he asks. 'Not Catalina any more?'

'I am Queen of England,' I say, thinking of Arthur saying these very words. 'I am Queen Katherine of England.'

'Oh, I say!' he exclaims, delighted at the idea of changing his name, as I have changed mine. 'That's good. We shall be King Henry, and Queen Katherine. They shall call me Henry too.'

This is the king but he is not Arthur, he is Harry who wants to be called Henry, like a man. I am the queen, and I shall not be Catalina. I shall be Katherine – English through and through, and not the girl who was once so very much in love with the Prince of Wales.

Katherine, Queen of England

Summer 1509

The court, drunk with joy, with delight in its own youth, with freedom, took the summer for pleasure. The progress from one beautiful, welcoming house to another lasted for two long months when Henry and Katherine hunted, dined in the greenwood, danced until midnight, and spent money like water. The great lumbering carts of the royal household went along the dusty lanes of England so that the next house might shine with gold and be bright with tapestries, so that the royal bed – which they shared every night – would be rich with the best linen and the glossiest furs.

No business of any worth was transacted by Henry at all. He wrote once to his father-in-law to tell him how happy he was, but the rest of the work for the king followed him in boxes from one beautiful parkland castle or mansion to another, and these were opened and read only by Katherine, Queen of England, who ordered the clerks to write her orders to the Privy Council, and sent them out herself over the king's signature.

Not until mid-September did the court return to Richmond and Henry at once declared that the party should go on. Why should they ever cease in pleasure? The weather was fair, they could have hunting and boating, archery and tennis contests, parties and masquings. The nobles and gentry flocked to Richmond to join the unending party: the families whose power and name were older than the Tudors, and the new ones, whose wealth and name was bobbing upwards on the rise of the Tudor tide, floated by Tudor wealth. The victors of Bosworth who had staked their lives on the Tudor courage in great danger found themselves alongside newcomers who made their fortunes on nothing more than Tudor amusements.

Henry welcomed everyone with uncritical delight; anyone who was witty and well-read, charming or a good sportsman could have a place at court. Katherine smiled on them all, never rested, never refused a challenge or an invitation, and set herself the task of keeping her teenage husband entertained all the day long. Slowly, but surely, she drew the management of the entertainments, then of the household, then of the king's business, then of the kingdom, into her hands.

Queen Katherine had the accounts for the royal court spread out before her, a clerk to one side, a comptroller of the household with his great book to another, the men who served as exchequers of the household standing behind her. She was checking the books of the great departments of the court: the kitchen, the cellar, the wardrobe, the servery, the payments for services, the stables, the musicians. Each department of the palace had to compile their monthly expenditure and send it to the Queen's Exchequer – just as they had sent it to My Lady the King's Mother, for her to approve their business, and if they overspent by very much, they could expect a visit from one of the exchequers for the Privy Purse to ask them pointedly if they could explain why costs had so suddenly risen?

Every court in Europe was engaged in the struggle to control the cost of running the sprawling feudal households with the newly fashionable wealth and display. All the kings wanted a great entourage, like a mediaeval lord; but now they wanted culture, wealth, architecture and rich display as well. England was managed better than any court in Europe. Queen Katherine had learned her housekeeping skills the hard way: when she had tried to run Durham House as a royal palace should be run, but with no income. She knew to a penny what was the price of a gallon loaf, she knew the difference between salted fish and fresh, she knew the price of cheap wine imported from Spain and expensive wine brought in from France. Even more rigorous than My Lady the King's Mother, Queen Katherine's scrutiny of the household books made the cooks argue with suppliers at the kitchen doors, and get the very best price for the extravagantly consuming court.

Once a week Queen Katherine surveyed the expenditure of the different departments of the court, and every day at dawn, while King Henry was out hunting, she read the letters that came for him, and drafted his replies.

It was steady, unrelenting work, to keep the court running as a well-ordered centre for the country, and to keep the king's business under tight control. Queen Katherine, determined to understand her new country, did not begrudge the hours she spent reading letters, taking advice from Privy Councillors, inviting objections, taking opinions. She had seen her own mother dominate a country by persuasion. Isabella of Spain had brokered her country out of a collection of rival kingships and lordships by offering them a trouble-free, cheap, central administration, a nationwide system of justice, an end to corruption and banditry and an infallible defence system. Her daughter saw at once that these advantages could be transferred to England.

But she was also following in the steps of her Tudor father-in-law, and the more she worked on his papers and read his letters, the more she admired the steadiness of his judgement. Oddly, she wished now, that she had known him as a ruler, as she would have benefited from his advice. From his records she could see how he balanced the desire of the English lords to be independent, on their own lands, with his own need to bind them to the crown. Cunningly, he allowed the northern lords greater freedom and greater wealth and status than anyone, since they were his bulwark against the Scots. Katherine had maps of the northern lands pinned around the council chamber and saw how the border with Scotland was nothing more than a handful of disputed territories in difficult country. Such a border could never be made safe from a threatening neighbour. She thought that the Scots were England's Moors: the land could not be shared with them. They would have to be utterly defeated.

She shared her father-in-law's fears of overmighty English lords at court, she learned his jealousy of their wealth and power; and when Henry thought to give one man a handsome pension in an exuberant moment, it was Katherine who pointed out that he was a wealthy man already, there was no need to make his position any stronger. Henry wanted to be a king famed for his generosity, beloved for the sudden shower of his gifts. Katherine knew that power followed wealth and that kings new-come to their throne must hoard both wealth and power.

'Did your father never warn you about the Howards?' she asked as they stood together watching an archery contest. Henry, stripped down to his shirtsleeves, his bow in his hand, had the second-highest score and was waiting for his turn to go again.

'No,' he replied. 'Should he have done so?'

'Oh no,' she said swiftly. 'I did not mean to suggest that they would play you false in any way, they are love and loyalty personified, Thomas Howard has been a great friend to your family, keeping the north safe for you, and Edward is my knight, my dearest knight of all. It is just that their wealth has increased so much, and their family alliances are so strong. I just wondered what your father thought of them.'

'I wouldn't know,' Henry said easily. 'I wouldn't have asked him. He wouldn't have told me anyway.'

'Not even when he knew you were to be the next king?'

He shook his head. 'He thought I wouldn't be king for years yet,' he said. 'He had not finished making me study my books. He had not yet let me out into the world.'

She shook her head. 'When we have a son we will make sure he is prepared for his kingdom from an early age.'

At once, his hand stole around her waist. 'Do you think it will be soon?' he asked.

'Please God,' she said sweetly, withholding her secret hope. 'Do you know, I have been thinking of a name for him?'

'Have you, sweetheart? Shall you call him Ferdinand for your father?'

'If you would like it, I thought we might call him Arthur,' she said carefully.

'For my brother?' His face darkened at once.

'No, Arthur for England,' she said swiftly. 'When I look at you sometimes I think you are like King Arthur of the round table, and this is Camelot. We are making a court here as beautiful and as magical as Camelot ever was.'

'Do you think that, little dreamer?'

'I think you could be the greatest king England has ever known since Arthur of Camelot,' she said.

'Arthur it is, then,' he said, soothed as always by praise. 'Arthur Henry.'

'Yes.'

They called to him from the butts that it was his turn, and that he had a high score to beat, and he went with a kiss blown to her. Katherine made sure that she was watching as he drew his bow, and when he glanced over, as he always did, he could see that her attention was wholly on him. The muscles in his lean back rippled as he drew back the arrow, he was like a statue, beautifully poised, and

353

then slowly, like a dancer, he released the string and the arrow flew – faster than sight – true to the very centre of the target.

'A hit!'

'A winning hit!'

'Victory to the king!'

The prize was a golden arrow and Henry came bright-faced to his wife to kneel at her feet so that she could bend down and kiss him on both cheeks, and then, lovingly, on the mouth.

'I won for you,' he said. 'You, alone. You bring me luck. I never miss when you are watching me. You shall keep the winning arrow.'

'It is a Cupid's arrow,' she responded. 'I shall keep it to remind me of the one in my heart.'

'She loves me.' He rose to his feet and turned to his court, and there was a ripple of applause and laughter. He shouted triumphantly: 'She loves me!'

'Who could help but love you?' Lady Elizabeth Boleyn, one of the ladies-in-waiting, called out boldly. Henry glanced at her and then looked down from his great height to his petite wife.

'Who could help but love her?' he asked, smiling at her.

That night I kneel before my prie-dieu and clasp my hands over my belly. It is the second month that I have not bled, I am almost certain that I am with child.

'Arthur,' I whisper, my eyes closed. I can almost see him, as he was: naked in candlelight in our bedroom at Ludlow. 'Arthur, my love. He says that I can call this boy Arthur Henry. So I will have fulfilled our hope – that I should give you a son called Arthur. And though I know you didn't like your brother, I will show him the respect that I owe to him; he is a good boy and I pray that he will grow to a good man. I shall call my boy Arthur Henry for you both.'

I feel no guilt for my growing affection for this boy Henry though he can never take the place of his brother, Arthur. It is right that I should love my husband and Henry is an endearing boy. The knowledge that I have of him, from watching him for long years as closely as if he were an enemy, has brought me to a deep awareness of the sort of boy he is. He is selfish as a child, but he has a child's generosity and easy tenderness. He is vain, he is ambitious, to tell truth, he is as conceited as a player in a troupe, but he is quick to laughter and quick to tears, quick to compassion, quick to alleviate hardship. He will make a good man if he has good guides, if he can be taught to rein in his desires and learn service to his country and to God. He has been spoiled by those who should have guided him; but it is not too late to make a good man from him. It is my task and my duty to keep him from selfishness. Like any young man, he is a tyrant in the making. A good mother would have disciplined him, perhaps a loving wife can curb him. If I can love him, and hold him to love me, I can make a great king of him. And England needs a great king.

Perhaps this is one of the services I can do for England: guide him, gently and steadily, away from his spoiled childhood and towards a manhood which is responsible. His father and his grandmother kept him as a boy; perhaps it is my task to help him grow to be a man.

'Arthur, my dearest Arthur,' I say quietly as I rise and go towards the bed, and this time I am speaking to them both: to the husband that I loved first, and to the child that is slowly, quietly growing inside me.

Autumn 1509

At nighttime in October, after Katherine had refused to dance after midnight for the previous three weeks, and had insisted, instead, on watching Henry dance with her ladies, she told him that she was with child, and made him swear to keep it secret.

'I want to tell everyone!' he exclaimed. He had come to her room in his nightgown and they were seated either side of the warm fire, on their way to bed.

'You can write to my father next month,' she specified. 'But I don't want everyone to know yet. They will all guess soon enough.'

'You must rest,' he said instantly. 'And should you have special things to eat? Do you have a desire for anything special to eat? I can send someone for it at once, they can wake the cooks. Tell me, love, what would you like?'

'Nothing! Nothing!' she said, laughing. 'See, we have biscuits and wine. What more do I ever eat this late at night?'

'Oh usually, yes! But now everything is different.'

'I shall ask the physicians in the morning,' she said. 'But I need nothing now. Truly, my love.'

'I want to get you something,' he said. 'I want to look after you.'

'You do look after me,' she reassured him. 'And I am perfectly well fed, and I feel very well.'

'Not sick? That is a sign of a boy, I am sure.'

'I have been feeling a little sick in the mornings,' she said, and watched his beam of happiness. 'I feel certain that it is a boy. I hope this is our Arthur Henry.'

'Oh! You were thinking of him when you spoke to me at the archery contest.'

'Yes, I was. But I was not sure then, and I did not want to tell you too early.'

'And when do you think he will be born?'

'In early summer, I think.'

'It cannot take so long!' he exclaimed.

'My love, I think it does take that long.'

'I shall write to your father in the morning,' he said. 'I shall tell him to expect great news in the summer. Perhaps we shall be home after a great campaign against the French then. Perhaps I shall bring you a victory and you shall give me a son.'

Henry has sent his own physician, the most skilled man in London, to see me. The man stands at one side of the room while I sit on a chair at the other. He cannot examine me, of course – the body of the queen cannot be touched by anyone but the king. He cannot ask me if I am regular in my courses or in my bowels; they too are sacred. He is so paralysed with embarrassment at being called to see me that he keeps his eyes on the floor and asks me short questions in a quiet, clipped voice. He speaks English, and I have to strain to hear and understand him.

He asks me if I eat well, and if I have any sickness. I answer that I eat well enough but that I am sick of the smell and sight of cooked meats. I miss the fruit and vegetables that were part of my daily diet in Spain, I am craving baklava sweetmeats made from honey, or a tagine made with vegetables and rice. He says that it does not matter since there is no benefit to eating vegetables or fruit for humans, and indeed, he would have advised me against eating any raw stuff for the duration of my pregnancy.

He asks me if I know when I conceived. I say that I cannot say for certain, but that I know the date of my last course. He smiles as a learned man to a fool and tells me that this is little guide as to when a baby might be due. I have seen Moorish doctors calculate the date of a baby's birth with a special abacus. He says he has never heard of such things and such heathen devices would be unnatural and not wanted at the treatment of a Christian child.

He suggests that I rest. He asks me to send for him whenever I feel unwell and he will come to apply leeches. He says he is a great believer in bleeding women frequently to prevent them becoming overheated. Then he bows and leaves.

I look blankly at Maria de Salinas, standing in the corner of the room for this mockery of a consultation. 'This is the best doctor in England?' I ask her. 'This is the best that they have?'

She shakes her head in bewilderment.

'I wonder if we can get someone from Spain,' I think aloud.

'Your mother and father have all but cleared Spain of the learned men,' she says, and in that moment I feel almost ashamed of them.

'Their learning was heretical,' I say defensively.

She shrugs. 'Well, the Inquisition arrested most of them. The rest have fled.'

'Where did they go?' I ask.

'Wherever people go. The Jews went to Portugal and then to Italy, to Turkey, I think throughout Europe. I suppose the Moors went to Africa and the East.'

'Can we not find someone from Turkey?' I suggest. 'Not a heathen, of course. But someone who has learned from a Moorish physician? There must be some Christian doctors who have knowledge. Some who know more than this one?'

'I will ask the ambassador,' she says

'He must be Christian,' I stipulate. *I know that I will need a better doctor than this shy ignoramus, but I do not want to go against the authority of my mother and the Holy Church. If they say that such knowledge is sin, then, surely, I should embrace ignorance. It is my duty. I am no scholar and it is better if I am guided by the ruling of the Holy Church. But can God really want us to deny knowledge? And what if this ignorance costs me England's son and heir?*

Katherine did not reduce her work, commanding the clerks to the king, hearing petitioners who needed royal justice, discussing with the Privy Council the news from the kingdom. But she wrote to Spain to suggest that her father might like to send an ambassador to represent Spanish interests, especially since Henry was determined on a war against France in alliance with Spain as soon as the season for war started in the spring, and there would be much correspondence between the two countries.

'He is most determined to do your bidding,' Catalina wrote to her father, carefully translating every word into the complex code that they used. 'He is conscious that he has not been to war and is anxious that all goes well for an English–Spanish army. I am very concerned, indeed, that he is not exposed to danger. He has no heir, and even if he did, this is a hard country for princes in their minority. When he goes to war with you, I shall trust him into your safe-keeping. He should certainly feel that he is experiencing war to the full, he should certainly learn how to campaign from you. But I shall trust you to keep him from any real danger. Do not misunderstand me on this,' she wrote sternly. 'He must feel that he is at the heart of war, he must learn how battles are won; but he must not ever be in any real danger. And,' she added, 'he must never know that we have protected him.'

King Ferdinand, in full possession of Castile and Aragon once more, ruling as regent for Juana who was now said to be far beyond taking her throne, lost in a dark world of grief and madness, wrote smoothly back to his youngest daughter that she was not to worry about the safety of her husband in war, he would make sure that Henry was exposed to nothing but excitement. 'And do not let your wifely fears distract him from his duty,' he reminded her. 'In all her years with me your mother never shirked from danger. You must be the queen she would want you to be. This is a war that has to be fought for the safety and profit of us all, and the young king must play his part alongside this old king and the old emperor. This is an alliance of two old warhorses and one young colt; and he will want to be part of it.' He left a space in the letter as if for thought and then added a postscript. 'Of course, we will both make sure it is mostly play for him. Of course he will not know.'

Ferdinand was right. Henry was desperate to be part of an alliance that would defeat France. The Privy Council, the thoughtful advisors of his father's careful reign, were appalled to find that the young man was utterly set on the idea that kingship meant warfare, and he could imagine no better way to demonstrate that he had inherited the throne. The eager, boastful young men that formed the young court, desperate for a chance to show their own courage, were egging Henry on to war. The French had been hated for so long that it seemed incredible that a peace had ever been made and that it had lasted. It seemed unnatural to be at peace with the French – the normal state of warfare should be resumed as soon as victory was a certainty. And victory, with a new young king, and a new young court, must be a certainty now.

Nothing that Katherine might quietly remark could completely calm the fever for war, and Henry was so bellicose with the French ambassador at their first meeting that the astounded representative reported to his master that the new young king was out of his mind with choler, denying that he had ever written a peaceable letter to the King of France, which the Privy Council had sent in his absence. Fortunately, their next meeting went better. Katherine made sure that she was there.

'Greet him pleasantly,' she prompted Henry as she saw the man advance.

'I will not feign kindness where I mean war.'

'You have to be cunning,' she said softly. 'You have to be skilled in saying one thing and thinking another.'

'I will never pretend. I will never deny my righteous pride.'

'No, you should not pretend, exactly. But let him in his folly misunderstand you. There is more than one way to win a war, and it is winning that matters, not threatening. If he thinks you are his friend, we will catch them unprepared. Why would we give them warning of attack?'

He was troubled, he looked at her, frowning. 'I am not a liar.'

'No, for you told him last time that the vain ambitions of his king would be corrected by you. The French cannot be allowed to capture Venice. We have an ancient alliance with Venice . . .'

'Do we?'

'Oh, yes,' Katherine said firmly. 'England has an ancient alliance with Venice, and besides, it is the very first wall of Christianity against the Turks. By threatening Venice the French are on the brink of letting the heathens into Italy. They should be ashamed of themselves. But last time you met, you warned the French ambassador. You could not have been more clear. Now is the time for you to greet him with a smile. You do not need to spell out your campaign. We will keep our own counsel. We will not share it with such as him.'

'I have told him once, I need not tell him again. I do not repeat myself,' Henry said, warming to the thought.

'We don't brag of our strength,' she said. 'We know what we can do, and we know what we will do. They can find out for themselves in our own good time.'

'Indeed,' said Henry, and stepped down from the little dais to greet the French ambassador quite pleasantly, and was rewarded to see the man fumble in his bow and stutter in his address.

'I had him quite baffled,' he said to Katherine gleefully.

'You were masterly,' she assured him.

If he was a dullard I would have to bite back my impatience and curb my temper more often than I do. But he is not unintelligent. He is bright and clever, perhaps even as quick-witted as Arthur. But where Arthur had been trained to think, had been educated as a king from birth, they let this second son slide by on his charm and his ready tongue. They found him pleasing and encouraged him to be nothing more than agreeable. He has a good brain and he can read, debate and think well – but only if the topic catches his interest, and then only for a while. They taught him to study, but only to demonstrate his own cleverness. He is lazy, he is terribly lazy – he would always rather that someone does the detailed work for him, and this is a great fault in a king, it throws him into the power of his clerks. A king who will not work will always be in the hands of his advisors. It is a recipe for overmighty councillors.

When we start to discuss the terms of the contract between Spain and England he asks me to write it out for him, he does not like to do this himself, he likes to dictate and have a clerk write it out fair. And he will never bother to learn the code. It means that every letter between him and the emperor, every letter between him and my father, are either written by me, or translated by me. I am at the very centre of the emerging plans for war, whether I want to be or no. I cannot help but be the decision-maker at the very heart of this alliance, and Henry puts himself to one side.

Of course I am not reluctant to do my duty. No true child of my mother's would ever have turned away from effort, especially one that led to war with the enemies of Spain. We were all raised to know that kingship is a vocation, not a treat. To be a king means to rule; and ruling *is always demanding work. No true child of my father's could have resisted being at the very heart of planning and plotting, and preparing for war. There is no-one at the English court better able than I to take our country into war.*

I am no fool. I guessed from the start that my father planned to use our English troops against the French, and while we engage them at the time and place of his choosing, I wager that he will invade the kingdom of Navarre. I must have heard him a dozen times telling my mother that if he could have Navarre he would have rounded the north border of Aragon and besides, Navarre is a rich region, growing grapes and wheat. My father has wanted it from the moment he came to the throne of Aragon. I know that if he has a chance at Navarre he will win it, and if he can make the English do the work for him he would think that even better.

But I am not fighting this war to oblige my father, though I let him think that. He will not use me as his instrument, I will use him for mine. I want this war for England, and for God. The Pope himself has ruled that the French should not overrun Venice, the Pope himself is putting his own holy army into the field against the French. No true son or daughter of the church needs any greater cause than this: to know that the Holy Father is calling for support.

And for me there is another reason, even more powerful than that. I never forget my mother's warning that the Moors will come against Christendom again, I never forget her telling me that I must be ready in England as she was always ready in Spain. If the French defeat the armies of the Pope and seize Venice, who can doubt but that the Moors will see it as their chance to snatch Venice in their turn from the French? And once the Moors get a toe-hold in the heart of Christendom once more, it will be my mother's war to be fought all over again. They will come at us from the East, they will come at us from Venice, and Christian Europe will lie at their mercy. My father himself told me that Venice with its great trade, its arsenal, its powerful dockyards, must never be taken by the Moors, we must never let them win a city where they could build fighting galleys in a week, arm them in days, man them in a morning. If they have the Venetian dockyards and shipwrights then we have lost the seas. I know that it is my given duty, given to me by my mother and by God: to send English men to serve the Pope, and to defend Venice from any invader. It is easy to persuade Henry to think the same.

But I don't forget Scotland. I never forget Arthur's fear of Scotland. The Privy Council has spies along the border, and Thomas Howard, the old Earl of Surrey, was placed there, quite deliberately I think, by the old king. King Henry my father-in-law gave Thomas Howard great lands in the north so that he, of all people, would keep the border safe. The old king was no fool. He did not let others do his business and trust to their abilities. He tied them into his success. If the Scots invade England they will come through Howard lands, and Thomas Howard is as anxious as I that this will never happen. He has assured me that the Scots will not come against us this summer, in any numbers worse than their usual brigand raids. All the intelligence we can gather from English merchants in Scotland, from travellers primed to keep their eyes open, confirms the earl's view. We are safe for this summer at least. I can take this moment and send the English army to war against the French. Henry can march out in safety and learn to be a soldier.

Katherine watched the dancing at the Christmas festivities, applauded her husband when he twirled other ladies around the room, laughed at the mummers, and signed off the court's bills for enormous amounts of wine, ale, beef, and the rarest and finest of everything. She gave Henry a beautiful inlaid saddle for his Christmas gift, and some shirts that she had sewn and embroidered herself with the beautiful blackwork of Spain.

'I want all my shirts to be sewn by you,' he said, putting the fine linen against his cheek. 'I want to never wear anything that another woman has touched. Only your hands shall make my shirts.'

Katherine smiled and pulled his shoulder down to her height. He bent down like a grown boy, and she kissed his forehead. 'Always,' she promised him. 'I shall always sew your shirts for you.'

'And now, my gift to you,' he said. He pushed a large leather box towards her. Katherine opened it. There was a great set of magnificent jewels: a diadem, a necklace, two bracelets and matching rings.

'Oh, Henry!'

'Do you like them?'

'I love them,' she said.

'Will you wear them tonight?'

'I shall wear them tonight and at the Twelfth Night feast,' she promised.

The young queen shone in her happiness, this first Christmas of her reign. The full skirts of her gown could not conceal the curve of her belly; everywhere she went the young king would order a chair to be brought for her, she must not stand for a moment, she must never be wearied. He composed for her special songs that his musicians played, special dances and special masques were made up in her honour. The court, delighted with the young queen's fertility, with the health and strength of the young king, with itself, made merry late into the night and Katherine sat on her throne, her feet slightly spread to accommodate the curve of her belly, and smiled in her joy.

Westminster Palace, January 1510

I wake in the night to pain, and a strange sensation. I dreamed that a tide was rising in the river Thames and that a fleet of black-sailed

ships were coming upriver. I think that it must be the Moors, coming for me, and then I think it is a Spanish fleet – an armada, but strangely, disturbingly, my enemy, and the enemy of England. In my distress I toss and turn in bed and I wake with a sense of dread and find that it is worse than any dream, my sheets are wet with blood, and there is a real pain in my belly.

I call out in terror, and my cry wakes Maria de Salinas, who is sleeping with me.

'What is it?' she asks, then she sees my face and calls out sharply to the maid at the foot of the bed and sends her running for my ladies and for the midwives, but somewhere in the back of my mind I know already that there is nothing that they can do. I clamber into my chair in my bloodstained nightdress and feel the pain twist and turn in my belly.

By the time they arrive, struggling from their beds, all stupid with sleep, I am on my knees on the floor like a sick dog, praying for the pain to pass and to leave me whole. I know that there is no point in praying for the safety of my child. I know that my child is lost. I can feel the tearing sensation in my belly as he slowly comes away.

After a long, bitter day, when Henry comes to the door again and again, and I send him away, calling out to him in a bright voice of reassurance, biting the palm of my hand so that I do not cry out, the baby is born, dead. The midwife shows her to me, a little girl, a white, limp little thing: poor baby, my poor baby. My only comfort is that it is not the boy I had promised Arthur I would bear for him. It is a girl, a dead girl, and then I twist my face in grief when I remember that he wanted a girl first, and she was to be called Mary.

I cannot speak for grief, I cannot face Henry and tell him myself. I cannot bear the thought of anyone telling the court, I cannot bring myself to write to my father and tell him that I have failed England, I have failed Henry, I have failed Spain, and worst of all – and this I could never tell anyone – I have failed Arthur.

I stay in my room, I close the door on all the anxious faces, on the

midwives wanting me to drink strawberry-leaf tisanes, on the ladies
wanting to tell me about their still births, and their mothers' still births
and their happy endings, I shut them away from me and I kneel at
the foot of my bed, and press my hot face against the covers. I whisper
through my sobs, muffled so that no-one but him can hear me. 'I am
sorry, so sorry, my love. I am so sorry not to have had your son. I don't
know why, I don't know why our gentle God should send me this great
sorrow. I am so sorry, my love. If I ever have another chance I will do
my best, the very best that I can, to have our son, to keep him safe till
birth and beyond. I will, I swear I will. I tried this time, God knows,
I would have given anything to have your son and named him Arthur
for you, my love.' I steady myself as I can feel the words tumbling out
too quickly, I can feel myself losing control, I feel the sobs starting to
choke me.

'Wait for me,' I say quietly. 'Wait for me still. Wait for me by the
quiet waters in the garden where the white and the red rose petals fall.
Wait for me and when I have given birth to your son Arthur and your
daughter Mary, and done my duty here, I will come to you. Wait for
me in the garden and I will never fail you. I will come to you, love.
My love.'

The king's physician went to the king directly from the queen's apartments. 'Your Grace, I have good news for you.'

Henry turned a face to him that was as sour as a child's whose
joy has been stolen. 'You have?'

'I have indeed.'

'The queen is better? In less pain? She will be well?'

'Even better than well,' the physician said. 'Although she lost one
child, she has kept another. She was carrying twins, Your Grace.
She has lost one child but her belly is still large and she is still with
child.'

For a moment the young man could not understand the words. 'She still has a child?'

The physician smiled. 'Yes, Your Grace.'

It was like a stay of execution. Henry felt his heart turn over with hope. 'How can it be?'

The physician was confident. 'By various ways I can tell. Her belly is still firm, the bleeding has stopped. I am certain she is still with child.'

Henry crossed himself. 'God is with us,' he said positively. 'This is the sign of His favour.' He paused. 'Can I see her?'

'Yes, she is as happy at this news as you.'

Henry bounded up the stairs to Katherine's rooms. Her presence chamber was empty of anyone but the least informed sight-seers, the court and half the City knew that she had taken to her bed and would not be seen. Henry brushed through the crowd who whispered hushed blessings for him and the queen, strode through her privy chamber, where her women were sewing, and tapped on her bedroom door.

Maria de Salinas opened it and stepped back for the king. The queen was out of her bed, seated in the window seat, her book of prayers held up to the light.

'My love!' he exclaimed. 'Here is Dr Fielding come to me with the best of news.'

Her face was radiant. 'I told him to tell you privately.'

'He did. No-one else knows. My love, I am so glad!'

Her eyes were wet with tears. 'It is like a redemption,' she said. 'I feel as if a cross has been lifted from my shoulders.'

'I shall go to Walsingham the moment our baby is born and thank Our Lady for her favour,' he promised. 'I shall endow the shrine with a fortune, if it is a boy.'

'Please God that He grants it,' she murmured.

'Why should He not?' Henry demanded. 'When it is our desire, and right for England, and we ask it as holy children of the church?'

'Amen,' she said quickly. 'If it is God's will.'

He flicked his hand. 'Of course it must be His will,' he said. 'Now you must take care and rest.'

Katherine smiled at him. 'As you see.'

'Well, you must. And anything you want, you shall have.'

'I shall tell the cooks if I want anything.'

'And the midwives shall attend you night and morning to make sure that you are well.'

'Yes,' she agreed. 'And if God is willing, we shall have a son.'

It was Maria de Salinas, my true friend who had come with me from Spain, and stayed with me through our good months and our hard years, who found the Moor. He was attending on a wealthy merchant, travelling from Genoa to Paris, they had called in at London to value some gold and Maria heard of him from a woman who had given a hundred pounds to Our Lady of Walsingham, hoping to have a son.

'They say he can make barren women give birth,' she whispers to me, watching that none of my other ladies have come close enough to overhear.

I cross myself as if to avoid temptation. 'Then he must use black arts.'

'Princess, he is supposed to be a great physician. Trained by masters who were at the university of Toledo.'

'I will not see him.'

'Because you think he must use black arts?'

'Because he is my enemy and my mother's enemy. She knew that the Moors' knowledge was unlawfully gained, drawn from the devil, not from the revealed truth of God. She drove the Moors from Spain and their magical arts with them.'

'Your Grace, he may be the only doctor in England who knows anything about women.'

'I will not see him.'

369

Maria took my refusal and let a few weeks go by and then I woke in the night with a deep pain in my belly, and slowly, felt the blood coming. She was quick and ready to call the maids with the towels and with a ewer to wash, and when I was back in bed again and we realised that it was no more than my monthly courses returned, she came quietly and stood beside the head of the bed. Lady Margaret Pole was silent at the doorway.

'Your Grace, please see this doctor.'

'He is a Moor.'

'Yes, but I think he is the only man in this country who will know what is happening. How can you have your courses if you are with child? You may be losing this second baby. You have to see a doctor that we can trust.'

'Maria, he is my enemy. He is my mother's enemy. She spent her life driving his people from Spain.'

'We lost their wisdom with them,' Maria says quietly. 'You have not lived in Spain for nearly a decade, Your Grace, you do not know what it is like there now. My brother writes to me that people fall sick and there are no hospitals that can cure them. The nuns and the monks do their best; but they have no knowledge. If you have a stone it has to be cut out of you by a horse doctor, if you have a broken arm or leg then the blacksmith has to set it. The barbers are surgeons, the tooth drawers work in the market place and break people's jaws. The midwives go from burying a man sick with sores to a childbirth and lose as many babies as they deliver. The skills of the Moorish physicians, with their knowledge of the body, their herbs to soothe pain, their instruments for surgery, and their insistence on washing – it is all lost.'

'If it was sinful knowledge it is better lost,' I say stubbornly.

'Why would God be on the side of ignorance and dirt and disease?' she asks fiercely. 'Forgive me, Your Grace, but this makes no sense. And

you are forgetting what your mother wanted. She always said that the universities should be restored, to teach Christian knowledge. But by then she had killed or banished all the teachers who knew anything.'

'The queen will not want to be advised by a heretic,' Lady Margaret said firmly. 'No English lady would consult a Moor.'

Maria turns to me. 'Please, Your Grace.'

I am in such pain that I cannot bear an argument. 'Both of you can leave me now,' I say. 'Just let me sleep.'

Lady Margaret goes out of the door but Maria pauses to close the shutters so that I am in shadow. 'Oh, let him come then,' I say. 'But not while I am like this. He can come next week.'

She brings him by the hidden stairway which runs from the cellars through a servants' passage to the queen's private rooms at Richmond Palace. I am wearily dressing for dinner, and I let him come into my rooms while I am still unlaced, in my shift with a cape thrown on top. I grimace at the thought of what my mother would say at a man coming into my privy chamber. But I know, in my heart, that I have to see a doctor who can tell me how to get a son for England. And I know, if I am honest, that something is wrong with the baby they say I am carrying.

I know him for an unbeliever the moment I see him. He is black as ebony, his eyes as dark as jet, his mouth wide and sensual, his face both merry and compassionate, all at the same time. The back of his hands are black, dark as his face, long-fingered, his nails rosy pink, the palms brown, the creases ingrained with his colour. If I were a palmist I could trace the lifeline on his African palm like cart tracks of brown dust in a field of terracotta. I know him at once for a Moor and a Nubian; and I want to order him away from my rooms. But I know, at the same time, that he may be the only doctor in this country who has the knowledge I need.

This man's people, infidels, sinners who have set their black faces against God, have medicine that we do not. For some reason, God and his angels have not revealed to us the knowledge that these people have sought and found. These people have read in Greek everything that the Greek physicians thought. Then they have explored for themselves, with forbidden instruments, studying the human body as if it were an animal, without fear or respect. They create wild theories with forbidden thoughts and then they test them, without superstition. They are prepared to think anything, to consider anything; nothing is taboo. These people are educated where we are fools, where I am a fool. I might look down on him as coming from a race of savages, I might look down on him as an infidel doomed to hell; but I need to know what he knows.

If he will tell me.

'I am Catalina, Infanta of Spain and Queen Katherine of England,' I say bluntly, that he may know that he is dealing with a queen and the daughter of a queen who had defeated his people.

He inclines his head, as proud as a baron. 'I am Yusuf, son of Ismail,' he says.

'You are a slave?'

'I was born to a slave, but I am a free man.'

'My mother would not allow slavery,' I tell him. 'She said it was not allowed by our religion, our Christian religion.'

'Nevertheless, she sent my people into slavery,' he remarks. 'Perhaps she should have considered that high principles and good intentions end at the border.'

'Since your people won't accept the salvation of God then it doesn't matter what happens to your earthly bodies.'

His face lights up with amusement, and he gives a delightful, irrepressible chuckle. 'It matters to us, I think,' he says. 'My nation allows slavery, but we don't justify it like that. And most importantly, you cannot inherit slavery with us. When you are born, whatever the condition of your mother, you are born free. That is the law, and I think it a very good one.'

'Well, it makes no difference what you think,' I say rudely. 'Since you are wrong.'

Again he laughs aloud, in true merriment, as if I have said something very funny. 'How good it must be, always to know that you are right,' he says. 'Perhaps you will always be certain of your rightness. But I would suggest to you, Catalina of Spain and Katherine of England, that sometimes it is better to know the questions than the answers.'

I pause at that. 'But I want you only for answers,' I say. 'Do you know medicine? Whether a woman can conceive a son? If she is with child?'

'Sometimes it can be known,' he says. 'Sometimes it is in the hands of Allah, praise His holy name, and sometimes we do not yet understand enough to be sure.'

I cross myself against the name of Allah, quick as an old woman spitting on a shadow. He smiles at my gesture, not in the least disturbed. 'What is it that you want to know?' he asks, his voice filled with kindness. 'What is it that you want to know so much that you have to send for an infidel to advise you? Poor queen, you must be very alone if you need help from your enemy.'

My eyes are filling with too-quick tears at the sympathy in his voice and I brush my hand against my face.

'I have lost a baby,' I say shortly. 'A daughter. My physician says that she was one of twins, and that there is another child still inside me, that there will be another birth.'

'So why send for me?'

'I want to know for sure,' I say. 'If there is another child I will have to go into confinement, the whole world will watch me. I want to know that the baby is alive inside me now, that it is a boy, that he will be born.'

'Why should you doubt your own physician's opinion?'

I turn from his inquiring, honest gaze. 'I don't know,' I say evasively.

'Infanta, I think you do know.'

'How can I know?'

'With a woman's sense.'

'I have it not.'

He smiles at my stubbornness. 'Well, then, woman without any feelings, what do you think with your clever mind, since you have decided to deny what your body tells you?'

'How can I know what I should think?' I ask. 'My mother is dead. My greatest friend in England . . .' I break off before I can say the name of Arthur. 'I have no-one to confide in. One midwife says one thing, one says another. The physician is sure . . . but he wants to be sure. The king rewards him only for good news. How can I know the truth?'

'I should think you do know, despite yourself,' he insists gently. 'Your body will tell you. I suppose your courses have not returned?'

'No, I have bled,' I admit unwillingly. 'Last week.'

'With pain?'

'Yes.'

'Your breasts are tender?'

'They were.'

'Are they fuller than usual?'

'No.'

'You can feel the child? He moves inside you?'

'I can't feel anything since I lost the girl.'

'You are in pain now?'

'Not any more. I feel . . .'

'Yes?'

'Nothing. I feel nothing.'

He says nothing, he sits quietly, he breathes so softly it is like sitting with a quietly sleeping black cat. He looks at Maria. 'May I touch her?'

'No,' she says. 'She is the queen. Nobody can touch her.'

He shrugs his shoulders. 'She is a woman like any other. She wants a child like any woman. Why should I not touch her belly as I would touch any woman?'

'She is the queen,' she repeats. 'She cannot be touched. She has an anointed body.'

He smiles as if the holy truth is amusing. 'Well, I hope someone has touched her, or there cannot be a child at all,' he remarks.

'Her husband. An anointed king,' Maria says shortly. 'And take care of how you speak. These are sacred matters.'

'If I may not examine her, then I shall have to say only what I think from looking at her. If she cannot bear examination then she will have to make do with guesswork.' He turns to me. 'If you were an ordinary woman and not a queen, I would take your hands in mine now.'

'Why?'

'Because it is a hard word I have to tell you.'

Slowly, I stretch out my hands with the priceless rings on my fingers. He takes them gently, his dark hands as soft as the touch of a child. His dark eyes look into mine without fear, his face is tender, moved. 'If you are bleeding then it is most likely that your womb is empty,' he says. 'There is no child there. If your breasts are not full then they are not filling with milk, your body is not preparing to feed a child. If you do not feel a child move inside you in the sixth month, then either the child is dead, or there is no child there. If you feel nothing then that is most probably because there is nothing to feel.'

'My belly is still swollen.' I draw back my cloak and show him the curve of my belly under my shift. 'It is hard, I am not fat, I look as I did before I lost the first baby.'

'It could be an infection,' he says consideringly. 'Or – pray Allah that it is not – it could be a growth, a swelling. Or it could be a miscarriage which you have not yet expelled.'

I draw my hands back. 'You are ill-wishing me!'

'Never,' he says. 'To me, here and now, you are not Catalina, Infanta of Spain, but simply a woman who has asked for my help. I am sorry for you.'

'Some help!' Maria de Salinas interrupts crossly. 'Some help you have been!'

'Anyway, I don't believe it,' I say. 'Yours is one opinion, Dr Fielding has another. Why should I believe you, rather than a good Christian?'

He looks at me for a long time, his face tender. 'I wish I could tell you a better opinion,' he says. 'But I imagine there are many who will tell you agreeable lies. I believe in telling the truth. I will pray for you.'

'I don't want your heathen prayers,' I say roughly. 'You can go, and take your bad opinion and your heresies with you.'

'Go with God, Infanta,' he says with dignity, as if I have not insulted him. He bows. 'And since you don't want my prayers to my God (praise be to His holy name), I shall hope instead that when you are in your time of trouble that your doctor is right, and your own God is with you.'

I let him leave, as silent as a dark cat down the hidden staircase, and I say nothing. I hear his sandals clicking down the stone steps, just like the hushed footsteps of the servants at my home. I hear the whisper of his long gown, so unlike the stiff brush of English cloth. I feel the air gradually lose the scent of him, the warm spicy scent of my home.

And when he is gone, quite gone, and the downstairs door is shut and I hear Maria de Salinas turn the key in the lock, then I find that I want to weep – not just because he has told me such bad news, but because one of the few people in the world who has ever told me the truth has gone.

Spring 1510

Katherine did not tell her young husband of the visit of the Moorish doctor, nor of the bad opinion that he had so honestly given her. She did not mention his visit to anyone, not even Lady Margaret Pole. She drew on her sense of destiny, on her pride, and on her faith that she was still especially favoured by God, and she continued with the pregnancy, not even allowing herself to doubt.

She had good reason. The English physician, Dr Fielding, remained confident, the midwives did not contradict him, the court behaved as if Katherine would be brought to bed of a child in March or April, and so she went through the spring weather, the greening gardens, the bursting trees, with a serene smile and her hand clasped gently against her rounded belly.

Henry was excited by the imminent birth of his child; he was planning a great tournament to be held at Greenwich once the baby was born. The loss of the girl had taught him no caution, he bragged all round the court that a healthy baby would soon come. He was forewarned only not to predict a boy. He told everyone that he did not mind if this first child was a prince or princess – he would love

377

this baby for being the first-born, for coming to himself and the queen in the first flush of their happiness.

Katherine stifled her doubts, and never even said to Maria de Salinas that she had not felt her baby kick, that she felt a little colder, a little more distant from everything every day. She spent longer and longer on her knees in her chapel; but God did not speak to her, and even the voice of her mother seemed to have grown silent. She found that she missed Arthur – not with the passionate longing of a young widow, but because he had been her dearest friend in England, and the only one she could have trusted now with her doubts.

In February she attended the great Shrove Tuesday feast and shone before the court and laughed. They saw the broad curve of her belly, they saw her confidence as they celebrated the start of Lent. They moved to Greenwich, certain that the baby would be born just after Easter.

We are going to Greenwich for the birth of my child, the rooms are prepared for me as laid down in My Lady the King's Mother's Royal Book – hung with tapestries with pleasing and encouraging scenes, carpeted with rugs and strewn with fresh herbs. I hesitate at the doorway, behind me my friends raise their glasses of spiced wine. This is where I shall do my greatest work for England, this is my moment of destiny. This is what I was born and bred to do. I take a deep breath and go inside. The door closes behind me. I will not see my friends, the Duke of Buckingham, my dear knight Edward Howard, my confessor, the Spanish ambassador, until my baby is born.

My women come in with me. Lady Elizabeth Boleyn places a sweet-smelling pomander on my bedside table, Lady Elizabeth and Lady Anne, sisters to the Duke of Buckingham, straighten a tapestry, one at each corner, laughing over whether it leans to one side or the other.

Maria de Salinas is smiling, standing by the great bed that is new-hung with dark curtains. Lady Margaret Pole is arranging the cradle for the baby at the foot of the bed. She looks up and smiles at me as I come in and I remember that she is a mother, she will know what is to be done.

'I shall want you to take charge of the royal nurseries,' I suddenly blurt out to her, my affection for her and my sense of needing the advice and comfort of an older woman is too much for me.

There is a little ripple of amusement among my women. They know that I am normally very formal, such an appointment should come through the head of my household after consultation with dozens of people.

Lady Margaret smiles at me. 'I knew you would,' she says, speaking in reply as intimate as myself. 'I have been counting on it.'

'Without royal invitation?' Lady Elizabeth Boleyn teases. 'For shame, Lady Margaret! Thrusting yourself forwards!'

That makes us all laugh at the thought of Lady Margaret, that most dignified of women, as someone craving patronage.

'I know you will care for him as if he were your own son,' I whisper to her.

She takes my hand and helps me to the bed. I am heavy and ungainly, I have this constant pain in my belly that I try to hide.

'God willing,' she says quietly.

Henry comes in to bid me farewell. His face is flushed with emotion and his mouth is working, he looks more like a boy than a king. I take his hands and I kiss him tenderly on the mouth. 'My love,' I say. 'Pray for me, I am sure everything will go well for us.'

'I shall go to Our Lady of Walsingham to give thanks,' he tells me again. 'I have written to the nunnery there and promised them great rewards if they will intercede with Our Lady for you. They are praying for you now, my love. They assure me that they are praying all the time.'

'God is good,' I say. I think briefly of the Moorish doctor who told

379

me that I was not with child and I push his pagan folly from my mind. 'This is my destiny and it is my mother's wish and God's will,' I say.

'I so wish your mother could be here,' Henry says clumsily. I do not let him see me flinch.

'Of course,' I say quietly. 'And I am sure she is watching me from al-Yan —' I cut off the words before I can say them. 'From paradise,' I say smoothly. 'From heaven.'

'Can I get you anything?' he asks. 'Before I leave, can I fetch you anything?'

I do not laugh at the thought of Henry — who never knows where anything is — running errands for me at this late stage. 'I have everything I need,' I assure him. 'And my women will care for me.'

He straightens up, very kingly, and he looks around at them. 'Serve your mistress well,' he says firmly. To Lady Margaret he says, 'Please send for me at once if there is any news, at any time, day or night.' Then he kisses me farewell very tenderly, and when he goes out they close the door behind him and I am alone with my ladies, in the seclusion of my confinement.

I am glad to be confined. The shady, peaceful bedroom will be my haven, I can rest for a while in the familiar company of women. I can stop play-acting the part of a fertile and confident queen, and be myself. I put aside all doubts. I will not think and I will not worry. I will wait patiently until my baby comes, and then I will bring him into the world without fear, without screaming. I am determined to be confident that this child, who has survived the loss of his twin, will be a strong baby. And I, who have survived the loss of my first child, will be a brave mother. Perhaps it might be true that we have surmounted grief and loss together: this baby and I.

I wait. All through March I wait, and I ask them to pin back the tapestry that covers the window so I can smell the scent of spring on the air and hear the seagulls as they call over the high tides on the river.

Nothing seems to be happening; not for my baby nor for me. The midwives ask me if I feel any pain, and I do not. Nothing more than the dull ache I have had for a long time. They ask if the baby has quickened, if I feel him kick me, but, to tell truth, I do not understand what they mean. They glance at one another and say over-loudly, over-emphatically, that it is a very good sign, a quiet baby is a strong baby; he must be resting.

The unease that I have felt right from the start of this second pregnancy, I put right away from me. I will not think of the warning from the Moorish doctor, nor of the compassion in his face. I am determined not to seek out fear, not to run towards disaster. But April comes and I can hear the patter of rain on the window, and then feel the heat of the sunshine, and still nothing happens.

My gowns that strained so tight across my belly through the winter feel looser in April, and then looser yet. I send out all the women but Maria, and I unlace my gown and show her my belly and ask if she thinks I am losing my girth.

'I don't know,' she says; but I can tell by her aghast face that my belly is smaller, that it is obvious that there is no baby in there, ready to be born.

In another week it is obvious to everyone that my belly is going down, I am growing slim again. The midwives try to tell me that sometimes a woman's belly diminishes just before her baby is born, as her baby drops down to be born, or some such arcane knowledge. I look at them coldly, and I wish I could send for a decent physician who would tell me the truth.

'My belly is smaller and my course has come this very day,' I say to them flatly. 'I am bleeding. As you know, I have bled every month since I lost the girl. How can I be with child?'

They flutter their hands, and cannot say. They don't know. They tell me that these are questions for my husband's respected physician. It was he who had said that I was still with child in the first place, not them. They had never said that I was with child, they had merely been called in to assist with a delivery. It was not them who had said that I was carrying a baby.

'But what did you think, when he said there was a twin?' I demand. 'Did you not agree when he said that I had lost a child and yet kept one?'

They shake their heads. They did not know.

'You must have thought something,' I say impatiently. 'You saw me lose my baby. You saw my belly stay big. What could cause that if not another child?'

'God's will,' says one of them helplessly.

'Amen,' I say, and it costs me a good deal to say it.

'I want to see that physician again,' Katherine said quietly to Maria de Salinas.

'Your Grace, it may be that he is not in London. He travels in the household of a French count. It may be that he has gone.'

'Find out if he is still in London, or when they expect him to return,' the queen said. 'Don't tell anyone that it is I who have asked for him.'

Maria de Salinas looked at her mistress with sympathy. 'You want him to advise you how to have a son?' she asked in a low voice.

'There is not a university in England that studies medicine,' Katherine said bitterly. 'There is not one that teaches languages. There is not one that teaches astronomy, or mathematics, geometry, geography, cosmography, or even the study of animals, or plants. The universities of England are about as much use as a monastery full of monks colouring-in the margins of sacred texts.'

Maria de Salinas gave a little gasp of shock at Katherine's bluntness. 'The church says . . .'

'The church does not need decent physicians. The church does not need to know how sons are conceived,' Katherine snapped. 'The church can continue with the revelations of the saints. It needs nothing more than scripture. The church is composed of men who are not troubled by the illnesses and difficulties of women. But for those of us on our pilgrimage today, those of us in the world, especially those of us who are women: we need a little more.'

'But you said that you did not want pagan knowledge. You said to the doctor himself. Your said your mother was right to close the universities of the infidel.'

'My mother had half a dozen children,' Katherine replied crossly. 'But I tell you, if she could have found a doctor to save my brother she would have had him even if he had been trained in hell itself. She was wrong to turn her back on the learning of the Moors. She was mistaken. I have never thought that she was perfect, but I think the less of her now. She made a great mistake when she drove away their wise scholars along with their heretics.'

'The church itself said that their scholarship is heresy,' Maria observed. 'How could you have one without the other?'

'I am sure that you know nothing about it,' said Isabella's daughter, driven into a corner. 'It is not a fit subject for you to discuss and besides, I have told you what I want you to do.'

The Moor, Yusuf, is away from London but the people at his lodging house say that he has reserved his rooms to return within the week. I shall have to be patient. I shall wait in my confinement and try to be patient.

They know him well, Maria's servant tells her. His comings and goings are something of an event in their street. Africans are so rare in England as to be a spectacle – and he is a handsome man and generous with small coins for little services. They told Maria's servant that he insisted on having fresh water for washing in his room and he washes every day, several times a day, and that – wonder of wonders – he bathes three or four times a week, using soap and towels, and throwing water all over the floor to the great inconvenience of the housemaids, and to great danger of his health.

I cannot help but laugh at the thought of the tall, fastidious Moor folding himself up into a washing tub, desperate for a steam, a tepid soak, a massage, a cold shower, and then a long, thoughtful rest while smoking a hookah and sipping a strong, sweet peppermint tea. It reminds me of my horror when I first came to England and discovered that they bathe only infrequently, and wash only the tips of their fingers before eating. I think that he has done better than me – he has carried his love of his home with him, he has re-made his home wherever he goes. But in my determination to be Queen Katherine of England I have given up being Catalina of Spain.

They brought the Moor to Katherine under cover of darkness, to the chamber where she was confined. She sent the women from the room at the appointed hour and told them that she wanted to be alone. She sat in her chair by the window, where the tapestries were drawn back for air, and the first thing he saw, as she rose when he came in, was her slim candlelit profile against the darkness of the window. She saw his little grimace of sympathy.

'No child.'

'No,' she said shortly. 'I shall come out of my confinement tomorrow.'

'You are in pain?'

'Nothing.'

'Well, I am glad of that. You are bleeding?'

'I had my normal course last week.'

He nodded. 'Then you may have had a disease which has passed,' he said. 'You may be fit to conceive a child. There is no need to despair.'

'I do not despair,' she said flatly. 'I never despair. That is why I have sent for you.'

'You will want to conceive a child as soon as possible,' he guessed.

'Yes.'

He thought for a moment. 'Well, Infanta, since you have had one child, even if you did not bear it to full term, we know that you and your husband are fertile. That is good.'

'Yes,' she said, surprised by the thought. She had been so distressed by the miscarriage she had not thought that her fertility had been proven. 'But why do you speak of my husband's fertility?'

The Moor smiled. 'It takes both a man and a woman to conceive a child.'

'Here in England they think that it is only the woman.'

'Yes. But in this, as in so many other things, they are wrong. There are two parts to every baby: the man's breath of life and the woman's gift of the flesh.'

'They say that if a baby is lost, then the woman is at fault, perhaps she has committed a great sin.'

He frowned. 'It is possible,' he conceded. 'But not very likely. Otherwise how would murderesses ever give birth? Why would innocent animals miscarry their young? I think we will learn in time that there are humours and infections which cause miscarriage. I do not blame the woman, it makes no sense to me.'

'They say that if a woman is barren it is because the marriage is not blessed by God.'

'He is your God,' he remarked reasonably. 'Would he persecute an unhappy woman in order to make a point?'

Katherine did not reply. 'They will blame me if I do not have a live child,' she observed very quietly.

'I know,' he said. 'But the truth of the matter is: having had one child and lost it, there is every reason to think that you might have another. And there should be no reason why you should not conceive again.'

'I must bear the next child to full term.'

'If I could examine you, I might know more.'

She shook her head. 'It is not possible.'

His glance at her was merry. 'Oh, you savages,' he said softly.

She gave a little gasp of amused shock. 'You forget yourself!'

'Then send me away.'

That stopped her. 'You can stay,' she said. 'But of course, you cannot examine me.'

'Then let us consider what might help you conceive and carry a child,' he said. 'Your body needs to be strong. Do you ride horses?'

'Yes.'

'Ride astride before you conceive and then take a litter thereafter. Walk every day, swim if you can. You will conceive a child about two weeks after the end of your course. Rest at those times, and make sure that you lie with your husband at those times. Try to eat moderately at every meal and drink as little of their accursed small ale as you can.'

Katherine smiled at the reflection of her own prejudices. 'Do you know Spain?'

'I was born there. My parents fled from Malaga when your mother brought in the Inquisition and they realised that they would be tormented to death.'

'I am sorry,' she said awkwardly.

'We will go back, it is written,' he said with nonchalant confidence.

'I should warn you that you will not.'

'I know that we will. I have seen the prophecy myself.'

At once they fell silent again.

'Shall I tell you what I advise? Or shall I just leave now?' he asked, as if he did not much mind which it was to be.

'Tell me,' she said. 'And then I can pay you, and you can go. We were born to be enemies. I should not have summoned you.'

'We are both Spanish, we both love our country. We both serve our God. Perhaps we were born to be friends.'

She had to stop herself giving him her hand. 'Perhaps,' she said gruffly, turning her head away. 'But I was brought up to hate your people and hate your faith.'

'I was brought up to hate no-one,' he said gently. 'Perhaps that is what I should be teaching you before anything else.'

'Just teach me how to have a son,' she repeated.

'Very well. Drink water that has been boiled, eat as much fruit and fresh vegetables as you can get. Do you have salad vegetables here?'

For a moment I am back in the garden at Ludlow with his bright eyes on me.

'Acetaria?'

'Yes, salad.'

'What is it, exactly?'

He saw the queen's face glow.

'What are you thinking of?'

'Of my first husband. He told me that I could send for gardeners to grow salad vegetables, but I never did.'

'I have seeds,' the Moor said surprisingly. 'I can give you some seeds and you can grow the vegetables you will need.'

'You have?'

'Yes.'

'You would give me . . . you would sell them to me?'

'Yes. I would give them to you.'

For a moment she was silenced by his generosity. 'You are very kind,' she said.

He smiled. 'We are both Spanish and a long way from our homes. Doesn't that matter more than the fact that I am black and you are white? That I worship my God facing Mecca and you worship yours facing west?'

'I am a child of the true religion and you are an infidel,' she said, but with less conviction than she had ever felt before.

'We are both people of faith,' he said quietly. 'Our enemies should be the people who have no faith, neither in their God, nor in others, nor in themselves. The people who should face our crusade should be those who bring cruelty into the world for no reason but their own power. There is enough sin and wickedness to fight, without taking up arms against people who believe in a forgiving God and who try to lead a good life.'

Katherine found that she could not reply. On the one hand was her mother's teaching, on the other was the simple goodness that radiated from this man. 'I don't know,' she said finally, and it was as if the very words set her free. 'I don't know. I would have to take the question to God. I would have to pray for guidance. I don't pretend to know.'

'Now, that is the very beginning of wisdom,' he said gently. 'I am sure of that, at least. Knowing that you do not know is to ask humbly, instead of tell arrogantly. That is the beginning of wisdom. Now, more importantly, I will go home and write you a list of things that you must not eat, and I will send you some medicine to strengthen your humours. Don't let them cup you, don't let them put leeches on you, and don't let them persuade you to take any poisons or potions. You are a young woman with a young husband. A baby will come.'

It was like a blessing. 'You are sure?' she said.

'I am sure,' he replied. 'And very soon.'

Greenwich Palace, May 1510

I send for Henry, he should hear it first from me. He comes unwillingly. He has been filled with a terror of women's secrets and women's

doings and he does not like to come into a room which has been prepared for a confinement. Also, there is something else: a lack of warmth, I see it in his face, turned away from me. The way he does not meet my eyes. But I cannot challenge him about coolness towards me when I first have to tell him such hard news. Lady Margaret leaves us alone, closing the door behind her. I know she will ensure no-one outside eavesdrops. They will all know soon enough.

'Husband, I am sorry, I have sad news for us,' I say.

The face he turns to me is sulky. 'I knew it could not be good when Lady Margaret came for me.'

There is no point in my feeling a flash of irritation. I shall have to manage us both. 'I am not with child,' I say, plunging in. 'The doctor must have made a mistake. There was only one child and I lost it. This confinement has been a mistake. I shall return to court tomorrow.'

'How can he have mistaken such a thing?'

I give a little shrug of the shoulders. I want to say: because he is a pompous fool and your man, and you surround yourself with people who only ever tell you the good news and are afraid to tell you bad. But instead I say neutrally: 'He must have been mistaken.'

'I shall look a fool!' he bursts out. 'You have been away for nearly three months and nothing to show for it.'

I say nothing for a moment. Pointless to wish that I were married to a man who might think beyond his appearance. Pointless to wish that I were married to a man whose first thought might be of me.

'No-one will think anything at all,' I say firmly. 'If anything, they will say that it is I who am a fool to not know whether I am with child, or no. But at least we had a baby and that means we can have another.'

'It does?' he asks, immediately hopeful. 'But why should we lose her? Is God displeased with us? Have we committed some sin? Is it a sign of God's displeasure?'

I nip my lower lip to stop the Moor's question: is God so vindictive *that He would kill an innocent child to punish the parents for a sin so venial that they do not even know that they have committed it?*

'My conscience is clear,' I say firmly.

'Mine too,' he says quickly, too quickly.

But my conscience is not clear. That night I go on my knees to the image of the crucified lord and for once I truly pray, I do not dream of Arthur, or consult my memory of my mother. I close my eyes and I pray.

'Lord, it was a deathbed promise,' I say slowly. 'He demanded it of me. It was for the good of England. It was to guide the kingdom and the new king in the paths of the church. It was to protect England from the Moor and from sin. I know that it has brought me wealth, and the throne, but I did not do it for gain. If it is sin, Lord, then show me now. If I should not be his wife, then tell me now. Because I believe that I did the right thing, and that I am doing the right thing. And I believe that You would not take my son from me in order to punish me for this. I believe that You are a merciful God. And I believe that I did the right thing for Arthur, for Henry, for England and for me.'

I sit back on my heels and wait for a long time, for an hour, perhaps more, in case my God, the God of my mother, chooses to speak to me in His anger.

He does not.

So I will go on assuming that I am in the right. Arthur was right to call on my promise, I was right to tell the lie, my mother was right to call it God's will that I should be Queen of England, and that whatever happens – nothing will change that.

Lady Margaret Pole comes to sit with me this evening, my last evening in confinement, and she takes the stool on the opposite side of the fire, close enough so that we cannot easily be overheard. 'I have something to tell you,' she says.

I look at her face, she is so calm that I know at once something bad has happened.

'Tell me,' I say instantly.

She makes a little moue of distaste. 'I am sorry to bring you the tittle-tattle of the court.'

'Very well. Tell me.'

'It is the Duke of Buckingham's sister.'

'Elizabeth?' I ask, thinking of the pretty young woman who had come to me the moment she knew I would be queen and asked if she could be my lady-in-waiting.

'No, Anne.'

I nod, this is Elizabeth's younger sister, a dark-eyed girl with a roguish twinkle and a love of male company. She is popular at court among the young men but – at least as long as I am present – she behaves with all the demure grace of a young matron of the highest family in the land, in service to the queen.

'What of her?'

'She has been seeing William Compton, without telling anyone. They have had assignations. Her brother is very upset. He has told her husband, and he is furious at her risking her reputation and his good name in a flirtation with the king's friend.'

I think for a moment. William Compton is one of Henry's wilder companions, the two of them are inseparable.

'William will only have been amusing himself,' I say. 'He is a heart-breaker.'

'It turns out that she has gone missing from a masque, once during dinner and once all day when the court was hunting.'

I nod. This is much more serious. 'There is no suggestion that they are lovers?'

She shrugs. 'Certainly her brother, Edward Stafford, is furious. He has complained to Compton and there has been a quarrel. The King has defended Compton.'

I press my lips together to prevent myself snapping out a criticism in my irritation. The Duke of Buckingham is one of the oldest friends of the Tudor family, with massive lands and many retainers. He greeted me with Prince Harry all those years ago, he is now honoured by the king, the greatest man in the land. He has been a good friend to me since then. Even when I was in disgrace I always had a smile and a kind word from him. Every summer he sent me a gift of game, and there were some weeks when that was the only meat we saw. Henry cannot quarrel with him as if he were a tradesman and Henry a surly farmer. This is the king and the greatest man of the state of England. The old king Henry could not even have won his throne without Buckingham's support. A disagreement between them is not a private matter, it is a national disaster. If Henry had any sense he would not have involved himself in this petty courtiers' quarrel. Lady Margaret nods at me, I need say nothing, she understands my disapproval.

'Can I not leave the court for a moment without my ladies climbing out of their bedroom windows to run after young men?'

She leans forwards and pats my hand. 'It seems not. It is a foolish young court, Your Grace, and they need you to keep them steady. The king has spoken very high words to the duke and the duke is much offended. William Compton says he will say nothing of the matter to anyone, so everyone thinks the worst. Anne has been all but imprisoned by her husband, Sir George, we none of us have seen her today. I am afraid that when you come out of your confinement he will not allow her to wait on you, and then your honour is involved.' She pauses. 'I thought you should know now rather than be surprised by it all tomorrow morning. Though it goes against the grain to be a tale-bearer of such folly.'

'It is ridiculous,' I say. 'I shall deal with it tomorrow, when I come out of confinement. But really, what are they all thinking of? This is *like a schoolyard! William should be ashamed of himself and I am surprised that Anne should so far forget herself as to chase after him. And what does her husband think he is? Some knight at Camelot to imprison her in a tower?'*

Queen Katherine came out of her confinement, without announcement, and returned to her usual rooms at Greenwich Palace. There could be no churching ceremony to mark her return her to normal life, since there had been no birth. There could be no christening since there was no child. She came out of the shadowy room without comment, as if she had suffered some secret, shameful illness, and everyone pretended that she had been gone for hours rather than nearly three months.

Her ladies-in-waiting, who had become accustomed to an idle pace of life with the queen in her confinement, assembled at some speed in the queen's chambers, and the housemaids hurried in with fresh strewing herbs and new candles.

Katherine caught several furtive glances among the ladies and assumed that they too had guilty consciences over misbehaviour in her absence; but then she realised that there was a whispered buzz of conversation that ceased whenever she raised her head. Clearly, something had happened that was more serious than Anne's disgrace; and, equally clearly, no-one was telling her.

She beckoned one of her ladies, Lady Madge, to come to her side.

'Is Lady Elizabeth not joining us this morning?' she asked, as she could see no sign of the older Stafford sister.

The girl flushed scarlet to her ears. 'I don't know,' she stammered. 'I don't think so.'

'Where is she?' Katherine asked.

The girl looked desperately round for help but all the other ladies in the room were suddenly taking an intense interest in their sewing, in their embroidery, or in their books. Elizabeth Boleyn dealt a hand of cards with as much attention as if she had a fortune staked on it.

'I don't know where she is,' the girl confessed.

'In the ladies' room?' Katherine suggested. 'In the Duke of Buckingham's rooms?'

'I think she has gone,' the girl said baldly. At once someone gasped, and then there was silence.

'Gone?' Katherine looked around. 'Will someone tell me what is happening?' she asked, her tone reasonable enough. 'Where has Lady Elizabeth gone? And how can she have gone without my permission?'

The girl took a step back. At that moment, Lady Margaret Pole came into the room.

'Lady Margaret,' Katherine said pleasantly. 'Here is Madge telling me that Lady Elizabeth has left court without my permission and without bidding me farewell. What is happening?'

Katherine felt her amused smile freeze on her face when her old friend shook her head slightly, and Madge, relieved, dropped back to her seat. 'What is it?' Katherine asked more quietly.

Without seeming to move, all the ladies craned forwards to hear how Lady Margaret would explain the latest development.

'I believe the king and the Duke of Buckingham have had hard words,' Lady Margaret said smoothly. 'The duke has left court and taken both his sisters with him.'

'But they are my ladies-in-waiting. In service to me. They cannot leave without my permission.'

'It is very wrong of them, indeed,' Margaret said. Something in the way she folded her hands in her lap and looked so steadily and calmly warned Katherine not to probe.

'So what have you been doing in my absence?' Katherine turned to the ladies, trying to lighten the mood of the room.

At once they all looked sheepish. 'Have you learned any new songs? Have you danced in any masques?' Katherine asked.

'I know a new song,' one of the girls volunteered. 'Shall I sing it?'

Katherine nodded, at once one of the other women picked up a lute. It was as if everyone was quick to divert her. Katherine smiled and beat the time with her hand on the arm of her chair. She knew, as a woman who had been born and raised in a court of conspirators, that something was very wrong indeed.

There was the sound of company approaching and Katherine's guards threw open the door to the king and his court. The ladies stood up, shook out their skirts, bit their lips to make them pink, and sparkled in anticipation. Someone laughed gaily at nothing. Henry strode in, still in his riding clothes, his friends around him, William Compton's arm in his.

Katherine was again alert to some difference in her husband. He did not come in, take her in his arms, and kiss her cheeks. He did not stride into the very centre of the room and bow to her either. He came in, twinned with his best friend, the two almost hiding behind each other, like boys caught out in a petty crime: part-shame-faced, part-braggart. At Katherine's sharp look Compton awkwardly disengaged himself, Henry greeted his wife without enthusiasm, his eyes downcast, he took her hand and then kissed her cheek, not her mouth.

'Are you well now?' he asked.

'Yes,' she said calmly. 'I am quite well now. And how are you, sire?'

'Oh,' he said carelessly. 'I am well. We had such a chase this morning. I wish you had been with us. We were half way to Sussex, I do believe.'

'I shall come out tomorrow,' Katherine promised him.

'Will you be well enough?'

'I am quite well,' she repeated.

He looked relieved. 'I thought you would be ill for months,' he blurted out.

Smiling, she shook her head, wondering who had told him that.

'Let's break our fast,' he said. 'I am starving.'

He took her hand and led her to the great hall. The court fell in informally behind them. Katherine could hear the over-excited buzz of whispers. She leaned her head towards Henry so that no-one could catch her words. 'I hear there have been some quarrels in court.'

'Oh! You have heard of our little storm already, have you?' he said. He was far too loud, he was far too jovial. He was acting the part of a man with nothing to trouble his conscience. He threw a laugh over his shoulder and looked for someone to join in his forced amusement. Half a dozen men and women smiled, anxious to share his good humour. 'It is something and nothing. I have had a quarrel with your great friend, the Duke of Buckingham. He has left the court in a temper!' He laughed again, even more heartily, glancing at her sideways to see if she was smiling, trying to judge if she already knew all about it.

'Indeed?' Katherine said coolly.

'He was insulting,' Henry said, gathering his sense of offence. 'He can stay away until he is ready to apologise. He is such a pompous man, you know. Always thinks he knows everything. And his sour sister Elizabeth can go too.'

'She is a good lady-in-waiting and a kind companion to me,' Katherine observed. 'I expected her to greet me this day. I have no quarrel with her, nor with her sister Anne. I take it you have no quarrel with them either?'

'Nonetheless I am most displeased with their brother,' Henry said. 'They can all go.'

Katherine paused, took a breath. 'She and her sister are in my household,' she observed. 'I have the right to choose and dismiss my own ladies.'

She saw the quick flush of his childish temper. 'You will oblige me by sending them away from your household! Whatever your rights! I don't expect to hear talk of rights between us!'

The court behind them fell silent at once. Everyone wanted to hear the first royal quarrel.

Katherine released his hand and went around the high table to take her place. It gave her a moment to remind herself to be calm. When he came to his seat beside hers she took a breath and smiled at him. 'As you wish,' she said evenly. 'I have no great preference in the matter. But how am I to run a well-ordered court if I send away young women of good family who have done nothing wrong?'

'You were not here, so you have no idea what she did or didn't do!' Henry sought for another complaint and found one. He waved the court to sit and dropped into his own chair. 'You locked yourself away for months. What am I supposed to do without you? How are things supposed to be run if you just go away and leave everything?'

Katherine nodded, keeping her face absolutely serene. She was very well aware that the attention of the entire court was focused on her like a burning glass on fine paper. 'I hardly left for my own amusement,' she observed.

'It has been most awkward for me,' he said, taking her words at face value. 'Most awkward. It is all very well for you, taking to your bed for weeks at a time, but how is the court to run without a queen? Your ladies were without discipline, nobody knew how things were to go on, I couldn't see you, I had to sleep alone . . .' He broke off.

Katherine realised, belatedly, that his bluster was hiding a genuine sense of hurt. In his selfishness, he had transformed her long endurance of pain and fear into his own difficulty. He had managed to see her fruitless confinement as her wilfully deserting him, leaving him alone to rule over a lopsided court; in his eyes, she had let him down.

'I think at the very least you should do as I ask,' he said pettishly. 'I have had trouble enough these last months. All this reflects very badly on me, I have been made to look a fool. And no help from you at all.'

'Very well,' Katherine said peaceably. 'I shall send Elizabeth away and her sister Anne too, since you ask it of me. Of course.'

Henry found his smile, as if the sun was coming out from behind clouds. 'Yes. And now you are back we can get everything back to normal.'

Not a word for me, not one word of comfort, not one thought of understanding. I could have died trying to bring his child into the world, without his child I have to face sorrow, grief and a haunting fear of sin. But he does not think of me at all.

I find a smile to reply to his. I knew when I married him that he was a selfish boy and I knew he would grow into a selfish man. I have set myself the task of guiding him and helping him to be a better man, the best man that he can be. There are bound to be times when I think he has failed to be the man he should be. And when those times come, as now, I must see it as my failure to guide him. I must forgive him.

Without my forgiveness, without me extending my patience further than I thought possible, our marriage will be a poorer one. He is always ready to resent a woman who cares for him – he learned that from his grandmother. And I, God forgive me, am too quick to think of the husband that I lost, and not of the husband that I won. He is not the man that Arthur was, and he will never be the king that Arthur would have been. But he is my husband and my king and I should respect him.

Indeed: I will respect him, whether he deserves it or not.

The court was subdued over breakfast, few of them could drag their eyes from the high table where, under the gold canopy of state, seated on their thrones, the king and queen exchanged conversation and seemed to be quite reconciled.

'But does she know?' one courtier whispered to one of Katherine's ladies.

'Who would tell her?' she replied. 'If Maria de Salinas and Lady Margaret have not told her already then she doesn't know. I would put my earrings on it.'

'Done,' he said. 'Ten shillings that she finds out.'

'By when?'

'Tomorrow,' he said.

I had another piece of the jigsaw when I came to look at the accounts for the weeks while I had been in confinement. In the first days that I had been away from court there had been no extraordinary expenses. But then the bill for amusements began to grow. There were bills from singers and actors to rehearse their celebration for the expected baby, bills from the organist, the choristers, from drapers for the material for pennants and standards, extra maids for polishing the gold christening bowl. Then there were payments for costumes of Lincoln green for disguising, singers to perform under the window of Lady Anne, a clerk to copy out the words of the king's new song, rehearsals for a new May Day masque with a dance, and costumes for three ladies with Lady Anne to play the part of Unattainable Beauty.

I rose from the table where I had been turning over the papers and went to the window to look down at the garden. They had set up a wrestling ring and the young men of the court were stripped to their shirtsleeves. Henry and Charles Brandon were gripped in each other's arms like blacksmiths at a fair. As I watched, Henry tripped his friend and threw him to the ground and then dropped his weight on him to hold him down. Princess Mary applauded, the court cheered.

I turned from the window. I began to wonder if Lady Anne had proved to be unattainable indeed. I wondered how merry they had been on May Day morning when I had woken on my own, in sadness, to silence, with no-one singing beneath my window. And why should the court pay for singers, hired by Compton, to seduce his newest mistress?

The king summoned the queen to his rooms in the afternoon. Some messages had come from the Pope and he wanted her advice. Katherine sat beside him, listened to the report of the messenger and stretched up to whisper in her husband's ear.

He nodded. 'The queen reminds me of our well-known alliance with Venice,' he said pompously. 'And indeed, she has no need to remind me. I am not likely to forget it. You can depend on our determination to protect Venice and indeed all Italy against the ambitions of the French king.'

The ambassadors nodded respectfully. 'I shall send you a letter about this,' Henry said grandly. They bowed and withdrew.

'Will you write to them?' he asked Katherine.

She nodded. 'Of course,' she said. 'I thought that you handled that quite rightly.'

He smiled at her approval. 'It is so much better when you are here,' he said. 'Nothing goes on right when you are away.'

'Well, I am back now,' she said, putting a hand on his shoulder. She could feel the power of the muscle under her hand. Henry was a man now, with the strength of a man. 'Dearest, I am so sorry about your quarrel with the Duke of Buckingham.'

Under her hand she felt his shoulder hunch, he shrugged away her touch. 'It is nothing,' he said. 'He shall beg my pardon and it will be forgotten.'

'But perhaps he could just come back to court,' she said. 'Without his sisters if you don't want to see them . . .'

Inexplicably he barked out a laugh. 'Oh, bring them all back by all means,' he said. 'If that is your true wish, if you think it will bring you happiness. You should never have gone into confinement, there was no child, anyone could have seen that there would be no child.'

She was so taken aback that she could hardly speak. 'This is about my confinement?'

'It would hardly have happened without. But everyone could see there would be no child. It was wasted time.'

'Your own doctor . . .'

'What did he know? He only knows what you tell him.'

'He assured me . . .'

'Doctors know nothing!' he suddenly burst out. 'They are always guided by the woman; everyone knows that. And a woman can say anything. Is there a baby, isn't there a baby? Is she a virgin, isn't she a virgin? Only the woman knows and the rest of us are fooled.'

Katherine felt her mind racing, trying to trace what had offended him, what she could say. 'I trusted your doctor,' she said. 'He was very certain. He assured me I was with child and so I went into confinement. Another time I will know better. I am truly sorry, my love. It has been a very great grief to me.'

'It just makes me look such a fool!' he said plaintively. 'It's no wonder that I . . .'

'That you? What?'

'Nothing,' said Henry, sulkily.

'It is such a lovely afternoon, let us go for a walk,' I say pleasantly to my ladies. 'Lady Margaret will accompany me.'

We go outside, my cape is brought and put over my shoulders and my gloves. The path down to the river is wet and slippery and Lady Margaret takes my arm and we go down the steps together. The primroses are thick as churned butter in the hedgerows and the sun is out. There are white swans on the river but when the barges and wherries go by the birds drift out of the way as if by magic. I breathe deeply, it is so good to be out of that small room and to feel the sun on my face again that I hardly want to open the subject of Lady Anne.

'You must know what took place?' I say to her shortly.

'I know some gossip,' she says levelly. 'Nothing for certain.'

'What has angered the king so much?' I ask. 'He is upset about my confinement, he is angry with me. What is troubling him? Surely not the Stafford girl's flirtation with Compton?'

Lady Margaret's face is grave. 'The king is very attached to William Compton,' she said. 'He would not have him insulted.'

'It sounds as if all the insult is the other way,' I say. 'It is Lady Anne and her husband who are dishonoured. I would have thought the king would have been angry with William. Lady Anne is not a girl to tumble behind a wall. There is her family to consider and her husband's family. Surely the king should have told Compton to behave himself?'

Lady Margaret shrugs. 'I don't know,' she says. 'None of the girls will even talk to me. They are as silent as if it were a grave matter.'

'But why, if it was nothing more than a foolish affair? Youth calls to youth in springtime?'

She shakes her head. 'Truly, I don't know. You would think so. But if it is a flirtation, why would the duke be so very offended? Why quarrel with the king? Why would the girls not be laughing at Anne for getting caught?'

'And another thing . . .' I say.

She waits.

'Why should the king pay for Compton's courtship? The fee for the singers is in the court accounts.'

She frowned. 'Why would he encourage it? The king must have known that the duke would be greatly offended.'

'And Compton remains in high favour?'

'They are inseparable.'

I speak the thought that is sitting cold in my heart. 'So do you think that Compton is the shield and the love affair is between the king, my husband, and Lady Anne?'

Lady Margaret's grave face tells me that my guess is her own fear.
'I don't know,' she says, honest as ever. 'As I say, the girls tell me nothing,
and I have not asked anyone that question.'
   'Because you think you will not like the answer?'
   She nods. Slowly, I turn, and we walk back along the river in silence.

Katherine and Henry led the company into dinner in the grand hall and sat side by side under the gold canopy of state as they always did. There was a band of special singers that had come to England from the French court and they sang without instruments, very true to the note with a dozen different parts. It was complicated and beautiful and Henry was entranced by the music. When the singers paused, he applauded and asked them to repeat the song. They smiled at his enthusiasm, and sang again. He asked for it once more, and then sang the tenor line back to them: note perfect.

   It was their turn to applaud him and they invited him to sing with them the part that he had learned so rapidly. Katherine, on her throne, leaned forwards and smiled as her handsome young husband sang in his clear young voice, and the ladies of the court clapped in appreciation.

   When the musicians struck up and the court danced, Katherine came down from the raised platform of the high table and danced with Henry, her face bright with happiness and her smile warm. Henry, encouraged by her, danced like an Italian, with fast, dainty footwork and high leaps. Katherine clapped her hands in delight and called for another dance as if she had never had a moment's worry in her life. One of her ladies leaned towards the courtier who had taken the bet that Katherine would find out. 'I think I shall keep my earrings,' she said. 'He has fooled her. He has played her for a fool, and now he is fair game to any one of us. She has lost her hold on him.'

I wait till we are alone, and then I wait until he beds me with his eager joy, and then I slip from the bed and bring him a cup of small ale.

'So tell me the truth, Henry,' I say to him simply. 'What is the truth of the quarrel between you and the Duke of Buckingham, and what were your dealings with his sister?'

His swift sideways glance tells me more than any words. He is about to lie to me. I hear the words he says: a story about a disguising and all of them in masks and the ladies dancing with them and Compton and Anne dancing together, and I know that he is lying.

It is an experience more painful than I thought I could have with him. We have been married for nearly a year, a year next month, and always he has looked at me directly, with all his youth and honesty in his gaze. I have never heard anything but truth in his voice: boastfulness, certainly, the arrogance of a young man, but never this uncertain deceitful quaver. He is lying to me, and I would almost rather have a bare-faced confession of infidelity than to see him look at me, blue-eyed and sweet as a boy, with a parcel of lies in his mouth.

I stop him, I truly cannot bear to hear it. 'Enough,' I say. 'I know enough at least to realise that this is not true. She was your lover, wasn't she? And Compton was your friend and shield?'

His face is aghast. 'Katherine . . .'

'Just tell me the truth.'

His mouth is trembling. He cannot bear to admit what he has done. 'I didn't mean to . . .'

'I know that you did not,' I say. 'I am sure you were sorely tempted.'

'You were away for so long . . .'

'I know.'

A dreadful silence falls. I had thought that he would lie to me and I would track him down and then confront him with his lies and with

404

his adultery and I would be a warrior queen in my righteous anger. But this is sadness and a taste of defeat. If Henry cannot remain faithful when I am in confinement with our child, our dearly needed child, then how shall he be faithful till death? How shall he obey his vow to forsake all others when he can be distracted so easily? What am I to do, what can any woman do, when her husband is such a fool as to desire a woman for a moment, rather than the woman he is pledged to for eternity?

'Dear husband, this is very wrong,' I say sadly.

'It was because I had such doubts. I thought for a moment that we were not married,' he confesses.

'You forgot we were married?' I ask incredulously.

'No!' His head comes up, his blue eyes are filled with unshed tears. His face shines with contrition. 'I thought that since our marriage was not valid, I need not abide by it.'

I am quite amazed by him. 'Our marriage? Why would it not be valid?'

He shakes his head. He is too ashamed to speak. I press him. 'Why not?'

He kneels beside my bed and hides his face in the sheets. 'I liked her and I desired her and she said some things which made me feel . . .'

'Feel what?'

'Made me think . . .'

'Think what?'

'What if you were not a virgin when I married you?'

At once I am alert, like a villain near the scene of a crime, like a murderer when the corpse bleeds at the sight of him. 'What do you mean?'

'She was a virgin . . .'

'Anne?'

'Yes. Sir George is impotent. Everyone knows that.'

'Do they?'

'Yes. So she was a virgin. And she was not . . .' He rubs his face against the sheet of our bed. 'She was not like you. She...' He stumbles for words. 'She cried out in pain. She bled, I was afraid when I saw how much blood, really a lot...' He breaks off again. 'She could not go on, the first time. I had to stop. She cried, I held her. She was a virgin. That is what it is like to lie with a virgin, the first time. I was her first love. I could tell. Her first love.'

There is a long, cold silence.

'She fooled you,' I say cruelly, throwing away her reputation, and his tenderness for her, with one sweep, making her a whore and him a fool, for the greater good.

He looks up, shocked. 'She did?'

'She was not that badly hurt, she was pretending.' I shake my head at the sinfulness of young women. 'It is an old trick. She will have had a bladder of blood in her hand and broke it to give you a show of blood. She will have cried out. I expect she whimpered and said she could not bear the pain from the very beginning.'

Henry is amazed. 'She did.'

'She thought to make you feel sorry for her.'

'But I was!'

'Of course. She thought to make you feel that you had taken her virginity, her maidenhead, and that you owe her your protection.'

'That is what she said!'

'She tried to entrap you,' I say. 'She was not a virgin, she was acting the part of one. I was a virgin when I came to your bed and the first night that we were lovers was very simple and sweet. Do you remember?'

'Yes,' he says.

'There was no crying and wailing like players on a stage. It was quiet and loving. Take that as your benchmark,' I say. 'I was a true virgin. You and I were each other's first love. We had no need for play-acting and exaggeration. Hold to that truth of our love, Henry. You have been fooled by a counterfeit.'

'She said...' he begins.

'She said what?' I am not afraid. I am filled with utter determination that Anne Stafford will not put asunder what God and my mother have joined together.

'She said that you must have been Arthur's lover.' He stumbles before the white fierceness of my face. 'That you had lain with him, and that . . .'

'Not true.'

'I didn't know.'

'It is not true.'

'Oh, yes.'

'My marriage with Arthur was not consummated. I came to you a virgin. You were my first love. Does anyone dare say different to me?'

'No,' he says rapidly. 'No. No-one shall say different to you.'

'Nor to you.'

'Nor to me.'

'Would anyone dare to say to my face that I am not your first love, a virgin untouched, your true wedded wife, and Queen of England?'

'No,' he says again.

'Not even you.'

'No.'

'It is to dishonour me,' I say furiously. 'And where will scandal stop? Shall they suggest that you have no claim to the throne because your mother was no virgin on her wedding day?'

He is stunned with shock. 'My mother? What of my mother?'

'They say that she lay with her uncle, Richard the usurper,' I say flatly. 'Think of that! And they say that she lay with your father before they were married, before they were even betrothed. They say that she was far from a virgin on her wedding day when she wore her hair loose and went in white. They say she was dishonoured twice over, little more than a harlot for the throne. Do we allow people to say such things of a queen? Are you to be disinherited by such gossip? Am I? Is our son?'

Henry is gasping with shock. He loved his mother and he had never thought of her as a sexual being before. 'She would never have . . . she was a most . . . how can . . .'

407

'You see? This is what happens if we allow people to gossip about their betters.' I lay down the law which will protect me. 'If you allow someone to dishonour me, there is no stopping the scandal. It insults me, but it threatens you. Who knows where scandal will stop once it takes hold? Scandal against the queen rocks the throne itself. Be warned, Henry.'

'She said it!' he exclaims. 'Anne said that it was no sin for me to lie with her because I was not truly married!'

'She lied to you,' I say. 'She pretended to her virgin state and she traduced me.'

His face flushes red with anger. It is a relief to him to turn to rage. 'What a whore!' he exclaims crudely. 'What a whore to trick me into thinking . . . what a jade's trick!'

'You cannot trust young women,' I say quietly. 'Now that you are King of England you will have to be on your guard, my love. They will run after you and they will try to charm you and seduce you, but you have to be faithful to me. I was your virgin bride, I was your first love. I am your wife. Do not forsake me.'

He takes me into his arms. 'Forgive me,' he whispers brokenly.

'We will never ever speak of this again,' I say solemnly. 'I will not have it, and I will not allow anyone to dishonour either me or your mother.'

'No,' he says fervently. 'Before God. We will never speak of this nor allow any other to speak of it again.'

Next morning Henry and Katherine rose up together and went quietly to Mass in the king's chapel. Katherine met with her confessor and kneeled to confess her sins. She did not take very long, Henry observed, she must have no great sins to confess. It made him feel even worse to see her go to her priest for a brief confession and come away with her face so serene. He knew that she was a woman of holy purity, just like his mother. Penitently, his face in his hands, he thought that not only had Katherine never been unfaithful to her given word, she had probably never even told a lie in her life.

I go out with the court to hunt dressed in a red velvet gown, determined to show that I am well, that I am returned to the court, that everything will be as it was before. We have a long, hard run after a fine stag who takes a looping route around the great park and the hounds bring him down in the stream and Henry himself goes into the water, laughing, to cut his throat. The stream blooms red around him and stains his clothes, and his hands. I laugh with the court but the sight of the blood makes me feel sick to my very belly.

We ride home slowly, I keep my face locked in a smile to hide my weariness and the pain in my thighs, in my belly, in my back. Lady Margaret brings her horse beside mine, and glances at me. 'You had better rest this afternoon.'

'I cannot,' I say shortly.

She does not need to ask why. She has been a princess, she knows that a queen has to be on show, whatever her own feelings. 'I have the story, if you want to trouble yourself to hear such a thing.'

'You are a good friend,' I say. 'Tell me briefly. I think I know the worst that it can be already.'

'After we had gone in for your confinement the king and the young men started to go into the City in the evenings.'

'With guards?'

'No, alone and disguised.'

I stifle a sigh. 'Did no-one try to stop him?'

'The Earl of Surrey, God bless him. But his own sons were of the party and it was light-hearted fun, and you know that the king will not be denied his pastimes.'

I nod.

'One evening they came into court in their disguises and pretended to be London merchants. The ladies danced with them, it was all very amusing. I was not there that evening, I was with you in confinement; someone told me about it the next day. I took no notice. But apparently one of the merchants singled out Lady Anne and danced with her all night.'

'Henry,' I say, and I can hear the bitterness in my own whisper.

'Yes, but everyone thought it was William Compton. They are about the same height, and they were all wearing false beards and hats. You know how they do.'

'Yes,' I say. 'I know how they do.'

'Apparently they made an assignation and when the duke thought that his sister was sitting with you in the evenings she was slipping away and meeting the king. When she went missing all night, it was too much for her sister. Elizabeth went to her brother and warned him of what Anne was doing. They told her husband and all of them confronted Anne and demanded to know who she was seeing, and she said it was Compton. But when she was missing, and they thought she was with her lover, they met Compton. So then they knew, it was not Compton, it was the king.'

I shake my head.

'I am sorry, my dear,' Lady Margaret says to me gently. 'He is a young man. I am sure it is no more than vanity and thoughtlessness.'

I nod and say nothing. I check my horse, who is tossing his head against my hands, which are too heavy on the reins. I am thinking of Anne crying out in pain as her hymen was broken.

'And is her husband, Sir George, unmanned?' I ask. 'Was she a virgin until now?'

'So they say,' Lady Margaret replies drily. 'Who knows what goes on in a bedroom?'

'I think we know what goes on in the king's bedroom,' I say bitterly. 'They have hardly been discreet.'

'It is the way of the world,' she says quietly. 'When you are confined it is only natural that he will take a lover.'

I nod again. This is nothing but the truth. What is surprising to me is that I should feel such hurt.

'The duke must have been much aggrieved,' I say, thinking of the dignity of the man, and how it was he who put the Tudors on the throne in the first place.

'Yes,' she says. She hesitates. Something about her voice warns me that there is something she is not sure if she should say.

'What is it, Margaret?' I ask. 'I know you well enough to know that there is something more.'

'It is something that Elizabeth said to one of the girls before she left,' she says.

'Oh?'

'Elizabeth says that her sister did not think it was a light love affair that would last while you were in confinement and then be forgotten.'

'What else could it be?'

'She thought that her sister had ambitions.'

'Ambitions for what?'

'She thought that she might take the king's fancy and hold him.'

'For a season,' I say disparagingly.

'No, for longer,' she says. 'He spoke of love. He is a romantic young man. He spoke of being hers till death.' She sees the look on my face and breaks off. 'Forgive me, I should have said none of this.'

I think of Anne Stafford crying out in pain and telling him that she was a virgin, a true virgin, in too much pain to go on. That he was her first love, her only love. I know how much he would like that.

I check my horse again, he frets against the bit. 'What do you mean, she was ambitious?'

'I think she thought that given her family position, and the liking that was between her and the king, that she could become the great mistress of the English court.'

I blink. 'And what about me?'

'I think she thought that, in time, he might turn from you to her. I think she hoped to supplant you in his love.'

I nod. 'And if I died bearing his child, I suppose she thought she would have her empty marriage annulled and marry him?'

'That would be the very cusp of her ambition,' Lady Margaret says. 'And stranger things have happened. Elizabeth Woodville got to the throne of England on looks alone.'

'Anne Stafford was my lady-in-waiting,' I say. 'I chose her for the honour over many others. What about her duty to me? What about her friendship with me? Did she never think of me? If she had served me in Spain we would have lived night and day together . . .' I break off, there is no way to explain the safety and affection of the harem to a woman who has always lived her life alert to the gaze of men.

Lady Margaret shakes her head. 'Women are always rivals,' she says simply. 'But until now everyone has thought that the king only had eyes for you. Now everyone knows different. There is not a pretty girl in the land who does not now think that the crown is for taking.'

'It is still my crown,' I point out.

'But girls will hope for it,' she says. 'It is the way of the world.'

'They will have to wait for my death,' I say bleakly. 'That could be a long wait even for the most ambitious girl.'

Lady Margaret nods. I indicate behind me and she looks back. The ladies-in-waiting are scattered among the huntsmen and courtiers, riding and laughing and flirting. Henry has Princess Mary on one side of him and one of her ladies-in-waiting on another. She is a new girl to court, young and pretty. A virgin, without doubt, another pretty virgin.

'And which of these will be next?' I ask bitterly. 'When I next go in for my confinement and cannot watch them like a fierce hawk? Will it be a Percy girl? Or a Seymour? Or a Howard? Or a Neville? Which girl will step up to the king next and try to charm her way into his bed and into my place?'

'Some of your ladies love you dearly,' she says.

'And some of them will use their position at my side to get close to the king,' I say. 'Now they have seen it done they will be waiting for their chance. They will know that the easiest route to the king is to come into my rooms, to pretend to be my friend, to offer me service. First she will pretend friendship and loyalty to me and all the time she will watch for her chance. I can know that one will do it, but I cannot know which one she is.'

Lady Margaret leans forward, and strokes her horse's neck, her face grave. 'Yes,' she agrees.

'And one of them, one of the many, will be clever enough to turn the king's head,' I say bitterly. 'He is young and vain and easily misled. Sooner or later, one of them will turn him against me and want my place.'

Lady Margaret straightens up and looks directly at me, her grey eyes as honest as ever. 'This may all be true; but I think you can do nothing to prevent it.'

'I know,' I say grimly.

'I have good news for you,' Katherine said to Henry. They had thrown open the windows of her bedroom to let in the cooler night air. It was a warm night in late May and for once, Henry had chosen to come to bed early.

'Tell me some good news,' he said. 'My horse went lame today, and I cannot ride him tomorrow. I would welcome some good news.'

'I think I am with child.'

He bounced up in the bed. 'You are?'

'I think so,' she said, smiling.

'Praise God! You are?'

'I am certain of it.'

'God be praised. I shall go to Walsingham the minute you give birth to our son. I shall go on my knees to Walsingham! I shall crawl along the road! I shall wear a suit of pure white. I shall give Our Lady pearls.'

'Our Lady has been gracious to us indeed.'

'And how potent they will all know that I am now! Out of confinement in the first week of May and pregnant by the end of the month. That will show them! That will prove that I am a husband indeed.'

'Indeed it will,' she said levelly.

'It is not too early to be sure?'

'I have missed my course, and I am sick in the morning. They tell me it is a certain sign.'

'And you are certain?' He had no tact to phrase his anxiety in gentle words. 'You are certain this time? You know that there can be no mistake?'

She nodded. 'I am certain. I have all the signs.'

'God be praised. I knew it would come. I knew that a marriage made in heaven would be blessed.'

Katherine nodded. Smiling.

'We shall go slowly on our progress, you shall not hunt. We shall go by boat for some of the way, barges.'

'I think I will not travel at all, if you will allow it,' she said. 'I want to stay quietly in one place this summer, I don't even want to ride in a litter.'

'Well, I shall go on progress with the court and then come home to you,' he said. 'And what a celebration we shall have when our baby is born. When will it be?'

'After Christmas,' Katherine said. 'In the New Year.'

Winter 1510

I should have been a soothsayer, I have proved to be so accurate with my prediction, even without a Moorish abacus. We are holding the Christmas feast at Richmond and the court is joyful in my happiness. The baby is big in my belly, and he kicks so hard that Henry can put his hand on me and feel the little heel thud out against his hand. There is no doubt that he is alive and strong, and his vitality brings joy to the whole court. When I sit in council, I sometimes wince at the strange sensation of him moving inside me, the pressure of his body against my own, and some of the old councillors laugh – having seen their own wives in the same state – for joy that there is to be an heir for England and Spain at last.

I pray for a boy but I do not expect one. A child for England, a child for Arthur, is all I want. If it is the daughter that he had wanted, then I will call her Mary as he asked.

Henry's desire for a son, and his love for me, has made him more thoughtful at last. He takes care of me in ways that he has never done before. I think he is growing up, the selfish boy is becoming a good man at last, and the fear that has haunted me since his affair with the Stafford girl is receding. Perhaps he will take lovers as kings always do, but perhaps he will resist falling in love with them and making the wild promises that a man can make but a king must not. Perhaps he will acquire the good sense that so many men seem to learn: to enjoy a new woman but remain constant, in their hearts, to their wife. Certainly, if he continues to be this sweet-natured, he will make a good father. I think of him teaching our son to ride, to hunt, to joust. No boy could have a better father for sports and pastimes than a son of Henry's. Not even Arthur would have made a more playful father. Our boy's education, his skill in court life, his upbringing as a Christian, his training as a ruler, these are the things that I will teach him. He will learn my mother's courage and my father's skills, and from me – I think I can teach him constancy, determination. These are my gifts now.

I believe that between Henry and me, we will raise a prince who will make his mark in Europe, who will keep England safe from the Moors, from the French, from the Scots, from all our enemies.

I will have to go into confinement again but I leave it as late as I dare. Henry swears to me that there will be no other while I am confined, that he is mine, all mine. I leave it till the evening of the Christmas feast and then I take my spiced wine with the members of my court and bid them merry Christmas as they bid me God speed, and I go once more into the quietness of my bedroom.

In truth, I don't mind missing the dancing and the heavy drinking. I am tired, this baby is a weight to carry. I rise and then rest with the winter sun, rarely waking much before nine of the morning, and ready to sleep at five in the afternoon. I spend much time praying for a safe delivery, and for the health of the child that moves so strongly inside me.

Henry comes to see me, privately, most days. The Royal Book is clear that the queen should be in absolute isolation before the birth of her child; but the Royal Book was written by Henry's grandmother and I suggest that we can please ourselves. I don't see why she should command me from beyond the grave when she was such an unhelpful mentor in life. Besides, to put it as bluntly as an Aragonese: I don't trust Henry on his own in court. On New Year's Eve he dines with me before going to the hall for the great feast, and brings me a gift of rubies, with stones as big as Cristóbal Colón's haul. I put them around my neck and see his eyes darken with desire for me as they gleam on the plump whiteness of my breasts.

'Not long now,' I say, smiling; I know exactly what he is thinking.

'I shall go to Walsingham as soon as our child is born, and when I come back you will be churched,' he says.

'And then, I suppose you will want to make another baby,' I say with mock weariness.

'I will,' he says, his face bright with laughter.

He kisses me goodnight, wishes me joy of the new year and then goes out of the hidden door in my chamber to his own rooms, and from there to the feast. I tell them to bring the boiled water that I still drink in obedience to the Moor's advice, and then I sit before the fire sewing the tiniest little gown for my baby, while Maria de Salinas reads in Spanish to me.

Suddenly, it is as if my whole belly has turned over, as if I am falling from a great height. The pain is so thorough, so unlike anything I have ever known before, that the sewing drops from my hands and I grip the arms of my chair and let out a gasp before I can say a word. I know at once that the baby is coming. I had been afraid that I would not know what was happening, that it would be a pain like that when I lost my poor girl. But this is like the great force of a deep river, this feels like something powerful and wonderful starting to flow. I am filled with joy and a holy terror. I know that the baby is coming and that he is strong, and that I am young, and that everything will be all right.

As soon as I tell the ladies, the chamber bursts into uproar. My Lady the King's Mother might have ruled that the whole thing shall be done soberly and quietly with the cradle made ready and two beds made up for the mother, one to give birth in and one to rest in; but in real life, the ladies run around like hens in a poultry yard, squawking in alarm. The midwives are summoned from the hall, they have gone off to make merry, gambling that they would not be needed on New Year's Eve. One of them is quite tipsy and Maria de Salinas throws her out of the room

417

before she falls over and breaks something. The physician cannot be found at all, and pages are sent running all over the palace looking for him.

The only ones who are settled and determined are Lady Margaret Pole, Maria de Salinas, and I. Maria, because she is naturally disposed to calm, Lady Margaret, because she has been confident from the start of this confinement, and I, because I can feel that nothing will stop this baby coming, and I might as well grab hold of the rope in one hand, my relic of the Virgin Mother in the other, fix my eyes on the little altar in the corner of the room and pray to St Margaret of Antioch to give me a swift and easy delivery and a healthy baby.

Unbelievably, it is little more than six hours – though one of those hours lingers on for at least a day – and then there is a rush and a slither, and the midwife mutters 'God be praised!' quietly and then there is a loud, irritable cry, almost a shout, and I realise that this is a new voice in the room, that of my baby.

'A boy, God be praised, a boy,' the midwife says and Maria looks up at me and sees me radiant with joy.

'Really?' I demand. 'Let me see him!'

They cut the cord and pass him up to me, still naked, still bloody, his little mouth opened wide to shout, his eyes squeezed tight in anger, Henry's son.

'My son,' I whisper.

'England's son,' the midwife says. 'God be praised.'

I put my face down to his warm little head, still sticky, I sniff him like a cat sniffs her kittens. 'This is our boy,' I whisper to Arthur, who is so close at that moment that it is almost as if he is at my side, looking over my shoulder at this tiny miracle, who turns his head and nuzzles at my breast, little mouth gaping. 'Oh, Arthur, my love, this is the boy I promised I would bear for you and for England. This is our son for England, and he will be king.'

Spring 1511

1st January 1511

The whole of England went mad when they learned on New Year's Day that a boy had been born. Everyone called him Prince Henry at once, there was no other name possible. In the streets they roasted oxen and drank themselves into a stupor. In the country they rang the church bells and broke into the church ales to toast the health of the Tudor heir, the boy who would keep England at peace, who would keep England allied with Spain, who would protect England from her enemies and who would defeat the Scots once and for all.

Henry came in to see his son, disobeying the rules of confinement, tiptoeing carefully, as if his footstep might shake the room. He peered into the cradle, afraid almost to breathe near the sleeping boy.

'He is so small,' he said. 'How can he be so small?'

'The midwife says he is big and strong,' Katherine corrected him, instantly on the defence of her baby.

'I am sure. It is just that his hands are so . . . and look, he has fingernails! Real fingernails!'

419

'He has toenails too,' she said. The two of them stood side by side and looked down in amazement at the perfection that they had made together. 'He has little plump feet and the tiniest toes you can imagine.'

'Show me,' he said.

Gently, she pulled off the little silk shoes that the baby wore. 'There,' she said, her voice filled with tenderness. 'Now I must put this back on so that he does not get cold.'

Henry bent over the crib, and tenderly took the tiny foot in his big hand. 'My son,' he said wonderingly. 'God be praised, I have a son.'

I lie on my bed as the old king's mother commanded in the Royal Book, and I receive honoured guests. I have to hide a smile when I think of my mother giving birth to me on campaign, in a tent, like any soldier's doxy. But this is the English way and I am an English queen and this baby will be King of England.

I've never known such simple joy. When I doze I wake with my heart filled with delight, before I even know why. Then I remember. I have a son for England, for Arthur and for Henry; and I smile and turn my head, and whoever is watching over me answers the question before I have asked it: 'Yes, your son is well, Your Grace.'

Henry is excessively busy with the care of our son. He comes in and out to see me twenty times a day with questions and with news of the arrangements he has made. He has appointed a household of no less than forty people for this tiny baby, and already chosen his rooms in the Palace of Westminster for his council chamber when he is a young man. I smile, and say nothing. Henry is planning the greatest christening that has ever been seen in England, nothing is too good for this Henry who will be Henry the Ninth. Sometimes when I am sitting on my bed, supposed to be writing letters, I draw his monogram. Henry IX: my son, the King of England.

His sponsors are carefully chosen: the daughter of the emperor, Margaret of Austria, and King Louis the Twelfth of France. So he is working already, this little Tudor, to cloud the French suspicion against us, to maintain our alliance with the Hapsburg family. When they bring him to me and I put my finger in the palm of his tiny hand, his fingers curl around, as if to grip on. As if he would hold my hand. As if he might love me in return. I lie quietly, watching him sleep, my finger against his little palm, the other hand cupped over his tender little head where I can feel a steady pulse throbbing.

His godparents are Archbishop Warham, my dear and true friend Thomas Howard, Earl of Surrey, and the Earl and Countess of Devon. My dearest Lady Margaret is to run his nursery at Richmond. It is the newest and cleanest of all the palaces near London, and wherever we are, whether at Whitehall or Greenwich or Westminster, it will be easy for me to visit him.

I can hardly bear to let him go away, but it is better for him to be in the country than in the City. And I shall see him every week at the very least, Henry has promised me that I shall see him every week.

Henry went to the shrine of Our Lady at Walsingham, as he had promised, and Katherine asked him to tell the nuns who kept the shrine that she would come herself when she was next with child. When the next baby was in the queen's womb she would give thanks for the safe birth of the first; and pray for the safe delivery of a second. She asked the king to tell the nuns that she would come to them every time she was with child, and that she hoped to visit them many times.

She gave him a heavy purse of gold. 'Will you give them this, from me, and ask them for their prayers?'

He took it. 'They pray for the Queen of England as their duty,' he said.

'I want to remind them.'

Henry returned to court for the greatest tournament that England had ever seen, and Katherine was up and out of her bed to organise it for him. He had commissioned new armour before he went away and she had commanded her favourite, Edward Howard, the talented younger son of the Howard house, to make sure that it would fit precisely to the slim young king's measurements, and that the workmanship was perfect. She had banners made, and tapestries hung, masques prepared with glorious themes, gold everywhere: cloth of gold banners and curtains, and swathes of cloth, gold plates and gold cups, gold tips to the ornamental lances, gold-embossed shields, even gold on the king's saddlery.

'This will be the greatest tournament that England has ever seen,' Edward Howard said to her. 'English chivalry and Spanish elegance. It will be a thing of beauty.'

'It is the greatest celebration that we have ever had,' she said, smiling. 'For the greatest reason.'

I know I have made an outstanding showcase for Henry but when he rides into the tiltyard I catch my breath. It is the fashion that the knights who have come to joust choose a motto; sometimes they even compose a poem or play a part in a tableau before they ride. Henry has kept his motto a secret, and not told me what it is going to be. He has commissioned his own banner and the women have hidden from me, with much laughter, while they embroider his words on the banner of Tudor green silk. I truly have no idea what it will say until he bows before me in the royal box, the banner unfurls and his herald shouts out his title for the joust: 'Sir Loyal Heart'.

I rise to my feet and clasp my hands before my face to hide my trembling mouth. My eyes fill with tears, I cannot help it. He has called himself 'Sir Loyal Heart' – he has declared to the world the restoration of his devotion and love for me. My women step back so that I can see the canopy that he has commanded them to hang all around the royal box. He has had it pinned all over with little gold badges of H and K entwined. Everywhere I look, at every corner of the jousting green, on every banner, on every post there are Ks and Hs together. He has used this great joust, the finest and richest that England has ever seen, to tell the world that he loves me, that he is mine, that his heart is mine and that it is a loyal heart.

I look around at my ladies-in-waiting and I am utterly triumphant. If I could speak freely I would say to them: 'There! Take this as your warning. He is not the man that you have thought him. He is not a man to turn from his true-married wife. He is not a man that you can seduce, however clever your tricks, however insidious your whispers against me. He has given his heart to me, and he has a loyal heart.' I run my eyes over them, the prettiest girls from the greatest families of England, and I know that every one of them secretly thinks that she could have my place. If she were to be lucky, if the king were to be seduced, if I were to die, she could have my throne.

But his banner tells them 'Not so.' His banner tells them, the gold Ks and Hs tell them, the herald's cry tells them that he is all mine, forever. The will of my mother, my word to Arthur, the destiny given by God to England has brought me finally to this: a son and heir in England's cradle, the King of England publicly declaring his passion for me, and my initial twined with his in gold everywhere I look.

I touch my hand to my lips and hold it out to him. His visor is up, his blue eyes are blazing with passion for me. His love for me warms me like the hot sun of my childhood. I am a woman blessed by God, especially favoured by Him, indeed. I survived widowhood and my despair at the loss of Arthur. The courtship of the old king did not seduce me, his enmity did not defeat me, the hatred of his mother did not destroy me. The love of Henry delights me but does not redeem me. With God's especial favour, I have saved myself. I myself have come from the darkness of poverty into the glamour of the light. I myself have fought that terrible slide into blank despair. I myself have made myself into a woman who can face death and face life and endure them both.

I remember once when I was a little girl, my mother was praying before a battle and then she rose up from her knees, kissed the little ivory cross, put it back on its stand and gestured for her lady-in-waiting to bring her breastplate and buckle it on.

I ran forwards and begged her not to go, and I asked her why she must ride, if God gives us His blessing? If we are blessed by God, why do we have to fight as well? Will He not just drive away the Moors for us?

'I am blessed because I am chosen to do His work.' She kneeled down and put her arm around me. 'You might say, why not leave it to God and he will send a thunderstorm over the wicked Moors?'

I nodded.

'I am the thunderstorm,' she said, smiling. 'I am God's thunderstorm to drive them away. He has not chosen a thunderstorm today, He has chosen me. And neither I nor the dark clouds can refuse our duty.'

I smile at Henry as he drops his visor and turns his horse from the royal box. I understand now what my mother meant by being God's thunderstorm. God has called me to be his sunshine in England. It is my God-given duty to bring happiness and prosperity and security to England. I do this by leading the king in the right choices, by securing the succession, and by protecting the safety of the borders. I am England's queen chosen by God and I smile on Henry as his big glossy black horse trots slowly to the end of the lists, and I smile on the people of London who call out my name and shout 'God bless Queen Katherine!' and I smile to myself because I am doing as my mother wished, as God decreed, and Arthur is waiting for me in al-Yanna, the garden.

22nd February 1511

Ten days later, when she was at the height of her happiness, they brought to Queen Katherine the worst news of her life.

It is worse even than the death of my husband, Arthur. I had not thought there could be anything worse than that; but so it proves. It is worse than my years of widowhood and waiting. It is worse than hearing from Spain that my mother was dead, that she died on the day I wrote to her, begging her to send me a word. Worse than the worst days I have ever had.

My baby is dead. More than this, I cannot say, I cannot even hear. I think Henry is here, some of the time; and Maria de Salinas. I think Margaret Pole is here, and I see the stricken face of Thomas Howard at Henry's shoulder; William Compton desperately gripping Henry's shoulder; but the faces all swim before my eyes and I can be sure of nothing.

I go into my room and I order them to close the shutters and bolt the doors. But it is too late. They have already brought me the worst news of my life; closing the door will not keep it out. I cannot bear the light. I cannot bear the sound of ordinary life going on. I hear a page boy laugh in the garden near my window and I cannot understand how there can be any joy or gladness left in the world, now that my baby has gone.

And now the courage I have held on to, for all my life, turns out to be a thread, a spider-web, a nothing. My bright confidence that I am walking in the way of God and that He will protect me is nothing more than an illusion, a child's fairy story. In the shadows of my room I plunge deep into the darkness that my mother knew when she lost her son, that Juana could not escape when she lost her husband, that was the curse of my grandmother, that runs through the women of my family like a dark vein. I am no different after all. I am not a woman who can survive love and loss, as I had thought. It has only been that, so far, I have never lost someone who was worth more than life itself to me. When Arthur died my heart was broken. But now that my baby is dead, I want nothing but that my heart should cease to beat.

I cannot think of any reason why I should live and that innocent, sinless babe be taken from me. I can see no reason for it. I cannot understand a God who can take him from me. I cannot understand a world that can be so cruel. In the moment that they told me, 'Your Grace, be brave, we have bad news of the prince,' I lost my faith in God. I lost my desire to live. I lost even my ambition to rule England and keep my country safe.

He had blue eyes and the smallest, most perfect hands. He had finger-nails like little shells. His little feet . . . his little feet . . .

Lady Margaret Pole, who had been in charge of the dead child's nursery, came into the room without knocking, without invitation, and kneeled before Queen Katherine, who sat on her chair by the fire, among her ladies, seeing nothing and hearing nothing.

'I have come to beg your pardon though I did nothing wrong,' she said steadily.

Katherine raised her head from her hand. 'What?'

'Your baby died in my care. I have come to beg your pardon. I was not remiss, I swear it. But he is dead. Princess, I am sorry.'

'You are always here,' Katherine said with quiet dislike. 'In my darkest moments, you are always at my side, like bad luck.'

The older woman flinched. 'Indeed, but it is not my wish.'

'And don't call me "Princess".'

'I forgot.'

For the first time in weeks Katherine sat up and looked into the face of another person, saw her eyes, saw the new lines around her mouth, realised that the loss of her baby was not her grief alone. 'Oh God, Margaret,' she said, and pitched forwards.

Margaret Pole caught her and held her. 'Oh God, Katherine,' she said into the queen's hair.

'How could we lose him?'

'God's will. God's will. We have to believe it. We have to bow beneath it.'

'But why?'

'Princess, no-one knows why one is taken and another spared. D'you remember?'

She felt from the shudder that the woman remembered the loss of her husband in this, the loss of her son.

'I never forget. Every day. But why?'

'It is God's will,' Lady Margaret repeated.

'I don't think I can bear it.' Katherine breathed so softly that none of her ladies could hear. She raised her tearstained face from her friend's shoulder. 'To lose Arthur felt like torture, but to lose my baby is like death itself. I don't think I can bear it, Margaret.'

The older woman's smile was infinitely patient. 'Oh, Katherine. You will learn to bear it. There is nothing that anyone can do but bear it. You can rage or you can weep but in the end, you will learn to bear it.'

Slowly Katherine sat back on her chair; Margaret remained, with easy grace, kneeling on the floor at her feet, handclasped with her friend.

'You will have to teach me courage all over again,' Katherine whispered.

The older woman shook her head. 'You only have to learn it once,' she said. 'You know, you learned at Ludlow; you are not a woman to be destroyed by sorrow. You will grieve but you will live, you will come out into the world again. You will love. You will conceive another child, this child will live, you will learn again to be happy.'

'I cannot see it,' Katherine said desolately.

'It will come.'

The battle that Katherine had waited for, for so long, came while she was still overshadowed with grief for her baby. But nothing could penetrate her sadness.

'Great news, the best news in the world!' wrote her father. Wearily, Katherine translated from the code and then from Spanish to English. 'I am to lead a crusade against the Moors in Africa. Their existence is a danger to Christendom, their raids terrify the whole of the Mediterranean and endanger shipping from Greece to the Atlantic. Send me the best of your knights – you who claim to be the new Camelot. Send me your most courageous leaders at the head of your most powerful men and I shall take them to Africa and we will destroy the infidel kingdoms as holy Christian kings.'

Wearily, Katherine took the translated letter to Henry. He was coming off the tennis court, a napkin twisted around his neck, his face flushed. He beamed when he saw her, then at once his look of joy was wiped from his face by a grimace of guilt, like a boy caught out in a forbidden pleasure. At that fleeting expression, at that brief, betraying moment, she knew he had forgotten that their son was dead. He was playing tennis with his friends, he had won, he saw the wife he still loved, he was happy. Joy came as easily to the men of his family as sorrow to the women of hers. She felt a wave of hatred wash over her, so powerful that she could almost taste it in her mouth. He could forget, even for a moment, that their little boy had died. She thought that she would never forget; never.

'I have a letter from my father,' she said, trying to put some interest into her harsh voice.

'Oh?' He was all concern. He came towards her and took her arm. She gritted her teeth so that she did not scream: 'Don't touch me!'

'Did he tell you to have courage? Did he write comforting words?'

The clumsiness of the young man was unbearable. She summoned her most tolerant smile. 'No. It is not a personal letter. You know he rarely writes to me in that way. It is a letter about a crusade. He invites our noblemen and lords to raise regiments and go with him against the Moors.'

'Does he? Oh, does he? What a chance!'

'Not for you,' she said, quelling any idea that Henry might have that he could go to war when they had no son. 'It is just a little expedition. But my father would welcome English men, and I think they should go.'

'I should think he would.' Henry turned and shouted for his friends, who were hanging back like guilty schoolboys caught having fun. They could not bear to see Katherine since she had become so pale and quiet. They liked her when she was the queen of the joust and Henry was Sir Loyal Heart. She made them uncomfortable when she came to dinner like a ghost, ate nothing, and left early.

'Hey! Anyone want to go to war against the Moors?'

A chorus of excited yells answered his holloa. Katherine thought that they were like nothing so much as a litter of excited puppies, Lord Thomas Darcy and Edward Howard at their head.

'I will go!'

'And I will go!'

'Show them how Englishmen fight!' Henry urged them. 'I, myself, will pay the costs of the expedition.'

'I will write to my father that you have eager volunteers,' Katherine said quietly. 'I will go and write to him now.' She turned away and walked quickly towards the doorway to the little stair that led to her rooms. She did not think she could bear to be with them for another moment. These were the men who would have taught her son to ride. These were the men who would have been his statesmen, his Privy Council. They would have sponsored him at his first communion, they would have stood proxy for him at his betrothal, they would have been godfathers to his sons. And here they were, laughing, clamouring for war, competing with each other for Henry's shouted approval, as if her son had not been born, had not died. As if the world were the same as it had ever been; when Katherine knew that it was utterly changed.

He had blue eyes. And the tiniest, most perfect feet.

In the event, the glorious crusade never happened. The English knights arrived at Cadiz but the crusade never set sail for the Holy Land, never faced a sharp scimitar wielded by a black-hearted infidel. Katherine translated letters between Henry and her father in which her father explained that he had not yet raised his troops, that he was not yet ready to leave, and then, one day, she came to Henry with a letter in her hand and her face shocked out of its usual weariness.

'Father writes me the most terrible news.'

'What is happening?' Henry demanded, bewildered. 'See, here, I have just received a letter from an English merchant in Italy, I cannot make any sense of it. He writes that the French and the Pope are at war.' Henry held out his letter to her. 'How can this be? I don't understand it at all.'

'It is true. This is from my father. He says the Pope has declared that the French armies must get out of Italy,' Katherine explained. 'And the Holy Father has put his own papal troops into the field against the French. King Louis has declared that the Pope shall no longer be Pope.'

'How dare he?' Henry demanded, shocked to his core.

'Father says we must forget the crusade and go at once to the aid of the Pope. He will try to broker an alliance between us and the Holy Roman Emperor. We must form an alliance against France. King Louis cannot be allowed to take Rome. He must not advance into Italy.'

'He must be mad to think that I would allow it!' Henry exclaimed. 'Would I let the French take Rome? Would I allow a French puppet Pope? Has he forgotten what an English army can do? Does he want another Agincourt?'

'Shall I tell my father we will unite with him against France?' Katherine asked. 'I could write at once.'

He caught her hand and kissed it. For once she did not pull away and he drew her a little closer and put his arm around her waist. 'I'll come with you while you write and we can sign the letter from us both – your father should know that his Spanish daughter and his English son are absolutely as one in his support. Thank God that our troops are in Cadiz already,' Henry exclaimed as his good fortune struck him.

Katherine hesitated, a thought forming slowly in her mind. 'It is . . . fortuitous.'

'Lucky,' Henry said buoyantly. 'We are blessed by God.'

'My father will want some benefit for Spain from this.' Katherine introduced the suspicion carefully as they went to her rooms, Henry shortening his stride to match hers. 'He never makes a move without planning far ahead.'

'Of course, but you will guard our interests as you always do,' he said confidently. 'I trust you, my love, as I trust him. Is he not my only father now?'

Summer 1511

Slowly, as the days grow warmer, and the sun is more like a Spanish sun, I grow warm too and become more like the Spanish girl I once was. I cannot reconcile myself to the death of my son, I think I will never reconcile myself to his loss; but I can see that there is no-one to blame for his death. There was no neglect or negligence, he died like a little bird in a warm nest and I have to see that I will never know why.

I know now that I was foolish to blame myself. I have committed no crime, no sin so bad that God, the merciful God of my childhood prayers, would punish me with such an awful grief as this. There could be no good God who would take away such a sweet baby, such a perfect baby with such blue eyes, as an exercise of His divine will. I know in my heart that such a thing cannot be, such a God cannot be. Even though in the first worst outpourings of my grief I blamed myself and I blamed God, I know now that it was not a punishment for sin. I know that I kept my promise, Arthur's promise, for the best reasons; and God has me in His keeping.

The awful, icy, dark fact of my baby's loss seems to recede with the awful cold darkness of that English winter. One morning the fool came and told me some little jest and I laughed aloud. It was as if a door had opened that had long been locked tight. I realise that I can laugh, that it is possible to be happy, that laughter and hope can come back to me and perhaps I might even make another child and feel that over-whelming tenderness again.

I start to feel that I am alive again, that I am a woman with hope and prospects again, that I am the woman that the girl from Spain became. I can sense myself alive: poised halfway between my future and my past.

It is as if I am checking myself over as a rider does after a bad fall from a horse, patting my arms and legs, my vulnerable body, as if looking for permanent damage. My faith in God returns utterly unshaken, as firm as it has ever been. There seems to be only one great change: my belief in my mother and my father is damaged. For the first time in my life I truly think it possible that they can have been wrong.

I remember the Moorish physician's kindness to me and I have to amend my view of his people. No-one who could see his enemy brought as low as he saw me, and yet could look at her with such deep compassion, can be called a barbarian, a savage. He might be a heretic — steeped in error — but surely he must be allowed his own conclusions with his own reasons. And from what I know of the man, I am certain that he will have fine reasons.

I would like to send a good priest to wrestle for his soul, but I cannot say, as my mother would have said, that he is spiritually dead, fit for nothing but death. He held my hands to tell me hard news and I saw the tenderness of Our Lady in his eyes. I cannot dismiss the Moors as heretics and enemies any more. I have to see that they are men and women, fallible as us, hopeful as us, faithful to their creed as we are to ours.

And this in turn leads me to doubt my mother's wisdom. Once I would have sworn that she knew everything, that her writ must run everywhere. But now I have grown old enough to view her more thoughtfully. I was left in poverty in my widowhood because her *contract was carelessly written. I was abandoned, all alone in a foreign country, because – though she summoned me with apparent urgency – in truth it was just for show; she would not take me back to Spain at any price. She hardened her heart against me and cleaved to her plan for me, and let me, her own daughter, go.*

And finally, I was forced to find a doctor in secret and consult with him in hiding because she had done her part in driving from Christendom the best physicians, the best scientists, and the cleverest minds in the world. She had named their wisdom as sin and the rest of Europe had followed her lead. She rid Spain of the Jews and their skills and courage, she rid Spain of the Moors and their scholarship and gifts. She, a woman who admired learning, banished those that they call the People of the Book. She who fought for justice had been unjust.

I cannot yet think what this estrangement might mean for me. My mother is dead, I cannot reproach her or argue with her now, except in my imagination. But I know these months have wrought a deep and lasting change in me. I have come to an understanding of my world that is not her understanding of hers. I do not support a crusade against the Moors, nor against anyone. I do not support persecution, nor cruelty to them for the colour of their skin or the belief in their hearts. I know that my mother is not infallible, I no longer believe she and God think as one. Though I still love my mother, I don't worship her any more. I suppose, at last, I am growing up.

Slowly, the queen emerged from her grief and started to take an interest in the running of the court and country once more. London was buzzing with the news that Scottish privateers had attacked an English merchant ship. Everyone knew the name of the privateer: he was Andrew Barton, who sailed with letters of authority from King James of Scotland. Barton was merciless to English ships, and the general belief in the London docks was that James had deliberately licensed the pirate to prey on English shipping as if the two countries were already at war.

'He has to be stopped,' Katherine said to Henry.

'He does not dare to challenge me!' Henry exclaimed. 'James sends border raiders and pirates against me because he does not dare to face me himself. James is a coward and an oath-breaker.'

'Yes,' Katherine agreed. 'But the main thing about this pirate Barton is that he is not only a danger to our trade, he is a forerunner of worse to come. If we let the Scots rule the seas then we let them command us. This is an island; the seas must belong to us as much as the land or we have no safety.'

'My ships are ready and we sail at midday. I shall capture him alive,' Edward Howard, the Admiral of the Fleet, promised Katherine, as he came to bid her farewell. She thought he looked very young, as boyish as Henry; but his flair and courage were unquestioned. He had inherited all his father's tactical skill but brought it to the newly formed navy. The Howards traditionally held the post of Lord Admiral, but Edward was proving exceptional. 'If I cannot capture him alive, I shall sink his ship and bring him back dead.'

'For shame on you! A Christian enemy!' she said teasingly, holding out her hand for his kiss.

He looked up, serious for once. 'I promise you, Your Grace, that the Scots are a greater danger to the peace and wealth of this country than the Moors could ever be.'

He saw her wistful smile. 'You are not the first Englishman to tell me that,' she said. 'And I have seen it myself in these last years.'

'It has to be right,' he said. 'In Spain your father and mother never rested until they could dislodge the Moors from the mountains. For us in England, our closest enemy is the Scots. It is they who are in our mountains, it is they who have to be suppressed and quelled if we are ever to be at peace. My father has spent his life defending the northern borders, and now I am fighting the same enemy but at sea.'

'Come home safely,' she urged.

'I have to take risks,' he said carelessly. 'I am no stay-at-home.'

'No-one doubts your bravery, and my fleet needs an admiral,' she told him. 'I want the same admiral for many years. I need my champion at the next joust. I need my partner to dance with me. You come home safely, Edward Howard!'

The king was uneasy at his friend Edward Howard setting sail against the Scots, even against a Scots privateer. He had hoped that his father's alliance with Scotland, enforced by the marriage of the English princess, would have guaranteed peace.

'James is such a hypocrite to promise peace and marry Margaret on one hand and license these raids on the other! I shall write to Margaret and tell her to warn her husband that we cannot accept raids on our shipping. They should keep to their borders too.'

'Perhaps he will not listen to her,' Katherine pointed out.

'She can't be blamed for that,' he said quickly. 'She should never have been married to him. She was too young, and he was too set in his ways, and he is a man for war. But she will bring peace if she can, she knows it was my father's wish, she knows that we have to live in peace. We are kin now, we are neighbours.'

But the border lords, the Percys and the Nevilles, reported that the Scots had recently become more daring in their raids on the northern lands. Unquestionably, James was spoiling for war, undoubtedly he meant to take land in Northumberland as his own. Any day now he could march south, take Berwick, and continue on to Newcastle.

'How dare he?' Henry demanded. 'How dare he just march in and take our goods and disturb our people? Does he not know that I could raise an army and take them against him tomorrow?'

'It would be a hard campaign,' Katherine remarked, thinking of the wild land of the border and the long march to get to it. The Scotsmen would have everything to fight for, with the rich southern lands spread before them, and English soldiers never wanted to fight when they were far from their villages.

'It would be easy,' Henry contradicted her. 'Everyone knows that the Scots can't keep an army in the field. They are nothing more than a raiding party. If I took out a great English army, properly armed and supplied and ordered, I would make an end of them in a day!'

'Of course you would,' Katherine smiled. 'But don't forget, we have to muster our army to fight against the French. You would far rather win your spurs against the French on a field of chivalry which will go down in history than in some dirty border quarrel.'

Katherine spoke to Thomas Howard, Earl of Surrey, Edward Howard's father, at the end of the Privy Council meeting as the men came out of the king's rooms.

'My lord? Have you heard from Edward? I miss my young Chevalier.'

The old man beamed at her. 'We had a report this day. The king will tell you himself. He knew you would be pleased that your favourite has had a victory.'

'He has?'

'He has captured the pirate Andrew Barton with two of his ships.' His pride shone through his pretence of modesty. 'He has only done his duty,' he said. 'He has only done as any Howard boy should do.'

'He is a hero!' Katherine said enthusiastically. 'England needs great sailors as much as we need soldiers. The future for Christendom is in dominating the seas. We need to rule the seas as the Saracens rule the deserts. We have to drive pirates from the seas and make English ships a constant presence. And what else? Is he on his way home?'

'He will bring his ships into London and the pirate in chains with him. We'll try him, and hang him on the quayside. But King James won't like it.'

'Do you think the Scots king means war?' Katherine asked him bluntly. 'Would he go to war over such a cause as this? Is the country in danger?'

'This is the worst danger to the peace of the kingdom of any in my lifetime,' the older man said honestly. 'We have subdued the Welsh and brought peace to our borders in the west, now we will have to put down the Scots. After them we will have to settle the Irish.'

'They are a separate country, with their own kings and laws,' Katherine demurred.

'So were the Welsh till we defeated them,' he pointed out. 'This is too small a land for three kingdoms. The Scots will have to be yoked into our service.'

'Perhaps we could offer them a prince,' Katherine thought aloud. 'As you did to the Welsh. The second son could be the Prince of Scotland as the first-born is the Prince of Wales, for a kingdom united under the English king.'

He was struck with her idea. 'That's right,' he said. 'That would be the way to do it. Hit them hard and then offer them a peace with honour. Otherwise we will have them snapping at our heels forever.'

'The king thinks that their army would be small and easily defeated,' Katherine remarked.

Howard choked back a laugh. 'His Grace has never been to Scotland,' he said. 'He has never even been to war yet. The Scots are a formidable enemy, whether in pitched battle or a passing raid. They are a worse enemy than any of his fancy French cavalry. They have no laws of chivalry, they fight to win and they fight to the death. We will need to send a powerful force under a skilled commander.'

'Could you do it?' Katherine asked.

438

'I could try,' he replied honestly. 'I am the best weapon to your hand at the moment, Your Grace.'

'Could the king do it?' she asked quietly.

He smiled at her. 'He's a young man,' he said. 'He lacks nothing for courage, no-one who has seen him in a joust could doubt his courage. And he is skilled on his horse. But a war is not a joust, and he does not know that yet. He needs to ride out at the head of a bold army, and be seasoned in a few battles before he fights the greatest war of his life – the war for his very kingdom. You don't put a colt into a cavalry charge on his first outing. He has to learn. The king, even though a king, will have to learn.'

'He was taught nothing of warfare,' she said. 'He has not had to study other battles. He knows nothing about observing the lie of the land and positioning a force. He knows nothing about supplies and keeping an army on the move. His father taught him nothing.'

'His father knew next to nothing,' the earl said quietly, for her ears only. 'His first battle was Bosworth and he won that partly by luck and partly by the allies his mother put in the field for him. He was courageous enough, but no general.'

'But why did he not ensure that Henry was taught the art of warfare?' asked Ferdinand's daughter, who had been raised in a camp and seen a campaign plan before she had learned how to sew.

'Who would have thought he would need to know?' the old earl asked her. 'We all thought it would be Arthur.'

She made sure that her face did not betray the sudden pang of grief at the unexpected mention of his name. 'Of course,' she said. 'Of course you did. I forgot. Of course you did.'

'Now, he would have been a great commander. He was interested in the waging of war. He read. He studied. He talked to his father, he pestered me. He was well aware of the danger of the Scots, he had a great sense of how to command men. He used to ask me about the land on the border, where the castles were placed, how the land fell. He could have led an army against the Scots with some hopes of success. Young Henry will be a great king when he has learned tactics, but Arthur knew it all. It was in his blood.'

Katherine did not even allow herself the pleasure of speaking of him. 'Perhaps,' was all she said. 'But in the meantime, what can we do to limit the raids of the Scots? Should the border lords be reinforced?'

'Yes, but it is a long border, and hard to keep. King James does not fear an English army led by the king. He does not fear the border lords.'

'Why does he not fear us?'

He shrugged, too much of a courtier to say any betraying word. 'Well, James is an old warrior, he has been spoiling for a fight for two generations now.'

'Who could make James fear us and keep him in Scotland while we reinforce the border and get ready for war? What would make James delay and buy us time?'

'Nothing,' he declared, shaking his head. 'There is no-one who could hold back James if he is set on war. Except perhaps only the Pope, if he would rule? But who could persuade His Holiness to intervene between two Christian monarchs quarrelling over a pirate's raid and a patch of land? And the Pope has his own worries with the French advancing. And besides, a complaint from us would only bring a rebuttal from Scotland. Why would His Holiness intervene for us?'

'I don't know,' said Katherine. 'I don't know what would make the Pope take our side. If only he knew of our need! If only he would use his power to defend us!'

Richard Bainbridge, Cardinal Archbishop of York, happens to be at Rome and is a good friend of mine. I write to him that very night, a friendly letter as between one acquaintance to another far from home,

telling him of the news from London, the weather, the prospects for the harvest and the price of wool. Then I tell him of the enmity of the Scottish king, of his sinful pride, of his wicked licensing of attacks on our shipping and – worst of all – his constant invasions of our northern lands. I tell him that I am so afraid that the king will be forced to defend his lands in the north that he will not be able to come to the aid of the Holy Father in his quarrel with the French king. It would be such a tragedy, I write, if the Pope was left exposed to attack and we could not come to his aid because of the wickedness of the Scots. We plan to join my father's alliance and defend the Pope; but we can hardly muster for the Pope if there is no safety at home. If I have my way, nothing should distract my husband from his alliance with my father, with the emperor and with the Pope, but what can I, a poor woman, do? A poor woman whose own defenceless border is under constant threat?

What could be more natural than that Richard, my brother in Christ, should go with my letter in his hand to His Holiness the Pope and say how disturbed I am by the threat to my peace from King James of Scotland, and how the whole alliance to save the Eternal City is threatened by this bad neighbourliness?

The Pope, reading my letter to Richard, reads it aright, and writes at once to King James and threatens to excommunicate him if he does not respect the peace and the justly agreed borders of another Christian king. He is shocked that James should trouble the peace of Christendom. He takes his behaviour very seriously and grave penalties could result. King James, forced to accede to the Pope's wishes, forced to apologise for his incursions, writes a bitter letter to Henry saying that Henry had no right to approach the Pope alone, that it had been a quarrel between the two of them and there is no need to go running behind his back to the Holy Father.

'I don't know what he is talking about,' Henry complained to Katherine, finding her in the garden playing at catch with her ladies-in-waiting. He was too disturbed to run into the game as he usually did and snatch the ball from the air, bowl it hard at the nearest girl and shout with joy. He was too worried even to play with them. 'What is he saying? I have never appealed to the Pope. I did not report him. I am no tale-bearer!'

'No, you are not, and so you can tell him,' Katherine said serenely, slipping her hand in his arm and walking away from the women.

'I shall tell him. I said nothing to the Pope, and I can prove it.'

'I may have mentioned my concerns to the archbishop and he may have passed them on,' Katherine said casually. 'But you can hardly be blamed if your wife tells her spiritual advisor that she is anxious.'

'Exactly,' Henry said. 'I shall tell him so. And you should not be worried for a moment.'

'Yes. And the main thing is that James knows he cannot attack us with impunity, His Holiness has made a ruling.'

Henry hesitated. 'You did not mean Bainbridge to tell the Pope, did you?'

She peeped a little smile at him. 'Of course,' she said. 'But it still is not you who has complained of James to the Pope.'

His grip tightened around her waist. 'You are a redoubtable enemy. I hope we are never on opposing sides. I should be sure to lose.'

'We never will be,' she said sweetly. 'For I will never be anything but your loyal and faithful wife and queen.'

'I can raise an army in a moment, you know,' Henry reminded her. 'There is no need for you to fear James. There is no need for you even to pretend to fear. I could be the hammer of the Scots. I could do it as well as anyone, you know.'

'Yes, of course you can. And, thank God, now you don't need to do so.'

Autumn 1511

Edward Howard brought the Scots privateers back to London in chains and was greeted as an English hero. His popularity made Henry – always alert to the acclaim of the people – quite envious. He spoke more and more often of a war against the Scots, and the Privy Council, though fearful of the cost of war and privately doubtful of Henry's military abilities, could not deny that Scotland was an ever-present threat to the peace and security of England.

It was the queen who diverted Henry from his envy of Edward Howard, and the queen who continually reminded him that his first taste of warfare should surely be in the grand fields of Europe and not in some half-hidden hills in the borders. When Henry of England rode out it should be against the French king, in alliance with the two other greatest kings of Christendom. Henry, inspired from childhood with tales of Crécy and Agincourt, was easy to seduce with thoughts of glory against France.

Spring 1512

It was hard for Henry not to embark in person when the fleet sailed to join King Ferdinand's campaign against the French. It was a glorious start: the ships went out flying the banners of most of the great houses of England, they were the best equipped, finest arrayed force that had left England in years. Katherine had been busy, supervising the endless work of provisioning the ships, stocking the armouries, equipping the soldiers. She remembered her mother's constant work when her father was at war, and she had learned the great lesson of her childhood – that a battle could only be won if it was thoroughly and reliably supplied.

She sent out an expeditionary fleet that was better organised than any that had gone from England before, and she was confident that under her father's command they would defend the Pope, beat the French, win lands in France, and establish the English as major landowners in France once more. The peace party on the Privy Council worried, as they always did, that England would be dragged into another endless war; but Henry and Katherine were convinced by Ferdinand's confident predictions that a victory would come quickly and there would be rich gains for England.

I have seen my father command one campaign after another for all of my childhood. I have never seen him lose. Going to war is to relive my childhood again, the colour and the sounds and the excitement of a country at war are a deep joy for me. This time, to be in alliance with my father, as an equal partner, to be able to deliver to him the power of the English army, feels like my coming of age. This is what he has wanted from me, this is the fulfilment of my life as his daughter. It is for this that I endured the long years of waiting for the English throne. This is my destiny, at last, I am a commander as my father is, as my mother was. I am a Queen Militant, and there is no doubt in my mind on this sunny morning as I watch the fleet set sail that I will be a Queen Triumphant.

The plan was that the English army would meet the Spanish army and invade south-western France: Guienne and the Duchy of Aquitaine. There was no doubt in Katherine's mind that her father would take his share of the spoils of war, but she expected that he would honour his promise to march with the English into Aquitaine, and win it back for England. She thought that his secret plan would be the carving up of France, which would return that over-mighty country to the collection of small kingdoms and duchies it once had been, their ambitions crushed for a generation. Indeed, Katherine knew her father believed that it was safer for Christendom if France was reduced. It was not a country that could be trusted with the power and wealth that unity brings.

May 1512

It was as good as any brilliant court entertainment to see the ships cross the bar and sail out, a strong wind behind them, on a sunny day; and Henry and Katherine rode back to Windsor filled with confidence that their armies would be the strongest in Christendom, that they could not fail.

Katherine took advantage of the moment and Henry's enthusiasm for the ships to ask him if he did not think that they should build galleys, fighting ships powered with oars. Arthur had known at once what she had meant by galleys; he had seen drawings and had read how they could be deployed. Henry had never seen a battle at sea, nor had he seen a galley turn without wind in a moment and come against a becalmed fighting ship. Katherine tried to explain to him, but Henry, inspired by the sight of the fleet in full sail, swore that he wanted only sailing ships, great ships manned with free crews, named for glory.

The whole court agreed with him, and Katherine knew she could make no headway against a court that was always blown about by the latest fashion. Since the fleet had looked so very fine when it set sail, all the young men wanted to be admirals like Edward Howard, just as the summer before they had all wanted to be crusaders. There was no discussing the weakness of big sailing ships in close combat – they all wanted to set out with full sail. They all wanted their own ship. Henry spent days with shipwrights and ship-builders, and Edward Howard argued for a greater and greater navy.

Katherine agreed that the fleet was very fine, and the sailors of England were the finest in the world, but remarked that she thought she might write to the arsenal at Venice to ask them the cost of a galley and if they would build it as a commission, or if they would agree to send the parts and plans to England, for English shipwrights to assemble in English dockyards.

'We don't need galleys,' Henry said dismissively. 'Galleys are for raids on shore. We are not pirates. We want great ships that can carry our soldiers. We want great ships that can tackle the French ships at sea. The ship is a platform from which you launch your attack. The greater the platform, the more soldiers can muster. It has to be a big ship for a battle at sea.'

'I am sure you are right,' she said. 'But we must not forget our other enemies. The seas are one border and we must dominate them with ships both great and small. But our other border must be made safe too.'

'D'you mean the Scots? They have taken their warning from the Pope. I don't expect to be troubled with them.'

She smiled. She would never openly disagree with him. 'Certainly,' she said. 'The archbishop has secured us a breathing space. But next year, or the year after, we will have to go against the Scots.'

Summer 1512

Then there was nothing for Katherine to do but to wait. It seemed as if everyone was waiting. The English army were in Fuenterrabia, waiting for the Spanish to join with them for their invasion of southern France. The heat of the summer came on as they kicked their heels, ate badly and drank like thirsty madmen. Katherine alone of Henry's council knew that the heat of midsummer Spain could kill an army as they did nothing but wait for orders. She concealed her fears from Henry and from the council but privately she wrote to her father asking what his plans were, she tackled his ambassador, asking him what her father intended the English army to do, and when should they march?

Her father, riding with his own army, on the move, did not reply; and the ambassador did not know.

The summer wore on, Katherine did not write again. In a bitter moment, which she did not even acknowledge to herself, she saw that she was not her father's ally on the chessboard of Europe – she realised that she was nothing more than a pawn in his plan. She did not need to ask her father's strategy; once he had the English army in place and did not use them, she guessed it.

It grew colder in England, but it was still hot in Spain. At last Ferdinand had a use for his allies, but when he sent for them, and ordered that they should spend the winter season on campaign, they refused to answer his call. They mutinied against their own commanders and demanded to go home.

Winter 1512

It came as no surprise to Katherine, nor to the cynics on the council, when the English army came home in dishonoured tatters in December. Lord Dorset, despairing of ever receiving orders and reinforcements from King Ferdinand, confronted by mutinying troops, hungry, weary, and with two thousand men lost to illness, straggled home in disgrace, as he had taken them out in glory.

'What can have gone wrong?' Henry rushed into Katherine's rooms and waved away her ladies-in-waiting. He was almost in tears of rage at the shame of the defeat. He could not believe that his force that had gone out so bravely should come home in such disarray. He had letters from his father-in-law complaining of the behaviour of the English allies, he had lost face in Spain, he had lost face with his enemy France. He fled to Katherine as the only person in the world who would share his shock and dismay. He was almost stammering with distress, it was the first time in his reign that anything had gone wrong and he had thought – like a boy – that nothing would ever go wrong for him.

I take his hands. I have been waiting for this since the first moment in the summer when there was no battle plan for the English troops. As soon as they arrived and were not deployed I knew that we had been misled. Worse, I knew that we had been misled by my father.

I am no fool. I know my father as a commander, and I know him as a man. When he did not fling the English into battle on the day that they arrived, I knew that he had another plan for them, and that plan was hidden from us. My father would never leave good men in camp to gossip and drink and get sick. I was on campaign with my father for most of my childhood, I never saw him let the men sit idle. He always keeps his men moving, he always keeps them in work and out of mischief. There is not a horse in my father's stables with a pound of extra fat on it; he treats his soldiers just the same.

If the English were left to rot in camp it was because he had need of them just where they were – in camp. He did not care that they were getting sick and lazy. That made me look again at the map and I saw what he was doing. He was using them as a counterweight, as an inactive diversion. I read the reports from our commanders as they arrived, their complaints at their pointless inaction, their exercises on the border, sighting the French army and being seen by them, but not being ordered to engage; and I knew I was right. My father kept the English troops dancing on the spot in Fuenterrabia so that the French, alarmed by such a force on their flank, would place their army in defence. Guarding against the English they could not attack my father who, joyously alone and unencumbered, at the head of his troops, marched into the unprotected kingdom of Navarre and so picked up that which he had desired for so long at no expense or danger to himself.

'My dear, your soldiers were not tried and found wanting,' I say to my distressed young husband. 'There is no question as to the courage of the English. There can be no doubting you.'

451

'He says . . .' He waves the letter at me.

'It doesn't matter what he says,' I say patiently. 'You have to look at what he does.'

The face he turns to me is so hurt that I cannot bring myself to tell him that my father has used him, played him for a fool, used his army, used even me, to win himself Navarre.

'My father has taken his fee before his work, that is all,' I say robustly. 'Now we have to make him do the work.'

'What do you mean?' Henry is still puzzled.

'God forgive me for saying it, but my father is a masterly double-dealer. If we are going to make treaties with him we will have to learn to be as clever as him. He made a treaty with us and said he would be our partner in war against France, but all we have done is win him Navarre, by sending our army out and home again.'

'They have been shamed. I have been shamed.'

He cannot understand what I am trying to tell him. 'Your army has done exactly what my father wanted them to do. In that sense, it has been a most successful campaign.'

'They did nothing! He complains to me that they are good for nothing!'

'They pinned down the French with that nothing. Think of that! The French have lost Navarre.'

'I want to court-martial Dorset!'

'Yes, we can do so, if you wish. But the main thing is that we still have our army, we have lost only two thousand men, and my father is our ally. He owes us for this year. Next year you can go back to France and this time Father will fight for us; not us for him.'

'He says he will conquer Guienne for me, he says it as if I cannot do it myself! He speaks to me as a weakling with a useless force!'

'Good,' I say, surprising him. 'Let him conquer Guienne for us.'

'He wants us to pay him.'

'Let us pay for it. What does it matter as long as my father is on our side when we go to war with the French? If he wins Guienne for us then that is to our good; if he does not, but just distracts the French when we invade in the north from Calais, then that is all to the good as well.'

For a moment he gapes at me, his head spinning. Then he sees what I mean. 'He pins down the French for us, as we advance, just as we did for him?'

'Exactly.'

'We use him, as he used us?'

'Yes.'

He is amazed. 'Did your father teach you how to do this – to plan ahead as if a campaign were a chess board, and you have to move the pieces around?'

I shake my head. 'Not on purpose. But you cannot live with a man like my father without learning the arts of diplomacy. You know Machiavelli himself called him the perfect prince? You could not be at my father's court, as I was, or on campaign with him, as I was, without seeing that he spends his life seeking advantage. He taught me every day, I could not help but learn, just from watching him. I know how his mind works. I know how a general thinks.'

'But what made you think of invading from Calais?'

'Oh, my dear, where else would England invade France? My father can fight in the south for us, and we will see if he can win us Guienne. You can be sure that he will do so if it is in his interest. And, at any rate, while he is doing that, the French will not be able to defend Normandy.'

Henry's confidence comes rushing back to him. 'I shall go myself,' he declares. 'I shall take to the field of battle myself. Your father will not be able to criticise the command of the English army if I do it myself.'

For a moment I hesitate. Even playing at war is a dangerous game, and while we do not have an heir, Henry is precious beyond belief. Without him, the safety of England will be torn between a hundred pretenders. But I will never keep my hold on him if I coop him up as *his grandmother did. Henry will have to learn the nature of war, and I know that he will be safest in a campaign commanded by my father, who wants to keep me on my throne as much as I want it; and safer by far facing the chivalrous French than the murderous Scots. Besides, I have a plan that is a secret. And it requires him to be out of the country.*

'Yes, you shall,' I say. 'And you shall have the best armour and strongest horse and handsomest guard of any king who takes the field.'

'Thomas Howard says that we should abandon our battle against France until we have suppressed the Scots.'

I shake my head. 'You shall fight in France in the alliance of the three kings,' I assure him. 'It will be a mighty war, one that everyone will remember. The Scots are a minor danger, they can wait, at the worst they are a petty border raid. And if they invade the north when you go to war, they are so unimportant that even I could command an expedition against them while you go to the real war in France.'

'You?' he asks.

'Why not? Are we not a king and queen come young to our thrones in our power? Who should deny us?'

'No-one! I shall not be diverted,' Henry declares. 'I shall conquer in France and you shall guard us against the Scots.'

'I will,' I promise him. This is just what I want.

Spring 1513

Henry talked of nothing but war all winter, and in the spring Katherine started a great muster of men and materials for the invasion of northern France. The treaty with Ferdinand agreed that he would invade Guienne for England at the same time as the English troops took Normandy. The Holy Roman Emperor Maximilian would join with the English army in the battle in the north. It was an infallible plan if the three parties attacked simultaneously, if they kept meticulous faith with each other.

It comes as no surprise to me to find that my father has been talking peace with France in the very same days that I have had Thomas Wolsey, my right-hand man, the royal almoner, writing to every town in England and asking them how many men they can muster for the king's service when we go to war in France. I knew my father would think only of the survival of Spain: Spain before everything. I do not blame him for it. Now that I am a queen I understand a little better what it means to love a country with such a passion that one will

betray anything – even one's own child, as he does – to keep it safe. My father, with the prospect on one hand of a troublesome war and little gain, and on the other hand peace, with everything to play for, chooses peace and chooses France as his friend. He has betrayed us in absolute secrecy and he fooled even me.

When the news of his grand perfidy comes out he blames it all on his ambassador, and on letters going astray. It is a slight excuse; but I do not complain. My father will join us as soon as it looks as if we will win. The main thing for me now is that Henry should have his campaign in France and leave me alone to settle with the Scots.

'He has to learn how to lead men into battle,' Thomas Howard says to me. 'Not boys into a bawdy house – excuse me, Your Grace.'

'I know,' I reply. 'He has to win his spurs. But there is such a risk.'

The old soldier puts his hand over mine. 'Very few kings die in battle,' he says. 'Don't think of King Richard, for he all but ran on the swords. He knew he was betrayed. Mostly, kings get ransomed. It's not one half of the risk that you will be facing if you equip an army and send it across the narrow seas to France, and then try and fight the Scots with what is left.'

I am silent for a moment. I did not know that he had seen what I plan. 'Who thinks that this is what I am doing?'

'Only me.'

'Have you told anyone?'

'No,' he says stoically. 'My first duty is to England, and I think you are right. We have to finish with the Scots once and for all, and it had better be done when the king is safely overseas.'

'I see you don't fear overmuch for my safety?' I observe.

He shrugs and smiles. 'You are a queen,' he says. 'Dearly beloved, perhaps. But we can always get another queen. We have no other Tudor king.'

'I know,' I say. It is a truth as clear as water. I can be replaced but Henry cannot. Not until I have a Tudor son.

Thomas Howard has guessed my plan. I have no doubt in my mind where my truest duty lies. It is as Arthur taught me – the greatest danger to the safety of England comes from the north, from the Scots, and so it is to the north that I should march. Henry should be encouraged to put on his most handsome armour to go with his most agreeable friends in a sort of grand joust against the French. But there will be bloody work on the northern border; a victory there will keep us safe for generations. If I want to make England safe for me and for my unborn son, and for the kings who come after me, I must defeat the Scots.

Even if I never have a son, even if I never have cause to go to Walsingham to thank Our Lady for the son she has given me, I shall still have done my first and greatest duty by this, my beloved country of England, if I beat the Scots. Even if I die in doing it.

I maintain Henry's resolve, I do not allow him to lose his temper or his will. I fight the Privy Council who choose to see my father's unreliability as another sign that we should not go to war. Partly, I agree with them. I think we have no real cause against France, and no great gains to make. But I know that Henry is wild to go to war and he thinks that France is his enemy and King Louis his rival. I want Henry out of the way this summer, when it is my intention to destroy the Scots. I know that the only thing that can divert him will be a glorious war. I want war, not because I am angry with the French, or want to show our strength to my father; I want war because we have the French to the south and the Scots to the north and we will have to engage with one and play with the other to keep England safe.

I spend hours on my knees in the royal chapel; but it is Arthur that I am talking to, in long, silent reveries. 'I am sure I am right, my love,' I whisper into my clasped hands. 'I am sure that you were right when you warned me of the danger of the Scots. We have to subdue the Scots or we will never have a kingdom that can sleep in peace. If I can have my way, this will be the year when the fate of England is decided. If I have my way, I will send Henry against the French and I will go against the Scots and our fate can be decided. I know the Scots are the greater *danger. Everyone thinks of the French – your brother thinks of nothing but the French – but these are men who know nothing of the reality of war. The enemy who is across the sea, however much you hate him, is a lesser enemy than the one who can march over your borders in a night.'*

I can almost see him in the shadowy darkness behind my closed eyes. 'Oh, yes,' I say with a smile to him. 'You can think that a woman cannot lead an army. You can think that a woman cannot wear armour. But I know more about warfare than most men at this peaceable court. This is a court devoted to jousting, all the young men think war is a game. But I know what war is. I have seen it. This is the year when you will see me ride out as my mother did, when you see me face our enemy – the only enemy that really matters. This is my country now, you yourself made it my country. And I will defend it for you, for me, and for our heirs.'

The English preparations for the war against France went on briskly with Katherine and Thomas Wolsey, her faithful assistant, working daily on the muster rolls for the towns, the gathering of provisions for the army, the forging of armour and the training of volunteers to march, prepare to attack, and retreat, on command. Wolsey observed that the queen had two muster rolls, almost as if she was preparing for two armies. 'Are you thinking we will have to fight the Scots as well as the French?' he asked her.

'I am sure of it.'

'The Scots will snap at us, as soon as our troops leave for France,' he said. 'We shall have to reinforce the borders.'

'I hope to do more than that,' was all she said.

'His Grace the king will not be distracted from his war with France,' he pointed out.

She did not confide in him, as he wanted her to do. 'I know. We must make sure he has a great force to take to Calais. He must not be distracted by anything.'

'We will have to keep some men back to defend against the Scots, they are certain to attack,' he warned her.

'Border guards,' she said dismissively.

Handsome young Edward Howard, in a new cloak of dark sea-blue, came to take leave of Katherine as the fleet prepared to set sail with orders to blockade the French in port, or engage them if possible on the high seas.

'God bless you,' said the queen, and heard her voice a little shaken with emotion. 'God bless you, Edward Howard, and may your luck go with you as it always does.'

He bowed low. 'I have the luck of a man favoured by a great queen who serves a great country,' he said. 'It is an honour to serve my country, the king . . . and,' he lowered his voice to an intimate whisper, 'and you, my queen.'

Katherine smiled. All of Henry's friends shared a tendency to think themselves into the pages of a romance. Camelot was never very far away from their minds. Katherine had served as the lady of the courtly myth ever since she had been queen. She liked Edward Howard more than any of the other young men. His genuine gaiety and his open affection endeared him to everyone, and he had a passion for the navy and the ships under his command that commended him to Katherine, who saw the safety of England could only be assured by holding the seas.

'You are my knight, and I trust you to bring glory to your name and to mine,' she said to him, and saw the gleam of pleasure in his eyes as he dropped his dark head to kiss her hand.

'I shall bring you home some French ships,' he promised her. 'I have brought you Scots pirates, now you shall have French galleons.'

'I have need of them,' she said earnestly.

'You shall have them if I die in the attempt.'

She held up a finger. 'No dying,' she warned him. 'I have need of

459

you, too.' She gave him her other hand. 'I shall think of you every day and in my prayers,' she promised him.

He rose up and with a swirl of his new cloak he went out.

It is the feast of St George and we are still waiting for news from the English fleet, when a messenger comes in, his face grave. Henry is at my side as the young man tells us, at last, of the sea battle that Edward was so certain he should win, that we were so certain would prove the power of our ships over the French. With his father at my side I learn the fate of Edward, my knight Edward, who had been so sure that he would bring home a French galleon to the Pool of London.

He pinned down the French fleet in Brest and they did not dare to come out. He was too impatient to wait for them to make the next move, too young to play a long game. He was a fool, a sweet fool, like half the court, certain that they are invincible. He went into battle like a boy who has no fear of death, who has no knowledge of death, who has not even the sense to fear his own death. Like the Spanish grandees of my childhood, he thought that fear was an illness he could never catch. He thought that God favoured him above all others and nothing could touch him.

With the English fleet unable to go forwards and the French sitting snug in harbour, he took a handful of rowing boats and threw them in, under the French guns. It was a waste, a wicked waste of his men and of himself – and only because he was too impatient to wait, and too young to think. I am sorry that we sent him, dearest Edward, dearest young fool, to his own death. But then I remember that my husband is no older and certainly no wiser, and has even less knowledge of the world of war, and that even I, a woman of twenty-seven years old, married to a boy who has just reached his majority, can make the mistake of thinking that I cannot fail.

Edward himself led the boarding party on to the flagship of the

French admiral – an act of extraordinary daring – and almost at once his men failed him, God forgive them, and called him away when the battle was too hot for them. They jumped down from the deck of the French ship into their own rowing boats, some of them leaping into the sea in their terror to be away, shot ringing around them like hailstones. They cast off, leaving him fighting like a madman, his back to the mast, hacking around him with his sword, hopelessly outnumbered. He made a dash to the side and if a boat had been there, he might have dropped down to it. But they had gone. He tore the gold whistle of his office from his neck and flung it far out into the sea, so that the French would not have it, and then he turned and fought them again. He went down, still fighting, a dozen swords stabbed him, he was still fighting as he slipped and fell, supporting himself with one arm, his sword still parrying. Then, a hungry blade slashed at his sword arm, and he was fighting no more. They could have stepped back and honoured his courage; but they did not. They pressed him further and fell on him like hungry dogs on a skin in Smithfield market. He died with a hundred stab wounds.

They threw his body into the sea, they cared so little for him, these French soldiers, these so-called Christians. They could have been savages, they could have been Moors for all the Christian charity they showed. They did not think of the supreme unction, of a prayer for the dead, they did not think of his Christian burial, though a priest watched him die. They flung him into the sea as if he were nothing more than some spoiled food to be nibbled by fishes.

Then they realised that it was Edward Howard, my Edward Howard, the admiral of the English navy, and the son of one of the greatest men in England, and they were sorry that they had thrown him overboard like a dead dog. Not for honour – oh, not them – but because they could have ransomed him to his family and God knows we would have paid well to have sweet Edward restored to us. They sent the sailors out in boats with hooks to drag his body up again. They sent them to fish for his poor dead body as if he were salvage from a wreck. They gutted his corpse like a carp, they cut out his heart, salted it down like cod, they stole his clothes for souvenirs and sent them to the French court. The butchered scraps that were left of him they sent home to his father and to me.

This savage story reminds me of Hernando Perez del Pulgar who led such a desperately daring raid into the Alhambra. If they had caught him they would have killed him, but I don't think even the Moors would have cut out his heart for their amusement. They would have acknowledged him as a great enemy, a man to be honoured. They would have returned his body to us with one of their grand chivalric gestures. God knows, they would have composed a song about him within a week, we would have been singing it the length and breadth of Spain within a fortnight, and they would have made a fountain to commemorate his beauty within a month. They were Moors; but they had a grace that these Christians utterly lack. When I think of these Frenchmen it makes me ashamed to call the Moors 'barbarians'.

Henry is shaken by this story and by our defeat, and Edward's father ages ten years in the ten minutes that it takes the messenger to tell him that his son's body is downstairs, in a cart, but his clothes have been sent as spoil to Madame Claude, the daughter of the King of France, his heart is a keepsake for the French admiral. I can comfort neither of them, my own shock is too great. I go to my chapel and I take my sorrow to Our Lady, who knows herself what it is to love a young man and to see Him go out to His death. And when I am on my knees I swear that the French will regret the day that they cut my champion down. There will be a reckoning for this filthy act. They will never be forgiven by me.

Summer 1513

The death of Edward Howard made Katherine work even harder for the preparations of the English army to leave for Calais. Henry might be going to play-act a war, but he would use real shot and cannon, swords and arrows, and she wanted them to be well made and their aim to be true. She had known the realities of war all her life, but with the death of Edward Howard, Henry now saw, for the first time, that it was not like in a story book, it was not like a joust. A well-favoured, brilliant young man like Edward could go out in the sunshine and come home, butchered into pieces, in a cart. To his credit, Henry did not waver in his courage as this truth came home to him, as he saw young Thomas Howard step up to his brother's place, as he saw Edward's father summoning his tenants and calling in his debts to provide troops to avenge his son.

They sent the first part of the army to Calais in May, and Henry prepared to follow them with the second batch of troops in June. He was more sombre than he had ever been before.

Katherine and Henry rode slowly through England from Greenwich to Dover for Henry's embarkation. The towns turned out to feast them and muster their men as they went through. Henry and Katherine had matching great white horses and Katherine rode astride, her long blue gown spread out all around. Henry, riding at her side, looked magnificent, taller than any other man in the ranks, stronger than most, golden-haired and smiling all around.

In the mornings when they rode out of a town they would both wear armour: matching suits of silver and gilt. Katherine wore only a breastplate and a helmet, made from finely beaten metal and chased with gold patterns. Henry wore full armour from toes to fingertips every day, whatever the heat. He rode with his visor up and his blue eyes dancing, and a gold circlet around his helmet. The standard bearers carrying Katherine's badge on one side, and Henry's on the other, rode either side of them and when people saw the queen's pomegranate and Henry's rose they shouted 'God Bless the King!' and 'God Bless the Queen!' When they left a town, with the troops marching behind them, and the bowmen before them, the townspeople would crowd the sides of the road for a good mile to see them ride by, and they threw rose petals and rosebuds on the road in front of the horses. All the men marched with a rose in their lapels or in their hats, and they sang as they marched: bawdy songs of old England, but also sometimes ballads of Henry's composing.

They took nearly two weeks to get to Dover and the time was not wasted, for they gathered supplies and recruited troops in every village. Every man in the land wanted to be in the army to defend England against France. Every girl wanted to say that her lad had gone to be a soldier. The whole country was united in wanting revenge against the French. And the whole country was confident that with the young king at the head of a young army, it could be done.

I am happier, knowingly happier, than I have been since the death of our son. I am happier than I had thought possible. Henry comes to my bed every night during the feasting, dancing, marching tour to the coast, he is mine in thought and word and deed. He is going on a campaign of my organising, he is safely diverted from the real war that I will have to fight, and he never has a thought, or says a word, but he shares it with me. I pray that in one of these nights on the road, riding south to the coast together, in the heightened tension that comes with war, we will make another child, another boy, another rose for England as Arthur was.

Thanks to Katherine and Thomas Wolsey the arrangements for the embarkation were timed to perfection. Not for this English army the usual delay while last-minute orders were given, and forgotten essentials desperately ordered. Henry's ships – four hundred of them – brightly painted, with pennants flying, sails ready-rigged – were waiting to take the troops to France. Henry's own ship, blazing in gold leaf with the red dragon flying at its stern, bobbed at the dock. His royal guard, superbly trained, their new livery of Tudor green and white, spangled with sequins, were paraded on the quay, his two suits of gold-inlaid armour were packed on board, his specially trained white horses were in their stalls. The preparations were as meticulous as those of the most elaborate of court masques and Katherine knew that for many of the young men, they were looking forward to war as they did to a court entertainment.

Everything was ready for Henry to embark and sail for France when in a simple ceremony, on the strand at Dover, he took the great seal of state and before them all invested Katherine as regent in his place, Governor of the Realm and Captain General of the English forces for home defence.

I make sure that my face is grave and solemn when he names me Regent of England, and I kiss his hand and then I kiss him full on the mouth to wish him God speed. But as his ship is taken in tow by the barges, crosses the bar of the harbour, and then unfurls her sails to catch the wind and sets out for France, I could sing aloud for joy. I have no tears for the husband who is going away because he has left me with everything that I have ever wanted. I am more than Princess of Wales, I am more than Queen of England, I am Governor of the Realm, I am Captain General of the army, this is my country indeed, and I am sole ruler.

And the first thing I will do – indeed, perhaps the only thing I will do with the power vested in me, the only thing that I must do with this God-given chance – is defeat the Scots.

As soon as Katherine arrived at Richmond Palace she gave Thomas Howard, Edward's younger brother, his orders to take the cannon from the armouries in the Tower, and set sail with the whole English fleet, north to Newcastle to defend the borders against the Scots. He was not the admiral that his brother had been but he was a steady young man and she thought she could rely on him to do his part to deliver the vital weapons to the north.

Every day brought Katherine news from France by messengers that she had already posted along the way. Wolsey had strict instructions to report back to the queen the progress of the war. From him she wanted an accurate analysis. She knew that Henry would give her an optimistic account. It was not all good news. The English army had arrived in France, there was much excitement in Calais and feasting and celebrations. There were parades and musters and Henry had been much congratulated on his handsome armour and his smart troops. But the Emperor Maximilian failed to muster his own army to support the English. Instead, pleading poverty but swearing his enthusiasm to the cause, he came to the young prince to offer his sword and his service.

It was clearly a heady moment for Henry, who had not yet even heard a shot fired in anger, to have the Holy Roman Emperor offering his services, overwhelmed by the glamorous young prince.

Katherine frowned when she read that part of Wolsey's account, calculating that Henry would hire the emperor at an inflated amount, and would thus have to pay an ally who had promised to come at his own expense for a mercenary army. She recognised at once the double-dealing that had characterised this campaign from the start. But at least it would mean that the emperor was with Henry in his first battle, and Katherine knew that she could rely on the experienced older man to keep the impulsive young king safe.

On the advice of Maximilian, the English army laid siege to Therouanne – a town which the Holy Roman Emperor had long desired, but of no tactical value to England – and Henry, safely distanced from the short-range guns on the walls of the little town, walked alone through his camp at midnight, spoke comforting words to the soldiers on watch, and was allowed to fire his first cannon.

The Scots, who had been waiting only until England was defence-less with king and army in France, declared war against the English and started their own march south. Wolsey wrote with alarm to Katherine, asking her if she needed the return of some of Henry's troops to face this new threat. Katherine replied that she thought she could defend against a border skirmish, and started a fresh muster of troops from every town in the country, using the lists she had already prepared.

She commanded the assembly of the London militia and went out in her armour, on her white horse, to inspect them before they started their march north.

I look at myself in the mirror as my ladies-in-waiting tie on my breastplate, and my maid-in-waiting holds my helmet. I see the unhappiness in their faces, the way the silly maid holds the helmet as if it is too heavy for her, as if none of this should be happening, as if I were not born for this moment: now. The moment of my destiny.

I draw a silent breath. I look so like my mother in my armour that it could be her reflection in the mirror, standing so still and proud, with her hair caught back from her face, and her eyes shining as bright as the burnished gilt on her breastplate; alive at the prospect of battle, gleaming with joy at her confidence in victory.

'Are you not afraid?' Maria de Salinas asks me quietly.

'No.' I speak the truth. 'I have spent all my life waiting for this moment. I am a queen, and the daughter of a queen who had to fight for her country. I have come to this, my own country, at the very moment that it needs me. This is not a time for a queen who wants to sit on her throne and award prizes for jousting. This is a time for a queen who has the heart and stomach of a man. I am that queen. I shall ride out with my army.'

There is a little flurry of dismay. 'Ride out?' 'But not north?' 'Parade them, but surely not ride with them?' 'But isn't it dangerous?'

I reach for my helmet. 'I shall ride with them north to meet the Scots. And if the Scots break through I shall fight them. And when I take the field against them I shall be there until I defeat them.'

'But what about us?'

I smile at the women. 'Three of you will come with me to bear me company and the rest of you will stay here,' I say firmly. 'Those

468

behind will continue to make banners and prepare bandages and send them on to me. You will keep good order,' I say firmly. 'Those who come with me will behave as soldiers in the field. I will have no complaints.'

There is an outburst of dismay, which I avoid by heading for the door. 'Maria and Margaret, you shall come with me now,' I say.

The troops are drawn up before the palace. I ride slowly down the lines, letting my eyes rest on one face and then another. I have seen my father do this, and my mother. My father told me that every soldier should know that he is valued, should know that he has been seen as an individual man on parade, should feel himself to be an essential part of the body of the army. I want them to be sure that I have seen them, seen every man; that I know them. I want them to know me. When I have ridden past every single one of the five hundred, I go to the front of the army and I take off my helmet so that they can see my face. I am not like a Spanish princess now, with my hair hidden and my face veiled. I am a bare-headed, bare-faced English queen. I raise my voice so that every one of them can hear me.

'Men of England,' I say. 'You and I will go together to fight the Scots, and neither of us will falter nor fail. We will not turn back until they have turned back. We will not rest until they are dead. Together we will defeat them, for we do the work of heaven. This is not a quarrel of our making, this is a wicked invasion by James of Scotland; breaking his own treaty, insulting his own English wife. An ungodly invasion condemned by the Pope himself, an invasion against the order of God. He has planned this for years. He has waited, like a coward, thinking to find us weak. But he is mistaken for we are powerful now. We will defeat him, this heretic king. We will win. I can assure you of this because I know God's will in this matter. He is with us. And you can be sure that God's hand is always over men who fight for their homes.'

There is a great roar of approval and I turn and smile to one side

469

and then the other, so that they can all see my pleasure in their courage. So that they can all see that I am not afraid.

'Good. Forward march,' I say simply to the commander at my side and the army turns and marches out of the parade ground.

As Katherine's first army of defence marched north under the Earl of Surrey, gathering men as they went, the messengers rode desperately south to London to bring her the news she had been expecting. James's army had crossed the Scottish border and was advancing through the rolling hills of the border country, recruiting soldiers and stealing food as they went.

'A border raid?' Katherine asked, knowing it would not be.

The man shook his head. 'My lord told me to tell you that the French king has promised the Scots king that he will recognise him if he wins this battle against us.'

'Recognise him? As what?'

'As King of England.'

He expected her to cry out in indignation or in fear, but she merely nodded, as if it were something else to consider.

'How many men?' Katherine demanded of the messenger.

He shook his head. 'I can't say for certain.'

'How many do you think?'

He looked at the queen, saw the sharp anxiety in her eyes, and hesitated.

'Tell me the truth!'

'I am afraid sixty thousand, Your Grace, perhaps more.'

'How many more? Perhaps?'

Again he paused. She rose from her chair and went to the window. 'Please, tell me what you think,' she said. 'You do me no service if, thanks to you, trying to spare me distress, I go out with an army and find before me an enemy in greater force than I expected.'

'One hundred thousand, I would think,' he said quietly.

He expected her to gasp in horror but when he looked at her she was smiling. 'Oh, I'm not afraid of that.'

'Not afraid of one hundred thousand Scots?' he demanded.

'I've seen worse,' she said.

I know now that I am ready. The Scots are pouring over the border, in their full power. They have captured the northern castles with derisive ease, the flower of the English command and the best men are overseas in France. The French king thinks to defeat us with the Scots, in our own lands, while our masquing army rides around northern France and makes pretty gestures. My moment is now. It is up to me, and the men who are left. I order the royal standards and banners from the great wardrobe. Flown at the head of the army the royal standards show that the King of England is on the battlefield. That will be me.

'You will never ride under the royal standard?' one of my ladies queries.

'Who else?'

'It should be the king.'

'The king is fighting the French. I shall fight the Scots.'

'Your Grace, a queen cannot take the king's standard and ride out.'

I smile at her, I am not pretending to confidence, I truly know that this is the moment for which I have waited all my life. I promised Arthur I could be a queen in armour; and now I am. 'A queen can ride under a king's standard, if she thinks she can win.'

I summon the remaining troops; these will be my force. I plan to parade them in battle order, but there are more comments.

'You will never ride at their head?'

'Where would you want me to ride?'

'Your Grace, perhaps you should not be there at all?'

'I am their Commander in Chief,' I say simply. 'You must not think of me as a queen who stays at home, influences policy by stealth, and bullies her children. I am a queen who rules as my mother did. When my country is in danger, I am in danger. When my country is triumphant, as we will be, it is my triumph.'

'But what if . . . ?' The lady-in-waiting is silenced by one hard look from me.

'I am not a fool, I have planned for defeat,' I tell her. 'A good commander always speaks of victory and yet has a plan for defeat. I know exactly where I shall fall back, and I know exactly where I shall regroup, and I know exactly where I shall join battle again, and if I fail there, I know where I shall regroup again. I did not wait long years for this throne to see the King of Scotland and that fool Margaret take it from me.'

Katherine's men, all forty thousand of them, straggled along the road behind the royal guard, weighed down by their weapons and sacks of food in the late summer sunshine. Katherine, at the head of the train, rode her white horse where everyone could see her, with the royal standard over her head, so that the men should know her now, on the march, and recognise her later, in battle. Twice a day she rode down the length of the line with a word of encouragement for everyone who was scuffing along in the rear, choking with the dust from the forward wagons. She kept monastic hours, rising at dawn to hear Mass, taking communion at noon, and going to bed at dusk, waking at midnight to say her prayers for the safety of the realm, for the safety of the king, and for herself.

Messengers passed constantly between Katherine's army and the force commanded by Thomas Howard, Earl of Surrey. Their plan was that Surrey should engage with the Scots at the first chance, anything to stop their rapid and destructive advance southwards. If

Surrey were defeated then the Scots would come on and Katherine would meet them with her force, and fling them into defence of the southern counties of England. If the Scots cut through them then Katherine and Surrey had a final plan for the defence of London. They would regroup, summon a citizens' army, throw up earthworks around the City and if all else failed, retreat to the Tower, which could be held for long enough for Henry to reinforce them from France.

Surrey is anxious that I have ordered him to lead the first attack against the Scots, he would rather wait for my force to join him; but I insist the attack shall go as I have planned. It would be safer to join our two armies, but I am fighting a defensive campaign. I have to keep an army in reserve to stop the Scots sweeping south, if they win the first battle. This is not a single battle I am fighting here. This is a war that will destroy the threat of the Scots for a generation, perhaps forever.

I too am tempted to order him to wait for me, I so want to join the battle; I feel no fear at all, just a sort of wild gladness as if I am a hawk mewed-up for too long and now suddenly set free. But I will not throw my precious men into a battle that would leave the road to London open if we lost. Surrey thinks that if we unite the forces we will be certain to win, but I know that there is no certainty in warfare, anything can go wrong. A good commander is ready for the worst, and I am not going to risk the Scots beating us in one battle and then marching down the Great North Road and into my capital city, and a coronation with French acclaim. I did not win this throne so hard, to lose it in one reckless fight. I have a battle plan for Surrey, and one for me, and then a position to retreat to, and a series of positions after that. They may win one battle, they may win more than one, but they will never take my throne from me.

We are sixty miles out of London, at Buckingham. This is good speed for an army on the march, they tell me it is tremendous speed for an English army; they are notorious for dawdling on the road. I am tired, but not exhausted. The excitement and – to be honest – the fear in each day is keeping me like a hound on a leash, always eager, straining to get ahead and start the hunt.

And now I have a secret. Each afternoon, when I dismount from my horse, I get down from the saddle and first thing, before anything else, I go into the necessary house, or tent, or wherever I can be alone, and I pull up my skirts and look at my linen. I am waiting for my monthly course, and it is the second month that it has failed to come. My hope, a strong, sweet hope, is that when Henry sailed to France he left me with child.

I will tell no-one, not even my women. I can imagine the outcry if they knew I was riding every day, and preparing for battle when I am with child, or even in hopes of a child. I dare not tell them, for in all truth, I do not dare do anything which might tilt the balance in this campaign against us. Of course, nothing could be more important than a son for England – except this one thing: holding England for that son to inherit. I have to grit my teeth on the risk I am taking, and take it anyway.

The men know that I am riding at their head and I have promised them victory. They march well, they will fight well because they have put their faith in me. Surrey's men, closer to the enemy than us, know that behind them, in reliable support, is my army. They know that I am leading their reinforcements in person. It has caused much talk in the country, they are proud to have a queen who will muster herself for them. If I were to turn my face to London and tell them to go on without me, for I have a woman's work to do, they would head for home too – it is as simple as that. They would think that I had lost confidence, that I had lost faith in them, that I anticipate defeat. There are enough whispers about an unstoppable army of Scotsmen – one hundred thousand angry Highlanders – without me adding to their fears.

Besides, if I cannot save my kingdom for my child, then there is little point in having a child. I have to defeat the Scots, I have to be a great general. When that duty is done, I can be a woman again.

At night, I have news from Surrey that the Scots are encamped on a strong ridge, drawn up in battle order at a place called Flodden. He sends me a plan of the site, showing the Scots camped on high ground, commanding the view to the south. One glance at the map tells me that the English should not attack uphill against the heavily armed Scots. The Scots archers will be shooting downhill and then the Highlanders will charge down on our men. No army could face an attack like that.

'Tell your master he is to send out spies and find a way around the back of the Scots to come upon them from the north,' I say to the messenger, staring at the map. 'Tell him my advice is that he makes a feint, leaves enough men before the Scots to pin them down, but marches the rest away, as if he is heading north. If he is lucky, they will give chase and you will have them on open ground. If he is unlucky he will have to reach them from the north. Is it good ground? He has drawn a stream on this sketch.'

'It is boggy ground,' the man confirms. 'We may not be able to cross it.'

I bite my lip. 'It's the only way that I can see,' I say. 'Tell him this is my advice but not my command. He is commander in the field, he must make his own judgement. But tell him I am certain that he has to get the Scots off that hill. Tell him I know for sure that he cannot attack uphill. He has to either go round and surprise them from the rear; or lure them down off that hill.'

The man bows and leaves. Please God he can get my message through to Surrey. If he thinks he can fight an army of Scots uphill he is finished. One of my ladies comes to me the minute the messenger has left my tent, she is trembling with fatigue and fear. 'What do we do now?'

'We advance north,' I say.

'But they may be fighting any day now!'

'Yes, and if they win we can go home. But if they lose we shall stand between the Scots and London.'

'And do what?' she whispers.

'Beat them,' I say simply.

10th September 1513

'Your Grace!' A page boy came dashing into Katherine's tent, bobbed a most inadequate, hurried bow. 'A messenger, with news of the battle! A messenger from Lord Surrey.'

Katherine whirled around, her shoulder strap from her halberk still undone. 'Send him in!'

The man was already in the room, the dirt of the battle still on him, but with the beam of a man bringing good news, great news.

'Yes?' Katherine demanded, breathless with hope.

'Your Grace has conquered,' he said. 'The King of Scotland lies dead, twenty Scottish lords lie with him, bishops, earls, and abbots too. It is a defeat they will never rise up from. Half of their great men have died in a single day.'

He saw the colour drain from her face and then she suddenly grew rosy. 'We have won?'

'You have won,' he confirmed. 'The earl said to tell you that your men, raised and trained and armed by you, have done what you ordered they should do. It is your victory, and you have made England safe.'

Her hand went at once to her belly, under the metal curve of the breastplate. 'We are safe,' she said.

He nodded. 'He sent you this . . .'

He held out for her a surcoat, terribly torn and slashed and stained with blood.

'This is?'

'The coat of the King of Scotland. We took it from his dead body as proof. We have his body, it is being embalmed. He is dead, the Scots are defeated. You have done what no English king since Edward the First could do. You have made England safe from Scottish invasion.'

'Write out a report for me,' she said decisively. 'Dictate it to the clerk. Everything you know, and everything that my lord Surrey said. I must write to the king.'

'Lord Surrey asked . . .'

'Yes?'

'Should he advance into Scotland and lay it waste? He says there will be little or no resistance. This is our chance. We could destroy them, they are utterly at our mercy.'

'Of course,' she said at once, then she paused. It was the answer that any monarch in Europe would have given. A troublesome neighbour, an inveterate enemy lay weakened. Every king in Christendom would have advanced and taken revenge.

'No. No, wait a moment.'

She turned away from him and went to the doorway of her tent. Outside, the men were preparing for another night on the road, far from their homes. There were little cook-fires all around the camp, torches burning, the smell of cooking and dung and sweat in the air. It was the very scent of Katherine's childhood, a childhood spent for the first seven years in a state of constant warfare against an enemy who was driven backwards and backwards and finally into slavery, exile and death.

Think, I say to myself fiercely. Don't feel with a tender heart, think with a hard brain, a soldier's brain. Don't consider this as a woman with child who knows there are many widows in Scotland tonight, think as a queen. My enemy is defeated, the country lies open before

me, their king is dead, their queen is a young fool of a girl and my sister-in-law. I can cut this country into pieces, I can quilt it. Any commander of any experience would destroy them now and leave them destroyed for a whole generation. My father would not hesitate; my mother would have given the order already.

I check myself. They were wrong, my mother and father. Finally, I say the unsayable, unthinkable thing. They were wrong, my mother and father. Soldiers of genius they may have been, convinced they certainly were, Christian kings they were called – but they were wrong. It has taken me all my life to learn this.

A state of constant warfare is a two-edged sword, it cuts both the victor and the defeated. If we pursue the Scots now, we will triumph, we can lay the country waste, we can destroy them for generations to come. But all that grows on waste are rats and pestilence. They would recover in time, they would come against us. Their children would come against my children and the savage battle would have to be fought all over again. Hatred breeds hatred. My mother and father drove the Moors overseas, but everyone knows that by doing so they won only one battle in a war that will never cease until Christians and Muslims are prepared to live side by side in peace and harmony. Isabella and Ferdinand hammered the Moors, but their children and their children's children will face the jihad in reply to the crusade. War does not answer war, war does not finish war. The only ending is peace.

'Get me a fresh messenger,' Katherine said over her shoulder, and waited till the man came. 'You are to go to my lord Surrey and tell him I give him thanks for this great news of a wonderful victory. You are to tell him that he is to let the Scots soldiers surrender their arms and they are to go in peace. I myself will write to the Scots queen and promise her peace if she will be our good sister and good neighbour. We are victorious, we shall be gracious. We shall make this victory a lasting peace, not a passing battle and an excuse for savagery.'

The man bowed and left. Katherine turned to the soldier. 'Go and get yourself some food,' she said. 'You can tell everyone that we have won a great battle and that we shall go back to our homes knowing that we can live at peace.'

She went to her little table and drew her writing box towards her. The ink was corked in a tiny glass bottle, the quill especially cut down to fit the small case. The paper and sealing wax were to hand. Katherine drew a sheet of paper towards her, and paused. She wrote a greeting to her husband, she told him she was sending him the coat of the dead Scots king.

In this, Your Grace shall see how I can keep my promise, sending you for your banners a king's coat. I thought to send himself to you, but our Englishmen's hearts would not suffer it.

I pause. With this great victory I can go back to London, rest and prepare for the birth of the child that I am sure I am carrying. I want to tell Henry that I am once again with child; but I want to write to him alone. This letter – like every letter between us – will be half-public. He never opens his own letters, he always gets a clerk to open them and read them for him, he rarely writes his own replies. Then I remember that I told him that if Our Lady ever blessed me with a child again I would go at once to her shrine at Walsingham to give thanks. If he remembers this, it can serve as our code. Anyone can read it to him but he will know what I mean, I shall have told him the secret, that we will have a child, that we may have a son. I smile and start to write, knowing that he will understand what I mean, knowing what joy this letter will bring him.

I make an end, praying God to send you home shortly, for without no joy can here be accomplished, and for the same I pray, and now go to Our Lady at Walsingham, that I promised so long ago to see.
Your humble wife and true servant,
   Katherine.

Walsingham, Autumn 1513

Katherine was on her knees at the shrine of Our Lady of Walsingham, her eyes fixed on the smiling statue of the Mother of Christ, but seeing nothing.

Beloved, beloved, I have done it. I sent the coat of the Scots king to Henry and I made sure to emphasise that it is his victory, not mine. But it is yours. It is yours because when I came to you and to your country, my mind filled with fears about the Moors, it was you who taught me that the danger here was the Scots. Then life taught me a harder lesson, beloved: it is better to forgive an enemy than destroy him. If we had Moorish physicians, astronomers, mathematicians in this country we would be the better for it. The time may come when we also need the courage and the skills of the Scots. Perhaps my offer of peace will mean that they will forgive us for the battle of Flodden.

I have everything I ever wanted – except you. I have won a victory for this kingdom that will keep it safe for a generation. I have conceived a child and I feel certain that this baby will live. If he is a boy I shall call him Arthur for you. If she is a girl, I shall call her Mary. I am Queen of England, I have the love of the people and Henry will make a good husband and a good man.

I sit back on my heels and close my eyes so the tears should not run down my cheeks. 'The only thing I lack is you, beloved. Always you. Always you.'

'Your Grace, are you unwell?' The quiet voice of the nun recalls me and I open my eyes. My legs are stiff from kneeling so long. 'We did not want to disturb you, but it has been some hours.'

'Oh, yes,' I say. I try to smile at her. 'I shall come in a moment. Leave me now.'

I turn back to my dream of Arthur but he is gone. 'Wait for me in the garden,' I whisper. 'I will come to you. I will come one day soon. In the garden, when my work here is done.'

Blackfriars Hall
The Papal Legate sitting as a court to hear the King's Great Matter, June 1529

Words have weight, something once said cannot be unsaid, meaning is like a stone dropped into a pool; the ripples will spread and you cannot know what bank they wash against.

I once said, 'I love you, I will love you forever,' to a young man in the night. I once said, 'I promise.' That promise, made twenty-seven years ago to satisfy a dying boy, to fulfil the will of God, to satisfy my mother and – to tell truth – my own ambition, that word comes back to me like ripples washing to the rim of a marble basin and then eddying back again to the centre.

I knew I would have to answer for my lies before God. I never thought that I would have to answer to the world. I never thought that the world could interrogate me for something that I had promised for love, something whispered in secret. And so, in my pride, I never have answered for it. Instead, I held to it.

And so, I believe, would any woman in my position.

Henry's new lover, Elizabeth Boleyn's girl, my maid-in-waiting, turns out to be the one that I knew I had to fear: the one who has an ambition that is even greater than mine. Indeed, she is even more greedy than the king. She has an ambition greater than any I have ever seen before in a man or a woman. She does not desire Henry as a man – I have seen his lovers come and go and I have learned to read them like an easy story book. This one desires not my husband, but my throne. She has had much work to find her way to it, but she is persistent and determined. I think I knew, from the moment that she had his ear, his secrets, and his confidence, that in time she would find her way – like a weasel smelling blood through a coney warren – to my lie. And when she found it, she would feast on it.

The usher calls out, 'Katherine of Aragon, Queen of England, come into court'; and there is a token silence, for they expect no answer. There are no lawyers waiting to help me there, I have prepared no defence. I have made it clear that I do not recognise the court. They expect to go on without me. Indeed, the usher is just about to call the next witness . . .

But I answer.

My men throw open the double doors of the hall that I know so well and I walk in, my head up, as fearless as I have been all my life. The regal canopy is in gold, over at the far end of the hall with my husband, my false, lying, betraying, unfaithful husband in his ill-fitting crown on his throne sitting beneath it.

On a stage below him are the two cardinals, also canopied with cloth of gold, seated in golden chairs with golden cushions. That betraying slave Wolsey, red-faced in his red cardinal's robe, failing to meet my eye, as well he might; and that false friend Campeggio. Their three faces, the king and his two procurers, are mirrors of utter dismay.

They thought they had so distressed and confused me, separated me from my friends and destroyed me, that I would not come. They thought I would sink into despair like my mother, or into madness like my sister. They are gambling on the fact that they have frightened me and threatened me and taken my child from me and done everything they can do to break my heart. They never dreamed that I have the courage to stalk in before them, and stand before them, shaking with right-eousness, to face them all.

Fools, they forget who I am. They are advised by that Boleyn girl who has never seen me in armour, driven on by her who never knew my mother, did not know my father. She knows me as Katherine, the old Queen of England, devout, plump, dull. She has no idea that inside, I am still Catalina, the young Infanta of Spain. I am a princess born and trained to fight. I am a woman who has fought for every single thing I hold, and I will fight, and I will hold, and I will win.

They did not foresee what I would do to protect myself, and my daughter's inheritance. She is Mary, my Mary, named by Arthur: my beloved daughter, Mary. Would I let her be put aside for some bastard got on a Boleyn?

That is their first mistake.

I ignore the cardinals completely. I ignore the clerks on the benches before them, the scribes with their long rolls of parchment making the official record of this travesty. I ignore the court, the city, even the people who whisper my name with loving voices. Instead, I look at no-one but Henry.

I know Henry, I know him better than anyone else in the world does. I know him better than his current favourite ever will, for I have seen him, man and boy. I studied him when he was a boy, when he was a child of ten who came to meet me and tried to persuade me to give him a Barbary stallion. I knew him then as a boy who could be won with fair words and gifts. I knew him through the eyes of his brother, who said – and rightly – that he was a child who had been spoiled by too much indulgence and would be a spoilt man, and a danger to us all. I knew him as a youth, and I won my throne by pandering to his vanity. I was the greatest prize he could desire and I let him win me. I knew him as a man as vain and greedy as a peacock when I gave to him the credit for my war: the greatest victory ever won by England.

At Arthur's request I told the greatest lie a woman has ever told, and I will tell it to the very grave. I am an Infanta of Spain, I do not give a promise and fail to keep it. Arthur, my beloved, asked me for

484

an oath on his deathbed and I gave it to him. He asked me to say that we had never been lovers and he commanded me to marry his brother and be queen. I did everything I promised him, I was constant to my promise. Nothing in these years has shaken my faith that it is God's will that I should be Queen of England, and that I shall be Queen of England until I die. No-one could have saved England from the Scots but me – Henry was too young and too inexperienced to take an army into the field. He would have offered a duel, he would have chanced some forlorn hope, he would have lost the battle and died at Flodden and his sister Margaret would have been Queen of England in my place.

It did not happen because I did not allow it to happen. It was my mother's wish and God's will that I should be Queen of England, and I will be Queen of England until I die.

I do not regret the lie. I held to it, and I made everyone else hold to it, whatever doubts they may have had. As Henry learned more of women, as Henry learned more of me, he knew, as surely he had known on our wedding night, that it was a lie, I was no virgin for him. But in all our twenty years of marriage together, he found the courage to challenge me only once, at the very beginning; and I walk into the court on the great gamble that he will never have the courage to challenge me again, not even now.

I walk into court with my entire case staked on his weakness. I believe that when I stand before him, and he is forced to meet my eyes, he will not dare to say that I was no virgin when I came to him, that I was Arthur's wife and Arthur's lover before I was ever his. His vanity will not allow him to say that I loved Arthur with a true passion and he loved me. That in truth, I will live and die as Arthur's wife and Arthur's lover, and thus Henry's marriage to me can be rightfully dissolved.

I don't think he has the courage that I have. I think if I stand straight and tell the great lie again, he will not dare to stand straight and tell the truth.

'Katherine of Aragon, Queen of England, come into court,' the usher repeats stupidly, as the echo of the doors banging behind me reverberates in the shocked courtroom, and everyone can see that I am already in court, standing like a stocky fighter before the throne.

It is me they call for, by this title. It was my dying husband's hope, my mother's wish and God's will that I should be Queen of England; and for them and for the country, I will be Queen of England until I die.

'Katherine of Aragon, Queen of England, come into court!'

This is me. This is my moment. This is my battle cry.

I step forwards.

Author's Note

This has been one of the most fascinating and most moving novels to write, from the discovery of the life of the young Katherine, to the great question of the lie that she told and maintained all her life.

That it was a lie is, I think, the most likely explanation. I believe that her marriage to Arthur was consummated. Certainly, everyone thought so at the time; it was only Dona Elvira's insistence after Katherine had been widowed, and Katherine's own insistence at the time of her separation from Henry that put the consummation into doubt. Later historians, admiring Katherine and accepting her word against Henry's, put the lie into the historical record where it stays today.

The lie was the starting place of the novel but the surprise in the research was the background of Catalina of Spain. I enjoyed a wonderful research trip to Granada to discover more about the Spain of Isabella and Ferdinand, and came home with an abiding respect both for their courage and for the culture they swore to overthrow: the rich tolerant and beautiful land of the Moslems of Spain, el Andalus. I have tried to give these almost forgotten Europeans a voice in this book, and to give us today, as we struggle with some of the same questions, an idea of the *conviviencia* – a land where Jews, Moslems and Christians managed to live side by side in respect and peace as 'People of the Book'.

A note on the double hearts

The double hearts at the chapter headings are the artist's impression of a carving said to have been found in Ludlow Castle in Arthur's chamber. The carving was sketched in 1684 but the original carving has been lost. They are a good example of the layers of reality that I often encounter: the carving is legend, the sketch is history, and the thought that they were carved by Arthur to show his love for Catalina, his young wife, is fiction.

A note on the songs

'Alas, Alhama!', 'Riders gallop through the Elvira gate . . .' and 'There was crying in Granada . . .' are traditional songs, quoted by Francesca Claremount in *Catherine of Aragon* (see book list below).

'A palm tree stands in the middle of Rusafa', is by Abd al Rahman, translated by D. F. Ruggles and quoted in Menocal, *The Ornament of the World* (see book list below).

The following books have been most helpful in my research into the history of this story:

Bindoff, S. T., *Pelican History of England: Tudor England*, Penguin, 1993
Bruce, Marie Louise, *Anne Boleyn*, Collins, 1972
Chejna, Anwar, G., *Islam and the West, The Moriscos, A Cultural and Social History*, State University of New York Press, 1983

Claremont, Francesca, *Catherine of Aragon*, Robert Hale, 1939

Cressy, David, *Birth, Marriage and Death, ritual religions and the life-cycle in Tudor and Stuart England*, OUP, 1977

Darby, H. C., *A new historical geography of England before 1600*, CUP, 1976

Dixon, William Hepworth, *History of Two Queens*, vol. 2, London, 1873

Elton, G. R., *England under the Tudors*, Methuen, 1955

Fernandez-Arnesto, Felipe, *Ferdinand and Isabella*, Weidenfeld and Nicolson, London, 1975

Fletcher, Anthony, *Tudor Rebellions*, Longman, 1968

Goodwin, Jason, *Lords of the Horizon, A History of the Ottoman Empire*, Vintage, 1989

Guy, John, *Tudor England*, OUP, 1988

Haynes, Alan, *Sex in Elizabethan England*, Sutton, 1997

Loades, David, *The Tudor Court*, Batsford, 1986

Loades, David, *Henry VIII and his Queens*, Sutton, 2000

Lloyd, David, *Arthur Prince of Wales*, Fabric Trust for St Laurence, Ludlow, 2002

Mackie, J. D., *Oxford History of England, The Earlier Tudors*, OUP, 1952

Mattingley, Garrett, *Catherine of Aragon*, Jonathan Cape, 1942

Menocal, *The Ornament of the World*, Little Brown and Co., 2002

Mumby, Frank Arthur, *The Youth of Henry VIII*, Constable and Co., 1913

Nunez, J. Agustia, (ed.), *Muslim and Christian Granada*, Edilux S.L., 2004

Paul, E. John, *Catherine of Aragon, and her Friends*, Burns and Eates, 1966

Plowden, Alison, *The House of Tudor*, Weidenfeld and Nicholson, 1976

Plowden, Alison, *Tudor Women, Queens and Commoners*, Sutton, 1998

Randall, Keith, *Henry VIII and the Reformation in England*, Hodder, 1993

Robinson, John Martin, *The Dukes of Norfolk*, OUP, 1982

Scarisbrick, J. J., *Yale English Monarchs: Henry VIII*, YUP, 1997

Scott, S. P., *The History of the Moorish Empire in Europe*, vol. 1 Ams Pr, 1974

Starkey, David, *Henry VIII: A European Court in England*, Collins and Brown, 1991

Starkey, David, *The Reign of Henry VIII, Personalities and Politics*, G. Philip, 1985

Starkey, David, *Six Wives, The Queens of Henry VIII*, Vintage, 2003

Tillyard, E. M. W., *The Elizabethan World Picture*, Pimlico, 1943

Turner, Robert, *Elizabethan Magic*, Element, 1989

Walsh, William Thomas, *Isabella of Spain*, London Sheed and Ward, 1935

Warnicke, Retha M., *The Rise and Fall of Anne Boleyn*, CUP, 1991

Weir, Alison, *Henry VIII, King and Court*, Pimlico, 2002

Weir, Alison, *The Six Wives of Henry VIII*, Pimlico, 1997

Youings, Joyce, *Penguin Social History of Britain*, Penguin, 1991

sion, he folds the cards down the middle ten minutes before game time and then slips them into the back pocket of his uniform. During a game, he pulls them out continually, almost like worry beads, peering at them as if in search of evidence that everything is fine, that he is doing exactly *what he needs to be doing*. More practically, he refers to them when deciding who to bring on in relief or who may be the best candidate to pinch-hit.

Matchups aren't foolproof to La Russa, perhaps because nothing is foolproof in baseball. They have their weaknesses, particularly if the statistics are several years old. But they do provide the best indicator of what the competition will be between a pitcher and a hitter. There are some hitters who, never mind their mediocre batting averages, simply tag the living crap out of some pitchers. Conversely, there are pitchers, despite soggy ERAs, who simply do well against particular high-stroke hitters.

But La Russa believes that in virtually all situations, human nature dictates results and that his role as a manager is to recognize the impact of human nature and take the best advantage of it. It sounds simple, maybe, but it isn't simple, because human nature isn't simple, and it's even less simple when applied to the twenty-five pieces of the puzzle. Some need to be left alone, some need a pat on the rump every so often, and some need a swift boot in the rear: fuzzy love or tough love or no love. To a certain degree, matchups are a compact reflection of the human psyche, in this instance the effect of confidence on performance. A hitter who has gained early success against a pitcher may simply continue to build on that. He *believes* he can see the ball better when it's thrown by that pitcher, even though there is no physical truth that he can. It's moot, immaterial; the octane of confidence itself is enough to propel him. It's the same with certain pitchers. Their curve may have less break, less tumble, less of that 12-to-6 plummet than their colleagues' curves, but they begin to succeed with it against a given hitter. They begin to feel, to *know*, that the poor little guy 60 feet and 6 inches down the road from them can't do anything with it. And it actually turns out that way.

But matchups also tell the truth about skill—the numbers, like the needle at the start of a lie detector test, are just the beginning of what will be revealed. So when La Russa looks at the matchup numbers that he has been handed, numbers he is familiar with because the Cardinals have already played the Cubs nine times before, it isn't the numbers he cares about as much as the stories behind them: ways to find a remedy for a hitter who has consistently lousy numbers against a sinkerballer (start hitting the ball the other way instead of always trying to pull it and roll over the ball with weak grounders), or the anomalies of right-handed relievers who, against the grain of baseball, actually do better against lefties and how to make use of that (instead of the conventional wisdom of putting in a lefty pinch-hitter, go with a righty). Of all the hours spent preparing before a game, many of them La Russa spends searching for the explanations of these matchup numbers, a slice of seemingly buried narrative that during the season can single-handedly change the outcome of the four or five games that—in La Russa's estimation—a manager can change.

The more La Russa scrutinizes these matchups, the less he likes them. Usually, they offer hope at some point in a series, but not this time. Over the next three nights, the Cards will confront three dominating pitchers. Adding to La Russa's anxiety, giving it the true crisp of darkness, is an acute animus: *the Cubs.*

The rivalry between the Cubs and the Cardinals is probably the oldest and perhaps the best in baseball, no matter how the Red Sox and Yankees spit and spite at each other. That's a tabloid-fueled soap opera about money and ego and sound bites. That's a pair of bratty high-priced supermodels trying to trip each other in their stilettos on the runway. But the Cards-Cubs epic is about roots and geography and territorial rights. It's entwined in the Midwestern blood and therefore refreshing and honest and even heroic. It isn't simply two teams throwing tantrums at each other but two feudal city-states with eternal fans far beyond their own walls, spread throughout not only the Midwest but also deep into the South and the West. The Cubs started amassing their empire through WGN, its crystal-clear radio waves sweeping out of Chicago into Iowa and

Wisconsin and the Dakotas. Until the Boston Braves moved to Milwaukee in 1953, no other National League team was in the upper Midwest.

As for the Cardinals, they were for a period of time baseball's *westernmost* team, and its *southernmost,* too, until the Dodgers moved to Los Angeles in 1958. The Cardinals' retort to WGN was KMOX, whose fifty thousand watts fed millions starved for big-league baseball. Carried by its powerful signal, Cardinals games rolled south from St. Louis, across Missouri into Arkansas and Mississippi, and west into Oklahoma and Texas and even beyond, if the night sky was right.

In Peoria and Decatur and dozens of smaller Illinois farm towns, factions developed, with half the population tuning in to WGN and half turning on KMOX. But the rivalry goes farther back than radio, deep into baseball's mythic youth.

It might have originated on June 24, 1905, when the Cubs' Ed Reulbach and the Cards' Jack Taylor each pitched eighteen-inning complete games before the Cubbies won 2–1. The mutual contempt was only sharpened by more recent heroics, such as the nine showdowns in the late 1960s and early 1970s between the Cubs' Fergie Jenkins and the Cards' Bob Gibson. In seven of these duels, both men pitched a complete game, four were decided by one run, and two of them produced a final score of 1–0. Once, in 95-degree St. Louis heat, as terrible a heat as this hemisphere can muster, both pitchers went the distance undaunted by the departure of homeplate umpire Shag Crawford, who found the weather so insufferable that even he quit in the middle of the game. St. Louis fans also hearken back to Bruce Sutter's split-fingered fastball, perhaps the greatest contribution to pitching since Mordecai "Three Fingers" Brown refined the curve ball. Cubs fans exult in the memory of Ryne Sandberg's stroking that splitter for two back-to-back homers in 1984, a deliciousness made more delicious because Sutter had once been a Cub himself before going over to the dark side.

The inevitable implosion of the Cubs—the sad fury of their futility—only gave the rivalry an added extra, with nothing more fun for a Cards fan than to watch the Cubs self-destruct with their own special brand of pathos. Their knack for misfortune has proved it-self thousands of times but rarely more eloquently than in "Brog-lio-for-Brock," a term synonymous in some circles with *idiocy, absurdity, ridiculousness,* and *senselessness.* Broglio-for-Brock was born in June 1964; at first, Cubs fans thought that they had gotten the better of the deal. They didn't mind at all when Lou Brock was sent to the Cardinals along with Jack Spring and Paul Toth in return for Ernie Broglio, Bobby Shantz, and Doug Clemens. Brock's statistics at the time were middling at best. He struck out often, got thrown out stealing nearly half the times he tried, and had an aggregate batting average with the Cubs of .255 over four years. Broglio, on the other hand, was a hard-throwing pitcher who had been 18 and 8 in 1963. The fact that he was only 3 and 5 in 1964, an indication of arm trouble, didn't seem to bother the Cubs' hierarchy.

As a Cardinal, Brock became one of the greatest players in the history of the game, leading the National League eight times in stealing, finishing five times in the top-ten voting for most valuable player, and getting inducted into the Baseball Hall of Fame in 1985. After the trade, Broglio subsequently won seven games and lost nineteen before leaving baseball two years later. Whether it's true or not, and it probably isn't, it is still considered to be the worst trade that has ever taken place in baseball. Cubs fans have never forgotten it, partially because Cardinals fans will never let them forget it, and it makes every series they play touched by trauma.

II

THIS SEASON, La Russa feels a special competitive edge against the Cubs because they're for real. He pays particular notice to the two pitchers who embody the team's newfound swagger and success: those punk rockers Mark Prior and Kerry Wood. They're the best 1-2 in the game this year, with psychoses that complement their skill. They both throw nasty stuff, and neither is afraid to go way up and way in on a hitter if that's what it takes to prevail.

Even more vital to the Cubs' resurgence is La Russa's counterpart, Dusty Baker. He's in his first season with the team; last year, he led the Giants to the National League Pennant. When Baker became available, La Russa was hoping that he would move over to the American League so that he might have to face him only in a World Series. But Baker dashed those hopes completely by settling in with *the Cubs.* Baker may not be the greatest strategist, but the way the sport and its players are evolving, La Russa also knows that how one manages during a game is becoming less important. What Baker is good at — superb at — is interacting with players. He can handle a ballclub as well as he handles the ever-present toothpick in his mouth; he knows better than anyone else in baseball how to manage the space between a player's ears. He is also masterful at deflecting attention to himself. He lets blunt and controversial remarks spill out of his mouth. But on closer analysis, they seem purposely designed to keep the media swarm buzzing around him. Better for him to get stung by clearly calculated outrageousness than his players.

The upshot is that the Cubs haven't done their annual cuddly collapse in the Friendly Confines. And the Astros, buoyed by the oak-barrel reliability of Craig Biggio and Jeff Bagwell, haven't fallen back either. On this last Tuesday in August, the Central Division standings reflect a race that's neck and neck as it heads into the summer embers:

ST. LOUIS	68–62	.523
HOUSTON	68–62	.523
CHICAGO	67–62	.519

By winning two of these next three games, the Cubs can overtake the Cardinals at a pivotal moment. Beyond that general worry are a lot of smaller, more specific concerns. Aside from the punk duo of Prior and Wood, there's the dark horse Carlos Zambrano, slated to go against the Cards in Game 3. Although few outside of Chicago know much about Zambrano, he is pitching better than Prior and Wood. He has, in fact, been the best pitcher in baseball the past month.

La Russa worries about how he will counter this trio with his own trio: Garrett Stephenson in Game 1, Woody Williams in Game 2, and Matt Morris in Game 3. It's not a shabby trio by any means; nor is it accidental that they'll be pitching in this three-game series. More than a month ago, La Russa and Dave Duncan mapped out their rotation all the way to the end of August to ensure that these would be the pitchers who went against the Cubs now. La Russa and Duncan purposely decided to backload the three-game series, sending the weakest of the three pitchers out first. As one of the many philosophies they have developed during two decades together, they would rather finish the series strong than begin it strong.

La Russa likes this rotation, but he doesn't love it. Each of his pitchers is hauling baggage. Stephenson has some kind of bipolar disorder on the mound. Williams, the staff workhorse, has hit a winless trough after an All-Star first half and may be mentally exhausted. Morris is still recovering from a recently sprained ankle that could well prevent him from pitching with any sustained effectiveness.

La Russa also frets over his hitters, particularly the top of the lineup, with two unpredictable neophytes. He's worried about Rolen's shoulder and neck, which have been hurting him ever since he slid headfirst into home plate at Fenway Park two and a half months ago. The injury restricts his mobility to get to certain pitches, not to mention that it's also painful. La Russa needs to give him a day off. But he can't give Rolen a day off, at least not for this series, anyway; even with a bad neck and shoulder, Rolen at third is still better than any other third baseman in the league, both defensively and offensively. La Russa is worried about Edmonds in center, whose shoulder has been cranky ever since the All-Star game in Chicago when he apparently did something to it during the Home Run Derby. La Russa is worried about Renteria at short, who collapsed in the shower with back spasms the previous game and will definitely be scratched from Game 1. La Russa worries too about the Cubs' lineup. There are Sammy Sosa and Moises Alou, the obvious game breakers, but he's even more worried about three ex-

Pirates who have given the Cubs enormous value down the stretch: Aramis Ramirez at third, Randall Simon at first, and Kenny Lofton in center.

As La Russa refines the little cheat-sheet cards in his tiny hieroglyphic handwriting, he spies a glimmer or two of possibility. The Cubs' starters make a lot of errors, and maybe it's an Achilles' heel he can exploit by bunting more than usual. And Prior, despite his prowess and his puffed-up attitude, still has never beaten the Cardinals. But La Russa takes little relief in any of this. Like most managers, he lives by adages and aphorisms, and the one he applies here resounds with his trademark joy: *Hope for the best; prepare for the worst.*

2

LOCKED IN

I

● ● ● WITH BATTING PRACTICE and the meetings that take place before every new series still a good hour away, the players mill about the clubhouse with an ease born of privilege. They pad across the carpeted floor in white slippers. They pass a little round table where a red batting helmet, destined for an army sergeant in Iraq, awaits their signatures. They tend to their bats, examine them for scuffs and imperfections, or in the case of Eddie Perez, strum the barrel of them like a banjo to ensure that they have the right pitch.

Other players scan a whiteboard just inside the entrance to see where their names are for batting practice, the groupings carefully constructed in terms of who gets to bat when and with whom, Pujols and Rolen getting to go last in the final embers of the afternoon, when the glare of the sun isn't so severe. At the opposite end of the clubhouse, past the little facsimile locker containing Stan Musial's itchy uniform and shoes that seem too small and flimsy for someone that fierce and good, players cluster around an oversized sheet that shows each team's lineups for tonight. Before game time, bench coach Joe Pettini will remove the sheet—now taped to a whiteboard—with a curator's care and retape it to the far corner of the dugout where La Russa resides. During the game, as players enter and exit, the sheet will precisely reflect their movements so La Russa can keep track of who is available and who has been excommunicated. By the last out, it will reflect a frenzy of activity:

crossouts, write-ins, cold diagonal lines through the first letter of a player's name, meaning that he's been rendered unavailable. But for now, the sheet is clean and pristine. It exudes hope, the vain suggestion that everything will proceed with ease and order.

A bit of adventure is always involved as the players scan the lineup sheet to see who is in tonight for the Cardinals, whether La Russa's analysis of the matchups has produced any last-minute surprises. Dusty Baker's not quite as itchy, but it's still an opportunity for the players to see whether he has any tricks of his own:

ST. LOUIS CARDINALS		CHICAGO CUBS	
Original Position	Change	Original Position	Change
Robinson RF		Lofton CF	
Hart 2B		Martinez 2B	
Pujols LF		Sosa RF	
Edmonds CF		Alou LF	
Rolen 3B		Simon 1B	
Martinez 1B		Ramirez 3B	
Cairo SS		Gonzalez SS	
Widger C		Bako C	
Stephenson P		Prior P	

ST. LOUIS CARDINALS   **CHICAGO CUBS**

Available Position Players

Left-Handed	Switch	Right-Handed	Left-Handed	Switch	Right-Handed
Palmiero		Perez	Goodwin		Glanville
		Matheny	O'Leary		Karros
		Taguchi	Womack		Miller
		Renteria			

ST. LOUIS CARDINALS   **CHICAGO CUBS**

Available Pitchers

Left-Handed	Right-Handed	Left-Handed	Right-Handed
Kline	DeJean	Guthrie	Alfonseca
Fassero	Isringhausen	Remlinger	Borowski
	Eldred		Farnsworth
	Simontacchi		

Tonight, for Game 1, the Cubs' lineup is straightforward. Sammy Sosa and Moises Alou, batting third and fourth, form the center of gravity, with forty-nine homers between them. Sosa's had a split personality this season, almost helpless the first half and now hitting with venom the second. Alou in particular is a Cardinals killer, so much so that Dave Duncan believes that they need to completely rethink how to pitch him: Simply stop feeding his first-pitch addiction. Alex Gonzalez, in the seventh hole, has seventeen homers. He strikes out a lot: 105 times already. But he likes to be a long-ball star, and he is the kind of dangerous low-end-of-the-lineup hitter who will kill you if you get lazy with him and let him be too comfortable, give him something too fat on the outside of the plate, something he thinks he can simply reach over and loose a swing at. Paul Bako, in the eighth spot, can't hit a lick: .213 coming into tonight. He's played with so many teams already in his brief career—this is his fifth in four years—he might as well keep his belongings in storage rather than risk the disappointment of setting down roots. He's in for his defense, a tough and uncompromising handler of pitchers that the Cardinals starter Brett Tomko distinctly remembers from their days together in the minors when he called time and came out to the mound to have a word with him.

"Are you really trying out here?"

"What do you mean?"

"Because your stuff is horrible today and if you don't try a little harder, you're not going to make it out of this inning."

The three Pirate expatriates—Lofton and Simon and Ramirez—have been equitably interspersed in the one-, five-, and six-holes, and it isn't pretty: A look at the matchups makes La Russa briefly wonder whether they'd been brought over from Pittsburgh specifically to torment Garrett Stephenson in Game 1. Against him, the three players are an aggregate 19 for 42—almost .500—with two home runs.

LOFTON	6-12-1
SIMON	8-18-1
RAMIREZ	5-12-0

As for the Cardinals' lineup, it's a patchwork because of injuries. Still, it features Pujols and Edmonds and Rolen in the thick of it, the best-hitting threesome in baseball right now. They have ninety home runs among them through 130 games, and each of them may well drive in more than a hundred runs. Despite a recent bout of the flu, Pujols has been in the stratosphere all season, contending for the Triple Crown and fresh off a thirty-game hitting streak. Edmonds has had stratospheric moments as well. If his shoulder hadn't turned cranky, he could have forty home runs instead of thirty-two, and he continues to play center field as if he's at the nastiest Texas Hold 'Em table at Binion's, betting the pot on every catch. Rolen, who is from a small farming town in southern Indiana and likes to draw as much attention to himself as you would expect from someone who is from a small farming town in southern Indiana, is humming along with typical incandescence. In the field, he doesn't have the gambler flair of Edmonds. Rolen's far more self-effacing, his style gritty and as determined as a linebacker without a single whiff of hey-look-at-me; it's easy to forget that he's already won three Gold Gloves and in all likelihood will win a fourth this season. As for his performance at the plate, he's once again on his way to another year, his fourth of seven in the major leagues, in which he will hit more than twenty-five homers and drive in more than a hundred runs.

These three players provide meat in the middle, but La Russa also likes danger at the top: a hitter in the one-hole who can get on base whether by hit or walk, followed by a hitter in the two-hole who can uncork power. He's felt that way at least since the early 1980s when Carlton Fisk came over to the White Sox from the Red Sox. In 1983, La Russa started putting Fisk at number two even though he was a prodigious home-run hitter. For virtually all his career, Fisk had hit in the three-, four-, or five-spot, and he didn't like the change in stature much at first, shunted into the space universally reserved for the little get-on-base piccolos. Given his immense New England pride, he didn't appreciate La Russa for much of anything at the beginning of the 1983 season. When the White Sox brought up catcher Joel Skinner from the minors without telling him, La Russa and Fisk started screaming and yelling at each other during stretching exercises before a doubleheader against the A's in June. But there were other frustrations. He was hitting under .200 at the time, and it was shortly afterward that La Russa, in trying to figure out something to get him unblocked, put him second in the order. He did it because of his thirst for power in the two-spot. He also did it because he knew he could, with his lineup strong enough in the middle to still pack pop. Fisk started blossoming at the plate afterward. He ended up hitting twenty-six home runs, his career high at the time. Placed ahead of Harold Baines, Greg Luzinski, and Ron Kittle, the foursome became an unorthodox murderers' row in the two- through five-holes, combining for 113 home runs, 380 RBIs, and 309 runs scored as the White Sox ran away with the division by twenty games.

Later, when La Russa managed the American League in the 1989 All-Star game, he took his theory of danger a step further when he put Bo Jackson in the one-hole. La Russa once again had the luxury to do so, because just about everybody on the team was a dangerous hitter. But still, Jackson wasn't your prototypical lead-off hitter. He had great wheels, but he struck out a lot: a natural-born cleanup hitter. His power carried danger, though: the ability to change the dimension of a game right away. When Jackson hit a 455-foot home run off Rick Reuschel in the bottom of the first, La Russa again saw what that danger can do to an opposing pitcher: rattle him and keep him rattled. When the next hitter up, Wade Boggs, who had everything but power, homered off Reuschel, it only confirmed to La Russa why explosive danger at the top is a good thing.

Another reason for explosion at the top—stacking the deck early—is to capitalize on the starting pitcher's uncertainty. In the first inning, even the best hurlers are still evaluating the feel of their fastballs and off-speed, no matter how well they warmed up. (Starting pitchers generally agree that there is little correlation between how well they warmed up before a game and how well they actually perform during it.) Sometimes, in the absence of classic power, its catalyzing effects can still be manufactured. In 2001, La Russa had

Placido Polanco bat second for part of the season. He was hardly a power hitter, but he was a great hit-and-run man, and toward the end of the year, La Russa almost always had him hit and run, both to push for a run and also to keep defenses on edge. But there is no sudden explosion tonight, even of the manufactured variety.

Normally, the veteran second baseman, Fernando Vina, would hit lead-off and the right fielder, J.D. Drew, hit second. But Vina is just coming off a torn hamstring that sidelined him for three months. He's played a few games in the minors to get the timing of his stroke back, but he looks lost at the plate and isn't ready yet, which leaves La Russa with Bo Hart, a last name straight out of central casting given the way he plays. He's the poster boy of scrappy, listed at 5'11" and 175 pounds, although he doesn't seem even as big as that. He's twenty-seven years old but looks in his late teens, with his nubby blond hair and a chin vainly struggling to grow something, as if he's not quite ready yet to grow something. When he's in the clubhouse on the road before a game, he likes to play cards—*cards*—as sweet as it gets in baseball.

His play at second since coming up from Triple-A in June has been exceptional, really. Into the middle of July, he was hitting over .350, and it's clear that he's one of those guys with average skills and above-average heart and fire. La Russa can't help but love players like that, but he also knows that stories like his rarely end the way they begin. Since mid-July, Hart has cooled off considerably. He's hitting .283 coming into the three-game series. With 240 at-bats, he's not the virgin he was when he came up, and every pitch Hart takes in the major leagues is one more chance for pitchers to discover and exploit the places he's having trouble getting to.

His stroke is compact, a delayed swing in which he lets the ball virtually get to the plate before he goes to hit it. He has good punch for a player that small, like a pinball smacking off a lever. But he has trouble with the breaking ball, which surprises La Russa because a swing like that should allow him to recognize a curve ball and react to it. Hart also tends to get too aggressive out of the strike zone, resulting in a quick strike 1 to put him into a hole. All this makes him a perfect hitter in the eighth spot, where that aggressiveness and punch would be a definite plus, making pitchers pause before thinking that they can simply go after him with high heat. But it's another La Russa adage that you can't dwell on what you don't have and can take advantage of only what do you have, so Hart is starting and batting second.

As for Drew, capable of launching the ball as far as anyone in both leagues, he went on the disabled list nine days ago. He's injured again, as he was at the beginning of the season. It's the sixth time he's been on the disabled list since coming into the league in 1998, surrounded by more anticipation than any other rookie since Mickey Mantle. Perhaps never in his managing career has La Russa had a player more tantalizing in terms of talent and more difficult to unleash. But like many young players, Drew came in with the advantages that only plot against you if your goal is the realization of what God gave you: a long-term contract, too many early millions, a billboard mystique about him before he had taken a single road trip.

To La Russa, there is a certain bittersweet tragedy to Drew, the embodiment of the best of times and the worst of times in baseball. The best of times for players because there is so much money out there and the ability to control your future. The worst of times because the money corrupts and compromises, makes it easy to play under your maximum and to reject the daily commitment that wins awards and World Series rings, because you can still make a ridiculous living at three-quarters speed. "A lot of young players fall into this trap where it's uncomfortable to push yourself on a daily basis," says La Russa. "They settle for some percent under their max. If you have the chance to be a two-million-dollar-a-year player, they might settle for 75 percent of that. In the case of J.D., if you have the chance to be a twelve-million-to-fifteen-million-dollar-a-year player, you settle for 75 percent of that."

The irony for La Russa—and what an irony it is—is that Drew may be *too* talented, that it comes too easily to him. He plays with little outward passion for the game, gliding through because even when he glides through, he still gets enough hits and enough home runs to make about three and a half million dollars a year. La Russa

knows that of all the qualities that a player possesses, outward passion is the most deceptive in terms of what it indicates. When
Harold Baines played for La Russa on the White Sox and in Oakland, he had no outward passion. He said little in the clubhouse and
even less to reporters; once, after hitting a prodigious home run to
win a game, his answer to the standard question "Guess you got a
piece of that, huh, Harold?" was expressed in one word: "Evi-
dently." But Baines was also a great competitor—one of the best
late-inning clutch hitters that La Russa has ever managed—with
no correlation between outward temperament and inward passion
for the game. La Russa doesn't feel the same about Drew.

He still believes in him, but he's also had ample opportunity
with him, and he wonders whether it would be better for someone
else to open himself up to the seduction of his limitless talent, find
what he never could.

When he thinks of Drew, La Russa inevitably thinks of another
player he once managed in the 1980s, Jose Canseco, the charming,
self-destructive, preoccupied poster boy of distraction. Once the
multiyear contract came Jose's way—once the money got into the
heavyweight millions—playing every day became nostalgic. "I'm a
performer, not a player," said Canseco, which in a lifetime of incredible comments from players, may well be the most incredible
one ever spoken to La Russa. But the comparison between the two
players goes only so far, because Canseco did work for the advantages he eventually got. He did turn in that MVP year with the
Oakland A's in 1988 when he became the first player ever to hit
forty or more home runs and steal forty or more bases. He loved
hitting with two strikes—half of his home runs that year were with
two strikes—which is about the discipline of getting a little wider
and not striding as much and working on reflexes through tedious
short-toss drills during early batting practice. Canseco had competitive passion before he pissed it away, only to have his body betray
him when he tried to recover what had once made him.

That leaves La Russa with Kerry Robinson in right field batting
first, and La Russa has significant concern about being left with

Robinson in right field batting first. It's the classic tension between manager and bench player: how much Robinson thinks he should be playing versus how much La Russa thinks he should be playing. Robinson aches and itches to be in the lineup every day. He sees himself in the same category as the Marlins' Pierre, who is on his way to stealing sixty bases this season, whereas Robinson is stuck on the bench most of the time. That's the way he feels about it — *he's stuck there* — and that infuriates La Russa, given his team-as-puzzle theory. He sees Robinson as a role player with a left-handed bat, good speed, and nice range in the outfield. All this means that Robinson can be vital in the right situations. But La Russa doesn't see him as another Pierre. As far back as spring training, he flat-out told Robinson that if he really thought he should be playing every day, he should go to the general manager, Walt Jocketty, and demand a trade. "Go find somebody who's going to give you the four or five hundred at-bats," La Russa said. "And I hope they're in our division so we can play against you."

Robinson accepted his fate; he had no choice. But he still doesn't like it, and he makes few bones about not liking it. He sulks when he is not in the lineup regularly — as when he sat on the outermost edge of the dugout by himself in Houston one day as if he were fishing off the end of a pier — and La Russa *hates* sulking. As for how Robinson will perform now that he is starting, La Russa doesn't really know. Robinson has played pretty well since replacing Drew — 8 for 14 in his last four games. He's getting it into the opposite field, which is a good sign, because it means that he's not trying to do too much by trying to power and pull the ball every time he's up. But as a lead-off hitter, Robinson is the antithesis of danger. He has no home runs in 165 at-bats so far this season and only three in his five-year career. Nor does he compensate for it with his on-base percentage, which is a meager .302.

The players continue to do what players do. They sit in front of their lockers and catch up on a little mail, which they never catch up on, given the torrents of letters that come in addressing them as "mister" and beseeching them with religious humility for autographs. They put on headphones because even they can't take the deafening sound of "P.I.M.P." stampeding through the locker room. They contend with the reporters already swarming, asking them the obvious so the obvious can be restated. They pad on those white slippers into the eating area, an oasis that provides not only sustenance but also a fine little hideout, as it is off-limits to the media. They make square little white-bread sandwiches from the trays of cold cuts. They help themselves to the private stock of ball-park hot dogs sunning on a metal grill. If they feel like having an omelet, an obliging cook will prepare one with fresh vegetables and finely diced cubes of turkey and ham and bacon. They read the sports pages of *USA Today* and the *St. Louis Post-Dispatch,* the other sections of the paper generally untouched by human hands. They grab from the plastic tubs of Butterfingers and Ding-Dongs and Twinkies and Kit-Kats and Snickers that have been laid out on a series of shelves. They dip into canisters of Bazooka and Double Bubble and individual sticks of Juicy Fruit that a clubhouse atten-dant has already unwrapped for them. They reach for the little packages of David's sunflower seeds that now come in four flavors: original, toasted corn, barbecue, and jalapeño hot salsa, for those who may need a little pick-me-up in the late innings. When they leave the kitchen, some go into the weight room to lift weights or to ride one of the stationary bikes. Some go into the training room where arms, in particular pitching arms, are salved and stretched and iced, in vain efforts to shield them from the inevitable attacks of time and extended use.

A steady flow of players leaves the clubhouse altogether and goes in two different directions. A trickle heads for the indoor cage to work on various drills: One is the basic hitting drill off the tee to hone the swing; a second is the short-toss drill in which batting coach Mitchell Page kneels about 15 feet away on one knee behind a screen and gets it in there with enough velocity and varied loca-tion to allow hitters to work on their two-strike reflexes as well as laying off the sinker or the high fastball; the third is a drill, invented by Pete Rose, in which first-base coach Dave McKay tosses the ball but the hitter purposely doesn't swing, instead simply watches the ball over and over as it comes in, to gain further intimacy.

A trickle heads through a nondescript red door. Inside is a dark little submarine of a room overstuffed with televisions and video consoles and satellite feed boxes and cable boxes and two computers and wires as criss-crossed as dreadlocks. Pipes leak in a corner, and several holes in one wall suggest something serious to do with rodents. Given that the Secret Weapon resides here—La Russa's own term for him—the place should have a little more flair, a little more style. Then again, Chad Blair doesn't look like much of a Secret Weapon, so maybe it's the right fit, after all.

Blair's standard-issue uniform—a T-shirt and shorts just above the cusp of some raw and ugly knees—gives no inkling of the contribution he makes. Nor do his glasses or his sweet, shaggy-dog voice. His physique is small and unimposing, entirely out of place beside those he works with. Blair also looks bleary-eyed *all* the time, maybe because his wife and he just had a baby girl, or maybe because his professional life is spent staring at grainy images, searching for the tiny differences that draw an unforgiving line between those who can and those who sometimes can and those who never will.

II

BLAIR IS the Cardinals' video coordinator, a vocation he stumbled onto in the early 1990s, when he was a freelance cameraman in the Bay Area and the Oakland A's built a video room for $100,000. It looked nice and had fancy equipment, but the team had no idea what to do with it, so Blair was asked to run it. It's been his life ever since: the compilation and dissemination of bite-sized chunks of video. At first, only coaches studied film, but it has become essential for players as well, or at least those players who want to remain competitive. Of all the changes in baseball over the past decade, the rise of video is the most significant. It has transformed the sport, showing hitters and pitchers how to refine their craft so minutely that their profession is no longer merely a game of inches. Now it's a game *of an inch* because of the ability of video to alert players and coaches to the slightest imperfections, and many franchises are spending millions for the latest in razzle-dazzle imaging technology.

Blair's Lair dazzles nobody. It's all of 750 square feet and has only one computerized editing system. It's dark even with the lights on. Its array of machines and screens has clearly been cobbled together since its humble start in 1996, when there were only two tape decks and a TV monitor. Now Blair can pull in cable or satellite feeds from virtually every team in both leagues; he can compile video on every player in the game. But it isn't simply the diligent collection of footage that makes Blair special; that's a technician's skill. He also has microscope eyes that can discern subtle patterns in the opposition. For Cardinals hitters, it's about identifying the repertoire of an opposing pitcher beforehand, seeing what he throws and how he throws it and where he throws it, so they can seize on a pitch when it comes or lay off of it. For Cardinals pitchers, it's about finding the hole that every hitter possesses somewhere in his swing and avoiding the wheelhouse.

Blair isn't a substitute for any of the coaches. He never says anything unless asked. But he's another detective on the never-ending trail of clues to how opponents can be exploited. Despite his ugly knees, players love the sharpness of his eyes and respect his analysis. They *listen* to him. So do La Russa and Duncan, no small acknowledgment from two men who between them have close to seventy-five years of experience in the game.

Blair's job imposes weird demands and limitations. As part of his duties, both at Busch or on the road, he charts pitches during the game by virtue of a center-field camera that feeds into a little video monitor in whatever clubhouse he happens to be in. It means that he is present for every game of the season yet never gets to see one in the flesh. His whole life is subterranean, spent beneath the steel skeleton of something. He is always squinting at something: a television monitor, an editing machine, a computer screen. He knows pitchers and he knows hitters solely by those pixilated images that come at him day after day, as if this is the only way baseball exists. It seems as though it should all blur together after a while: the difference in movement between one fastball and another too imperceptible to matter, one hitter's sinker hole no different from a dozen other hitters' sinker holes. But Blair's eyes are just *different*. Sinker holes are like fishing holes, each one unique and worthy of discovery. As for pitchers, he picks up on the slivers of gradations that make home plate, relative to its size, the most hotly contested piece of real estate mankind has ever known: a million battles fought over terrain that measures 17 inches across at its widest point.

As part of his preparation for a three-game series earlier in the month, Blair watched Dontrelle Willis of the Marlins and noticed that his high herky-jerky leg kick, beyond being something cute for broadcasters to talk about, is an essential factor in his remarkable success this season as a rookie. Blair realized that it enables him to hide the ball up to the moment he delivers it, which gives him one of those fastballs that sneaks up on hitters, gets in on them real quick so that a pedestrian velocity of 92 mph seems a lot faster when a hitter tries to catch up with it. He watched the Marlins' Brad Penny and noticed that it isn't only his 95-mph fastball that kills a hitter but also the way Penny plays havoc with the hitter's line of sight: the high-heat fastball traveling the ladder up and the big-break curve ball traveling down.

Before every three-game series, the Secret Weapon creates three basic sets of videos. For the Cubs series, he first compiled recent performances of Cubs hitters for Duncan and bullpen coach Marty Mason to dissect and then disseminate to the pitching staff before Game 1. Blair chooses only a handful of at-bats per hitter, because Duncan and Mason don't need more than that to make their findings. Another compilation features the Cubs starting triumvirate against both the Cardinals and other recent opponents. The third features pitchers with styles *similar* to this series' Cards' starters who have done well against the Cubs. Certainly, the Cardinals hurlers can look at videos of their own performances. But the theory behind this compilation is that it helps pitchers enormously to see other examples of success besides their own.

With game time about three hours away, more players file in to Blair's Lair. They sit on gray-backed swivel chairs, staring at a row of four Panasonic monitors on a black Formica table. They prop their feet up and thumb little remote controls to push the tapes back and forth. They settle in comfortably before the TVs: potato chips and beer the only things missing. Some stay for only a few minutes. Some like to linger. Pujols, in a swivel chair at the end, is a lingerer. So is Mike Matheny.

Matheny typically lingers so much in Blair's Lair before a game that he often takes on the same bleary-eyed look as Blair himself: a head too full with video snippets. He is inordinately hard on himself—too hard, in La Russa's judgment—beating himself up for failure when teammates will tell you that he is as diligent and rock-solid as any player in the game today. When you see him in the video room, it's clear that he is simply watching too much of the stuff: a digital overdose. Even he admits that he watches too much of the stuff, until you consider that Matheny's job—catcher—is the most demanding in all of sports and maybe the worst. It's the equivalent of going both ways in football, because of the offensive demands of it and, in the eyes of La Russa, actually more important defensive demands of it. La Russa places a high premium on what a catcher does behind the plate: not only blocking it and preventing pitches from going wild but also the very style with which a catcher calls a game, the ability to be creative within the context of knowing what his pitcher is capable of and what opposing hitters are incapable of. It's an act of tremendous balance and feel and intelligence, so much more than simply throwing down fingers behind the plate and hoping for the best.

By these exacting standards, Matheny is as conscientious as any catcher La Russa has ever had. His contribution behind the plate is so valuable that La Russa couldn't care less if he hit .000. But Matheny cares profoundly about his defense *and* his offense. So he screens more video than any other player. He watches it from both perspectives, fretting over what pitchers are likely to throw at him, fretting over what opposing hitters are hoping to see. You can feel his burden, click, rewinding, then playing a snippet of video again, click, rewinding, then playing the snippet again, click, rewinding, then playing the snippet again until all the swivel-backed chairs are empty except his.

• • •

The players trot out of Blair's Lair around 4:15 P.M. They leave the clubhouse and work their way through the tunnel that leads to the dugout and the field beyond. The tunnel is carpeted with artificial turf so splotched and stained it looks like the product of a kindergarten painting class. They pass an ancient floor fan that vainly tries to cut the St. Louis heat so thick that even the Mississippi wilts. For men who among them make over $80 million a year, it's an incongruously low-rent backdrop. Around the corner and down another hundred feet, they come to the back end of the dugout. Inside the tunnel by the dugout entrance, several rows of cubbyholes resembling old-fashioned mail slots hold batting helmets. A bat rack underneath has also been divided into cubbyholes so nobody gets confused and picks up a bat that isn't his. It's all once again hierarchical; the bench players and the on-the-cusp players leave their equipment here, and the regulars put their tools in compartments located in the dugout itself.

They hit the field for batting practice, wearing bright red warm-up jerseys: cherries baking in the sun. Stephenson goes first because he's tonight's starting pitcher. He gets five minutes. Then he slips back into the clubhouse for the pitching meeting with Duncan, perhaps the most important element of Game 1, although the game itself hasn't even begun.

3

"I'M GONNA KILL YOU!"

I

● ● ● DAVE DUNCAN IS the kind of man who in the storm at sea would simply lash himself to the mast; he'd wait out the hurricane by reading the paper, hold the putter steady in the tornado. His nothing-gets-to-me look is the same in the dugout whether the Cardinals are up 5–0 in the top of the ninth with the bases empty or 1–0 in the top of the ninth with the bases loaded. La Russa wears tension like a catcher wears a face mask, but Duncan wears nothing on his lean Texas-flat features except that deadpan. It makes him a source of reassurance to pitchers and La Russa alike: the coach who won't crack.

In twenty years together in the claustrophobic hothouse of the dugout, Duncan and La Russa have never once argued; they have yet to share a bad vibe, except when La Russa gives some stock complaint about ineffective pitching during a game and Duncan studies him and says, "Here we go again." The two men know each other as well as any two men possibly can, honoring the boundaries of each other's baseball knowledge and the equally vast continents of their silences. La Russa gets through to Duncan whenever it's necessary. But there is something eternally inscrutable about Duncan—a safe that can't be cracked—hours spent before his computer with a pinch of Skoal in his cheek as ample companionship. Words emerge from his mouth like reluctant bubbles that barely

ping the surface. You can sit in the same room with him for sizable stretches and he'll utter nothing beyond, "How's it going?"
The only reason he'll divulge this much is that someone has said,
"Hey, Dunc," and courtesy dictates saying *something* back. When
he does expound into a sentence or two in his slivery voice, it's
never for pleasure, which is maybe why one of his prize pupils,
Todd Stottlemyre, refers to him as "The Deacon" and calls his
words "biblical."

In addition to the two decades Duncan and La Russa have
shared in the dugout, their history goes back another twenty years
before that when they were teenagers coming up in the Kansas City
A's organization. They first played together in the winter instructional league in Bradenton in 1964, then in the minors over the
next three years. Most of the players on those teams were still
"kids," as La Russa put it, still "trying to figure it all out." But Duncan was different, with a steadiness and maturity even in his late
teens and early twenties. Advancing through the A's system as a
catcher, making it to the major-league team in 1968, he also dis-
played another quality: bullwhip bluntness, regardless of the repercussions.

In the 1972 World Series, Duncan caught Game 7 for the A's
against the Cincinnati Reds, not the least bit nervous even though
this was his first start. In the bottom of the ninth, baseball's top reliever, Rollie Fingers, got two outs to bring up the Reds' Pete Rose
in a last-chance gasp with the score 3–2. When A's manager Dick
Williams headed for the mound, Duncan knew his intent: to replace Fingers with starter Vida Blue and turn the switch-hitting
Rose around from the left side to the right. Duncan thought that
it was a bad idea, putting Blue into a situation he wasn't used to,
taking Fingers out of a situation that he conquered better than any
other reliever in baseball at the time. He more than thought it was
a bad idea: Joined by A's captain Sal Bando on the mound, he told
Williams that it was a *bad idea,* even though he was a twenty-seven-
year-old catcher and Williams was a forty-three-year-old manager
with 793 games of experience. Williams did what Duncan suggested: He left Fingers in, then watched along with the rest of

America as Rose hit a shot toward the outfield wall in left center. Now Duncan got *nervous*, proof of the existence of blood in his veins. But Joe Rudi snagged the ball to save Duncan and the series.

After the season, the irresistible force of A's outfielder Reggie Jackson went against the immoveable object of A's owner Charley Finley in a salary dispute. Duncan publicly sided with Jackson, which led to a predictable reaction, equal parts cheap and cantankerous, from Finley: He traded Duncan from the world champion A's to the arctic outpost of the Cleveland Indians.

Duncan became the bullpen coach for the Indians after his playing days were over. In 1982, he moved to the Seattle Mariners as the pitching coach with Rene Lachemann as the manager, taking a weak and watery staff and turning it around to finish second in the American League in strikeouts and saves. He thought he deserved a $5,000 raise for his efforts, but the Mariners' owner thought otherwise, so Duncan quit and joined up with La Russa on the White Sox.

Over the years, La Russa has found that a lot of hitting and pitching coaches are ineffective because they refuse to put themselves on the line. They don't want to tell a player what to do, in case it backfires. So they deal in open-ended aphorisms or dish out moral support, a steady stream of claps and "C'mon, baby" from the dugout. But that's not Duncan: the brevity of a news bulletin, maybe, but never reticent. He has the laser eye for mechanical flaws and where to make adjustments. He has given performance makeovers to dozens of pitchers over the years by adding a pitch to the repertoire or modifying one. Just as important, he bases his ideas not on ethereal wisdom but on hard data that he continually examines: breaking down video of opposing hitters, analyzing by computer to further ferret out the best pitch to throw in the best situation, and compiling his own legendary pitching charts.

La Russa cedes little territory to his coaches. He takes their input, but he shoulders the decisions. The one exception is Duncan; if La Russa approaches anyone during a game, it's almost invariably him. He knows of Duncan's penchant for solitude, to work out problems on his own. But he will never confuse his deadpan for inaction. When Duncan caught for the A's, his nickname was the

Quiet Assassin, and it still rings true today. When pressed for proof, La Russa gets a little Cheshire cat smile on his lips, clearly recalling one of his most beautiful baseball moments ever: George Bell of the Toronto Blue Jays charging one of Duncan's pitchers, and Duncan leaping out of the dugout and chasing him around the field, screaming, "I'M GONNA FUCKING KILL YOU!!!!"

Duncan's attitude toward his pitchers is fatherly: He protects them against attack, and he holds himself responsible for their improvement. He gives his starters detailed plans for dealing with every opposing batter in the starting lineup. He teaches his pitchers to think differently on the mound; he'll lessen the burden of a bases-loaded-and-one-out situation by going to the mound and pointing out to the pitcher that he's *one pitch* away from getting out of the inning with a double-play ball. He specializes in rescuing pitchers at precarious points in their careers, pitchers who are on the skids and have bounced around too much or have lost too much confidence or have broken up with a pitch they need to woo back. He did it with Dennis Eckersley, whom nobody wanted in 1987 when the A's plucked him from the Cubs after a season in which he'd gone 6 and 11 with a 4.57 ERA. He did it with Mike Moore, who went 19 and 11 with Oakland in 1989 after two seasons with Seattle, when he'd been an aggregate 18 and 34. He did it with Stottlemyre, a .500 Blue Jays pitcher who went 14 and 7 in his first season with Oakland. He did it with Kent Bottenfield, who had gone from one mediocre season to another before he won eighteen with the Cardinals in 1999, equaling his total number of major-league wins until that point. He did it with Darryl Kile after a disastrous season in Colorado, where he'd gone 8 and 13 with a 6.61 ERA. La Russa told Kile to "place his career in Duncan's hands," and Kile did so, building a record of 20 and 9 the next year.

Most notably, he did it with Dave Stewart, out of baseball altogether in 1986, when the A's picked him up as little more than a curiosity. Stewart had played around with a forkball for a little bit during his career, but in Texas and Philadelphia, he had been discouraged from using it amid the widespread belief that throwing a forkball could hurt your arm. But Duncan encouraged him to rediscover it, convinced that Stewart needed a change in style. Duncan understood that the pitch had to be executed properly, and he showed Stewart how to throw it with the right motion, retaining a loose wrist. Duncan got him to stop making mistakes that caused it to go up. It didn't take long before Stewart was throwing a filthy little forkball. It became his second-best pitch after his fastball, pushing the slider to third, and suddenly Stewart *was* a different pitcher. He finished the year 9 and 5. Over the next four years, from 1987 to 1991, Stewart won twenty games or more each season. His forkball was a hitter's temptress, slow and sweet before the bottom went to hell.

II

TONIGHT, DUNCAN'S TRYING to do it with Garrett Stephenson. Stephenson has tools. Because he's a major leaguer, he has tools, and his one breakout season, in 2000, shows what he can do with them:

W	L	ERA	G	GS	IP	H	HR	BB	SO
16	9	4.49	32	31	200.1	209	31	63	123

This season, going into tonight's game, the numbers are different:

W	L	ERA	G	GS	IP	H	HR	BB	SO
7	12	4.41	27	25	159.1	148	26	57	83

Obviously, they reflect a losing record, but they also reflect Stephenson's schism: He has given up fewer hits than innings pitched, an increasing rarity among starting pitchers. At this point in the season, he has an even better ERA than he had in 2000. It means that he has pitched at certain moments with effectiveness this year. But the numbers also reflect that he has given up twenty-six home runs, a horrific number. Which means that there are times when he ends up challenging hitters with that fastball that simply doesn't pose enough of a challenge, particularly when he throws it high.

He lacks one of those Bugs Bunny sliders that stops at home plate, catches some bennies for a split second, and then exits in a vapor. He doesn't have one of those wicked Mariano Rivera cutters that against lefties should be declared a WMD. As a result, he has the problem shared by many starting pitchers: a macho refusal to accept that pitching is not only about speed. Speed is considered God in baseball. Speed sells in baseball. Virtually every scoreboard now has a little square section showing the velocity of each pitch. Fans ooh and ah, nudge each other in the ribs the faster a pitch gets. But it's a false God, in La Russa's eyes, a fastball in the high eighties with movement and location far preferable to a flat fastball in the nineties. Speed alone can kill, at least kill a pitcher's perform-ance. To offset this obsession, La Russa once ordered the speed section of the scoreboard juiced up a few miles per hour because he could tell that his pitcher was paying as much attention to it as the fans were.

To make the best use of his tools tonight, Stephenson *has* to mix location and mix speeds. He needs to use his lumbering fastball al-most as a flirtation, to get the Cubs hitters looking for it, craving it, only to confound them with his off-speed curve and changeup on the edges of the plate. It's a mental art as much as it is a physical one, every pitch a product of conscious deliberation: *What am I going to throw and where am I going to put it?* It's exhausting to have to con-centrate this much, far easier simply to get up on that mound and wing it. And sometimes, Stephenson likes to do just that: be a ma-cho man, dare opponents to hit his fastball. Which they often do.

Using a little portable DVD player, Duncan has spent several hours reviewing the disc of Cubs' hitters that Chad Blair made for him. He has seen the Cubs nine times already this season, but Dun-can is looking for the slightest little slice that may be new, ways they may be covering the plate better or adjusting to inside pitches better or handling curves in the strike zone better. He's also pa-trolling for new weaknesses that might have developed in making those very improvements, every tiny patch creating another tiny hole. He also has a red binder in front of him. This particular one is marked "Cubs," but he has one for every team in the league. He stores them in a red steel case that goes on the road with him. It looks a little bit like a vault on wheels, maybe because the knowledge it holds is priceless.

The binders contain his charts, a packet for every opposing player, a remarkable Rorschach in which he has tracked every pitch each batter has been thrown by his pitchers and what that batter did with it. Using a system of grids, three up and three across dividing the hitting zone into nine sections, he has made small notations that record the type and location of every pitch. The charts also track any trends that have emerged in particular situations—where a Cardinals pitcher has given up first-pitch hits and where he has gotten first-pitch outs, where he has given up hits with two strikes, and where he has gotten outs with two strikes. Duncan is looking for patterns, a cluster of notations together in a certain spot, almost like tiny cracks in a frozen lake, to detect spots that a given hitter is getting to.

He sees those clusters with the Cubs hitters. They tell stories, much like La Russa's matchups tell stories. In the quiet of the clubhouse, he is trying to make Stephenson heed the morals of what they say, the same as he does with every starting pitcher and catcher two hours before the start of every game.

The meeting takes place in the room that Duncan uses when he is in the clubhouse. It's next to La Russa's office, with a common doorway in between, affording the two men easy access to each other, although each stays in his own sphere. The room is small and Spartan: a bookcase filled mostly with the current media guides of opposing teams, a rudimentary copier, several utilitarian desks of beige metal favored by police stations and mental asylums. Its only function is the microscopic grist of baseball, the captivating and strange science of pinpointing pitches, anything else an unwelcome distraction.

Duncan respects his pitchers and knows that they have their own set views on how hitters should be handled. He appreciates that they have earned their opinions the hard way, out there on the mound, the most isolated spot in sports, even when things are going well. He also has his own back story, the handling of six Cy Young pitchers between his playing days as a catcher and his years as a pitching coach—Catfish Hunter and Blue and Jim Palmer on the playing side and La Marr Hoyt, Bob Welch, and Eckersley on the pitching side.

He wants to hear from Stephenson on how he wants to handle the Cubs hitters. "Okay, Garrett," Duncan says, and Stephenson starts in with the lead-off hitter, Kenny Lofton. He talks about mixing it up and using both sides of the plate, then quickly repeats the part about using both sides of the plate. "Can I make a suggestion?" interrupts Duncan. Based on his charting, he has made the analysis that most of Lofton's hits off Stephenson have come on "sloppy breaking balls" that were either up or over the plate, whereas most of the outs he has gotten have been on changeups down in the zone after fastballs. From this moment on, with that voice even softer and lower to the ground than La Russa's, Duncan takes over the meeting.

He points out a general truth: Almost all the Cubs hitters tonight are aggressive. They have a tendency to seize on pitches early in the count, so more than normal attention has to be paid *not* to put the ball over the plate. Which means, as another general truth, that Stephenson must establish the inside on hitters. Going inside has two purposes. The first is that it marks Stephenson's turf, making the Cubs "inside conscious" to prevent them from effortlessly reaching to the outside for pitches. The second is that it will intimidate them by playing on the understandable fear all hitters have of getting jammed.

If he doesn't establish the inside on Lofton in the lead-off spot, Duncan predicts, "he'll just hang out over the plate." Stephenson must do it with Sammy Sosa in the third hole for much the same reason, because it's the only way of rearranging Sosa's focus so he's not totally locked on getting something up over the plate. He needs to do it with Moises Alou, because Duncan's charts on Alou show a first-pitch jackpot against Cardinals pitching—first-pitch slider for a home run, first-pitch middle-high fastball for a home run, first-pitch high-away fastball for a home run, first-pitch sinker high middle for a home run. And he needs to do it most of all with Randall Simon, the greatest of Stephenson's three ex-Pirate nemeses.

"This guy *kicks* my ass on off-speed," says Stephenson in a gust of frustration. "He hits every off-speed I've *thrown.*" It doesn't matter whether Simon gets three good inside fastballs in a row, Stephenson notes. Presumably, the steady stream of those fastballs and their location should speed up Simon's bat enough, make him expect the fastball enough, so that when Stephenson comes with something slower, Simon's timing should be completely off. But he *still* gets to it.

Duncan, based on his charts and Blair's DVD, has another explanation for what ails Stephenson: *location.* It's not what he's throwing or what sequence he's throwing it in as much as it is *where* he's throwing it.

"Garrett, let me make this real simple for you," says Duncan, using the past history of his charts as potential prologue. "Hit: high-and-away fastball. Put in play: high away. Struck him out: low and in. High and away: base hit. High and away: base hit." The point is obvious.

"Everything that he has hit against you has been up."

So Duncan's first lesson for Stephenson is not to give Simon anything up, even on the outside, because video analysis has shown that Simon has an ability to get to these pitches, especially if he doesn't think he has to worry about the inside.

"First time up," Duncan advises, "I would pound this guy [inside] with every pitch."

On it goes like this for about ten minutes, Duncan providing Stephenson with a concise MapQuest on how to get past each Cubs hitter. Stephenson listens intently; he wants to do well. But Duncan has had such meetings with Stephenson before, when he seemed to be listening. La Russa has had some as well. And then . . .

It came to a head in July, after Stephenson gave up a home run and double to the Dodgers' Hideo Nomo—a pitcher, for God's sake—out of what Duncan termed sheer "carelessness": You can't simply roll it out there even if it is the *pitcher.* Stephenson was demoted from the starting rotation and sent to the bullpen. He was indignant, blaming poor run support and lousy defense for his misfortune.

La Russa was indignant at Stephenson's indignation. In a closed-door meeting, he adopted the increasingly frequent role of psychiatrist, telling Stephenson that the only way he could be an effective major-league pitcher—get back to the groove of 2000—would be to concentrate better and stop blaming everyone around him for his problems. La Russa complimented his fearlessness, his conviction that "whoever the guy is, you can pitch to him." He liked that Stephenson had the guts to keep hitters inside conscious, as many pitchers don't like to throw inside, for the very reason that they may hit someone. But, La Russa pointed out, Stephenson had started challenging people at the wrong time with that fastball of his, which never rose above the high eighties. Like Brian Giles of the Pirates, whom Stephenson treated as if he hadn't hit a single dinger this season, when he'd hit thirteen of them and was the ultimate aggressive fastball hitter. Then there was Stephenson's general failure to respect the bottom third of an opponent's order, feeding them too many fastballs on the plate, giving these guys an undeserved feast. He had been careless all season long about keeping the ball down, and La Russa advised him rather strenuously to stop worrying about defense and run support and to pay attention to the only thing he could control: his pitching.

The result was a 3–1 win against the Braves in early August; Stephenson kept the ball down and went all the way into the eighth. Five days later, he gave up only one earned run in eight innings against the Pirates. Based on those recent performances, it's likely that he *can* keep the ball down. He *can* use his fastball to set up the curve and change, hit those edges. He *can* go inside. Duncan still believes in him—tells him as much—as the meeting nears an end.

"If you concentrate and really just get locked in out there, you'll pitch good against these guys. If you get careless—that's what they are—they're mistake hitters. And we need a game, so get your game face on and be ready to stick it in their ass."

As Stephenson heads out the door, Duncan leaves him with one final thought: He reminds him that the most successful pitchers are not mistake free—because every pitcher makes mistakes—but are those who don't fall apart after they do make one.

"And hey, don't get frustrated out there if something doesn't go right. Don't lose your concentration and make a couple of bad pitches before you get it back."

III

THE PLAYERS finish up batting practice around 5:45 P.M. and travel back through the tunnel to the clubhouse. As a matter of league rule, the clubhouse is now closed to outsiders, so none of the players find themselves hopelessly outnumbered by the wolf pack of print and television and radio reporters who were there before batting practice. Back in the clubhouse, they immediately pump up the sound system, and they continue to loiter, loose and carefree. But the music soon gives way to two meetings. The first is for the relievers, in Duncan's office. It's run by Marty Mason, in an Alabama treble of such perfect down-home pitch, you long for the Confederacy even if you're from the North. The information is largely the same as what Duncan went over with Stephenson but with a slightly different emphasis. Relievers, unlike starters, almost never face a batter more than once, so they are much more inclined to go with their strength rather than try to whittle away at a hitter's weakness. La Russa is there, his chair straddling the open door that connects his office to Duncan's. He says little, except when it comes to Aramis Ramirez in the sixth hole and the terrible price you might pay for giving him a breaking ball in the strike zone: "He'll launch it."

The meeting is followed quickly by a gathering of the hitters in La Russa's office. Hitting coach Mitchell Page goes through the Cubs pitchers, beginning with Mark Prior. "First thing you gotta do, boys, lay off the high fastball," he offers, admittedly easier said than done. The meeting has more of a war room feel as hitters trade their own intelligence back and forth. The consensus on Prior's fastball, as Orlando Palmeiro puts it, is that it's "sneaky," exploding in on you at the last moment. The hitters also trade tidbits about the Cubs relievers. How Joe Borowski, the closer, isn't above a back-door slider; how the lefty set-up man, Mike Remlinger, has no fear when it comes to his changeup and will throw it in any situation to any hitter, righty or lefty. La Russa speaks only at the end, urging his hitters to work up the pitch count on Prior, so Dusty Baker is pushed earlier than he would like to where La Russa wants him: the tender meat of the Cubs' bullpen.

"It's the end of August. I don't think Baker is going to let Prior throw a bunch of pitches like he would at the end of September. Make him work for every out he gets."

The players trickle out of La Russa's office after the meeting. There's now about a half hour left until the start of Game 1. The music ignites again, "Shake Your Tailfeathers" from the soundtrack of *Bad Boys II* spewing fury and testosterone. Jeff Fassero sits in front of his locker, reading the paper. Tino Martinez, so struggling at the plate in the shadow of his former Yankee self that it's become a perpetual cloak, adjusts his uniform pants. Scott Rolen emerges from the shower, then goes to the indoor cage for one final run-through. Jim Edmonds, typical of his Hollywood roam in center field, dons a series of bright red wristbands like strips of neon. From the two television consoles that hang from the ceiling of the locker area, video loops show Prior's most recent outing against the Cardinals in early July. Bo Hart watches raptly, so hungry for improvement, joined by Eddie Perez, who gets there just in time to see the three-run bomb he banged off Prior in the second. "That was so much fun!" he says, then trots off with a beatific smile.

With twelve minutes to game time, after most of the players and coaches have already left for the dugout, La Russa puts on his uniform shirt and pants and begins his ritual. He closes his closet door. He neatens up his desk, moving wayward papers into right angles. He gathers up the information that he has carefully inscribed on the fronts and backs of several scorecards: the matchups as well as an additional reference guide to the Cubs hitters and how they should be pitched, in little two- or three-word capsules. He folds and creases them so they make that perfect fit in his back pocket. He adjusts his cap. He turns off the lights. And then he strides out toward the dugout and Game 1.

4

THE PEEKER

● ● ● KENNY LOFTON leads off for the Cubs. He is what he is: a sneaky pest with good speed and a veteran hitter's instinct for survival. No shame in simply staying with the ball and slapping it to the opposite field for itsy-bitsy singles if that's the best a pitch can offer. A single gold chain nestles neatly under the collar of his gray uniform. "CHICAGO" wraps across his shirt in bright and muscular red. His hands, swathed in white gloves, heft a black bat. He gently taps it on the plate as if it's a divining rod in search of water —plentiful abundance around that plate if he can just find it.

Cheers go up from the thousands of Chicago fans who have made the pilgrimage for the three-game series and taken over downtown St. Louis like Cossacks in Cubbie Blue, overrunning hotels and restaurants with their meaty fists and happy beer bellies and this-is-our-year swagger. Unlike his teammate Sammy Sosa, who enters the batter's box with a puffed-up presence so grand he might as well be the pope, Lofton draws no particular attention to himself when he settles in. It's more a glum matter-of-factness, a business, the business of batting—*hey, been there, done that*—with just the slightest oregano of arrogance, the implication that he knows he has Garrett Stephenson's number and has no reason to get all herky-jerky and hyperventilated.

The first pitch is a fastball on the far side of the plate. It's a smart pitch: not too fat, not too fine. It carries the outside corner for a strike as Lofton looks it in with curiosity, as if a car of make and model he's not sure he has seen before has just sped by him. Dave Duncan has to be smiling inwardly, because it abides by his belief in the power of the first-pitch strike. Of all the pitches in a given at-bat, it is by far the most important, and Duncan has more than merely sentiment on his side. In addition to his binders full of pitching charts, he does his copious computer analyses, inputting every pitch a Cardinal throws to see what kind of predictors emerge beyond hunch and gut instinct. He's looking for trend lines, just like mutual fund managers look for reliable indicators of a stock's performance. Based on that analysis, the value of a first-pitch strike is so overwhelming he calls it "almost goofy." During spring training, Duncan trotted out his theory of the value of strike 1 for pitchers. To make the point, he was equipped with statistics for several past Cardinals seasons in which he had tracked each op-posing batter faced, roughly 6,100 per year. His analysis showed that in 2002, for example, Cardinals hurlers threw first-pitch strikes 59 percent of the time. Of that number, 17 percent were put in play, with the actual yield of hits equivalent to a batting average of .059.

The first pitch also ignites the game's smallest subplot and one of its more intricate ones—what La Russa is fond of calling "the war" of each at-bat. As Duncan's stats demonstrate, who draws blood first forms a remarkable barometer of who will win this lit-tle war: a pitcher who goes 1 and 0 now peering at a plate with a smaller-than-ever margin of error because he doesn't want to fall even further behind, and a hitter who goes 1 and 0 getting pumped because nibbling has just been curtailed. Like everything else in baseball, the barometer isn't foolproof. There are exceptions that define greatness, pitchers such as Greg Maddux and Curt Schilling, who still have the confidence to work the wisps of the plate even when the count is 1 and 0, and hitters such as Pujols, who even when they fall behind 0 and 1, refuse to chase in the face of a strike zone suddenly widened by the pitcher's advantage.

Duncan has come to conclude that many pitchers pitch back-ward, try to be too *fine* on that first throw—aim for something per-fect on the elusive black of the plate—because they think that they have some room to maneuver with a virginal count. But once they get behind, they have no choice but to come with something too fat over the plate. In Duncan's experience, the exact opposite approach is the most effective: Don't be too fine. Instead, use a portion of the plate to get that first strike. If the hitter puts it into play, so be it. If he doesn't, the pitcher still has an enormous advantage: Now he can nibble at the black without pinpoint precision, as hitters, made nervous by their 0 and 1 deficit, are far more inclined to go after pitches that aren't strikes.

Baseball is a game primarily of firsts in terms of who wins and who loses: getting the first strike in an at-bat, getting the first out of an inning, scoring the game's first run to gain momentum and tempo. Like Duncan, La Russa believes fervently in the importance of firsts, but the game's first first doesn't comfort him. He's nervous, anxious for a zero here because the worst thing you can give a pitcher the caliber of Mark Prior is an early lead, the aura of intimidation that surrounds him to begin with now a full galaxy. So he's obsessively watching Stephenson to see whether he's doing what he needs to do, not being some heavy-metal rocker out there with an instrument that's strictly acoustic.

In the dugout, La Russa stations himself near the entrance to the tunnel, so far to the left that he sometimes spills over into the concrete square reserved for the cameras that televise games locally on Fox SportsNet. He is standing alone, with a hand on the railing of the steps that lead up to the field. Some managers like company during a game. They like to chat back and forth, if nothing else to deflect the anxiety onto someone who at least can provide a little companionship. Joe Torre of the Yankees has had his Pagliacci, Don Zimmer, for years. Bobby Cox of the Braves has pitching coach Lee Mazzone, their jowls working in unison. But except for the occasional whisper to Duncan, La Russa refuses such relief. Instead, he occupies a self-imposed foxhole, big enough for only one, in which he alone must fend off all present and future crises. Even after one pitch, his face is clenched and closed off.

With the count 0 and 1 to Lofton, he's not inspecting only Stephenson for signs of which persona is on the mound tonight. He's also eying Lofton, the pesty part of Lofton, the shameless part of

Lofton that would steal first if it were legal. Lofton isn't above trying a bunt to third base. Both Duncan and Marty Mason discovered the trend of it when they broke down the Secret Weapon's
DVD, so La Russa is making sure that Rolen is sufficiently guarding against it at third. La Russa also knows that Lofton, like most
hitters, is a creature of irresistibility, who can be brought down
through his chase hole—the spot he thinks he can get to but can't.
La Russa hopes that Stephenson will recall Duncan's advice to go
above the strike zone for Lofton's chase hole—the high fastball.
When the next pitch is a fastball in, La Russa is encouraged even
though it's a ball. It's still a smart place to spot a pitch, particularly
effective against hitters such as Lofton, who has a tendency to
make a big fuss when the ball is inside. He makes no bones about
the indignity, glaring at the pitcher, beseeching the umpire with a
look—*Did you see what they just did to me?*—his histrionics guaranteeing only that he's going to see even more pitches inside than
usual for the very reason he makes such a show.

Stephenson throws another fastball, this time down and away.
La Russa thinks that the location is good, *really good,* another
smart pitch: three in a row, if you're keeping score at home. Lofton
simply slaps at it, stays with it just enough to hit an easy two-hopper
to short.

La Russa does say repeatedly that baseball is a cruel game.
Much of that has to do with decisions you make as a manager that
seem like no-brainers and still devolve into disasters. But the ball
itself is sometimes cruel, not simply a benign layering of twine and
rubber and leather but a little organism with a perverse love of tur-
moil: *Where can I go to create the most disruption? Who needs to be
tested right away?*

Edgar Renteria usually plays shortstop. He was a Gold Glover
last year and will probably get another one this year, so this would
be a routine play for him. But two days before, after a grinding 3–0
win against the Phillies in which he made several wonderful defensive plays, he hobbled into the clubhouse. It was suddenly cleared
of all outsiders, even reporters on tight deadlines—an unheard-of
step. In the dignity of privacy, Rolen and Edmonds each wrapped

an arm around their teammate and helped him out of the shower; wrenching back spasms prevented him from walking by himself. By now he has partially recovered, but he's still unavailable.

In Renteria's place at shortstop is Miguel Cairo, a consequence of consequences, as Cairo, a valuable utility infielder, has little experience at short. Which is why the ball determinedly seeks him out on the very first play of the game. It bounces directly to Cairo, and he scoops it into his glove. But his throw to Tino Martinez at first is off target, lacking assurance. It comes to Martinez on a hop far more devious than the one that settled into Cairo's glove. Although he's thirty-three, Lofton still has a sweet set of wheels. He's hustling, really hustling, his hustle suggesting what it usually suggests in players who have had rocky mood-swing careers regardless of prodigious talent and impressive numbers: It's the free-agency year, and good behavior has far more rewards than American Express. Martinez tries to keep his right foot pinned to the corner of the bag as he fields the hop. But he can't.

Lofton is safe at first. Instead of one away in the top of the first, there is only potential chaos in the top of the first.

Lofton is nowhere close to the golden season he had with the Indians in 1996, when he led the league with seventy-five stolen bases, but he is still a threat to steal second. He's already stolen nine bases since he came over to the Cubs in mid-July, and the mere suggestion of it sets all sorts of plot subtexts in motion. He's jittery at first, not a huge lead. One arm is folded, and the other hangs between his knees. He's being coquettish, a professional flirt, what he may *not* do as important as what he *may* do: *Will he or won't he?*

The plot turns on the speed of Stephenson's delivery to the plate. Joe Pettini, the bench coach, is timing it with a stopwatch, and the results are pretty good. It's taking 1.3 seconds from the start of Stephenson's wind-up to Chris Widger's getting the ball in his catcher's mitt. It's the Maginot Line of base stealing, 1.3 seconds or less making it difficult for a gifted runner to steal with any smugness.

He's going to have to factor in at least six other complexities:

the arm strength of the catcher, the quality of the pitcher's move to first whether it's a snap throw or long-armed, the hardness or softness of the base path, whether the pitcher is altering the timing of his delivery from one pitch to the next, whether the hitter is right-handed or left-handed—since a left-handed hitter shields the catcher's line of sight to second—and the pitcher's repertoire—since a forkballer or sinkerballer forces the catcher to drop his mitt low for the pitch and therefore have a more difficult throw.*

If video is the greatest revolution in baseball over the past twenty years, the running game is its greatest crushed revolution. In the 1960s and 1970s, Wills and Lou Brock each stole more than a hundred bases in a season. Into the 1980s, when La Russa was cutting his teeth as a manager, Rickey Henderson stole a hundred or more bases in three different seasons. All over both leagues, good base stealers were running wild, out of control, taking second base like their birthright. Except against teams managed by Gene Mauch. Legendary for his strategy, acclaimed by his peers as the shrewdest tactician to grace the dugout in modern times, Mauch had gotten tired of the base-stealing revolution; he became determined to quell it once and for all.

La Russa saw that Mauch's pitchers weren't going to the plate in what was the standard threshold then: 1.4 or 1.5 seconds. They were going even more quickly—1.2 or 1.1 seconds—in an effort to make stealing second a far more risky venture. La Russa also noticed that Mauch had gone a clever step further. Good base stealers try to pick up a pitcher's pattern in his delivery—the so-called mind switch—the moment when his attention shifts from the base

---

* Altering the playing surface to dampen fast runners and base stealers is not nearly as common today as it was when La Russa first came up as a player in the early 1960s. When the Dodgers came to town, groundskeepers would give the dirt in front of the plate and on the base paths between first and second a healthy soaking to make it soupy and beachlike, to help prevent Maury Wills and Willie Davis from simply slapping the ball high to get on first and then stealing second. Conversely, the Dodgers packed their own surface to resemble concrete, to make it as easy as possible for Wills and Davis to slap the ball high to get on first and then steal second.

runner on first to the batter at the plate. Base runners are taught to look for it, and the great base stealers, such as Henderson, had developed a feel for it that let them get a good jump and steal regardless of how quick the delivery.

So Mauch worked with his pitchers to break their patterns. One way was to simply hold on to the ball or make a throw over to first or step off the rubber. All this made it more difficult for a base runner to pick up the mind switch, and eventually, Mauch countered the base-stealing revolution. La Russa copied Mauch's tactics. So did other managers, and by the 1990s, the stolen base had lost much of its impact as an offensive weapon.

Lofton obviously knows that Stephenson isn't going to display an easily recognizable pattern. Also, Lofton is a "peeker," and "peekers" do what the name implies. They are voyeurs—alleyway window watchers—peeking from first at the catcher as he puts down his signs and trying to figure out the one for the curve ball, a better pitch to steal on than the fastball because it takes longer to get to the plate. Which means that from the dugout, La Russa is instructing Widger to put on all sorts of decoy signs to make sure that the one for the curve ball is sufficiently buried.

Lofton continues to flirt off of first. He's still jittery: *Will he or won't he?* But he isn't going anywhere. Stephenson is maintaining the essential benchmark of delivering to the plate in 1.3 seconds. As a further impediment, Stephenson is also throwing fastballs to the number two hitter Ramon Martinez instead of slower off-speed stuff, the last a nasty jam that he hits harmlessly to Kerry Robinson in right field for the first out.

It brings up Sosa, who, much like Stephenson, has been suffering from a bipolar disorder this season. When the Cards faced him in May, it was pretty clear to Duncan and Mason, watching the DVD on him, that he was going through *something*. He was flinching on curve balls as if he were afraid he might get hit, and he began to develop a sizable hole in his swing on pitches down and away.

To La Russa, the explanation was embedded in human nature. In May, Sosa had gotten beaned by a pitch, his batting helmet splintering like a dropped glass of water. It was clear that he had gotten tentative after that, with good reason. Few things in sports are more terrifying than a pitch hurtling at a hitter's head with no time for reflexes, the incident only reinforcing to La Russa the urgency of the commissioner's office to stop ignoring the increasing problem and do something about it, such as an automatic three-week suspension for the pitcher involved.

Sosa had become intimidated, as every hitter in the history of the game has become intimidated, after such a frightening moment. He suffered a lapse of courage, and the question was how long it would last, since La Russa has seen such varied reactions: It could be an at-bat, a game, a series, a season, even, in some cases, an entire career.

When Sosa drives the ball into center and right center, it means that he's getting to balls away. But after he got hit, he became reluctant to dive over the plate to get to them. One of his hitting strengths is good plate coverage, but he was almost turning from the ball, as Duncan and Mason had discovered. Over the past several weeks, however, the old Sosa has re-emerged. It's the one who "sticks his nose in there," as La Russa puts it, staying on the ball wherever it is thrown, once again showing the courage that all great hitters possess. The result has been thirteen home runs in July and another seven in August to give him thirty for the season leading up to the three-game series. He's also made an adjustment: He's moved his stance closer to the plate because once the word was out that Sammy wasn't the same Sammy anymore — couldn't get to it anymore unless it was down the pipe where anybody could hit it — he had been fed a steady diet of pitches away.

He gets three fastballs from Stephenson. All of them are high. The count goes to 3 and 0. But that's okay, because Sosa has a chase hole up, and there's also no point giving him something in his wheelhouse that he can turn on. Widger sets up outside on the 3-0 count. Sammy, still being Sammy, has the green light to swing. He hits the pitch with power, but he gets under it a little bit, and the result is a high fly to Robinson in right for the second out.

Lofton is still at first when Moises Alou comes up in the cleanup spot with two outs. Lofton has been effectively hog-tied there, enabling Stephenson to focus on Alou and try to avoid the first-pitch pitfalls that have made him so dangerous. Stephenson comes in with a fastball. Alou goes for it in his unbridled aggressiveness. He gets a swing on it, a pretty good swing—a damn good one, actually. He fouls it straight back, meaning that he missed driving it by a matter of only inches. Stephenson throws another fastball, this one better located on the inside. Alou gets a swing on it, a pretty good swing—a damn good one, actually. He hits it sharply to third. Rolen backhands it, his reflex action so sublimely quick, it seems like a natural extension of him—the way the rest of us pick up a fork to eat—and makes one of his lightning-bolt throws to first to end the top of the first.

It's a twelve-pitch inning for Stephenson. Every pitch he has thrown has been a fastball, which could be a recipe for implosion if he keeps it up and doesn't mix his pitches. And maybe it means that not a word of what La Russa and Duncan have preached to him all season has sufficiently spread through his 6'5" frame. But Stephenson, like many pitchers, tends to rely almost exclusively on the fastball the first time through the lineup. And La Russa has no problem with that, particularly if it means that he's using the fastball as a setup for something else, lulling the Cubs batters into complacency, getting them to chirp up and down the gossipy line of the dugout that all he's throwing out there is fastballs, only to shut them up with off-speed.

In every game that La Russa manages, he conducts a running conversation with himself, a *Waiting for Godot* dialogue to keep the pressure on and make sure that he doesn't miss anything, mining for gold even though it's the top of the first, because sometimes, it's those little nuggets that can win a game. Lofton didn't go anywhere, which is good. Sosa's ego on 3 and 0 caused him to try to drive an outside fastball, which is good. Stephenson threw first-pitch strikes to three of the four batters he faced, which is very good. And he likes what he is seeing from Stephenson, the fearlessness and big balls folding into a pitcher tonight, glimpses of that 16 and 9 season in 2000 returning.

Between halves of the inning, La Russa retires to the dugout bench. He sits by himself. He's still nervous, because he's always nervous and his patented glower is not some pose. The stakes are high in every game, since one game can prove the difference between the playoffs in October or golf in October. The best managers—the ones La Russa has modeled himself after—ground their way through every at-bat, unlike some others he knew who believed that their job really didn't begin until the last three innings, when moves became more readily apparent. La Russa's inability to smile also goes to the very nature of the game: capricious, mean, sneaking up on you with accumulated vengeance if you let down even for a moment. "Unless you pay it respect, it's gonna spank you, and the fact is that even when you do pay it respect, it's gonna spank you, just not as often or as hard," he says. The feeling he wants after every game, whether it's a 1–0 win or a 10–0 loss, is that everything he had was left in the dugout—he had nothing else to give. It's his nature, what comes with the territory when you spend so much of your life alone in a dark and subterranean place. But whatever fear he feels, whatever anxieties envelop him, there's a supreme confidence to the decisions he makes, probably because there's no way he could have survived for almost a quarter century if he weren't.

It was different at the beginning. When he started his managing career with the White Sox in the middle of the 1979 season, the prevailing sentiment was that he had been hired by owner Bill Veeck because he came cheap; his only experience was a little more than a year of managing in the minors with Knoxville and Des Moines. He was thirty-four years old and scared for his life. Self-doubt rattled through him—*Do I really know what I'm doing?*—and he became a whipping boy for the radio broadcast duo of Harry Caray and Jimmy Piersall, who offered the almost daily critique that he managed with his head squarely up his ass. In the insular world of baseball, where newness was anathema and crustiness a work of art, La Russa was a typical Veeckian choice, playing so far against type that he could have been sold as a novelty at the concession stand. His general manger, Rollie Hemond, tried to warn La Russa that few in the game were rooting for him.

"You have five things going against you," Hemond told him. "You're young. You're handsome. You're smart. You're getting your law degree. You have a nice family—

"I don't think you're going to last very long."

Given that La Russa was also bilingual in English and Spanish, as well as a strict vegetarian in a church of meat eaters, there may well have been seven strikes against him. La Russa also from the outset showed a streak of defiance, stubbornness in the face of a second guess. Early on in his career against the Yankees, he tried a hit-and-run in the top of the ninth with a man on first and no outs and the White Sox losing by a run. Goose Gossage was in his prime then. He threw 95-mile-an-hour fire, fire that exploded high, making it impossible, in La Russa's estimation, for a hitter to successfully bunt the runner over to second. Few things in baseball are more difficult than trying to bunt with heat like that rising up on you. So he went with a hit-and-run. The runner on first tipped off the play with his lead: The Yankees pitched out and nailed him, killing any chance to tie the game. Predictably, Caray and Piersall went nuts in the broadcast booth. Within the same series he had the exact same situation and did the exact same thing: a hit-and-run that also failed when the batter popped out. Caray and Piersall went nuts again, prompting Charley Lau, then the hitting instructor for the Yankees, to remark, "I don't know if you have enough brains to be a manager, but you have the balls."

La Russa finished that first season of managing in 1979 by guiding the White Sox to a .500 record, twenty-seven wins and twenty-seven losses. It was a nice performance given that the team was in disarray, still feeling the effects of the single worst promotion in baseball in the considerable history of them, the so-called Disco Demolition night. Intended as a gentle condemnation of disco in which fans were encouraged to bring disco records for destruction in between games of a doubleheader, it turned instead into a full-scale riot. Thousands of White Sox fans poured onto the field and began to tear it up. Genuine revulsion of disco no doubt had something to do with how the fans reacted. But after twenty years of watching the Sox without a pennant in the grime and gloom of old Comiskey Park, where the sightlines in certain places were worse than in the Cook County jail, this was their liberation. Sharp-edged vinyl discs were lasered across the field, perhaps intended only to insult disco but injuring many fans in the process. The collected waft of marijuana became a nuclear cloud over the South Side. The White Sox were forced to forfeit the second game, and soon La Russa was put in to finish out the rest of the season.

When it was over, Hemond made a point of taking La Russa to the World Series: the Pirates versus the Orioles. It was the first World Series that La Russa had ever attended, and he suddenly found himself in the company of all these men, all these *baseball men,* who knew more about the game that he could ever hope to know. They all rode in a bus together from the hotel to the game. They took the same bus back to the hotel afterward and congregated for a party. There were managers—Gene Mauch and Sparky Anderson and Whitey Herzog—and gun-slinger scouts—Hugh Alexander of the Phillies and Bobby Mattick of the Blue Jays. On the bus back from every game, they were already taking a blow-torch to how Earl Weaver had managed the Orioles and Chuck Tanner had managed the Pirates—*Weaver gave Flanagan too early a hook when he took him out after six down only by a run; Tanner put his ass on the line when he brought in Blyleven in relief for four*—evisceration, condemnation, and, of course, *what they would have done instead.* Nobody, nothing escaped their attention. They were brutal in their critiques. They were passionate, so unbelievably passionate, the game their animus, and the sound of it to La Russa, with his fifty-four games of major-league managerial experience, was gorgeous. "I mean, it was beautiful baseball," he remembered, that favorite phrase again. He was in awe, but he was also slightly terrified. If they were doing this to Weaver and Tanner, two legends who between them had won 1,871 regular-season games, what would they do to him if he ever made it to the postseason—hardly a legend—and even worse, *a vegetarian, a vegetarian with a law degree?* He honestly wasn't sure he could stand up to the scrutiny.

But as critical as the grand masters were, many of them were also benevolent. Managers such as Anderson and Tanner and Dick Williams and Billy Martin and John McNamara adopted an almost paternalistic stance toward La Russa—as did Earl Weaver, after a probationary year to see if the neophyte had any real clue. On the field before a game, when La Russa started in with his incessant riff of strategic questions, they took the time to answer. Along with the steady patience of new White Sox owner, Jerry Reinsdorf, who stood by La Russa as the team continued to chug and churn in the early 1980s, he somehow survived.

In 1983, he did arrive in the Promised Land—he took the White Sox to the playoffs for the first time in his career, against the Orioles. No matter how kind the grand masters were, he also knew everything he did would still be subject to their not-so-tender postgame party mercies. He emerged with an undesirable conclusion, a loss of three games to one to Baltimore. In the last game, he made a typically controversial balls-to-the-wall decision by taking his starter, Britt Burns, into the tenth, when he finally faded, and the Orioles broke through a drought of nine scoreless innings for three runs and the victory.

But even in the aftermath of his loss, La Russa found something valuable within himself. He realized that he had passed a test, withstood the scrutiny of those he cared about the most, by traveling deeply into the psychic tunnel of the dugout, so locked on the game that he had been oblivious to everything else—the fans in the stands, the millions watching on TV, even the very baseball men he knew were riding back to the postgame party to machete his every move. *Burns? How could you stay with Burns in the tenth? What's he thinking there? It's a damn good thing this guy got his law degree, because he's gonna need it.* He wasn't brilliant or close to brilliant— he didn't have every answer no matter how much he tried to act outwardly as though he did—but he had achieved the crucial art of hearing only his own voice. He learned that the variables of the game can overcome you, overwhelm you, if you don't figure out a way to slow it down. He developed a catch phrase for himself, a way of mental discipline:

Slow it down by staying ahead of it to stay on top of it.

It was the mantra he repeated to himself after every half inning. The mantra he used then and the mantra he uses now. *Slow it down by staying ahead of it to stay on top of it.* A minimum of seventeen times a game. The dual responsibility of focus on the present and anticipation of the future, sometimes playing out scenarios a full inning or two ahead so nothing will take him by surprise.

He pulls the little cheat sheets from his back pocket and looks at them even though they can't give him much advice so early in the game. Thoughts travel through his mind in those little Godot blips.

Does what he normally does, which is throw a lot of fastballs early . . .

Showed good command . . .

Got the ball inside good . . .

Away pretty good . . .

There should be some relief in those blips; they suggest that Stephenson's got game tonight, the head rejecting the heart. But La Russa feels no respite, because of what awaits the Cards: the most talented pitcher in baseball right now.

5

THE PITCHER'S TALE

I

● ● ● IT'S MARK PRIOR, standing on those thick redwood legs, peering at the plate with that blank stare of beneath-me contempt. But Prior's stuff is what gives La Russa the most trouble. Because Prior has the stuff — first and foremost a nasty fastball with what hitters call "late life." It has a little extra *pop* at the end that makes a really good fastball far more than simply a function of how fast it measures off the radar gun.

Orlando Palmeiro, who spot-starts and makes a careful study of pitchers, will tell you that there are some fastball pitchers who barely get out of the eighties. But that *pop,* that little point underneath the exclamation, makes them difficult to hit. But Prior *does* throw in the nineties. And he brings it smoothly and effortlessly all the way up from those redwoods, like the steady spout of water from a fountain where you can't quite grasp the mechanics of how it can flow so easily yet so forcefully.

And it's not only his fastball. He's got that curve with the nice tight break. If he ever gets that changeup going — the last dab of paint in crafting the perfect portrait of a power pitcher — the demands on hitters will become impossibly intense, forced to respond to the middle nineties on one pitch and the low eighties on the next, without knowing when the downshift is coming and having four-tenths of a second to react to it.

Kerry Robinson enters the batting box to begin the bottom half of the first. He's overmatched here, as is every Cardinal tonight except the great Pujols. Prior gets the sign from Paul Bako. Prior shows no emotion—not a speck, no anticipation, no excitement —just the machinery of his motion, exquisite, almost without exertion.

He comes with a fastball to begin the night's journey. It sails high to give Robinson the comfort of a 1-and-0 advantage in the count. In his foxhole, La Russa paces back and forth a little bit. There's a distinct pattern to it: three paces out, three paces in, three paces sideways. Part of it is habit, and part of it is a highly developed sense of superstition, the belief that any break in the routine will bring a hex. Early in his career with the White Sox, he had to wear a flak jacket as the result of a death threat. The threat passed, but La Russa wore the jacket for another month because his team was winning.

There isn't much to learn from that first pitch. But the fact that it was high might indicate that Prior, despite his outward presence, is acutely aware of what's at stake in this series and is maybe overthrowing a little bit, a heart that does beat madly under pressure. So La Russa lets himself hope that maybe this first pitch bodes poorly for Prior, just like Garrett Stephenson's first pitch of the game, a fastball strike, was a good omen.

But Prior settles down after that. He comes in with two nasty fastballs down and away in the zone to push Robinson into a 1-and-2 hole. He comes with a fastball, his fourth in a row. It's high and inside; Robinson takes a cut at it and manages to foul it off. Prior comes with a fifth straight fastball, clearly thinking that he can dominate Robinson with his strength: no need to break up the pattern with anything off-speed. It jams Robinson. He puts a swing on it, but there's no authority to it, and the result is an easy liner near the bag at second for the first out.

It brings up Bo Hart, second in the ersatz lineup that injuries have forced on La Russa. Hart approaches the plate with an infectious earnestness, bouncing and bounding in: *Let's go, let's go!* The Cardinals fans, red-soaked in their own regalia to counterbalance the machine gun nests of Cubs supporters, love him for it, live through him; he treats his at-bats as they might if they were suddenly told to get in there and hit major-league pitching, grab a stick of wood and plug their ass off. His uniform is usually dirty and his body outstretched, diving for something, getting to something, fighting off something. Now the Cards fans cover him with cheers as he arrives at the plate, bellowing his name: *Hart.*

Prior throws a curve that catches him looking for strike 1. It's obvious that the Cubs have been studying their own video compilations; this is an area where Hart has been having increasing trouble. He swings through an inside-and-low fastball to make the count 0 and 2, and now he's in baseball hell, so helpless and lonely, the plate metastasizing because of the hitter's desperate impulse to flail at anything that might remotely get him out of his hole. Prior can feel the kill shot. He throws a curve that buckles down and away on the outside corner. In the parlance of the players, it's a *filthy* pitch. Hart has no choice but to swing at it.

He actually gets something on it. He hits it hard, and it skips past Prior's foot and past second base for a single. It's a sweet piece of hitting, a suggestion that Hart's War—his battle against the curve—will someday be won. Prior threw filth at him, and he spanked it right back.

Up comes Pujols, who takes two fastballs for an immediate 0-2 count. Normally, this *would be* baseball hell all over again, but neither Pujols nor Prior is normal, so the at-bat has just begun to have narrative. There is no better matchup in all of baseball right now: the perfect storm. Certainly, La Russa is eager for Pujols to emerge as the hero, but even he can't help but relish the mano a mano between the two, the beautiful game between pitcher and hitter.

There is Prior, as if he's been at it for a decade—in on the black, out on the black, up on the black, low on the black—trying to tempt with something nasty and offering nothing plump. As his performance shows tonight, he has exceptional location. He works both sides of the plate with his fastball. His curve, because of its tightness, doesn't hang like a fat apple on a tree. And he's smartly situational with it—with a "get me over" breaking ball early in the count for strike 1, and then a bounce-in-the-dirt breaking ball that a hitter will chase with two strikes. He isn't afraid to go inside, as many young pitchers are, either because they fear hitting someone or because they've been burned too many times by those springy aluminum bats that allow high school and college players to send even an inside pitch with authority to the outfield. But what is most prodigious about Prior is his combination of maturity and mechanics. Even before he had thrown a major-league pitch, one ranking had Prior fifth in efficiency after Nolan Ryan, Curt Schilling, Randy Johnson, and Roger Clemens.

As for his maturity, it isn't exactly the serene, modest, old-soul kind. He's cocky as hell, like many young athletes La Russa has seen in recent years who at the first sign of prowess are singled out by parents and coaches and teammates and lose all link to the grace of humility. His maturity has more to do with how he husbands his most precious resource: his arm. The fluidity of his delivery protects it, of course, but so does his attitude, his willingness to throw breaking balls in clutch two-strike situations instead of the more typical alpha-male fastball. Unlike most young pitchers, he does not believe that the solution to all problems is more juice on the ball. For now, his cockiness serves instead of impedes, never a sure thing in baseball.

Pujols also has an uncommon maturity, hitting as though he's been at it for a decade, with his own disciplined command of the strike zone, refusing temptation, trying to force Prior to throw the ball in a meaty part of the plate, where he can drive something with his own mechanically sublime stroke that *launches* the ball off the bat. Pujols comes into Game 1 with his statistical set and the heels of that thirty-game hitting streak:

G	AB	R	H	2B	3B	HR	RBI	BB	SO	SB	AVG.
125	473	110	171	43	1	34	108	54	50	1	.362

Prior comes into Game 1 with his statistical set, which has only gotten better as the season has progressed. In the last four games, he's given up two runs in thirty-one innings:

W	L	ERA	G	GS	SHO	IP	H	R	ER	HR	BB	SO	Opp. Avg.
12	5	2.54	23	23	1	159.2	134	55	45	11	37	179	.225

Pujols so far has Prior's number: unafraid and unabashed. He simply tags him, with a .556 average against him and two home runs. Prior, who considers Clemens and Ryan his role models, pitchers notorious for going up and in, is not about to back down by overtly pitching around him, an intentional walk without making it look intentional. Given that both players are still in their twenties, La Russa can sense the beginning of something memorable. "It's gonna be a war," was the description he once again used. There was a crease of excitement in his voice as he said it—not simply a manager's appreciation but also a fan's appreciation—something to look forward to in the way that DiMaggio versus Feller and Mays versus Gibson and Aaron versus Drysdale were something to look forward to, moments when the eight other players on the field might as well return to the dugout so they too can have the joy of watching.

So Pujols isn't going to wilt on the 0 and 2—go away with some halfhearted slap swing—just as Prior isn't going to wilt on it with some breaking ball in the dirt. Pujols is all steel, and Prior looks more impenetrable than ever. He's not afraid of Pujols—he's not afraid of anyone—which is the way every twenty-three-year-old should be.

You know he's going to bring it. He does bring it. And Pujols puts a swing on it. There is that sweet-sounding *crack* as the ball flies off the bat and launches into right with the speed of expectation. The red-drenched faithful come out of their seats, and so do the blue-drenched faithful, colors colliding all over the stadium. From his corner in the dugout, La Russa bolts forward a few steps, willing it with his eyes and a slight opening of the lips as if what he really wants to do is scream his head off—just bloody *scream* —savoring the prospect of a 2–0 lead in the bottom of the first off Prior, the anticipation on his face the anticipation he's had a million times as a manager when a ball starts off like lightning: Will it *carry?*

It's just a little too much off the end of the bat. Sammy Sosa in right makes the catch as it dies, and all that anticipation gives way to the reality that Jim Edmonds is up with two outs and Hart still on first.

Prior runs the count to 1 and 2. It puts Edmonds at a clear disadvantage, but the count also opens up a small sliver of possibility that La Russa may try to exploit. Because of the count in Prior's favor, La Russa figures that the next pitch will be one of two choices: a high fastball or a curve in the dirt, something out of the strike zone that still induces Edmonds to chase. He's also calculating that with the upper hand in the count, Prior's focus is going to be on Edmonds anyway, not paying attention to whether Hart tries to steal second.

As Prior goes into his wind-up, Hart takes off on La Russa's sign. It's a classic manager strategy, so classic that most managers now routinely look for a steal with two outs, on the theory that it's better to make the third out at second than at the plate. If the ball is a curve out of the strike zone, he'll probably steal it. If it's the high fastball, he probably won't, because of the greater velocity and the quality of Bako's arm. It's an aggressive play to try so early; other managers might wait for the game to settle in a little bit. But for La Russa, it meets the threshold of aggression with common sense. It's a push for a run with two outs in the bottom of the first against a pitcher who has thrown first-pitch strikes to the last three batters he's faced and has been virtually unhittable his last four games. It's the only way to deal with a pitcher this good: be proactive, *make something happen.* If Hart succeeds, he can now score off a single. That's obviously the preferred result. But if Hart is thrown out, it's not the end of the world, because it gives Edmonds a fresh count to start the next inning, a baseball mulligan.

Hart hauls down the line toward second. He's gotten a good jump and has decent speed. It still hinges on whether La Russa has guessed right that Prior will come after Edmonds with a curve.

It is a curve in the dirt. Edmonds doesn't chase, and Bako doesn't even bother to throw. An inning that seemed dead may have something left to it after all, particularly when Edmonds pushes the count to 3 and 2. Suddenly, Prior needs to make a pitch in the strike zone. He doesn't want to walk Edmonds, not with Scott Rolen up next and capable of hitting something for extra bases with his natural-born power. Because of the count, it's an obvious fastball situation, when a pitcher cornered like this goes to his strength. But Prior elects maturity instead. He comes with a curve, but it's not one of his best ones. It's middle of the strike zone, belt-high. From the dugout, La Russa can see its voluptuousness. It's such a peach for Edmonds, something he can drive. But he's not looking for it. His assumption, the common hitter's assumption, is that Prior is going to come after him with the fastball, which means that he has to adjust. It is virtually impossible to adjust to a fastball when you're looking for a curve, although it is possible to adjust to a curve when you're looking for a fastball. But Edmonds's timing is still off a little bit. He taps a three-hopper to first and the inning is over.

There is no particular tumult in the dugout as the first inning ends. Opportunities in baseball come and go all the time, and dugouts early in the game resemble luncheonettes where all the diners know one another and have formed little cliques and talk amiably until one of them has to go to work, and it may take hours before that even happens. Farthest right are the bench players, who may or may not get into the game. La Russa rarely ventures into this territory, perhaps because he may hear them talking about hunting or cars instead of baseball, which would drive him crazy, just as it drives him crazy when a hitter gets a single and starts chatting it up with the first baseman as if they're distant cousins at a family reunion. He shares the fan's view that it simply doesn't look good: Baseball is meant to be a game of competition, not a game of *whassup dawg?* In the middle are the starting pitchers who won't get into the game because, like an extended Sabbath, these are their days of rest. Stephenson sits on the bench in back, left alone to ponder the next inning, with Simon and Ramirez, the remaining two heads of the monster, due up. As Hart and Edmonds file back into the dugout to end the inning, Stephenson comes out of his reverie, gets his glove, and heads back out to the mound.

II

STEPHENSON THROWS a solid second inning. He gets Simon out on a 1-1 fastball in. It's a good location pitch, banging Simon inside, just like Duncan told him to do. Stephenson comes back from a 3-1 liability to Ramirez for an easy fly out to center. He uses his head against Alex Gonzalez, working him in so he gets antsy that he better protect the inside of the plate, the *inside conscious* thing, then works him outside and fools him so badly that he awkwardly lunges at the ball for a weak foul out.

Prior answers in the bottom of the second with his own 1-2-3 dispensing of Rolen and Tino Martinez and Miguel Cairo in twelve pitches. So far, La Russa hasn't seen anything from Prior that surprises him. He's spotting the ball well. He's showing excellent command. If there's anything that buoys La Russa, it may be the pitch count. Rolen took a seven-pitch at-bat against Prior before flying out. Edmonds went seven pitches in the first before that weak tapper on the stealth curve. Through two innings, Prior has thrown thirty pitches, which would put him right around a hundred in the seventh and maybe force Dusty Baker to consider the purgatory of the bullpen.

La Russa watches Prior with professional admiration. But in emotional terms, Prior gets under his skin. It isn't Prior personally that bothers him but what Prior represents: the young player with the big talent who instead of being circumspect his first few years in the league routinely rises to the media bait so prevalent today and gives answers to *everything,* when he hasn't been around long enough to have the answer to *anything.* He doesn't like the intemperate out-of-the-blue comments Prior makes about the Cardinals, how he hates them. He doesn't think he needs to make comments about Barry Bonds, how he isn't afraid of him, when this is Prior's first full year in the league and this is Bonds's eighteenth. *I think he needs to be doing this a while* is the way La Russa thinks about it when he watches him pitch. It's an old-fashioned comment, said by a manager who believes in circumspection among young players because that's the way he came up: Your first couple of seasons, no matter how good you are, you should be in the corner, shutting up and soaking it in.

Prior can rank up there with Schilling and Maddux and Johnson by the time he's through. With his rare mix of stuff and smarts, he is that dominant. But he's also that young. He has the swagger that is the hubris of youth, taking his invincibility for granted when nobody ever should, receiving too much early attention and slathering in it.

La Russa has seen a procession of pitchers over the years who have broken down and busted out because of arm problems and high expectation problems and personal problems and, perhaps most of all, problems making the distinction between being a thrower and being a pitcher. He has seen young pitchers done in by their need for speed. He has seen pitchers done in by the fear of coming into the majors even though they have major-league-caliber stuff. He has seen young pitchers done in by being rushed to the big leagues, as every team is hungry for pitching. Time after time, he has seen the fall from the stratosphere, the burnup. No player in baseball is more vulnerable than a pitcher, the physical and psychic requirements for sustained success not only monumental but also fragile. The line between success and implosion is so terribly thin. Climbing a sheet of ice has more job security, as evidenced over the past thirty years by the number of number-one picks in the baseball draft who were highly touted, highly ballyhooed pitchers but flamed out without ever getting close to the majors.

And even when you do make it—even when the world seems sun-kissed, as Prior's world seems sun-kissed at this very moment as he mows down the Cardinals through two—something can happen, something you don't expect or could ever imagine. And La Russa knows it vividly.

III

THEY SIGNED HIM right out of high school, and pretty soon afterward the Cardinals brought him into Busch Stadium one Sunday so he could pitch batting practice, get a feel for what the big-league atmosphere was like, let him dress in the clubhouse and wear a uniform that bore his name.

A-N-K-I-E-L. It spread between the shoulder blades like neon. Rick Ankiel was eighteen. And he didn't seem to have a care in the world. The ball simply sizzled. It had that *pop* into the catcher's mitt, that sweet sound of a guy who was simply bringing it. And it moved—*oh, man,* did it move—the way it always seems to move a little bit more when a lefty is pitching. People gathered around the cage to watch this kid who had it. *Sizzle. Pop. Sizzle. Pop.* And nobody dared to say it then, because there's no way you say something like that about an eighteen-year-old kid. But here was *Sandy Koufax.*

He became the Prior of 2000, the kid with the golden arm. He came to the Cardinals, touted as the best young pitcher in the country. He was happy and carefree because there couldn't possibly be anything better than to be pitching in the major leagues at twenty-one. And he had good stuff, just like Prior three years later would have good stuff. He competed his ass off. He had a cool cockiness on the mound. And he was soaking up the game, learning it like a baseball prodigy, just as Prior would later learn it. Working almost exclusively with Mike Matheny as his catcher, he started with a fastball that smoked in the low- to mid-nineties. But then he developed a sinker that moved down and away from right-handed hitters. He threw it about four or five miles per hour slower than his other fastball. It was almost like a batting-practice fastball, but the change of speeds between the two pitches, combined with that sinking movement on the slower one, drove hitters to despair. They didn't know what was coming. They didn't know where it was coming. And they didn't know how fast it was coming. "He had a fastball that jumped up on you and he had that sinker that would get groundballs," La Russa remembered. He also had a curve ball that he wasn't afraid to use as an out pitch. With a little more refinement, the next pitch in the repertoire would have been a more consistent change, just like it would be for Prior.

In their twenty years together, La Russa and Duncan had seen their share of golden pitchers—La Marr Hoyt and Richard Dotson and Tom Seaver with the White Sox, Dennis Eckersley and Dave Stewart and Bob Welch with the A's, bulldog Darryl Kile and the eventual coming of Matt Morris with the Cards. Outward excitement is not something the two men would ever be confused with, Duncan the Quiet Assassin and La Russa always in the dark clench of his internal intensity. Riding in some Hertz Rent-a-Car together on the way to the ballpark five or six hours before game time, they spoke in short syncopation as if the other one weren't there — Duncan making some soft-as-a-feather short-sentence pronouncement as La Russa mumbled off into the windshield — yet both men understanding *exactly* what the other one was saying. They had the kind of relationship that men in baseball develop when they're together eight months out of the year for two decades. They spoke in the Morse code of the game: turbo sinkers, get-me-over curves, middle in versus middle away, nasty shit. They did *know* what each other was thinking without having to articulate it, so why bother to articulate it, and if you had to articulate it, why make some sloppy mess of it.

But when it came to Ankiel, they got excited. They got excited because of what he was doing on the mound, developing that nasty sinker to righties, watching him advance right past thrower to pitcher at such a tender baseball age. They got excited because a lefty like that comes up once in a millennium. He was the *real deal,* and the world, the entire world, was Rick Ankiel's, blowing away the game with that arm born and bred in the Florida sun, able to do whatever he wanted to do whenever he wanted to do it and nothing more Wild West in all of sports, a pitcher on a mound simply blessed with it.

Down the stretch run of the 2000 season in August and September, Stephenson's arm got sore and so did Andy Benes's knee. Pat Hentgen simply wore down. The rotation became a two-man show starring Kile and Ankiel, and Ankiel won his last four games to finish the year 11 and 7.

The Cardinals won the Central division. Their opponent would be the Braves, and before the playoffs started, La Russa made a decision that perhaps haunts him more than any he has ever made.

Aware that he had only two healthy starters and wanting to maximize their appearances, he discovered a potential edge in the play-off schedule. Ankiel needed four days' rest in between starts, but by pitching him in Game 1, he could still pitch Game 4 if necessary, whereas Kile, able to go on three days' rest, could go in Games 2 and 5. It meant giving two pitchers four of the five starts, and it meant that Ankiel would pitch that first game even though Kile, a twenty-game winner and the clear ace of the staff, would ordinarily get that honor. It also meant that Ankiel would be facing Maddux, who had gone 19 and 9 and would be starting his twenty-fourth playoff game, more games than Ankiel had started in his entire life.

Aware also of what that would mean in terms of media exposure and not wanting to subject Ankiel to any more pressure than there already was, he pulled a bait-and-switch with reporters the day before the series began. He had Ankiel do his pitching work and then got him out of the clubhouse. He then told Kile to go into the interview room to take the obligatory questions from the national media, as if he were pitching in Game 1. And Kile played the role perfectly, because although he acted as if he were pitching in Game 1, he never explicitly said that he *was or wasn't*. It was only after the interview ended and the reporters had left for the day that La Russa announced the switch. He did it to protect Ankiel, keep him away from the self-evident questions that are the bane of the professional athlete: *What about the pressure of facing Maddux in Game 1? How does it feel as a rookie to go against the best pitcher in baseball in Game 1? Any butterflies, Rick, any butterflies?* La Russa knew the media were pissed and had a right to be pissed. But his responsibility was to his team. And he had protected Ankiel. He had reduced the pressure on him, so all he needed to do was go out and pitch. Everything seemed to line up in Ankiel's favor, except for Mike Matheny's birthday.

The Thursday before the end of the regular season, Kile had won his twentieth game in San Diego. It was a strange and wild affair. La Russa got thrown out when he protested a balk call, throwing down his glasses and stepping on them, to the disgust of the umpire and the adoration of his players. He was in the runway behind the dugout, trying to manage with the Cards down by a run in the eighth, 6–5. He sent up three pinch hitters and each of them got hits and the Cards went ahead 7–6 and Kile, for the first time in his career, got to the twenty-game-win plateau.

It was a joyous moment, and it lasted until the next morning when La Russa was on his way to the ballpark and got a call from Barry Weinberg—always a bad sign when the trainer called like that. Matheny had cut his hand with a hunting knife he had gotten as a birthday gift. He would be out for the rest of the regular season and the playoffs.

The first playoff game took place in Busch Stadium. Right away, the crowd of nearly 53,000 could tell that something stunning was unfolding.

The Cardinals got *all over* Maddux in the first. Staying back on the ball, they countered the movement on his pitches by hitting to the opposite field: nothing fancy, no heroics trying to pull the ball for a home run. It was one of those days when the ball simply knew where to go, a grounder by Fernando Vina to the right side hitting the bag for a single, a broken-bat single by J.D. Drew, the usually seamless Andruw Jones muffing Edmonds's fly to left center, singles to center and right center by Will Clark and Placido Polanco. The score was 6–0 after the first. *Six runs* against Maddux. Could you believe it? *Six,* what La Russa called the "crooked number" when runs explode on the board rather than the usual trickle.

Ankiel had given up two walks in the top of the first to the Braves, as well as a single, but he got out of the inning when Brian Jordan popped up to Clark in foul territory. He began the second by striking out Reggie Sanders. Walt Weiss doubled on a 1-1 pitch, but then Edgar Renteria made a spectacular play on Javy Lopez's liner and flipped to Vina to turn the double play.

The score was still 6–0 when the Braves came to bat in the top of the third. The line score for that half-inning tells what happened:

Braves 3rd: Maddux walked; Furcal popped to Clark in foul territory; Ankiel threw a wild pitch (Maddux to second); Ankiel threw a wild pitch (Maddux to third); A. Jones walked; Ankiel threw a wild pitch (A. Jones to 2nd); C. Jones was called out on strikes; Gallarraga walked (Maddux scored on wild pitch by Ankiel; A. Jones to 3rd); Jordan singled to Lankford (A. Jones scored, Gallarraga to 2nd); Ankiel threw a wild pitch (Galarraga to 3rd, Jordan to 2nd); Sanders walked; Weiss singled to Lankford (Galarraga scored, Jordan scored, Sanders to 2nd; JAMES REPLACED ANKIEL; Lopez popped to Vina; 4 R, 2 H, 0 E, 2 LOB. Braves 4, Cardinals 6.

With Matheny out with those torn tendons, Carlos Hernandez was catching. He wasn't the defensive force that Matheny was, and he also had a bad back, further limiting his mobility. Matheny's strong and quiet presence had done wonders for Ankiel, as it had for many pitchers. Despite his quiet, self-effacing exterior—no bluster to be seen anywhere—he didn't take crap from pitchers. He knew their foibles and petty pouts, how to a certain degree they were spoiled prodigies who in truth had a far worse idea of what they should throw and when they should throw it than he did. Or sometimes they didn't pay attention to the signs he gave but instead threw whatever the hell they wanted.

There had been slight bouts of wildness before from Ankiel, as in the game against Cincinnati, when he had thrown four wild pitches in five innings, or the time, two months later, when he had thrown three in five innings, once again against the Reds. But Matheny's superb coverage behind the plate—nobody in baseball could block the plate better—had minimized the impact of Ankiel's wildness and helped settle him down. They had a rhythm together, the same rhythm that Tim McCarver had when he caught Steve Carlton with the Phillies and the same rhythm that Jorge Posada had with Orlando Hernandez with the Yankees, even though they seemed to be arguing most of the time.

But Matheny wasn't in the first game of the playoffs. And La Russa, in trying to explain what will be forever inexplicable, wonders whether Ankiel began to panic without Matheny there to reel in some of his errant pitches. And in panicking, Rick Ankiel began to think about what he was doing and how he was doing it. What had always seemed such a natural gift now seemed forced, as if he had never done it before. The terror of self-consciousness set in and drowned out muscle memory. Because of the situation he had been thrust into—a rookie in the first game of the playoffs—he also had no experience to carry him through, no keys to draw on to determine whether what was happening was mechanical or emotional.

He laughed off the performance against the Braves at first, noting that, if nothing else, he had set a record for most wild pitches in a game in the history of the postseason with five, a record that he had actually broken in that one half-inning in the top of the third. He was loose and relaxed as the first wave of media buzzards started rubbernecking, smelling the burning rubber of a really juicy car wreck on the mound. And they were clearly enjoying themselves. There had been other mound meltdowns in baseball. Steve Blass with the Pirates. Mark Wohlers with Atlanta. But nothing this public, right smack in the playoffs. Nobody knew, or perhaps really wanted to know, the extent of what was happening yet.

The Cardinals ended up sweeping the Braves, and La Russa slated Ankiel to start the second game of the National League Championship Series against the Mets. His first pitch was a 91-mph fastball to Timo Perez that just missed beaning him. Of the twenty pitches he threw before he was taken out, five went to the backstop. And it was then that Ankiel, two weeks before described as a phenom and a wonder, began to have other labels applied to him by the media: *meltdown, crazy tosses.*

It was over after that. He came back the next season, and La Russa and Duncan did what they could to shield him from the rubberneckers determined to document every pitch of his ongoing disintegration. They had him work out at sunrise in spring training in the Cardinals' compound in Jupiter when it was cool and quiet and empty. Early in the regular season, they had him warm up in a tunnel underneath the stadium so no one could watch. Ankiel, who had initially reacted to his predicament with humor, now became hard and defensive and reticent. He turned down most interview requests, because who in their right mind would *want* to talk about something like that, but there seemed to be a joy among certain writers in goading him, seeing whether they could get to him:

C'mon, Rick, just a few questions about what it's like to crack up on the mound. And there was also a certain school suggesting that Ankiel had only gotten what he deserved—signing for too much money out of high school, hiring an agent in Scott Boras who always went for too much money, floating through life without the requisite suffering that they went through—*You want to know what pressure is, Rick, try writing for peanuts on deadline*—too damn golden for his own good with that fat contract and all those threats that he was going to go to the University of Miami if he didn't get the money he wanted.

In the Thursday afternoon sun at Busch in May 2001, Ankiel threw the final pitch he would throw that season against Pat Meares of the Pirates. The ball went to the screen, and Duncan went out of the dugout. Ankiel hung his head as he made the baseball equivalent of a perp walk, and then he put on his jacket in the dugout and headed down the tunnel toward the clubhouse.

He went to spring training a year later but was put on the disabled list with a sore elbow and did not pitch the entire year. He came back to spring training the season of 2003 with La Russa's hope that he could make the team as a reliever. It created yet another media deathwatch, the careful chronicling of his every pitch: how many were strikes and how many were balls and how many sailed wild and how many almost hit someone.

On a Thursday morning at the end of March in the clubhouse in Jupiter, Duncan came into La Russa's office to tell him that a decision on Ankiel's fate had been made by Walt Jocketty: how he would stay with the club until spring training broke and then go down to the minors where those in charge of minor-league development for the Cardinals would take over and determine the best course.

"How much influence do we have on where he's sent?" asked La Russa.

"I assume we'll have input," said Duncan.

Duncan wanted him to go down to Double-A, where there would be less pressure, but La Russa worried about the bus trips.

"He'll be fine," said Duncan. "There's less travel in Double-A than in Triple-A."

And then he added something else, perhaps what—in the best of worlds, where there is time to develop young pitchers physically and mentally and the economies of the game don't demand immediate results—should have happened all along.

"He's twenty-three years old. He should be in Double-A."

Two days later, the team left Florida to make its way north. There was a delicious sense of renewal and anticipation to it, the slate wiped clean, the arduous tedium of spring training over with its rote drills and games that don't count, every team in both leagues starting off fresh in first place with exactly the same record, each of them still believers in the beautiful delusion that it will come together. Two Bekins moving trucks pulled up outside the Jupiter clubhouse, and soon they were filled with the tools of the game: satchels crammed with batting helmets, canvas cylinders built for bats, red bags virtually overflowing with baseballs like a slot jackpot in Vegas, the trunk containing Duncan's pitch-chart binders.

The players and the coaches got onto two buses that would take them to the airport in Palm Beach, then off to St. Louis for the opener. La Russa was the last to get on. He was dressed in a black sport coat and blue jeans, a pair of sunglasses hanging by one of its stems out of the breast pocket. There was a smile on his face because it was finally going to start now, the season, the regular season, every question and anxiety about his ballclub to be answered now. In the rigid hierarchy of the team, he took the first seat of the first bus, and then off the team went. A clump of loyalists clapped as the caravan rolled through the black metal gate, and it was as American as America ever gets.

The clubhouse, relieved of its occupants, suddenly seemed sodden, flooded with the sad, slow weight of south Florida humidity, the constant chirp of ballplayers replaced by the void of departure. Lockers—once filled with uniform shirts and practice jerseys and bats and fresh batting gloves in shiny plastic packets and virginal hats without a crease and baseball cards to be signed and packets of protein powder—were now virtually empty, except for white plastic hangers and the nameplates of those who were now on their way north:

Robinson Renteria Pujols Drew Fassero Rolen Edmonds
Martinez Girardi Matheny Eldred Marrero Palmeiro Painter
Tomko Hermanson Perez Morris Cairo Isringhausen Simon-
tacchi Delgado Springer Stephenson Williams Taguchi

A box of scuffed baseballs stood in one corner, rejects that
hadn't made the cut. A stack of pizza boxes bore the pockmarks of
their half-eaten cargo. There was a FedEx slip on the carpet and a
picture of somebody's baby and a baseball card of the old Giant
great Juan Marichal with that leg kick poking a hole in heaven and
a stack of unopened fan mail and a twenty-dollar coupon for Guis-
seppe's restaurant. One player, Al Levine, a righty reliever cut
toward the end of camp, had even left behind a copy of his contract, as if the compensation he was receiving for being released,
$600,000, wasn't worth the paper it was printed on, probably be-
cause he knew he would find enlistment papers somewhere else.
The only people in the clubhouse were the attendants scurrying
about, throwing blue towels into metal shopping basket bins, collecting soiled stirrup socks, removing peels of tape. And then Rick
Ankiel walked in to gather his things, as if he had waited for this
moment when no one would be there to see him.

La Russa still believes in Rick Ankiel. He still believes that he can
get it back if he's left alone for a little bit without the rubberneckers
smelling flesh, rediscover the muscle memory of what once was
there. "He still has it in him to pitch well," says La Russa.

But whatever happens, there is the image of somebody trying to
make a comeback—not in his forties or fifties or even his thirties,
but at the age of twenty-three. Which is why, as La Russa watches
Prior on the mound in Game 1 with his impervious strut and thinks
to himself: *Maybe he needs to be doing this a while,* he's thinking it
as much for Prior's benefit as he is his own. Because nobody, no
matter how good you are already and how much better everyone
thinks you will become, is ever immune to the vagaries of what can
happen when your life depends on throwing a baseball.

6

PRAYING FOR CHANGE

I

● ● ● LA RUSSA FEELS gratified by Stephenson's performance so far. He's put two zeros on the board. He didn't float something up and over for Randall Simon. He used both sides of the
plate with Alex Gonzalez. He has kept the ball down.

It's too early to make predictions, but La Russa wonders
whether this might be a pivotal moment not only in Stephenson's
season but also for his career, the moment when a pitcher realizes
who he is and what he is and what he's capable of and drops the
action-hero pretensions that get him into trouble. Maybe it's like
the epiphany Todd Stottlemyre experienced when he came over to
the A's from Toronto in the early 1990s and placed himself at the
mercy of Duncan.

Stottlemyre, by his own admission, suffered from the big-balls
delusion. La Russa understood that attitude and to a certain degree
embraced it. He had been around pitchers enough to know what
egotistical creatures they had to be because of the very nature of
what they did, alone on that little hill with the outcome of the game
in lockstep with their performance. "They're starting pitchers," he
said. "They *need* to be heroes." Now he didn't even bother to ask a
starter how he was feeling when he visited the mound, as the only
one he had ever encountered in a quarter century who didn't flat-
out lie, admitted to being out of gas if he was out of gas, was Tom

Seaver. The rest said they felt great even if they no longer had any feeling left in their arms.

Stottlemyre was the ultimate mound warrior. But under Duncan, he harnessed his drive and competitiveness so that each batter became a potential out, not a rite of ego. He learned how to kill with location. He realized that if you toss in the right mix of pitches —think of yourself as a chef making a soufflé with varied ingredients—the hitter's timing, his most precious commodity, is stolen from him. Stottlemyre fell in love with command, which even when you don't have good stuff on a certain night can still get you through. He became something he had never really been before— a pitcher—and he credits Duncan for that transformation, the first pitching coach who taught him more than mechanics. The Deacon got inside his head because of the meticulousness of those charts, proved to him with hard-core data what he was doing wrong, and fixed the circuitry to turn him from an inconsistent .500 pitcher into a pitcher with a consistent winning record.

So maybe here's where Stephenson crosses the border from thrower to pitcher and never crosses back. He's had his moments before, moments when it's worked on all cylinders and moments, terrifying moments, when he himself has acknowledged that he has no idea where his fastball is going. Now would be a lovely time to do it, against a young gun like Prior with first place in the Central on the line. The only thing La Russa hasn't seen from Stephenson is off-speed. Twenty-seven pitches thrown through seven batters and all of them fastballs. But that's okay as long as Stephenson ultimately starts mixing in his curve and changeup. Also, with the eighth and ninth hitters coming to the plate in the top of the third before Kenny Lofton's up again, there's a little relief in the lineup. Given the way Stephenson is pitching, the third inning should be easier than the first two.

The catcher Bako leads off for the Cubs. He's hitting .213 with no home runs and eleven RBIs. Finally, Stephenson has a matchup that favors him; in four at-bats, Bako's never gotten a hit against him.

Stephenson comes with a low-and-away fastball that Bako

swings through to get the first-strike advantage. Stephenson's next pitch, his twenty-ninth straight fastball, is up and in for a ball to make the count 1 and 1. In the dugout, a queasy feeling comes over La Russa: *Where are the curve and the changeup? Where is the deception? Why give the eighth-place hitter who isn't hitting two and a quarter a gift like this by throwing nothing but fastballs?*

Stephenson comes with another fastball. He is hoping to locate the pitch inside, but he doesn't, at least not inside enough. Bako hits it sharply into right. Kerry Robinson reaches into the corner, cutting the ball off before it goes to the wall, and saves it from becoming a double.

Now La Russa begins to worry. Stephenson's bipolar disorder is showing definite signs of relapse. In the Cubs dugout, a vicious yet accurate rumor is no doubt spreading: *He's throwing nothing but fastballs up there.* No pitcher should ever let a hitter feel comfortable, and if Stephenson keeps throwing heat, the Cubs will come to the plate with a bat and a Mai Tai.

Stephenson faces Prior next and jams him, with the result a harmless pop-up to the infield. It gives Stephenson his first out, and maybe La Russa's agitations are the agitations of a man who agitates over everything, even the little crushed paper cups that procreate on the dugout floor: La Russa walks the length of the dugout, kicking them into neat little piles. The reality is that Stephenson, after working his way through the Cubs lineup, has given up only *the one hit,* to Bako. But La Russa still frets, waiting for the game to sucker-punch him, his only defense to *agitate.* He went into the inning hoping to catch a break. With the lowest spots in the order due up first and second, he harbored the expectation that Lofton, coming up with two outs and nobody on, would be neutralized. But that fastball to Bako has set off a potentially wicked chain, because Lofton now settles in with a man on first and only one out.

Stephenson digs himself a hole with three straight balls, then gets back into the at-bat with two strikes to make the count full at 3 and 2.

It's another sumptuous subplot: The hitter has an assumed advantage because of the likelihood that the pitcher will come with a fastball, rather than risk a walk with something too fine that will put runners on first and second. But La Russa and Duncan will often try to screw up that assumption if they figure it's likely that the runner on first is going for second off the 3-2 count. They encourage their pitchers and catchers to treat the situation as if the runner is *already* on second, with first base open, to lessen the usual tendency to give in to the full count with a fastball. Instead, they preach off-speed here; a walk that puts runners on first and second is still better than the hitter getting the fastball he thinks he is going to get. La Russa himself will further encourage the antifastball philosophy by conveying to the catcher through signs what pitch the pitcher should throw. But he makes no sign here. He believes that both Stephenson and Chris Widger have been sufficiently coached on fastball danger. He believes the pitch will be a curve or a changeup to muck up Lofton's anticipation.

It's a fastball. A *high* fastball. The kind of pitch that keeps Lofton in gloves and gold chains. He slaps it the other way into the corner in left, Pujols scampering after it. Bako scores easily from first. Lofton reaches second standing up. The Cubs lead 1–0.

The next batter, Martinez in the two-hole, singles on a fastball to drive in Lofton: 2–0 Cubs. That pitch was in but also up, the kiss of death. In the foxhole, La Russa's inner voice pleads with Stephenson: *Mix in something different!* Stephenson obliges with a changeup to begin the at-bat against Sosa. At this point, La Russa is almost shocked to see it.

Finally. But it's moot anyway, as Stephenson, after building to 0 and 2, loses Sosa to a walk to put runners on first and second with, still, one out. The last thing Duncan had told Stephenson in their meeting—the moral he left him with—was not to get frustrated and lose concentration if things started to go a little sour. But the back-to-back hits by Lofton and Martinez have obviously flustered Stephenson, and La Russa has the feeling that he is slipping away, a crooked number in the works with all that potential damage approaching in the four-, five-, and six-spots.

It's a great situation for Alou in the cleanup—he usually kills Cardinals pitching with his RBI aggressiveness—but he flies to left for the second out. There are still runners on first and second. Stephenson has given up three hits, a walk and two runs; he suddenly looks scraggly and rattled. It's been a bumpy inning, an ugly inning. Yet he can still walk away with minor scratches if he gets the next out.

The object that blocks Stephenson's escape from the inning is Simon, the very Simon who, Stephenson acknowledged, *kicks his ass*. This is the key at-bat of the inning, probably of the entire game, and La Russa's inner voice is succinct: *You get Simon out. You got a game.*

Stephenson knows it too. If he retires Simon here, it's the Cardinals who get the crucial psychological lift because the Cubs should have done more damage. It's also a crucial mental victory for Stephenson, a bad matchup that he turned in his favor, an at-bat that can propel a pitcher the rest of the way.

Simon offers no pretext of discipline. He plays the game the way Bernie Mac might play it: sweet and fun and just a wee bit devilish. His shirt billows like an America's Cup jib, his girth ample enough to scare Bigfoot. He likes getting up there, guessing the pitch, and then taking an El Niño swing. He has no clean stride into the ball, just a little baby step, and after he swings, he looks even more disheveled, as if he just exited from one of those roller coasters where you hang upside down.

His ebullience does sometimes get him into trouble. He has actually earned a little piece of baseball lore already this season, not for anything he did while playing but for using a bat to trip up an unsuspecting mascot dressed up as a bratwurst during the run-around-the-field race the Milwaukee Brewers put on at each home game. The poor bratwurst—it actually may have been an Italian sausage—collapsed in a tottering heap. The video image of it went around the world, and Simon paid a $432 fine for disorderly conduct. When he is playing, he has good bat speed. He can drive something deep, and as Duncan pointed out to Stephenson, he likes his meat up.

The first pitch is a curve low in the zone. Simon is way out in front of it, terribly fooled.

He fouls off the next pitch to make the count 0 and 2. Stephenson's in control now, and from the stands comes a rumbling murmur that yes, *yes!* he is going to squirm his way out of this thing with only two runs.

He throws a fastball outside, then a fastball inside. They're chase pitches, considerably off the plate but appropriate. Simon doesn't bite and the count is squared at 2 and 2.

Before the next pitch, La Russa sees Stephenson shaking off the sign from Chris Widger. He knows what *that* means: Widger wants Stephenson to go with a breaking ball, particularly because Simon doesn't hit curve balls well. Stephenson, however, still wants his fastball, feels most comfortable with it. Widger sets up inside to at least get the right location.

The ball floats up and away. Simon hits the bejesus out of it. He smacks it hard to the opposite field in left. Stephenson turns and watches and thinks, or maybe just prays, that it's carrying foul. Pujols goes into the corner in left to see what kind of play he can make if it stays fair: get a good carom off the wall and *maybe* hold the runner at first from scoring. He's on the run, readying for the zigzag off the bumpers. But then he stops and simply gazes at the ball as it opts for early retirement.

Simon has just hit a three-run homer. The Cubs lead 5–0.

Duncan squints in the dugout. There's a look of bemused irony on his face, as if to say, *Now, Garrett, what did I tell you about getting the ball up to Simon? What did I tell you?* As for Stephenson, he's visibly upset. He isn't thinking at all now—to hell with the game plan. With Aramis Ramirez up, he throws another fastball— a particular kind of fastball that pitchers in this situation often throw—a fastball that La Russa recognizes as a *first-pitch pissed-off fastball,* a fastball that invariably causes regret. Ramirez hits a home run four rows beyond the Budweiser sign in left center: 6–0 Cubs.

As Duncan trots out to the mound, La Russa opens the little black box in the right corner of the dugout just inside the tunnel entrance. He pulls out the phone and speaks to Marty Mason, who in turn gets Sterling Hitchcock up and throwing in the bullpen. Over in the Cubs dugout, Dusty Baker takes a healthy guzzle from a green Gatorade cup, then chases it with a healthy spit as a little toast to the Cubs' crooked number. Prior, with a white towel around his pitching arm, sits on the bench as implacable as ever, his hair barely matted even in the heat, his sideburns so long and straight, you could land a plane on them.

Stephenson glumly listens to Duncan. His head is down, awkwardly cocked, the goatee around his chin thin and insubstantial. He's getting a terse baseball lecture here, the look on *his* face like a child who knows that trying to throw the eraser past the teacher's head was stupid once and inexcusable twice. He will be punished for this. There will be another demotion to the bullpen.

He manages to strike out Alex Gonzalez to end the inning, and even that's scary, as Gonzalez rips the first two pitches foul into left field, pulling them just a little bit too much. But the damage is done —nine batters, five hits, six runs, two home runs—to raise Stephenson's death toll to twenty-eight. He is through for the night after three. He relied on his fastball too much, and he couldn't control it. He paid the price, exactly what La Russa predicted would happen if he pitched this way. His matchups now seem prescient given the collective performance of those three ex-Pirates in all of three innings: Six at-bats. One double. Two home runs. Three runs scored. Five RBIs. And Stephenson's hastening into oblivion.

II

THE DUGOUT is quiet after the top of the third ends. La Russa hasn't given up yet. A 6–0 disadvantage this early in the game is not insurmountable. Things simply happen to the Cubs because of the handcuffs of their history, and they particularly happen in St. Louis. Since 2000, the Cubs have won only four of twenty-seven games at Busch. And in the back of their minds must be the time last year when the Cards overcame a 9–4 deficit in the ninth to win 10–9 on a three-run homer by Edgar Renteria. But Prior is pitching tonight, and although this is nowhere close to the best game he's pitched this season—his fastball doesn't have the location that it usually does—he still has the *it*. He has what Scott Rolen describes as "presence," an intangible confidence. It may be impossible to quantify, but as Rolen puts it, "The difference between a 3-and-1 fastball fouled back or lined to center is who has the most confidence."

He easily dispenses with the Cardinals in the third and fourth, the only hit a go-nowhere single by Edmonds. In the foxhole, La Russa has trouble purging the top of the third out of his mind. The home runs bother him less than the very first at-bat of the inning when Bako, who doesn't even hit *two and a quarter*, got that gift pack of three straight fastballs. But he still refuses to become dispirited, pushes himself to grind away even harder whatever the reality. The game in 2001 between Houston and Pittsburgh—when the Astros lost after being ahead 8–2 with the Pirates batting with two outs and nobody on in the bottom of the ninth—creases his mind. Anything can happen in baseball: the beauty or the brutality.

But by the end of the fifth, with the score now 7–0 Cubs, thoughts of a comeback are fading. Prior has given up only two hits. He's thrown first-pitch strikes to eleven of the eighteen batters he has faced. No Cardinals runner has gotten beyond second base. The St. Louis faithful recognize the plodding, futile rhythm of a rout. The air was sucked out of them in the third with Simon's swing. They've uttered little since, and as they scan the out-of-town scoreboard, they find more bad news:

	1	2	3	4	5	T
LOS ANGELES	3	0	0	0	0	3
HOUSTON	2	1	1	0	6	10

If the Astros keep it up and the Cardinals keep it up and the Cubs keep it up, the dogfight atop the Central will produce a complete flip-flop in the space of one game:

HOUSTON	69–62	.527
CHICAGO	68–62	.523
ST. LOUIS	68–63	.519

In the bottom of the sixth, the crowd emerges from its funk when Pujols appears at the plate for another war against Prior. He got just under one in the first, and then he walked in the fourth. But Prior has nothing to lose now. He has a 7–0 score on his side and *you know what, Albert, let's put down the switchblades and go straight to sabres. My best against your best. Deal?*

Deal. Prior comes with a fastball on the first pitch. It rides the radar gun at 93 mph.

Pujols counters. He flicks his bat toward the dugout as if it's too hot even for his own hands, follows the ball with his eyes as it cracks the ozone layer and heads for some telecommunications satellite. It reenters earth with an innocent plop on the grassy knoll behind center field, 414 feet from where it originated. It's a meaningless run in the flow of Game 1. The Cardinals will still end up losing 7–4 on a three-run ninth-inning rally that fizzles. But as Pujols encircles the implacable Prior on the mound in his pulled-up blue stirrup socks covering up calves so big that his nickname is Calfzilla, there is the comfort that at least one score has just been settled.

III

LA RUSSA FACES the media after the game, just outside the clubhouse. His hair is damp and his uniform sticky from the breezeless heat. The small, harsh lights on top of the television cameras glare into his eyes, like being inches away from a truck's headlights, making him even more uncomfortable-looking than he already is. He answers the obligatory questions with obligatory brevity.

Once the press conference is over, he retreats immediately to his office. In the locker area, Stephenson, showered and in street clothes, finds himself surrounded by a circle of reporters and offers no excuse for what happened. "When you leave the ball up, more bad things are gonna happen than good things. And it's my fault."

Afterward, several reporters go into La Russa's office. One of them, reiterating a question posed to him in the press conference, asks his opinion of Stephenson's pitch selection. La Russa cracks, unable to conceal his irritation, convinced that the intent of the question is to provoke him, get him to say something publicly negative in the heat of the moment. "I have no problem with the way he went about it. Did you hear me say that? So why would you ask that question? I have no problem with the way he went about it. He just didn't pitch well. Why would you ask that?"

He won't show up a player publicly. But privately, he's deeply frustrated with Stephenson's ill-fated dependence on the fastball. He checks with the Secret Weapon to get an accurate tally of how many off-speed pitches Stephenson threw during his three innings: only twelve out of sixty-five, an unhealthy ratio. "The way he gets guys, he's got to be somewhere around even with his curve ball and his changeup," says La Russa as he unpeels his uniform. "But he kept going fastball, fastball, fastball . . ."

By the time he changes into his street clothes, the clubhouse will be empty. He will eat in silence at J Bucks restaurant several miles from the stadium. He will have a book with him, *Flags of Our Fathers,* by James Bradley, about the battle of Iwo Jima. He will climb into his Cardinals-red Cadillac Escalade. He will return to where he lives in St. Louis, a residential suite in a hotel in the city's west end. And he will follow the routine that he has followed since he first went into the foxhole. He will pull out the little lineup cards that he uses to keep score during the games. They help him keep track and stay ahead when he manages, and now he's reviewing certain situations the players faced—the count, an RBI situation or a steal situation or a hit-and-run situation—and whether he reacted appropriately. He uses the cards to learn something about his team that may be of help in the future, just as he uses them to learn something about his opponent that may be of help in the future: little glints of their personalities that came out in pivotal plays. The cards may also reveal something about baseball he has never noticed before, a slice of insight in a game that, after 3,767 of them, still has the capacity to humble him.

As he manages, he also makes tiny little lists of opportunities lost and not lost, moments when maybe he could have stolen a run or prevented one: how, for example, the Expos' Jose Vidro likes to punch it in the hole between first and second with a runner on first, so you shade the second baseman to take away the hole, even if it makes a normal double play more difficult, or that Expos pitcher Tomo Ohka is one of those inverse righties who pitches better against lefties, so you better stock your lineup accordingly. He learned to keep a list from Dick Williams, the manager of the A's when they won world championships in 1972 and 1973. Williams told him that if you don't make notes about a game as it's occurring and review them afterward, you will forget what happened, because of the daily grind of the season. But there aren't many notes here because, let's face it, the game was over by the floodgates of the third when Simon hit the three-run dinger into left.

He will project ahead to Game 2, when Kerry Wood is slated to go for the Cubs. His matchup numbers against the Cardinals are similar to Prior's, cause enough for brooding. But the style with which Wood pitches creates an anxiety for La Russa more terrible than anything else he faces as a manager. He will ponder the lineup. There's not much he can do about the neophytes Bo Hart and Kerry Robinson at the top except stick with them, but he hopes he'll be able to restore Renteria to shortstop. He will pore over every detail.

"I've been able to devote more concentration than most to it," he acknowledges. "My life revolves around the score." And then he admits, "I've had an incredible advantage at a terrific price."

IV

FOR EIGHT MONTHS a year, La Russa lives by himself. During spring training, he stays at a condominium near the Cardinals' complex in Jupiter. When the team moves north for the regular season, he stays in the residential hotel suite while his wife, Elaine, and their two daughters remain 2,000 miles away in Alamo near San Francisco. The support of La Russa's family has enabled him to focus his life 100 percent on baseball during the season. But the number of times he sees them during the season can be counted on two hands—a couple of series against the Giants and the occasional off day when he steals a plane to Oakland for a twenty-four-hour reunion. A plaque on a wall in the La Russas' home sums up their relationship: "We interrupt this marriage to bring you the baseball season."

Their first daughter, Bianca, was born in September 1979, a month after her father had started managing the White Sox. Their second daughter, Devon, was born in August 1982. Their births came when La Russa was most vulnerable, or felt he was most vulnerable—still cutting his teeth as the White Sox' manager. Living in Des Moines, where La Russa had the Triple-A job with the White Sox, Elaine begged her husband not to make the move to the parent club in Chicago. She was eight months pregnant and the timing was beyond bad. Since their marriage on New Year's Eve in 1973, they had moved nearly forty times, shuttling between spring training and the baseball season and Tony's law school studies in the off-season. Most of their possessions were in storage, bed sheets often served as drapes, plants inevitably froze in the car on the way to some strange and faceless apartment filled with the sour odors of transience. The thought of moving again, when Elaine was about to give birth, filled her with dread. *A child, Tony. We're having a child.* But they moved anyway.

Elaine played the baseball wife at first, quietly nursing Bianca in the stands soon after she was born. She loved the game—at least at first she loved it—and she loved even more to keep score. After the games, White Sox owner Bill Veeck held court at a bar called the Bard's Room in the upper reaches of Comiskey Park. Her husband's attendance was mandatory, so Elaine dutifully followed with Bianca, even though they weren't allowed in the actual bar itself, because women simply were not allowed: an unwanted governor on the bawdy, off-color atmosphere with which baseball defined itself back then. Instead, they sat in an adjacent room, falling asleep arm-in-arm until two or three or four in the morning, whenever Veeck, basically an insomniac, had had enough baseball talk for the night.

Elaine also took her husband's intense temperament in stride, even when his body language, after a loss, said *get the hell away from me.* All coaches take losses hard. But Jim Leyland, who coached under La Russa and then went on himself to manage four-teen years for the Pirates and Florida and Colorado, believes that La Russa magnified the impact. "Losing hurts all of us, but it probably hurt Tony too much," said Leyland. And it hurt others as well.

"I was paranoid about not doing the job right," said La Russa of those early years, paranoid about not being prepared, paranoid about missing some millimeter edge there for the taking if he could only find it. He found himself consumed by the philosophy of Paul Richards, who had managed in the big leagues for twelve years, was considered a master innovator, and was the director of the farm system for the Chicago White Sox when La Russa took over: *It's your ass. It's your team. It's your responsibility. There's a strategy for every situation. So start making some decisions.*

Early in the 1983 season, Elaine was taking care of their daughters in Sarasota. The White Sox had just broken spring training there, and she planned to bring the children north to Chicago in late May or early June so the family could be together. One night, she called from Florida: She had just been diagnosed with pneumonia and required hospitalization. La Russa responded to the news with a fateful decision, one that would cement his status as a baseball man but would also define him in another way.

Based on a strong finish in 1982, the expectations were high for the White Sox in 1983. But the season got off to a wretched start, mired at 16 and 24. Floyd Bannister was having trouble winning anything. La Marr Hoyt had a record of 2 and 6 and Carlton Fisk was a mess at the plate. In the middle of May, the team lost eight of nine games. Toronto swept them; then Baltimore swept them. La Russa found himself fighting for his life, or what he mistook for his life. He had a team that was supposed to win, that had spent money on free agents and had good pitching and still wasn't winning. The only reason he was still around was because of the vision of White Sox owner Reinsdorf, who continued to stand by him. So he did what he thought he had to do: He called his sister in Tampa and asked whether she would take care of the kids so he could take care of baseball.

Only with the benefit of hindsight, twenty years of it, did he realize that the right decision was the one he hadn't made. "How was I stupid enough? I should have left the team and taken care of my wife and kids. I've never forgiven myself for that and they've never forgotten."

Looking back on it, Elaine remembers feeling "terribly hurt" when her husband failed to come to Florida. But she also thinks that he was so overwhelmed by the myriad responsibilities of managing—so scared by it on the one hand and so determined on the other to succeed at it—that he lost all sight that there was more to life than his professional life. "I think at that time he was basically clueless," she said. She also believes she enabled his pursuit by taking care of everything that was family-related, so he never had to assume any responsibility. "Don't worry about me," she said to him over the phone when he elected to stay with the team. "Do what you have to do, because I know it's tough for you." She wanted to be supportive, but she believes now that she made a mistake in not demanding more of him personally: insisting upon it. "I know it helped him become what he is and where is he now," she said. "But on a personal level, I should have been more of a Scarlett O'Hara. In retrospect, if I hadn't been so efficient, it would have forced him to become more of an equal partner. He knew that everything would be taken care of. I think it just fed into the monster."

When La Russa moved to the Oakland A's in 1986 after getting fired by the White Sox, the dugout became a further entrapment. He joined the A's in the middle of the season—again carrying the weight of his enormous expectations—and the team responded to him. There came a game in August against the Yankees, one of those no-justice, manage-your-ass-off games in which the A's scratched back from a 6–5 deficit and brought an 8–6 lead into the top of the ninth, when all sorts of weird hell broke loose, the Yankees scoring three times on three singles and two walks and a sacrifice fly.

His wife and daughters were at the game that night. He made them wait an hour and a half before he came out of the clubhouse. He drove home from the stadium silent and stone-faced. He started to give the girls a bath, but he lost his temper and his voice rose and Elaine finished bathing them.

The A's played a night game the next day. It ended relatively early, and after it was over, he called Elaine and asked how long the girls were going to be up. Occasionally, if there was a night game followed by a day game, La Russa had slept in the clubhouse rather than get home late and head back to the park the next morning at 7:30. Elaine told him that the girls wanted to know how the A's had done: If they'd lost, she told her husband, the girls would prefer that their father spend the night at the clubhouse.

When the A's later played the Detroit Tigers, La Russa told Tigers manager Sparky Anderson, whom he also admired deeply, what had happened. Anderson dressed him down and told him that he had to keep his priorities straight. La Russa knew that Anderson was right, but by his own admission, "I still didn't fix it enough. I just got better at hiding it. I still got to the park too early. I still stayed too late."

Gradually, Elaine stopped taking the girls to the games; she didn't want them to become captive to the team's fortunes and their father's moods. "As I got more and more into it, more caught up, dumber and dumber," said La Russa, "she realized that the girls were not going to have a life."

Elaine still loved baseball, but she felt she had to step away from it. She began to feel that baseball ruined families, not simply in terms of the eight months it kept a man from his family, but also in terms of its antifamily rituals. "Baseball is wonderful for separating families," she said. "They are real good at that. Back in Sarasota [during spring training with the White Sox], they still had a stag night. Families were not allowed." She became increasingly independent in the raising of her children: schooling them at home, encouraging their love of dance through the Oakland Ballet. She also saw that even when her husband was at home in body during the season, he was never there in spirit, so consumed by achieving success in Oakland that he went into a place all his own. There could be no balancing work life with home life, particularly because a manager's obligations, unlike a player's, were ceaseless. She had first met Tony in 1972 in Richmond, Virginia, when he was a minor-league player, and his focus then was simple: He wanted to hit .300. But when he became a manager, it was like a tidal wave hit:

strategic responsibilities, off-the-field responsibilities, responsibility for players as needy and mercurial as they were so blessedly talented. When Tony had been a player, he and Elaine had shared everything, talked about everything. But as a manager, the last thing he wanted to talk about when he came home was his job after twelve nonstop hours of it each day, every day, from February to October.

In 1996, when La Russa went to the Cardinals, Elaine elected to stay behind with the children to lead their own lives while he led his. It wasn't for want of love, because the love in the family was intense, but because it was best for everyone involved, a division of labor that made sense in terms of what was important to each of them: Elaine in charge of parenting Bianca and Devon on the West Coast, her husband in the Midwest with nothing between him and baseball. From her origins as a dutiful baseball wife, Elaine realized how crucial it had become for both her and her children to have an identity beyond what her husband and their father did for a living, that he was the only one with his name spread across his shoulders. Back in the days when she had gone to the games, she had always noticed the other baseball wives huddled around in their enclave in the stands. Without being dismissive, she came to the conclusion that they were little more than fans with better seats and greater entitlement. *Where do you go beyond that?* she wondered. *What do you do? What is your life about?* She also noticed something else: how many marriages fell apart once the baseball stopped. It wasn't something she wanted, just as she also knew that if she and the kids simply followed Tony to St. Louis, they would have only ended up resenting him for the disruption he had caused, for the fact that he still would be the man who wasn't there.

"I know to somebody on the outside looking in, it must be strange and different and weird," she said of their separation for two-thirds of every year, "but it's what you have to do to make it work." And it had worked. It had kept their lives intact and made their marriage whole; the separation eased by phone calls to each other every night after every game. But it wasn't perfect, since few things ever are. "It's not the ideal. If I had written about my life and what I expected it to be, even in baseball, it would not be any way like it has been."

As for La Russa himself, there is the hindsight of what didn't have to be, the excess of obsession and the toll it must take. "I have huge regrets about it because I could have done just as well in my job with less significant time spent apart," said La Russa. But what's been done can't be undone. The truth of that particularly struck him one weekend during spring training in the 2001 season, when he saw Mike Matheny and Matheny's wife, Kristin, walking hand in hand.

When Matheny is disappointed with the way he plays, he gets a certain look in his eye, what La Russa knows too well as the "lost look" of someone thrashing himself for something he felt he should have done. When he glimpsed Matheny away from the game simply holding hands with his wife, it so affected him that he did something he almost never does as a manager—he gave unsolicited advice that had nothing to do with baseball.

"Look, you're not asking for this advice but I'm giving it to you. Ignore it. Tell me to shut up," La Russa said. "But it moved my heart to see you holding your wife's hand. Just before you held hands, you had that lost look because of something you did on the field—getting too hard on yourself. I made enormous mistakes with my wife and kids; now I have terrific regrets and it's too late to do much about it."

He admired Matheny's willingness to take responsibility in an era when fewer and fewer athletes ever take responsibility. He didn't want Matheny to lose his capacity for self-critique, but he also urged him not to let those thoughts spill over into his family. "The more you think about it, it only gets worse," he told him. "And when you're with your family, there's nothing you can do about it until you get to the park tomorrow."

He hoped that Matheny would listen to what he had to say, even though he knew it was something he was not remotely capable of himself. Which is why, as the clubhouse quickly empties out after Game 1 and the players attend to their lives beyond baseball—because there is life beyond baseball—La Russa is still there.

GAME
TWO

....

7

GONZALEZ MUST PAY

I

● ● ● BY ELEVEN on Wednesday morning, when he arrives at the clubhouse, La Russa has sublimated the sour memories of Game 1. Although he had hoped for the best before the game yesterday, he'd prepared for the worst. There's no use dwelling on it, although the simple reality is that the Cards have to win the next two to take the three-game series.

During batting practice in the watery afternoon light, La Russa walks the field with a red fungo bat in hand. The tapestry of batting practice is elaborately stitched, an ingenious workmanship behind the strategically placed cages and nets that rim the basepaths. Inside the empty stadium, its rhythm has deceptive leisure; it's the only time ever in baseball when all the puzzle pieces are simultaneously engaged: hitting, running, fielding, throwing. La Russa takes it all in, roaming here, roaming there, seeking omens.

He watches Edgar Renteria scuttling along the sandy apron of the infield, tucking the ball into his glove and then making the throw to first. Will his ailing back keep him out of another game at shortstop? La Russa needs Renteria tonight because he is a superb hitter, and he needs him because of his golden glove, his footwork as light and fluid as a ballet dancer's, able to reach deep into the canyon crevice between second and third.

There's also Renteria's attitude, the combination of competition and puckish joy that spills onto the other players. Team chemistry is its own odyssey, and different players contribute different catalysts. Rolen leads largely on the basis of his grinding performance; outside the field he's as careful with his words as he is with his emotions, no air leaking out of the tires. Albert Pujols leads because he is the great Pujols. Woody Williams leads because beneath his Texas twang is a pitcher who simply guts it out.

Renteria leads with *joie de vivre,* developing handshakes for each player on the team, customized to his own idiosyncrasies, ending hitters' meetings with his Latin hip-hop chirp of *Let's go play, dawg!!* He is the favorite of his fellow teammates, but his sense of the game makes him more than just another clubhouse cutup. He doesn't wilt when the heat is on. At the age of twenty-two in the eleventh inning of Game 7 of the 1997 World Series, he delivered the game-winning single for the Marlins off a breaking ball from the Indians' Charles Nagy. It was a feat for anyone that young, but behind it was an untold story of baseball intelligence: Jim Leyland, the Marlins' manager at the time, is convinced that Renteria set up Nagy with a deception worthy of a fifteen-year veteran, jumping out of the way of a first-pitch Nagy breaking ball to suggest that he was mystified by it, when he only wanted Nagy to *think* he was fooled so he would get another breaking ball on the next pitch.

Renteria gathers up a few more grounders; then he takes his turn hitting in the cage, fifteen at-bats. He turns to La Russa afterward and gives a thumbs-up. Renteria doesn't look 100 percent to La Russa, but he appreciates the determination Renteria's gesture implies. He's managed players who, given any reason to take a free pass because of the threats posed by tonight's opposing pitcher, would ride the entire bus system with it. So Renteria's decision has meaning to him, gives him a lift.

A few minutes later, La Russa's mood is yanked back to half-mast when he hears that Dusty Baker has juggled the Cubs' pitching rotation in anticipation of another series against the Cards starting Monday. The timing of it — on the heels of Prior's effortless victory last night even without his usual sharpness — only taunts him.

"Prior's starting on Monday," a reporter informs La Russa.

"Says who?"

"Dusty."

"The *Tribune* had him starting Sunday."

"Dusty said it today."

"I hope they get their *ass* beat on Sunday," he snaps like a door slamming shut.

Back at his desk, La Russa feels even more tense than he usually feels before a game. As he mulls the matchups, he knows that the Cards cannot lose tonight if they want to remain in the division race. There is still ample baseball left to be played: thirty-one games. But Game 2 is a rarity: It emits psychological reverberations capable of dictating the rest of the season. Beating the Cards tonight will guarantee the Cubs a series win at Busch Stadium, imbuing them with more confidence than ever that their time has finally come.

At least tonight's matchups offer the hope of a more even contest than in Game 1. The Cards' starter, Williams, has the better record — 14 and 6 — and earned his first stint as an All-Star this season. Kerry Wood, on the hill for Chicago, has struck out 208 batters in 168 innings. Tonight's game also promises to be one of memorable and beautiful contradiction because the starters' styles are so different: Dada versus minimalist, surfer versus swimmer, punk rocker versus song stylist. Williams was drafted in the twenty-eighth round as a shortstop out of college. Wood was picked fourth in the first round, already a bit of a legend because of his smoke artistry at Grand Prairie High School in Texas, with the inevitable comparisons to those other Lone Star legends: Ryan and Clemens. Williams knocked around the minors for five years and hardly became a household word when he finally made it to the majors. Wood stayed in the minors for only two seasons and in 1998, as a rookie, struck out twenty Astros to tie a major-league record. Williams is methodical on the mound, plugging away. Wood, five inches taller, with a small, punched-in face and a sneer across the lips, looks like the kind of guy who cuts you off on the Interstate and then gives you the finger. Williams wins with command and location. Wood wins by letting it rip.

One of three different Woods will take the mound tonight.

There's Wild Wood, who has no idea where any of his pitches is going and walks too many batters to be effective. There is Controlled Wood, who consciously tries to keep the ball around the strike zone and not walk batters. Then there's Effectively Wild Wood, with enough pitches in and around the strike zone to make him consistent but a few every now and then where he's simply not sure where they're going to go.

Williams has no similar dramatic aspirations. Like a lot of major-league pitchers, he's plain-looking, really, with a trim beard and no outward hint of the physique that can harness a ball on the mound. The stuff he throws is low-octane, but it leaves a trail of baffled hitters. This is a guy they *should hit,* should just *get to.* But they don't, because Williams has learned how to pitch; he's a textbook example of how finesse can trump velocity.

When asked to describe Williams, Dave Duncan uses one word —"pitchmaker"—and, as is his style, doesn't elucidate further. He goes back to his computer in his Spartan office, as if maybe he's already said too much. But coming from Duncan, it speaks volumes, the ultimate compliment from teacher to pupil. Williams throws three kinds of fastballs: the straight four-seamer, the cutter, and the sinker. The four-seamer is about speed; the cutter and the sinker, about movement and location. With the cutter going one way and the sinker the other, his fastball works both sides of the plate, creating particular havoc for right-handed and left-handed hitters. They don't know whether it'll run in on them or away from them, which makes them off-balance. They lose their senses in a fog of uncertainty. When he strikes out hitters, they retreat to the dugout, bitching about how in hell could they just have struck out against a guy who throws so slow—*90! Are you kidding me, I haven't seen 90 since Little League.* It addles them beyond a particular at-bat. Next time up, they arrive at the plate frustrated, and Williams's style only breeds more frustration: *The son-of-a-bitch just did it to me again.* Compounding the frustration are his three quality off-speed pitches—a curve, a slider, and a changeup—all of which he can locate with precision.

Williams is also the ultimate survivor, proof that heart still counts for something, that behind the dizzying array of statistical predictors and indicators is the exquisite mystery of flesh and blood. With San Diego in 2000, he opened the season with a 3-2 record. He was off to a good start, the only hindrance an odd numbness in the fingers of his pitching hand. He let it go—simply the price of doing business, he figured—and it hardly hampered him when he went eight and a third innings against Florida in early May. But the numbness persisted. A series of medical tests found an aneurysm near his right armpit. Had it gone untreated, it could have meant the amputation of his pitching hand. He underwent successful surgery in early June and was back in the Padres' rotation by July.

The essence of Williams—why La Russa and Duncan coveted him—could be seen in how he performed on his return. He pitched four complete games and recorded the best ERA of his career as a starter. As a Cardinal, he's become another of Duncan's prodigies, an ex-.500 pitcher whose winning percentage has increased by nearly a hundred points. In the days before he starts, Williams spends hours watching tape of past performances, feeding a video addiction almost as intense as Mike Matheny exhibits as catcher. He watches what he did with the hitters, how he got to them, and he compares his outings with the Cardinals to what he did in San Diego to make sure he doesn't fall into any bad habits. When he meets with Duncan before Game 2 to go over the Cubs hitters, he already has formulated a strategy to use against them. It relieves Duncan of the need to plot out the game plan entirely on his own, as he had to do with Garrett Stephenson. This meeting is much more productive than yesterday's—all the fat trimmed. Williams leaves with a pinpoint sense of what needs to be executed, how Ramon Martinez in the two-hole is susceptible to the slider, how Alex Gonzalez at the seven-spot likes sitting on curve balls late in the game, particularly if he has seen a lot of them, how Damian Miller at the eight-spot can't resist high heat, even if it's over his head.

Williams also won't be daunted by Stephenson's three nemeses. Kenny Lofton and Aramis Ramirez are a combined 9 for 40 against him, with only one dinger. Randall Simon's numbers are so lackluster that he isn't even starting tonight. In fact, the matchups throughout the Cubs' lineup benefit Williams nicely:

LOFTON	5-20-0
MARTINEZ	2-10-0
SOSA	2-14-1
ALOU	6-26-1
KARROS	8-29-1
RAMIREZ	4-20-1
GONZALEZ	3-14-0
MILLER	7-14-0

When La Russa looks at them, he doesn't smile, but he also doesn't grimace. The biggest threat comes from Miller in the eight-spot, which, if you're the opposing manager, would appear to be just the spot where you want a batter who has a bead on your pitcher. But La Russa perceives a potential danger there, obscure to the baseball layman but ominous to La Russa. He obviously fears Miller's coming up with men on base and maybe driving them home. But what also worries him is Miller's coming up with *two outs* and the *bases empty,* which seems like the very scenario a manager would want: Even if Miller does get on base, Wood comes up next in the pitcher's spot. But La Russa doesn't want to end the inning with Wood, because that might give the Cubs an insidious advantage when they start the next frame with the top of their order. So it's not only that Miller gets hits off Williams; Miller may get a hit tonight that imperceptibly tilts the game—as delicate a system of pulleys and levers as has ever been created—toward the Cubs.

La Russa frets over that behind his desk. But another sheet of stats reminds him of how meticulously ruthless Williams can be against the Cubs, the ball zigzagging all over the plate, like a pesky fly. The last time he faced them, about seven weeks ago, Williams went seven and two-thirds innings in a 4–1 Cardinals win to run his record to 11 and 3.

Of course, Wood's matchups against the Cardinals hitters also benefit him nicely:

ROBINSON	4-16-0
HART	1-2-0
PUJOLS	7-23-3
EDMONDS	8-27-2
ROLEN	3-16-1
MARTINEZ	3-17-2
RENTERIA	5-27-0
MATHENY	1-13-0

There are homers to be had, but with the exception of Pujols and Edmonds, nobody is hitting above .250 against Wood. Once you get past the cleanup spot, nobody is hitting above .200 against him.

If the two pitchers are on tonight, Williams pitching like Williams and Wood pitching like Effectively Wild Wood, the game will be taut and low scoring, an edge-of-the-seat nail biter from the top of the first to wherever it ends. But there's something else gnawing away at La Russa. Wood's past performance hints that tonight, the Cardinals' manager may have to make what he calls the "most gut-wrenching decision of all" in twenty-five years of making them, an agony affecting him even worse than losing.

II

WHAT WILL HE DO if he thinks that Wood is intentionally throwing at one of his hitters? Wood has already plunked fourteen batters this season. He not only leads the league but also is on a pace to hit more batters than any National League pitcher since 1907. There's certainly no love lost between him and Pujols after he brushed him back with a pitch on July 4 at Wrigley Field. His blazing high-and-tight fastball, which keeps hitters uneasy, may well be his most effective weapon. Which is why La Russa is feeling so on edge.

"There are so many conflicting emotions," he says, when your batter gets hit. Because how do you sort it out? How do you know for sure that the pitcher acted intentionally? Pitchers themselves, even his own, were generally mum about it, their own version of

Omerta. Throughout baseball in general, the whole subject was taboo, never honestly discussed, never acknowledged, although it is deeply embedded in the game.

Some managers ignored it. They expected the players to take care of it themselves. But La Russa knew that such inaction bred enormous ill will down the length of the dugout, the possibility of a silent but corrosive insurrection against a weak manager who wouldn't defend his own guys. A player took it personally when he got hit. The results could be lethal, not only physically but also mentally, in the form of a persistent fear that accompanied him on every trip he made to the plate. So at the very least, hitters expected their pitchers to protect them against that arrogant son-of-a-bitch on the mound who had just used them for target practice because his stuff wasn't good enough on its own. And if they thought they couldn't rely on their pitchers to defend them, they would sit in the dugout and become more angry and upset than they were already. But if a pitcher did respond on his own, he might pick the wrong victim or a strategically inopportune moment.

La Russa was managing Double-A in Knoxville in 1978 when Harold Baines, a beautiful hitter and the first pick of the 1977 draft, arrived there on his way up the White Sox farm system. From his own years of managing, Paul Richards, then the farm system director for the White Sox, knew only too well what pitchers might do when confronted with young hitters capable of launching a moon shot. So he gave La Russa some instructions on how to manage: "You must make sure Harold Baines doesn't get abused."

If a pitcher hit Baines, Richards told La Russa, don't let it fester. Don't let it spread beyond your control. Don't let the players determine how to retaliate. If Baines did get plunked, Richards added, it mightn't be such a bad policy to pick the best hitter on the opposing team and make sure your pitcher plunked him. A batter for a batter in the Hammurabi Code of baseball, a deterrent against future attacks.

La Russa took Richards's advice to heart. Over the years, he made it clear to his players that the Hammurabi Code was in his hands, not theirs. He told his teams: "If you think you should be protected, and there's no retaliation, you don't go to your pitcher. You come to me." La Russa would determine whether the plunk had been intentional and how to respond.

In determining whether a pitcher had behaved with malice aforethought, La Russa always checked with Duncan. As a pitching coach, he could be more dispassionate, could better tell the difference between a pitch that had simply wandered off course and one that had found its target.

Duncan's input helped, but the feelings that swirled through him were still agonizing, still worse than losing—the most difficult feelings he ever had to face in baseball. In virtually every case of a batter getting hit by a pitch, La Russa and most other managers went through a traumatic struggle to determine real intent. Much of the uncertainty had to do with teams needing to pitch inside to be successful. In ratcheting down an opponent's offense, the advantages of pitching inside were too numerous to avoid: the very reason Duncan had tried to pound the philosophy into Garrett Stephenson the night before. It was undeniable that by making a hitter "inside conscious," the plate then widened for a pitcher to make a pitch away. It was also undeniable that hitters, in combating pitches inside so they wouldn't get jammed, tended to start their swing early, which in turn made them susceptible to slower off-speed pitches. In today's style of baseball, where more and more hitters are able to reach the outside of the plate and get the thick head of the barrel on the ball, the only way to move them off that territory is to pitch inside.

Because pitchers do pitch inside, batters inevitably are going to get hit, and therein lay La Russa's dilemma. Was it simply a pitch that had gotten away? Was the pitcher trying to intimidate by going inside? Or was the pitcher taking a cheap shot and deliberately plunking someone? Other variables had to be considered as well: the pitcher's own reputation as a cheap-shot artist, and the club he was pitching for (some teams hit batters often enough to suggest that they'd made a policy of it). La Russa was also aware of his own innate bias, the same bias that all managers have: It was *intentional* if one of his batters got hit, *accidental* if one of his pitchers hit a batter. If sparks flew during a game, it was often this built-in bias that caused them. It's also why, when La Russa's batters were on the receiving end, he went to Duncan for help.

But once you were convinced of malicious intent, deciding how to respond got only more fraught. Because this wasn't about playing a hit-and-run. This wasn't about putting on a bunt. This wasn't about pushing for a run or saving one. This was about *hitting* someone. "If you put yourself in the manager's shoes, the responsibilities and the consequences are huge," La Russa points out. "You're telling someone on your club to hit someone on the other side." Thrown baseballs had ended careers; one had killed a major-league player. In meetings with pitchers during spring training, he issued clear guidelines: Any kind of message had to be aimed at the ribs or below, and nothing above the shoulder would be tolerated.

III

LA RUSSA KNEW that over the years, he had gained a reputation for being vengeful when perhaps vengeance wasn't necessary. He was also known as something of a headhunter himself, but La Russa says that he has never told a pitcher to throw at a hitter simply because he was too dangerous at the plate and needed to be quieted down. "If a guy is hitting good against us, I have never told a pitcher to go out and drill him. I have said, 'Pitch the guy tough, pitch the guy different.' If a pitcher does something on his own, I will take him out. I will not hesitate. You can pitch a hitter inside. You can try to open up the plate on him, get him to speed up the bat. But you do not drill him."

In July 1995, the A's played the Blue Jays at the Coliseum in Oakland. In the second inning, Mark McGwire, batting for the A's, got to a tough slider away and blasted a home run. The next day, David Cone, pitching for the Blue Jays, hit McGwire in the head, and McGwire had to go to the hospital with a possible concussion. Cone pitched into the eighth inning without giving up a walk, bringing La Russa to what he considered an obvious conclusion —other than beaning McGwire, Cone had exhibited no control problems whatsoever. He was furious, convinced that McGwire had been hit, *in the head,* as retribution for his home run the night before.

Taking the Hammurabi Code into his own hands, La Russa ordered Mike Harkey to hit the Blue Jays' Joe Carter. Harkey did so, literally bending over backward to obey the rule laid down in spring training. He hit Carter in the buttocks, an act of fleshy mercy compared to what La Russa believed Cone had done. But Carter didn't like it. He pointed to La Russa glowering in the dugout and yelled at him.

"*You* caused all this!"

Which brought La Russa steaming out toward Carter.

"We have a guy in the hospital with a concussion, and you're whining about a *bee sting!*"

Will Clark was more matter-of-fact than Carter when *he* got hit in retaliation for a pitcher again drilling McGwire. Clark had once signed a bat for the animal rescue foundation La Russa had formed so it could be auctioned off to raise money, and he sent a message back afterward:

"Tell the manager, no more autographs."

In older days, verbal histrionics rarely intruded on the quiet cause-and-effect of a pitcher punishing a hitter for some perceived slight. Pitchers like Bob Gibson and Don Drysdale laid down a clear-cut rule: In the fight for the Gaza Strip of the plate, middle away belonged to them, and middle in belonged to the hitter. As long as you didn't venture over into the pitcher's territory, you were okay. But if you did, you were going to get banged, and you had no one but yourself to blame. Naiveté, rookie eagerness, ignorance of the rule—none of it could excuse you from your fate.

Umpires, on the directive of major-league baseball, have become far more vigilant about keeping the game from devolving into a dogfight. When a hitter gets drilled, umpires are more inclined to warn both teams that any retaliation will get the offending pitcher and his manager ejected. But no amount of vigilance can erase the Hammurabian compulsion toward justice.

Early this season in Colorado, the pitcher on the mound for the

Rockies, Dan Miceli, threw one at Edmonds's legs in the twelfth, forcing him to dance out of the way. La Russa wasn't quite sure how it was intended. Pitchers have to throw inside at Coors Field more than at any other major-league stadium because the ball carries so far in the mile-high air. If you don't, hitters simply whack it like a tee ball. Which is pretty much what Edmonds had been doing all night, 4 for 6 with a homer, two doubles, and five RBIs.

In the second game of the series, Nelson Cruz's first pitch to Edmonds was up and in; he went down to dodge it. The second pitch hit him in the shoulder. Now La Russa had an answer to the question he had been agonizing over the night before.

He waited for the right time and the right batter to make what he considered the right move, in this case, a message. In the third inning, Cards pitcher Brett Tomko threw behind Todd Helton, the Rockies' best hitter—a shot across his bow that responded to Cruz's assault, while keeping Tomko in the game. Home plate umpire Mike DiMuro promptly put the warning into both benches. But La Russa wasn't so sure it was over.

"This guy Cruz thinks he's John Wayne," he told DiMuro. "He's gonna take another shot." And in the top of the seventh, he hit Tino Martinez. Cruz and Clint Hurdle, the Rockies' manager, were immediately ejected. But their ouster did little to soothe La Russa, still furious over what he saw as the original gutlessness of hitting Edmonds in the first inning because his bat had been so hot the night before.

The Rockies' bench coach was Jamie Quirk. In the early 1990s, Quirk had played for La Russa. He later went into coaching, and La Russa had recommended him as a manager. He considered Quirk a friend. But he also felt that Quirk had crossed a line, that he had played a role in what had happened, or at least could have done more to prevent Edmonds from getting drilled in the first place. He had Quirk's cell phone number and he left a message after the game. "You don't take cheap shots," he told him. "Just because Edmonds is swinging good, you just don't go out and drill him."

After the next-day's game, La Russa was heading to the team bus when he saw Quirk in the hallway that leads to the Coors Field parking lot. By now, La Russa had had twenty-four hours to pon-der what had happened. He'd learned the hard way not to confront someone too soon after he had done something during a game that upset La Russa. One night in 1996, after the Cardinals had dropped a close game to the Braves, he zeroed in on John Mabry as a sym-bol of the loss because he played first and had been laughing at something with Fred McGriff after McGriff had gotten on base. Immediately after the game, La Russa went off on Mabry, accused him of not caring enough—too busy chatting with McGriff—to give the game the competitive focus it demanded. As soon as the words left his mouth, he knew he had made a mistake—looking for someone to kick after a tough loss and finding the wrong target in Mabry, who was a competitor. La Russa apologized the next day, but their relationship had been affected. Mabry began to mistrust his manager; his performance suffered. He ended up going else-where, and La Russa believes that his impromptu outburst caused Mabry's decline with the Cardinals.* As a result, La Russa began to enforce a twenty-four-hour gag order on himself: He would keep his mouth shut for a full day to assess how much of his anger might be legitimate and how much might be caused by the fresh pain of losing. If he still felt agitated, the twenty-four-hour rule also gave him time to figure out something constructive to say.

With a full day of distance from the current skirmish, La Russa could do something like that with Quirk here. They were friends. He had recommended *Quirk* for jobs. *Quirk* had played for him. Seeing Quirk in the hallway, he had the opportunity to chalk up what had happened to the passion that sometimes overtakes the game. Instead, still disappointed, he looked right through him as if he weren't there.

Less than two weeks later, the Cards were playing the Dia-mondbacks at Busch. It was a pitcher's duel between Tomko and Miguel Batista, scoreless into the fifth when Arizona scratched out a run on doubles by Craig Counsell and David Dellucci. In the bot-

---

* Mabry subsequently returned to the Cardinals for the 2004 season. He hit .296, an indication that he accepted La Russa's apology.

tom of the fifth, Tino Martinez led off for the Cardinals. Batista threw him a ball. Then he hit him in the right shoulder blade, and then he stared at him after he hit him, rubbing it in: Take that, you *son-of-a-bitch.*

Before the game, La Russa had felt the fluttering in his stomach over the prospect of facing Batista and what could occur. He was in that category of pitcher who had gained a reputation for plunking batters. But La Russa didn't anticipate it happening, not with the score 1–0. Now that it had, a shot near Martinez's head, the fluttering rose into the dread of how to respond. It was the stare-down that led La Russa to believe that he had acted on his own, that there might have been bad blood between Martinez and Batista left over from the 2001 World Series between the Diamondbacks and the Yankees. So now the gut-wrenching question arose again: *What do you do about it?* La Russa took up his inner Godot dialogue:

We've gotten hit a lot.

It's not coincidental that we lead the league in hitting and getting hit by pitches.

We don't see Arizona again until the end of the year.

Tino has been hit four times this season, and the first three times, I didn't do squat.

We have to send the right message.

La Russa scanned the Diamondback lineup and immediately found the appropriate subject for retaliation against, given the situation. It was Luis Gonzalez, who had hit fifty-seven home runs two seasons earlier in 2001 and had so nobly gutted it out against Mariano Rivera's rapier cutter in the ninth inning of the seventh game with two outs, blooping it into center like a falling Easter egg to win the World Series for the Diamondbacks. On the basis of talent alone, Gonzalez was the obvious candidate. But the choice was complicated by personal entanglements.

Gonzalez, Martinez, and La Russa were all from Tampa. They had all gone to the *same* high school, Jefferson High, in Tampa. And Gonzalez was one of the classiest guys in the league, doing frequent charity work in the off-season because it meant something to him and not because some agent told him that he should do it for his image. One of those charity events had been a special appearance of behalf of La Russa's foundation.

There were strategic complications too. Once La Russa decided that he had to do something and that Gonzalez was the guy he had to do something to, the score was 1–0 Arizona in the eighth. Given where Gonzalez fell in the order, he might not get another at-bat, and justice might be denied.

So when the Diamondbacks' Junior Spivey singled and stole second with two outs, it was, oddly, a blessing for La Russa, the opening he needed. The count had run to 1 and 2 on the batter at the plate, Chad Moeller, when Spivey stole. Suddenly, La Russa gave the sign to intentionally walk Moeller. With first base open, it appeared as if he had simply decided to pitch around Moeller. But that was just the cover: Moeller's free ride to first had nothing to do with thinking that the next batter would be an easier out.

He didn't want Moeller to end the eighth inning with an out, because that might put Gonzalez out of reach in the ninth, as he would be batting fourth. So he put Moeller on even though the count had run to 1 and 2. He took a chance on runners on first and second in a 1–0 nail biter, just to make sure that Gonzalez would definitely come up in the ninth.

The score was still 1–0 going into the top of the ninth when La Russa brought in Jeff Fassero. He told the reliever that he hoped he could get the first two batters out. And then he told him to do what is standard in a situation such as this—throw a breaking ball away so it looks like he's having a little control problem, then hit Gonzalez in the ribs with the next pitch. Fassero executed it perfectly. Gonzalez got hit. Fassero and La Russa were both ejected, and the Cards ended up losing 1–0.

La Russa knew that he had possibly affected the game's outcome for the sake of retaliation. He also realized that his friendship with Gonzalez might suffer. That bothered him immensely because Gonzalez, in a game so littered with go-through-the-motion fakes, was the real thing both professionally and personally. After the game, he left him a message on his cell phone, just like he had done with Quirk, trying to explain his reasoning:

"You can think what you want, but you check with anybody who has played with me. We don't hit someone just because they're hitting good against us."

He still didn't like what he had done. He sifted through the layers of his decision deep into the night and through the off day on Monday before the team chartered out to Atlanta. He knew that if he didn't protect his players, didn't stand up for them, the respect they gave him—a porous bond to begin with in the distracted world of the modern athlete—would crumble away. Richards had once told him that sometimes, you have to be willing to lose a game to win more later. And this, La Russa concluded, had been one of those times.

La Russa isn't sure that Wood intentionally pitches up into the danger zone as much as he doesn't quite know where the ball will land when he throws inside. Wood himself insists that his victims have been plunked by innocent curve balls that simply got away from him. But Wood's role models are Ryan and Clemens, pitchers without qualms about drilling batters. La Russa also believes that Wood is susceptible to the media frenzy that occurs over the prospect of beanball wars, stories that only encourage young power pitchers to take the bait and feel compelled to strut their machismo. Because Wood is normally so aggressive—trying to reach the mid- and upper nineties with his fastball—he tends to hurry and fall out of his delivery, which causes the ball to sail even more than usual into uncharted territory. But to La Russa, that's not much of an excuse when the result is a batter getting hit. It's still a dangerous headball, which is why La Russa is also so adamant that the baseball commissioner's office give out automatic suspensions in all but obviously accidental circumstances. If major-league baseball is not proactive, he is convinced, more and more players will get seriously injured. "The key," he explains, "is whether or not a club is trying to pitch inside just for effect. That's okay if they have command. But if they're pitching without command and guys keep getting hit, then at some point, they should quit doing it. We're not gonna be targets."

8

LIGHT MY FIRE

I

● ● ● IT QUICKLY becomes clear that Kerry Wood and Woody Williams are waging the pitchers' duel La Russa anticipated tonight. Each stays within the sphere of his respective strengths and style: Wood flailing about like a restless child; Williams so economical he's almost invisible.

In the top of the first, Williams dispatches the Cubs with fourteen pitches, unfazed by a double that Ramon Martinez, batting in the two-hole, strokes into the right-field gap. Wood follows with a style whose only constants are unpredictability and success. His fastballs fly so high that the Cubs' catcher, Damian Miller, reaches for them as though he's scurrying up a stepladder. His breaking balls fall off the plate because he finishes his delivery in such haste. Then he uncorks a rat-a-tat of nasty stuff in and around the zone, striking out Bo Hart and Scott Rolen. He seems all confusion on the mound: *Hey, it's not my fault the ball won't tell me where it's going.* But it's misleading. La Russa can already tell that they're facing Effectively Wild Wood tonight — hitters at the mercy of his orchestrated whimsy.

Through three innings, Williams is achieving the same end by the opposite means. He's thrown only thirty-nine pitches, including a five-pitch second inning. By the bottom of the third, when Kerry Robinson comes to bat for the Cardinals with one out and nobody on, Wood's flailing has already produced four strikeouts. Robinson's in the lineup by default because of the injury to J.D. Drew, and it looks like that way when Wood sends him a nasty slider, and he responds by weakly swinging through it. Wood comes next with a fastball outside and away on the black. The pitch is more difficult to handle than the first one, that lethal combination of high-heat velocity and location you see sometimes on the Autobahn. But Robinson stays with it and slaps a single past third base, going the opposite way with it. In the dugout, La Russa has a lovely thought about Robinson: *That was a great piece of hitting.*

It proves to him what Robinson can do if he sets aside his sulkiness about not playing every day and accepts his place in the puzzle, not some tiny piece, but of ample size because of what a strong bench can do for a team beyond trying to capitalize on occasional playing time. It is a difficult role, and La Russa readily concedes the difficulty. But the spirit of bench players is as essential to the chemistry of a team as the spirit of a star player. You have a star player who treats his colleagues like inferiors; that's an essential edge your team has lost. You have a bench player who sulks; that's a valuable edge lost as well. Which is why La Russa wishes that Robinson would follow the lead of Eddie Perez and Miguel Cairo, bench players who not only do the obvious—make the most of their playing opportunities—but also act as assistant coaches for the very reason that they can soak up the game. They can often figure out an opposing pitcher's pitch beforehand because of the way he holds the ball in the glove. They can offer subtle advice to infielders who are getting into the habit of laying back on the ball instead of charging, or sweetly scold fellow hitters who are getting pull-happy and flying open at the plate.

Certainly Robinson's approach to the game has improved since an episode several weeks ago against the Phillies when he was pinch-hitting and took a pitch pretty much down the pipe for a strike instead of swinging, then ultimately struck out. La Russa likes his hitters to be aggressive on the first good strike they get in an RBI situation. Especially pinch hitters, because they often get only *one* good strike in the entire at-bat. La Russa and his coaches inculcate this philosophy into players from the earliest stages of spring training, and Robinson's failure to apply it irked the manager. After the game, he summoned Robinson into the visiting manager's office in the penal colony of Veterans Stadium to discuss why he wasn't following such a basic precept.

"As a general run-producing philosophy," he reminded Robinson, "you have to be aggressive and ready to swing at the first good strike. It's true for most hitters. Especially true for pinch hitters."

"No, no. I don't challenge that philosophy," said Robinson.

"Well, that's good because it's been developed by watching too many guys produce."

Case closed. Meeting over. Since then, Robinson seems to have given the basics more of the respect they deserve.

To Robinson, this hit against Wood is further proof that he should be playing *every day,* that with a little faith, he can be another Juan Pierre. He knows he's no slugger, but he has speed; he can steal and stretch doubles into triples. And he believes that he can handle the bat better when he plays every day, because he admits that it's difficult for him to get into any kind of rhythm coming off the bench, a cold can of soup barely heated up. On a visceral level, coming off the bench profoundly contradicts his self-image. "This is my third year in the big leagues, and I don't want to just be labeled as a bench guy without even having an opportunity to start at the big-league level," he says.

He has impressive local lineage, a heralded three-sport St. Louis high school athlete who set school records in 1991 for the highest batting average (.557) and for the most goals scored in hockey (twenty-nine). His first year with the Cardinals in 2001 was the first time he had ever been on the bench in his athletic life. During the following season and this one as well, he has made a deliberate attempt not to think about baseball except when he has to —when he's taking batting practice or loosening up in the cage in the fourth or fifth because he may go in at some point or on those rare occasions when he's in the game from the beginning. Otherwise, he would only dwell on not starting. "If I go there and think about it all the time, I'll drive myself crazy," he confesses. And now that he is getting a chance to play regularly, he does wonder whether his moment has arrived. "Maybe this is my time now, for all I know," he muses.

La Russa would like nothing better than for now to be Robinson's time, although one sweet hit is still a single. It's not stealing home in the bottom of the ninth. It's not a bases-clearing double. It's pretty much what you should expect from Robinson under the circumstances that he is not an everyday player.

Because it should be Drew in there, the pivotal series in the pivotal point in the season with first place at stake and the possibility of one of those momentum surges that pushes you through September and into the shadowy, sublime October light when playoff games are waged. It is the reason to play baseball—getting to that moment where, as Dusty Baker put it just before tonight's game, the "leaves turn to brown and somebody wears the crown."

History is here. Finely aged rivalry is here. Tension is here. Competition is here. Everything you want in baseball is here, everything you can still hope for in this era of narrowing expectations. Except for Drew, the parable of the modern-day athlete.

II

DREW ROCKS FIREBALLERS like Prior and Wood. He rocks anybody who thinks he can throw fire by him. Like he did earlier this season when he hit a 514-foot dinger, the longest home run ever recorded at Busch by a left-handed hitter, blocked in its flight by the scoreboard or it would have gone even farther. He's pressure-proof, like the home run he hit in the eighth inning off Curt Schilling's forkball in the deciding fifth game of the 2001 playoffs to tie the game at 1–1. It's why the Cardinals spent $7 million on Drew as a first-round pick in the 1998 draft. It's why, when they got their first look at him in the uniform—saw the speed, the fluid left-handed stroke, the way the ball just launched off the bat—they thought *Mickey Mantle,* as dangerous, maybe, as thinking *Sandy Koufax* when they saw Rick Ankiel.

But his talent was that big, and La Russa wonders whether perhaps it still is that big, submerged within that remote exterior like other great players have been remote, wearing a Cardinals uniform but never really a part of the team, alone in the clubhouse most of the time, shunning membership in any of the cliques, saying little in his southern accent as thick as an Irish brogue, shuffling to the cage during batting practice like a tired old man, taking his cuts in silence and then shuffling away in silence. And then he does something prodigious and spectacular and beautiful because his swing is so beautiful, tight and compact and as effortless as walking. But La Russa has resigned himself to wondering whether he'll ever get to *it,* whatever that *it* is at this point. And as much as he believes that there is nothing he can do—that he can't create fire—part of him knows that his very job as a manager is to create fire, whatever its temperament. And it pulls at him that his best wasn't good enough.

Like others, La Russa's early hopes for him were maybe too heady; there's no surer doom for anyone than great expectations. In the history of intercollegiate baseball, it was difficult to find someone with more of a can't-miss pedigree. In his junior year at Florida State in 1997, Drew recorded the first 30-30 season in NCAA Division One history, with thirty-one homers and thirty-two steals, but that was just a small part of the almost supernatural epic told by his statistics:

G	AB	R	H	2B	3B	HR	RBI	BB	SO	SB	AVG	OBP	SLG.
67	233	110	106	15	3	31	100	84	37	32	.455	.599	.961

The irresistible comparisons came out—that here, after all those years and all that sifting in the dust of some diamond for gold—was a true find, a natural stroke as pure as Musial and Mantle and Aaron and Mays. The references put him under a cloud from the very beginning, the notion that he was bound for the Hall of Fame before he'd had a single big-league at-bat.

As such, he was the *unsuperstar.* Other players talked about him, much of it disparaging, much of it along the lines of *Who the hell does this kid think he is?* and *Who cares how many homers he hit at Florida State?* He won few admirers when the Phillies made him the first-draft pick and he scoffed at their record-setting offer: $2.6 million signing bonus and $6 million overall for a five-year contract. Through his agent, he said that he was thinking more in terms of a $5 million signing bonus and $11 million overall. Drew ultimately refused to sign with the Phillies, an act that drew headlines and condemnation around the country. Fairly or unfairly, he was portrayed over and over as selfish, the personification of everything wrong with the modern young athlete. He played for the St. Paul Saints in the Independent League and re-entered the draft in 1998. The Cardinals made him the fifth pick overall and signed him to a four-year deal worth $7 million guaranteed and as much as $9 million, including various bonuses and incentives. The signing was announced with much fanfare and ballyhoo, particularly because the Cardinals had done what the Phillies could not. In the euphoria of it, only one question remained: How good was he?

He came up to the Cardinals in September 1998 after a mere forty-five games in the minors at Arkansas and Memphis. In his first eight games, he batted .350, with three homers, seven RBIs, and a .900 slugging percentage. La Russa said that he hadn't seen a better first week in the majors since 1985, when Jose Canseco had played against his White Sox. "Let's take it easy," La Russa also cautioned at the time. "He doesn't need more notoriety. He needs less." Even that first week, as good as it was, contained the tiny hint of something to watch for when he was scratched from the lineup in one game because of back stiffness. It became a leitmotif of his career, the rhythm of his performance continually broken by injury.

His first full season in the majors, 1999, was not the stuff of immortality but the stuff of a mortal player still trying to get a handle on the potential humiliations of a big-league curve. He hit .242, with thirteen home runs and nineteen steals. He played in only 104 games, spending six weeks on the sidelines because of an injury to his quadriceps.

The next two seasons—2000 and 2001—were improvements. He hit .295 in 2000, with eighteen home runs. In 2001, he rose to .323, with twenty-seven home runs. But he still made frequent trips to the disabled list. His average number of at-bats in both those seasons was less than four hundred, and in 2002 he slipped badly:

G	AB	R	H	2B	3B	HR	RBI	BB	SO	SB	AVG	OBP	SLG.
135	424	61	107	19	1	18	56	57	104	8	.252	.349	.429

There were also more injuries, this time a tendon in his knee. He had surgery in the off-season to repair it, meaning that he would start this current season on the disabled list. Injuries are part of baseball; there's no way to avoid them. But something else about Drew began to concern La Russa, something trickier and more elusive than a damaged knee or a strained quadriceps.

Increasingly, La Russa wondered whether Drew's underlying ailment, like it was for so many young players coming into sudden millions, was an absence of sustained passion that had no medical remedy. Did he simply lack the will to play in a way that would fulfill all those auguries? La Russa urged him to not be satisfied with what he had done, that there was so much more he could do if he committed himself to doing it. La Russa knew that Drew was making $3.6 million this season and told him that he could probably pull in double that in future seasons if he put some added heat into his game, went into it with the same kind of relentlessness that Albert Pujols did on every at-bat. He even offered to put Drew into the same batting practice grouping as Pujols from the very first day of spring training in the further hope that the great Pujols would rub off on him. He told Drew that he could make the kind of money in baseball that could guarantee a lifetime of security. But as he spoke, it dawned on him that for a small-town boy from Georgia who still lived where he had grown up, $3.6 million a year was already ample bounty. He told Drew that it was a waste for him to simply go along like this when he could be so much more. They'd had these talks more than once, but La Russa knew that he had never gotten through to him, except when he threatened to bench him if he didn't choke up with two strikes to better defend himself against striking out.

During spring training this year, when Drew couldn't play because of his knee rehabilitation, he left the dugout in the middle of a contest against the Expos to head back to the clubhouse. La Russa had no problem with the regulars doing that once they were done playing for the day. It was a little bit of the special treatment that a regular got, the extra care and stroking. But Drew wasn't a regular at this point. It upset La Russa, because if Drew couldn't play, the least he could do was watch, see what a pitcher was up to, put it in the back pocket somewhere for the regular season. Williams was in the dugout even though he wasn't pitching. So was Matt Morris. And even when Drew had been physically there, his whole body language suggested to La Russa, *Why am I here?* His head lolled back and he seemed to be looking at everything he could except for the game on the field. La Russa's feeling was, *You're in the big leagues. Watch and learn.*

The next morning, La Russa called Drew into his office in the Jupiter compound. "If you come, you stay the full nine, that's the deal," he scolded, and then he fined him $250. Drew left the office, looking like most players do when they leave the manager's office, the look of a pained little boy suddenly unsure how much he really likes his mother because of all these rules she makes you follow. But because the fine came out of his meal money check, it didn't even dent his $3.6 million salary. And even if it had, it would amount to approximately .00015 percent of his compensation. To La Russa, the issue wasn't money. It was the message he was sending, maybe an ultimatum, about what he expected of Drew and what Drew should expect of himself.

Drew returned to the lineup toward the end of April. He struggled, as any player will struggle coming back from knee surgery. Against the Expos in early May, with first place on the line and the score 3–1 Cards in the bottom of the eighth, La Russa tried a delayed double steal with Drew on third, Jim Edmonds on first, and Rolen at the plate. It was a daring play—on the surface, managerial aggressiveness *without* common sense—but the Expos' third baseman, Fernando Tatis, was playing so deep, almost on the outfield grass, that La Russa saw an opening and went for it. With Tatis too far off the bag to pick him off, Drew could take an unusually long lead off third. He should have broken for home with fury once it became apparent that the catcher's throw was going straight to second, where Edmonds was heading, instead of being cut off by the pitcher. But Drew took a short lead off third, despite Jose

Oquendo's urgings, and then got a lousy jump off the throw. He was caught in a rundown, and instead of scrambling for his life to avoid it, he simply surrendered.

God damn, J.D.! The words coursed through La Russa in the dugout, but he said nothing to Drew as he sheepishly returned with his head ducked down. The play was as blown and ugly as it gets, and now La Russa would have to explain to Rolen why he'd put more faith in a misplaced fielder than in Rolen's dependable bat.

Later that night, La Russa had dinner at Dominic's in suburban St. Louis with one of the Cardinals owners. Despite winning the game 3–1, he was brooding about Drew, wondering once more whether there was some way to get to him, let that talent pour out in terrific torrents. He pulled out an index card and began to write down possible things to say to him, all of which he realized he had said already. He put the card back in his breast pocket after several minutes. The conversation turned to how many players La Russa had managed who have had that rare combination of talent and fiery heart, refused to settle for good as long as there was the horizon of greatness. La Russa approached it methodically, combing carefully through each of the three teams he had managed. He deliberated carefully because it was an interesting question that required an interesting answer. It was easy to think of players who had one or the other. *Most* players who had hit the big leagues had one or the other. But *both* was rare, very rare. As he gave out a name, it got written down on a list.

Seventeen. That's what it came out to when he was finished. He looked at the names to make sure he hadn't missed anyone. Seventeen. In twenty-four years of managing, seventeen players who had willed themselves to put it all together. It was a small number—depressing, really—reflective of how many ballplayers are content to coast along on the basis of the talent they have when they could do so much more. As La Russa looked at the makeshift list, he wondered how many more there could have been had he done a better job of managing, had he figured out a way to punch through. The conversation circled back to Drew, and the nagging question arose in La Russa's mind once again: Was it J.D.'s fault that he wasn't playing to his level, or was it the fault of the manager he played for?

In the weeks since, Drew has shown glimmers of the magic that set apart those seventeen. He continued to play according to his own mercurial rhythm, such flashes of brilliance you still knew that it was all going to pour out one day; other moments when he was slowed down or stopped completely by injury. Which meant that four months down the road in the three-game series against the Cubs, he would not play at all, replaced by a player who would never match fire with fire on a fastball but who was consumed by the burning desperation to play each and every day.

III

WITH ROBINSON on first after that slapped single into left, Hart comes up to bat, and one of baseball's most controversial plays becomes a possibility: *hit-and-run.* Some managers loath it because the swing that puts the ball in play usually costs a precious out and the dividend—moving the man on first to second—often doesn't materialize. Other managers embrace the *hit-and-run* because they believe that it's worth giving up an out to put a runner in scoring position and stay out of the double play. Plus, if it's executed properly and the ball finds a hole, the play has created a run-scoring opportunity, maybe even a crooked number because of the *hit-and-run's* unique momentum.

When La Russa was a novice manager with the White Sox, he spent a great deal of time at the Bard's Room. It was the kind of place that doesn't exist in baseball anymore, a seedy, stinky hole in the wall, where baseball men congregated to drink and smoke and debate the game's intricacies into the small hours. La Russa showed up just about every night, finding the back-and-forth dialogue tantamount to "getting your Ph.D. in baseball." So did luminaries from the White Sox front office, such as general manager Rollie Hemond and Paul Richards. So did Billy Martin and Sparky Anderson, skippers who would attend when their teams were in town, as well as some of the game's greatest scouts. Presiding over all of it was the one-in-a-millennium Bill Veeck, with a beer in one hand and a cigarette in the other.

Veeck made it a point of his life to never view himself, or anyone else, with too much pomp and circumstance. He titled his memoir *Veeck as in Wreck,* and he brought a similar mindset to baseball, which he saw above all as entertainment. In gauging his life in baseball, inevitable disputes arise as to which of his promotions was the most inspired. It may have been the one in 1951, when, as owner of the St. Louis Browns, he sent 3'7" Eddie Gaedel to the plate for his only major-league appearance. His uniform bore the number ⅛ and he drew a walk, even though the catcher, trying to frame the proper strike zone, dropped to his knees. Or it could have been the one later that season when he sat the Browns' manager in a rocking chair next to the dugout and invited the fans to manage by consensus. Browns' coaches showed placards suggesting various options — bunt, hit-and-run, pinch-hit — and the spectators delivered their verdict by holding up cards showing either yes or no. Or maybe the one in which he had six midgets race from the outfield to home plate in Cleveland, with Bob Hope as the emcee. Less successful, however, was the infamous Disco Demolition Night right before La Russa's arrival.

But not all of Veeck's stunts were designed to work laughs. He hated the stuffy sanctimony of the game, but he also revered the game. It was Veeck who planted the ivy on the outfield wall of Wrigley. It was Veeck who first put the names of players on the back of their uniforms. It was Veeck who invented the exploding scoreboard, and it was also Veeck who in 1947, half a century before it would become reality, first suggested interleague play.

The White Sox were his last hurrah, the hiring of La Russa one of his final acts. The sheer surprise of it was typical of him, for La Russa was far too young — only thirty-four — and unproven by anyone's standards except Veeck's. But bringing him in was no stunt; Veeck could see that La Russa more than loved the game — he thirsted for it, studied it voraciously, couldn't get enough of it. Veeck also liked the fact that La Russa was studying law in the off-season. Before hiring him, Veeck made him promise that he would pass the bar and get his license.

An important part of La Russa's baseball indoctrination was the Bard's Room, where Veeck purposely pitted him against dyed-in-the-wool baseball men to see how he handled himself, how he struck the balance between deference to the elders and defending his convictions. He loved to see arguing, and one of the best ways to achieve that was simply to mention the phrase *hit-and-run*. Before you knew it, Richards and La Russa would be debating with each other, La Russa thinking it worthy in certain circumstances, his mentor thinking it worthless in all circumstances. Richards saw it in much the same way that Woody Hayes at Ohio State viewed the forward pass: Three things could happen, and two of them were bad. In the middle would be Veeck, adding saucy comments just to keep the debate going — *it's smart, it's stupid, it can work, it can't work* — his only break from stoking the fire when he flicked his cigarette ash into a little hole he had built into his wooden leg.

In this particular moment in Game 2, with a runner on first and one out in the bottom of the third, La Russa is weighing the matchup between Hart and Wood as a reason to consider the *hit-and-run*. It's not a great matchup for Hart, given Wood's nasty curve. So if he can *hit-and-run* Robinson to second, it will give Pujols a better opportunity to drive in the run, which, in La Russa's mind, makes it worth any potential sacrifice.

Because La Russa believes in the *hit-and-run*, he has his players work on it exhaustively during spring training and throughout the season during batting practice. The goal he sets for them is simple: to hit the ball on the ground as hard as you can. He does not advocate guiding the ball toward a certain location, because trying to do that only takes away from how hard a hitter can sting it. If the ball is middle in on the plate, you try to pull it. If the ball is middle away, you take it to the opposite field. La Russa also believes that by practicing the *hit-and-run*, you can dramatically increase the number of hits you get out of it: from five out of fifty to possibly fifteen.

It is a winning play if the result is a hit. But even at 15 out of 50, it's still not a great percentage. The other problem is that the more successful you are with it, the more opposing managers look for it and try to defend against it, the Darwinian evolution of baseball working much like it did when steals were getting out of hand.

Opposing managers will pay obsessive attention to the kind of lead a runner is taking off first base, trying to glean whether it's a true base-stealing lead or the slightly less precocious *hit-and-run* lead. In a base-stealing lead, the runner must explode toward second at some point in the pitcher's delivery, commit himself to swiping the bag, which is why most managers, faced with the choice between a runner's getting picked off first or getting thrown out at second, will take the pick-off because at a minimum, it implies aggressiveness. In a *hit-and-run* lead, the runner must not risk the possibility of a pick-off, so there is no similar explosion: Once he takes his lead, he's just a little bit more stable.

Opposing managers will also scrutinize the divinations coming from the third-base coach and see whether their own code breakers on the bench can decrypt them. If they think they have sniffed right on the *hit-and-run,* they may call for a pitch out, which for the offense can result in a hitter's swinging through a lousy pitch *and* the runner's getting thrown out at second, a terrible result and yet not even the worst one, precisely why Richards hated it so much.

A manager contemplating the *hit-and-run* continually struggles to evade detection. So many eyes are watching him all the time, his only recourse is to bury himself in the corner of the dugout as deeply as possible. For La Russa, one of the subtle benefits of day games is the opportunity they give him to wear sunglasses, and La Russa likes wearing sunglasses because they make it impossible for an opposing manager to read his eyes. But most games are played at night.* And in some dugouts—Wrigley, for example—it's impossible to hide effectively, because the layout ensures that a manager remains in view. So managers often resort to other measures. The highly respected Tom Kelly, when he was managing the Twins in the early 1990s, purposely picked lousy *hit-and-run* counts— 0-1, for example, when the batter was already at a deficit—to work the play and preserve the element of surprise. The gamble worked for a while, until other managers got wise to Kelly's *hit-and-run* pattern and began to pitch out. La Russa himself will put a *hit-and-*

---

* In 2004, La Russa switched from regular glasses at night games to tinted ones. The reason for the switch was to shield his eyes from code breaking.

run on from the bench without even telling all the parties involved. The way it works, the number two batter due up in the inning is told before the inning starts that he is going to *hit-and-run* on the first pitch if the hitter ahead of him gets to first. But the initial batter isn't told anything unless he makes it to first. Then the first-base coach tips him off in the kind of casual chitchat that occurs throughout the game, and the spontaneity of the information prevents him from making his lead too obvious. In these situations, of course, there are no signs, because the last thing you want to do is alert an opposing manager with signs, particularly if it's a runner you don't normally *hit-and-run* with.

Such a strategy has worked effectively, as it did against the Pirates earlier in the season. But the overriding problem with the *hit-and-run* is that it can blow up beyond all belief by making a complete fool out of the normally reliable line drive. Earlier this month, when the Cardinals were playing Atlanta, La Russa put on a *hit-and-run* with runners on first and second, no outs, and pitcher Woody Williams hitting. The likely play here was a bunt to advance the runners with the score tied 1–1 in the fifth. Williams did indeed show bunt on the first two pitches. But he is also a superb hitting pitcher, one of the best in the game, and with the count 1 and 1, La Russa pulled the trigger.

Williams swung away with the runners going. He hit a line drive to the left of the second-base bag. Shortstop Rafael Furcal leaped to catch it. First out. Second baseman Marcus Giles yelled to Furcal to give him the ball so he could step on the bag and double up Matheny at second. But Furcal had a certain moist look in his eye. He told Giles he could handle it all by himself. He stepped on the bag to double up the catcher Matheny. Second out. He tagged out Orlando Palmeiro as he vainly tried to get back to first. Third out. An unassisted triple play. Only the twelfth in major-league history. Thanks, *hit-and-run.* Go screw yourself.

It was the second triple play the Cardinals had hit into during the season on the basis of La Russa's *hit-and-run* fetish, the first against Colorado. It said something about La Russa's love of the play. It also showed how little he had moved from what coach

Charley Lau—impressed by La Russa's balls if not necessarily his brains—had said about him twenty-five years earlier when La Russa had first begun to manage.

The memories make using the *hit-and-run* here fraught with implications. As soon as Hart settles in at the plate, La Russa starts flashing signs to the third-base coach, Oquendo. He knows that Baker and the other Cubs coaches are vivisecting Oquendo, asking themselves what's up with all those scratches and sweeps and ear squeezes. La Russa wants Baker to ask what's up, just as Baker wants La Russa to think that maybe he's thinking, *C'mon, Tony, I wasn't born in a barn. I know your style, so I know all you're trying to do is fool me into thinking that something is up,* a diagonal back and forth from one dugout to the other, tracer bullets of dekes and feints and sucker punches.

Hart swings through a slider. Nothing's on: 0 and 1, a tough *hit-and-run* count. If Baker wants to go with a pitchout, 0 and 1 is a good time to do it, as there is little harm done even if he guesses wrong, the count moved only to 1 and 1. The 0-and-1 count also favors Wood. He can afford something nasty here off the plate that will be difficult to hit, which in turn only makes a successful *hit-and-run* that much more difficult to achieve.

Hart takes an up fastball. Nothing's on. The count goes to 1 and 1 as La Russa continues to flash signs to Oquendo. Simultaneously, Robinson takes an antsy lead off first base, not enough to show flat-out steal, but enough to suggest the flirtation of something. It's back to Baker, because maybe he should pitch out here. Or maybe that's exactly what La Russa wants him to do—*think* something is on so he does pitch out and drives the count back toward the hitter's favor to 2 and 1.

Baker does nothing. La Russa makes his move.

Robinson goes on the pitch. Wood throws a fastball that sails high, very high. It's a difficult pitch to hit: It defies all natural order to even touch it. Hart takes a kind of punchy tomahawk swing at it, a wondrous reflex action, and he gets it into the hole between first and second for a single. Robinson easily advances to third; this time, the *hit-and-run* has paid off handsomely. Suddenly, in the bottom of the third, it's gotten interesting, the ersatz top of the lineup working singles off Wood on two great pieces of hitting, with the heart of the order due up.

Pujols walks on four straight pitches, La Russa wincing only slightly when he takes an up curve ball on 1-0, because it's a hittable pitch and one that maybe he should have swung at. But now the bases are loaded and Edmonds is up, still with only one out.

No one can carry a team like Edmonds can when he's on his stroke. Since coming over to the Cardinals from Anaheim in 2000, he's averaged more than thirty home runs and a hundred RBIs a season. But he has been bothered by shoulder soreness lately, and possibly no hitter gets pounded inside as much as Edmonds, causing him to flinch and bail out even when pitches come nowhere close to the inside.

La Russa is familiar with the theory, promoted to gospel by *Moneyball,* that the most important hitting statistic today is on-base percentage. He doesn't dispute the value of players who can work walks in any situation and have a diamond merchant's eye for the strike zone. But he also sees it as akin to the latest fashion fad —oversaturated, everybody doing it, everybody wearing it, until you find out the hard way that stretch Banlon isn't quite as cool as originally perceived. And he tries to teach his players that the better decision is to play the scoreboard.

If you're leading off an inning, it makes sense to push the count into your favor, to be "really fine" in searching out that good strike. You might take a ball right over the plate, even if you think you can hit it hard, in the hope of drawing a walk. But if you're coming up with the bases loaded and one out, as Edmonds is now, the table obviously is *set.* You don't want patience here. You want aggression, which is what he pounded into Robinson after that game against the Phillies. You need to expand the zone in which you're willing to swing. Don't wait around like some haute couture stylist to get something perfect—be ready to go on that first good strike.

Edmonds has a nice advantage here. With three Cardinals aboard, Wood can't be too fine about what he brings. Which means that in the continual back and forth between hitter and pitcher, Ed-

monds now has the power. Wood throws a slider middle down on
the plate. It's there for Edmonds, right in his "happy zone," as La
Russa later puts it.

Edmonds takes it, looking for 0 and 1, clear that he was hoping
for something else and had no intention of swinging. Wood comes
in with a slider on the outside corner. Edmonds takes it, looking
again for 0 and 2.

Now the power returns to Wood; he can pick Edmonds to death
with nothing more than temptation. Forget a good strike in the
zone, because Wood has no use for them. He threw one, the first
one, and one is enough, and he finishes Edmonds off a pitch later
with a chest-high fastball. It brings up Rolen, with two outs and the
bases, of course, still loaded.

Wood comes in with a slider low, almost at Rolen's ankles. He
swings and misses and La Russa can almost hear the chorus of crit-
ics asking themselves why he chased at a pitch like that. But La
Russa prefers his aggressiveness here, would rather see it than
not, convinced that this aggression will produce more runs over the
course of the season. The only problem is that Rolen strikes out
four pitches later to end the inning. The Cards have just squandered
one of the stronger scoring opportunities baseball ever offers.

La Russa knows that they should have put a run on the board
here, maybe even a crooked number with the bases juiced and
one out and your four and five hitters up. He mourns the wasted
chance, and he worries about the emotional momentum that has
just swung over to Wood's favor. Escaping a jam like that will give
him a dangerous spillover of confidence, make him fall more
deeply in love than ever with the quality of his stuff, think he can
do anything and maybe actually do it. If the Cardinals had gotten a
couple of runs here, Wood's emotions might have gotten to him. He
might have gotten pissed off, overthrowing so much that he'd
morph from Effectively Wild Wood to plain old Wild Wood. Instead, he just tucked the killer knot of the order into bed in the bottom of the third without a peep of protest.

9

WHODUNIT

I

● ● ● SAMMY SOSA leads off the top of the fourth by grounding out to second on a breaking ball from Williams. Moises Alou strikes out on a breaking ball from Williams. Eric Karros flies out to center on a breaking ball from Williams. It's a fourteen-pitch inning. He is moving deeper and deeper into that zone of pure performance, each inning better than the previous. Unlike many pitchers, his stuff gets, as La Russa says, "more oiled" as he progresses further into a game. Because he is a pitchmaker rather than a thrower, he has to feel out his pitches, make sure that the cutter has bite and that the curve isn't too fat. So he often does in the first inning what Darryl Kile did: checks out his equipment like an auto racer to see what is working and what may need a little bit more fine-tuning. After the first two or three innings, the location and command of his pitches only improve, and he tends to sail ever more smoothly on to the seventh or eighth.

It's beautiful to watch a pitcher who can work a ball like this, somehow make the plate seem spacious and roomy and easy to target when it measures less than 20 inches across. In his foxhole, behind the camouflage of his get-away-from-me grimace, La Russa entertains an effusive thought: *He's nailing it.* And against Kerry Wood, he has to nail it if the Cardinals are to hang on long enough to force Dusty Baker to resort to his bullpen. There is no margin for carelessness or frustration or mental lapse.

Williams has done yeoman work in speeding up right-handed hitters' bats with the fastball inside so that they're way out in front when he comes in with his curve. His best side of the plate is the first-base side, the away side for righties, but tonight he's also been effective pitching inside to them. Which means that he's working both sides of the plate, so vital to the success of any pitcher. He's showing the kind of stuff that took him to a 12-and-3 record before the All-Star break.

He fell into a rut after the break and lost some confidence; tonight marks his sixth straight attempt to push his win total to fifteen for the season. La Russa and Duncan noticed that after the All-Star break, Williams had changed his style, trying to pitch everybody as if they were Babe Ruth. Instead of going after hitters to get strike 1, he tried to be too fine with his pitches, even with nobody on when a get-me-over fastball or curve would have the least consequences. The culprit, they suspected, was fatigue. Because of the crisis in the bullpen the first half of the season, Williams went deep into virtually every game he pitched. La Russa and Duncan needed him, and he responded beautifully, but the use wore on him. His arm inevitably got tired, which led to a lack of confidence in the sheer quality of his stuff, which then led to a greater urge than usual to pinpoint the ball in the perfect location. Which ironically only created even more fatigue because he might throw as many as twenty pitches in an inning in which he got a zero. Aware of the cycle, La Russa and Duncan have made a deliberate effort in Williams's recent starts to not overuse him. They have let him regain his strength, and it's showing tonight in the style that made him an All-Star, the proper symbiotic balance of aggression and pitch mixture.

Wood's parry to Williams in the bottom of the fourth confirms La Russa's premonition that getting out of the bases-loaded jam the inning before, neutering Jim Edmonds and Scott Rolen with strikeouts, has only added to his hubris. On the mound, he stares down batters with eyes that seem almost dead, no spark or sparkle at all: flat, cold executioner's eyes. Tino Martinez takes a curve ball looking for a strikeout. Edgar Renteria strikes out on a high fastball.

Mike Matheny strikes out on a slider that follows a 97-mph fastball. He threw first-pitch strikes to all three hitters, not to mention that he now has five strikeouts in a row. After four innings, the line score of Game 2, slotted into the center of the dark green score-board of Busch with its barebones essentials, reads like chapters in an unfolding thriller:

	1	2	3	4	R	H	E
CUBS	0	0	0	0	0	2	0
CARDINALS	0	0	0	0	0	3	0

The continuing contrast in style between Wood and Williams only accentuates the drama. Wood with that big kick and follow-through. Wood with those dead-fish eyes. Wood with that scraggle-haired Fu Manchu. Wood stepping off the mound after a strikeout and encircling it in a little warrior stomp. Wood picking up the rosin bag and heaving it down like it's a black barbell at a weight-lifting competition. Williams with a demure kick. Williams with the trim beard. Williams taking the ball after a strikeout and going right back to work. Williams picking up the rosin bag and putting it down like it is, after all, a rosin bag.

Williams builds a quick 0-2 count on Aramis Ramirez with a fastball and a sinker to begin the top of the fifth. He throws three straight balls, trying to get him to chase something high. But he comes back with a fastball low and away on the full count to strike him out. Alex Gonzalez grounds out to Williams in a three-pitch at-bat. Up comes Damian Miller in the eight-hole with two outs—Miller, who is 7 for 14 against Williams before tonight and has had more success against him than any other Cub.

It's the precise scenario that La Russa fretted over at his desk before the game, the possibility of Miller's getting on with two outs, failing to score before the third out is made but affecting the lineup so that the Cubs start off the following inning at the top. If Williams gets Miller out here, the pitcher, Wood, leads off the following in-ning, a major difference in terms of momentum.

Williams goes to 1 and 1 on Miller with two sinkers. Then he comes with a slider. From the foxhole, La Russa can see that the location is perfect, just perfect. It's down and away to the right-handed Miller, a sweet chase pitch. You can't throw a better slider in that situation. It's not humanly possible. Miller takes an embarrassed half-swing and manages to flare it into the outfield for a yappy little double: further proof that baseball *is* the cruelest game, that the best execution can still produce an unfair outcome.

Batting in the ninth spot, Wood pushes Williams to 2 and 2 before he grounds out to short to end the inning. It means a zero for the top of the fifth, a relatively easy zero, but that little fear La Russa nurtured has come to pass. The Cubs will start off the sixth with Kenny Lofton, the top of their order. But with Williams pitching the way he is, La Russa's fear might border on paranoia. Lofton has a meaningless hit tonight. So does Martinez in the two-hole. After them, the three-, four-, and five-hole hitters are a combined 0 for 6 against Williams, with two strikeouts. Sosa and Alou haven't even gotten it out of the infield. And Williams is getting better as the game continues, his impassivity belying the competitiveness that ticks inside him like an old-fashioned alarm clock; nothing can muzzle its insistent beat. On the dark green scoreboard, another chapter has been slotted into the whodunit:

	1	2	3	4	5	R	H	E
CUBS	0	0	0	0	0	0	3	0
CARDINALS	0	0	0	0		0	3	0

Leading off the bottom of the fifth, Williams burnishes his reputation as a great hitting pitcher by singling on a 1-and-1 curve that hangs a little high. It brings up Kerry Robinson, the Cards' lead-off man pro tem, and now La Russa has another crucial decision to make. But it won't sneak up on him, the very panic of indecision because a decision is demanded. In keeping with his mantra that the only way to keep up with the game is to stay ahead of it, he started playing out different what-ifs before the Cardinals came to bat in the fifth, the same as he does before every offensive inning. Leaving the foxhole and retreating to the back bench in the left corner of the dugout, pulling out his cheat sheets to make sure no nugget of prior information is missed, he considers the possibility of having Robinson bunt if Williams gets on base. By examining the scenarios this way, La Russa will be ready for the moment whatever moment arises—putting out his signs quickly to the players involved so there is no confusion or hesitation. The variable here, because in baseball there is always a variable, boils down to this in the bottom of the fifth: how hard to push in a 0–0 game that shows no signs of yielding runs without a fight.

First, La Russa considers Wood's pitch count. It stands at seventy-nine, which hardly suggests that the Cardinals are about to get rid of him, particularly as Baker is infamous for taking his starting pitchers deep into games. No one in the major leagues did it more last season; nineteen times he kept his starters in for more than 120 pitches. But once Wood's pitch count creeps over 100, even Baker has to think about calling the bullpen. The Cubs' bullpen is their soft spot; their setup men are greeted with relief by opposing hitters, vulnerable fill-ins after starters as good as Prior and Wood and Zambrano, their closer, Joe Borowski, getting through on grit without classic closer material. So, from La Russa's perspective, the most exploitable aspect of Wood's performance tonight is his pitch count. The best way to win against any top-shelf pitcher is not always trying to rack up runs against him, because however much you try, you may not rack up any. Instead, the most effective path is to work the count, resist the itch to chase after junk food off the plate, realize that a foul ball sometimes has more value than a fair one because it lengthens your at-bat.

If Wood's count were a little bit higher—if La Russa could look over at Baker in the visitor's dugout and know that he was thinking *bullpen*—pushing for a run now might not matter much. With Wood gone, a run would be easier to come by. But he'll be around for a while.

So pushing is important to La Russa, but *how important?* Because doing so entails some likely sacrifice. A successful bunt by Robinson moves Williams to second, with Hart and Pujols up next to try to drive him in. With Williams standing on first now, La Russa's internal debate takes up the antibunt argument in full drive:

Robinson got a base hit last time.

It's only the fifth, and you want to do a little something more than get the runner over.

There's something else unsettling him: who's on first. If Robinson bunts, Williams will have to dig for second. He's fully capable of doing that, but La Russa doesn't want him to run hard and chance an injury when he's pitching so well. (For the same reason, La Russa is also leaning away from putting on a *hit-and-run* here.) He juggles all these variables in a couple of seconds. No amount of pre-inning planning could buy him any time here; baseball follows its timepiece, not his, and he has to pull the trigger.

He places his faith in Robinson's bat: His fine piece of hitting last time up takes precedence. Wood throws a fastball high to make the count 1 and 0. He does the exact same thing on the next pitch to make the count 2 and 0. It's a hitter's count, and if Robinson gets a pitch to hit, he's going to get it now. Wood no longer has the luxury of trying something nasty off the plate. He's going to go with his strength, which is his fastball.

It's a 95-mph fastball. But lacking movement or location, the fastest fastball has all the subtlety of a streaker—little to it beyond the gainly flab of the buttocks. This fastball is down the pipe, just like that pitch the Phillies threw at him was down the pipe, about belt-high. It is *the* pitch to hit.

Robinson doesn't lift his bat. Everything that favored him suddenly dissolves. Wood, knowing that he got away with something and feeling good about it, hits the outside corner for a strike to make it 2 and 2. That gives him a little breathing room to expand the zone, which he does by throwing a 12-to-6 curve for strike 3.

Hart bounces up to the plate and hits a little nubber down the first-base line, slow enough so that the only play is to first for the second out. That summons Pujols, with Williams on second. La Russa draws a breath, wondering whether this is the moment of headball he's been dreading, particularly with first base open. Wood throws a fastball a little bit up in the zone, and Pujols swings through it.

It gives Wood the crucial first-pitch strike, but against Pujols, it has the effect only of making things a little more balanced for the pitcher. Wood knows this, as this is the twenty-fourth time he has faced Pujols, with the outcome seven hits and three homers. The other Cubs know this. The fans know this. And so does La Russa. Although he has managed Harold Baines and Carlton Fisk and Jose Canseco and Rickey Henderson and Mark McGwire, and although he is not prone to gratuity, La Russa calls Pujols the best player he has ever managed. He is loathe to ever single a player out, but he is also convinced that Baines and Henderson and all the rest—given the opportunity to play with Pujols season after season—would also conclude that he is the best. Pujols has the consummate qualities that every manager looks for in a player: good hands, a strong and accurate arm, instinctive hitting reflexes. But it's more than just the skill: In the best of times and the worst of times of baseball, the constant thundercloud of money overhanging the game, Pujols tries to exploit his skills *every* day through *every* at-bat.

He has achieved the status of superstar. His statistics are too irrepressible for him to be treated otherwise. But because he plays in a small media market, he is a superstar of unknown portfolio, rarely mentioned in the same breath as Alex Rodriguez or Barry Bonds, although the numbers he has put up his first two seasons are the best that any player in the history of the game has ever put up:[*]

AB	R	H	2B	3B	HR	RBI	BB	SO	AVG.	OBP.	SLG.
590	112	194	47	4	37	130	69	93	.329	.403	.610
590	118	185	40	2	34	127	72	69	.314	.394	.561

This season his numbers are even better, on a pace once again to hit thirty or more homers, drive in a hundred or more runs, score a hundred or more runs, and hit well over .300.

Wood follows his fastball with a curve up and away. Pujols doesn't chase, and the count goes to 1 and 1. It's typical of Pujols to

---

[*] Rodriguez hit 59 home runs, scored 241 runs, drove in 207 runs, and averaged .329 his first two seasons. Bonds hit 49 home runs, scored 196 runs, drove in 117 runs, and averaged .272. Pujols hit 71 home runs, scored 230 runs, drove in 257 runs, and averaged .321 his first two seasons.

lay off the pitch, his whole approach a remarkable combination of preparation, concentration, adjustment, and self-discipline. It is a combination that La Russa has seen before but never quite like this, the thick mix of all these different portions. It also explodes the supposition that hitting is fundamentally some inexplicable natural talent that cannot be substantially refined or perfected, something either you have or don't have. For Pujols, talent is where he begins.

II

HE SLIPPED IN out of nowhere. He wasn't a big-time bonus baby. He wasn't a first-round pick or even a tenth-round pick. At the outset, he seemed like nothing beyond a guy with a pretty good bat and an interesting glove who could tell people in twenty years around the grill that he once had a shot.

He was born with the real first name of Jose in Santo Domingo in the Dominican Republic. His family came to New York, where he was raised by his grandmother. After he saw a man get shot outside a grocery store as a teenager, she moved the kids to Missouri. He went to Fort Osage High School in Independence, then to Maple Woods Community College. A highly respected college coach who watched him play in a summer league over in Hays never thought that Pujols would make it, and he wasn't singing a solo. Pujols's body was soft. He was considered slow, never better than 4.6 or 4.7 seconds to first. His bat was slow as well, and he rarely pulled the ball. In a world buzzing with scouts and the coming of the next new thing—in which promising players are tracked from the age of twelve by the publication *Baseball America*—Pujols was the antithesis of the prodigal player. Before he was drafted, he was mentioned only once in the *St. Louis Post-Dispatch,* in 1997, as a "player to watch" in the Class 4A Missouri high school baseball tournament, alongside such unfamiliar names as Chris Francka and Eric O'Connor.

The Cardinals made him a thirteenth-round pick in the 1999 draft, the 402nd player taken overall, signing him for around

$30,000. In the annual "Down on the Farm" story in the *Post-Dispatch* in April 2000, he was listed as a future possibility for the Cardinals at third base, although the story made it clear that Chris Haas was considered to have the rosier prospects. He was still obscure, another player in the minor-league shuffle of Johnson City and Peoria and Potomac and New Haven and Memphis. But then he took off, first in Peoria, then in Potomac, ending up the season in Triple-A Memphis, where he clinched the Pacific Coast League playoffs over Salt Lake City with a homer in the thirteenth inning. He went to the Arizona Fall League afterward, and although he hit well, there was continued concern about his weight. The Cardinals set him up with a nutritionist and a strength coach. He came to spring training in 2001 with a body toned and svelte. On a Wednesday afternoon during a throw-away intrasquad game at Roger Dean Stadium, he hit a pitch that went over the left-field wall and smashed into the adjacent offices of the Montreal Expos—perhaps the most exciting thing that had happened to the Expos in their history—and La Russa wondered just what kind of prospect he had on his hands.

Younger players, particularly those who had spent most of the previous season at Class A ball, viewed spring training as a vacation because they figured they had no shot to make it. They floated through the bunt drills and the cut-off drills and the soft-toss drills in the mesh of the neatly laid-out batting cages with sweet smiles on their faces, just happy to be there and waiting for the next roster cutdown when they would be returned to the hinterland for further tenderizing. A manager, at least a manager with a clue, went out of his way to give a prospect a positive spring by keeping him out of difficult situations, to nurture his head a little bit. But Pujols was different, so different that La Russa did the exact opposite, had him bat cleanup, put him in day in and day out against the best pitchers, because he had to see what was really there. "He has a serious, mature approach," La Russa told reporters at the time. "He's almost too good to be true."

But he still felt compelled to test Pujols, unwilling to give him a spot on the club if there wasn't ample opportunity for playing time. Shortly before spring training ended, the Cardinals played Atlanta at the Braves' complex in Disneyworld in Orlando. La Russa didn't have Pujols in the lineup that day, instead making sure that the regulars got in some final at-bats before the regular season began. Mark McGwire started at first, took his three cuts, then headed for the shower and stood behind La Russa in the dugout runway in his street clothes. The game was tied in the ninth when La Russa called on Pujols to pinch-hit against Matt Whiteside. Amid all the curiosity about his immediate future, Pujols didn't just hit the ball, he hit it over the scoreboard in center field. From behind, La Russa suddenly felt McGwire's huge hand smacking him across the back, a little bit like being hit with the wing of a 747. "Dude, I told you, he's on the club!" McGwire said to his manager. While La Russa knew at that moment that McGwire was right, he still subjected himself to second-guessing when the Cards ended up losing that game. His father was there that day, and afterward, when he saw his son, his comment was succinct and to the point: "You should have played Pujols the whole game."

Since then, he has only gotten better, his determination unwavering despite the fact that every day, he gets more and more attention—his performance this season at the All-Star Home Run derby in Chicago, where he hit fourteen home runs in the semifinals, a kind of coming-out party for him—a nation discovering what only a few truly knew before.

Just like pitching well, hitting well is a mental act masquerading as a physical one. A lot of hitters become afraid to consistently do well because it creates expectation and extra pressure—the curse of responsibility to perform. So they disengage their higher faculties and simply guess what a pitcher might throw. They don't go through the admittedly laborious study of video beforehand to try to pick up patterns, which is why some of them keep the bat on their shoulders when they should swing and swing when they should keep the bat on their shoulders. They also feel the creep of self-satisfaction, willing, if they get two hits in the first two or three at-bats, to let it go at that, 2 for 4 a perfectly nice day's work in the big leagues, the tired truism that if a hitter went 2 for 4 every day, he would be the greatest hitter ever.

But Pujols *was* different from the beginning and stayed that way.

"He has this relentless ability about not throwing at-bats away," says La Russa. "A lot of players throw an at-bat or two away every couple of games. They don't concentrate the same way."

Like other players who routinely hit over .300, Pujols is equipped with what La Russa calls "high batting average mentality." Going into each at-bat, he has a specific war room strategy for countering the pitcher's likely line of attack. He also works continually on what La Russa calls a "very productive high average stroke." After developing a relationship with Alex Rodriguez through a mutual friend, he traveled to Rodriguez's home in Miami one winter, and together they worked on about fifteen different drills off a batting tee that Rodriguez had developed, further advancing a hitting style to all parts of the field that isn't just pull-happy. He's perfected a stroke in the mold of the revolutionary batting instructor Charley Lau, passed down from generation to generation of great hitters from George Brett to Hal McRae to Fisk to Wade Boggs to McGwire and now to Rodriguez and Pujols.

Lau was the batting instructor for the White Sox when La Russa managed there after having already left his trademark on the Yankees and the Kansas City Royals. Lau died tragically of cancer in 1984, but he left a profound legacy. La Russa believes that Lau single-handedly influenced the game of baseball more than any other individual in the past quarter century, because of the way he used video when nobody really knew what video was. He broke down the swing frame by frame, saw that great hitters have certain absolutes. He studied the swing, examined it, instead of simply assuming the mechanics of it, and he figured out a new approach for it, saw the similarities between hitting and a golf swing but also made sure that the absolutes of the great hitters were never shed. Head on the ball at all times. Weight shift from back to front. An inside path to the ball that, if you're a righty, aims for center and right center. Top to bottom swing with no uppercut. And great extension, which is why the top hand comes off the bat of some hitters as they finish to give them the right arc through the ball. Pujols inherited the Lau style without ever meeting him, of course. So have hundreds of other hitters.

Before every game, Pujols keeps to himself in the clubhouse. He is not a talker. He makes himself available to his teammates, but he views reporters with sulky perspective, as if he is suddenly being encircled by a large cluster of dermatologic oddities that don't spread infection but do cause copious itching if they hover around too long. His face seems hung with a "do not disturb" sign. He has no time for the obvious answers to the obvious questions from the radio and television boys looking for their soundbites. He is busy in these moments, intensely busy, shuffling back and forth between the clubhouse and the blessed off-limits-to-reporters sanctuary of the darkened little video room where the Secret Weapon is screening tape of today's opposing starter. It is difficult to characterize Pujols's expression as he watches one of the monitors. It isn't rapaciousness or blood lust or any kind of particularly strong emotion. In baseball, less on the outside is usually more on the inside. But there is the glimmer of desire, almost a kind of dreaminess, the eyes narrowing ever so slightly as he watches, a big cat who, when the time is right, will consume the mouse who needs a mound to stand tall.

He showed that look four days earlier in preparation for Kevin Millwood, the Phillies' starting pitcher. He watched Millwood pitch against the Brewers, reacquainting himself over and over with the cutter away that Millwood deploys against righties. He showed that look when he watched footage of his own two homers in one recent game against Cincinnati, the first on a sinker that seemed impossible to hit, much less tattoo, almost surfing the dirt. He replayed the first homer in slow motion, silently following the trajectory of the pitch followed by the trajectory of his bat with that high-finish stroke, the reaffirming of mechanics and muscle memory. He showed that look when he hit a home run against Prior earlier in the season in the bottom of the eighth to tie the game at 1–1.

As good as his swing is, Pujols still treats it as a work to be meticulously refined, studied, examined, pulled apart, mercilessly critiqued. He adjusts it continually, bearing in mind the natural human tendency toward entropy and the fact that no two pitchers are any more perfectly alike than any two snowflakes or two fingerprints are alike. He has sustained periods of Zen, such as the thirty-game hitting streak that ended only the week before. But on certain days, in quiet conversation with Chad Blair, he assesses the complex components of his swing that have failed a little bit: too down on his legs, moving around too much, too *busy* at the plate.

Pujols's obsession over video isn't relegated simply to the small hours before a game. He has also retreated to the clubhouse for a fix during games, disappearing from the dugout to confer with the Secret Weapon about what has gone wrong with the at-bat he has just taken. In early May against the Expos, Claudio Vargas was pitching and beforehand was talking it up a little bit, telling a mutual friend of Pujols's that he was coming to town to strike him out. And in fact Vargas had done just that on the first at-bat in the minimum three pitches. "He got me that time, but I got three more at-bats," he said to Blair, meticulously charting the game pitch by pitch with the perfect vantage point of that camera in center field. Pujols watched what Vargas had done to him, how he had gotten him out. He studied his hands, his stride in reaction to Vargas and made the adjustments he thought necessary. But actually he had it all wrong: He didn't need three more at-bats to right the equation. He needed only one more, when he hit a 452-foot shot to center field.

As a manager, La Russa couldn't help but luxuriate in Pujols's search-and-destroy approach to hitting. During his career, he has felt lucky and blessed to have been placed in situations that provided him with the tools necessary to win. On each of the three teams that he has managed, he has had supportive owners—Bill Veeck and Jerry Reinsdorf in Chicago, Walter Haas in Oakland, and Bill DeWitt in St. Louis—unafraid to spend when spending was needed. He has had strong front offices. The result has been the one ingredient a manager must have for success regardless of how clever and crafty he is: players.

But still, there was nothing quite like Pujols. Players like that don't come along once in a lifetime; they never come along. Yet Pujols had another quality that La Russa treasured even more, maybe because he himself had come of age in the game during the 1960s. It was selflessness in this ultimate age of selfishness, a joy in others' accomplishments that exceeded whatever joy Pujols took in his own accomplishments. He liked baseball, all of baseball, didn't condescend to it. He was the first one to leap to the dugout's top step to celebrate someone else's hit. He took a walk when he needed to take a walk. He liked the challenge and surprise of bunting with men on. It made Pujols a new old-fashioned superstar, in the mold of other Cardinals greats such as Red Schoendienst and Stan Musial and Lou Brock. "The numbers and the money take care of themselves," said La Russa of him. "He's just out there playing to win. That's why I admire him."

III

WITH THE COUNT evened at 1 and 1, Wood comes in with a fast-ball. It's slightly up and inside. It hits Pujols, nicking his shirt. As he heads to first, he mutters something to Wood in Spanish, his first language. Wood, who doesn't speak Spanish, doesn't know what he said and doesn't particularly care. "Imagine that," he will remark later. "It stinks to get hit."

From the corner of the dugout, La Russa glares at Wood, as that sickening feeling he has felt so many times already this season comes over him again, the agony of what to do worse than losing. He isn't convinced that Wood meant to hit Pujols. Trying to be dis-passionate about it, he acknowledges that the ball wasn't too high and tight and was considerably below head level. But Wood's intent matters less than the fact of yet another hit batsman. It's a problem that all managers share, and it means that a message must be sent. He sifts through possible candidates, although the choice is clear. An eye for an eye. A Sosa for a Pujols. But this game isn't against Arizona in April, when La Russa could risk losing in return for winning the hearts and minds of his players. This is late August against the Cubs in a division firefight. The cost of a message is still potentially huge, because of what the home plate umpire may do. The best antidote would be the Cardinals scoring a run here. But Edmonds flies out to left on a fastball to strand runners at first and second, and another chapter is published:

	1	2	3	4	5	R	H	E
CUBS	0	0	0	0	0	0	3	0
CARDINALS	0	0	0	0	0	0	4	0

Williams works Kenny Lofton with cutters and straight four-seam fastballs to begin the top of the sixth. The ball moves around the plate like jazz music: up, down, in, out, arrhythmic, no opportunity for Lofton to anticipate the next note. There is no youthful swagger here between Williams and Lofton, just two pros in their midthirties with a collective thirty-two years of professional experience trying to outfox, outthink, outmaneuver the other.

With the count 1 and 1, Williams comes in with a cutter so high and inside that Matheny can barely get to it. But it's a little piece of catnip, the next pitch a fastball to the other side of the plate that Lofton slaps at and fouls. Williams goes the other way on his next pitch, back inside. Lofton slaps it again and fouls it off again because it's down to gut-level survival now, trying to outlast Williams and maybe get something reasonably hittable. With the count 2 and 2, Williams throws a slider down and in. It's a jam pitch in on Lofton's hands, right where he doesn't like the ball. It's the spot Williams wants to get to, the spot Duncan pinpointed for him during the pregame meeting, *in on the hands because Lofton doesn't like it there.*

Lofton swings. It's one of those defensive just-trying-to-make-contact swings. He gets a little piece without any particular inspiration. The ball meanders in the air, a halfhearted ennui, the kind of existentialist hit that would keep Camus or Sartre in the money if they had played baseball, before it simply runs out of energy and plops into right field well ahead of Robinson. The ball is bored, so tired of itself, it doesn't even roll once it plops. Lofton stretches the weary little thing into a double when Robinson, again building a bigger, better doghouse for himself, fails to get to it quickly.

It brings up Ramon Martinez. Williams's first pitch to him is a curve that sails above Matheny to the backstop. Lofton advances to third with no outs, and now La Russa faces the issue of what to do with the infield. His split-second deliberations begin with the basic question: *How much will this run hurt us?*

Then he resumes the internal dialogue. He weighs the inning: *top of the sixth*. He weighs who is pitching: *Wood*. He weighs how he's pitching: *lights out*. He decides that this run could hurt quite a bit. So it does mean playing the infield in. It sounds easy enough once the strategy is decided on, just wave the boys in and wish them luck, but given all the variables, it isn't simple at all.

Option A puts all the infielders in on the grass. It affords an infielder the best opportunity of stopping a runner on third from scoring if he can get to the ball, but his range is obviously limited because he has less time to get to any ball that's out of his immediate reach. Option B would be to place the infielders halfway in. It would make it slightly more difficult for some punky grounder to get through, and it would give the infielders more room to roam than the naked exposure of option A. It's effective against slow runners, but Lofton isn't slow, so option B is unlikely. Option C plays mind games a little bit by starting the infielders back and then having them charge as the pitch is thrown. The advantage of option C is that it can confuse the third-base coach, who is responsible for sending the runner and may not be prepared for a suddenly charging infield. Another advantage is that all the sudden movement can distract the hitter just enough so that he doesn't make good contact if he hits it. The disadvantage is that it doesn't allow the infielders any time to get set. There's also option D, which is a variation of option C. It's basically a half-charge; within option D are two suboptions: option D-1 in which only the second baseman charges, and option D-2, in which only the shortstop charges. If the hitter is right-handed, you charge only with the second baseman. Because of the natural line of sight of a right-handed hitter, a charging second baseman offers the maximum in terms of distraction, and he still has a chance to make a play since balls to the opposite field are not hit as sharply. Vice versa if it's a left-handed hitter; you send the shortstop.

The complexities are dizzying, the effort to prevent something perhaps encouraging the very thing you want to prevent, the system of pulleys and levers vengeful and sadistic, damned if you do and, given the normal shelf life of a major-league manager—about four years—damned if you do anyway. They are small choices, tiny ripples in the game, but they can also save a win. After examining them, La Russa decides to go with the most comprehensive version, option A, in which *all* the infielders are playing in. With no outs, it's a strategy that has to succeed twice to keep Lofton from scoring, and the odds of such success aren't very good. But La Russa can find no alternatives. He doesn't want that run to score. There is major risk involved: If playing the infield in backfires, the Cubs are set up for a crooked number to put the game out of reach. But he simply doesn't want it. Not with Wood pitching the way he is tonight: ninety-four pitches after five innings. If his ceiling is around 120, he could easily last into the eighth, precisely what La Russa didn't want to happen.

Williams comes in with a curve on the 1 and 0. Martinez hits it hard toward second base. Hart dives for it on the infield grass, getting to the ball quickly and getting it out of his glove fast enough to throw out the runner and hold Lofton at third. The infield-in strategy pays off, and now it has to pay off again with Sosa up.

Sosa approaches the plate in his usual style, more decked out than an overeager groom, tight blue batting gloves stretched tight, a guard to protect his right shin, plus the strangest-looking bat in history, even minus the cork that popped out earlier in the season. From the bottom of it hangs an oversized knob that, as one Chicago sportswriter put it, looks like an ever-expanding goiter. He also has something working in his mouth, gum or tobacco, that seems to grow exponentially the closer he gets to the batter's box — a complement to that goiterish knob. But all his trappings can't distract anyone from his 529 home runs to date. He'll pound any pitch that ventures into his wheelhouse.

Williams works Sammy with four straight fastballs. But three of them go high: 3-1. It's a hitter's count, and Sammy makes his living off counts such as this, seizing on vulnerability. The expectation is fastball, something that can't afford to be too nasty, too in love with the edges. Walking Sammy would put runners on first and third with Alou up, and Alou wears out the Cardinals. As for plunking Sammy in retaliation for Wood's plunking Pujols, now's not a good time, for the same reason that it puts runners on the corners and moves the Cubs closer and closer to the possibility of a crooked number. So Williams has to give him something. But if he gives him too much of something . . .

He comes with a curve. It's a smart pitch on 3 and 1, unexpected. But it hangs a little bit, not quite where Williams wanted to put it. And Sammy gets a swing on it, a good swing.

He singles sharply into left. Pujols takes the ball and, still not taking any chances with his cranky elbow, shuttles it to Edmonds, like a screen pass, so he can make the throw in just in case Sammy has any ideas about going to second. Sammy stays put, but Lofton trots home: 1–0 Cubs.

Williams engages Alou with heart-pounding symmetry. Curve. Foul. Curve. Foul. Curve. Foul. Curve. Foul. Until a fifth curve in a row, the best one Williams has thrown in the at-bat, gets him on a dribbler back to the box. Williams gets out of the inning two batters later. He nicely puts down a first-and-second jam, turns a possible crooked number into a footnote. But because this is baseball—so much decided by who does what first—the fact of the damage is still undeniable: The Cubs have struck first.

10

BEING THERE

I

● ● ● WITH TWO OUTS in the bottom of the sixth and Mike Matheny at bat in the eighth spot with nobody on, La Russa opens the black box mounted on the wall beside him. He picks up the phone and tells Marty Mason to get Cal Eldred up in the bullpen.

Just because he's warming up doesn't mean that Eldred will see any action tonight. If Matheny gets on base, La Russa may decide to pinch-hit for Williams here, which would mean Eldred's entering in the top of the seventh. It's the right place for Eldred, who has generally been used as a middle-inning reliever. But Williams handles a bat as well as any pitcher can. Besides, he's still pitching exquisitely, so it's likelier that La Russa would bring in Eldred sometime later in the seventh, if Williams falters then. If he makes it through the seventh, Eldred may never get in the game, with other relievers in the Cardinals bullpen more suited to the down-to-the-short-hair moment of the eighth and ninth.

It's the fate of the modern-day reliever to live an unrequited life: get up, never mind, sit down, get up, never mind, sit down, just wait for my call, actually we just found someone we like better now. Eldred is inured to this, as is everyone in the Cardinals bullpen, because of La Russa's penchant for tossing relievers in or pulling then out at a moment's notice, guided by his matchups. The blunt truth is that Eldred shouldn't even be here tonight—he should be home in Iowa, in retirement, yet another of those pitchers who burned too brightly and then fell to earth. Which makes the sight of him reassuring, restorative. He is special to La Russa in the same way that Pujols is special to La Russa beyond the skills applied to the field. He represents something that La Russa takes comfort in and admires, a reminder of what still persists in this age of narcissism and personal stat building.

When you have spent so much of your life in baseball that it becomes your life — when you have managed thousands of games and thousands of players — you see the timeline and transformation of the game from a unique point of privilege. You see the changing strike zone and the current mania over pitch count that never existed when Koufax and Gibson and Ryan were going at it during your own formative years. You see the dawn of sweet little cookie-cutter parks where a guy can hit a home run into the short porch in left simply by flicking his wrists. You see the rise of the sinker as the preferred pitch and the neglect of the forkball like an old widow. You see hitters routinely milking the count, whereas when you came up, hitters came to the plate to swing because that was the very point. But what you see most of all is the changing attitudes.

La Russa saw the old attitude on the 1983 White Sox, whom he managed to a division championship, where veterans Jerry Koosman and Greg Luzinski embraced their roles as team leaders. They relished spending money on pizza and beer for team parties at which baseball talk would fill the androgynous, interchangeable hotel rooms in Seattle and Milwaukee and Boston and Cleveland until sunrise. Carlton Fisk joined those same White Sox as a free agent after all his fame with the Red Sox and jettisoned his pride in favor of work ethic. Under the eye of Charley Lau, Fisk reconstructed his swing and contributed with the freshness of a rookie yearning to prove something to the game instead of the game proving something to him. Like Fisk, Tom Seaver came to the White Sox after a career that had already guaranteed him a plaque in Cooperstown. He was past his sublimity with the Mets, that seven-year stretch from 1969 to 1976 when he won twenty or more four

times. But he could still handle a game from the mound in a way
that La Russa still talks about with the starry eyes of seeing magic.
In 1984 against Toronto, Lloyd Moseby came up in the late innings,
with the White Sox clinging to a one-run lead and runners on second and third with two outs. Still in the habit of inquiring over the
inevitable, La Russa came out to the mound to ask Seaver how he
felt. But Seaver refused to sugarcoat it:

"I don't have much else left."

And then he proceeded to tell La Russa precisely how he was
going to pitch to Moseby: purposely run the count on him to 3-1 to
lull him into a false sense of superiority, give him a hitter's count,
then get him out with a changeup.

"Don't worry about it," he told La Russa.

La Russa trotted back to the dugout, trying not to worry about
it. He watched as Seaver threw a fastball in and off the plate to
run the count to 3-1. Then he watched as Seaver threw Moseby a
changeup that was down and away but still fat enough to desire.
Moseby swung, his timing upset by the fastball Seaver had just
thrown. He popped the ball up behind third base to end the inning.

La Russa and Seaver ultimately parted, La Russa to the A's and
Seaver to the end of his career with the Red Sox. But La Russa's respect for Seaver never diminished, only became stronger when he
learned that Seaver turned down an extra year he was entitled to
by contract because he didn't have it anymore and didn't want to
take something he no longer felt he deserved.

The old attitude showed itself after the hideously painful loss in
Game 4 of the 1992 American League Championship series to the
Toronto Blue Jays, when A's pitcher Dave Stewart stood in the
silent and crestfallen clubhouse and told his teammates to have
their bags packed for a return to Toronto, because there was no
way he was going to lose Game 5 to let the Blue Jays walk away
with the ALCS. You just knew he'd keep his promise, because of
that angry take-it-personal fire in his eyes, and he did, pitching a
complete game in a 6–2 win. The old attitude could also show itself
in defeat, as when Eckersley refused to flinch from the fury of reporters' questions in the clubhouse after he gave up The Home
Run to Kirk Gibson in the 1988 World Series against the Dodgers

on that fateful back-door slider that went through the front door instead.

There are occasional splendid throwbacks, such as Pujols, and La Russa has had more than his fair share because of the situations in which he has managed. But he also believes that no aspect of the game has changed more profoundly in the last twenty-five years than the values of the players—what turns them on and turns them off and whether some of them can be turned on at all.

He spends more time than ever now schooling players on the value of competition. He explains to them in spring training the challenge and magnificence of getting a World Series ring, because "it won't happen accidentally. You gotta tell 'em to want it." He sees how quickly clubhouses empty out regardless of how sweet the win or how tough the loss, suburbanites hoping to catch the 5:05 home, all-night talk of baseball replaced by simply wanting to get to wherever they're going. He wishes there were more team parties, but when so many players are glancing impatiently at their Rolexes because it's almost ten o'clock, no party could generate much esprit de corps.

In recent years, La Russa has noticed that many players' careers run on either of two settings. Most seasons, players do what they have to do and plug along because when you have talent, you can plug along. During the *free-agency* year, their intensity picks up, and they're like hungry rookies again, eager to prove themselves and to avoid injury. Certain players display increased selfishness, free-swinging on the first pitch because they're 0 for 2 and frantic to get a hit when they really should be working the pitcher for a walk. The only scoreboard they're watching is the one in their head, tracking their stats that may mean nothing during a game but could be worth millions at arbitration. In La Russa's playing days, and during his first years in the foxhole, a manager's tactical ability was the greatest determinant of his shelf life. The psychiatric component of the game—urging players along with pleas and prods and love and tough love—getting them to play hard all the time and focus on competition, was only an occasional duty. The biggest problem that players had in the 1960s and 1970s was, according to Duncan, insecurity: the knowledge that if they didn't perform, they would be up and out. It was a merciless environment for players. But now the problem is overconfidence, the job security they have earned over the years breeding, as he puts it, "a different monster." La Russa calculates that for today's players, winning is "third or fourth on their list behind making money and having security and all that other BS."

Over two and a half decades, La Russa's job description has drastically changed. The strategy is still crucial, but the ability to coax players now is just as important, if not more so.

He was aware of Jose Canseco, the most talented player he has ever managed, sitting with teammates around a hotel pool in Texas in 1990, complaining about the rigors of the baseball season. The A's had been to the World Series the last two years and had clinched the division the night before, but Canseco admitted to a certain ambivalence. "Why is it always us that has to go to the play-offs?" he asked without irony. The A's realized his fears by getting all the way to the World Series against the Reds. But Canseco clearly wanted to be somewhere else—weary of the red, white, and blue bunting and all that other hype. He was still a prodigious hitter when he wanted to be, but what was the point of making a man play in the World Series who didn't want to play in the World Series? He dogged a play in the outfield in Game 2 that cost the A's a victory, so La Russa benched him in Game 4. He tried to cover for Canseco by claiming that he had an injury, and Canseco did in fact have an injury, the crippling baseball disease of disinterest that comes with too much security and too much money and too much attention. Of all the players La Russa ever managed, no one ever had a more virulent case of it.

After the great season of 1988, in which he set the baseball world on fire, Canseco had become a portrait only of distraction. In the middle of the 1990 season, he signed a multiyear, multimillion-dollar contract, but it didn't result in better play. It resulted in the opposite—flailing at pitches nowhere close to the plate, playing the oufield with all the vigor of waiting for a bus—so La Russa called him into his office.

"What the hell are you doing? You're not playing the game. This is not how we play."

"Tony, people would rather watch me take three big swings and try to hit the ball into the upper deck and strike out than shorten up with two strikes and try to play the game."

"You're kidding me?"

"No, I'm serious."

"You're serious but you're wrong. You're a baseball player."

"I'm a performer."

Canseco was also dogged throughout his career by rumors that his prodigious feats on the field were enhanced by taking steroids off the field. During the 1988 American League Championship series against the Red Sox, Boston fans chanted "Ster-oids! Ster-oids!" as Canseco took his spot in right field. Rather than ignore the taunts, he turned, pulled up his sleeve, and flexed his biceps, perhaps just a taunt of his own, given that he hit three home runs in the A's four-game sweep of the Sox. On the eve of the 1988 World Series, Tom Boswell of the *Washington Post* accused Canseco of being on the juice. La Russa had established his own criterion to determine whether a player was taking steroids—a dramatic, bloatlike increase in size and strength in the off-season, without any previous dedication to strength training. But Canseco did not fit the criterion in 1988. Instead, La Russa saw him working out nearly every day in the clubhouse gym under the tutelage of first-base coach Dave McKay, who as a player had been one of the first to discover the fruits of weight training and aerobics. Canseco was stronger than he had been when La Russa came to the A's in 1986, but his tall physique was still relatively lean.

But by 1992, before the A's traded Canseco to Texas, his body was notably different. He had the bloated look—as if he could be popped by a pin—and he wasn't the only player who looked that way during the early 1990s. "That's when it became clear to baseball people that we have something developing here that's not right or normal," said La Russa. But word was out that steroids did make a competitive difference, whatever the medical risks or the illegality (the federal government had classified them as controlled substances). La Russa suspected several players on his teams were juiced, although he also believes that steroid use on his clubs was "not excessive" when compared to other teams.

By the late 1990s, La Russa saw something even more troubling: a widespread pattern of steroid use in the minor league. "Minor leaguers became convinced that to compete they had to do some form of steroids because they were looking at other guys in the minors going from .270 to .300 and fifteen homers to twenty-five." La Russa approached various minor-league players in hopes of discouraging their steroid use: Most were still in their teens, which made the health risks even more acute. They were also spending money they didn't have on juice. But their responses to his warnings only further defined the horror of the situation that organized baseball had created by not testing players for steroids. "How am I gonna make it if I don't?" they asked him. "I'm gonna be released. I got to do it to have a chance. Guys are going right by me."

Of course, steroids were only the latest in a line of enhancers that players had taken over the years to improve performance. In the 1960s, there was "red juice," a liquid stimulant that players of that era favored. Then came "greenies," culminating in a criminal trial in which a doctor admitted he had supplied amphetamines to various members of the Phillies in the early 1980s. After greenies disappeared, it was inevitable that ballplayers would find something else rather than, in the parlance of the game, "play naked."

If it was evident by the late 1990s that taking steroids improved performance, it was also evident that the one entity that could curtail it most effectively—the Major League Baseball Players Association—would not do so. "In each case where any of us would approach a player, what ended up happening was that the union made it clear that you're not going anywhere with this one," said La Russa. So he and other managers and coaches were left to deal with the problem on their own. During spring training, La Russa talked to the team generally about steroid use, pointing out the health risks as well as the consequences of getting caught, because it was a federal crime to use them. He instructed his training staff and coaches never to suggest a player use them. But he didn't make a stump speech about the issue, aware of how little his harangues could achieve in the absence of league testing.

Baseball's owners could have exerted their clout on the players' union to agree to testing, but every time the issue was raised, the union said it was a violation of players' privacy and sealed off further discussion. The owners may have had their own motivations to let the problem continue to escalate. In the late 1990s, the owners—desperate to reclaim the game's fan base after the strike of 1994 that had cancelled the World Series—latched on to the home run as a marketing tool. Fans liked it, and if steroids helped fuel the home-run frenzy, so be it. The tacit sanctioning of steroids upset La Russa and other managers and coaches, and their unease wasn't simply altruistic. Throughout the 1990s, several innovations had gradually shifted the game in the hitters' favor: a lowered mound, added expansion teams (which enlarged and diluted the pool of pitching talent), new teacup-sized ballparks, a tighter strike zone. Add steroids to the list, because they gave strength to drive balls farther, and it was like "piling on," as La Russa put it; crooked numbers became almost effortless in certain parks.

Home-run hysteria peaked in 1998 when the Cards' Mark McGwire and the Cubs' Sammy Sosa battled to break perhaps the most sacred record in all of baseball, Roger Maris's sixty-one home runs in a single season. Both players didn't just break it; they shattered it: McGwire hitting seventy home runs and Sosa sixty-six. La Russa managed McGwire when he broke the record, and McGwire admitted that during the season he had taken a steroid precursor known as "Andro," short for androstendione. Andro was available over the counter at the time, although the NFL and the Olympics had banned it. McGwire made no attempt to hide his use of it. He kept a bottle on the shelf of his locker in plain view, and La Russa does not believe that McGwire ever used anything other than Andro (he also stopped taking it in 1999 and still hit sixty-five home runs). He was big when he came into the league in 1986 and over time became dedicated to working out as often as six days a week in order to prevent further injuries. In the early 1990s, he actually lost weight to take pressure off a chronically sore heel; weight loss runs counter to the bloated look of someone on steroids. But the same could not be said of Canseco. Despite a body that ultimately metamorphosed into an almost cartoonish shape—Brutus meets Popeye—he denied throughout his career that he ever had taken steroids, until his playing days ended in 2002. Two weeks later, ever the performer, he admitted with much ballyhoo that he had indeed been on the juice.

Rickey Henderson was another high-profile player who moved to his own brooding rhythms. In all of La Russa's years of managing, no player in baseball has ever been more dangerous than Henderson with his combination of on-base percentage and base-stealing skills and power. Impervious to pressure unlike any player La Russa had ever seen before, he became a marked man around the league because he could beat you in so many ways, and he still starred for almost the entire decade of the 1980s. Henderson was a popular teammate, friendly and respectful. But he could be difficult.

In 1991, he started turning to La Russa before games and saying that he could not play because of hard-to-pinpoint injuries. La Russa appreciated Henderson's talent and knew that his own job was to tap into the pool of it. He understood that Henderson always believed that he was being taken advantage of, screwed with. It had driven him nuts in 1990 when the A's, after saying that they could not pay any single player more than $3 million a year, signed Canseco to a $5-million-a-year contract. Henderson was pissed and rightly so, La Russa felt, given that he was having an MVP year.

Henderson became convinced that Canseco was getting preferential treatment and watched obsessively for evidence. By 1992, Henderson made sure that Canseco got nothing over him, including the disabled list. When Canseco went, Henderson went. If Canseco said he couldn't play for a couple of days, Henderson said he couldn't play for a couple of days. As the manager, La Russa could insist that Henderson play if there was no apparent injury. But what good would that do? When Henderson said he couldn't go and La Russa put him in anyway, he'd simply stand in the outfield "like a cigar store Indian. Balls would bounce here, bounce there, all around him."

La Russa established a rule: When Henderson felt he couldn't play, he had to tell him directly instead of relaying it through the trainer, as players usually did. That way, at least, La Russa and Henderson could discuss why he couldn't play. This system worked well; Henderson opted out only a few times, until one game against Baltimore around the All-Star break in 1993. The A's were trying to stay in the divisional race, and there were rumors that Henderson might be traded for a pitcher.

"I can't go today," he told La Russa.

"What do you mean you can't go?"

"I'm telling you, Tony. If I tell you I can't go, I can't go."

"Rickey . . ."

"Rickey's head's not right."

"What do you mean your head's not right?"

"I hear I'm being traded. So my head's not right. I can't go."

In the decade since then, La Russa has had dozens of such conversations, conversations that can steal his faith.

And then there's Eldred, warming up in the bottom of the sixth of Game 2. And La Russa's faith returns.

II

HE WAS a phenom once—a first-round pick of the Brewers in the June 1989 draft. He had the label in the late 1980s as he rolled through Beloit and Stockton and El Paso and Denver. His face— sweetly round and soft—contained a corn-fed quality that people liked to associate with a big, strapping 6'4" kid from Cedar Rapids who could bring it. He had a four-seam let-it-rip fastball, and he liked letting it go. The notes from the Cardinals media guide about Eldred, one of those elliptical athlete's biographies, testified to its power:

1989—. . . named the No. 2 College Prospect in the country by *Collegiate Baseball.*

1990—Struck out a season high 15 batters on 5/10 vs. San Jose . . . opened the season at Stockton with a one-hit, 14-strikeout performance.

1991—. . . led Class AAA pitchers in strikeouts, IP and games started . . . was named the Brewers' Minor League Player of the Year . . . made his ML debut on 9/24 vs. NYY, becoming the first Brewers rookie since Rickey Keaton (1980) to win his starting pitching debut.

1992 — Was named AL Rookie Pitcher of the Year by *The Sporting News* . . . posted an 11-2 record with a 1.79 ERA . . . set club record with a .846 winning percentage surpassing Moose Haas (.813 in 1983) . . . tied club record with 10 straight wins from 8/8 to 9/29 . . . limited opponents to a .207 BA, best among AL starting pitchers . . . was named AL Pitcher of the Month for September after going 5-0 with a 1.17 ERA and two complete games.

Following that sublime rookie season in 1992, Eldred established himself as the Brewers' workhorse. In his first full season in 1993, at the age of twenty-five, he led the American League in innings pitched, with 258. He finished third in the same category in 1994. After all, he was a big kid from Iowa, and that's what big kids from Iowa are supposed to do, work on the mound just like they're working back on the farm. Myth became reality and reality became myth. Had they not been keeping him so busy pitching, the Brewers might have put Eldred in a milking contest during the seventh-inning stretch against some western Wisconsin magic-fingers udder expert. During both years, he tied for the league lead in games started. And then the media guide begins to read differently:

1995 — . . . was placed on the disabled list on 5/19 and missed the remainder of the season after having Tommy John surgery on 6/23.

1996 — . . . began the season on the 60-day disabled list . . .

1998 — . . . was placed on the 15-day disabled list on 7/27 with a small fracture in his right elbow and missed the rest of the season . . .

1999 — . . . began the season on the 15-day disabled list recovering from a small fracture in his right elbow . . .

2000 — Injuries to his right elbow cut short one of his best major-league seasons . . . did not pitch from 7/15–9/26 . . . left his first start of the second half on 7/14 vs. STL in the fifth inning after experiencing discomfort in his right elbow . . . injury was later

diagnosed as ulnar neuritis . . . was placed on 15-day disabled
list on 7/17 . . . allowed four runs in 2.0 IP in his second rehab
start on 9/3 before experiencing pain (diagnosed as a stress
fracture below his right elbow) . . . had a five-inch screw surgically inserted near his elbow on 9/7 by White Sox senior team
physician Dr. James Boscardin . . .

2001—Made two starts, both against Cleveland, before missing
the rest of the season with an injury to his right elbow . . . was
placed on the 15-day DL on 4/12 and did not pitch again . . .

2002—Sat out the entire season as he continued to rehab his injured right elbow.

From 1995 to 2002, there was only one season in which Eldred
had not been sidelined by injuries involving his right elbow. He was
on the disabled list six times. He missed large chunks of the 1995,
1998, 2000, and 2001 seasons. He went through Tommy John surgery. He suffered a small fracture in his right elbow and then a
stress fracture below his right elbow, requiring the insertion of
the 5-inch screw to somehow patch it back together. It isn't unusual
for a pitcher to miss an entire season because of arm troubles and
then come back. Arm troubles are to pitchers what girl troubles are
to country singers. But Eldred didn't miss one season; he basically
missed *two,* his last game on April 11, 2001, when he was with
the White Sox and pitched two innings against Cleveland before
knowing the elbow still wasn't right. In 1992, he'd been named
AL Rookie of the Year. Nine years later, his arm was useless; he
couldn't pick up one of his children, much less pitch. Hindsight suggested that the Brewers had done him no favors by working him so
hard early in his career.

He went back home to Cedar Rapids. His wife was pregnant
with their fourth child, and Eldred realized that there were certain
things about baseball he didn't miss at all, such as the travel or the
time away from his family. In August 2001, he had the *fourth* surgery on his right elbow, to remove the screw that had been inserted.
When the next baseball season rolled around, Eldred was still in
Iowa. And then he felt something, or more precisely the absence of
something, and he thought it was worth telling his wife:

"My arm doesn't hurt."

For the first time in what seemed like forever, he could do household chores without pain. And then came the usually catastrophic thought that comes to every former pro athlete—*Do I have something left?* This too was worth telling the wife:

"I think I'm gonna try to pitch again."

Eldred missed the competition. He missed being part of a team. Those are the things that you expect an athlete to mention when you ask what he misses. But there was something else. He knew that his wife might have a difficult time truly understanding it, as would anybody who hasn't done it. It was the feeling of what it felt like to grip a baseball, know the grip felt right in the fingers because you were coming with a full-heat hothouse four-seamer, throw that four-seamer to the very spot you intended, then watch it *pop* into the back of the catcher's glove as the hitter swings through it. It wasn't a macho feeling to Eldred. It was simply one worth trying to have again.

His wife, slightly more detached about it all and therefore less sanguine, advised him:

"If it hurts again, stop."

Eldred mentioned his intention to a trainer he was friendly with, Mitch Doyle, at nearby Coe College. Doyle was surprised, maybe a little dubious about the ability of a pitcher to come back from *four* elbow surgeries. But if that's what Eldred wanted, Doyle was willing to help.

They started by playing catch around the Coe College campus. Bit by bit, Eldred's tosses became a little stronger. He threw with a little more authority, although the worst thing to do was to overdo it, so he didn't. In September, he went to a clinic in Tempe to further rehab his arm. At the end of September, just before he returned to Iowa, he got up on the mound for the first time in nearly two years. He was nervous and excited and also practical. *Well, if it works, it works.*

He wasn't throwing anything close to fire—his old fire was long gone, and he knew it would not come back. But he was exquisitely pain free, the most beautiful term there is to a pitcher who has felt pain, the roots of something still there. About a month later, he went back to Arizona to throw again, this time in front of about twenty scouts. One of them was Marty Keough of the Cardinals, dispatched by Walt Jocketty, the general manager. Keough was interested in Eldred's control, as the lack of it would indicate a physical problem that forced him to push the ball instead of throwing naturally. Eldred's control was excellent.

The Cardinals signed him as a minor-league free agent. He came to spring training as a nonroster invitee, a thirty-five-year-old rising from the dead. He threw off the mound in the spring training complex, lined up in a row beside kids who had been thirteen when he had won his first major-league game. When Dennis Eckersley visited the Jupiter complex and heard that Eldred was in camp, he told La Russa:

"Hope he doesn't break down."

La Russa and Duncan watched Eldred carefully, refusing at first to let him throw a curve because of the arm stress it could cause. They watched him in his first appearance of the spring against the Marlins, the first game he had pitched in 690 days. He went two innings and struck out three and gave up one run on three hits. They watched him five days later, again facing the Marlins, when he gave up no hits in four innings and struck out four. And they watched him again five days later when he threw four scoreless innings for the second time in a row to lower his ERA to .90. His next two outings were wobbly, more than wobbly, nine runs and sixteen hits in eight innings.

He was on the cusp. As the Cardinals began to trim their payroll to somewhere around $83 million, they questioned the efficacy of keeping Joey Hamilton and Al Levine, who had been signed in the off-season as relievers. In the best of all possible worlds, they would have kept them, but baseball is not the best of all possible worlds except for the Yankees, and by dumping them in the spring, they could save on their salaries. The Cards let them go, and the space they vacated allowed Eldred a spot on the opening-day roster as a right-handed setup reliever.

La Russa admired his guts. He admired his professionalism. He admired the way he went about his business, one of those guys you never had to sit down with to remind him why he was playing. But La Russa also knew that he had made it by omission. Had there been no need to pare payroll, he might well have been back in Iowa. The team's right-handed relief pitching, particularly with the closer Jason Isringhausen on the shelf until June, scared the hell out of La Russa and Duncan. And although there had been moments of shine in Eldred's performance so far, La Russa had been through enough springs to know one thing:

"Never fall in or out of love too early in the spring."

In the ninth inning of the opening game of the season, with the Cardinals nursing an 11–7 lead against the Brewers, La Russa put in Eldred to get him reacclimated, give him a margin of error if there was error. The results did not inspire confidence:

IP	H	R	ER	BB	SO	HR	ERA
0	3	2	2	0	0	1	Infinity

He put Eldred in three days later, in the last game of the four-game series against the Brewers:

IP	H	R	ER	BB	SO	HR	ERA
⅓	3	3	3	0	0	1	135.00

Not much confidence there either. But Duncan worked with Eldred. He encouraged him to develop a two-seam sinker as a complement to his four-seamer. He helped him to modify his breaking ball so it had more of a side-to-side movement across the strike zone. In keeping with his belief in the value of the first-pitch strike, he urged him not to cut it too sharp on the first pitch, just throw something get-me-over and then nibble. Five days after his outing against the Brewers, Eldred came in to relieve in the twelfth in the pitcher's punishment of Coors Field in Denver:

IP	H	R	ER	BB	SO	HR	ERA
2	0	0	0	0	2	0	19.29

It was his first win in the major leagues in 1,014 days.

His ERA started to resemble an Internet stock bubble, plummeting from that high of infinity and confirming the wisdom of the investment: scoreless inning against the Rockies on April 10—13.50. Two scoreless innings against the Astros on April 13—8.44. Three scoreless innings against the Marlins on April 27—5.06. Scoreless inning against the Mets on May 1—4.63. Scoreless inning against the Cubs on May 16—3.94. Scoreless inning against the Red Sox on June 10—3.46.

He was prone to the ill-timed dinger. Sometimes the cutter slipped a little bit, landing over the plate when he wanted it more inside. Sometimes when Matheny wanted to go back away, Eldred shook him off and went inside, with the result a double pulled down the line. But he had appeared in fifty games during the season up until this moment in the bottom of the sixth. He had thrown fifty-one innings and struck out an equal number. He led the Cardinals relievers in wins with seven. And sometimes, when he threw the four-seamer and it went to the spot he intended and it exploded with a pop in the back of the catcher's glove as the hitter swung through it, he knew exactly why he was here: not for money, not for glory, not to build up his own statistical package, but because it was still where he belonged.

III

WHILE ELDRED gets loose, Matheny continues to gut it out against Kerry Wood. He fends off two fastballs foul before he flies out to left on a tough curve low and outside. It puts down the Cardinals in the bottom of the sixth, still behind 1–0, and it brings out Woody Williams for the seventh, as he didn't come up to bat in the previous inning. Eldred remains in his holding pattern, La Russa delaying any decision until he sees how Williams fares.

He has an eleven-pitch inning, retiring the Cubs in order, even his nemesis Damian Miller. He's shown remarkable economy so far through seven: 104 pitches, 74 strikes, and 30 balls. He's thrown 13 first-pitch strikes to the twenty-seven batters he's faced and his line score up to now is about as good as it gets, all you could possibly want from him:

IP	H	R	ER	BB	SO
7	5	1	1	1	6

Which is probably why he slams down a bat in frustration in the back of the dugout when he learns that he is being lifted for a pinch hitter in the bottom of the seventh. He's pitching well, more than well, but the decision is easy for La Russa, given a fresh bullpen that should be able to hold the Cubs at bay for the eighth and ninth. Conversely, there are only nine outs left offensively, and when he pinch-hits for Williams, his thinking is clear: *We need to start the rally.*

He picks the right-handed So Taguchi. Actually, he's already picked him; while Williams was still pitching the seventh, La Russa moved down the dugout and whispered into Taguchi's ear to get ready.

Taguchi is from Japan. He starred for the Orix Blue Wave in the Japanese Pacific League after a distinguished career at Nishinomyia Kita High School and Kansai Gakuin University in Osaka. He won five Gold Gloves for his defensive play, generally ranked around the top fifteen in batting average, was a teammate of Ichiro, and signed as a free agent for a million dollars. He is still a star in Japan, and when he's up with the Cardinals—he's been back and forth between St. Louis and Triple-A Memphis—a little knot of Japanese reporters follows his every move, seeking ways to extol his contributions even when all he does is pinch-run. He speaks little English, is polite to a fault, smiles to those he sees while offering a little self-effacing nod, and spends most of the time in the clubhouse, studying video. He first started playing baseball when he was three and it shows; his fundamentals are beautiful, a purer foundation of the game than with most American players. There is only one major flaw to him—he's had trouble hitting major-league pitching with consistency. It's why he has spent much of the season at Triple-A.

Like every move that La Russa makes, this is not some seat-of-the-pants calculation, which isn't to say that it also won't fizzle: At the very least, he has some prior logic for it. Before each game, La Russa prioritizes his bench players, subject to the matchups they have against an opponent's pitching, and the crucial explanations of performance those numbers reveal. The choice of Taguchi here means not choosing Miguel Cairo or Eddie Perez or Orlando Palmeiro, pinch hitters La Russa feels he must save for the eighth or ninth innings, given that nobody is on base right now and the game is still close. That may make the decision easier, but it becomes complicated again since Taguchi has never faced Wood before, which means there are no matchup numbers to provide a glimmer of the future.

In evaluating Taguchi, however, La Russa has discovered several key attributes about him. One is that he has never been in awe of the major-league baseball scene ever since coming over from Japan, which means that he won't be a deer in the headlights against Wood. Whatever his abilities—and they are not limitless—they will not disappear late in the game: take a leave of absence in the face of Pinch Hitter Madness, a hitter who by mandate is cold —thrust against a pitcher who has had seven innings to get hot and stay hot. La Russa has also seen Taguchi make a greater effort as of late not simply to stay inside the ball and hit the opposite way, but also to use the pull side of the plate. It means he's starting to cover both sides of the plate, crucial against a pitcher such as Wood, given that he is throwing to both areas tonight.

Just like Williams, Wood has gotten sharper as the game has progressed. He's given up one hit since the third inning, and he's already struck out ten. He comes with a fastball low and on the outside, and Taguchi fouls it off for 0 and 1. Wood throws a slider that nibbles low and outside, and Taguchi hits another foul for 0 and 2. Wood throws a waste pitch nowhere close to make the count 1 and 2, but then he gets serious again. Taguchi's helplessness is palpable.

Wood comes with a slider on the outside black, and Taguchi fouls it off. Wood comes with a curve that bites low, and Taguchi has no choice but to protect himself because of the count, and he *fouls* that off too, his fifth in six pitches. He's hanging in there in a decided pitcher's count, the reason La Russa went to him. Finally, on the seventh pitch, a fastball on the inside of the plate, Wood puts Taguchi away with a fly out to right.

It goes down in the record books as a failure, of course, an 0 for

1. But to La Russa, it is a beautiful at-bat, a testament to Taguchi's deceptive grit and his obsessive scrutiny of video. Even though he's a bench player who's never faced Wood before, Taguchi is familiar enough with his pitches that he could at least battle them off. He won the at-bat without ever leaving the plate. It's also the most important at-bat the Cardinals have had thus far, because it took Wood to seven pitches at a time when each pitch he throws is a precious commodity, one more drop from a drying well.

His count is up to 116 after Taguchi worked him for all those fouls. Kerry Robinson follows with a grounder to second, but he doesn't go down gently either, pushing Wood for six more pitches. Bo Hart doesn't do as well. He strikes out in three pitches to end the inning.

Another agonizing chapter is slotted into the scoreboard with few pages left to figure out the whodunit:

	1	2	3	4	5	6	7	R	H	E
CUBS	0	0	0	0	1	0	0	1	5	0
CARDINALS	0	0	0	0	0	0	0	0	4	0

But Wood's count stands at 125. Even though he retired the side in order, and even though he's pitching a finer gem than Williams, Baker must now ask the very question that La Russa has been waiting for: *Will Wood pitch the eighth?*

11

UNDER PRESSURE

I

● ● ● *Wood's at 125.*

La Russa doesn't envy Dusty Baker here, facing one of those decisions that, if it doesn't pan out, will have half the sports talk of Chicago saying he blew it because *Whaddya crazy, how can you take Wood out of the game when he's pitching like he is, and look, don't get me wrong, Dusty's been really nice for the Cubs, but let's face it: He handles pitching about as well as he handled his little kid when he was the batboy for the Giants and almost got run over in the World Series* and the other half saying, *Whaddya crazy, it'd blow out Wood's arm, and look, don't get me wrong, Dusty's been really nice for the Cubs, but let's face it: He handles pitching about as well as he handled his little kid when he was the batboy for the Giants and almost got run over in the World Series.*

No decision has more public glare for a manager than when—or whether—he should remove the starting pitcher in a close game. In other sports, starters and substitutes routinely slip in and slip out. A coach makes a mistake and gets a chance to rectify it. It's a momentary lapse at worst. But in baseball, when you're out, you're out.

Last inning, it was the scoreboard that pushed La Russa to hook Woody Williams, down 1–0 with only nine outs left. He knew he had to make a move, the only question was what move to make. As usual, he began with the matchup numbers of the Cardinals relievers against the top of the Cubs' lineup coming to bat in the eighth, then excavated behind them. It came down to a choice between Cal Eldred and Mike DeJean, the new arrival from Milwaukee. La Russa elected to go with DeJean, based on the fact that his out pitches—a running fastball to the third side of the plate and a forkball—would be more effective here than Eldred's out pitch, a cutter to the first-base side. Eldred has been working on a two-seamer to the third-base side, but he has yet to develop full confidence in it, which is another vote for DeJean. It all sounds smart and wise, but baseball doesn't care right now. DeJean gets Lofton on a fly ball to left for the first out. Then he gives up a single to Martinez, followed by a double by Sosa.

Sosa's hit burns even more, since this was supposed to be the moment when DeJean sent a little message to Sosa in return for Wood's nicking Pujols's shirt, suitable retaliation for La Russa under the circumstances that Wood's act was probably inadvertent. At least make him dance a little bit, feel the heat. But the message got mixed up. His first pitch was a fastball way outside, off the plate. Then he left his second pitch, which was meant to be inside, on the center of the plate. Sosa killed it into the gap and Martinez easily scored for the added cushion of a 2–0 lead.

That doesn't help with Baker's pitching choice, though; because it rotates around the noose of the pitch count, the extra run gives Wood and the bullpen equal room to maneuver. The bullpen is fresh; Wood is not. So that's a vote for the bullpen. But Wood only looks stronger, not weaker, and the Cubs bullpen, even when it gets the desired result, is best watched with both eyes closed. So that's a vote for Wood. Baker can use his bullpen to match up the Cardinals hitters to death, a pursuit he relishes almost as much as La Russa does. But Wood is overpowering tonight. But . . .

Wood's at 125.

Pitch counts are another part of the Darwinian evolution of the game, ignored for the first one hundred years, creeping into the consciousness over the next twenty, and now a sacred commandment. In the late 1950s and early 1960s, pitchers threw somewhere around 155 pitches a game. But one manager, Paul Richards, was beginning to consider the wear and tear on a pitcher's arm. When he was running the Orioles, he put Milt Pappas on a seventy-pitch count to nurture his arm, with the net result a seventeen-year career for Pappas and 209 wins despite the nickname of "Gimpy." It made sense to Richards, just as it made sense to him when, tired of watching Gus Triandos failing repeatedly to catch Hoyt Wilhelm's evil knuckleball, he invented an odd-looking catcher's mitt—as oversized as a clown bowtie—because there was nothing in the rules saying you couldn't. Close to twenty years later, Richards introduced La Russa to the concept of pitch count when he told him as a minor-league manager to place a strict hundred-pitch threshold on the arms of White Sox up-and-comers Steve Trout, Richard Dotson, and Britt Burns.

Today, that threshold is the golden rule, the moment when managers instinctively start to make appointments with the bullpen. But Richards, when he first started keeping track, was an anomaly. In the 1970s, when pitch counts were not recorded with the religiosity that they are today, Nolan Ryan once threw 235 pitches in thirteen innings against the Red Sox.* In addition, the relief game, of which La Russa may well be the key cultural anthropologist, had yet to evolve. The ninth-inning closer was not yet born, never mind the legions of setup specialists, each of whom might be called in just to get one out. Situational matchups between hitter and pitcher in the late innings, which La Russa probably relies on more than any manager ever has, weren't remotely contemplated. Counts eventually did begin to drop, among increasing suspicion that starters, particularly young guys, would inevitably blow out their arms if subjected to the rigors of the past.

Like other aspects of baseball, a significant evolution was also taking place in the use of the bullpen. In the early 1970s, when La

---

* Ryan struck out nineteen Red Sox hitters in the game, on June 14, 1974. Chief among them was Cecil Cooper, who struck out six times in a row. He also walked ten batters before being lifted, achieving a rare baseball double-double. The Angels won in the fifteenth 4–3.

Russa was playing at Triple-A in Des Moines and Wichita, he noticed a manager in the league named Vern Rapp, in Indianapolis. Rapp's team maintained a stoked bullpen far beyond the traditional setup guy and closer—he had his own little legion of relievers—which set off La Russa's curiosity. Rapp said that it had become obvious to him that hitters, faced with the choice between seeing an effective starter in the late innings or a fresh reliever of good but hardly lights-out vintage, would still opt for the starter. Familiarity didn't breed contempt for a starter as much as it did comfort, Rapp noticed; a hitter, even if he were 0 for 3 against a starter with three strikeouts, would still rather face him because of the considerable value of having seen his full repertoire of pitches. Also, unlike a starter, a reliever could rely almost exclusively on his best pitch, and air it pitch after pitch because he knew he would be in on only a limited basis. Unlike a starter, he never had to worry about fatigue and pacing himself.

If it made life even more miserable than usual for a hitter, it also made life easier for a reliever, particularly one who knew the rigors of starting. Eckersley, for example, after a career of starting, chafed at being sent to the bullpen by Oakland in 1987 after his trade there. He considered it banishment, purgatory for lesser pitchers, an absolute affront to his machismo. Until he realized the joy of being able to come into a game and throw whatever you wanted as hard as you wanted, just let it rip and not fret too terribly much over pitch selection. Along with his imperviousness to pressure, it's what made Eckersley a Hall of Fame reliever, the luxury of concentrating his stuff into ten or twelve pitches.

Beginning in the 1990s, the role of the bullpen was refined even further so that hitters weren't routinely facing a reliever or two in the late innings but virtual swarms of them, each with a speciality pitch, each one able to simply let it go because they knew they would not be hanging around for very long, maybe only one batter. Managers, if they were holding a lead into the small hours of the game, also began to break down the last third into *individual* outs, nine opportunities to make life as miserable as possible for every hitter coming to the plate. Hence greater use of relievers than ever for only one at-bat.

The change in bullpen use had an obvious effect on pitch counts. By 1989, the average pitch count for a starter had fallen to ninety-four, according to the *Cultural Encyclopedia of Baseball.* By 1991, it was down to eighty-two. In 1987, 106 pitchers had games in which they threw 140 pitches or more. The number had dwindled to thirty-six by 1995. Even nearer extinction was the complete game, plummeting from 40 percent in 1950 to 4 percent in 2001.*

Some former managers—Jim Leyland, for example—believe that the one-hundred-pitch threshold too often becomes a crutch. He's worth listening to, perhaps, as La Russa credits him with having a better instinct for when to take a pitcher out than any other manager he has ever played against. "Just because a pitcher has thrown extra pitches doesn't mean he's done," says Leyland. "One of the areas where a manager falls into a trap is when he worries about who he will have to answer to after the game."

He believes that pitch count is as much a function of greed as it is keeping young arms safe and strong. "You got agents involved. You got big money at stake. You got lawsuits. Trainers are scared to death." For him, the irony of reduced pitch counts is that today's pitchers are much better conditioned than the men who routinely threw 150 a game back in the 1960s and 1970s. "These guys are in better shape and they run more and half of them have home gymnasiums and strength trainers. I think managers baby them." Nor, Leyland believes, do they ever effectively learn their trade in the minor leagues. "They used to have to get out of their own jams. Now someone else there does it for them."

Baker, who doesn't think much of the one-hundred-pitch threshold, would no doubt be heartened by Leyland's comments. When he came up as a player in the 1970s, the pitch count that most managers went by was an occasional glance at the mound to make sure that the guy's arm was still connected to his shoulder. Despite withering criticism in the media and the sports talk shows that he

---

* The last major-league pitcher to throw thirty complete games was Catfish Hunter of the A's in 1975, and the last to throw twenty was Fernando Valenzuela of the Dodgers in 1986. In 2001, Curt Schilling was the National League leader with six, the lowest complete game total ever.

doesn't know how to preserve pitchers, Baker has had only two during his ten-year managing career who required arm surgery. But it still doesn't solve the immediate problem of what to do:

Wood's at 125.

Baker has managed against La Russa enough to know what La Russa would like him to do: pull Wood and let the Cardinals finally get a shot at the bullpen. He knows that Wood is pitching as well as he's pitched all year. He knows that Wood has thrown more than 125 pitches in a game already this season, going as high as 141 against the Cardinals in the hitter's Club Med of Wrigley. And all he needs is *six outs.* Granted, it is *six outs* against the meat of the Cardinals lineup, with Pujols followed by Jim Edmonds followed by Scott Rolen. But Wood has been *blowing them away.* They are an aggregate 1 for 6 against him today with three strikeouts.

But Wood is one of those young pitcher poster boys who developed arm trouble early in his career. He exceeded 118 pitches in twelve of his twenty-six starts as a rookie and once threw 175 pitches in a single game in high school, because if you think major-league managers are tough on arms, you should take a look at high school and college coaches. It's true that Edmonds is a lefty, and late in the game, that's a matchup you would probably rather avoid because Edmonds can go downtown with the pressure on. And all the bullpen needs is *six outs.* It's why you have those guys sitting around back there doing nothing for most of the game, and if you don't have a bullpen that can't get *six outs,* there's no point even pretending you're going to get anywhere near October.

Wood's done at 125.

He's been hooked. Antonio Alfonseca has come out of the bullpen to face Pujols to begin the bottom of the eighth. He's big, 6'5", and unlike other pitchers that tall, there is nothing string bean about him. His chest is large, very large; it barrels beyond his uniform. His physique makes you think of a small-town sheriff who likes his barbecue big and doesn't mind confrontation. He's also an anomaly, with six fingers on his pitching hand, which may help to explain why he has dominated Pujols more than virtually any other pitcher, getting him out five of the six times he has faced him.

He's in the classic role of specialty reliever, probably in only for this one at-bat, with a lefty due up next, so he can flaunt his out pitch with impunity because he doesn't have to worry about seeing the hitter again. His strength is hard and down to the third side of the plate, which for a hitter means "cheating" a little bit—getting the bat head out early—or keeping his hands inside the ball. Alfonseca has no need to save up strength and pace himself, think down the line. He comes in throwing hard and leaves throwing hard, and the whole time he's in, he exudes contempt and swagger. To La Russa, someone like Alfonseca is perhaps the most difficult pitcher in the game to do something against. The worst approach for a hitter to take here is the misguided heroism of going for the bomb.

With only six outs left for the Cardinals, with first place, maybe the division championship, at stake, the pressure is enormous. Sabermetricians—those numbers-crunchers who have come to dominate thinking about strategy over the past few years—believe that they have debunked clutch situations as statistically irrelevant. La Russa has read the various studies. Based on his own forty years plus of experience, he believes those studies to be bunk of their own. To say that players don't react differently to the tension of a clutch situation is to deny the existence of human nature. He has seen thousands of players under pressure, and he knows that they have varying but distinct reactions to it: some so pumped up that you must remind them to breathe, some rendered tentative by it, a distressing number not wanting to deal with it at all. "Players can make a lot of money on their stats alone. They can play below their optimum and still make a very good living," says La Russa. "There are a lot of players that don't really want to dig deep enough to try to win."

Some coaches think that the best way to deal with pressure is to ignore it, treat every moment of a game the same so as not to heighten the tension even more. La Russa believes that players need to openly acknowledge pressure—literally embrace it as "your friend," in his words—because the more they embrace it, the less it can intimidate them. He teaches hitters that the best way to deal with pressure is to prepare for it, come into the at-bat with a keen sense of what the pitcher is likely to throw and how you should handle it. Most important, when you're up there, focus on the process and not the result; don't project into the future. Forget about the noble but irrational concept of going for broke. Put away the hero complex and simply try to get something started. But don't hesitate, either: In clutch moments, you're unlikely to get your perfect pitch, so don't wait around for it. Be aggressive.

Nobody lives these principles better than the great Pujols. Alfonseca serves him a sinker low and inside to start the inning. It's a good first pitch: difficult to drive, difficult to get into the gap. Pujols stays inside of it with his hands. He doesn't try to do too much with it; he simply makes contact, and the ball scoots up the middle, past the shipwreck hulk of Alfonseca. It's a single, an Oscar-worthy short-form documentary on focusing on the process and not the result.

Edmonds is due up next, but before he gets to the plate, Baker goes to the mound and makes a quick little jab signal to the bullpen, like a New Yorker hailing a cab. Alfonseca is hooked, replaced by the lefty Mark Guthrie. It's a good matchup for Baker, as Edmonds is a negligible 2 for 11 against him. Guthrie's stuff is not as good as it used to be; he has to stay away from the strike zone, or he'll get tattooed. Nowadays, he lives off chase pitches, and he's been pretty good at it. If he's not as strong as he once was, he's also smarter.

He comes with a curve low and away on the first pitch. Edmonds swings through it, and Guthrie has the coveted first-pitch strike. He throws a forkball high. Edmonds holds off, and the count evens to 1 and 1. He follows with a sweet curve on the outside black, and Edmonds is now 1 and 2 and not looking very good in the process, Guthrie tying him into knots with effective junk. He comes with a forkball, and this pitch is even better than the curve he just threw: sweeter, nastier. Edmonds holds up, but this is strike 3. In the foxhole, even La Russa concedes that it's strike 3. In fact, the only person who doesn't think it's strike 3 is the home plate umpire. He calls it a ball. Guthrie comes with a curve that sails outside to make the count 3 and 2. He follows with another curve, close enough to the strike zone that Edmonds can't afford to hold up on it. It's in on the hands a little bit so that Edmonds's only alternative, which isn't much of one, is to fight it off and see whether he can turn it over just enough into the outfield. It drops for a single to right.

Rolen is now due up, with runners on first and second and no outs. But before he gets to the plate, Baker goes to the mound again and hails another cab. Guthrie is hooked in favor of Kyle Farnsworth because righty-versus-righty would be a better matchup for the Cubs.

Pacing back and forth in the foxhole, La Russa privately debates about putting on a bunt. But it feels like too defensive a play right now, given that Rolen has the power to turn the game into a 3–2 lead with one swing. Looking ahead, he begins to consider the possibility of pinch hitters after Rolen. J.D. Drew's presence as a bench player would be enormous if Baker sticks with Farnsworth. Drew *kills* Farnsworth; La Russa has it written down on the little cheat sheets he keeps in his back pocket:

DREW   5-7-3

But Drew isn't here, and La Russa can't dwell on what he doesn't have.

The count runs to a quick 3 and 0 on Rolen. But Farnsworth fights back with two strikes, and the count is full. La Russa thinks about trying a double steal to break up the double play that might result if Rolen hits the ball on the ground. But he worries that the runner going from second to third might distract Rolen at the plate, upset his timing or maybe push him to swing at a bad pitch. Even though Rolen has swung and missed twice, they were two good swings, so he's not looking cold at the plate. La Russa also figures that even if he puts the ball on the ground, Rolen has just enough speed to possibly beat it out and hold the Cubs to a force-out. He keeps the runners where they are. Farnsworth throws his fifth straight fastball. It's high, and the bases are loaded with no-body out.

Tino Martinez is now due up. Because he's a lefty, La Russa waits for Baker to hail a cab. Surely he'll send in a lefty pitcher to face the lefty hitter. When he does, La Russa may counter with his own move to push the matchup back his own way. He may remove Martinez for a pinch hitter, but it's not an easy emotional decision for him. He knows that Martinez has four World Series rings from his days as a Yankee. He knows the way in which, all his career, he has accepted the responsibilities of being a key hitter in key situations. That's the Martinez the Cardinals signed for $21 million after the 2001 season. But La Russa also knows the struggling Martinez, and in clutch situations with runners in scoring position, Martinez has been struggling terribly. So the question for La Russa, the one he will have to make in a matter of moments, is to somehow try to glean which Martinez is going to come to the plate.

II

MARTINEZ'S RESPONSE to pressure has been like a 45-rpm record, a timeless hit on one side and the flip side maybe best forgotten. When La Russa needs an example of how to deal with tension, he points to the bottom of the ninth inning of Game 4 of the 2001 World Series between the Yankees and the Diamondbacks at the Stadium, fifty days after September 11. Martinez was up with two outs against Byung-Hyun Kim and the Yankees down by 3–1 with a runner on first. He remembers what anyone who has ever watched baseball will remember: that game-tying two-run homer into right field that didn't simply shake Yankee Stadium to new levels of hysteria but unleashed torrents of pride through a suffering city. La Russa was curious about what had gone through Martinez's mind in the ultimate clutch situation: whether he was thinking home run or at the very least trying to pull the ball. Tino said no; he knew that Kim was a fastball pitcher, so that's what he was looking for, a fastball that he could put his best swing on. To La Russa, it was the perfect answer: putting his best swing on the pitch—not his home-run swing, not his pull swing—just his best one. Focusing on the process and not the result.

The flip side could be seen once Martinez came to St. Louis after the 2001 season. He signed a fat three-year deal, which placed the noose of expectations on a player who many around the league thought was losing bat speed, nowhere close to hitting the forty-four home runs he'd hit for the Yankees in 1997. Martinez also had to fill the shoes of Mark McGwire at first base, an expectation no man could fulfill given McGwire's season-breaking seventy home runs in 1998. Martinez immediately became a fall guy for St. Louis fans who, by this season, had begun doing something they almost never did: booing a Cardinal when he came to the plate. Because Cards' fans are the most knowledgeable and loyal in all of baseball, they booed almost reluctantly, polite as booing goes, what would have passed for a standing ovation in Philly.

But in this moment in the bottom of the eighth with the bases loaded and no outs, Martinez is hitting .225 against left-handed pitching. Coupled with his performance the prior season, .262 with twenty-one home runs and seventy-five RBIs, it is clear that Martinez's pride is increasingly at odds with his output. He felt burned when La Russa pinch-hit for him against the lefty Dan Plesac in the Phillies series just prior to this one. He felt humiliated, and in the clubhouse, he had become privately snappish, telling others his problems at the plate were largely the fault of La Russa's incessant tinkering. He *should* feel burned, as any man animated by competitive spirit should. La Russa likes such qualities in a ballplayer, but he also knows that players are often unrealistic about their situations. Earlier this season, Martinez complained about hitting sixth or seventh in the Cardinals lineup; he said that when he played for the Yankees, Joe Torre never juggled him around but always batted him fourth. The comment rankled La Russa, so he pursued the substance of it and found that Torre did indeed have Martinez hit sixth or seventh in the Yankee lineup. It indicated to La Russa there were times that Martinez struggled as a Yankee and was dropped in the lineup, just as he is struggling now. Which is only further incentive for La Russa to lift him if Baker calls in for the lefty.

But Baker stays put. He doesn't head to the mound to hail a cab. Martinez won't be burned this time, unless it's by Farnsworth.

Martinez hasn't faced him much: two at-bats, no hits. Given his .203 average with runners in scoring position this season, this is not an optimum situation for him with the bases juiced. It only gets worse when Farnsworth gets a favorable call from the umpire for a first-pitch strike. Farnsworth follows with another fastball. It's clearly a ball if Martinez holds up on it, and all year long, even in troubled times, he has always maintained savvy plate discipline, more than willing to squeeze a walk here, not succumb to visions of immortality. But he doesn't.

La Russa would be content with a sacrifice fly to right, and so would Martinez. It would send Pujols home and put the next batter, Edgar Renteria, in the situation he thrives in — two runners on and only one out, a seventh-hole hitter with seventy-eight RBIs. But it's a grounder to the right side. It's going somewhere, but it's unclear *where,* in that uncertain zone between sharp and not sharp enough, just out for a little summer-night stroll. Cardinals fans don't know whether to cheer or groan. Cubs fans don't know whether to cheer or groan.

It could be a single. Or it could be a double play. Rolen, who has taken a healthy, smart lead off first, is off on contact to try to avoid the latter. As he's going, the ball skitters by and almost hits him. He dodges it somehow without breaking his momentum. The ball has opted for the path between first and second, with just enough force that the Cubs infielders on the right side can't quite get to it.

Pujols comes home: 2–1. Edmonds comes home: 2–2.

Martinez stands exultant at first, just the little trace of a smile, basking in the kind of adoration he has so rarely enjoyed in St. Louis. He has tied the game on a gritty piece of hitting, getting to a pitch up and out of the zone and simply staying with it. It is beauty under pressure. But even more beautiful to La Russa is Rolen's base running. It's a lost art because there's no money in it; no incentive clause rewards you for doing it well, so those who actually do it want something from the game other than money. They play it right because it was meant to be played right.

Rolen is a superb athlete, the ingredients still there of someone who was good enough back in Jasper High School to be offered basketball scholarships from the University of Georgia and Oklahoma State. He looks too big to play third base the way he does, an outside linebacker in a baseball uniform. Yet he's quick down the line with his backhand scoops, and nobody ever in baseball, at least nobody La Russa has ever seen, comes in better on the ball bare-handed with that big right hand of his, followed by such a punishing throw it's a wonder that Martinez at first doesn't end up head over heels in the stands. The one thing he's not, however, is lightning fast. But a base runner's skill has to do only in part with speed, in La Russa's mind. The more essential ingredient is how well you maximize your opportunities relative to your speed, which is why Rickey Henderson was a great base stealer—where wheels matter —but not a great base runner. When he wasn't stealing a base, he tended to relax, as many great base stealers do: no joy in the mundane and certainly no Benjamins. La Russa could only watch helplessly as Henderson took a few halfhearted steps off first and kind of plopped there. Much slower players got from first to third more often than Henderson did, the ultimate example the bottom of the ninth in Game 6 of the 1993 World Series when Henderson, then playing for the Blue Jays, somehow failed to get from first to third on a dumpy single by Paul Molitor hit slow enough so that there was ample room to run. He made it only to second, and were it not for the epic three-run homer against the Phillies by Joe Carter—a batter later to win the World Series—Henderson's lackadaisical attitude could have well made him the goat.

But Rolen took a good primary lead off first. Then he extended it into a secondary lead, pushing out more and more, all the while zeroed in on what was happening at the plate, ready to explode off the bat. And he was agile enough to keep his stride even while evading the ground ball. Brains and focus propelled him to third.

With Renteria up, Baker continues to stick with Farnsworth. The pitcher responds to the vote of confidence by throwing a wild pitch that makes Rolen's base running more than simply an instructional video. Because he's on third, he easily trots home, the system of pulleys and levers rewarding him for his quiet savvy: 3–2 Cardinals.

Farnsworth is a wreck at this point. He walks Renteria to put runners on first and second, and suddenly, improbably, the Cardinals are in the land of the crooked number on the basis of three singles, two of which were of the seeing-eye-dog variety, two walks and a wild pitch. They are scoring because they are lucky, and they are lucky because they are scoring. There are still *no* outs. Now La Russa and Baker are going mad with moves, like men frantically emptying a suitcase, racing to find the one item that actually fits.

La Russa's move: He brings in Miguel Cairo to pinch-run for Martinez at second, having already decided that he's going to have the next batter, Mike Matheny, bunt here. So he wants a quicker runner at second, as it's slightly easier for a team on defense to make a force play to third on a bunt. For a split second, he toys with a *hit-and-run* but then rejects it, as the speed of Farnsworth's fastball, in the mid-nineties, would make it more difficult than usual to get something on the ground. So he sticks with the bunt, which Matheny successfully executes to move the runners to second and third.

Baker's move: With the pitcher due up and knowing that he isn't going to hit, Baker hails another cab. He hooks Farnsworth in favor of the lefty Mike Remlinger, the *fourth* pitcher he has used this inning.

La Russa's move: He anticipates Baker's move to bring in Remlinger. But he still counters with Orlando Palmeiro to pinch-hit, even though he's a lefty, because he knows from his cheat sheets that Remlinger is one of those inverse pitchers who gets out righties better than lefties. Because of this slight advantage, he thinks that it gives Palmeiro, a good contact hitter, a decent chance of getting something on the ground and moving another run home. Also, he figures that if he had gone to the righty Eddie Perez off the bench, Baker would have pitched around him, with first base open, to set up for a force at home or a double play. This way, Palmeiro at least has the chance of getting something to hit. But Remlinger is all over the place. He walks Palmeiro. The bases are once again loaded.

Baker's move: He hails yet another cab. He benches Remlinger and brings in Joe Borowski, his ninth-inning closer, even though it's the bottom of the eighth with one out. It's the *fifth* pitcher he has used in the half-inning, a National League record.

La Russa's move: He sends Perez to the plate to pinch-hit for Robinson at the top of the order as he's gritty in the clutch with nine home runs and thirty-three RBIs in only 219 at-bats. With the bases loaded, Baker doesn't have the luxury of pitching around him. Perez has a swing as free as his laugh, capable of driving one into the seats. It would be a marvelous result, but La Russa's decision to use Perez here, lifting the number one hitter in the lineup, even though he's a lefty and Borowski a righty, goes far beyond home-run hope. Perez may be a free swinger, but he's also a smart one, who spends requisite time before each game studying prospective relievers; he knows what Borowski likes to throw and can recognize his pitches off the delivery. Borowski's main pitch to a right-handed batter is his slider, and it's more of an out-and-over-the plate slider. It matches Perez's own hitting strength, making him in La Russa's evaluation more likely to have a productive at-bat than Robinson.

Perez hits a puny little ground ball. It should be an easy double play to get the Cubs out of the inning, down by only one run. But Martinez at second base bobbles it, the pressure of the moment tapping him on the shoulder just as he fields the ball to ask him whether everything is okay. He recovers the ball. He does that much as the volume at Busch tops 100 decibels, fans going delirious in the best chapter yet in this thriller. He manages to make the play to first. He does that much. But Cairo comes home. The Cards lead 4–2.

III

LA RUSSA still looks all steel from the foxhole in the top of the ninth, no change in the glare. But it's a front. His head throbs with what feels like a migraine. His throat is so dry, he can't swallow. His stomach is flipping so much, he feels he's going to vomit, only he knows he can't, because of the dryness in his throat. He is inevitably thinking to himself, *Why am I doing this for a living?* just as he also knows that if he somehow gets the third out here in the top of the ninth, he will inevitably think to himself, *What a great way to make a living!* He occasionally turns back to look at the lineup sheet posted on the wall. He's also dipping his head down after every batter to keep score in his little runic scribblings. But it's more force of habit than anything else, because the game has basically left his hands. It would be easier emotionally if the score were more crooked in the Cards' favor, but La Russa is still where he wants to be, the journey of his managing in Game 2 of three getting him to the right crescendo.

It's why his favorite player on any team is always the closer, if he's a real-deal closer and not some knock-off closer, the only player piece of the puzzle who can guarantee a win if he does what he is paid to do. He believes that he has the real deal in Jason Isringhausen. He was hurt at the beginning of the season, a situation that La Russa knew would make almost every game a psychological circus. The Cardinals hit the burrito out of the ball, but their record in one-run games was abysmal: 2 and 14 in one-run games through the end of May.

One of the few philosophical disagreements between him and Dave Duncan is the greater premium he places on the bullpen; Duncan believes that the starters matter more. In La Russa's opinion, Duncan can do enough things with a starter—get him to see the rewards of mixing speed and location, offer him up a new pitch to make hitters uncomfortable—to keep him going for six innings. You can elevate a starter. But it's his view that a reliever, whether he's setting up or closing, must have an effective out pitch. And that's difficult to teach—a rare instance in which preparation and hard work can't improve much on innate baseball talent.

Since Isringhausen's return in June, there is every indication that his stuff has returned with him, hard cutter—his out pitch—backed up by a good hook:

W	L	ERA	G	SV	IP	H	R	ER	HR	BB	SO	Opp. Avg.
0	0	2.36	26	14	26.2	20	10	7	1	10	26	.198

With the score 4–2 here, Izzy has some insulation. The Cubs are slotted to send up Ramirez and Gonzalez and Miller, and La Russa's cheat sheets show that the matchups are good, but not great, because of Gonzalez and that home run:

RAMIREZ	0-3-0
GONZALEZ	1-3-1
MILLER	0-1-0

Baker has carte blanche now. He can use his bench to drive the matchups however he wants, as La Russa isn't going to budge off Izzy. No situational relief here by countering a lefty hitter with a lefty pitcher. For eight innings, La Russa has slowed the game down by staying ahead of it, but now the game has caught up.

La Russa knows what Izzy has been thinking as he was warming up: *We've just gone eight innings in this hugely meaningful game, and we've had this great comeback, and it's all on me to get three outs.* He knows that not just anybody can do that, has that combination of guts and attitude and stuff. La Russa himself is thinking about the single thing that separates the highest-caliber closers from the next level: *Keep the ball out of the middle.*

It's also why he gave his little conspiratorial laugh in spring training when he heard of the Red Sox plan, based on analysis by statistical guru and team consultant Bill James, to have rotating closers instead of one designated pitcher. James, in part because of what he felt was the inflated statistic of the save (you get one even with a three-run lead), believed that it wasn't always necessary to bring in a classic closer to pitch the ninth. La Russa repected James, but based on managing nearly 4,000 games, was convinced James was wrong. La Russa was also right: the Red Sox ultimately dumped the idea when it became clear that closer-by-committee was no-closer-by-committee.

Of all the ways to lose in baseball, none is more painful to La Russa than failing to hold on to a close lead going into the ninth. If it happens enough, it creates a cycle of frustration and discouragement that can unravel a season. Hitters, aware that the only way to win is to score unrealistic bunches of runs to neuter the ninth, can't shoulder the burden after a while.

Izzy has the face for what he does: impish, suggesting good times, with a softness about the chin and cheekbones, a certain buoyancy to it without the weight of self-reflection and overanalysis. He also has the requisite balls. He loves working the ninth. It has become his domain when he is healthy, although staying in one piece has been an issue with Izzy since birth. Some of his ailments have been downright scary, well beyond the typical arm sufferings. But his medical history also implies a sure-fire way of identifying future relievers, based on a childhood propensity to almost get themselves killed in small towns. The lefty setup reliever Steve Kline also exhibited such pathology when his brothers, in the name of what passed for science in the central Pennsylvania town he grew up in, tried to electrocute him.

Izzy's wounds were more of the self-inflicted variety. As a child growing up in Brighton in southern Illinois, he enjoyed jumping off the roof of the family's two-story house to see what the chances were of flying (not good). On a long car ride to Virginia when he was twelve, he occupied himself with counting up his scars and got pretty close to 115. During his career in the big leagues, he has undergone surgeries on his elbow and shoulder. He was diagnosed with tuberculosis, and he once fell off a third-floor balcony in spring training, cracking his sternum and several toes.

He began his career as a starter and had nice success with it, a 9-2 season for the Mets in 1995. But recurring shoulder and elbow problems made him a natural candidate for the bullpen. Izzy remembers the first time he ever came in in the ninth. It was against the Yankees in 1999, when he was with Oakland; he had never pitched in the stadium before. He didn't feel fear. He felt *total fear,* as he put it, the way the façade, like one of those Tim Burton sets in *Batman,* just seemed to go straight up for miles and miles to the lip of the moon. He finished the game that night and notched a save. "I succeeded, and the first rush came about," he said, even better than jumping off the roof of his house and seeing whether he could fly; on this night, he really could fly. The next year, he took the mound in a similar situation, with a one-run lead in the bottom of the ninth, and gave up back-to-back homers to Bernie Williams and David Justice—just about the same as jumping off the roof and landing with a thud. It was then that Izzy learned the other crucial component of being a closer, besides keeping the ball out of the middle: "A short memory."

Izzy takes a little journey off the mound after his warm-ups. He removes his red cap to wipe the heat off his brow, draws in a breath. He gives a little whisper to Rolen and returns to the top of the mound. He's casually chewing gum as if to say, *It's no big deal coming into the game like this to either preserve it or destroy it, be a well-paid hero for very little work or a complete asshole.*

He comes in with a hard cutter against the lead-off batter, Ramirez. It's similar in style to the one that Mariano Rivera throws, bearing in on you with ninety-plus velocity so that the only thing you can do is use your bat as a weapon of meager defense. Ramirez hits it meekly foul, readjusts his blue batting gloves, and settles back in to the plate. Izzy counters next with a nice curve low and away. Ramirez hits it to the right side, one hop, two hops, three hops, four hops, each hop smaller and thinner than the previous. Hart at second has to come in for it, a nasty little nubber. He's almost on the infield grass when he gets to it, then has to make the throw in a fast and fluid motion across his body. It's hit softly enough for Ramirez to have a chance even though he's a lumberer. It all depends on the throw.

La Russa watches Hart from his corner. Baker watches from his corner, leaning forward slightly, peering through the green-padded bars on the top and bottom of the dugout. He has a slightly shocked look, unable to cleanse his mind of the surreal ugliness of the bottom of the eighth when a 2–0 lead became a 4–2 deficit on the basis of three puny singles rolling into the outfield like little winks, three walks, a wild pitch, and a bobbled grounder. Izzy no longer faces the plate, because he's watching Hart too.

Ramirez is out by several steps. One away.

Izzy steps off the mound to get a new ball from the home plate umpire. He works it in, rubbing his palms and fingers over it to add his own imprint. He takes off his glove to touch the peak of his cap. He flexes his shoulders. Then back to work with Gonzalez up.

La Russa has the right fielder, the so-called off outfielder because Gonzalez is right-handed, shade in two or three steps from his usual depth. With the tying run on deck, he's trying to take away what he thinks is the most probable hit, a line drive or bloop single the opposite way. Like the infield-in options, shading outfielders has a dizzying set of variables, so much so that La Russa often puts his outfielders in almost continuous motion in the late innings. If the hitter is right-handed and gains the count in his favor, La Russa will immediately shade the outfield to guard against the likely tendency of the hitter to pull the ball. If the count goes even or to the pitcher's advantage, La Russa will then immediately shade the outfield to straighten up within the same at-bat. He also takes into account the minute knowledge of hitters gained through scouting and video and Duncan's pitching charts, as there are some who, even in classic pull counts of 1-0 and 2-0, still simply try to cover the plate and put the ball in play.

Izzy knows that he has a great defense behind him with three Gold Glovers in Renteria and Rolen and Edmonds. So the thing he's fixated on, the only thing besides the muscle memory of throwing hard and hitting different halves of the plate, is not giving up a home run. He didn't do that once in sixty games last season, and he's given up only one this season. *Keep the ball out of the middle.*

He works Gonzalez over with cutters, none of them center-cut over the plate. Gonzalez swings through the first, resists the second because it's outside, then breaks his bat fouling off a hellacious one down to make the count 1 and 2. A piece of it splinters toward first base. He goes to get a new bat from the batboy, and La Russa is thinking *finishing curve ball here.* Izzy's stuff is too good not to try overpowering Gonzalez with it. He's got a big hook, so *throw the big hook.* But instead, he flips a *do-somebody-a-favor* curve.

Gonzalez loops a single to left center. The Cubbies are alive.

With a man on first and one out, Baker sends Troy O'Leary to pinch-hit in the eighth spot for Miller. La Russa switches to a no-doubles defense in which all three outfielders play deep. Izzy goes with his cutter against O'Leary on the first pitch. It's inside for 1 and 0.

It's never the best way to start, but beyond simply the count is another exposure. With the first baseman positioned deep to provide more range, Gonzalez isn't even being held. La Russa is obviously aware of that, just as he's aware that Izzy normally doesn't have a quick move to the plate and is easy to run on. Gonzalez could be running early as a result to take away the possibility of the double play; it's an almost sure steal. But Baker doesn't make the move, at least not now.

Izzy comes with a fastball on the next pitch to even the count. Gonzalez still stays put at first. Izzy throws a cutter inside. O'Leary has to dance out of the way a little bit, but Gonzalez *still* stays put. He throws another cutter. It comes in low. O'Leary chops at it.

It bounces in front of the plate, takes another bounce toward the left side. Izzy stabs at it, but it's simply a reflex action; the ball is way over his head. It comes in to Renteria several steps from second base. It's fitting justice, given the ball's well-established pleasure and penchant for perversity: In Game 1, it immediately sidled up to Cairo, playing in place of Renteria because of his ailing back, and Cairo threw wide for an error. Now in Game 2, it has fixated on Renteria in a potential game-ending double-play situation to see just how that ailing back is really feeling. He sidesteps toward the bag at second, the footwork smooth and gliding except for a little baby step at the end to make sure he touches the base. He keeps his motion going as he throws to first. *Double play.*

Izzy opens and closes his glove in a little jawlike snap, his own private victory salute. He steps off the mound and is immediately swarmed by acolytes. High-fives are tossed about like prom-night bouquets as Cardinals players blanket the infield. The Cubs walk the line of the dugout into the tunnel with the joy of prisoners being led back into the dim-bulb fortress after recreation. Their bench empties out quickly, except for Remlinger, who lingers there after everyone else has left. He's staring glassy-eyed at the field, no doubt wondering what everybody else on the Cubs is wondering, with no sensible answer except that it is, after all, the Cubs: *What just happened?*

GAME
THREE

12

D.K.

I

● ● ● THE LOWEST MOMENT of the season for La Russa came eleven days before the Cubs series started, in the androgyny of a Hertz rental car heading south on Broad Street in Philadelphia. He was on his way to the closest thing in baseball to a rat-infested sewer-spewing urine-stinking public-housing high-rise, when he got a call from Barry Weinberg, the trainer. It was bad enough going to the Vet, where the pipes routinely leaked and the clubhouse carpet was a deep purple momentarily popular during the tie-dye heyday of the 1960s, when LSD was considered a dietary supplement. But a call from Weinberg at eleven in the morning?

Weinberg was the ultimate grim reaper when it came to unexpected phone calls. He was Rasputin in red Banlon, the angel of death in a Polo shirt with little red birds on the front. Nothing was worse in a rental car on the way to the ballpark than a call from Weinberg. It meant that whatever Weinberg had to tell him couldn't wait for the clubhouse, just like the time Weinberg had called him to tell him in 2000 that Mike Matheny had cut his hand and wouldn't be able to catch in the playoffs.

"Morris turned his ankle. I'm taking him for an x-ray."

"How serious is it?"

"It's got a chance to be a problem."

La Russa hung up. He continued driving in his soundproof

silence. By the time he got to the visiting clubhouse of the Vet, his mood was even more foul, disappointment mixed with disbelief. Because there went the Thing of Beauty that he and Dave Duncan had worked so hard on just the night before. Forget the three-game series against the Cubs, with Matt Morris scheduled for the third game, the perfect coda. For that matter, forget the season if the ankle was as serious as Weinberg was indicating it might be by trying not to indicate anything.

Morris had come into this year as the deserved ace of the pitching staff. In the previous two years, he had put together numbers as good as anyone in baseball, not only wins and losses but also innings pitched, a two-hundred-plus inning workhorse:

W	L	Pct.	ERA	G	GS	CG	IP	H	R	ER	BB	SO
22	8	.733	3.16	34	34	2	216.1	218	86	76	54	185
17	9	.654	3.42	32	32	1	210.1	210	86	80	64	171

But this season had been star-crossed, almost freakish. It had started out brilliantly, peaking in two back-to-back complete-game shutouts in the middle of May: the first against the Cubs, and the next against Pittsburgh. The one against the Cubs was achingly beautiful: first-pitch strikes to twenty-three of thirty batters, fourteen groundball outs, a fastball combination of straight four-seamer and sinker, a wicked 12-to-6 curve he had such confidence in he threw it on 2-0 counts, eighty-two strikes out of 117 pitches.

If there was *anything* that marred the performance against the Cubs, it was that last number, the ball and chain of pitch count, not because of anything Morris had done wrong but because of a disturbing trend. La Russa kept track of pitching performances as he kept track of everything, with pencil and ruler and lined legal-size paper that went wherever he went. In the case of Morris, the series of numbers looked like this:

```
7/8/5/106  8/3/0/103   8.2/6/3/122  6/5/0/104  7/5/2/73   6/5/2/115
9/6/2/124  8/10/3/111  6/5/4/77     9/4/0/117  9/9/0/123  7.1/6/3/107
```

La Russa wasn't adverse to computers, although he has never used one for baseball. He knew that he could rely on Duncan—

who in another life would have made a fine hacker, given his ability to tunnel inside without leaving a trace—and was up-to-date on all the latest technology trying to predict player trend lines. La Russa appreciated the information generated by computers. He studied the rows and columns. But he also knew they could take you only so far in baseball, maybe even confuse you with a fog of overanalysis. As far as he knew, there was no way to quantify desire. And those numbers told him exactly what he needed to know when added to twenty-four years of managing experience. Each line was a concise history of Morris's twelve outings through the end of May, and the numbers within each line reflected the following: innings pitched, hits allowed, runs given up, and pitches thrown. They told La Russa a story just like his matchups did, and this particular one contained dark foreshadowing.

They showed that, out of Morris's twelve starts through the end of May, he'd exceeded the 100-pitch threshold ten times, including three games in which he had thrown more than 120. It was a lot of pitches early in the season. Woody Williams's numbers were similar, but there was little La Russa could do about it, given the bullpen's nightmarish performance without Jason Isringhausen. Pushing them was the only way to stay alive, just as figuring out a solution to Pujols's elbow had been the only way to stay alive. He worried that if they both kept it up at this pace, it was only a matter of time before they would get physically drained. But the alternative to not taking his two primary starters deep was no alternative if the Cards wanted to stay up with the Astros and the Cubs. The team had to win games somewhere.

In June, Morris developed some crankiness in his arm because of a knot behind his right shoulder. It wasn't enough to put him on the disabled list, but it forced him to alter his mechanics, which can be beneficial as well as risky, as so much of pitching, like love, is about feel and therefore as elusive as it is beautiful. It was also enough for La Russa to start juggling the rotation to give Morris more rest in between starts. Because the rotation is scheduled out roughly six weeks ahead, with a key pitcher, such as Morris, placed into as many key games as possible, La Russa's pencil and eraser took a beating as he swapped starts and reslotted. In July against the Dodgers, Morris wobbled through five innings. He did some things well, but he threw nothing fastballs to several hitters and the result was a five-run inning. His fastball velocity was down into the high eighties, and he was suffering the worst slump of his five-year career, with thirty-four earned runs given up in thirty-three and two-thirds innings. An MRI on his shoulder failed to reveal any structural problems.

But *something* was wrong, a loss of concentration that could be fatal to the team if it kept up and something that, as a manager, La Russa had to figure out how to pinpoint and handle. Of course, the early rigors of the season had taken a physical and mental toll on Morris, but La Russa suspected that more fundamental aspects of human nature had greater influence. Morris's record stood at 8-6 heading into the All-Star break: not terrible but not great. His ERA had ballooned from 2.37 at the end of May to 4.19, a numerical indicator of mental health for a pitcher as good as Morris. In his multiple roles of Doctor Phil, Doctor Ruth, and Doctor Seuss, La Russa wondered whether what Morris felt was pretty simple.

The season had just gotten messed up, 8 and 6 exactly what it sounded like—barely above mediocre—when with any help from the bullpen, it could have been 11 and 3 and on the way to the twenty-win grail. He privately acknowledged to Morris the tragedy of the bullpen early in the season and how it had screwed the starter. He emphasized his crucial place in the rotation, that he still had an easy shot at fifteen wins. He pointed out that if the team made it into the playoffs, Morris would have another opportunity, as in the previous two seasons when the team had gotten there, to show millions that he was in the highest echelon of pitchers. It all sounded good, but La Russa backed up his pep talk with pragmatism, giving Morris a full ten days off, including the All-Star break, before his next start, against San Diego.

But maybe something else altogether was wrong, an absence as literal as it was emotional—a permanent vacancy at the locker two down from Morris's. It was empty except for the uniform shirt of the player who had once worn it, a shirt of deep Cardinals red hung on a white plastic hanger, the name across the back in proud capital-letter symmetry like a highway sign announcing the next town.

It was unaffected by its surroundings and would forever be unaffected, and there was terrible cruelty in that. And Morris still felt it, not as much, maybe, as at the beginning. But something like that didn't simply tick away. The player who had once worn that shirt had been a mentor to him, helped teach him not only the rigors of pitching but also the rigors of the baseball life: the road trips, how much to tip the clubhouse attendant, the pacing, the mental art that must go in lockstep with the mechanics.

D.K. It's what his teammates called him.

II

SOMETHING had been bothering Darryl Kile in June 2002. He was off his stride, and La Russa knew that he was off his stride, the psychological challenges of pitching impacting the mechanics and the mechanics impacting the psychological challenges. He was working his ass off. He always worked his ass off. But he was languishing at the .500 mark, the last two seasons when he had gone a combined 36 and 20 feeling more and more like a lost horizon. Something was up, and La Russa felt that he had to take it on, fathom the inside of Darryl's head a little bit.

Darryl wanted to win as much as ever, hated it when he had taken back-to-back no-decisions against the Astros, even though he had pitched well and deep — a *no-decision,* as if you hadn't even been there. But Darryl was distracted, preoccupied in a way La Russa hadn't seen before, and it worried him. A pitcher's head is far more precious than his arm and far more inscrutable. An arm could show you it was tired. It could exhibit shoulder crankiness or elbow crankiness. It could be balmed, rubbed, bandaged, iced. It could demand rest or even surgery: *Stop treating me like this.* But a pitcher's head wasn't always so clear. And during the two and a half years that Kile had been with the Cardinals, his head had been so focused, so absent the clouds that can cause temporary insanity in any pitcher at any time. His performance reflected it — the ace of the staff — so what was happening now was more than simply a blip.

He had been something of an enigma when he came over to the

Cardinals in 2000 in an off-season trade with the Rockies. He had put together one spectacular year with the Astros in 1997, going 19 and 7. But then the Astros didn't want to pay him. So he signed with the Rockies, willing to endure the Bataan Death March of Coors Field, so littered with the skeletal psyches of pitchers who started the first and got to the fourth with the score 8–7 and men on second and third and no outs and the ball frolicking in its freedom. Because the ball carried like a space capsule in the thin air, outfielders tended to play deep, meaning that bloopers blooped. The thin air also took some of the snap out of your curve ball, a killer 12 to 6 morphing into a very mortal 12 to 3. Sinker ballers did okay there. So did guys who weren't afraid to live with their changeups. But Kile had a good fastball and a curve that did go 12 to 6 when it was snapping right, and this wasn't the right place for him.

He went 8 and 13 with an ERA of 6.61, four runs more than the 2.57 he had put up during that sensational year with the Astros. The Cards ended up getting him after the season, La Russa and Duncan wondering whether that 19-and-7 season in Houston had merely been some first act with no second one but believing that there were grounds for replication.

Spring training is valuable for La Russa in assessing new pitchers; he closely observes how they respond to the absolute pull-your-hair-out tedium of it. Before the start of exhibition games, they throw only every other day, so there isn't much to do other than the same drills over and over, pick-off drills, fielding-bunt drills, hitting drills in the cage. How a new guy reacts to it — gets after it or sloughs through it — tells La Russa a great deal. He keenly watched Kile, trying to gauge that elusive quality called professionalism. He watched one day. He watched another. He got reports from the other coaches handling the drills, including Duncan, of course. And what he said to Duncan about Kile was crisp and pointed because he almost couldn't believe how serious Kile was about everything:

"I hope this is not a façade. I hope he's not fooling us."

Kile went 20 and 9 for the Cardinals in 2000. Along the way, working with Duncan, he developed a forkball. The more he used it, the more he seemed to like it, with its wicked downward tumble. On many days, it became an equally effective out pitch for him as his fastball and curve. In 2001, he went 16 and 11, polishing his reputation as a bulldog worker, maybe the toughest in the National League. It marked the fourth season out of five in which he had been in the top ten in the league in innings pitched, games started, and batters faced. In fact, Kile took great pride in never having been on the disabled list, *never*, a truly Herculean feat for a starting pitcher.

Kile had other qualities that marked him as far more than a power pitcher who had thrown $232\frac{1}{3}$ innings in 2000 and $227\frac{1}{3}$ innings in 2001 and seemed destined to do the same in 2002. He was a wonderful husband to his wife, Flynn, and she was a wonderful wife to him. They had three children together: the twins, Kannon and Sierra, who had turned five in January, and the little son, Ryker, who was less than a year old. They were a gorgeous American family, blond and floppy-haired. You looked at them and wished that everybody in the entire world, including your own family, looked that way. They stood together during picture day at Busch in a tight little rainbow, everybody holding on to one another.

There was also Kile the teammate. *Teammate* is a hackneyed term like so many terms, overused and overwrought. But it still can be beautiful, two powerful words that under the right conditions can take on even more powerful significance when merged together. A ballclub is a family, the most forced and unnatural family imaginable—players passing through like container cargo in the continual money juggle of baseball. How it comes together or splits up, takes in its newest members or spits them out, struggles through hard times or splinters apart, is a crucial element of its success. To be successful, it must have steadying influences, particularly in the emotional trough of late June and early July, when you look around the clubhouse and see faces that maybe you already wish you didn't ever have to see again. Nerves get frayed. Egos become hypersensitive: a pitcher pissed off because he got an early hook, a batter plotting insurrection because he got pinch-hit for. Even the question of what video to slip in the clubhouse VCR in the slow hours before a game can produce a shouting match, comedy versus drama. Cliques form. An ever-widening language gap separates the Latino players, who speak mostly Spanish, and American-born players, who speak English, and the lone Japanese player, who doesn't speak either.

Kile was a great teammate, the ultimate bonding agent. He was a mentor to Rick Ankiel and Morris as they rose and struggled and struggled and rose. He gave Matheny, who caught him, a Rolex watch after he won his twentieth. He put his arm around Jason Simontacchi when he was a rookie pitcher, still dazzled by the intimidating wonder of it all, and took him out for dinner. He was always digging into his pocket and paying for meals, although just about everybody at the table made at least a million or two or three or four. Then there were the little things he did in the clubhouse, the rituals that made everyone laugh: announcing like a lighthouse foghorn three hours before game time that there were three hours to game time, singing in the summer heat that ridiculous little song about "let it snow, let it snow, let it snow."

Kile was about more than comic relief, though. La Russa knew that the best clubhouses don't have a single team leader; they have a small cadre of guys you can count on to cosign what you say and convince their teammates to accept what you say, assuming, of course, that what you have said makes sense. You could not function without their support; they could empower a manager, or they could sink him by letting the inevitable disgruntlements elevate into mutinies.

Kile belonged to that cadre, a key component. It was essential for Kile to buy into what La Russa said. It was essential because of the impact that Kile had in the clubhouse, not just the presence of personality that players felt comfortable with but a competitiveness that they admired and rubbed off on them. He considered nothing in life more insulting than the intentional walk, went toe-to-toe with La Russa on several occasions because of his recalcitrance to throw one. La Russa worried that other pitchers, wanting to emulate their leader, would kick up their heels as well when the order came from the foxhole to put pride aside and simply put the damn guy on first. But La Russa had trouble getting too terribly upset with Kile, because as much as he loved talent in a player, it was the add-on of competitiveness that created the possibility of the spectacular.

Kile's influence stretched past the players to the entire extended family that also make a clubhouse different from any place on earth: the equipment managers, the attendants, the guys running the video, those who ensure order but toil in obscurity underneath the surface glamour of working for a big-league ball club. It was easy to condescend—the upstairs-downstairs mentality, those who play and those who never will. But Kile made sure that the guys coming up never took them for granted, never acted with entitlement when their own presence here was just a matter of genes and the blessings of fortune that came and went. Because who knew what could happen? Who really knew . . . ?

III

LA RUSSA SIMPLY liked talking to Kile as he made his floating rounds during spring training. He liked probing him about the Astros, because, ever since coming over to the National League in 1996, La Russa had admired how the Astros had played. He wanted to know what made their clubhouse tick, and Kile told him about the influence of Craig Biggio and Jeff Bagwell, the steady tone they set and how their steadiness spilled over onto the field. Then one day, Kile asked La Russa to name the ten people in his life who had truly put it all together: the blend of talent and heart and work ethic. The question came up in the context of an article in which La Russa had been quoted in *Time* on the greatness of Michael Jordan. It was a deep question, almost philosophical, a player probing beyond mechanics and the downward tumble of a forkball into something perhaps unfathomable. La Russa appreciated the depth of it. He told Kile that a question as serious as that deserved an equally serious answer, which meant that La Russa would take it and play with it in the quiet hours when men who should be sleeping are sleepless. As he mused on the question, he was struck by what it suggested about Kile, a player who knew he was on the cusp of greatness and wanted to map out the final steps.

Which is what made June 2002 so troubling. Kile had had arthroscopic surgery on his shoulder during the off-season. It had thrown a whack into his spring-training regimen, curtailing the amount of work he could put in. A lot of pitchers simply would have stayed down in Florida once the team moved north, get in four or five starts to put the wheels back in motion and then rejoin the club on May 1. But Kile didn't like the idea of putting his team in the hole like that.

"Who are you gonna pitch in my place?" he asked La Russa.

"That's not the way we look at it, Darryl. It's a six-month season. You come back May first ready to go, we'll still be in contention."

Kile refused the opening offered to him. He had never spent a day on the disabled list, and he wasn't about to start now. He was a starting pitcher. He was paid to start. And that's what he did right from the beginning of the season. He pitched well, incredibly well given how much of the spring he had missed. But as much as he hated to admit it, because it implied some excuse, and he was from the old-time school where any excuse was just that, he was still recovering. By the beginning of June, his record was 2 and 3, including those two no-decisions against Houston. He pitched well against Pittsburgh—six hits in seven innings and one run—to get to .500. Although he struggled in his next start against Kansas City, he still got the win to push up to 4 and 3. La Russa and Duncan liked the way he was coming back physically from the surgery. They were pleased with his progress. They admired his progress. He was beginning to look right. But something wasn't right inside. He was quiet. He really wasn't saying anything, no foghorn blast to the assembled three hours before game time, not even that stupid little song about snow.

"You okay?" they separately asked him.

"I'm okay. Just trying to get my stuff right."

And that's all he said. La Russa talked to Duncan about it, and Duncan thought that Kile's moody silence was simply an expression of frustration, that it was June and he wanted to be pitching great all the time and was barely over .500. La Russa let it go, but then came the Seattle game. His stuff was pretty good, but "within the ears," as La Russa described it, he simply didn't seem to be there. In the pregame meeting, Duncan had stressed several crucial points to Kile, including not to throw anything soft and breaking to John Olerud. But during the game, Kile was doing the exact opposite of what Duncan had told him. It happened a couple of times. From the dugout, La Russa, who had sat in on the meeting, watched and thought, *What the hell was that? Why did he do that?*

Then Olerud came up, and Kile threw exactly what Duncan had told him not to throw, a soft breaking ball, and Olerud hit it out for a two-run homer. It was abundantly clear to La Russa that Kile's head simply wasn't into it. So in the fifth, he came out to the mound and took Kile out. Kile was surprised. He made a bid to stay, but it was too late.

"I've already signaled from the bench. I've already got a guy coming in. Give me the ball."

Kile gave him the ball, an act of surrender even more humiliating than an intentional walk. After the game, on the plane back to St. Louis, La Russa went back to talk to some of the players. He tried to make eye contact with Kile, but the pitcher turned away. La Russa let it go, because he knew that Kile was hard-wired with pride. A hook in the fifth was more than some glancing blow.

Over the next several days, La Russa and Kile continued their dance of avoidance. When the pitcher saw the manager, he went the other way. Then Duncan called La Russa and said that something was wrong with Kile.

"I tried to talk to him about a couple of things. He's not being rude. But he's not listening. He's not into it."

He simply wanted to get his pitching in, which was entirely uncharacteristic of him. "He's bothered about something," said Duncan.

There was a game against Kansas City that Sunday. La Russa waited until all the reporters had gotten their quotes and left the clubhouse. Then he tapped Kile on the shoulder and asked him to come into his office.

"Look, you get the ball Tuesday and there's an off day tomorrow," said La Russa. "For you and for us, I want to have this conversation."

Most times, La Russa would start off a conversation with a player by asking a question and listening to the player's response. But now he began differently.

"I got three things I want to say to you, and I'd like to get all three things out. Then you can say anything you want to. Or say nothing if you want to. But I'd like to say those three things." Kile nodded.

First, La Russa reaffirmed the fact that nobody believed in him more as a pitcher than La Russa and Duncan did and that nothing had happened this season, *nothing,* to change that. His second point had to do with why he'd hooked Kile in the fifth inning in Seattle. It wasn't to humiliate the pitcher but because of the mental mistakes Kile had made.

"As a manager, there is only one way a player and a team improves—if something gets done wrong, you address it, unless it's a hiccup. It's common sense but it's hard to accept if you're the individual involved.

"Do you think that's a bad philosophy?" he asked rhetorically. "If it was you, would you just let mistakes happen?"

La Russa's third point, and perhaps the most important one, was to let Kile know just how important he was to the team—a core player, a core leader—and the responsibility that implied. "That means if you're in Seattle and something happens and you get taken out of the game, you can react however you want. This is America. You can get mad at me. You can dispute my decision. What I would challenge you to dispute is my intention to do the right thing for the team and for you. I think it's real important that you walk out of here today knowing that you're a key guy and that any decision I'm trying to make is for us and for you."

Finished with what he felt he had to say, he asked Kile for his response. "This is totally about me," said Kile. "It's not about you guys. You address things. You work on stuff. You don't ignore things."

"That means I can't ignore it when it involves you."

"I understand that."

"Well, you understand that you're a key guy?"

"Tony, this is totally about me," he repeated. "It's been really hard for me to struggle like I've been struggling."

At that moment, La Russa understood what was eating at Kile, and he respected him more than ever for it. "Darryl, do you understand how few pitchers could have gone through what you did with the arthroscopic surgery and would be determined not to miss a start?"

"I just go out there," Kile lamented. "I pitch four innings. I pitch three innings. I pitch five innings."

La Russa pulled out the legal sheet showing that Kile had also pitched six innings, seven innings, including those two no-decisions against Houston where he had worked his ass off.

"Darryl, we still have four months to play. It's all in front of us."

"It's hard for me. It's just hard."

"Your arm strength is good. Your stamina is good. Cut yourself some slack. You've already gone through the hardest part."

"I'm bouncing back good. I feel strong. Then I get these no-decisions."

La Russa looked at him and said the only thing that was left to say, because no matter how much money you made and how much adulation you received for doing what you did, you could never hear it enough.

"We can't make it without you."

IV

KILE PITCHED two days later against the Angels on a star-crossed night marked by the passing of Cardinals broadcaster Jack Buck. He went seven and two-thirds innings, his longest outing of the season. He gave up six hits and one earned run. He was lights out, his best performance of the season, and the 7–2 win put the team into undisputed possession of first place. On a sad and painful evening—because losing Buck was to St. Louis like losing the Mississippi—Kile had been magnificent.

Five days later, in mid-June, he was set to go against the Cubs at

Wrigley. Flynn Kile felt that something was amiss as she talked to her husband in those days leading up to the start in Chicago. He suddenly asked her to remarry him. He seemed overly emotional and affectionate, as if he were preparing for something, getting ready for something, even if he had no idea what it was. That Friday night, from his hotel room at the Westin off Michigan Avenue, he talked with her for an hour. He didn't want to get off the phone. She remembered him saying that. *I don't want to get off.* But he did because there was a game the next day, and Kile, just as he prided himself on never missing a start, also prided himself on never being late to the ballpark.

There were so many things that happened the next morning, images that could not be erased no matter how much you wanted to erase them. You could see Mike Matheny urging someone, anyone, to check on Kile's whereabouts when he still hadn't shown up in the cubbyhole of the visitor's clubhouse of Wrigley after the team bus had arrived. You could see the head of security for the Westin breaking into room 1102 after repeated phone calls had gone unanswered and finding him there, still in his bed, wearing the black eyeshades that helped him sleep, with one arm across the pillow and the other across his upper torso. You could see Barry Weinberg rushing off the field with Walt Jocketty after a phone call. You could see Buddy Bates, then the equipment manager, fall into a chair in the clubhouse and cup his head in his hands. You could see reliever Dave Veres whispering, "They found D.K. They can't wake him up," then retreat into the tiny equipment room to sob in private. You could see Matheny pleading with Bates to tell him what was wrong, asking him, *Is Darryl still alive?* and lifting Bates by the collar when Bates didn't know what to say because how do you say something like that until he just nodded no and Matheny pulled off his jersey because baseball simply didn't matter anymore. You could see Tony La Russa standing in the middle of a circle of players and saying softly, *"They found Darryl. He's dead."* You could see Joe Girardi, then playing for the Cubs, come out onto the field of Wrigley and announce to the sold-out crowd with tears in his eyes, almost unable to speak, that the game would be postponed because of "a tragedy in the Cardinals family." You could see all those things and so many more things and still not believe it: a player, a teammate, there with you the night before doing the things players do on the road—grabbing dinner with friends at Harry Caray's, getting back to the hotel at 10:30 to call his wife, rejecting Morris's invitation shortly after midnight to have a drink in the hotel bar—because *you know what, Matty Mo, I feel a little tired. I just feel a little tired.*

You could think of Darryl, the way he competed and the impatience with which he treated himself, not cutting himself any slack, because that's what quitters did and baseball had enough quitters in it already, and when you thought of Darryl, it was impossible not to think of his wife and those three beautiful children. You could grope for things to say, ways of realizing it, or somehow making it less real.

You could listen to Tony La Russa in a closed-door meeting that night on the sixteenth floor of the Westin, recounting that last conversation he'd had with Darryl, how he had told him how important he was to the team, how he had said, *"We can't make it without you."* And then you could listen to Dave Duncan, Duncan the Quiet Assassin, Duncan the Deacon, Duncan whose words were so sparse they were called biblical. You could see the tears well up in his eyes as he spoke about his fallen pitcher who had died of a heart attack in his sleep at the age of thirty-three. You could see him stop to steady himself. And then you could listen to him in the sterile antiseptic wash of that hotel conference room when he talked about what a privilege it had been to work with Darryl Kile. You could listen to him describing how wonderful it had been to talk the bittersweet beauty of pitching with him, the timeless and impossible science of trying to figure out what precisely made it work, which was why it was always worth talking about. And you could listen to him when he said that for now and forever, he would use Darryl Kile as a model in his own life, to attain the same professional heights and more than just that because there was so much more than just that: the humanity of Darryl Kile, the exquisite humanity.

• • •

The Cardinals foundered in the immediate aftermath. There was the incomprehensible loss of Darryl Kile and beyond that, the soul-searching every player went through as they privately wondered, maybe for the first time ever, just how important baseball really was anymore. They knew that Darryl had left behind a wife and three children, and they also thought of their own families: the vulnerability of them, how everything in life could change so very much from one day to the next, there and then not there. The team was still in the thick of a race for the division, and as the manager, La Russa's mandate was to get them to compete. But he also did not want to trample on those who asked themselves, because it was worth asking themselves, why the race for the division mattered. In the week following Kile's death, the team won only two of seven games, and the atmosphere in the clubhouse was ghostly even in the rare victories, players walking in quietly and then showering and then leaving as fast as they could.

La Russa continued to search for the right thing to do. He mourned as they mourned, but he was still a manager. In the past, he had always relied on the advice of his mentors, but they were of no help now because nothing they had been through was parallel to what he and his team were going through. Then he read a column by Bernie Miklasz in the *St. Louis Post-Dispatch*. And it hit him: a way maybe, just maybe, to recapture the hearts and minds of his players back to where he felt they should be.

Several hours before the game to be played that night, he gathered the team into the eating room in the clubhouse. "We're all examining what's right in our lives and what's right for our families," he said. "We mourn Darryl and we worry about his wife and kids and it's not like you can go to the office and hide since we all compete in front of each other." He acknowledged that he wasn't sure what to do, how the coaches weren't sure what to do, how appropriate was it now to get after a player who didn't hustle, to seize on the very things that had once been so automatic before Kile's death. Then La Russa pulled out a piece of paper in which he had copied down a small portion of Miklasz's column, actually something that Kile himself had once written about the death of his own father. "This is what helps me," La Russa told his players. And while he wasn't sure it would help them, he also felt it was worth reading aloud:

> I don't think I'll ever get over it, but my father was my best friend. But in order to be a man, you got to separate your personal life from your work life. It may sound cold, but I've got work to do. I'll never forget my father, but I'm sure he'd want me to keep on working and try to do the best I can do.

The pall began to lift after La Russa read those words. A team that had stopped competing discovered that it was okay to compete again because of what their teammate was telling them: letting them know, just as he had once learned, that there *was* still work to do, that the very definition of a professional *was* to separate out the personal. Which is why, when the Cardinals went on to win ninety-seven games and the division title that year—when they beat Randy Johnson and Curt Schilling of the Diamondbacks in back-to-back games to win the division series, when they came within a breath of going to the World Series—it was a performance in every way remarkable for the sorrow that had been overcome, except maybe to Darryl Kile.

It would have to be enough. For every teammate who had known him, heard that silly and comforting foghorn reminding them that it was three hours before game time, watched him pitch his ass off and argue with Matheny like a stubborn old woman to the point that Matheny would just as soon strangle him and stuff him in a box except that he loved him in the way that only a catcher can love a pitcher.

Whatever they felt and remembered would have to endure. For La Russa and Duncan. For Matheny and Williams and Bates and Veres. For Pujols and Simontacchi and Renteria. For Morris, whose locker, so stoked with the stuffing of the game it looked like Santa's sack, was just down the row from the one that was bare except for the uniform shirt hanging on the white plastic hanger, there long after the last light had been turned off and Morris and everyone else had gone home knowing, as much as they ever knew anything in life, that they would be back at it the next day three hours before game time.

13

THING OF BEAUTY

I

● ● ● SAN DIEGO WAS the perfect place for Matt Morris to get back into the groove after the All-Star break. The very name of its stadium—Qualcomm—sounded like an over-the-counter herbal remedy guaranteeing sweet dreams, the fans equally relaxed so there would be no extra burden on his performance beyond the burden of performance itself.

He came back strong, the ten days' rest clearly of benefit. His delivery and mechanics were smooth. His composure was in place, essential for Morris because he tended to fall out of his delivery and rush his throws when he got excited. In his brief absence from the game, he had rediscovered love.

As La Russa watched him in that first inning against the lead-off hitter, Ramon Vazquez, he couldn't help but feel that a huge obstacle had been overcome. The Cardinals could not win without Morris. His prolonged absence would affect the club like an oil spill, an ecological catastrophe whose black ooze would eventually touch everybody, not only the pitchers who would have to fill in for him but also hitters who would feel the extra burden to attain crooked numbers without his regular presence on the mound.

Morris struck out Vazquez on a 92-mph fastball, and there was *baseball* to La Russa, just *beautiful baseball*. It had that pop, that sweetest sound, the same sound that had moved Cal Eldred to defy

216

the laws of nature with his patched-up pothole of an elbow and return to the game. Morris threw a curve to start the cat-and-mouse against the second-place hitter, Mark Kotsay. He swung through it, not simply a curve but one of those curves that almost genuflects by the time it's through, and there was *baseball* to La Russa, more *beautiful baseball.* Kotsay was able to turn on the next pitch, lining it up the middle. It was the ninth pitch of the game for Morris. And then came a different sound altogether, the sound of ball against bone.

The ball hit Morris's right hand. La Russa and Duncan and the assistant trainer, Mark O'Neal, ran to the mound to try to assess the seriousness. Morris threw a warm-up toss that hit the backstop, and that was it. He was lifted, and even the home plate umpire told La Russa that it was a shame, because Morris had been *on,* his fastball clocking at 92 and 93 and 94 mph. A resulting CT scan showed a nondisplaced fracture of his pitching hand, above his right index finger, that would sideline him anywhere between three and six weeks.

In desperate times, men of course do strange and desperate things. In La Russa's case, the urgency was exacerbated by another bedrock theory of his: When in doubt, *try something.* Jeff Fassero was thrust into the starting rotation in the hope that this jumper cable would give him some spark. He had been a starter for most of his career with Montreal and Seattle, and he responded. He liked the challenge of starting, which is why La Russa threw him up there. Garrett Stephenson needed a different path. La Russa gave him a carefully designed whacking—*We're sending you to the bullpen*—the only words a starter fears more than *Can I talk to you a minute?* And, later, when he was promoted again to the starting rotation, he too responded. Brett Tomko, the number three starter, was so laid back on the mound that he confessed to actually feeling sleepy on his pitching day, despite stuff of such quality that Duncan in spring training pegged him for eighteen wins. He also got whacked with the threat of long-term banishment, and he started winning. Danny Haren was promoted out of Double-A, even though he probably wasn't ready yet, and he started winning. Pujols embarked on a thirty-game hitting streak. Bo Hart, who during the previous off-season had worked in a department store to make ends meet, was still hitting the flying crap out of the ball after his send-up from the minors.

When they came into Philly from Pittsburgh in early August, they were tied for first after dropping three and a half back in the immediate aftermath of Morris's injury. They had gone 14 and 8 in his absence. They had played four three-game series, and they had taken the rubber game of each, and now Morris was coming back. It had the same uplift of a midsummer trade in which the Cards had landed a great number one starter without giving up anything.

Anticipating his return, La Russa and Duncan went to work in the plane to Philadelphia on the Thing of Beauty. The most pressing question was where to fit Morris within it. The last game of the three-game series against the Phillies was also the Sunday night Game of the Week on ESPN, and both men wondered how fair it would be to throw Morris into the fire like that when he hadn't pitched for three weeks. The alternative was Tomko, and they worried about Tomko in a situation like this. In high-pressure moments on the mound, you could see the confidence drain from Tomko's body. He lost faith in the curve in these moments. He pretty much lost faith in everything. So Duncan walked to the back of the plane to tell Morris that he would start the Sunday night game and also to tell Tomko that he wouldn't start the Sunday night game.

Then they went back to work on the Thing of Beauty. La Russa penciled in and erased and then penciled in some more and erased some more, the tricky goal to maximize starts for Morris and Woody Williams while ensuring that they also pitched in the pivotal series left on the schedule, in particular the three games against the Cubs at the end of August. By the time the plane landed in Philly, they had the Thing of Beauty worked out. They had mapped out the rotation for the team's remaining forty games, and it *was* a Thing of Beauty, the defining document for the rest of the season, their Magna Carta. Morris would be getting eight starts and Williams nine. Their presence would be guaranteed in the Cubs series, as well as series against the Astros in August and September. It was the first time all season that La Russa and Duncan had felt excited about their chances to compete and win from here until the end. They looked at each other on finishing the Thing of Beauty—without saying a word, of course—but thinking the same lofty thought: *Man, maybe we can pull this thing off.*

Until the phone call from Weinberg.

II

ON THURSDAY NIGHT after dinner with several teammates in Philadelphia, Morris had slipped on a small set of marble stairs in the lobby of the Four Seasons hotel. He didn't think much of it at the time and headed for the elevators. His ankle felt a little tender, but he wrapped it and went to sleep; when he woke up the next morning, it was sizably swollen. Which is when Weinberg was called. Which is when Weinberg called La Russa on the way to the hospital for an x-ray. Which is when La Russa's mood, tentative on game day to begin with, crashed.

The word was that Morris would be out a minimum of *two weeks,* maybe *three.* The ankle was significantly sprained, and the injury had occurred on his landing foot, meaning that every pitch he threw might exacerbate it. The Thing of Beauty was worthless now. It would have to be completely reworked; the immediate repercussion was that Tomko, after being told he wouldn't start Sunday night, would now be told that he would be starting Sunday night, akin to parents saying that they want to adopt you and then deciding against it and then taking you anyway because nobody else was left at the orphanage.

Morris came into the clubhouse, limping noticeably. Steve Kline looked at him.

"How'd you do that?" he asked. It was a question requiring an answer that Morris clearly didn't want to go into.

"The lobby," he curtly replied. And then he limped into the asylum of the trainer's room, which was off-limits to reporters.

For La Russa, it was a pivotal moment, one of those moments in which managing the team *mentally* was more important than managing *strategically*. He was adamant that none of what was happening would defeat them. The team had regrouped and rebounded when Morris had gotten hurt against San Diego, and they would do the same now. He was trying to be positive, but it wasn't easy. He couldn't help but agonize over the upcoming series against the Cubs, knowing that Morris, slotted for Game 3, could not pitch it. He also knew that the Cubs were about to embark on a hellacious road trip, nine games in ten days, culminating in the series against the Cards. He hoped they would go 0 and 6 before they arrived in St. Louis, because wouldn't that be lovely, send the punky boys packing. But what if they broke even, or they went 4 and 2? What if they came into Busch thinking they could win because they could win? What if they threw Prior and Wood and Zambrano at them versus Stephenson and Williams and Tomko? What if what if what if what if?

And *what now* . . .

The Phillies three-game series was a disaster, an accumulation of miseries. Williams couldn't keep the ball down in Game 1. Matheny failed on a *hit-and-run*. Haren was great until the sixth of Game 2, when he challenged and lost and gave up two home runs. Edmonds turned an inside-the-park homer into a double when he ambled to first, thinking he'd hit it out of the park; if he'd hustled like he should have, he could have made it home when the ball landed in an unpopulated portion of the outfield. Martinez left eight men on base. Tomko was as shaky as La Russa had feared in Game 3 with six runs and two homers in three innings. Even Pujols wasn't immune. He got the flu and missed one game entirely. The series ended on a fitting note when La Russa got ejected in the ninth for exhorting the umpire to eject Phillie pitcher Turk Wendell for hitting a Cardinal after several Cardinals had already been hit. In doing so, he pulled his little cheat sheets out of his back pocket and ripped them up, and while the fluttering of those little torn pieces to the artificial turf might have made him feel momentarily calmer, it also meant that he would now have to do them all over again because the Phillies were coming to St. Louis the following weekend.

But the three-game series is the perfect drug; by definition, it leaves the system quickly. It is over, finished, and then on to the next one. Pittsburgh was in next for three games, and something stunning happened during that series: the setback that had occurred five days ago now offset by such amazing news that it sent La Russa dancing out of his office in what looked remarkably like an imitation of Jackie Gleason on his old variety show. Which was almost as amazing as the news itself.

III

"MORRIS LOOKED pretty darn good. I was really surprised."

La Russa, still in his uniform after an ugly first-game win against the Pirates, smiled for the first time all season when he heard those words from team doctor George Paletta.

"Hallelujah."

Paletta thought it was possible for Morris to go against the Cubs in Game 3, as it was still nine days off. The biggest risk was making sure that his mechanics were proper, in particular that he took a normal stride and landed correctly on his follow-through. A bullpen session with Morris had been scheduled for the next day. Paletta cautioned Duncan and La Russa to scrutinize him closely. He also advised that the only way to tell for sure how his ankle was healing would be to have him pitch at game-level intensity.

Paletta left, and La Russa pounced. Because Morris had to pitch at game-level intensity anyway to make sure he was okay, La Russa sounded out Walt Jocketty on the prospect of letting Morris pitch Saturday against the Phillies on a limited pitch count, instead of heading down to the minors for a rehab game or, worse yet, waiting until the Cubs' series. Pitching against the Phillies would give Morris all the intensity he needed, La Russa reasoned, and, more important, would give him a start before jumping into the fire against the Cubs.

Jocketty was dubious. But before he finished his sentence, La Russa was doing his *away-we-go* Jackie Gleason move to the trainer's room to talk to Weinberg. Jocketty could have canceled the idea, but what La Russa was suggesting made sense, as Morris would have to pitch somewhere before the Cubs' series.

When La Russa came back a few minutes later, he was smiling as broadly as the kid who got the train set for Christmas and the lifetime subscription to *Penthouse*. He pulled out the Thing of Beauty that had become so ugly in the immediate aftermath of Morris's ankle.

"Let's go to work now," he said.

He continued to toil in his uniform, the clubhouse emptied out until the only person left was the assistant equipment manager, Buddy Bates, rattling through with a set of white plastic hangers. He slotted in Morris for Saturday against the Phillies. He slotted him in for Game 3 on Thursday against the Cubs. He restored the initials MM in six other places so that he and Williams had fourteen starts of the games still remaining. "That looks better," he said when he was done. Then he said what he always said when something worked, or at least looked like it *might* work: "*Son of a bitch.*"

Morris went five innings that Saturday, his pitch count recorded in the dugout like the heartbeat monitor of a hospital patient:

Eighteen in the first. Up to twenty-nine by the second. Up to forty by the third. Up to fifty-seven by the fourth. Up to seventy-five by the fifth. If you push it any more, he's going to need a defibrillator.

He threw fifty-two strikes out of those seventy-five pitches. He gave up six hits and left on the short end of a 1–0 Phillies lead. He kept his team in it, and an inning later, the Cardinals turned the tables into a 5–1 lead that held up. If his ankle hurt—and it must have, given what it had looked like a few days earlier, a sight so gnarly that Morris himself regretted looking at it right after eating lunch—he didn't give in to it. He threw mostly fastballs and sinkers, but he didn't try to overthrow. His mechanics were smooth. His curve ball was still pissed at him for that month of rust, doing what curve balls so often do when they've been slighted, refusing any immediate offers of conciliation. His competitiveness was his kill shot, and you couldn't help but wonder if something private and indescribable had passed through to him from someone else who had pitched the exact same way.

He had done what he had been asked to do, just as five days later he would be asked again, this time against the Cubs in the rubber game.

14

KISS MY ASS

I

● ● ● LA RUSSA REMEMBERED the first time he had ever heard the mention of Morris's name. It was late in 1995, and after a ten-year run with Oakland, La Russa was thinking about his future. He was trying to figure out where to go next—maybe Baltimore—when he found himself sitting at a dinner banquet next to Walt Jocketty.

Jocketty had become the general manager of the Cardinals in 1994 after spending almost all of his major-league, front-office career with Oakland, so he knew La Russa well. He was from Minneapolis originally, and the combination of that Minnesota accent, where every answer still seems in the form of a curious question, along with the white hair as finely woven as pasta, exuded Rotarian solidity. He didn't seem like someone who tried to BS his way through as a general manager—make up complete lies about the talents of players who needed to be traded—when some would argue that the whole point of being a general manager was to lie, make your BS better than the other guy's BS. Almost uniquely, he had survived, and survived well, by telling the truth.

Jocketty's style also reflected something else—an increasing anachronism in baseball today. He believed that direct communication with a manager and coaches on personnel decisions could only *enhance* the quality of a ballclub. He showed none of the tendency to treat the manager as *middle* manager, there to be seen in the dugout but never heard, a few steps up from batboy. He listened carefully to the evaluations of La Russa and Duncan on possible players coming in and possible players to be shipped out. He respected their expertise and intuitions, which isn't to say that he always agreed with them or only listened to them exclusively. The decisions were Jocketty's, but La Russa—similar to his experiences with Rollie Hemond on the White Sox and Sandy Alderson on the A's—never felt deserted. But Jocketty was still a general manager.

He was by nature a hyperbolist, an enthusiast who could put a good spin on anything, find truth and justice in a three-card monte. At the table that night, he told La Russa and Duncan, who was there as well, about all the great young pitchers the Cardinals had coming up in the system. Alan Benes was mentioned, and so was someone named Matt Morris. He argued convincingly that the Cardinals had a strong pitching core, and he got La Russa and Duncan fired up, as they had been through enough to know that no matter how prodigious a team's hitting, it is pitching that always carries a team into the October light.

It was pretty much on the basis of that dinner that La Russa and Duncan, traveling in loyal tandem as usual, decided to make St. Louis their next stop. When they got down to spring training in 1996, they liked what they saw not only in Alan Benes but also brother Andy, who had signed as a free agent. But there was this other kid, Morris, even younger, whom the Cardinals had taken in the first round out of Seton Hall. The pitchers were throwing off the mound, and La Russa and Duncan were watching them. They looked up and down the row, and their eyes kept coming back to this 6'5" kid with the delivery, the way he arched his back, the way he got over on his front leg, the way the ball left his hand so *beautifully.* "Everything was so gorgeous," La Russa remembered. And although La Russa knew enough to heed his own admonition—*Never fall in and out of love too early in the spring*—forget it.

He was smitten, and by and large the love has been rewarded. But tonight in Game 3 is different. Different because of Morris's still uncertain ankle. Different because the Cardinals are going against a pitcher who has won six of his last seven starts and last time out, six days ago, carried a no-hitter into the eighth. Besides his competitive heart, Morris is also going to need the return of his stuff. He has to keep the ball down, and his curve—unhittable when it's on, because of its vengeful drop at the plate—must drop the picket signs and get back to work. It's also the rubber game of the three-game series, and in the 162-game season of baseball, trying to make it manageable, winning the rubber game of every three-game series is the way La Russa stays in contention. It's why he tells his players to think of it as if it's the seventh game of the World Series.

Morris is long and spindly on the mound, almost bow-legged. He likes to work quickly, sometimes too quickly when he's excited, which he obviously is tonight in Game 3, given the stakes. The Cardinals' win last night, coupled with Houston's victory over Los Angeles, have only perpetuated the seesaw torture of the standings: three teams separated by 11 one-hundredths of a percentage point:

HOUSTON	70-62	.530	—
ST. LOUIS	69-63	.523	1
CHICAGO	68-63	.519	1½

It only adds to the pressure on Morris tonight, and there's something else to watch for besides his ankle. It's a concern for Duncan and La Russa every time Morris pitches, as baseball may be the only organized profession in the world where theft is perfectly legal. There are virtually no rules about it. Instead, like suspected cattle rustling, it's taken care of with an impromptu code of justice much like a batter getting hit by a pitch. It is not tolerated if discovered, and there are some who will resort to the threat of death. But everyone is up for grabs—the pitcher, the catcher, the third-base coach, the first-base coach, the manager, the bench coach—because of a tendency to inadvertently spill secrets.

In recent years, since so many major-league pitchers are moved up before they've learned the subtler aspects of the game, La Russa has noticed a new twist on baseball theft. Preying on that virginity, players sit on the bench watching for whether a pitcher is tipping off his pitches in the process of his wind-up by the way he reaches in for a forkball or fans the glove on a curve; the wider the glove, the easier the detection. It's a burgeoning phenomenon because so many pitchers, with so little experience in the minors, haven't learned how to conceal what they're throwing. Some players, like Shawn Green of the Dodgers, can figure out a pitcher's pitches with uncanny accuracy. And this is only one of an assortment of attempted thefts that La Russa has seen in his managing career.

There are also the "peekers"—runners on first who try to peek into the catcher's glove to see what he is throwing as a basis for whether or not to try to steal second. There are runners on second who, with their bird's-eye view of the catcher, will try to tip location or the type of pitch to the batter with how they lead off second. There are relief pitchers in the bullpen who will communicate location to the batter by how they drape their arms over the bullpen wall. There are first-base coaches who will tip location with a series of sudden movements. There are coaches who will spend hours staring into dugouts to see if they can figure out the pitchout sign, like Cardinals bench coach Pettini did when he broke the Pirates earlier in the season.

There are ways to combat all of this. A manager, knowing he is surrounded by all these cat burglars, will act like he's putting on a sign when it's simply a series of dekes. La Russa does that sometimes when he goes to his leg or touches his hat, much ado about nothing. Aware that an opponent may be watching on television with its intimate camera angles, a catcher such as Matheny may have as many as six different sets of signs for a starter that he will change with a tap on his mask or a thump on his chest. Outright threats are effective as well—like the one Roger Clemens once gave to a runner on second whom he suspected of tipping. He called time, walked up to the runner, and stated succinctly that "somebody was going to get killed" if he kept it up. But attempted thefts still go on throughout a game, an underworld of deceit and deception. Early in his career, when he was with the White Sox, La Russa learned the value of sign stealing from a third-base coach named Joe Nossek. Nossek was the Willie Sutton of his day—he stole signs because they were there—and rare was the sign he couldn't crack. He got La Russa to pay attention to the science, and La Russa was a good student.

In 1983, as the White Sox were making their run to a division championship, they played the Yankees in a three-game series at the Stadium in August. Suddenly La Russa realized that he had figured out the steal sign from the Yankees' third-base coach Don Zimmer after it had been conveyed to Zimmer by manager Billy Martin from the dugout. The White Sox bench was fond of Zimmer. Everybody in baseball was fond of Zimmer. To not be fond of Zimmer was un-American. But the White Sox coaches also knew that Yankee manager Billy Martin had a reputation for being tough on his coaches, calling them out after games if he thought they had done something wrong.

So La Russa set up a decoy to use against Martin so he would not figure out that the White Sox theft had come from Zimmer. La Russa parked coach Eddie Brinkman in the front of the dugout with strict instructions to do nothing but stare at Martin. During the game, the Yankees tried a steal of second and it failed because the White Sox knew it was on. As ordered, Brinkman just stared at Martin and Martin glared back. Late in the game it happened again, another Yankee thrown out attempting to steal, this time Omar Moreno. Brinkman just kept on staring. Martin threw up his hands in disgust, now thoroughly convinced that he was the one whose steal sign had been filched. And Zimmer was saved from getting scalded.

During Game 3 tonight La Russa will pay close attention to a runner on second to see if his movements off the bag are coordinated to where Matheny is setting up behind the plate. If the runner takes a little jab step to third, does that mean he's signaling to the batter at the plate that the ball is coming in on the third-base side? If he takes a little jab step back toward second, does that mean the ball's coming into the first-base side? La Russa wants Matheny to give a good target to the pitcher. It's an essential component of a pitcher making his pitches. The best way for the catcher to set up the target is to frame the pitch nice and early. But because of a concern that the runner on second is telegraphing pitches to the batter, the catcher will move around, or he may purposely not set up early. Which combats the telegraphing but also deprives him of giving the most effective target. So for every plus there's a minus, and for every minus a plus, those pulleys and levers working overtime yet again.

Maybe it's simply paranoia on La Russa's part, one more thing to look for and worry about. But this is not a new issue between the Cubs and the Cardinals. There is some history to it. The prior season, the two teams almost engaged in hand-to-hand combat over suspicions of theft. It happened in May when the Cards were facing the Cubs at Wrigley. Sosa hit a home run in the first inning off Morris; as far as the Cardinals bench was concerned, something wasn't right about it, the way Sosa just seemed to know what was coming. And come to think of it, what exactly was the Cubs' first-base coach Sandy Alomar doing over at first? Why was he *falling* to his knees like that? Why was he *coughing?* The Cards became convinced that Alomar was tipping location to Sosa. When the inning was over, the third-base coach Oquendo ran over to Alomar as he was coming off the field and asked him *what the hell* was going on. Alomar said nothing, but the belief only grew deeper that there was something rotten. Angry words were traded after the game. The Cubs issued denials and the Cards made continued affirmations. There was no resolution beyond the war of words, but the suspicion still lingers, which is why La Russa will have his eyes peeled tonight.

Kenny Lofton comes up to begin Game 3 in his customary role as the Cubs' lead-off hitter and incessant rabble-rouser. He's 4 for 9 in the series, and he's been at the center of just about all the offense the Cubs have been able to muster. He hits Morris for better average than any other hitter in the Cubs' lineup tonight, the matchups in La Russa's back pocket revealing a subplot of 6 for 15. But there's an even more tangled subplot between the two, dating back to the fifth and final game of last year's National League Championship series against San Francisco, when Morris hit Lofton with a pitch in the bottom of the fourth. Given the circumstances of what was at stake, this wasn't some payback plunk, but in Game 1 of the series, Lofton hit a homer off Morris. He paused at first base to admire his prowess, and Morris silently stared at Lofton as he continued around the bases with the subtlety of a rifle scope.

All this adds considerable intrigue to the first at-bat, in addition to the already considerable intrigue imposed by Morris. There's the ankle factor. There's also the excitement factor, which can cause him to fall all over the place on the mound in his hurried delivery, which sends balls that should be located down into the sweet hitting zone of up. There is the tipping factor.

Morris begins the game by throwing a nasty sinker to Lofton on the outside corner for a called strike. If there is still bad blood between the two, Morris is not going to draw it. Tonight is about pitching, not the settling of Hatfield-and-McCoy baseball feuds. He comes back with a sinker to the other side of the plate, and Lofton hits it harmlessly to Scott Rolen at third for an easy popout. He uses another one to get the second-place hitter, Martinez, on a ground out to Edgar Renteria at short. He's notched two outs in five pitches. From the foxhole, La Russa looks into Morris's eyes and feels confident that he has the right look tonight: focused, suitably anxious to get it on, but not rushing his pitches to his own detriment.

Sammy Sosa comes up in the third spot. Morris goes after him with a sinker. Sosa looks it in without lifting the bat. It's just outside for 1 and 0. Morris comes in with another sinker, clearly the pitch that he is favoring tonight. Sosa cocks the bat, ready to swing, but he lays off. Strike on the outside corner for 1 and 1. Morris throws another sinker the other way, working the inside of the plate. Sosa takes a whiplash swing, visions of the 402-foot sign in center field swirling in his head. He misses for 1 and 2.

Morris has him where he wants him. It's a perfect waste-pitch opportunity: Try to get him to chase, prey on Sosa's ego to go downtown. He throws another sinker, up and away, to even the count at 2 and 2. But it's still a pitcher's count. There's no reason to risk anything here, still a situation in which you can get Sosa to go for something he doesn't really like, still ample room to prey on his feelings of omnipotence. Morris throws his fifth straight sinker. It's up and out over the plate.

From the dugout, La Russa cringes as he sees it, a slight bracing as if he is readying for some terrible explosion. His arms are still folded, his eyes still locked, but his lips have clamped down more tightly than usual, as if this is it, the final heartbreak out of the thousands of them that he has experienced in all those years of managing. He's never going to open his mouth again, say another word.

Morris has made a mistake. All pitchers make them, and they often get away with them. But Morris has made a mistake with Sosa, and Sosa is a mistake hitter. On the scorecard La Russa keeps, he will make a one-word notation to describe what has just happened: *stupid.* No tipping of location here.

Sosa gives a little cha-cha dance step as he hits it, as if maybe the move will propel the ball a few extra feet. In center field, Edmonds turns on his heels and runs back. He keeps running, ever closer to the western front of the warning track. He has his head on the ball as he runs back. He has a bead on it. He knows where it is. Nobody in baseball right now, maybe nobody in the history of baseball, goes back better on a ball than Edmonds does. He makes spectacular over-the-fence grabs look so routine that he's expected to make them. But now he slows to a trot and lifts his head back to watch the ball sail over him, over the 402-foot sign in deep center, landing on a little patch of berm with the silence of a tee shot plump on the fairway.

Morris steps off the mound and walks a few feet as Sosa rounds the bases, not dawdling, but not setting any speed records, adding his own tenderizer to the slab of beef that Morris just served up. Morris removes his glove and wipes his hand, as if to preoccupy himself with anything besides the fact that Sosa just tagged the living crap out of him; the last thing he's going to do is watch Sammy's eternal victory lap. Sosa rounds third and gives a little fist to the third-base coach. Then he touches home and gives a little kiss to the heavens. 1–0 Cubs.

II

KERRY ROBINSON leads off the bottom of the first for the Cardinals, fresh from building another addition on his doghouse, this time for his positioning in right field in Game 2. First-base coach Dave McKay, who handles the positioning of the outfielders, had trouble getting Robinson's attention: Before the start of Game 3, La Russa called Robinson into his office and flat-out told him he'd bench him if there were any more communication problems. In La Russa's mind, it's just another example of Robinson's wobbly fundamentals. His failure to be aggressive in an RBI situation against the Phillies still burns, and it's difficult to think that the relationship between the two can go any lower. The only way for Robinson to redeem himself would be with a spectacular at-bat, and the odds of that plummet as he strikes out on three pitches, all sinkers, groping with late, punchless swings.

Carlos Zambrano is the least known of the Cubs' formidable starting trio, barely a glimmer behind the punky aura of Prior and Wood. Zambrano has neither the redwood thighs nor the sneer. Nor does he have the lineage, signed as a nondrafted free agent out of Venezuela when he was sixteen. But he is hardly some add-on. Prior is Prior, and nobody on the Cardinals disputes that Prior is Prior, a limitless future *if* he stays injury free. Wood is also Wood, tough because he's nasty and nasty because he's tough, and nobody disputes that, either. But at the age of twenty-two, Zambrano has already developed an instinct on what to throw and when to throw it. At certain times during the season, he has been the Cubs' most effective pitcher, and August has been one of those times.

"I'm surprised at how quickly he's become a pitcher," says the Secret Weapon, who from his blurry-eyed sessions in front of the monitor knows the difference between those who have stuff and those who have Zen and those who have both. Blair means it as the ultimate compliment. He's seen countless clips of Zambrano's splitter, his hard slider, his straight powerball four-seamer, and his lights-out two-seamer sinker that clocks in the low nineties with late movement, resulting in a plethora of weakly hit groundballs.

He comes in with a record of 12 and 9 and an ERA of 2.94. His ERA since the All-Star break has been 1.51, and his last three performances give La Russa particular agita:

DATE	OPP.	IP	H	R	ER	HR	BB	SO	GB	FB	PIT
Aug. 12	Houston	9	5	0	0	0	2	10	12	4	121
Aug. 17	Los Angeles	7	5	2	2	0	3	5	14	2	105
Aug. 22	Arizona	9	3	1	1	0	2	4	18	7	93

Nobody in baseball has put together recent numbers like that, the ratio of groundballs to fly balls a remarkable 3 to 1. It makes him the best unknown pitcher in the game right now, an anonymity defined by the little putt-putt green of a partial goatee, centered on his chin, that has become standard equipment among pitchers.

He gets Hart to fly to right; after five pitches, he has two outs. Pujols works a single—the eighth consecutive plate appearance in which he's gotten on base: reason 10,456 why he is the best hitter in the game. But then Edmonds strikes out to end the inning. Zambrano has thrown twelve pitches, nine of them strikes, including first-pitch strikes to three of the four batters he faced.

Morris settles down in the top of the second. He dispatches Simon, Ramirez, and Gonzalez in only six pitches.

Zambrano handles his half of the second by working Rolen and Martinez for easy grounders to third and second. Zambrano shows his precocity with his first pitch to Renteria, a get-me-over slider that most hitters, including Renteria, wouldn't look for. He doesn't lift the bat, and Zambrano has the 0-and-1 advantage. He continues to work Renteria with a combination of sliders and sinkers. The count goes to 1 and 2. Renteria is almost up on his tiptoes as he adjusts to the batter's box, delicate and storklike. Zambrano comes with a nasty sinker inside and low. Renteria simply stays with it, doesn't try to do too much with it, and singles a liner to right.

Matheny, who hasn't had a hit in the entire series so far, lines a single into left. It puts runners on first and second with two outs, a scoring opportunity, but baseball, just a mean bitch sometimes, places Morris into the batter's box.

Morris carries a pretty good bat. But he is clearly overmatched by Zambrano, who is throwing free and easy in the midnineties, his strength rising from thick thighs and chunky buttocks. Even if Morris does manage to make contact, running on that bad ankle subjects him to far more pain and jeopardy than pitching does. On a 3-and-2 count, he hits a slow chopper to the left side, not slow enough for a guaranteed infield hit, not hard enough for an easy out, but exactly in between. Meaning that there will be a play. Meaning that the outcome will hinge on Morris's ability to get down the line to first.

The ball bounces once, twice, past the mound as Zambrano lunges for it and fails. It's heading into that patch of no man's land on the infield grass between third and short, where the lines of personal responsibility between third baseman and pitcher blur. Morris is hustling his buttocks off to get to first because the Cardinals rally will stay alive if he makes it in time, and he will perhaps atone for his mistake with Sosa. The ankle is hurting him like hell. He isn't openly limping, but his stride, with no natural serenity, is halting and choppy, as if he's running against the tide.

Ramirez at third moves toward short to get it on the third bounce. He makes the throw, but the angle is awkward. Simon at first has to dive to get it. He falls off the bag like a skyscraper toppling, and here comes Morris, and it's going to be close, real close. Simon finishes toppling. Because he's big and hardly a garden of coordination, you can almost hear the thud. Morris is on top of the bag. The umpire sees what he sees in the chaos.

He's out. The Cards are still down 1–0 after two.

Morris makes another mistake in the top of the third, rushing a curve ball to Zambrano as if it's a chore, the pitching equivalent of your mother's telling you to take out the garbage and you leave half of it in a paper-towel trail through the house. Zambrano, looking almost surprised to get a cookie like this, slaps it into left to put runners on first and third. If you seek omens, and baseball is all about omens, you can find one in the fact that Zambrano produced a hit, whereas Morris couldn't in his first at-bat. Another omen is Morris's tendency to get the ball up this inning. It's never a good thing, and La Russa is worrying more than ever that Morris's ankle, still throbbing from the close play at first, is definitely starting to affect his concentration and mechanics.

With runners on the corners, Lofton lines a scorcher up the middle, but Hart at second doesn't have to move an inch to get it. It's a blessed break—maybe even an omen that favors the Cardinals—because if the ball goes a foot one way or a foot another, it would carry the Cubs into the land of the crooked number. Morris jams the next hitter, Martinez, with a sinker. It's a nasty pitch, but he gets enough of it to send it into center for a sacrifice fly that ushers home the man on third.

Sosa follows, but Morris handles him far more surgically than he did last time. He bears in on him with a sinker to go 0 and 1 and open up the outside of the plate for himself because Sosa, now inside conscious, is looking for something in the same location. He hits a weak grounder to short for a force-out, ending the top of the third. La Russa is buoyed by the Cubs' failure to reap the crooked number. But the score is still 2–0.

III

IN THE ENTIRE three-game series, the Cardinals have managed exactly one run against the Cubs' starters. It's a horrible trend, and it shows no signs of improvement when Robinson grounds out to short with another overmatched swing and Hart follows by striking out. It brings up Pujols in the three-hole, who finally squeezes out a walk on the seventh pitch of the at-bat when Zambrano's fastball wanders a little high. It's the ninth straight appearance in which he has gotten on base: reason 14,988 why he is the best hitter in baseball.

La Russa, still looking sour, paces forward and back and sideways in the parameters of his foxhole. His habits have become superstitions and his superstitions have become habits. He glances every now and then at the lineup sheet. He takes the little cheat sheets out of his back pocket and puts them back, takes them out and puts them back. He's searching for a spark now, however tiny, to get a fire going, Paul Richards's advice resting on his shoulder: *Make something happen.*

So he tries to sneak a steal, an unlikely moment to try it with the cleanup hitter at bat and Pujols, no speedster, on first. But the unlikelihood of the situation makes him try it. Zambrano can be quick to the plate when he's in the mood, but he gets slow—about 1.5 seconds—when he's not concerned about the runner on first. He doesn't seem particularly worried about Pujols's going anywhere; he's loosing a high, mighty leg kick that speeds up his throw but slows down his overall delivery. He's focused on the batter, so La Russa makes his move. With a dozen pairs of eyes always on him, deconstructing his every gesture, the sign to steal does not come directly from him. Instead, he communicates it to someone else in the dugout, who in turn communicates it to Pujols. Edmonds himself does not know that the steal is on, because the batter can sometimes inadvertently tip something. He swings away as Pujols goes. He fouls the pitch off, and La Russa takes the steal off after that because the element of surprise, the best thing going for his ploy, has evaporated. After Edmonds hits an easy tapper back to the pitcher to end the third inning, La Russa's conviction only strengthens that a run will be a rarity tonight. Zambrano is pitching well with nice rhythm. He's thrown fifty pitches, hardly a taxing amount, and he's gotten first-pitch strikes on nine of the thirteen batters he's faced. The Cardinals have responded with three singles, and nobody has made it past second.

Morris moves easily through the fourth. Five pitches dispense with Alou, Simon, and Ramirez.

Zambrano handles his half of the fourth in thirteen pitches.

Morris takes ten pitches to put away Gonzalez and Bako and Zambrano in the top of the fifth. He's retired nine in a row. With the game now more than half complete, he's thrown a remarkably economical forty-eight pitches. But he's still behind 2–0, and La Russa thinks about pinch-hitting for him here in the bottom of the fifth because there's no way of knowing how much he has left or when that ankle might give way. But how he retired the side in order in the top of the fifth tells La Russa something, so Morris leads off the bottom of the inning. He fouls the first pitch toward the third-base side. He steps out of the box, takes a breath, steps back in. Zambrano comes with a nasty sinker low and away.

Morris reaches for it and clips it down the right-field line into the corner. Again he'll have to run like hell on his bad ankle, and it's agonizing to watch. He makes it around first with a noticeable limp, and his pace slackens as he nears second, catching a slight break when the ball caroms into the corner and Sosa has to root around for it. That saves him from having to slide, which might just wreck his ankle altogether.

Robinson, up next, has a simple task. With no outs, he needs to advance the runner to third. La Russa has his players work on this maneuver religiously during batting practice. Robinson's options have been clearly delineated. He can either try to pull the ball into right, as that placement, far from third base, gives Morris the best chance to advance. Or he can bunt down the first-base line for the same reason.

A smart pitcher like Zambrano might know what Robinson's up to and sink the ball away, making it more difficult for him to pull it to right field. But this simplifies the hitter's task, as now he need only choose between:

1. Taking the pitch.
2. Bunting toward first base.

But Robinson settles on a third choice when Zambrano wisely throws a sinker away. Robinson tries to pull it to right, even though doing so flouts the laws of physics.

He hits it to left field, *short left field,* the very worst place to put the ball if you want to advance the runner from second. Alou comes in from left to make the easy catch. Morris remains at second. La Russa seethes in the dugout. Robinson has failed to apply the lessons of Baseball 101, and his relationship with his manager, which really couldn't go lower, has now gone lower. Few things infuriate La Russa more than the modern player's steadfast refusal to play the game right. It irks him all the more as a reflection on his own managerial abilities; he can imagine a baseball man in the stands turning his head in disgust as he watches a play like that and saying to himself, *This is simply bad baseball,* a basic move-the-runner-over play that doesn't come out close to right.

Hart is up with one out and goes down swinging on four straight sinkers from Zambrano. Where once there was a runner on second with no outs, there is now a runner on second with two outs.

Pujols is up and, with first base open, Zambrano pitches around him for the walk. Edmonds walks as well and the bases are loaded for Rolen. It's the best scoring opportunity the team has had all day, and the fans' chorus rises to its feet in a pleading swell, making it clear that this is it. The game's karma will be determined right here.

In the dugout, the knotted cliques draw tighter, except for the hermit J.D. Drew, who sits alone on the stairs at one end of the dugout, staring blankly from the familiar detachment of the disabled list. The dugout is quiet, perhaps because the players feel the same queasy expectation that the fans do.

Zambrano grips the ball behind his back, then shifts it to his glove for one final readjustment of fingers on seams. Rolen comes to the plate and performs the same ritual he performs before every pitch, gently touching his bat to the border of dirt just outside of the plate and then the center of the plate itself and then the inside border, an expectant magician warming up his wand. In an obvious RBI situation like this, La Russa preaches aggressiveness — take a swing at the first good pitch — and Rolon embraces the dogma zealously.

Zambrano throws a sinker inside and low. Rolen swings. He launches a foul toward the seats past the dugout on the first-base side. He watches as it hangs. Players pop out of the Cards' dugout like a collective jack-in-the-box — Perez and Palmeiro and Williams and Tomko and Haren — all saying the same thing with their outstretched necks: *How far will it carry?*

Simon runs from first to make a play. The ball is definitely headed into the seats past first base, a row back, maybe a row and a half. He's already earned his keep today when he fell to earth to get Morris by a step. Now he has to bend and gyrate and stick his glove into a morass of goopy hands and see whether he can pull something out. He dips his clam-digger-sized glove into the goop. For a moment, it's buried, submerged. Then he scoops it out of the muck to see what it contains.

He has the ball. The inning's over, and the karma has declared itself:

	1	2	3	4	5	R	H	E
CUBS	1	0	1	0	0	2	3	0
CARDS	0	0	0	0	0	0	5	0

Eight men left on base through five. Robinson so deep in the doghouse for not advancing the runner that La Russa turns to the third-base coach Oquendo and snaps without charity: *"If that son of a bitch starts another game this year, I'll kiss your ass."*

15

THREE NIGHTS IN AUGUST

I

● ● ● MORRIS RETIRES the side in order in the sixth, the final pitch a sweet 12-to-6 curve that Sosa misses by so much, even the Arch smiles. He has now retired twelve in a row, no Cubs batter reaching base since Zambrano got that cookie in the third. He has thrown only sixty-one pitches.

But the game continues to play wicked mischief, the primary motivation to make Morris run on that gimpy ankle as much as possible. He comes to the plate in the bottom half of the sixth, with Edgar Renteria on first and two outs. This seems like the place for La Russa to bring in the lefty Palmeiro to pinch-hit, as Morris has done more on the mound than anybody had a right to expect. La Russa further forecasts that possibility by having Cal Eldred already warming up to take the seventh.

But La Russa is juggling the variables here and looking ahead to the ninth. Palmeiro is the only left-handed bat on the bench, and La Russa needs to save him for the ninth, on the assumption that Dusty Baker will inevitably give the ball to his right-handed closer, Borowski. So Palmeiro stays put for now. The other option would be pinch-hitting for Morris with a righty to go against the righty Zambrano. But the bottom line in La Russa's mind is that Morris has the best chance of anyone on the staff of getting three outs in the seventh because of the way he is pitching.

So he lets Morris hit with the two outs, even though there is a man on. Given what he has already been through on the basepaths tonight, simple human compassion begs that Morris quietly pop up on the first pitch or simply strike out. Please, don't run any more.

Zambrano throws a sinker on the inside corner for 0 and 1 as Morris doesn't swing. He comes in with a sinker on the next pitch. It's a fat pitch, almost dead center on the plate. Morris pops it foul to the first base, and now he's in the 0-and-2 trough.

Baker calls for a pitchout on the next pitch. It's an effective move even if nothing is on, as it has a tendency to shut down an opponent's running game. Baker has also seen La Russa in action for more than twenty years. He even played for him briefly in Oakland. He knows that La Russa has a thieving heart behind that Mount Rushmore façade. He's already tried it once before in a less likely situation than this. Renteria at first is a good base stealer. He is capable of going at any time. If he makes it, he's in scoring position. If he doesn't, it's really no bad thing. It ends the inning, thereby preventing Morris from having to finish the at-bat and risk any more agony to his ankle. He can go out and pitch the seventh, which will definitely be his last inning. Assuming that he gets through it, La Russa can then pinch-hit for him in the bottom of the inning, with the world fresh and uncomplicated and three outs available.

Renteria stays put: 1 and 2. Zambrano throws a slider that viciously slides outside. Morris gets the tiniest sliver of it to foul it off: still 1 and 2.

Zambrano comes with a sinker to the other side of the plate. Morris taps a slow roller to the left side of the infield, slow enough that *here we go again.* Baseball has produced yet another seemingly impossible moment, nothing quite like it in all the vast statistical annals that could fill the Atlantic and the Pacific: a pitcher with a bad ankle, barely able to run, comes to bat *three times* and puts the ball in play *three times* with the game's potential outcome on the line *three times.*

Morris's ankle basically gives out on him, causing him to slip as he leaves the batter's box. He's going as fast as he can, but the ankle is killing him, and everybody in Busch can virtually feel his pain every time he lands on it as he makes his choppy run down the line. Zambrano fields the ball on one hop. He has plenty of time to make the throw. But he takes a little bit off it. As Morris chugs closer and closer to the bag, the ball bounces in front of Simon at first. Can he handle it?

He can't. Morris is safe at first.

Robinson comes up, with Renteria now on third and Morris on first and with two outs. Robinson takes the first pitch for a strike. It's a sinker that doesn't come close to sinking, so it's down the pipe. La Russa mouths obscenities from the dugout, because *Haven't we been through this before, Kerry, haven't we? HAVEN'T WE!!!! IN AN RBI SITUATION, YOU MUST SWING AT THE FIRST GOOD PITCH!!*

The ball is right on the plate. It's right down the middle. It's an urban garden in the wasteland of garbage that a good pitcher like Zambrano relies on. So it's a fait accompli—another wasted scoring chance, ten men now left on base with only nine chances left—because Robinson won't get a better pitch than that.

He doesn't. The next pitch is a sinker away. Its location is devilish, but Robinson swings and slaps it down the left field line for a double.

Renteria scores to close the gap to 2–1. Morris winces his way around second and heads for third. The dugout, so tongue-tied all night, finally expresses itself. The separate cliques of coaches and pitchers and position players momentarily dissolve. A line forms to greet Renteria, as if he's been away on an epic journey, with the usual assortment of fist kisses and helmet smacks and butt pats.

But the joy is short-lived; there's trouble at third. Morris managed to make it to the bag without sliding, but he arrived in a noticeable limp. La Russa runs out to see whether he's seriously injured. So does Barry Weinberg. La Russa takes his glasses off.

"You don't look too good. You're hobbling. How sore is it?"

"Pitching is the part that hurts me the least. The running hurts much more."

Morris gives La Russa enough reassurance to leave him in

there. But as La Russa runs back to the dugout, he's fretting, the system of pulleys and levers pumping away. He let Morris bat because he wanted him to pitch the seventh, but now he has to face the consequences of Morris as a base runner. If there's a wild pitch, Morris will not only have to break for home on that ankle but also slide. He could put in a pinch runner, but if he doesn't give Morris the seventh, the game could slip away, because he's pitching so well. But, realistically, how much does Morris have left?

Hart grounds out to end the inning, which alleviates the wild-pitch worry. Morris trots gingerly back to the dugout, gets his glove, and heads back to the field. Now La Russa can focus on worrying about how much his starter has left. With one out in the top of the seventh, he gives up a single to Simon and walks Ramirez.

Duncan runs out to the mound to review the MapQuest against the next batter, Gonzalez: how he has a tendency to sit on breaking balls late in the game. La Russa reaches into his back pocket, pulls out his cheat sheets, and finds a little relief: Gonzalez is 0 for 11 against Morris coming into the game. With a ground out and fly out in his two previous at-bats, he's now 0 for 13. It's a perfect matchup. He works Gonzalez into a 0-2 deficit on two pitches, the second the best curve ball he has thrown all night.

Pitch no. 3: Gonzalez is sitting on a fastball. He gets a fastball and fouls it straight back, an indication that he missed pulverizing it by an inch. Still 0 and 2.

Pitch no. 4: A sinker low and away. Gonzalez lifts it foul to the right side. Still 0 and 2.

Pitch no. 5: A curve inside and high for a ball. It suggests that Morris is tired: It's nowhere near where it was supposed to go. A band of sweat has formed on his cheekbone. It's still sultry hot, the mighty river pushing out cookie tins of humid heat. His ankle has gotten a workout that no one could have cooked up, worse than any reality show. Morris simply wants to get Gonzalez out here, finish him off: The last thing he needs right now is this cat-and-mouse torment. He steps off the mound, then hauls himself back on those spindly legs.

Pitch no. 6: Another curve. Foul behind home plate. Still 1 and 2.

Pitch no. 7: A sinker inside. Another *foul.* Still *1 and 2.*

Morris is exhausted now. He knows it. La Russa knows it. The dugout knows it. Everybody knows it.

Pitch no. 8: A sinker on the inside of the plate. Gonzalez hits it fair on the ground. It's a shot. He got to it. It's also right at Rolen, who doesn't have to move as he makes the throw to Hart at second. Who makes the throw to first. A double play to end the inning.

Morris is done for the night after this. With the score 2–1, he may still end up the losing pitcher, and he won't even have a chance to get the win, unless the Cardinals mount an immediate rally. The agate in the box score the next day will show that he gave up four hits in seven innings, an outstanding quality start. On the batting side, he will be listed as 1 for 3 with a double. No statistic will show what he did on the basepaths, the war he waged with his ankle with every step he took. If the Cardinals lose, the focus won't be on Morris's performance at all but on the Cubs' finally conquering the jinx of Busch by taking two out of three. His heroism tonight will evaporate.

Working the bottom of the seventh, Zambrano jams Pujols on a sinker to induce an easy ground out to third, then strikes out Edmonds in a fricassee of forkball and fastball and curve ball and finishing sinker. The three and four hitters in the Cardinals' lineup have just gone down without defiance, and Zambrano looks as sharp as he has all night. It brings up Rolen, who is hitless not only tonight but also in the entire series. His back hurts. His neck hurts. His whole body hurts. He needs a day off. He's chasing high fastballs. He hasn't hit a home run in more than two weeks.

But he hits one now into the right-field seats: 2–2.

II

STEVE KLINE comes in to relieve in the top of the eighth. The fans go crazy at the sight of him, his hurdy-gurdy style on the mound with all those tics and jerks, one step away from hyperventilating into a heap or body slamming the home plate umpire because he didn't give him the corner. He's a left-handed reliever who went to the University of West Virginia, so he's profoundly crazy, but that's normal for a left-handed reliever. He is never dressed before the start of a game, not even his jock strap, on some occasions. He likes walking around the clubhouse in the buff, then stretching out on a couch behind Chad Blair, offering largely irrelevant commentary as the Secret Weapon watches the game on his little monitor and keeps the pitching chart, doing six things at once and keeping his equilibrium. Kline apparently thinks of the clubhouse as a nude beach; it's his way of staying loose, not letting nerves overcome him, something to preoccupy him for a couple of hours anyway, as his life has no real meaning until the late innings.

The fans love Kline for his lack of pretense. He loves the fans back, in that regard a throwback to a different era in which players soaked up the whole atmosphere of it all like sun worshippers, or at least pinched themselves before and after each game as a reminder that what they did for a living would never be confused with work.

Kids particularly like Kline. They edge the front row of the stands before games like starving refugees, yelling his name as if they have some special relationship, even though they've never met him—*Steve! Steve! Over here! Kliner! Kliner! Over here!* He returns the favor by signing the balls and the pictures and the baseball cards that pour out of their bottomless pockets like rabbits out of a hat. Then he lets them smell the peak of his hat, the smudgy stinky smelly odiferous hat filled with rosin and sweat and horsehide and leather that Kline insists on wearing the entire season. The kids crinkle up their noses when they smell it, but they also close their eyes when they smell it, because they are kids and therefore savvy enough to know that they are taking in the scent of something pure regardless of its reek.

The situation is set up nicely for him here, coming in as a lefty to face the lefty Bako. He gets him on a grounder to Hart for the first out in the top of the eighth.

Baker brings in Doug Glanville to pinch-hit in the ninth spot, It's an expected move, as Glanville is a righty and Kline a lefty. La Russa could bring in another pitcher here, and he's certainly not above doing it. But with Lofton the lefty on deck, Kline is staying right where he is. In addition, the presence of Kline prevents Baker from going to the lefty bats he has lying in wait on the bench.

He throws a good slider that tails away. Glanville swings and makes contact. He hits it hard on the ground. If he had hit it to the right spot, it would have been an easy single through the infield. But it's straight at Hart. He comes up on the ball. And the ball stays down, skittering through Hart's legs into the outfield. Glanville is on first on the error, and bad karma once again soaks the night. Because now Lofton is up. And it isn't simply that Lofton is a pain in the ass, at his age still able to get on base and advance chaos in his shuffling glide.

He is Kline's eternal nemesis, the psychotic ex-girlfriend who sends you creepy notes through the mail to remind you she's still around. Some pitchers truly do have Kung Fu serenity. They react to nothing; that blank stare when they give up a homer is a two-way mirror into the blankness inside them, blessedly free of any and all memory. Kline is not like that. He remembers every pitch he has ever thrown in the major leagues since he first came up with Cleveland in 1997. He catalogues them in his head like an anal-compulsive librarian. And he remembers what Lofton did to him in the ninth inning of the 2002 National League Championship series, when there were two outs and runners on first and second and Kline came in specifically to face Lofton, and Lofton hit a hanging slider on the first pitch to right center to win the game and the pennant.

Now he's facing Lofton again, this time in the top of the eighth of a 2–2 game with a runner on first and one out. Regardless of past history, La Russa has the lefty-versus-lefty matchup he wants. But it's the late innings of a razor-close game, one of those games in which nothing ever turns out to be entirely harmless.

Kline throws a slider on the first pitch, a nice crispy slider tailing to the outside. Lofton takes it. A called strike: 0 and 1.

Kline throws another slider. It goes into the sweet spot of the plate, not only against the wishes of Kline but also Matheny, who has set up outside. La Russa has seen this pitch before; it's the same pitch he threw Lofton in the National League Championship series.

Lofton nails it. He tags it, drills it, creams it, drives it, powers it, powders it, smokes it, kills it, commits every baseball cliché of hitting and then some.

It's headed for the gap in right center between Robinson and Edmonds: The only thing they can do is to vainly chase after it. Glanville is easily around third and on his way to home, and Lofton will have a stand-up triple out of this thing. It's a disaster, a 3–2 Cubs lead with one out and a man on third and the meat of the order coming up.

Until the ball bounces off the dirt of the warning track and into the stands. It's a ground-rule double. Which means that Glanville has to go back to third instead of scoring the go-ahead run. It's a potentially enormous break, and Lofton has only himself to blame; he was so eager to humiliate Kline once again that he simply hit the ball too damn hard.

Kline is out, replaced by the righty DeJean, with Martinez due up. He's a righty, so it only makes sense for Baker to bring in a left-handed pinch hitter. He has several on the bench, but Baker doesn't make the move, and La Russa assumes it's because Baker knows his team better than anyone else.

La Russa signals for the infield to play in. The count goes to 1 and 1 on Martinez. DeJean throws a forkball that doesn't tumble down. Martinez gets a piece of it and lines it to center field.

Edmonds is playing shallow. He likes to play shallow, a reflection of his confidence and penchant for drama. He takes two steps in and catches the ball high in the glove, glancing for a split second in the stitch of the webbing to make sure he caught it. He has his momentum going for him, and he's going to need it because Glanville is tagging up from third and trying to score and here comes the best craziness in all of sports.

He's running full bore and he's quick and Matheny moves two steps up the line, awaiting the throw, and Edmonds makes an over-the-top throw with beautiful carry and La Russa can see it and so can Duncan and so can Morris as he leaps off the back bench because it's gonna be close, it's gonna be really close, and while it's all happening fast, very fast, there's also a slow-motion quality to it as Edmonds throws the ball and Matheny awaits the ball and Glanville comes down the line, hoping he gets there before the ball and who will intersect with what when?

The throw is dead solid perfect. It gives Matheny time to take those two steps up the third-base line and set up in a stoic crouch. It's going to be a wreck at home plate, a serious wreck. Sosa, due up next, leaves the on-deck circle and, like a bystander vainly trying to ward off a car crash, motions to Glanville with his hands to *get down, get down.* But the throw is too far ahead of Glanville, his only choice to go for the high-impact head-on collision. He barrels into Matheny, using his forearm to hit him in the face. He uses the rest of his body to try to flatten him. Matheny does a full 360-degree pirouette. His glove goes flying, and if the ball is still in there, Glanville is safe, and the Cubs will win because there's no way you lose after a play like this.

It takes a second, maybe two, the crowd going berserk and two entire dugouts up on their toes and the home plate umpire bending his neck into this Bill Gallo cartoon swirl of arms and legs and what belongs to whom and who belongs to what, charged with answering everybody's question: *Where is the ball?*

Where is the ball? It's in Matheny's bare hand. He switched it from his glove right before impact. Glanville is out.

HE'S OUT!!!

The crowd goes more berserk, the mix of love and relief and maybe a few I-told-you-sos, although nobody could have ever told you so, a double play like this to end the inning. Edmonds trots in from center field into the dugout into a sea of high-fives led by Rolen and Renteria. He sits in the back of the dugout with his cap off, sweaty and luxuriant, his hair, so carefully slicked back before each game in his Hollywood style, now standing at attention in certain spots. It's a great play, so great that La Russa leaves his foxhole to congratulate him, an almost surreptitious shake of the hand because he believes that this is a player's moment to be shared by other players and that the last place a manager should be is in the middle of it, as if he somehow had something to do with it. Then he goes back to the foxhole because it's still not over, one of those games that just might reach into infinity, the karma meter flopping so wildly, there's no point in trying to glean anything from it, except that whatever happens, it's not going to be emotionally simple.

III

REMLINGER GETS the call from Baker in the bullpen to replace Zambrano. He retires the side in order in the bottom of the eighth.

DeJean answers in the top of the ninth by retiring Sosa and Alou and Simon.

Remlinger is still there in the bottom of the ninth, with Robinson due to lead off. It makes sense for Baker to leave Remlinger in there, as he's getting a lefty-versus-lefty matchup. La Russa knows that, of course, but he doesn't counter off the bench with a pinch hitter. Because of Remlinger's anomaly, better against righties than his own kind, he's leaving Robinson in the game. But the decision should not be confused with a newfound faith in Robinson after his last at-bat, when he doubled and drove in a run. One double does not demolish a doghouse. Robinson himself has no illusions. Between halves of the inning, when La Russa went to Cairo on the bench and told him to get ready to pinch-hit, Robinson assumed that Cairo was going in for him.

"No, no, no," La Russa told him. "You go ahead and hit."

He's hoping that Robinson can use his speed to his advantage here and maybe get on even if it's weakly hit. He's actually thinking less about Robinson than about what moves he will make if Robinson does get to first. It suggests an opportunity to have Cairo bunt him over to second when he pinch-hits for the next batter. But if Robinson advances to second, it will also mean that first base is open, which will take the bat out of Pujols's hands, as Baker will surely walk him. Which in turn will make the matchup between Edmonds and Remlinger the key matchup of the inning. So he isn't quite sure what to do here, and he won't know for sure until Robinson's at-bat is over.

Remlinger is in the Popeye mold of a pitcher, squat and short-looking, even though he's listed at 6'1". His physiognomy suggests power but his best pitch is his changeup, and he will use it anywhere in the count.

The Cubs are thinking that Robinson will want to use his speed here; they're playing him in at the corners and conceding him the right-field line, as he never pulls it that far. He's thinking about using his speed, too, showing bunt on the first pitch but pulling off and taking a strike looking for 0 and 1. He fouls off the next pitch to dig himself an immediate 0-and-2 dungeon. La Russa, one hand on the staircase railing, has a feeling that he can stop musing over whether to have Cairo bunt Robinson to second, because Robinson isn't going to make it out of the batter's box.

Remlinger throws a curve ball a little low to make the count 1 and 2. He throws a fastball up and in to make the count 2 and 2. He throws another fastball high to make the count 3 and 2. Robinson doesn't walk very much, but maybe he can squeeze a walk here, keep the spigot open for the bigger boys. Bako, the catcher, wants a changeup. But Remlinger shakes off the sign; he wants a fastball, so a fastball is what he's going to throw. He comes with it, and Robinson makes contact.

He pulls it into right the exact way he should have pulled it in the fifth when he needed to advance Morris to third. At the very least, La Russa will have to give him credit for getting to the fastball and putting a good swing on it.

But suddenly, everybody in the dugout rises in synch. They're watching and watching and watching because he just hit the living hell out of it, and they're watching some more because it always seems to take forever and every pair of eyes is turned the same way and willing it the same way, with those eyes stretched north because *Can you really believe this, is this really happening?*

And then the catch is made in right field. By Simontacchi, in the bullpen, with his cap.

3–2 Cardinals. It's over.

Players pour onto the field as if there's a fire drill. They run to home plate and form a line like a wedding party. Robinson jumps on the plate and is enclosed, buried beneath Pujols and Rolen and Edmonds and Hart and Matheny and Renteria and Morris and Williams and a dozen others. They form a circle around Robinson and start jumping up and down in lovely unbridled joy, their faces bent and bursting: thirty-year-olds, some of them with the exuberance of fifteen-year-olds. It lasts for a few seconds, this circle bouncing up and down to its own beat, and you really wouldn't mind if it lasted the whole night. You could simply sit back and watch, because it shows you what baseball can still be when it wants to be: a game for little boys that grown men are lucky enough to play.

La Russa hugs Robinson when he finally escapes from beneath the bodies, making it clear that under certain circumstances, managers have even shorter memories than relievers. Robinson runs off to do the postgame TV interview because he is the star this night, maybe the star of the season in some utterly improbable way. Then Oquendo whispers something to La Russa that has nothing to do with his coaching responsibilities at third base. La Russa laughs, actually *laughs,* so you know that whatever Oquendo just said has to be worth something.

"When are you gonna kiss my ass?" Oquendo asks him.

For the first and only time during these three nights in August, La Russa is out of moves.

The spontaneous combustion ends once Robinson escapes. The players disengage and trot down the steps of the dugout into the tunnel that winds under the ratty pipes to the clubhouse. They are still excited, still chatty. They have taken the rubber game of the three-game series. They have taken two out of three against the Cubs. They are tied for first place in the division on a summer night that should always have baseball somewhere within it. They are also tied for first in the traffic jam of the Wild Card. With one victory, they've earned two possible trajectories to the playoffs.

The effects of this experience will linger, stay in the blood of these players: a few of them stars and a few of them recognized outside of the city in which they toil but most of them only anonymous pieces in the vast puzzle of the game that will go on and on after their spaces are taken up by other puzzle pieces. They will think about the three-game series they have just played. Robinson will think about it, the way in which he traveled from the doghouse to heaven at the same velocity as the home run he just creamed to right. Morris will think about it, a performance that no doubt brings a smile to the face of the silent protector who stays near him wherever he goes. Williams will think about it, the way he went head to head against Wood and outpitched him with quiet verve. Martinez will think about it, the momentary relief of standing on first just having done what maybe, just maybe, you weren't sure you could do anymore, although you would never admit that to anyone. Drew will think about it, knowing that by not playing in a single inning these past three nights, his days in a Cardinals uniform are probably numbered, better for him to start over somewhere else, unburdened by burdens. Eldred will think about it, how he shouldn't be here at all. Stephenson will think about it, the unforgiving repercussions of pitching with too much of your heart and not enough of your head, although come to think about it, Stephenson *probably* won't think about it. Rolen will think about it, quietly, very *very* quietly. Pujols will think about it, wondering why he didn't get a hit on *every* at-bat. Kline will think about it, continued nightmares of being told to kiss the bride and lifting up the veil and seeing that it's frigging Lofton, Lofton at the register when he's in the checkout line searching for his bonus card, Lofton in the car next to him when he stops at a red light, Lofton asking him whether he prefers a window seat or an aisle, Lofton, Lofton, Lofton, smiling in such a way that it does resemble a hit into the gap.

La Russa will think about the three-game series. So will Duncan. So will Oquendo, who probably knows, despite unimpeachable witnesses, that La Russa will never dole out what he so emphatically promised in the bottom of the fifth in his impassioned vow *never ever* to start Robinson again.

Player or coach, star or invisible man, hustler or somebody who simply hustles, happy to be there or unhappy to be anywhere, the future in front of you or the future behind you, it doesn't really matter right now. Each and every one of them will let the three-game series just played continue to sit and settle for a little bit. They will allow themselves the pleasure, for at least as long as it takes to strip off the uniform to grab the shower to change into the street clothes to go to the airport to fly on the charter to sleep in the hotel room to arrive at the ballpark to start another one beginning tomorrow, still what it is despite so many efforts to make it feel like something else, still a part of us even when we say never again, what La Russa believes it to be and will always believe it to be because a quarter century in the foxhole of the dugout, if it has taught him anything, has taught him this.

Beautiful. Just beautiful baseball.

EPILOGUE

● ● ● TONY LA RUSSA waited in the dugout after the game was over. Dignity and professionalism required it no matter what he felt inside: an almost surreal deflation. He waited to see whether Red Sox manager Terry Francona would look over from the Busch visitor's dugout to acknowledge him so that La Russa in turn could give his own acknowledgment, the silent language of the victor and the vanquished.

The Red Sox had done it in 2004. They had won the World Series, not in seven games or six or even five, but in a four-game sweep over the Cardinals. La Russa waited for a minute or so—although the dugout was the last place he wanted to be, just a further rub-it-in reminder of the scene of the crime—the bearlike bodies of the Red Sox with their mountain-men beards and grizzly hair in a Rubik's Cube hug less than a hundred feet away. But Francona was understandably busy, caught up in the joy of his players. So La Russa left, walking by himself into the tunnel, passing beneath the exposed pipes on the way to the clubhouse, which right now had to be the saddest single place in the world. He walked toward a terrible coda on what by any measure had been a fantastic season for the Cardinals, maybe the most special team that La Russa had ever managed.

Even after that delicious third night in August, the Cardinals still lost the Central Division to the Cubs in 2003. As for 2004, none of the pundits had any faith in St. Louis. With the Astros making moves for starting pitchers Roger Clemens and Andy Pettitte, with the Cubs still stoked by the triumvirate of Prior and Wood and Zambrano, the Cardinals were universally picked to finish third. Their starting pitching wasn't good enough. Their bullpen wasn't good enough. With J.D. Drew traded to Atlanta, there was a problem in right because J.D. at 75 percent was still better than many right fielders at 100 percent. There was also a problem at second, because Bo Hart, as valiant as he was, could not sustain the rigors of a full season as a starter. In the off-season, the Cardinals looked on like envious children as the superbrats made the multimillion-dollar moves that still define the game—Schilling to the Red Sox and everyone else to the Yankees.

In the middle of May, the Cardinals were mired at 16 and 16 after losing two out of three to the Montreal Expos. They were lurching along, vainly trying to find a way. La Russa's contract was up for renewal after the season. The front office approached him then about re-upping, but he didn't want to negotiate, in part because he thought it would look bad to players who were potential free agents and wanted their own contracts negotiated, but also because he wasn't convinced that the Cards would even want him back if the team continued in its mediocrity. It was his ninth year with the team, and the history of managing suggested that nine years with one team was maybe too long.

But then, at the end of the month, something happened, and the twenty-five pieces of the puzzle became a team. Using the unit of the three-game series as a yardstick, the Cardinals played twenty-one of them from June to the end of August. They swept eight, lost only three, and had a record of 87-44 going into September in running away with the division. Their record at the end of the season—105 wins and only 57 losses—was the best in baseball.

The Cardinals opened the playoffs by beating the Dodgers three games to one to advance to the National League Championship series against the Astros. In the aura of the irresistible "reverse the curse" narrative as the Red Sox improbably prevailed over the Yankees in the ALCS by winning four straight games after falling behind 3–0, the Cardinals-Astros series was barely noticed.

But it too was brilliantly played, filled with the flip-flop of drama, the Cardinals going ahead two games to nothing at Busch, then losing three in a row to Houston in their boisterous house, then returning to St. Louis to win the next two, including the final seventh game against eventual National League Cy Young Award winner Roger Clemens.

Then came the World Series and the Red Sox thrashing. First and foremost, La Russa believes that Boston deserved to win because they were the better team, got the pitching they needed when they needed it, got the timely two-out hits by making pressure their friend. But he also believes that there is no way—at least no rational way—the Cardinals should have gotten swept. The team was too gifted for that to happen. Except that it did happen.

After his typical sleepless search for pragmatic explanations to unintended results, he now wonders if it all moved a little bit too quickly, a film at fast-forward where everything just became blurred. After the epic win in Game 7 against Clemens, La Russa tried to tell his team that there was still work to be done. "We just earned a ring, but it's not *the* ring," he said. But he also honored human nature; for various players who had been on the team for several years, finally winning the NLCS—after two failed tries in 2000 and 2002—was a huge monkey off their backs. The same was true for La Russa himself: an end to the local media's intimations that he clutched in the clutch.

The team celebrated hard that night, lingering in the clubhouse until three or four in the morning, feeling both the joy and the relief that destiny was still theirs. They got to their respective homes late, stole a little sleep, began to make travel arrangements for their families, heard from people they hadn't heard from in a thousand years yearning for World Series tickets, arrived at a hotel parking lot near the airport at 11:30 A.M., and by noon were on a plane to a cold, sodden Boston to face a Red Sox team buoyed by both talent and mythology.

If it wasn't the World Series, La Russa would not have had the team work out that day. But because it was the World Series, they were required to make an appearance. They arrived in Boston at

4:45 P.M., then got a police escort to Fenway Park because they were late. They were supposed to start working out at 5:00, but didn't arrive until 5:15 and had to wait for the equipment. After their workout ended, the last bus left Fenway at 8:15 P.M. and made its way to the hotel the Cardinals had been placed at by the Red Sox—since it was the home team's responsibility—located not downtown near Fenway, but forty minutes away in Quincy. The Cardinals were told that there were several large conventions in Boston that had taken up all premium downtown hotel space.

When a team loses, and loses badly, all explanations sound like excuses. The fact of the matter, as La Russa put it, is "that either you do or you don't and we didn't." But he did feel that in the rush to the World Series, the team lost an edge.

Game 1 the following night, in contrast to the sweet spectacle of both the American League and National League Championship series, was like a sloppy Little League game. The chilly weather made the ball slick, which in turn made it difficult for starter Woody Williams to ever get the right feel and establish effective command. Early in the game, when Matheny set up down and in against Orlando Cabrera and Williams ended up hitting him on the shoulder, La Russa could feel the curse of his own Bambino. Cardinals pitchers gave up eight walks. Red Sox pitchers gave up six of their own, and the Boston defense made four errors.

In the top of the eighth, the Cards scored twice to tie the score at 9–9. They had the bases loaded and only one out with Rolen due up followed by Edmonds. During the season, the two of them had combined for seventy-six home runs and 235 RBIs while each hitting over .300. But in what may have been the most pivotal at-bats of the World Series, Rolen popped out to third. Edmonds then struck out looking to end the inning. A superb chance to steal a win at Fenway had been lost, and what it portended was even worse. Rolen would ultimately go 0 for 15 in the World Series and Edmonds 1 for 15. (Throw in Reggie Sanders, who batted sixth in the first three games, and the Cardinals four-, five-, and six-hitters went a combined 1 for 39.) When Mark Bellhorn hit a two-run homer off reliever Julian Tavarez in the bottom of the eighth to give the Sox an 11–9 lead that would hold up, it really did seem that the Bambino had simply switched sides.

The eerie fate of indignity only continued in Fenway's parking lot, where the Cardinals' last bus sat idle for twenty minutes because it was blocked by a security guard's car. The bus arrived at the Marriott in Quincy at 1:45 A.M. The hotel had agreed to keep its restaurant open an hour after the last bus arrived. The hotel staff was less specific about what kind of food would be served; when La Russa walked into the dining room, he saw players and their families eating hamburgers and pizza: basic junk food. This *wasn't* a World Series *moment*. It was dreary and depressing, and La Russa blamed himself because he should have seen it coming. In the aftermath, arrangements were made for one of Boston's better downtown restaurants to stay open after Game 6 so players and their families could feel as if they were in the World Series, instead of the high school state playoffs. But there would be no Game 6.

In Game 2, Matt Morris retired the first two batters, then walked the next two to face Jason Varitek. Duncan had told Morris and Matheny in the pregame deconstruction of the Red Sox hitters not to throw a changeup to Varitek. But with the count 1 and 2, Morris still threw a changeup because he thought he had Varitek set up for the pitch. Varitek stroked a two-run triple.

In the same game, Reggie Sanders missed second base on his way to third on a successful *hit-and-run* and had to go back to second. It was the kind of fundamental miscue the Cardinals had almost never committed during the season, and the ecosystem of baseball wouldn't tolerate it now. A batter later, La Russa pulled a run-and-hit with Matheny at the plate. The runners went early and Matheny hit the ball sharply. But third baseman Bill Mueller, coming toward the bag to cover Sanders' attempted steal, serendipitously found himself in perfect position to snag the ball and easily put the tag on Sanders for a double play, because Sanders was coming right at him. The irony was that Mueller's positioning would have been different had Sanders made it to third in the first place; Mueller wouldn't have been racing to the bag to cover a steal because there would have been no steal, which would have meant

Matheny's line drive snaking down the line instead of being caught, which would have meant a possible crooked number instead of an inning-ending double play.

Schilling was on the mound for the Red Sox in Game 2. La Russa had seen him enough to know that this wasn't vintage Schilling. His Frankenstein ankle, the tendon held together by stitches blotched with blood, was clearly bothering him. He was hittable, but he also made pitches when he needed them, particularly with his off-speed. When he needed to get his forkball down, he didn't miss by throwing it over the plate—an example of how to compete under pressure that the Cardinals starters could not emulate.

The Cards lost the second game 6–2 to fall behind in the World Series two games to zero. La Russa assembled the team afterward. What he told them was similar to what he had told them after Game 5 of the NLCS, when the Astros had risen from the dead to win three straight at home and take a 3–2 series lead. "Listen, nobody controls what we think and how we are going to act. You are going to get blistered right now and overwhelmed with people in the media trying to tell you how you should feel. How you guys are getting ready to mug a great season. But we control. The big thing is we control how we feel and how we act and how we play." La Russa knew his team had not been itself in the first two games at Fenway. But they were going back to Busch Stadium now, and Busch had been the postseason Promised Land for the team. They hadn't yet lost a playoff game there, and they were too good to fold up now. Which made what happened at Busch—the Cardinals scoring a total of one run in the next two games, while losing both—the part of the World Series that haunts him the most. Because what did happen? Where did the offense—the best in the major leagues—go? Why for the first time all year, with the possible exception of a three-game series sweep by the Pirates at the end of June, did the Cardinals start taking poor at-bats—uppercut fly-ball swings—instead of hitting through the ball hard to take advantage of a Red Sox defense that had made *eight* errors in the first two games?

Beyond the strategy and the psychological head games, managing is the art of survival: learning somehow not to become crippled by the decisions that even when you make them right, still turn out to be wrong, not to mention all the things you cannot control no matter how much you want to control them. Over the past quarter century, La Russa had learned to survive in the foxhole by examining his own actions first: a detached clinical examination to avoid wallowing in the mud of what just occurred. As he stood in the corner of the dugout waiting for Francona, he knew that his team had just played its worst baseball of the entire season: silent bats, poor base running, over-the-plate pitching. He also knew that he had just lost his eighth straight World Series game; the last time he had been to the Series, fourteen years earlier in 1990, had also been a four-game sweep.

In fact, La Russa's whole managerial experience in the Fall Classic had the pallor of Greek tragedy. He had been in the Series four times and the number of games he had managed, seventeen, was only one more than the *minimum* of sixteen. In 1988, he had lost in five games, after the Kirk Gibson home run that had rocked the world. In 1990 and 2004, his teams had been swept. In his one World Series win in 1989, his Oakland A's had swept the Giants, but even this victory had been improbably upstaged: interrupted by an earthquake and the indelible image of players on the field with their families just before Game 3, frozen with the terror of not knowing if Candlestick Park would hold together.

That kind of history could eat away at a man. He could become spooked, jinxed, irreparably tortured. But La Russa hearkened back to Paul Richards and the most enduring piece of advice he has ever received, as much about life as about managing: *It's your ass, it's your team, so take responsibility.* The fault was not his players, because they had been too brilliant all season long to simply collapse like this. He concluded instead that the fault was his, something he didn't do—a breakdown of his obligation to prepare his players, never mind how hard he had tried. But he also knew that simply taking the blame, an act of ultimately meaningless self-flagellation, wasn't enough.

So the day after the Series ended, as players flushed out a season's accumulation of balls and bats and gloves from their lockers, he met with his coaches to constructively delineate what had happened, why the bats had gone silent, why the pitchers couldn't find the black of the plate. They mused over the edge that had been lost in the fast-forward rush to the World Series. They wondered if the euphoria of winning the pennant, beating no less a force than Clemens, had been *too* euphoric. La Russa himself wondered if maybe the team had over-prepared, affected by a comment ESPN announcer and Hall-of-Famer Joe Morgan made to him afterward that in his own World Series experience, he didn't want a lot of information, just the bare bones of how hard a particular pitcher threw and how he used his off-speed. La Russa and his staff also discussed personnel changes, because it was inevitable that some players who had been cornerstones of the Cardinals in 2004 would be gone in 2005, either through free agency or salary realities or trade.

The questions came easier than the answers, but during the off-season, La Russa would be determined to find them. And the one thing he would *not* do is let the World Series overshadow a magnificent season. There were the obvious proofs: winning more games than any team in baseball, taking the division by thirteen games, winning the National League Pennant. There was the team itself, with its stoked lineup and vintage five-man rotation and fine mix of relief with two lights-out lefty specialists: a team that hit hard and ran hard and defended hard and gave pleasure to rival scouts and front-office men and managers who always thirst for baseball played right. But there were also the smaller subtleties, the little edges, not as apparent to the outside world perhaps but just as important and maybe even more memorable.

When the Cardinals clinched the NLCS, Elaine La Russa and the La Russas' daughter Devon were there. As soon as the game ended, their husband and father looked up to the stands and beckoned them to join him. They descended along with the players' families, a flood onto the field. Bianca, their elder daughter, hadn't come because she had nobly agreed to stay behind in California to take care of the house and the large brood of pets. Elaine thought of her in that instant, wished she could be here. But it was still a joyous moment for Elaine—no, a perfect moment—a long way from the stag-night parties and men-only restrictions of the Bard's Room of Comiskey. For the first time in a long time, she fell in love with baseball again, felt the beauty of it. As she looked at her husband, she also felt something else, something that she hadn't always felt during the preoccupation of his career. She felt that he was thrilled she and Devon were there, that as much as he reveled in the joy of winning the National League Pennant, there was something else he reveled in more, and that was his family.

Two days later, when the Cardinals conducted their workout before Game 1 of the World Series in the frigid froth of Boston, La Russa wanted his players to do what they had to do on the field and then get back to the clubhouse as quickly as possible. Like a mother hen, he walked the outfield shooing his players inside. But Cal Eldred lingered despite the cold. Standing before the Green Monster of Fenway, he had a huge smile on his face, soaking in every second of the fact that after fourteen years of ups and downs and too many elbow reconstructions for any elbow to bear, he had arrived. He didn't want to leave no matter how cold it was, so La Russa let Cal Eldred be. He just let him be, in the shadow of the Green Monster.

Six days later, after the World Series ended and La Russa walked through the tunnel to the clubhouse, he saw his players for what would be the last official time. There was nothing to say, all the bullets spent. If they were complicated men, they were also professionals, and no empty words of solace from a manager would do any good anyway.

In a couple of minutes the media would burst into the clubhouse with their predictable stream of hard questions. But for now, the clubhouse was sacred, intimate, a team and only a team. The players stood in front of their lockers in silence, perhaps because they were still expecting their manager to give some little speech. Instead, La Russa did something he had never done before. He had his coaches and all the clubhouse personnel form two lines. Then one of the lines went to the right and the other to the left to shake hands with each player, circling until they were done. La Russa knew what his players had done during the season. He loved them for that—took great pride in them as a manager and as a man—and this was the best way he could think of to tell them he would never forget it.

POSTSCRIPT

THE CARDINALS

Rick Ankiel, following rehabilitation from reconstructive elbow surgery, pitched in the major leagues for the first time since 2001, after being activated by the Cardinals in September 2004. He gave up one walk over ten innings in five relief appearances. In October 2004, he won his first major-league game since April 8, 2001, surrendering one run in four innings to the Milwaukee Brewers.

Chad Blair continued in his role as the Cardinals' video coordinator in 2004.

Miguel Cairo, after hitting .245 for the Cards in 2003 as a utility player—in which he played first base, second, shortstop, third, and the outfield—became a free agent and signed with the Yankees in 2004. He emerged as the team's regular second baseman and hit .292.

J.D. Drew was traded after the 2003 season, along with Eli Marrero, to the Braves for pitchers Jason Marquis, Ray King, and prospect Adam Wainwright. La Russa's feeling about Drew—that he might thrive with a different manager—was proven true. Healthy most of the season in his free-agent year, Drew had over 500 at-bats for the first time in his career, hitting .305 with thirty-one home runs and ninety-five RBIs. But the trade was one of those rare ones in baseball that benefited both sides. Marquis established himself as a bona fide starting pitcher at the age of twenty-five, going 15 and 7. Coming out of the bullpen, the lefty King had an ERA of 2.61 and gave up only forty-three hits in sixty-two innings. Despite Drew's breakout year, the Braves still chose to let him test the free-agent market. He signed a five-year, $55 million contract with the Dodgers.

Dave Duncan, in his twenty-second season as La Russa's pitching coach, had perhaps his most satisfying year ever in 2004, guiding a staff that before the season had been doomed for mediocrity by virtually every baseball pundit. The team's ERA, 3.75, was second in the National League and nearly a run less than in 2003.

Jim Edmonds was the subject of trade rumors after the 2003 season, because of a lackluster second half in which he batted only .214. After shoulder surgery in the off-season, he returned to the Cardinals and hit .301 in 2004 with forty-two home runs and 111 runs batted in.

Cal Eldred, after leading Cardinals relievers in wins in 2003 with seven, appeared in fifty-two games in 2004 with a record of 4 and 2 and an earned run average of 3.76. After the season, Eldred was among ten Cardinals players eligible for free agency. He elected to remain in St. Louis.

Bo Hart started on the Cardinals in 2004 but was sent down to Triple-A after thirteen at-bats.

Jason Isringhausen, healthy all year in 2004 as the closer, tied for the league lead in saves with forty-seven.

Walt Jocketty was named major-league Executive of the Year by the *Sporting News,* based on the myriad moves he made as general manager in shaping the 2004 Cardinals without ballooning the team's payroll.

Steve Kline had his best year in the majors as a lefty specialist out of the bullpen in 2004, recording an ERA of 1.79 in sixty-seven games. In keeping with his personality, he also gave La Russa the finger from the bullpen during a game in June when he became upset at not being used. When La Russa found out about it afterward, he steamed into the shower to confront Kline. "I don't think he'll be mad," Kline later told reporters. "He loves me too much." He became a free agent after the season and was not re-signed by the Cardinals. He inked a two-year deal with the Baltimore Orioles.

Tony La Russa, after an 85-77 finish in 2003, managed the Cardinals to a 105-57 record in 2004 and a franchise-record 112 wins including the playoffs. If he wins eighty-one games in 2005, he'll move into third place on the all-time list of managerial wins, behind Connie Mack and John McGraw. He has 2,114.

Tino Martinez was traded after the 2003 season to the Tampa Bay Devil Rays for a minor-league player. The Cardinals also agreed to pay $7 million of the $8.5 million due on his contract. He hit .262 with twenty-three home runs and seventy-six runs batted in.

Mike Matheny won the Gold Glove as catcher in 2004, just as he had in 2003. He became a free agent at the end of the season, and signed with the San Francisco Giants.

Matt Morris went 15 and 10 in 2004 but was plagued by inconsistency. His velocity was noticeably down and his record in the postseason—0 and 2 with an earned run average of 5.91—was disappointing. A free agent, with an uncertain future after once being heralded as one of the best young pitchers in baseball, Morris had arthroscopic surgery last November on his pitching shoulder. Rather than test the market, Morris re-signed a one-year contract for $2.5 million with incentive clauses. The amount was $10 million less than what he had made in 2004, a rare case in baseball of a player opting for honest reappraisal instead of greed.

Orlando Palmeiro, after hitting .271 with the Cardinals in 2003 as a role player, signed with the Houston Astros. He appeared in 102 games and hit .241.

Eddie Perez, after hitting .285 with eleven home runs in 2003 off the bench, signed with the Tampa Bay Devil Rays. He tore his Achilles tendon early in May 2004 and missed the remainder of the season.

Albert Pujols, after leading the National League in hitting in 2003 with a mark of .359, in 2004 became the first player in major-league history to hit thirty or more home runs his first four seasons. He also joined Joe DiMaggio and Ted Williams as the only players to drive in 500 runs or more their first four seasons. Pujols hit .331 with forty-six home runs and 121 runs batted in.

Edgar Renteria hit .287 at shortstop in 2004 and drove in seventy-two runs. He became a free agent at the end of the season and signed with the Boston Red Sox.

Kerry Robinson was traded by the Cardinals shortly before the 2004 season to the San Diego Padres for outfielder Brian Hunter and shuffled back and forth between Triple-A and the parent club. He appeared in eighty games for the Padres, with four extra-base hits in ninety-two at-bats, all of them doubles. He hasn't hit a home run since the one described in this book.

Scott Rolen had his best year in the majors in 2004, hitting .314 with thirty-four home runs and finishing second in the National League in runs batted in with 124, despite missing much of September because of a strained calf muscle.

Garrett Stephenson did not pitch in major-league baseball in 2004 because of an injury.

So Taguchi continued to improve as a player off the bench for the Cardinals in 2004, hitting .291.

Woody Williams, bothered by shoulder tendinitis in spring training, got off to such a terrible start in 2004 that he contemplated retirement. But he finished strong to go 11 and 8 and was chosen as the Cardinals starter for the first game of the World Series. He filed for free agency after the season and signed with the Padres.

THE CUBS

Mark Prior, after going 18 and 6 in 2003 and finishing third in the National League Cy Young voting, discovered his own mortality in 2004 in his second full season in the major leagues. He missed the first two months with a sore Achilles tendon and elbow, and finished with a record of 6 and 4 and an ERA of 4.02.

Sammy Sosa had his worst year ever for the Cubs in 2004, hitting .253 with thirty-five home runs and only eighty RBIs. He was fined $87,400 for arriving late to the Cubs' season finale at Wrigley and then leaving fifteen minutes after the game had started. Sosa, who makes around $17 million, then accused the Cubs of mistreating him.

Kerry Wood missed several weeks of the 2004 season because of tendinitis in his triceps, only adding to the injury woes Wood has experienced since breaking into the major leagues. He went 8 and 9 with an earned run average of 3.72. He also hit eleven batters in 140 innings, including three Astros in a single game.

Carlos Zambrano emerged in 2004 as the most effective starter of the Cubs triumvirate, going 16 and 8 with an ERA of 2.75 in 209 innings.

The Cubs, based on their finish in 2003 in which they advanced to the National League Championship series, were picked by many pundits to make it to the World Series in 2004. Plagued by injuries, they did not live up to expectations, but were still contending for the NL wild card late in the season. Then at the end of September, a one-and-a-half game lead turned into dust when they lost seven of eight games. As only the Cubs could do and only baseball could do to them, the slide began when they lost to the Mets in extra innings after being ahead 3–0 with two outs in the ninth.

A NOTE ON SOURCES

Close to 90 percent of what appears in *Three Nights in August* was based on personal observation and interviews. I spent several weeks with the St. Louis Cardinals during spring training in 2003 and attended about fifty regular-season games. In the depictions of various players and personalities in the book, I also used written sources. The archives of the *St. Louis Post-Dispatch* were invaluable. I also utilized articles from *Baseball America,* the *Chicago Tribune,* the *New York Times,* the *Sporting News,* and *USA Today.* In writing of the events leading up to and following the death of pitcher Darryl Kile, an article in the St. Louis Cardinals' publication *Gameday Magazine* was particularly helpful, as was an interview with Flynn Kile on ESPN. This book also could not have done without the historical box scores compiled by the Web site Retrosheet.org, which go back more than a hundred years. The Web sites of Espn.com and Mlb.com were enormously helpful as well. Below is a list of selected bibliography.

Baseball America 2003 Almanac. Durham, North Carolina: Baseball America Inc., 2003.

Baseball America 2004 Almanac. Durham, North Carolina: Baseball America Inc., 2004.

Baseball Register 2003 Edition. St. Louis: Sporting News Books, 2003.

Baseball Register 2004 Edition. St. Louis: Sporting News Books, 2004.

Birnbaum, Phil, Deane, Bill, and John Thorn. *Total Baseball: The Ultimate Baseball Encyclopedia, 8th Edition.* Toronto: Sport Media Publishing, 2004.

Castle, George, and Jim Rygelski. *The I-55 Series: Cubs vs. Cardinals.* Champaign, Illinois: Sports Publishing Inc., 1999.

Gentile, Derek. *The Complete Chicago Cubs.* New York: Black Dog & Leventhal Publishers, 2002.

Golenbock, Peter. *Wrigleyville.* New York: St. Martin's Press, 1999.

———. *The Spirit of St. Louis.* New York: HarperCollins, 2000.

Holtzman, Jerome, and George Vass. *Baseball, Chicago Style.* Chicago: Bonus Books, 2001.

Honig, Donald. *The Man in the Dugout.* Chicago: Follett Publishing, 1977.

James, Bill. *The Bill James Guide to Baseball Managers: From 1870 to Today.* New York: Scribner, 1997.

Koppett, Leonard. *The Man in the Dugout.* New York: Crown Publishers, 1993.

Lau, Charley, with Alfred Glossbrenner. *The Art of Hitting .300.* New York: Penguin Books, 1991.

Lewis, Michael. *Moneyball.* New York: W. W. Norton, 2003.

Libby, Bill. *Charlie O. and the Angry A's.* Garden City, New York: Doubleday, 1975.

Light, Jonathan Fraser. *The Cultural Encyclopedia of Baseball.* Jefferson, North Carolina: McFarland, 1997.

Logan, Bob. *Miracle on 35th Street: Winnin' Ugly with the 1983 White Sox.* South Bend, Indiana: Icarus Press, 1983.

Myers, Doug. *Essential Cubs.* Chicago: Contemporary Books, 1999.

The Scouting Notebook 2004. St. Louis: Sporting News Books, 2004.

Smith, Curt. *Voices of the Game.* New York: Simon & Schuster, 1992.

Will, George. *Men at Work.* New York: HarperCollins, 1991.

ACKNOWLEDGMENTS

There are many people to thank for the creation of *Three Nights in August,* but first and foremost is my editor at Houghton Mifflin, Eamon Dolan. A few lines of praise are inadequate to describe the seminal role that Eamon played from beginning to end with patience, support, love, tough love, a few necessary head slaps to the overly fragile psyche, and everything else that counts in the creative process. He demanded with a quiet relentlessness, dedicated to making this book as good as it could possibly be. In a profession in which the invaluable art of editing is becoming a lost art, he proved himself to be a Picasso.

Among the St. Louis Cardinals, the list is long because of the graciousness that was consistently shown. Pitching Coach Dave Duncan must be highlighted not only because he unfailingly answered all my questions despite continual interruptions to his concentration but also because he helped me fix my laptop when it became besieged by a virus one terrible morning in Houston. Bench Coach Joe Pettini provided valuable help on the Zen of just about everything that was baseball related. Bullpen Coach Marty Mason provided valuable help on the Zen of pitching, and of course there is the Secret Weapon, Video Coordinator Chad Blair. Traveling Secretary C.J. Cherre made my life infinitely easier in trying to keep up with the blistering seasonal schedule of the Cardinals during 2003. Equipment Manager Rip Rowan and assistant Buddy

Bates made me feel like a welcome presence in the clubhouse despite working twenty-five hours a day. So did Head Athletic Trainer Barry Weinberg and Bullpen Catcher Jeff Murphy.

Other members of the Cardinals organization who must be thanked include Chairman of the Board and General Partner Bill DeWitt, Jr., Vice Chairman Fred Hanser, Limited Partner Dave Pratt, General Manager Walt Jocketty, Assistant General Manager John Mozeliak, and team media gurus Brain Bartow, Brad Hainje, and Melody Yount. Among the Cardinals players, all of them were giving of their time despite continual demands by the media. Several in particular went above and beyond the call of duty during the 2003 season: Steve Kline, Cal Eldred, Mike Matheny, Orlando Palmeiro, and Eddie Perez.

Outside the Cardinals family, a tip of the hat to Joe Strauss, who covered the team in 2003 for the *St. Louis Post-Dispatch.* The same to Rick Hummel of the *Post-Dispatch,* who may well know more about baseball than any other person in the history of the game. On the broadcast side, television announcers Al Hrabosky and Dan McLaughlin always made for interesting bus trips from the hotel to the ballpark, and it's difficult to think of anybody in life who has more character and more stories than the radio voice of the Cardinals, Mike Shannon. There is also Ed Lewis and Jim Leyland and Rollie Hemond and Jerry Reinsdorf, baseball men to the core.

Last but not least, thanks to agent David Gernert for putting Tony La Russa and me in the same room together at the outset. And, of course, there is La Russa himself, a manager of unique distinction, but more important, a man with qualities of loyalty and honor and decency as rare as they are gratifying.

INDEX